JACKIE COLLINS

Dear Readers,

"Hollywood Wives" was the book that really made my name. The wives of Hollywood were furious that I had WRITTEN about them, and yet they took a great deal of delight in recognizing all their closest friends! On the day of publication in Los Angeles, the ladies of Hollywood had their drivers and housekeepers lining up at the bookstores to get an early copy! Yes, "Hollywood Wives" rocked their very perfect world! The guessing game took over – and what fun that was as they all recognized their worst enemy! "Hollywood Wives" topped bestseller lists across the world. What a TRIP!

Jackie C.

Praise for Jackie Collins

'Sex, power and intrigue – no one does it better than Jackie'
heat

'A tantalising novel packed with power struggles, greed and sex. This is Collins at her finest.' *Closer*

'Bold, brash, whiplash fast – with a cast of venal rich kids, this is classic Jackie Collins' *Marie Claire*

'Sex, money, power, murder, betrayal, true love – it's all here in vintage Collins style. Collins's plots are always a fabulously involved, intricate affair, and this does not disappoint'
Daily Mail

'Her style is pure escapism, her heroine's strong and ambitious and her men, well, like the book, they'll keep you up all night!' *Company*

'A generation of women have learnt more about how to handle their men from Jackie's books than from any kind of manual . . . Jackie is very much her own person: a total one off' *Daily Mail*

'Jackie is still the queen of sexy stories. Perfect' *OK!*

'Cancel all engagements, take the phone off the hook and indulge yourself' *Mirror*

Also by Jackie Collins

The Power Trip
Married Lovers
Lovers & Players
Deadly Embrace
Hollywood Wives – The New Generation
Lethal Seduction
Thrill!
L.A. Connections – Power, Obsession, Murder, Revenge
Hollywood Kids
American Star
Rock Star
Hollywood Husbands
Lovers & Gamblers
Hollywood Wives
The World Is Full Of Divorced Women
The Love Killers
Sinners
The Bitch
The Stud
The World Is Full Of Married Men
Hollywood Divorces

THE SANTANGELO NOVELS

Goddess of Vengeance
Poor Little Bitch Girl
Drop Dead Beautiful
Dangerous Kiss
Vendetta: Lucky's Revenge
Lady Boss
Lucky
Chances

Jackie Collins

HOLLYWOOD WIVES

SIMON &
SCHUSTER

London · New York · Sydney · Toronto · New Delhi

A CBS COMPANY

First published in Great Britain by William Collins & Co. Ltd, 1983.

This edition published by Simon & Schuster UK Ltd, 2012
A CBS COMPANY

1 3 5 7 9 10 8 6 4 2

Simon & Schuster UK Ltd
1st Floor
222 Gray's Inn Road
London WC1X 8HB

Simon & Schuster Australia, Sydney
Simon & Schuster India, New Delhi

www.simonandschuster.co.uk

A CIP catalogue record for this book is available from the British Library

ISBN 978-1-84983-625-8

Typeset by Hewer Text UK Ltd, Edinburgh
Printed and bound in Great Britain by CIP Group (UK) Ltd,
Croydon, CR0 4YY

For Tracy, Tiffany and Rory
with all my love

Nobody is allowed to fail within a two-mile radius of the Beverley Hills Hotel.

Gore Vidal

Prologue

He stood in the living room of the small house in Philadelphia. He stood and stared at the three of them. Three pigs. Three laughing faces. Teeth and eyes and hair. Three pigs.

There was a black rage within him. A rage which beat at his head from the inside.

The television was on in the room. Archie Bunker mouthing futile jokes. Canned studio laughter.

And more laughter. In the room with him. More inane laughter.

His mother. Mousy wisps of brown hair. A sagging body and a sagging mind.

His father. Balding. Skinny. False teeth that clicked in and out at will.

Joey. He had thought she was different.

Three pigs.

He walked to the television set and raised the sound.

They took no notice. They were too busy laughing. At him. Yes. They were laughing at him.

The rage was in his head, but outwardly he was calm. He knew how to make them stop. He knew . . .

Fast and fluid. Before they had time to stop laughing and start thinking . . .

Fast and fluid. The machete swung in a lethal circle.

Fast and fluid as the blood spurted. His mother and father felled with the first lethal sweep.

But Joey. Swifter, younger. Her eyes bulging with horror as, clutching at her wounded arm, she staggered towards the door.

You've stopped laughing now, Joey. You've stopped laughing now.

He swung the machete again, felling her before she could progress further.

They did not scream. Not one of them.

He had taken them by surprise, just like soldiers were trained to do. Only he wasn't a soldier was he? He wasn't a soldier . . .

Sobs began to shake him violently. Strange silent sobs which convulsed his body as he wielded the machete. Dealing with all three of them equally. Indulging in a frenzy of grisly death blows.

The television drowned out the sounds of the carnage. Archie Bunker. Canned laughter.

And the machete continued to whirl and slash as if powered by some demonic force.

Book One

Chapter One

Elaine Conti awoke in her luxurious bed in her luxurious Beverly Hills mansion, pressed a button to open the electrically controlled drapes, and was confronted by the sight of a young man clad in a white T-shirt and dirty jeans pissing a perfect arc into her mosaic tiled swimming pool.

She struggled to sit up, buzzing for Lina, her Mexican maid, and at the same time flinging on a marabou trimmed silk robe and pressing her feet into dusty pink mules.

The young man completed his task, zipped up his jeans and strolled casually out to view.

'Lina!' Elaine screamed. 'Where *are* you?'

The maid appeared, inscrutable, calm, oblivious to her mistress's screams.

'There's an intruder out by the pool,' Elaine snapped excitedly. 'Get Miguel. Call the police. And make sure all the doors are locked.'

Unperturbed, Lina began to collect the debris of clutter from Elaine's bedside table. Dirty Kleenex, a half-finished glass of wine, a rifled box of chocolates.

'Lina!' Elaine yelled.

'No get excited, Señora,' the maid said stoically. 'No intruder. Just boy Miguel sent to do pool. Miguel sick. No come this week.'

Elaine flushed angrily. 'Well why the hell didn't you tell me before?' She flung herself into her bathroom, slamming the door so hard that a framed print sprang off the wall and crashed to the floor, the glass shattering. Stupid maid. Dumb ass woman. It was impossible to get good help anymore. They came. They went. They did not give a damn if you were raped and ravaged in your own home.

And this *would* have to happen while Ross was away on location. Miguel would *never* have dared to pretend to be sick if Ross was in town.

Elaine flung off her robe, slipped out of her nightgown, and stepped under the invigorating sharpness of an ice cold shower. She gritted her teeth. Cold water was best for the skin, tightened everything up – and God knows – even with the gym and the yoga and the modern dance class it still all needed tightening.

Not that she was fat. No way. Not a surplus piece of flesh on her entire body. Pretty good for thirty-nine years of age. Pretty damn good.

When I was thirteen I was the fattest girl in school. Etta the Elephant they called me. And I deserved the nickname. Only how could a kid of thirteen know about nutrition and diet and exercise and all that stuff? How could a kid of thirteen help it when Grandma Steinberg stuffed her with cakes and latkes, lox and bagles, strudle and chicken dumplings. Constantly.

Elaine smiled grimly. Etta the Elephant, late of the Bronx, had shown them all. Etta the Elephant, former secretary in New York City, was now slim and svelte. She was called Elaine Conti, and lived in a six bedroomed, seven bathroomed, goddamn Beverly Hills palace. On the flats too. Not stuck up in the hills or all the way over in Brentwood. On the flats. Prime real estate.

Etta the Elephant no longer had a sharp nose, mousy hair, gapped teeth, wire rimmed glasses and flat tits.

Over the years she had changed. The nose was now retroussé, cute. A perfect Brooke Shields in fact. The mousy hair was a rich brown, cut short and tipped with golden streaks. Her skin was alabaster white and smooth, thanks to regular facials. Her teeth were capped. White and even. A credit to Charlie's Angels. The unbecoming glasses had long been replaced with soft blue contact lenses; without them her eyes were slate grey and she had to squint to read. Not that she did a lot of reading. Magazines of course. *Vogue*, *People*, *Us*. She skimmed the trades, *Variety* and *Hollywood Reporter*, concentrating on Army Archerd and Hank Grant. She devoured *Women's Wear Daily*, but was not really into what she termed hard news. The day Ronald Reagan was elected President was the only day she gave a passing thought to politics. If Ronald Reagan could do it how about Ross?

The tits, while being nowhere in the Raquel Welch class, were a perfect 36B, thanks to the ministrations of her first husband, Dr. John Saltwood. They stuck defiantly forward, no pull of gravity would ever harm *them*. And if it did, well . . . back to good old Johnny. She had found him in New York, wasting himself doing plastic surgery for a city hospital. They met at a party and she recognized a plain lonely man not unlike herself. They married a month later, and she had her nose and tits fixed within the year. Then she talked him into going to Beverly Hills and setting up in private practice.

Three years later he was *the* tit man, and she had divorced him and become Mrs Ross Conti. Funny how things worked out.

Ross Conti. Husband. Movie star. First class shit.

And she should know. After all they had been married ten long years and it hadn't all been easy and it wasn't getting any easier and she knew things about Ross Conti that would curl the toes of the little old ladies who still loved him because after all he was hitting fifty and his fans were not exactly teenagers and as each year crept by it was getting more and more difficult and God knows financially things were not as good as they had been and each film could be his last and . . .

'Señora.' Lina hammered on the bathroom door. 'The boy, he go now. He want pay.'

Elaine stepped out of the shower. She was outraged. He wanted paying – for what? Pissing in her pool?

She wrapped herself in a fluffy terrycloth robe and opened the bathroom door. 'Tell him,' she said grandly, 'to piss off.'

Lina stared blankly. 'Twenny dollar, Meesus Conti. He do it again in three day.'

* * *

Ross Conti swore silently to himself. Jesus H. Christ. What was happening to him? He couldn't remember his frigging lines. Eight takes and still he was screwing up.

'Just take it easy, Ross,' said the director calmly, placing a condescending hand on his shoulder.

Some frigging director. Twenty-three if he was a day. Hair hanging down his back like a witch at Halloween. Levis so tight the outline of his schlong was like a frigging beacon.

Ross shook the offending hand off. 'I'm taking it easy. It's the crowd – they keep on distracting me.'

'Sure,' soothed Chip, signalling to the first assistant. 'Calm them down for crissakes, they're background – not auditioning for Chorus Line.'

The first assistant nodded, then made an announcement through his loud speaker.

'Ready to go again?' questioned Chip. Ross nodded. The director turned to a suntanned blonde. 'Again, Sharon, sorry babe.'

Ross burned. *Sorry babe. What the little prick really means is sorry babe but we gotta humour this old fart because this old fart used to be the biggest thing in Hollywood.*

Sharon smiled. 'Right on, Chip.'

Sure. Right on, Chip. We'll humour the old schmuck. My mother used to love him. She saw all his movies. Creamed her panties every time.

'Make-up,' Ross demanded, then added, his voice heavy with sarcasm, 'That's if nobody minds.'

'Of course not. Anything you want.'

Yeah. Anything I want. Because this so-called hotshot needs Ross Conti in his film. Ross Conti means plenty at the box office. Who would line up to see Sharon Richman? Who has even heard of Sharon Richman except a couple of million television freaks who tune in to see some schlock programme about girl water ski instructors. Glossy crap. Sharon Richman – a hank of hair and a mouthful of teeth. I wouldn't even fuck her if she crawled to my trailer on her hands and knees and begged for it. Well . . . maybe if she begged.

The make-up girl attended to his needs. Now *she* was all right. She *knew* who the star was on this picture. Busily she fussed around him, blotting out the shine of sweat around his nose with an outsize powder puff, touching up his eyebrows with a small comb.

He gave her a perfunctory pinch on the ass. She smiled appreciatively. *Come to my trailer later, baby, and I'll show you how to give a star head.*

'Right,' said Chip the creep. 'Are we ready, Ross?'

We are ready asshole. He nodded.

'Okay. Let's go then.'

The scene began all right. It was a simple bit of business which involved Ross saying three lines to Sharon's six, then strolling nonchalantly out of shot. The trouble was Sharon. She stared blankly, making him blow his second line every time.

Bitch. She's doing it purposely. Trying to make me look bad.

'Jesus H. Christ!' Chip finally blew. 'It's not the fucking soliloquy from Hamlet.'

Right. That's it. Talking to me like some nothing bit player. Ross turned and stalked from the location without a backward glance.

Chip grimaced at Sharon. 'That's what happens when you're dealing with no talent.'

'My mommy used to love him,' she simpered.

'Then your mommy is an even bigger moron than her daughter.'

She giggled. Chip's insults did not bother her. In bed she had him under control, and that was where it *really* mattered.

* * *

Elaine Conti drove her pale blue Mercedes slowly down La Cienega Boulevard. She drove slowly so as not to spoil her nails which she had just had done at a senational new nail clinic called The Nail Kiss of Life. Wonderful place. They had wrapped her broken thumb nail so well that even *she* couldn't tell. Elaine loved discovering new places, it gave her a tiny shot of power. She pushed in a Streisand tape and wondered – as she had wondered countless times before – why dear Barbra had never had her nose fixed. In a town so dedicated to the perfect face . . . And God knows she had the money . . . Still . . . It certainly had not harmed her career . . . nor her love life for that matter.

Elaine frowned and thought about her own love life. Ross hadn't ventured near her in months. Bastard. Just because *he* didn't feel in the mood . . .

Elaine had indulged in two affairs during the course of her marriage. Both of them unsatisfactory. She hated affairs, they were so time consuming. The highs and the lows. The ups and the downs. Was it all worth it? She had decided no, but now she was beginning to wonder.

The last one had taken place over two years previously. She blushed when she thought about it. What absurd risks she had taken. And with a man who could do her absolutely no good at all except fix her teeth, and they were already perfect. Milton Langley, her dentist – and probably everyone else's with money in Beverly Hills. How indiscreet of her to have picked him. But really he had picked her. He had sent his nurse scurrying off on an errand one day, climbed aboard the chair, and made fast and furious love to her. She remembered the day well, because he had climaxed all over her new Sonia Rykiel skirt.

Elaine giggled aloud at the thought, although she hadn't giggled at the time. Milton had poured mouthwash over the damaged garment, and when his nurse returned sent her over to Saks to purchase a replacement. After that they had met twice a week in some dreadful motel on Santa Monica for two hot months. One day Elaine had just decided not to go. End of *that* little episode.

The other one wasn't even worth thinking about. An actor on one of Ross's films. She had slept with him twice and regretted both times.

Whenever she mentioned their lack of a sex life to Ross he flew into a rage. 'What the frig do you think I am? A machine?' he would snarl. 'I'll get it up when *I* want to – not just because you've read some crap sex magazine that says you should have ten orgasms a day.'

Chance would be a fine thing. She was lucky if she got ten a year. If it wasn't for her trusty vibrator she would be climbing walls.

Maybe his erection would return if the movie he was doing turned out to be a hit.

Yes. That was what Ross needed – a massive shot of success. It would be good for both of them. There was nothing like success for putting the hard-on back in a man's life.

Carefully she made a left on Melrose. Lunch at Ma Maison was a must on Fridays. Anybody who was anybody and in town invariably showed up. Elaine had a permanent booking.

She made a right into the small parking lot, and left her car in the hands of a parking jockey.

Patrick Terrail, the owner of Ma Maison, greeted her at the entrance to the small outdoor restaurant. She accepted a kiss on each cheek, and followed a waiter to her table, keeping an eagle eye out for anyone she should acknowledge.

Maralee Gray, one of her closest friends, was already waiting.

She nursed a spritzer and a sour expression. At thirty-seven Maralee maintained more than a shadow of her past prettiness. In her time she had been voted the most popular girl in high school *and* Miss Hot Rod 1962. That was before she had met, married and divorced Neil Gray – the film director. Her father – now retired – owned Sanderson Studios. Money had never been Maralee's problem. Only men.

'Darling. I'm not late am I?' Elaine asked anxiously, brushing cheeks with her friend.

'Not at all. I think *I* was early.' They exchanged 'You look wonderfuls', admired each other's outfits, and cast their eyes around the restaurant.

'And how's Ross making out on location?' Maralee inquired, extracting a long black cigarillo from a wafer thin gold case.

'You know Ross – he makes out wherever he is.'

They both laughed. Ross's reputation as a cocksman was an old Hollywood joke.

'Actually he hates everything,' she confided. 'The script, the director, the crew, the food, the climate – the whole bug-ridden set-up as he so charmingly puts it. But Maralee, believe me—' She leaned confidentially towards her friend, 'He's going to be dynamite in this movie. The old Ross Conti – full force.'

'I can believe it,' Maralee murmured. 'I've never counted him out, you know that.'

Elaine nodded. Maralee was a true friend, there weren't many of them around. In Hollywood you were only as hot as your last hit – and it had been a long time between hits.

'I'm going to have my eyes done,' Maralee announced dramatically. 'I'm only telling you, and you mustn't mention it to anyone.'

'As if I would!' Elaine replied, quite affronted. 'Who's going to do it?'

Maralee laughed. 'The Palm Springs connection, of course. I'll spend a couple of weeks there – after all I have the house

– then I'll come back and nobody will know the difference. They'll just think I was vacationing.'

'Wonderful idea,' Elaine said, thinking to herself was Maralee stupid or what? Nobody took a vacation in Palm Springs – even if they did have a house there. They either weekended or retired. 'When?' she asked, her eyes flicking restlessly round the restaurant.

Maralee shrugged. 'As soon as possible. Next week if he can fit me in. He's so busy.'

They both stopped talking to observe the entrance of Sylvester Stallone. Elaine threw him a perfunctory wave but he did not appear to notice her. 'Probably needs glasses,' she sniffed. 'I met him at a party only last week.'

Maralee produced a small gold compact and inspected her face. 'He won't last,' she remarked dismissively, removing a smudge of lipstick from her teeth. 'Let's face it – Clark Gable he's not.'

* * *

'Oh yeah, that's it . . . Don't stop . . . don't ever stop. Oh yeah, yeah . . . Just keep on going, sweetheart, keep right on going.'

Ross Conti listened to the words pouring from his mouth and wondered how many times he had uttered them before. Plenty. That was for sure.

On her knees, Stella, the make-up girl, worked diligently on his weak erection. She sucked at him like he was a water pump. Her technique could do with some improvement. But then – in his time – Ross had had some of the best little cocksuckers in the business. Starlets, whose very livelihood depended on doing a good job. Hookers, who specialized. Bored Beverly Hills housewives who had elevated cocksucking to an art.

He felt his erection begin to deflate, and he dug his fingers hard into the girl's scalp. She yelped with pain and stopped what she was doing.

He wasn't sorry. Quick as a flash he tucked himself out of sight and firmly zipped up. 'That was great!'

She stared at him in amazement. 'But you didn't come.'

He could hardly lie. 'Sometimes it's better this way,' he mumbled mysteriously, reaching for a bottle of tequila on the side table in his hotel room.

'It is?' She continued to stare.

'Sure. Keeps all the juices inside. Keeps me buzzing. That's the way I like it when I'm working.' If she believed that she'd believe anything.

'I think I know what you mean,' she began enthusiastically. 'Sort of like a boxer before a fight – you mustn't release that precious energy. Instead you have to make it work for you.'

'Right! You got it!' He smiled, took a slug of tequila straight from the bottle, and wished she would go.

'Would you like me to . . . do anything?' she questioned expectantly, hoping that he would ask her to undress and stay.

'There's a million things I'd like you to do,' he replied. 'But the star has got to get some sleep. You understand, don't you?'

'Of course, Mr Con . . . Ross.'

He hadn't said she could call him by his first name. Mr Conti would do nicely. Women. Give them nine inches and they frigging moved in. 'Goodnight, Sheila.'

'It's Stella.'

'Right.'

She finally left, and he switched on the television set. Just in time for The Tonight Show. He knew that he should call Elaine in L.A. but he couldn't be bothered. She would be furious when she heard he had blown his lines and walked off the set. Elaine thought he was on the way out. She was always nagging him about keeping up with what the public wanted. He had done his last movie against her advice, and it had bombed at the box office. God, that had pissed him off. A fine love story with a veteran director and a New York stage actress as his leading lady. 'Old fashioned garbage,' Elaine had announced baldly. 'Sex, violence and comedy, that's what sells tickets today. And you've got to get in on the act, Ross, before it's too late.'

She was right of course. He did have to get in on the act because he was no longer Mr Box Office, not even in the frigging top ten. He was on the slide, and in Hollywood they could smell it.

Johnny Carson was interviewing Angie Dickinson. She was flirting, crossing long legs and looking seductive.

Abruptly Ross picked up the phone. 'Get me the bell captain,' he snapped.

Chip had come grovelling to his trailer after his walk-out earlier. 'Nothing we can't sort out, Ross. If you want to quit today we can schedule to reshoot the scene first thing in the morning.'

He had agreed. At least they knew they were dealing with a star now, and not some nothing has-been.

'Yes, Mr. Conti. This is the bell captain. How may I help you?'

Ross balanced the phone under his chin and reached for the tequila bottle. 'Can you be discreet?'

'Of course, sir. It's my job.'

'I want a broad.'

'Certainly Mr Conti. Blonde? Brunette? Redhead?'

'Multi-coloured for all I care. Just make sure she's got big tits – and I *mean* big ones.'

'Yes *sir*!'

'Oh – and you can charge her to my account. Mark it down as room service.' Why should *he* pay. Let the film company pick up the tab. He replaced the receiver and walked to the mirror. Fifty. He was soon going to be fifty. And it hurt. Badly.

* * *

Ross Conti had lived in Hollywood for thirty years. And for twenty-five of those years he had been a star. Arriving in town in 1953, it had not taken long before he was discovered hauling boxes in a food market on Sunset Boulevard by an ageing agent's young wife. She was entranced by his blond good looks, and set about persuading her husband to handle him. In the meantime she was handling him herself – twice a day – and loving every minute.

Her husband discovered their affair on the day Universal decided to sign his young client. In a fit of fury the old agent negotiated the worst deal he possibly could, waited until it was signed, then dropped Ross, and badmouthed him as an untalented stud all over town.

Ross didn't care. He had grown up in the Bronx. Spent three years kicking around New York grabbing bit parts here and there, and a Hollywood contract seemed just perfect to him, whatever the terms.

Women adored him. For two years he worked his way through the studio, eventually picking on the pretty mistress of a studio executive, who promptly saw to it that Ross's contract was dropped.

Two years, and all he had done were a few small parts in a series of beach party movies. Then suddenly – no contract, no prospects, no money.

One day, lounging around Schwabs drugstore on the strip he got talking to a girl called Sadie La Salle, a hard working secretary with the most enormous knockers he had ever seen. She was not a pretty girl. Overweight, suspicions of a moustache, short of leg. But oh those magnificent tits! After talking for a while he surprised himself by asking her for a date. She accepted readily, and they went to the Aware Inn, ate health burgers and talked about him. He loved every minute of it. How many girls were prepared to discuss him and only him for five solid hours?

Sadie was very smart – a quality Ross had not encountered in a woman before. She refused to go to bed with him on their first date, slapped his hands away when he went after the magic tits, gave him sound advice about his career, and on their second date cooked him the best meal he had ever had.

For six months they had a platonic relationship. Seeing each other a couple of times a week, speaking on the phone daily. Ross loved talking to her, she had an answer for every problem. And oh boy, did he ever have problems! He told her about the girls he was screwing, the trouble he was having finding work. Going on interview after interview and getting nowhere was depressing, not to mention terrible for his ego. Sadie was a wonderful listener, plus she cooked him two great meals a week and *did his washing.*

One night he had a narrow escape while visiting a nubile girlfriend. Her out-of-town husband returned home sooner than expected, and Ross was forced to drop out of her bedroom window desperately clutching his pants. He decided to pay Sadie an unexpected visit and tell her the story, sure that she would love it.

When he arrived at her small apartment on Olive Drive he was shocked to discover her entertaining a man, the two of them sitting at her candlelit dining table finishing off a delicious smelling pot roast. There was wine on the table, fresh cut flowers and her best cutlery. Sadie was wearing a low cut dress and looked flustered to see him.

It had never occurred to him before that she had boyfriends, and for some unknown reason he was extremely pissed off.

'Ross, I want you to meet Bernard Leftcovitz,' she said primly, eyeing Ross's crumpled clothes and mussed hair with distaste.

He flung himself familiarly into a chair and threw a brief silent nod in Bernard Leftcovitz's direction. 'Get me a drink, hon,' he said to Sadie, reaching out to slap her on the ass. 'Scotch, plenty of ice.'

She glared, but did as he asked. Then he outsat Mr Leftcovitz who finally left an hour later.

'Thanks a lot!' Sadie exploded, as soon as the door shut behind him.

Ross grinned. 'Wassamatter?'

'You know *what's the matter. Walking in here like you own the place, treating me like one of your . . . your . . . goddamn women!' She was spluttering with anger. 'I hate you, Ross, you know that? I really hate you! You think you're such a big deal. Well, let me tell you—'*

He grabbed her fast. Moved in for the kill – for he knew that's what it would be – a killer scene, all thighs and heat and those amazing mountainous tits enveloping him.

She pushed him away. 'Ross—' she began to object.

He wasn't about to listen to any reason why they shouldn't. Sadie La Salle was going to be his and only his – screw the Bernard Leftcovitzes of this world.

She was a virgin. Twenty-four years old. A resident of Hollywood and a virgin.

Ross could not believe it. He was delighted. Ten years of solid fucking and she was his first.

The next day he packed up his things and moved in with her. He was two months overdue with the rent on his apartment anyway, and money was becoming a definite problem. Moving in with Sadie seemed like a great idea, plus she loved having him in her life. She said goodbye to Bernie without a second thought and devoted all her time to taking very good care of Ross indeed. 'We have to find you an agent,' she fretted, because she knew his failure to land a part in a movie was upsetting him more than he cared to admit. Unfortunately all the agents he visited seemed to have got the message – Ross Conti equals bad news.

One day she made a major decision. 'I'll *be your agent,' she stated quite seriously.*

'You'll what*?' he roared.*

'I'll be your agent. It's a good idea. You'll see.'

The next week she gave up her job, withdrew her savings from the bank, and soon found a tiny little room in a seedy building on Hollywood Boulevard. She stuck a notice on the door – Sadie La Salle – Agent to the Stars. Then she had a phone installed, and was in business.

Ross found the whole thing hysterically funny. What the hell did Sadie know about being an agent?

What she didn't know she soon found out. For six years she had worked as a secretary in a large law firm which specialized in show business work. Sadie had the legalities down pat. And the rest wasn't difficult. She had a product. Ross Conti. And when the women of America got a good look at him they were going to want to buy.

'I have a great idea,' she told him one day, 'and I don't even want your opinion of it because it'll work. I know *it's going to work.'*

As it happened he loved her idea – although it was a little crazy, and very expensive. She borrowed the money she needed from her former boss, an uptight jerk named Jeremy Mead who Ross suspected wanted to ball her. Then she had Ross photographed by the Pacific Ocean in just faded Levi cut-offs and a smile. And she had the picture blown up and placed on as many billboards as she could afford all across America, with just the words – 'WHO IS ROSS CONTI?'

It was magic time. Within weeks everyone was asking, 'Who is *Ross Conti?' Johnny Carson began making cracks on his show. Letters started to arrive by the sackload, addressed to Ross Conti, Hollywood. (Sadie had prudently informed the post office where to forward them.) Ross was stopped in the street, mobbed by adoring women, recognized wherever he went. The whole thing took off like a rocket just as Sadie had predicted it would.*

At the peak of it all Sadie flew with her now famous client to New York, where he had been invited to do a guest appearance on The Tonight Show. They were both ecstatic. New York gave Ross the feel of what it would be like to be a star. Sadie was thrilled that it was she who had done it for him.

He was marvellous on the show – funny, sexy, and magnetically attractive. By the time they got back to Hollywood the offers were piling up. Sadie sifted through them and finally negotiated an ace three picture deal for him with Paramount. He never looked back. Success as a movie star was instantaneous.

Six months later he dumped her, signed with a big agency and married Wendy Warren, a rising young star with impressive thirty-nine inch breasts. They lived together in much photographed luxury on top of Mulholland Drive, five minutes from Marlon Brando's retreat. Their marriage lasted only two years and was childless. After that Ross became the *Hollywood bachelor. Wild stories, wild pranks, wild parties.*

Everyone was delighted when in 1964 he married again. This time to a Swedish starlet of seventeen with, of course, wonderful tits. The marriage was stormy. Lasted six months. She divorced him claiming mental cruelty and half his money. Ross shrugged the whole thing off.

At that time his star was at its peak. Every movie he appeared in was a winner. Until 1969, when he made two disastrous films in a row.

A lot of people were not sorry to observe his fall from superstardom. Sadie La Salle for one. After his defection from her loving care she had faded from sight for a while, but then she had resurfaced and slowly but surely built herself an empire.

Ross met Elaine when he went for a consultation with her husband. At thirty-nine he thought that maybe he needed a little face work. He never got the surgery, but he did get Elaine. She moved in on him without hesitation, and she was just what he needed at that time in his life.

He found her sympathetic, supportive and an excellent listener. The tits were nothing to get excited about, but in bed she was accommodating and warm, and after the aggression of the usual Hollywood starlet he liked that. He decided that marriage to Elaine was just what he needed. It did not take a lot of persuasion for her to divorce her husband. They married a week later in Mexico, and his career took a sharp upwards swing. It stayed up for five years, then slowly, gradually, it began to slip. And so did their marriage.

* * *

Forty-nine. Heading full speed towards fifty. And he didn't look a day over forty-two. The blond boyish good looks had aged nicely. Although he could do without the greying hair that had to be carefully bleached, and the deep indentations under his piercing blue eyes.

Still . . . he was in excellent shape. The body was almost as good as new. He stared at his reflection, hardly hearing the discreet knock on the door.

'Yes?' he called out, when the knock was repeated.

'Room service,' crooned a feminine voice.

Room service was twenty-five and stacked. Ross made a mental note to tip the bell captain royally.

Chapter Two

'He was never a normal boy, Deke Andrews wasn't, always a strange one.'

'Yeah? How so?'

'You know . . . Not interested in television, movies or girls. Not like the other kids round this street – even when he was growin' up.'

'What *was* he interested in?'

'Cars. First job he got he went right out and put a down payment on an old Mustang. Loved that car. Polished it, tuned it, worked on that old jalopy for hours on end.'

'What happened to it?'

'Got sold. Don't know why. He never did get another one.'

'You sure about that?'

'Sure about what?'

'That he never got another car.'

' 'Course I'm sure. I know everything goes on in Friendship Street. I've sat lookin' out this same window for thirty years. Did I tell you 'bout my accident? Had heavy machinery collapse on my legs. I ain't never walked a step since. Compensation? You think I got money? I got *nothing* for all the stinkin' time I put in at that lousy plant. Have you any idea . . .' The old man went red in the face as his voice rose and shook with anger.

Detective Leon Rosemont rubbed the bridge of his large

nose and stared at a cheap framed print on the wall. Who could ever figure people out? This old man was more interested in what had happened to him thirty years previously than what had happened only hours before in the house across the street. As a witness he was useless. He had heard nothing. Seen nothing. Knew nothing.

Soon the newspapers would be screaming their banner headlines. SAVAGE TRIPLE KILLING. MURDER HORROR IN SUBURBIA. BLOOD MASSACRE. How the press loved a good juicy mass murder. Three people brutally murdered in a small house on Friendship Street in a respectable suburb of Philadelphia. Jesus! How he wished he could wipe the morning's carnage from his mind. Bile rose in his throat, and he swallowed it down sharply.

Detective first grade Leon Rosemont. A heavy-set man in his early fifties, broad shouldered and powerfully built, with a mass of thick grey hair, shaggy eyebrows, and sharp, kindly brown eyes. He looked like an out-of-condition football star. And that's exactly what he had been in college – the hero of the field. He had been twenty-nine years on the force. Twenty-nine years of mutilations, sex killings and vicious slayings.

How he hated all the shit that came his way.

They gave all the pretty ones to him, but this was the prettiest in a long while. Three people hacked to pieces for no apparent reason. No sexual assault. No robbery. No nothing. And not a good goddamn thing to go on. Except maybe Deke Andrews, the son of the household who seemed to be missing.

So – was this just another nice old-fashioned family murder?

Deke Andrews wasn't around to tell. But then perhaps he was away on a trip, staying with friends, or shacked up with some girl. After all, it was only Saturday afternoon, and according to forensic the killings could have taken place any time between eleven p.m. Friday and four a.m. Saturday.

Deke Andrews. Twenty-six years old. A loner who kept to himself.

But then how many people had been questioned about him? Four? Five? The investigation hadn't even started yet. These were early days.

'Niggers!' the old man stated fiercely. 'They're causin' trouble all over.'

'What?'

'It's these niggers moved in down the street. I wouldn't be surprised if they did it,' he snorted. 'I keep my doors locked now – not like the old days – why I can remember when you didn't hafta *have* locks.'

Detective Rosemont nodded curtly. There was a sour taste in his mouth, and the memory of the early morning tableau danced horrifically before his eyes. His head ached, his lips were parched and his eyes felt sunken and dry. He wished he was at home in bed with his wife, sweet black Millie, and wouldn't *that* give this old bigot something to think about.

'They should stay on South Street where they belong,' muttered the old man ominously. 'Comin' to live among decent folk. It ain't right, there should be a law . . .'

Detective Rosemont pushed himself heavily out of the overstuffed armchair he was sitting in and headed towards the door. Screw it. He was beginning to feel suffocated. 'Thank you, Mr Bullen,' he said tightly. 'We'll be needing a formal statement of course. One of my men will be back later —'

'Niggers!' screeched the old man hysterically, warming to his subject. 'They shoulda been left in Africa runnin' around naked. That's what I think. That's what all decent folk think.'

Angrily Leon Rosemont let himself out of the small house. It was raining, a bleak relentless drizzle. The television trucks were blocking the end of the street, and some ghoulish sightseers huddled in a group behind a police barricade. What did they come for? What was so exciting about the outside of a house where violent deaths had occurred? *Just what the hell did they expect to see?*

He shook his head. People. He would never understand them.

Grimly he pulled up the collar of his old English raincoat and hurried across the street.

In all his years of hard grind service he had never had to deal with a murder case where he knew one of the victims. This was a horrible sickening first. And in a chilling way he wondered if any of the guilt was his . . .

Chapter Three

Montana Gray gazed at her husband, Neil, as he studied himself in the dressing room mirror of their Coldwater Canyon house. His obsession with his appearance whenever he wore a suit amused her. She waited patiently for the inevitable question.

He did not disappoint. 'Do I look alright?' he asked, quite secure in the fact that he looked fine, but anxious for her approval anyhow.

She grinned. 'How come you're always so insecure when you know you look terrific?'

'Me? Insecure. Never,' he replied, sounding more like Richard Burton than the original article. 'I merely enjoy your praise.'

She loved his English accent, it had always been a turn-on. 'Hmmm . . .' She regarded him quizzically. 'Later – in bed – I'll praise you 'til your hair stands on end.'

'Only my hair?' he mocked.

'And anything else you can think of.'

'Oh, I'll think of something.'

She laughed. 'I'm sure you will, not only are you the greatest movie director around, but your imagination ain't bad either!'

He grabbed her and they began to kiss.

Montana was twenty-nine. Neil fifty-four. During a year of living together and four years of marriage the twenty-five year age gap had never bothered either of them, although it still bothered a lot of other people. Neil's ex-wife, Maralee. Some of his friends, and *all* of their wives.

'Hey.' Gently she pushed him away. 'We have a whole bunch of guests anxiously awaiting our illustrious presence at the Bistro. We'd better shift ass.'

He sighed theatrically.

'Don't go giving *me* any heavies about tonight. This whole celebration bit was *your* idea, Neil.'

He mock bowed and ushered her to the door. 'Well madam, in that case let us – as you so succinctly put it – shift ass!'

* * *

Montana. Five feet ten inches tall. Waist length black hair. Direct gold-flecked tiger eyes. A wide sensual mouth. An unusual and striking beauty.

Montana. Named for the state she was born in by parents who were unconventional to say the least. Her father was a geologist. Her mother a folk singer. They both loved to travel, and by the time Montana was fifteen she had been around the world twice, had two short affairs, spoke fluent French and Italian, could water ski, snow ski and ride horses like a cowboy.

Her parents were strong, independent people who instilled in their only child a fun sense of confidence and self-worth. 'Believe in yourself and you can do anything,' her mother often said.

'Never be frightened in life,' was her father's motto. 'Face whatever comes your way with dignity and strength.'

It was alright for them, they had each other, and although they loved her very much, she often felt like an intruder, so when they finally decided to settle down on a ranch in Arizona, she knew the time had come to move out into the world on her own. She took off with their blessing and a small amount of money to keep her going. It was 1971, she was seventeen years old and filled with all the energy and enthusiasm of extreme youth.

First she went to stay with an older cousin in San Francisco.

He gave her pointers on sex, drugs and rock 'n' roll and left her to her own devices. She was inquisitive and anxious to learn, trying out a series of jobs – everything from waitressing to making silver jewellery and selling it on the street.

This kept her busy until she met a rock musician who talked her into India and meditation. They ended up in Poona, sitting at the feet of the celebrated guru, Rajneesh. She tired of this sooner than her companion, and travelled on to London alone, where she stayed with friends in Chelsea, mixing with photographers, models and writers. She tried a little of everything until eventually she moved to New York with a radical journalist and began to do what she had decided really interested her most of all – writing. The pieces she turned out were both cynical and stylish, and it wasn't long before she developed a name for herself, and a regular page in Worldly, *an avant garde magazine. It was on a working trip to Paris that she first met Neil.*

A party on the Left Bank. Crowded. Noisy. Montana arrived with a sometime boyfriend – Lenny. Neil was already there, stoned on a mixture of Jack Daniels and Acapulco Gold. A wasted looking man with intense eyes, a well lived in face, and a mass of unruly greying hair, he was sitting in a corner holding court while a group of admirers hung on to his every word.

'You know – I really want to meet that guy,' Lenny said. 'He's better than Altman.'

'Nobody's better than Altman,' she replied dismissively, heading in the direction of friends.

It was hours later when she finally wandered over to the group still gathered around Neil Gray. Lenny introduced her.

By this time Neil was so drunk he could hardly speak. But he did manage, 'What kind of a bullshit name is Montana?'

She ignored him, smiled sweetly at Lenny and said, 'Let's split.'

Two days later, while browsing magazines in the American Drug Store on the Champs Elysées, a voice said, 'Montana. What kind of a bullshit name is that?'

She turned, and for a moment did not remember him. Then he breathed whisky fumes in her face and she recalled the party.

'Want to have a drink?' he asked.

'Not particularly.'

Their eyes locked and for a brief moment something sparked. She was intrigued enough to change her mind, although older men had never been her scene.

He took her to a bar where he was obviously a regular patron, and proceeded to get totally smashed. Before doing this he impressed her with sharp, knowledgeable and witty conversation, and she began to wonder why he had this need to obliterate the present.

She took the trouble to find out more about him. He was a complex man bent on self-destruction. A talented director, he had alienated many people along the way with his drinking and erratic behaviour, and he was now reduced to shooting television commercials for large sums of money which he used to support his ex-wife, Maralee, who lived in great style in Beverly Hills.

In Paris he seemed to enjoy his celebrity, starting off each day sober, but by early afternoon becoming hopelessly drunk.

Montana postponed her return to New York and began spending more and more time with him. Neil Gray was a challenge, and that excited her. Her father would have said she had the hots for him. Sex had always been a very open subject when she was growing up, and the only advice her parents had ever given her on the subject was to do whatever she felt was right. Something told her that Neil Gray was right, although he made no move to get her into bed, which intrigued her even more. She finally invited herself, and to his drunken amusement he couldn't get it up.

Montana did not find this funny. She thought that maybe the time had come to do something about Mister Neil Gray, so she hired a car, borrowed a friend's chateau in the country, and persuaded him to spend the weekend. He agreed, expecting a two day binge of booze and fun.

The chateau was isolated and empty, Montana had made sure it housed no spirits. She hid the keys of the car, pulled the connection on the phone, and kept him there for three delirious weeks. Well, after the first few days it was delirious, when she calmed him, stopped his furious ravings, and finally got him into bed in *a sober state. He was a devastating lover when he didn't have alcohol slowing him down. No young stud, but a man who she felt very comfortable with indeed.*

By the time they returned to Paris they had both decided togetherness was the name of the game. They stayed in Paris for only a few months. By that time Montana managed to convince Neil he was wasting his talent, and he finally agreed to return to America. Word was out he was sober and straight, and by the end of their first year together, he was back in action shooting a low-budget thriller movie on the streets of New York. The film was a mild hit, and once more Hollywood beckoned. They headed west. 'You'll hate *Beverly Hills,' he warned her. 'There's more shit per square inch than a sewage plant.'*

She grinned and busied herself with her own projects. She had an idea for a television series, and there was a book she wanted to write about Hollywood in the thirties. Neil encouraged her all the way. He also insisted that they get married. She would have been happy leaving things the way they were, but he was not prepared to risk losing her. She was special. She had dried him out, got him working again, and given him a whole new outlook on life.

They got married in Hawaii, and from then on commuted between a permanent suite at the Beverly Wilshire Hotel and a New York apartment.

Montana wrote her television series – which was quite successful. She collaborated on the book about Hollywood, and drawn towards the movies, she wrote, produced and directed on offbeat, short film about children in the Watts area of Los Angeles. It won two awards.

Neil was proud of her accomplishments, he had more than encouraged her on the next project she became involved in – a gritty screenplay titled 'Street People' *which she wrote in six weeks flat. When he first read the script he was thrilled. As a director he felt it had the potential to be an exciting and important movie. And he knew at once that he wanted to do it. He was hot again due to the fact that his previous two movies had made money, and several studios were ready to back anything he cared to do. But he wanted control, so after discussing it with Montana, he took the script to Oliver Easterne Productions. Oliver was a snake, but Neil knew he would give them the deal they were after.*

Now everything was agreed, and as of that very morning contracts were signed.

It was an excellent deal. Total artistic control – which meant that no one could mess with Montana's script or with what Neil planned on putting up there on the screen. As long as they stayed under budget and on schedule, no interference from anyone. They were both delighted.

Final cut. Total control. *Magic words, and now a special dinner to announce the project to their friends.*

* * *

Montana stared moodily out of the car window as three hours later they drove home. As far as she was concerned, the entire evening had been one big waste of time. Friends. She could manage quite nicely without them thank you very much. As long as she had Neil of course, because *he* didn't give a damn about anybody, and she admired that quality in a town full of ass kissers. In fact it was one of the qualities that had attracted her to him in the first place.

'Cigarette?' He shook one out of the pack while he guided his red Maserati across Santa Monica, up Beverly towards Sunset.

She accepted it without a word, and thought yet again about the reaction to their news from Neil's so-called friends. They had all said, 'Wonderful!' 'Congratulations!' Then one by one they got their little digs in.

Bibi Sutton, *the* social pacesetter of Beverly Hills. Chic, French wife of one of filmland's biggest stars, Adam Sutton. 'Sweetie? Neil? He *really* do film *you* wrote?' Her obvious amazement was hardly disguised.

Chet Barnes, a talented screen writer with two Oscars to prove it. 'Writing for movies is a very specialized art, Montana.

It's not like hacking it out for T.V.' *And fuck you too, Mr Barnes.*

Gina Germaine, thirtyish sex symbol trying to be taken seriously and looking like an overgrown Barbie Doll. 'Did you have a ghost writer, Montana? You can confide in me, I won't tell. As a matter of fact I do a little writing myself . . .'

And so on and so on. One crack after another. People were just plain jealous, and that was the truth. Good looking women had roles in life and they were supposed to stick to them. They could be movie stars, models, housewives, hookers, but God forbid they should skirt onto what was strictly regarded as Big Boy's Territory. Writing a major movie for a major director was Big Boy's Territory. And in their own pretty little way everyone wanted to let her know that. She felt soured by their jealousy. But then, what had she expected?

'Sometimes I hate people!' she exploded.

Neil laughed. 'Don't waste your energy, my love.'

'But they were all so—'

'Envious.'

'You noticed it too?'

'I could hardly help it. Karen Lancaster kept on asking me to admit that I wrote the bloody movie myself.'

'That spoiled bitch!'

'And then Chet insisted on telling me I'd ruin my career. Oh, and even Adam Sutton wanted to know why I was helping you this way.'

'Christ! Friends!'

He took his hand from the steering wheel and patted her on the knee. 'I told you when I first brought you here never to take any of them seriously. Hollywood's a funny town with funny rules. You break them all.'

'I do, huh?'

'Most certainly.'

'How?'

'Well . . . let's see now. You don't shop on Rodeo Drive. You don't give catered parties. You don't lunch with the girls.

You don't employ a maid. You don't have impeccable fingernails. You don't gossip. You don't spend my money at a speed faster than sound. You don't—'

She held up her hand, still laughing. 'Enough already! Let's go home and make out.'

'*And* you don't wait to be asked.'

Her hand slid across the gear lever and settled on his crotch. 'Aren't *you* the lucky one.'

The Maserati swerved across the street. 'Who, my love, is arguing?'

* * *

Montana slept soundly as Neil crept quietly from their bed early in the morning. He found that the older he got the less sleep he needed, so he showered, did a few half-hearted push ups, then walked out to the patio and admired the view. When the smog wasn't in action you could see for miles, sometimes as far as the ocean. It was one of the main reasons they had purchased the house several months previously. A lot of people put Los Angeles down – but Neil had a genuine love for the city. Born and raised in England, he found he never missed the place. America was his home, and had been for over twenty years.

* * *

Neil Gray first came to Hollywood in 1958. He was a young brash director who thought he knew it all. The studio who brought him over after his first big English film treated him royally. A bungalow at the Beverly Hills Hotel, a parade of beautiful starlets, and an endless expense account.

The movie he made for them died at the box office. A woman slapped him with a paternity suit which he hotly denied, and, suitably chastised, he fled back to England.

However, American fever was in his blood, he wanted more,

and early in the sixties he returned to Hollywood – this time with no studio to back him. He rented a room at the Chateau Marmont, a modest old-fashioned hotel above the Strip. There he tried to get a script he had optioned off the ground. The going was hard, until one day, round the pool, he quite literally bumped into Maralee Sanderson. She was a pretty, spoiled teenager whose mother had died when she was fourteen, and who had been raised by her father, Tyrone, the founder of Sanderson Studios. At the time Maralee was having an affair with a New York method actor, but she took an immediate fancy to Neil and switched affections. He had no choice. What Maralee wanted – she got. Besides, he was flattered. She was young, gorgeous and rich. And daddy owned a studio. What more could an out-of-work film director want?

'Daddy'll put up the money for your movie,' she remarked casually one day. 'If I ask him, that is.'

'What the hell are you waiting for?' he yelled.

'A little thing called marriage,' she replied innocently.

Marriage. The very word scared him. He had tried it once at nineteen and found it sadly lacking. But now . . . seventeen years later . . . many women later . . . much booze later . . .

Marriage. He thought about it for a week. Then decided why not? It was about time he took the big step again, and besides, it seemed to be the only surefire way to get his movie off the ground.

An inner voice nagged him constantly: 'What about integrity? Making it on your own? Love?'

Fuck it – he thought. I want to make this film. I want a little clout in this town. Fuck it.

'Yes,' he told Maralee.

'Good,' she replied. 'Daddy wants to meet you.'

Tyrone Sanderson had not got where he was by charm. He was short and thick set. He smoked outsize cigars and favoured starlets with outsize attributes. He was desperate to marry his daughter off. She had bedded half of Hollywood but Neil Gray was the first man she had shown any permanent interest in.

'You wanna do a movie – do it,' Tyrone growled at their first meeting.

'I have a script for you to read—'

'Who reads? Do it.'

'Aren't you interested in what it's about?'

'I'm interested in you marrying my daughter. Period.'

Maralee and he were married on the terrace of Tyrone's Bel Air estate two weeks later. Most of the big names in Hollywood attended the wedding. They honeymooned in Acapulco, and returned to live on Rodeo Drive in the house daddy bought them as a wedding present. Neil went straight to work.

His first film was a success, both artistically and financially. From being referred to as just 'the son-in-law' he became the new wonder kid in town. Every studio was after him, and since Tyrone Sanderson had not signed him to a contract he was free to do whatever he wanted.

'You have to stick with daddy,' Maralee insisted. 'He gave you your first chance.'

'Screw daddy,' Neil replied. 'I took *my first chance, he never* gave *me anything.'*

Neil made a succession of hot movies, while Maralee indulged in a succession of hot affairs. Neil drank, Maralee spent money.

Then came the flops. Suddenly Neil was bad news. He took off for Europe after a major fight with Maralee which ended when she summoned her father to the house. 'If you bring him into our life it's over,' he threatened.

'So goodbye,' she snapped. 'You no-talent-pain-in-the-ass-English-has-been!'

Montana turned up at just the right moment.

Divorcing Maralee had not been easy. Although she didn't want him, she didn't want to not have him either.

The divorce was messy and expensive. But worth every cent.

* * *

Neil gazed out at the sweeping view and thought about Montana. She was strong, intelligent and sensual. And he had been faithful to her for longer than he had ever thought possible. But in the last year he had disgusted himself with the occasional bird brain he took to bed. Fluffy blondes with low I.Q.s.

If Montana ever found out she would walk, just like that. He knew his wife.

So why did he do it? He honestly didn't know. Maybe the risk element was exciting. Or the fact that sometimes he felt the need to have a woman underneath him who wasn't his equal. A full breasted piece – who was just that – a piece. No conversation. No intellectual meeting of the minds. Just a lay.

Not that Montana wasn't the best. In bed she was as stimulating as ever. But she was always his equal and sometimes he felt this burning desire to bed a woman who wasn't. Sometimes all he wanted was a hot impersonal uninvolved fuck. He was fifty-four years old. Life goes on and you never learn a goddamn thing.

He left the patio and went indoors to the kitchen where he fixed himself a cup of tea and a dish of cereal.

Gina Germaine. Fluffy. Blonde. Dumb. And worse. A movie star.

He had bedded her twice and was going back for more. It was madness, but he couldn't help himself.

Chapter Four

Getting lost in the city of New York was no problem for Deke. Burying his anger in a small room in the Village. Thinking. Brooding. Working things out.

Got a job. Changed his name.

No sweat.

Altered his appearance. It was easy. A pair of scissors was all it took to cut off his shoulder length hair. A barber finished the job, shearing his scalp until all that remained was a light sprouting – less than a crew cut – more like a delousing.

Could not do anything about the eyes. They burned black and angry in a pale nondescript face.

He was tall, thin, built like a million other young men who wore the uniform of Levis, shirt and lumber jacket.

He was obsessively tidy. Everything in his room was neat. Not that there was much to mess up: when he left Philadelphia he had taken nothing except a small carryall.

He worked in a seedy hotel in Soho. The afternoon shift – twelve noon until six p.m. He sat behind a desk and handed out room keys to a strange assortment of customers. Visitors to the city with an obvious lack of money, hookers, eccentrics, businessmen who didn't want to be seen on an afternoon tryst with their secretaries.

For the first six weeks he took a regular trip to the newstand in Times Square which carried the Philadelphia papers. Back in his room his eyes devoured the newsprint from front to back, missing nothing. When he was finished he neatly clipped out all the stories on the Friendship Street murders and studied them intently. Finally, when he was satisfied that he was missing no details of the investigation, he hid the news clips between the pages of a racing auto magazine which he then stuffed under his mattress.

Gradually the stories petered out. After all, there was nothing *that* sensational about the case. An ordinary middle aged couple. Mr and Mrs Willis Andrews. Who cared? Joey Kravetz. A tough street tramp who had been in and out of reform school since she was fourteen. Who cared?

THE POLICE WOULD LIKE TO INTERVIEW DEKE ANDREWS. THE ANDREWS' TWENTY-SIX YEAR OLD SON WHO HAS BEEN MISSING SINCE THE DAY OF THE CRIME.

How polite.

DETECTIVES ARE URGENTLY SEEKING DEKE ANDREWS, LONG HAIRED SON OF THE SLAUGHTERED COUPLE.

Less polite.

THIS MONSTER MUST BE FOUND.

A woman writer of course.

NO LEADS ON THE WHEREABOUTS OF DEKE ANDREWS. POLICE ARE BAFFLED.

He allowed himself a smile at *that* one.

New York was perfect. The streets had accepted him and swallowed him up just like one of its own. He could relax and go about his business.

And soon he would be ready to make his next move.

Chapter Five

The Safeway supermarket on Santa Monica Boulevard was packed. Angel Hudson selected a cart and gave a little sigh as she glanced at the long lines waiting at each checkout.

A boy, busy packing groceries into strong brown bags, could not take his eyes off her. She had that effect on the male sex. Even gays couldn't resist checking her out.

Angel certainly was something. Nineteen years old. Five feet five inches of smooth creamy skin, long lashed aquamarine eyes, small straight nose, full pink lips, natural long blonde hair, rounded breasts, a handspan waist, narrow rear, and endless legs. There was nothing trampy or obvious about her startling good looks.

As usual she wore very little make-up, and a simple outfit of pink sweater and baggy white overalls. It did not stop the stares.

Slowly she guided her cart down the crowded aisles, stopping occasionally to check out the price on certain items. Hmmm, she thought, Safeway or not everything sure costs a lot. All she had was thirty-five dollars, and that was supposed to keep her and Buddy going for a week. She smiled when she thought of him. She blushed when she thought of them in bed together that very morning. His hands everywhere . . . His tongue exploring hidden places . . .

Thinking about him gave her the shivers. He was so

wonderful and worldly. So good looking. She shivered again. He was her husband and had been for two great and glorious days.

'Hi,' a voice said.

She glanced up at a muscled man in a red open-neck shirt and carefully pressed pants.

'Didn't we meet the other night at a party?' he questioned, edging round the side of her cart until he was standing quite close.

'I'm sorry,' she said quickly, 'but I only got into town yesterday.'

Now why was she apologizing? Buddy had told her about it a hundred and one times. *Don't go around saying sorry to everyone. You gotta learn to be more aggressive in life.*

'Well . . .' the man said, 'if you only got into town yesterday maybe I can buy you dinner tonight. Whaddya say to that?'

'I'm sor—' she began, then quickly stopped herself.

'I'm married,' she stated primly.

He laughed suggestively. '*I* don't mind if *you* don't.'

Why did they always have to pick on her? Ever since she could remember strange men had been sidling up and talking to her. On the street. At the movies. On the bus. She pushed the cart firmly down the aisle hoping to lose him, but he followed, mumbling one or the other of a hundred lines.

She stopped and fixed him with her devastating eyes. 'Please leave me alone,' she murmured softly. 'I told you, I'm married. My husband wouldn't like you talking to me. He wouldn't like it one little bit.'

She had not meant it as a threat. But it seemed to work, and the man retreated.

She had not lied. Buddy did hate other men looking at her. If he only knew how they approached her all the time he would go crazy. But it wasn't *her* fault was it? She gave them no come on. Never wore form-fitting clothes or short skirts. She kept herself to herself and could not remember ever having given any man an inch of encouragement. Buddy was the first man who had ever done more than kiss her goodnight. And that was only since their marriage. Instinctively she had known it was right to wait, and Buddy's appreciation on their wedding night had been worth all the slapped hands and frustrations of her past. How very lucky she was to have found him, he was a man in a million.

'Excuse me, miss,' mumbled a tall gangly boy in a torn baseball shirt, 'but I think you dropped these.'

She stared blankly at the box of crackers he held out. 'I'm sorry, they're not mine,' she apologized.

'No? I thought I saw them drop off your cart.'

'Sorry.'

He nervously scratched at a pimple. 'If I get in front of you in the line I can help you take all your junk out to your car.'

'No, thank you.' She moved quickly down the aisle. Safeway was teeming with them. Maybe next time Buddy would come with her.

* * *

Frances Cavendish leaned back in the chair behind her modern chrome desk and sucked greedily on a joint cunningly fitted into a roach holder. She held the rich smoke down in her lungs for a count of ten, then exhaled with a deep sigh of obvious satisfaction. She did not offer the contraption to Buddy Hudson, who slouched moodily on the other side of the desk, uncomfortable on a small straight-back chair.

'You've got your goddamn nerve walking in here,' she said.

'Huh?'

'Don't act like you don't know what I'm talking about. I got you that T.V. pilot, and with the help of that old crone you were shacked up with you blew the whole thing.'

'Hey, Frances. That was then. Now I need a job. I really do. I just got married.'

'Sorry, Buddy.' She waved her hand dismissively. 'But you must know how it is right now. Things are tight. I can't help you.'

She could help him if she wanted to. She was one of the most powerful casting agents in town.

'Hey – Frances,' he wheedled. 'You gonna tell me you haven't got *anything*? This is Buddy Boy you're rappin' with. I thought we had somethin' special.'

Frances picked up a pair of rhinestone trimmed glasses and perched them on her long pointed nose. 'Didn't you just tell me you got married?'

'Yeah, I told you that.'

'Well, dear boy, I do think that makes a difference to our . . . relationship. Don't you?'

What relationship? He had escorted her to a few events. She had thrown a little work his way. It wasn't like he had ever balled her.

'Why?' he demanded sulkily, wishing he had never told her.

She glared at him. 'I haven't seen you for eight months. Then you just amble in here and casually announce you're married. What makes you think I should give *you* special treatment?'

He stood. 'So don't.'

She took off her glasses and narrowed flinty eyes. Buddy Hudson was the best looking male animal she had seen in months. It would be a shame to just let him walk out. 'I can send you up for a commercial,' she sighed.

'Shit! I don't want to do any more commercials. I've been in Hawaii for six months singing up a storm – they couldn't get enough of me there. What I want now is a classy guest shot on some television show. Little acting, little singing, I'll knock 'em on their fat cat asses.'

Frances picked up a pen and tapped it impatiently on her desk. 'You want to go for a commercial or not?'

He thought about his situation. Two hundred bucks to his name, a beat up old Pontiac, and a one room apartment off the Strip he had borrowed from a friend.

Some situation. And a wife of two days named Angel. Beautiful, soft, innocent, and all his. He had brought her back from Hawaii like a conquering hero. She thought he was a successful actor with jobs just lining up for him. Wouldn't do to disillusion her so early on in their married life.

'Yeah, I'll go,' he decided.

She scribbled something on a card and handed it to him. 'Four o'clock tomorrow, don't be late.'

He glanced at the card, then back at her. 'Frances,' he said, 'Aren't you at least going to give me a toke?'

* * *

Angel sang softly to herself as she unpacked the groceries. She could hardly believe how happy she was. So much had happened in such a short period of time. And everything had fallen into position perfectly.

To think – that only a year and a half earlier she had graduated from high school in Louisville, Kentucky, gotten a job as a receptionist in a beauty salon, and one idle day entered a competition in a movie magazine. In her wildest dreams she had never imagined winning. But she had, and the prize was a thousand dollars and a week's paid trip to Hollywood with a companion.

* * *

Hollywood. *A magic place Angel had only ever read about.* Hollywood. *A dream come true!*

Without hesitation she packed a bag and headed west with her best girlfriend, Sue-Ann. Taking off was no problem. Angel was a foster child in a large family, and the extra space in the small house they all shared was more than welcome.

A week in Hollywood at the Hyatt Hotel on the famous Sunset Boulevard. She and Sue-Ann barely had time to catch their breath. The magazine arranged for them to be photographed doing everything from exploring Disneyland to lunch with Burt Reynolds.

Burt Reynolds!! Angel thought she would faint. But he was very nice and made her laugh – even put his arms around her and Sue-Ann for a photo.

The week raced by, and when it was over she did not want to return to dull old Louisville. There were no real ties to pull her back. The family she lived with had never mistreated her, but she had always felt like an outsider, an intruder. Sometimes no more than just a maid. When she was growing, it had seemed natural to fetch and carry for everyone – but as she reached puberty and her beauty developed, it seemed she was resented more and more by the family.

Getting away had been on her mind for as long as she could remember, and this seemed like the perfect opportunity. 'I'm going to stay,' she told Sue-Ann, her eyes shining with the light of the converted. 'This is where I belong. I'm going to be an actress!'

Sue-Ann remonstrated with her friend, but to no avail. Angel had made up her mind. After all, every man she met in Hollywood had told her that she should be in the movies, so why not give it a try? She had the thousand dollar prize money, and if she was careful it should last her for several months at least.

First of all she needed somewhere to live, for she had no plans to waste money staying on at the hotel. The photographer gave her the phone number of a girl he knew who rented rooms. 'Call her,' he said, winking. 'An' don't forget, beautiful, if she's got no bed for you there's always a place in mine.'

She ignored his suggestive remark, called, and within an hour was installed in the back room of a large rambling house off Fairfax.

'Two minutes from May Co. an' a block from Farmers Market. How lucky can you get?' questioned the flashy redhead who rented out. 'You new in town, honey?'

She nodded. 'I'm going to be an actress.'

'Sure you are. An' the Pope got married yesterday.'

'What?'

'Forget it.'

Becoming an actress was not easy, but who had ever said it would be? First she found out that she needed photographs and an agent, and then Daphne, the redhead, told her, 'Ya gotta join some kinda stupid union. Sure ya wanna bother? There's easier ways of makin' a buck. A chick that looks like you . . .' She trailed off and stared.

Professional photographers cost a hundred dollars, although the photographer did suggest there were ways she could pay other than cash. She pretended she didn't know what he was talking about, but of course she did.

After visiting several agents she decided on a fatherly type with an office on Sunset. He seemed better than the younger ones who she instinctively knew would be trouble.

In six weeks he sent her on four interviews, none of them resulting in a job, but plenty of propositions. He then said he could get her the second lead in a porno movie, and she left his office in tears.

'Dirty old bastard,' Daphne sympathized. 'Tell you what, I'm gonna treat ya to a trip to Hawaii, all expenses paid.'

'What about your job?' Angel asked tentatively. Daphne had told her she was some kind of sales representative, always running off to appointments day and night.

'Screw the job. I need a vacation.'

Angel could hardly believe how lucky she was to have found a friend as nice as Daphne. What did it matter if she wore too much make-up and flashy clothes. She was a nice person. And anyway – the thought of visiting Hawaii was too tempting to turn down.

They arrived late at night after a turbulent flight. A twenty minute cab ride took them straight from the airport to the Hawaiian Village Hotel. Daphne, who had managed to consume quite a few drinks on the five hour journey, fell into a drunken sleep. Angel paid the cab fare and shook her awake, all the while staring around, her wide eyes taking in every new sight.

'Shit!' mumbled Daphne. 'We here already?'

Angel glanced at the cab driver to see if he had heard, but he stared impassively ahead.

They entered the lobby and approached the reception desk. 'You go in an' sit down while I register,' Daphne instructed.

She waited patiently, wishing that her friend didn't drink so much, maybe cut down on the swearing. Still . . . she wasn't in Louisville anymore . . . Daphne wasn't Sue-Ann. And it was so good to be out in the world and free.

'All set!' Daphne swooped down on her. 'Honey – I am one tired person, let's hit the old sack right away.'

The room was clean, with colour television, a view over the pool and a double bed. Angel hardly relished the thought of sharing. The heavy perfume Daphne wore failed to conceal the pungent body odour she exuded.

'Give the guy a tip,' Daphne ordered, indicating the bellboy who was placing their two suitcases on the floor.

Angel fished in her purse, thinking that her money was not lasting as long as she had hoped. Out of the thousand dollars she only had four hundred left. She gave the boy a dollar which didn't seem to thrill him.

By the time he was out of the room Daphne had stripped off her red dress and was heading for the bathroom clad only in a pair of brief purple panties.

Angel did not see how she could object to the double bed without feelings being hurt, so she gave a small sigh, opened up her suitcase and extracted the blue baby doll nightdress she had purchased at the May Co. Her one extravagance, but it was so pretty she had been unable to resist it.

Daphne emerged from the bathroom stark naked, and placed both hands on her hips while shimmying her large breasts. 'Not bad, huh? An' all mine, honey.'

Angel hurried into the bathroom where she showered, and pondered on the fact that maybe coming to Hawaii wasn't such a good idea after all.

Back in the bedroom all was quiet. Daphne was under the sheets and the lights were off. Angel crept into the other side of the bed, closed her eyes, and thought about her attempts at becoming an actress. She had to get a job to keep her afloat. Perhaps she could be a receptionist . . . in a film studio . . . or maybe Burt Reynolds needed a secretary . . . or Richard Gere . . . or . . .

At first, the hand creeping up her leg was just an irritation. She didn't realize what was happening until the hand dived between her thighs and suddenly Daphne was upon her, huge bosoms flopping in her face. 'Oh, no!' she gasped in horror. 'What are you DOING!'

'Well I ain't playin' tennis,' replied Daphne, trying to ease her fingers under the tight elastic of Angel's panties.

'Stop it! Stop it at once!' She kicked out.

'Oh. A playful chickie, huh? Tell you the truth, hon, I ain't averse to a few games myself.' The elastic tore, and Daphne's fingers were quick to touch the warm triangle of fluff.

'WILL YOU STOP IT!' screamed Angel, scrambling from the bed. 'What's the matter *with you?'*

'What's the matter with me*? Why the heck do you think I brought you to Hawaii?'*

'For . . . a . . . a . . . vacation,' she stammered shakily.

'For a fuck, sweetheart. For a little bit of soft pussy instead of hard cock. Makes a change, doncha know.'

Her hand flew to her mouth. 'Oh my God! I feel sick.'

'Go puke somewhere else,' blazed Daphne. 'You don't want to play – take your bag an' get the hell out of here.'

'But . . . but I've got nowhere to go.'

Daphne was not interested. 'Tough tit,' she spat.

Fifteen minutes later Angel stood forlornly in the lobby pleading with the surly desk clerk who told her repeatedly that there were no vacant rooms in the hotel.

Buddy Hudson, fresh from an energetic scene with an Australian tourist, could not help noticing the delectable blonde. He checked out women automatically, and this one was something. When she turned away from the reservation desk he moved right in. 'Trouble?' he questioned sympathetically.

She gazed at him and quite literally felt her legs go weak. 'Oh!' she murmured.

'Oh – what? Trouble or no trouble?' He had to have this one. She was Christmas six months early.

'I . . . er . . . I can't get a room here.' She couldn't stop staring. Buddy Hudson was the most handsome man she had ever seen. A combination of her two favourite movie stars – Richard Gere and John Travolta. But better than both of them, with tight black curly hair, smoky ebony eyes, and a body that was both muscular and thin. She gazed up at him; he was over six feet tall, and his very closeness made her feel small and helpless.

'Hey – hey. That's not good. Didn't you make a reservation in advance? This is tourist seasonville.'

'I did . . . but . . .' Her wide eyes brimmed with tears. 'I just had the most horrible experience.'

This was going to be easy. 'Want to talk about it?'

'I couldn't!'

'Sure you could. Talking always helps. Come on – I'll buy you a drink.' He guided her to a nearby lounge, where the waitress greeted him by name. 'What'll it be?' he asked, wondering how long it would take to get her into bed.

'A fruit punch, please.'

'With a shot of rum to liven it up?'

'Plain.'

He looked surprised. 'You don't drink?'

She shook her head.

'Smoke?'

Again she shook her head.

He wondered if he dared . . . No . . . Why even make a joke of it – they all did.

'So . . .' he began, 'tell me what happened. Some jerk giving you a hard time?'

She didn't know why she trusted him, she just did. Soon she was confiding everything – from the moment she first set foot in Hollywood to her recent vile scene with Daphne. 'I feel so . . . dirty. Can you imagine a girl *wanting to do something like that?'*

Could he imagine? Oh boy – if he only had a buck for all the chicks he'd watched making it together. This little fox was either putting him on or she was a real innocent. 'I got a bed you can use,' he remarked casually.

Quickly she remembered he was a man. And men only wanted One Thing. 'No thank you.'

He didn't push. Just said mildly, 'You have to park it somewhere for tonight.'

'No I don't. I'm going to the airport and waiting for a plane to Los Angeles.'

'That's the dumbest thing I ever heard.'

'Why?'

'Because, sugar, you are here on one of the most beautiful islands in the world. And I am not letting you go anywhere *until I have personally shown you around.'*

'But—'

He placed a finger on her lips. 'No buts. I have a friend who owns a small hotel. We'll get you a room there.'

'But—'

'Rule one. Never argue with Buddy Boy.'

Three weeks sped by, and true to his word Buddy showed her the island. Not only did he give her a guided tour of Honolulu, but another friend of his who operated a tourist shuttle plane took them on day trips to Maui, Lanai and Molokai.

They explored white deserted beaches, coral reefs alive with exotic tropical fish, rain forests, and the dramatic Paradise Park.

Angel had never felt so excited and alive. Buddy created feelings in her she had not known existed. Installed in a cosy room at his friend's hotel, she waited anxiously each day for him to pick her up. He tried a few times to have her spend the night at his place, but each time she explained very carefully that she wasn't 'that kind of girl'.

He laughed when she said that. But his laughter did not weaken her resolve. Although secretly she had to admit that she did *want him. She yearned for his hard strong body to possess her totally. When he kissed her goodnight it took every ounce of will power to push him away.*

Buddy sang in a piano bar. 'I'm really an actor,' he explained. 'But I needed a rest – so I left L.A. – an' I've been down here a few months. I was working nonstop in Hollywood. Y'know – movies, television shows. You name it, I've been on it.'

'Really?' Her eyes widened.

'Sure. Didn't you recognize me when we first met?'

She shook her head. 'I don't watch much television . . .'

'Ha! An' I thought that's why you let me talk to you in the first place. I'm famous, kid!'

He allowed her, only once, in the place where he worked. She sat at the bar gazing lovingly at him while he warbled everything from 'My Way' to 'Chicago'.

'They like the old fashioned stuff,' he explained rather sheepishly. 'My real bag's more Billy Joel and rock. But I gotta make a buck.'

One day, lying on a quiet beach, he rolled over on top of her and began kissing her harder and faster than he ever had before. 'You know you're drivin' me crazy,' he muttered. 'No way can I go on like this.'

She could feel his hardness digging into her thigh, and instinctively her body pushed towards his.

'Oh baby!' he mumbled, burying his head in her golden hair. 'Oh baby . . . baby . . . baby . . . I got to have you. You understand what I'm sayin'? Got to.'

She wanted him as much as he wanted her. He was everything she had ever dreamed of and more. He could be the family she had never had. Someone to care for . . . Someone who would look after her . . . Someone to belong to.

'We could get married,' she whispered timidly.

He backed off. Fast. Then later he reconsidered. So what was so terrible about marrying the most beautiful girl in the world? 'You got it, kid,' he told her, and a week later they were married. A simple ceremony. Buddy in a borrowed suit, and Angel in a white lace dress she purchased with the last of her money.

'You know what?' Buddy announced excitedly, the day after their wedding. 'We're headin' back to Hollywood. You and I kid – that's where we're both gonna make it so big they won't even know what's hit 'em!'

* * *

Dreamily Angel finished unpacking the groceries and hoped that Buddy would approve of what she was fixing for dinner. Hamburgers, green beans, baked potatoes and apple pie.

She smiled softly to herself and thought about *after* dinner. She and Buddy alone together . . . In bed together . . . making love together . . .

Thank you Daphne, for you changed my life and made me the happiest girl in the world!

* * *

Buddy was able to jazz Frances up to at least smiling before he left her office. She even let him have a couple of drags on her joint. Not enough to get him high – but who needed drugs with Angel in his life? Just looking at her gave him a shot of adrenaline – enough to take him right through the day with no trouble at all.

Who would have thought Buddy Hudson would ever get himself caught? Not him for sure.

Buddy Hudson. Answer to every girl's prayers. Stud. Hero. Superstar. Well jeez – if *he* didn't think positive who would? One of these days he'd make it . . . one of these days.

* * *

Buddy Hudson. Twenty-six years old. Brought up in San Diego by a mother who adored him, perhaps too much. She kept him by her side at all times and only relinquished her hold to allow him to attend school.

When he was twelve his father died, and although they were left in good financial shape his mother was distraught. 'You will have to look after mommy now,' she wailed. 'You must be my big big man.'

Young as he was her words frightened him. Her closeness was already oppressive, and now with his father gone it could only get worse.

It did. She insisted that he share her bed at night. 'I'm frightened,' was her excuse.

He hated the way she stifled him, and looked forward to school and a friend called Tony, who also had problems at home. The two of them fantasized about getting a little freedom. 'Why don't we make a break for it?' Tony suggested one day.

The idea appealed to Buddy. He was already fourteen, tall and well built, with a strong desire to get out into the world and see what was going on. 'Yeah,' he agreed. 'Let's do it.'

A few days later he borrowed twenty dollars from his mother's purse and during lunch recess he and Tony skipped out of school. They raced down the street laughing and yelling with relief.

'What shall we do?' Buddy asked.

Tony shrugged. 'I dunno. What'd'y' think we should do?'

Buddy shrugged. 'I dunno.'

Finally they decided on the beach and a movie. The beach was hot. The movie was The Thomas Crown Affair, *and Buddy fell in love with Faye Dunaway, and decided that if Steve McQueen could be an actor, why couldn't he? The seeds of ambition were firmly planted.*

They rolled out of the movie with no clear idea where to spend the night, and found themselves drifting down towards the harbour. Buddy thought about his mother alone in her big bed, and he wasn't sorry, just delighted that he had managed to escape.

They hung around outside a bar, bumming cigarettes from emerging sailors, until eventually an older man in civilian clothes approached them. 'You want to go to a party?' he asked, his small eyes darting shiftily this way and that.

Buddy looked at Tony, and Tony looked at him, and they both nodded enthusiastically.

'Follow me,' said the man, walking down the street to a large foreign car.

The two boys jumped obediently into the back seat.

'I think it's a Bentley,' Tony whispered.

'More like a Rolls Royce,' Buddy whispered back.

Now that the man had the boys in his car, he ignored them, and drove silently and swiftly. After about ten minutes Buddy leaned forward and tapped him on the shoulder. 'Excuse me, mister, where exactly is *this party?'*

The man braked sharply. 'If you want to get out say so now. Nobody's forcing you to go anywhere. Just remember that.'

The words made Buddy uneasy, he nudged Tony. 'Let's split,' he whispered.

'No,' argued Tony. 'We got nowhere else to go.'

Very true. Suddenly Buddy wished he was home. Only he couldn't lose face and let Tony know that.

Another ten minutes or so and they pulled into a private driveway, then finally slid to a stop in front of a brightly lit mansion. The drive was full of other expensive cars.

'Whew!' Tony whistled. 'Some place!'

'Follow me,' said the man, leading them through the front door into a spacious hallway. 'What are your names?' he hissed.

'I'm Tony, he's Buddy,' Tony replied amiably. 'And we're both real hungry. Any food?'

'Of course. All in good time. This way.'

He threw open the double doors of a sunken living room filled with people. The room was abuzz with conversation and the clink of glasses. They stood in the doorway until they were noticed and the noise tapered off.

'Gentlemen,' their escort announced formally. 'I'd like you to meet Tony and Buddy.'

Every eye in the room fixed upon them and there was a deathly silence for only a moment. 'No sailors, Freddie?' An effeminate voice broke the hush, and laughter filled the room. A short butterball of a man in a bright orange kaftan detached himself from a group and approached them holding out a bejewelled hand. 'Welcome to my party, boys. What can I get you?'

Tony took the fat man's hand. 'Food!' he said, grinning, loving every minute of their adventure.

Buddy still felt uneasy. If he had wanted out before, now he felt doubly so. However he was drawn into the room along with Tony, realizing it was too late to make an escape. Besides, when he got a load of the table full of delicious food he wasn't sure that he still wanted to.

They were given drinks. Not hard liquor, but frothy concoctions in tall glasses that tasted more like milk shakes than anything else. Then they were served plates of rich food. Everyone fussed around them – not like they were a couple of kids – but nicely – asking their opinion on this and that – filling their glasses whenever they were half full – and giving them cigarettes.

Buddy felt pretty good after a while.

'Here, try this.' Butterball passed him a different kind of cigarette.

He managed only a short drag before Tony grabbed it from his hand and said, 'Is that grass? Let me try it.'

Butterball smiled; he had sharp, ferret-like teeth. 'So try it.'

Tony pursed his lips and drew deeply on the cigarette. Then he began to cough frantically.

Butterball laughed aloud, and even the man who had picked them up allowed himself a smirk.

Tony's eyes narrowed as he dragged on the cigarette again, this time managing not to choke, holding the smoke in his lungs for a while then exhaling triumphantly.

'You learn fast,' murmured Butterball.

'Sure I do,' boasted Tony. 'What else you got for me to try?'

Butterball's eyes gleamed. 'Are you big enough to sample a little cocaine?'

'I'm big enough to sample anything!'

By this time Buddy was feeling distinctly sick. 'Gotta go to the bathroom,' he mumbled, staggering from the room. Nobody took any notice. Tony was the centre of attention as he prepared to snort the white powder Butterball was lining up on a glass table.

Buddy found the can and took an endless pee. The relief was great, but he still felt ill. He wandered into the hall and spotted an open window right at the back. What he needed was a few big gulps of fresh air. He opened the window wide and leaned out. Coordination deserted him, and before he knew what was happening he lost his balance and fell, landing hard on a patch of grass.

He remembered nothing more until awakening in the early hours of the next morning, the daylight harsh in his eyes, his body stiff and cramped. He had no idea where he was. Panic swept through him. His head throbbed and the taste in his mouth was disgusting. Desperately he tried to think as he stood up in the unkempt garden and looked around.

Tony. Me and Tony. Running away. The movies. The harbour. Man in car. Faggots. Food. Drink.

My mother will kill me. For sure she will kill me.

He brushed down his clothes and made his way around the front of the house. There were no cars in the driveway. The place was deserted, and in the revealing light of day it looked run-down and dilapidated, not at all the magnificent mansion of the previous evening.

Buddy frowned. The front door was locked, but he was able to peer through a window and was amazed to see the few pieces of furniture in sight covered with dust sheets. The place looked like nobody had lived there in months.

He hung around for a bit, hoping that Tony would show up, all the while skirting round the house searching for a place of entry. But everything was securely locked. Tony had obviously split – and why not? He probably thought that Buddy had run out on him.

Suddenly leaving home did not seem like such a smart idea anymore. Not when you were on your own, cold, tired and hungry. His mother would kill *him, but returning home did seem the only answer. He set off in what he hoped was the right direction.*

The events of the next twenty-four hours still haunted him. Sometimes he would wake in the middle of the night bathed in a cold clammy sweat, and the memories would be there – as sharp as if it had all happened the day before.

Arriving home. His mother hysterical. The police . . . Questions . . .

Tony's body had been thrown from a car in the Bay Area at five a.m. Battered, sexually abused, and very very dead.

The cops pounced on him as if he *had done it. He was taken to the police station and grilled continuously for seven straight hours, until his mother managed to drag him out of there with the help of the family lawyer.*

He was taken home, given a sedative and slept a straight ten hours. Then the cops were back, requesting that he guide them to the house where the party had taken place. He was driven round in a squad car for hours, but he couldn't remember where it was.

'Are you sure there was a party?' questioned a suspicious detective. 'Are you certain there was a house?'

After three fruitless hours they drove him back to the police station where he was given book after book of mug shots to look through. He didn't recognize one face.

Finally the detective decided he should see the body. Together they went to a cold tiled room that smelled of formaldehyde and death. The ghastly smell made Buddy's nostrils twitch and his stomach churn uneasily.

The detective was casually matter-of-fact as he instructed a white-coated pathology assistant to show them the body.

A steel locker in the wall was pulled out, and there lay Tony, naked and dead. His lifeless body covered with purple bruises and weals.

Buddy stared, unable to believe that he was being made to look. Then he started to cry, great racking sobs. 'I'm gonna throw up,' he mumbled. 'Get me out of here – please – get me away.'

The detective made no move. 'Take a good long look. That could've been you, boy. And don't you forget it.'

Buddy threw up all over the floor.

The detective gripped him by the arm. 'Let's go find that house. Maybe seeing your friend has jogged your memory.'

He was never able to locate the house, or identify any of the men at the party. Tony was buried, and after a flurry of outraged publicity the case faded from the headlines. Just another unsolved murder.

Only this particular unsolved murder changed Buddy's life. Whereas before, life with his mother had been smothering – now it was impossible. She did not leave him alone for a second, all the while smoothing his hair back, stroking his face, clinging to his hand.

He slept uneasily in her bed, keeping as far away as he could from her fussing petting hands.

She questioned him constantly. 'Did those men try to put their things near you?' 'Did they undress you?' 'You know it's not normal – two men together.'

How dumb did she think he was? He knew it wasn't normal. In fact he knew what was normal. He was beginning to eye the girls in class, and getting a hard-on just thinking about what he would like to do to them.

No chance, there was no escape from his mother. He couldn't even jerk off at home. He had to content himself with furtive sessions locked in the can at school with a faded Playboy centrefold for company.

By the time he reached fifteen he had his eye on a girl called Tina. He wanted to ask her for a date, but it was impossible. His mother allowed him no freedom, and when he complained, she just fixed him with a hurt expression, and mournfully said, 'Remember Tony?'

So it was down to grabbing what opportunities he could. Tina was not averse to his attentions. Buddy was certainly the best looking boy in school. They indulged in heavy petting sessions during lunch recess. Tina had pert breasts that he loved to feel, and in return she massaged him to orgasm on a pile of Kleenex. This all took place in the science lab, which was never used at that time of day.

'I think I love you, Buddy,' Tina sighed, after several months of this activity.

'I think I love you, too,' he dutifully replied, hoping that this meant she was finally going to let him do 'it'. He had her blouse and bra off, and now he fiddled with the catch on her skirt while she gazed passionately into his eyes.

Her skirt dropped to the floor and quickly she said, 'I've never done this before. Have you?'

'No,' he replied truthfully, rapidly pulling down her panties before she changed her mind.

'Oh!' She shivered. 'Take your clothes off too.'

He left in the early hours of the morning while she still slept. Only this time he was smart. He cleared her purse of two hundred dollars and took several pieces of expensive jewellery which she kept hidden.

This time he was really going. And no way was he ever coming back.

* * *

Outside Frances' office he extracted a wad of gum from his pocket and checked out a tall redhead walking into the building. An out of work actress, he could tell. They all had that same half-desperate look in their eyes as if they would do anything for a role. And most of them did.

He rolled the gum over his tongue, and walked slowly to the parking lot in back. Buddy had the perfect Hollywood stud walk – part Travolta in *Saturday Night Fever* – and part Gere in *American Gigolo*. He knew he looked great. He should – he worked hard to capture that lazy horny hip swaying thrust. He could have played the hell out of the guy in Gigolo. He had lived the part for Christ sakes. In the eleven years he had been on his own he had lived most parts.

'Hey – Buddy. How ya doin' man?' Quince, a black actor friend of his, slapped palms as they passed. 'Frances in a good mood today?'

Buddy shrugged. 'She's gettin' there – but I wouldn't do handstands.'

'When you get back, man?'

'A day or two ago.'

'So stay around – we'll share a cappuccino – I got a *wild* new fox nibblin' at my breakfast crunchies – one you gotta meet – a real peach. *And* she has a sister.'

'Some other time. I havta go see a guy about a T.V. series.'

'Sure, so like later. Give me a buzz and we'll get it together. Drop by Maverick's one night.'

'Yeah, I'd like that.'

They slapped palms once again and went their separate ways.

Buddy pulled up the collar on his leather jacket and headed for his car. Why hadn't he old Quince he was married? Why did he wish he hadn't told Frances? He wasn't regretting it was he?

Hell, no. But a guy had to promote a certain image, and *his* image was that of a sexy macho stud ready to do anything and go anywhere at a moment's notice.

Somehow a wife just didn't fit the picture.

He started the old car and tuned into a rock station. Angel was hardly a wife to be ashamed of. She was young, beautiful and *pure.* Kind of a funny word – but how else could you describe a girl like Angel? Most of the stuff runnin' around Hollywood was into everything and everyone by the time they hit twenty. Angel was different – but how to keep her that way in a town crawling with slimy creeps?

Right now that wasn't the problem. The immediate problem was scoring some bucks. Angel thought he was a winner – and no way was he going to let her think otherwise. Even if it meant falling back into bad habits – only on a temporary basis of course.

Buddy put his foot hard down on the accelerator and headed towards Beverly Hills.

Chapter Six

Millie Rosemont mumbled in her sleep, and threw her left arm restlessly across her husband.

Leon lay on his back and stared unseeingly at the ceiling. Carefully he moved his wife's arm and turned to look at her, willing her to wake up so that they could talk. She did not budge.

Silently he slid from the bed and padded into the kitchen where he opened the refrigerator and stared mournfully at the contents. Six eggs, a bowl of apples, some skim milk and a dish of cottage cheese. Some feast. But then he *was* supposed to be on a diet and Millie was only helping him keep to it.

Over a three month period he had put on twenty-four pounds. A steady two pounds a week. He felt big and ungainly, not to mention the fact that the waist on his pants had had to be let out three times, and his jackets and shirts were bursting at the seams.

It was Millie's fault. She was a sensational cook.

It was his fault. He ate like a pig – especially when he had something on his mind.

He took out the cottage cheese, a spoon from the drawer, and sat himself down at the kitchen table. There was no denying it. He *did* have something on his mind. The Friendship Street murders. Three people hacked to death in a small suburban house for no apparent reason. And one of those people was Joey Kravetz. Pathetic little Joey.

The newspapers had described her as 'beautiful teenage model'. But what did they know? If a victim was under thirty and female she was automatically described as beautiful. It made better headlines.

Model, my ass. And he should know. He felt the anger rising in him. Anger combined with the sense of frustration he felt every time he thought of Joey and her bloody mutilated body. Joey, who was only a kid . . .

He remembered their first encounter.

* * *

'Lookin' for some games, mister?'

Leon could not believe he was being propositioned. He glanced around, convinced the baby-faced hooker in the black fake-leather mini-dress and ridiculous high wedges was talking to someone else.

The street was deserted.

'How old are you?' he asked incredulously.

'Old enough!' She winked cheekily, and he noticed a distinct cast to her left eye. She couldn't be more than fifteen, sixteen at the most.

'So – waadya say, cowboy?' She placed her hands on her hips and grinned at him. 'I can show ya paradise!'

'And I can show you my I.D. I'm a detective.'

The grin faded from her face. 'A cop? Aw shee . . . t.' She cocked her head to one side. 'You're not gonna pull me in are ya? I mean we was just talkin'. I didn't offer you nothin'.'

'Where do you live?'

She wasn't sure if he was accepting her original offer or planning to book her. 'I gotta go,' she whined.

'You live with your parents?'

'I ain't got no parents, man. I'm eighteen. I can do what I want.'

'And I can take you to the station and have you for soliciting if I want.'

She stared down the street and contemplated making a run for it. But he was a big guy and would probably catch her, so she stuck a finger in her mouth and chewed on the nail. 'Tell ya what. I'll give ya a freebee,' she said after a moment or two.

He wondered if he should take her in. Not that rounding up under-age hookers was his job. But Jesus! He was a cop. You had to have some sense of responsibility, and she was only a child.

'I think you'd better come with me,' he said wearily, and gripped her by the skinny arm.

'Motherfucker!' She kicked him hard on the shin, wrestled her arm free and ran.

He rubbed his ankle, watched her clatter wildly down the street, then limped to his car and sat thoughtfully behind the wheel. He would give the information to Juvenile, they'd pick her up in no time.

* * *

Angrily Leon spooned bland cottage cheese into his mouth. Joey. What a terrible waste.

In his mind he reviewed the case on the vanished Deke Andrews.

So many people interviewed. So many different opinions. Deke Andrews was remembered as smart, dumb, rude, polite, aggressive, a troublemaker, a loner . . .

The list went on and on, and no two people agreed.

Fact: He was a car nut.

Fact: He had shoulder length hair. Big deal – he probably cut that off the moment he ran.

Fact: He was sallow of complexion, six feet two inches tall, thin but strong.

Fact: He was not successful with women. Of the four girls tracked down he had dated, not one would admit to sleeping with him. Indeed, not one had even ventured on a second outing.

'Why?' Leon had questioned.

'Dunno.' Girlish shrugs. 'He was just sort of . . . weird.'

They all had variations on the same theme. So add weird to his list of outstanding qualities. A young apparently healthy male, and they could not find one girl he had screwed. Logical conclusion – he slept with hookers or was gay. So that must be where Joey came in . . . But why had he taken her home with him? And why had he indulged in such a passionate orgy of killing?

As the days turned into weeks and the weeks into months, Leon tried to get a picture in his mind of Deke. But there were so many contradictions it was impossible. Only the facts were clear. The Andrews family had moved into the house on Friendship Street over twenty years before. Their background was a mystery. They seemed to have sprung up from nowhere.

Deke went to junior high, graduated from high school, took a job in a garage, and stayed there until the murders. Then he vanished. Taking nothing but a carryall and the secret of what had precipitated his acts of violence.

Inevitably new cases came along and the Friendship Street murders became less important. The press stopped mentioning them because all at once they were old news.

At police headquarters the file was still open but it was no longer hot. Other cases came and went. But Leon was not prepared to let the case fade away and become just another dusty file. Most of all he was not prepared to forget about Joey.

Millie walked into the kitchen, her face swollen with sleep. She swooped on the dish of cottage cheese as though it was contraband. 'And what do you think you're doin', Leon Rosemont?' she demanded sternly.

Millie slept naked. For her trip to the kitchen she had not bothered to put clothes on her comely black body. Leon felt his first arousal in weeks. He grinned and rose from the table.

Her eyes were immediately drawn to his erection. 'My, oh, my!' she drawled. 'So *that's* what I gotta do to get you sexy. Just take me some cottage cheese to bed!'

He laughed with her, followed her into the bedroom, and was not embarrassed by the roll of fat around his middle as they began to make love. With Millie everything was natural, she was the warmest human being he had ever encountered.

He remembered the first time he had set eyes on her. She was a school teacher then, and she had brought a group of youngsters to the precinct for an outing. Some outing. Hookers screaming obscenities. A pickpocket or two getting booked. A few gang members with their heads busted open. And pimps and pushers and undercover cops and muggers and car thieves and junkies and rape victims.

Just a normal day on the job.

She was dark of skin and soft of voice. Her eyes were brown and kindly. Her lips wide and sensual . . . He was fifty years old and he had been divorced from his first wife, Helen, for years, so there was no reason why he shouldn't find out her number and call her. A month later they were married. And for three years they had been very happy indeed.

Millie sighed and rolled over. 'That was real gooood!'

'It was real fast too,' he apologized.

'Not my fault!'

True. What had happened to his control? Millie didn't seem disappointed, in no time at all her breathing was deep and even and she was asleep.

Leon lay there wide awake, his mind back on Deke Andrews. He was out there somewhere. Somewhere in the black night. Somewhere . . .

And he, Leon Rosemont, would have to find him. For Joey's sake.

Chapter Seven

'Str . . . eee . . . tch. That's it ladies. Put something into it. One more time. Come on now – str . . . eee . . . tch.'

Elaine thought she might have done herself permanent damage. She lay on her stomach in a large work-out studio with thirty other women, most of them in impeccable shape. Her right arm was behind her clutching desperately on to the ankle of her left leg. Every muscle in her body was on Air Force One alert. It felt terrible.

'Okay everyone. Let it go. Relax,' the instructor said. As Elaine slumped flat on her face she wondered if he was gay. He certainly enjoyed inflicting pain. She stared up at him from her supine position. He wore a yellow leotard, black leg warmers, and a striped scarf. His crotch bulged disconcertingly. 'Is he gay?' she whispered to Karen Lancaster, who lay beside her.

'I expect so,' Karen answered. 'All the pretty ones are nowadays.

'Okay,' said the instructor. 'Now I want you to join me in a little something called the Snake.'

'The one-eyed variety I hope,' murmured Karen wistfully.

Disco music blared out as thirty almost perfect bodies writhed across the floor on their stomachs.

Elaine joined in and inexplicably began to feel incredibly horny. All that pressure on the clit. And no action from Ross in God knows how long, although he was due back from location that very afternoon, and maybe . . . if she was very very lucky . . . and played the perfect wife . . .

I want to come she thought *right here and now*. She gazed at that impossible crotch and shuddered and wriggled to a quite satisfactory climax while the music blared and the slight smell of sweat filtered in amongst the heavy scent of Joy and Estee and Opium.

'Oh God!' she exclaimed.

'Sorry?' questioned Karen.

'Nothing,' she giggled, feeling very liberated.

'Okay ladies. That's it for today. Did you enjoy it?'

He had to be kidding. She would come every day. The double entendre almost made Elaine laugh aloud, and feeling very pleased with herself she got up and headed for the showers.

Ron Gordino's health and exercise class. The latest and the best. Bibi Sutton had discovered it. Where Bibi went others followed.

Elaine stripped off in a tiny cubicle, then, naked, stepped boldly into the communal shower. Very un-Beverly Hills. But right now very in. Anyone who was frightened to show everything they had at Ron Gordino's was immediately suspect. Nudity and letting it all hang out were *the* thing to do.

Perfumed soap oozed from a wall faucet at the press of a button. Elaine soaped herself thoroughly, her eyes darting this way and that checking out the other bodies on display. Karen had the largest nipples she had ever seen. Big brown buttons, like giant knobs on a transistor radio. Elaine decided that if she were a man she would probably find them quite repulsive.

'Have you heard about the new Neil Gray film?' Karen asked. She was tall, with a supple tanned body, thick copper coloured hair and carefully chiselled features. Her connections were the best, she knew everyone and everything – since her father was George Lancaster, a giant superstar who had retired five years previously to marry Pamela London, the third richest woman in

America. He now lived in Palm Beach, and Karen visited him often. She was in her early thirties and twice divorced.

'No. What's he doing?' Elaine soaped under her arms, and tried to stop staring at her friend's awful nipples.

'A movie that his *wife* wrote. Can you imagine?'

For a moment Elaine was confused. 'Maralee?'

'No, not his ex-wife, silly. His *wife*. Montana. El big pain in the necko.'

'Oh. Her.' Elaine was silent for a moment while she digested this information. She always thought of Maralee as Neil Gray's wife although they had been divorced for years. Elaine had never met Montana, although of course she had heard enough about her.

'Neil sent the script to daddy in the hope that he would want to do it,' Karen continued. 'He told me it's very good. Of course nobody believes that Montana actually wrote it. Neil must have written it himself and decided to give her credit.'

'Is George interested?' Elaine asked curiously, wondering what Karen was leading up to.

'Of course not. No way would daddy do a movie – not even if it was guaranteed to be another *Gone With the Wind*. He's *had* the picture biz, just adores doing nothing. Being married to Pamela London suits him fine. I mean they *own* Palm Beach.'

Together they stepped from the showers, wrapping themselves in giant fluffy bath sheets.

'The thing is,' Karen continued pointedly, 'that daddy says the part is perfect for Ross – you know he's always liked him.'

That was news to Elaine. Ross had only ever had bad things to say about George Lancaster, calling him everything from a ham actor to a hood. They hadn't even received an invitation to the Palm Beach wedding – one of *the* social events of the year. Karen had explained apologetically at the time – 'Can't invite too much show biz. Pamela's orders.' So how come everyone from Lucille Ball to Gregory Peck had been present? Elaine had burned with fury for weeks.

'Who *is* Ross's agent?' Karen inquired artlessly.

Elaine stared at her friend and wondered why she was taking this sudden interest in her husband's career. 'He's with Zack Schaeffer.'

Karen frowned. 'You know, I just can't understand why he isn't with Sadie La Salle. She really *is* the best.'

Elaine couldn't understand it either – but every time she brought the subject up, Ross muttered something about he and Sadie not getting along. At parties they studiously ignored each other, and he vetoed Elaine's suggestion of ever inviting the powerful Ms De Salle to their home. It was a well known fact that Sadie had discovered Ross years and years ago – but apparently that meant nothing to either of them. It really infuriated Elaine, because Sadie La Salle *was*, as Karen said, the absolute best.

'I hear they're talking Tony Curtis or Kirk Douglas now,' Karen continued. 'Why don't you get Zack on it right away? I think it's called *Street People*. Oliver Easterne's producing. You know Oliver, don't you?'

Yes, she knew Oliver. He was What Makes Sammy Run reincarnated. A hot shot hustler who got lucky. Ross couldn't stand him either. And anyway, if George Lancaster thought Ross was so perfect, why hadn't *he* suggested him?

'Ross has got so much lined up . . .' she murmured vaguely. 'And if they're talking Curtis and Douglas they're hardly talking big time.'

Karen laughed softly. 'Come *on*, Elaine. Don't snow-job *me*. I know where every single body is buried in this town. Ross needs a good film, and this could be it.'

* * *

'Ninety-two . . . ninety-three . . . ninety-four . . .' The words shot out of Buddy's mouth as his arms propelled his body up and down, up and down. Push-ups. One hundred a day. Kept him in the greatest shape in town. '. . . Ninety-eight . . .

ninety-nine . . . one hundred.' He leaped energetically off the floor, barely out of breath.

Angel clapped her hands in admiration. She watched him every day, it was the highlight of her morning – that was if they hadn't made love. Sweet love which every time took her on a roller coaster ride of joy. 'Buddy, I love you!' she sang out. 'I totally *love* you!'

'Hey – hey.' He grinned. 'What's with the outburst?'

'I just feel so happy!'

She ran to him and he opened up his arms to receive her. Angel liked to be cuddled more than anything else in the world. With Buddy it always turned into something more, but she didn't mind that either.

This time he pushed her gently away and stretched his arms high above his head. 'Gonna take a fast swim, then I've got me that important interview. Remember? I told you yesterday.'

She didn't remember. But maybe that was because he was always busy running here, there, and everywhere. They had been in Hollywood for two weeks and during the day she hardly ever saw him. 'Business,' he had explained. 'Y'know kid, I bin away. It'll take a few weeks before everything falls into position.'

She hoped it would fall into position soon. She could just see the movie magazines – *Mrs Buddy Hudson visited her husband on the set of his latest movie today, what a cute couple they make! Angel Hudson, an aspiring actress, says that Buddy and their home life together come first.*

She imagined a four page colour photo spread of them together. Jogging in matching track suits. Feeding each other ice cream. Laughing in a hot tub.

'Buddy?' She ran after him as he headed for the door. 'Do you think you'll be doing a movie soon?'

He stared at the upturned face, the wide eyes, the adoring expression. Maybe he had convinced her a little too thoroughly that he was hot shit in the movie world. But then he hadn't expected her to believe him so absolutely. 'Well . . . I sure hope so, babe. Like I told you, I *have* been away, an' this town's got a real short memory.'

'Oh.' Disappointment clouded her face.

'But you can bet on old Buddy Boy pullin' off somethin' real big an' juicy soon. Like I just turned down a guest shot on *Taxi*. The part wasn't big enough – I gotta come back with somethin' special. Right, sugar?'

'Right, Buddy.' She was glowing again.

He contemplated postponing his swim. Making love to Angel was like taking a ride to heaven. But then he thought – no – gotta get my act together – gotta get my muscles in shape – gotta swim off some of the anger and frustration that are beginning to creep into every pore of my body.

Back in town two stinking weeks and nothing. No goddamn action whichever way he turned. Commercial. Movies. Television. Zilch.

Six interviews.

Six turndowns.

He was Buddy Hudson. He had everything going for him. Why weren't they hanging out flags?

He ran down two flights of stairs to what was laughingly referred to as the pool area. There were twenty-two apartments, each of which housed at least two people. Every day forty-four bodies splashed and revelled in the slimy twenty foot pool which never seemed to get cleaned. The only good thing about the apartment was that it cost nothing – courtesy of Buddy's good friend Randy Felix, who was currently in Palm Springs shacked up with a wealthy widow and her daughter.

It was early so the pool was deserted. A thin film of oil formed a slick on top of the water. He dived straight in – if you stopped to think about it you were lost. Then he churned up and down like a frenetic dolphin confined in too small a space. When he hit it, man, he would get the biggest and the best pool in the whole of the city. Something with space, and cool clear water, and a diving board, and Italian tiles, and a filter that worked, and . . .

‘ ’Morning.’ A girl stood by the side watching him. She had orange hair frizzed into tight little curls on top of her head, and she wore the smallest string bikini he had ever seen. It barely covered her large breasts, and merely skimmed her crotch.

He continued to swim.

She settled herself on a towel and began to oil her body.

Before Angel he would have hit on her. Immediately. He always had the best lookers, and this one – while being nowhere near Angel – *was* – in her own particular way – a very choice number.

‘My name’s Shelly,’ she announced. ‘Who’re you?’

He hauled himself from the pool and began doing leg bends. ‘Buddy. Buddy Hudson.’

‘You live here alone?’ she asked pointedly, unhooking the clasp of her bikini top and taking it off.

He couldn’t help staring at her large firm breasts. ‘No. I live here with my wife.’

She hooted with laughter. ‘*You’re* married?’

What was so funny about that? ‘Yeah. *I’m* married.’ Furiously he worked on his legs – four more pulls on each thigh and then straight back into the pool for further punishment. He did the crawl for thirty lengths before emerging again.

Shelly lay on her back, legs spread and nicely oiled, tits pointing skyward like two polished aubergines. Dark shades covered her eyes, and a transistor radio was tuned to *KIIS F.M.*

Buddy picked up his towel and walked into the building. On his way upstairs he checked out the mailbox. Three bills for Randy. A leaflet urging all and sundry to *join Jesus.* And a brochure from an enthusiastic exterminator – *You got mice we deal with ’em nice.*

In the one room apartment Angel was busying herself with a vacuum. She switched off the machine when he entered and grinned. ‘I borrowed it from the lady next door. She said I could use it anytime. Isn’t that nice?’

‘Sure is.’ Angel was a nut. Why waste time vacuuming this dump? He pulled off his wet shorts and dropped them on the floor before walking to the closet they called a bathroom. There, he attempted to shower with a hand attachment that fitted onto the bathtaps – not an easy exercise.

When he emerged Angel was busy squeezing fresh juice for him behind the bar which doubled as a kitchen. The whole apartment, with no trouble at all, would fit neatly into two medium sized suitcases.

He opened the closet and selected black slacks, his one and only silk shirt, and a lightweight Yves Saint Laurent jacket. Fortunately, in Buddy's case, clothes did not make the man. Whatever he put on looked good and he knew it. This puzzled him. If he always looked so good how come he wasn't a star?

He dressed and gulped the juice Angel handed him. 'I'll be back around six or seven. What are you goin' to do today?'

'Go to the market I guess . . . Only I'll need some money . . .'

'Oh yeah, sure.' He was embarrassed. He had no goddamn money. He was down to his last hundred. Dragging some bills from his pocket, he gave her two tens. 'Don't spend it all at once.' Corny old clichéd joke. Sometimes he hated himself.

She smiled. 'I'll try not to.'

He grabbed her, ran his hands over her gorgeous body, kissed her on the mouth. 'Later, sugar.'

* * *

Pre-production was in full swing. Since *Street People* was to be shot mainly on location there was much to get organized. The availability of the crew Neil usually worked with was of prime importance, and so far everything was falling into position – no big problems. He was out early most days with his lighting cameraman and first assistant scouting for locations. Some directors employed location scouts, but he preferred to do it himself.

Montana was busy casting. She had settled into an office in Oliver Easterne's building on the Strip and gone straight to work. She could have got an agency to sift through the hundreds of possibles, or indeed hired a first rate casting director like Frances Cavendish, but she wanted to see everyone herself, then present her selections to Neil for his full approval. It was her movie, and she planned to see it stayed that way.

The excitement of actually launching into the pre-production period was heady. She knew she was lucky because she was married to Neil, and he loved her script and wanted to do it. But even if he had hated it . . . Well she was quite confident it was good enough to take to any studio or independent and get them interested. It was the best thing she had ever done, and she had no intention of employing false modesty. *Street People* was good because it was real. She had based it on scenes of life that were happening all around. Mostly she had based it on the characters she had observed while shooting her children's film on the streets of Los Angeles. Neil's enthusiasm was a real plus, but deep down she couldn't help wondering if he hadn't of grabbed the property – maybe – just maybe – she might have got the opportunity to direct it herself.

Bullshit. Since when did women get opportunities like that? Wise up kid and be grateful your old man's doing it so at least you get a fifty per cent say.

There were three star roles plus thirty-two speaking parts to be cast. Some of them were only one line, but they mattered. Montana didn't want to see actors who were in every dreary television show, she wanted new talent – and she was enjoying every minute of finding the perfect actor or actress for each role.

They came in their hundreds. Smiling, surly, eager. Old, young, pretty, ugly. All carried their portfolios filled with photos, lists of credits and résumés.

Agents assaulted her from all sides. The good and the bad.

'You wanna Marilyn Monroe type? I gotta girl that'll rouse every cock from here to the Valley!'

'This boy I'm sending you is James Dean. I'm telling you he's Dean – only better.'

'A young Brando . . .'

'An older Brooke Shields . . .'

'A sexy Julie Andrews . . .'

'A taller Dudley Moore . . .'

'An American Michael Caine . . .'

She was swamped with every type possible. But gradually she began to pick and choose, getting more excited with each find.

In the evenings she worked on the script – adding scenes, changing lines. Neil told her about the locations he had found, and she told him about some of the characters she had interviewed. Their personal lives got swept to one side while together they lived, breathed and ate *Street People*. It became the focus of both of their lives.

Occasionally they fought. The three main roles were not cast. Oliver Easterne wanted at least two bankable stars and Neil was hotly pursuing retired superstar, George Lancaster. 'If we get George,' he pointed out, 'the other two can be unknowns.'

'*If* we get the asshole,' Oliver agreed. To him all actors were assholes, be they stars or bit players. 'Which doesn't seem likely the way things are going.'

'I'll fly to Palm Beach this weekend,' Neil decided. 'He likes the script, I think I can convince him.'

'I hope so. Time's running tight. I have some ideas myself . . .'

Neil knew about Oliver's ideas. Half-assed star names that were wrong wrong wrong. He had no intention of even considering them.

Montana was not mad with enthusiasm about George Lancaster. 'He can't act,' she stated flatly.

'He will. With me.'

She was unconvinced, but realistic enough to know that certain concessions had to be made. 'What do you think? Should I come with you?'

Neil shook his head quickly. 'No. You've got enough to take care of here. I can handle George.'

She nodded, her mind filled with faces. 'There's a couple of actors I think we should test for the part of Vinnie.'

'*If* we land George Lancaster. Otherwise we're going to have to go with a name.'

'I don't know why.'

'Yes you do. It's called playing the box-office game.'

'I never did like playing games.'

'Learn.'

'Screw you,' she said amiably.

'Ah, if there was only time,' he replied.

She grinned. 'I'll make time, when you get back.'

* * *

Elaine's day.

After Ron Gordino's exercise class, a visit to The Nail Kiss of Life, then four hours at Elizabeth Arden having her legs waxed, her eyebrows shaped, a facial, and her hair washed and blow dried. She got home in time to change into green Norell lounging pyjamas before Ross arrived back from location. Even if she did say so herself she looked wonderful. 'You look divine!' she whispered to her bedroom mirror. *Eat your heart out, Etta the Elephant.*

She strolled into the living room and was about to fix herself a drink when glancing through the huge plate glass windows she was horrified to see him at it again. Pissing in her pool!

'Lina!' she yelled, striding to the glass doors and stepping outside. 'Lina!'

The boy lazily zipped up without – it seemed – a care in the world. 'Afternoon ma'am,' he drawled.

'You filthy pig!' she shouted. 'I saw what you did!'

He was now bending over the hose which gushed fresh water into the pool. 'Huh?'

'Don't huh *me*. You know what I mean.'

Lina appeared at that point, wiping her hands on an apron tied firmly round her waist and frowning. 'What ees it Señora? I try make dinner.'

Elaine pointed a perfectly manicured finger at the boy. 'I

do not want him here again. You understand me, Lina? Not anymore.'

He continued to fiddle with the hose while Lina heaved a dramatic sigh. 'Miguel – he sick—' she began.

'I don't care about Miguel,' Elaine screamed. 'I don't care if he drops dead on the job. But I do not – and please understand me – I do not want this . . . this . . . person here *ever* again. You got that, Lina?'

Lina gave another dramatic sigh and raised her eyes to heaven. 'Sure,' she said. 'I got.'

'Good. Then get him out of here right now.' Elaine stalked back into the house and headed straight for the bar where she fixed herself a double shot of vodka with one token ice cube. Unbelievable! Help these days! Impossible!

An old pick-up truck flashed past from the back of the house just as a long black limousine pulled up at the front. Ross! Quickly Elaine checked out her appearance in the antiqued mirror behind the bar. She looked good. Wouldn't it be nice if he noticed for once?

He didn't. He strode into the house wearing mud caked boots over faded Levis, and a checked shirt with an old leather jacket. Lately Ross had taken to dressing young. It didn't suit him. He looked like an over-the-hill cowboy.

'Darling!' Dutifully she pecked at his cheek, and was rewarded with rough stubble.

'Hot damn!' he exclaimed. 'Am I glad to be out of *that* pisshole.' He flopped down on a white brocade sofa which Elaine had just had recovered at great expense and put his legs up, boots and all. 'I'm friggin' exhausted! Get me a drink – before I fuckin' faint!'

The movie star was home.

* * *

Buddy whistled as he ran down the stairs from the apartment. Angel with the trusting eyes. She never bugged him, complained about the apartment or their lack of money. She never questioned him when he came home, or insisted that he tell her what he was doing every minute of the day. She was perfect. Golden lady. One day he would swamp her with furs and jewels and stereos and cars. Whatever she wanted – it would be hers.

When? That was the question. When would it all happen for him? He had been in Hollywood ten years now . . . Ten years was a long time . . . a real long time . . .

* * *

Running away from his mother the second time was easy. Especially with two hundred dollars to help him on his way. Sixteen years old, wary as a fox, and determined not to be caught. He got out of San Diego as quickly as he could, jumping a bus to Los Angeles, then hitching his way down to the beach where he hung out sleeping rough, scrounging food, and making friends. There were a lot of kids in the same position as him. Runaways with nothing to do with their time except the five big Ss – Surf, Swim, Sunbathe, Sleep and Sex. With a few drugs thrown in whenever they could afford it. Buddy didn't hesitate, he got into sex in a big way. There was no lack of partners among the girls – even the boys – but that was definitely not his scene.

His first score was a big freckled girl who liked it rough. She loved to roll on the beach with sand penetrating every crack. He had her two or three times a day until she ran off with a fat man in a Cadillac who promised her Acapulco. Next came a little redhead whose speciality was 'sucking dick', as she called it. He didn't like that, it made him feel too vulnerable, like her sharp white teeth were going to clamp down and ruin his future. He moved on to a Swedish starlet who visited muscle beach to develop her pectorals. She taught him to drive her pale pink Thunderbird, and to give head. He enjoyed both.

He got himself a job slinging hamburgers at a beach hangout, and that gave him just enough money to rent a room. A friend showed him how to play the guitar, and he wasn't bad. He worked on his voice, getting together a repertoire of songs. Occasionally he landed himself a gig singing and strumming the guitar and that was a help financially.

The five big Ss remained constant. He was tanned all over, strong from surfing, muscled from working out. He had all the sex he ever wanted, plenty of sleep, and he never once thought of his mother. She was dead as far as he was concerned.

Buddy was a loner. He wanted it that way.

He palled up with a would-be actor named Randy Felix, and once in a while he'd hitch a ride into Hollywood and hang around the class Randy attended. Joy Byron's Method Acting School. Joy Byron was an old English broad with a voice like a hacksaw. She wore flowered dresses and carried a parasol at all times – even indoors. Her students adored her, and worshipped regularly twice a week in a disused warehouse on the wrong side of Wilshire. When Randy dropped out to pursue other interests, Buddy continued to go on his own. He loved every minute of the two hour classes, and soon he was performing everything from Stanley Kowalski in A Streetcar Named Desire *to Jay Gatsby in* The Great Gatsby.

Joy Byron said he was good, and she should know – for in her day she had acted with the very best. Olivier, Gielgud – all the English greats, or so she said, and Buddy was inclined to believe her.

As acting fever struck, so the beach lost its appeal. A move seemed logical, and Randy, who was sharing a house with two girls in West Hollywood, said there was always room for a fourth. Just before he hit twenty Buddy moved in.

The house was a dump, the girls were dykes, but living in Hollywood was living in Hollywood. Buddy felt at home in no time at all. Only problem. No money. No car. Getting by at the beach was one thing. Making out in town was another. Randy always seemed to be reasonably flush, so Buddy asked him how he did it.

'By gettin' paid for what you're *givin' away for free,' Randy explained. 'I got me an agent takes twenty percent an' arranges everythin'. No hassle. No sweat. I sell dick – to ladies – it sure as hell beats shovellin' hot dogs!'*

'You sell what?'

'Give it a try, Buddy. I get commission on every stud I bring in.'

They both started to laugh. 'Really?' Buddy asked between bouts of mirth. 'Really?'

Randy nodded. He was five feet nine inches tall, pleasant looking but nothing special. He had a large nose, small eyes and no back teeth. When he laughed this was very noticeable.

'Well I'll be a son of a bitch!' Buddy exclained. 'Who would believe it?'

Randy took Buddy to meet his agent, a black homosexual dressed from head to toe in tight white leather.

'No . . . er . . . male customers,' Buddy mumbled, hardly believing what he was getting himself into.

'No males?' sniffed the agent, affectionately known as Gladrags by his stable of active young studs. 'What are you – some kind of a weirdo freak?'

So began his life as a hustler.

The first time he wasn't sure if he could get it up. He met the woman at a designated time at an apartment Gladrags had arranged. She turned up twenty minutes late, a middle-aged lady in a severely cut business suit. 'You're new,' she remarked casually, as if she was familiar with every one of Gladrags' boys. 'I don't take my clothes off,' she announced, hitching her skirt around her waist, and removing sensible white panties. 'But I want you *naked. Strip.' She lay down on the bed and watched him as he fumbled his way out of his clothes.*

Jeez! He felt like he was en route to the dentist! No way could he get a hard-on until desperately he remembered Randy's advice – 'Close your eyes an' use your imagination.' Quickly he flashed onto a memory of a girl he had balled recently. Nineteen. Pretty. With a trick of licking his balls until he felt he could shoot his stuff twenty feet in the air.

It worked. Suddenly he was in business.

He never looked back. Servicing women for money was no problem. It paid the bills and enabled him to pursue an acting career.

Joy Byron fixed him up with an agent, and he got some pictures together and began going on interviews. Almost immediately he landed a two liner in a Starsky and Hutch, *followed by a small part in a Burt Reynolds block buster. He was on his way! He was going to be a star!*

It didn't exactly work out that way. There followed a lean patch, during which time the Starsky and Hutch *episode aired and he was not in it. And the Burt Reynolds movie played and he was not in that either!*

The humiliation of ending up on the cutting room floor twice was too much.

'Never mind,' Joy Byron consoled. 'Something else will come along.'

She was a funny old bird who had taken to inviting him to her house for 'extra coaching'. He was kind of flattered, and he certainly enjoyed acting out scenes from all the great plays with her, although sometimes, in the dusty living room of her Hollywood Hills house, when they were in the middle of a seene, she would move a little too close for comfort. He was servicing women for money regularly, but the thought of getting it on with Joy Byron was not to be relished. For a start she had to be at least seventy years old. And he respected her. She was a great actress. She was his teacher *for crissakes.*

One night she said to him, 'Buddy. I have a wonderful idea. The workshop will put on a special performance of Streetcar. *I will invite agents, casting directors, studio executives. I know these people, and if I invite them they will come. You – of course – will play Stanley Kowalski. A perfect showcase for you.'*

'Hey . . . terrific . . .' he began.

She grabbed him before he could finish the sentence.

It wasn't that bad.

It wasn't that good.

He got to give up whoring. He moved into Joy's freaky house and she took care of all the bills.

He got to act day and night, night and day. Joy was always ready. He zipped through all the great playwrights. He zoomed through a stack of old screenplays. He emoted until he was blue in the face.

Joy Byron taught him plenty about the business. Everything from make-up to lighting and the best camera angles. She coached him in mime, and diction, and posture. She kept him very busy, and true to her word she starred him in a student production of Streetcar.

Several important people actually did turn up. Frances Cavendish was one of them. The flinty-eyed casting agent was one of the best in town because she never missed an opportunity to view new talent.

Buddy looked sensational. Torn T-shirt. Skin tight jeans. Marlon Brando move over. He had seen the 1951 movie many times on television. He had studied every nuance and gesture of the great actor's performance. Now he had it down perfectly and he knew he was good. It did not surprise him when Frances Cavendish sent back a note for him to drop by and see her.

He waited a week. Did not want to appear too anxious. Then he sauntered into her office, perched on the side of her desk, and mumbled, 'I hear ya wanna make me a movie star.'

She adjusted her glasses and stared at him. 'Shift your buns off my desk, sonny. They're casting a horror movie at Universal. I think you might be right. Get yourself over there pronto.'

He got the part. Three days. No lines. There followed a series of similar bits. A week on a gangster movie. Two days on Police Woman. *A shaving cream commercial. A two part* Vegas *– his best role yet. Finally – his shot.*

'I think you're right for the lead in a new pilot,' Frances said, and actually smiled. 'This might *be it, Buddy.'*

He was floating. The producers liked him. He ran home to Joy with a script and a stomach that wouldn't lie down. He was going to play the lead in a new pilot. He was going to be a star.

Joy Byron read the script and pronounced it 'Crapshit!' She could be very salty for an old lady. 'We'll shape it into something worthwhile,' she told him with a long theatrical sigh.

They worked long and hard. Joy gave him motivations, she told him exactly *what to do and when to do it. She even accompanied him to the set to make sure he changed none of her instructions.*

On the second day, directly after the producers had viewed the previous day's shooting, he was fired.

'So what?' snorted Joy Byron. 'I told you it was crapshit!'

He left her house in the middle of the night while she slept. He was sick with disappointment and anger and frustration. When was Buddy Boy going to become a star?

He drifted right back into his old way of living. Only now he began to drink too much, and take too many drugs. A girlfriend introduced him to Maxie Sholto, an unsavoury agent who was into arranging Hollywood *Parties – the kind where the hired help performed for an audience. At least he was getting* seen. *So what if it was with two bimbos crawling all over him? He was on show. And the women at the parties loved him.*

One day he bumped into his friend, Randy. 'You're gonna be dog turd in this town if you don't watch it,' Randy warned.

Buddy was flying. 'I'm makin' big bucks. Y'want some of my action?'

'Where's your big bucks gettin' you? All I see is snow up your nose an' grass down your throat. Straighten out, or you'll be finished.'

He straightened out. Three nights later. In the middle of an orgy with come streaming down his face from a fat record producer, and a thin girl riding pony on his joint.

He caught his reflection in a mirror, and he also caught a camera in action which pissed him no end.

He threw the girl off him, smashed the camera, beat up the record producer, and stormed out of the place. He was Buddy Hudson. He was going to be a star, and nothing would stop him.

The next day he hopped a plane to Hawaii where he dried out, got himself a job singing in a piano bar, and met Angel.

* * *

So – Buddy thought to himself, as he climbed in his wreck of a car. What to do now? Returning to L.A. with new bride in tow all ready to set the town on fire was one thing. Reality was another. He needed money. And there was only one sure way he knew how to get it.

* * *

Neil Gray glanced around the VIP lounge. He nursed a large Jack Daniels on the rocks, his second.

Across the room sat Gina Germaine. Blonde, bubbly, bosoms and bum. Surrounded by admiring airline personnel tripping over each other to grant her every wish. He had greeted her briefly when she entered. Two people who knew each other only vaguely. Christ! But his balls were aching for her. He couldn't wait to be with her on the plane, maybe jam it to her in the toilet if she would let him . . .

If she would let him indeed! Gina Germaine would let him fuck her in Trader Vics on a Sunday night if he told her that's what he wanted.

God! Was he getting senile? Why this obsession with some blonde movie star? There was definitely something the matter with him. Had to be. Taking her to Palm Beach with him was sheer lunacy. The risk of getting found out . . .

The risk was giving him the best erection he'd had all year.

Chapter Eight

New York could turn you schizo. If you weren't already.

What mean streets. Dirt and grime and low down filthy reality. Rats. Cockroaches. The streets were crawling with them – the human kind too. A walk through the city could guarantee no end of meetings with the insane.

Deke kept himself to himself. He walked with a purposeful stride, his chin tucked down, his bleak eyes hooded and watchful.

Once two kids tried to jump him on the corner of 39th and Seventh Avenue. It was not yet dark, and people were plentiful on the street. No one came to his aid as he struggled with the two crazed teenagers, one of them armed with a knife.

Deke fought back. He thrust and lunged and clawed. Until he was able to grab the knife from his assailant and shove it into the boy's chest, surprise spilling out of the boy's stoned eyes as blood spilled out of his body.

The other attacker ran, and Deke strolled casually off while passersby scurried along the street, eyes studiously averted.

It gave him such a good feeling. A tremendous surge of power. It reminded him of Philadelphia . . . that night . . . that special night . . .

His step quickened as he remembered . . .

The machete he had bought from a pawnshop for twenty bucks because he liked the look of it. It had hung on the wall of his bedroom unused for two years, although occasionally he had taken it down and struck a pose in front of his dresser mirror. He had never imagined the day would come when he would use it for real.

He thought of Joey. Of her squat body, spiky hair, and wide red mouth.

Joey Kravetz . . .

* * *

'Hey – hey. You lookin' for some fun, buster?'

Deke attempted to walk past, but she blocked his way, planting herself firmly in his path. She cocked her head on one side and winked lasciviously. 'I don't wanna rip ya off, nothin' like that. I just wanna get in your pants an' give ya the hottest bounce y'had all year. Can y'dig it?'

He stared at her. She was almost pretty, but her nose was off centre, one eye had a slight cast, her lipstick was smudged over a red cavern of a mouth. 'How much?' he muttered.

'A buck a minute. Can't be fairer than that.' She squinted up at him, for he was much taller than her five feet three inches. 'Ya won't regret a dime of it, cowboy!'

Cowboy. He had never been called that before. It made him feel good. 'Okay,' he mumbled, knowing the event would take no longer than five minutes. 'Where?'

'I got me a little jive ass palace.' She grabbed him by the arm. 'Two blocks down, ya can tell me the story of y'life on the way. My name's Joey, what's yours?'

He had never met a girl like her before. Sure, plenty of hookers with sour mouths and empty eyes; and girls he had dated, who smiled politely and never let him so much as touch them. Joey was different. She seemed to want to be with him as they walked along the rain soaked streets.

Her 'palace' was a small room two flights up with a sink in the corner, a bed lounged on by a fat white cat, and one lamp draped with a singed pink chiffon scarf.

She shooed the cat off the bed, threw off her plastic raincoat, and said, 'Nice, huh? Sure beats my last dump.'

He stood hesitantly in the doorway and wondered if it would be as usual. Money out first. Then a furtive hump against a silent piece of meat.

Joey undid the side zip on her tight black mini skirt and wriggled out of it. Underneath she wore bikini panties with TUESDAY embroidered in red. It was Friday.

Deke groped in his pocket for some money.

'Put it away, y'don't know how long ya gonna stay,' she giggled. 'Sure y'don't wanna change the deal? Fifty bucks for as long as ya like?'

He shook his head negatively.

'Suit yourself, buster,' she said, pulling her sweater over orange spiky hair and flinging it on the floor.

She had very small breasts with cheaply rouged nipples. The colour had smudged, so had the mascara under her lazy eye.

She brought her fingers up and played with her nipples until they stood to attention. 'Now ain't that worth a buck an' a half,' she giggled. 'I got lotsa tricks like that, cowboy.'

He coughed dryly.

'You're really nice,' she said, continuing to play with her rouged nipples. 'I like you. I think you an' I could be friends – y'know – real close friends. You've got the kinda eyes I like, horny eyes. I could get off just lookin' into your eyes, cowboy – just lookin'.'

He stayed two hours. It cost him one hundred and twenty dollars and was worth every cent.

* * *

In the distance Deke could hear the familiar whine of police sirens. He quickened his pace. It was definitely time to move on. New York had been a good resting place, a city to get lost in while the murders faded away. Another day or so and he would be off. He had things to do, places to go.

Chapter Nine

So – the big movie star was home. Bitching and complaining about everything.

They were in bed, Ross propped up on four pillows, eyes firmly glued to the television, when Elaine decided the time was right to mention the movie Karen Lancaster had told her about. 'I think you should get Zack on it right away.'

'Ha! The great George Lancaster turns something down and *you* think I should call my agent,' sneered Ross. 'Jesus, Elaine! You really get to me sometimes.'

'If the part was offered to George it has to be good,' she insisted stubbornly.

'Bull*shit*! George made more crap than a laxative factory.' Irritably he changed the television channels with the remote control. 'And – George frigging Lancaster is fifteen frigging years older than me. Don't you forget *that*.'

'Twelve,' corrected Elaine. She knew everyone's age to the exact day.

Ross raised his ass from the bed and let forth a rampant fart.

Elaine was enraged. Oh, if his fans could only see him now! 'If you have to do that kindly do it in the bathroom,' she snapped.

In reply he farted again and switched channels.

'How come, before we were married, you always managed to control your bodily functions?' she asked coldly.

He mimicked her voice, 'How come, before we were married, you never nagged?'

'God! You're impossible!' She got out of their king-sized bed and pulled on a turquoise silk negligee.

'Where are you going?' he demanded.

'To the kitchen.'

'Get me some ice cream. Vanilla and chocolate, with some hot fudge sauce.'

'You're supposed to be on a diet.'

'I don't need a diet.'

'Everyone over the age of twenty-five needs a diet.'

He weakened. 'Get me the ice cream and I'll call Zack.'

'Promise?'

He grinned the famous Conti grin. 'When have I ever lied to you, sweetheart?'

* * *

Montana sat in her office and stared at the young actor sitting across the room. He was hitting on her and she knew it. She lowered her eyes and studied the list of credits he had handed her. The usual rota of crap television and bad movies.

'I never expected to walk into this office today and find someone like you behind that desk,' he said in a low husky voice.

He was hitting on her with his eyes again. A penetrating stare which she found most disconcerting, because in those eyes she could read stark desperation, and she understood the look only too well. 'It says here that you're twenty-two. I'm really looking for someone a little older,' she said briskly.

'How much older?' he countered.

She hesitated. Let him down easy. Rejection was never easy to dish out.

'Well . . . er . . . twenty-five, six.'

'I can look older. I'm really twenty-four.' He had a facial twitch which sprang into action spoiling his bland good looks.

'Fine,' she said, handing him back his résumé. 'I'll keep that in mind. Thanks for coming by.'

'Is that all?' He sounded surprised. 'Don't you want me to read or anything?'

'Not today.'

'Does that mean I'll be coming back?'

She smiled in what she hoped was a non-committal fashion. 'Thank you, Mr Crunch.' *Crunch.* What kind of a name was that? 'We'll be in touch with your agent.'

He stood up and sauntered towards her. 'Can I see you sometime?' he asked, the desperate eyes and the twitch going full force.

She felt sorry for him and all the hundreds of other young actors just like him. 'Look,' she said patiently, 'don't sell yourself short.'

'Huh?'

'You're probably a very good actor, but not right for this movie – so stop pushing it.'

He reddened, bit down hard on his bottom lip, but still kept trying. 'You an' I could make some beautiful things happen. Give me a try?' he leered suggestively. 'I come highly recommended, y'know what I mean?'

She was getting annoyed. 'Why don't you just go. Okay?'

'Lady – you have no idea what you're missing,' he muttered.

Her patience snapped. 'Hey – I've got a feeling I know *exactly* what I'm missing.'

Reluctantly he slouched from the room.

She sighed. Hollywood. City of ambition. A town where success was the name of the game. If you had it you were top of the heap. If you didn't . . . goodbye Charlie – you were less than nothing.

Hollywood. To be an actor or an actress you really had to be a masochist. *That* was for sure.

Come to think of it being a writer was no picnic either. She recalled her first efforts with the original outline on her television series. Nobody had taken her seriously at first. She had done the rounds of agents and the so-called network executives. *Who are you? What are your credits? Baby, you got two strokes against you. One – you're from the East Coast. Two – you're a woman.*

Oh, really?

Wanna climb in the sack and discuss it?

She had never used Neil's influence to achieve anything. The television idea was good. Eventually it had sold. Then came the book on old-time Hollywood, and writing that had been bliss because she was her own boss and didn't have to answer to anyone. Doing the film on children was the biggest challenge of all. She had put it together herself. No small achievement. Especially for a woman, she thought cynically.

She buzzed for the next actor to be sent in, and lit up a cigarette, inhaling deeply. How was Neil doing in Palm Beach with the wonderful George Lancaster? Not that it bothered her either way. If they got him it would be good box office. If they didn't then they could go with a real actor – someone who would make the character of the old cop come alive. A far more exciting prospect.

She opened the script which lay on her desk and flicked through the pages. It could be a great movie. With Neil directing she was sure it would be.

* * *

So what was a guy supposed to do? Let his new bride starve? Because that's what was going to happen if he didn't score some bucks soon.

Buddy sat disconsolately behind the wheel of his car and thought it all out. Yet again. He had been doing so much thinking lately that his head felt like it wanted to bust right open and let all the crap out.

He was an actor. That was his trade. Couldn't land one job. So? What other job paid enough to keep him afloat, and still available to go on interviews? He wasn't about to park cars for a living. No way.

The answer was simple. No big deal when you really thought about it. Half an hour in bed with some faceless woman, a hundred in the pocket, free time to spend with Angel. Sex was like taking a piss. Get it out, do what you have to do, zipper up and vroom . . . long gone. And what Angel didn't know . . .

His mind was made up. He checked out his appearance in the rearview mirror, ruffled his hair and hooded his smokey black eyes. Satisfied with his appearance he leapt out of the car, and with his thrusting walk in overdrive, headed towards the men's store Gladrags owned on Santa Monica Boulevard. Six years before it had been a hole in the wall selling leather accessories. Since that time Gladrags had bought the buildings on either side and expanded. Now the store had glass windows which extended for a quarter of a block, and sold everything from Cerrutti suits to cashmere jock straps. Buddy was impressed. He wondered if he could get a discount.

Inside the store a perfumed transvestite hurried over to greet him.

'He-*llo*,' the lame clad creature gushed in a disturbingly masculine voice. 'And what can I do for *you*?'

Buddy took an involuntary step backwards. Gays. They always made him nervous.

'Your boss around?' he questioned.

Transvestite fluttered long false lashes. 'Do you mean Mr Jackson?'

'Is that Gladrags?'

'I *beg* your pardon?'

'Black guy. Tall. Wears lots of leather.'

'*Sounds* like Mr Jackson.'

'Tell him Buddy's here.'

'I would simply *love* to. But Mr Jackson *never* comes in before one.' He put a manicured nail pensively to his chin. 'Perhaps you'd like to wait.'

'Hey,' snapped Buddy. 'I can't wait. I got things to do.'

'I'm *sure* you have.' Transvestite was in love. Amber eyes swam with promise of devotion.

'Where can I reach him now?'

'I really can't say.'

'Force yourself.'

'Oh, dear. You see, Mr Jackson has strict rules about giving out his home address and phone number.'

Buddy narrowed his eyes tough guy style. 'An' I have strict rules about *always* getting what I want.'

Transvestite fluttered sensitive hands. 'What do *you* think I should do?'

Buddy winked. 'Give me the address and nobody will be any the wiser 'cept the two of us. Our secret. Right?'

Transvestite smiled nervously. 'If *you* say so.'

* * *

It was no wonder George Lancaster loved living in Palm Beach. In Beverly Hills or Palm Springs he was just another retired superstar. There were dozens of them around. Sinatra, Astaire, Kelly, Hope. You could trip over them every time you ventured out of the house or onto the golf course. In Palm Beach, George Lancaster reigned supreme. He was King. Or at least Prince Consort to his wife, Pamela London, the third richest woman in America.

Neil Gray sniffed around the two of them warily at a special luncheon in his honour. Pamela was a woman to be wary of. She was known for her sharp tongue and acid wit. She had been married four times, George was her fifth. 'A husband a decade,' she was fond of saying. 'None of them could keep it up longer than that. With the exception of George, of course.'

She was fifty-four years old. A large boned woman over six feet tall, with a wild mass of red frizzy hair.

George was an extremely well preserved sixty-two. He had been married twice before. The first time to a childhood sweetheart for thirty-two years, the result of that union being his daughter, Karen. And the second to a Hollywood bitch for nine months three days and two minutes exactly.

Pamela and George made an imposing couple. During five years of marriage they had forged an amicable animosity towards each other. Insults ruled the day, but togetherness was the name of the game.

'So,' Pamela said, cornflower blue eyes raking Neil. 'You want old George to get his big fat rump back to work. Is that it?'

Neil smiled and glanced down the other end of the long table where George was deep in conversation with a sun-baked cosmetic queen. Trust Pamela to seat him as far away as possible, she *knew* it was George he had come to see. 'If he wants to,' he said easily.

'If he wants to,' she sneered. 'If *I* want him to, you mean.'

Neil had known Pamela for years. At one time she had been married to a movie producer friend of his, lived in Beverly Hills, and they had moved in the same social circles. She didn't intimidate *him*. He kept smiling. 'George likes the script, he likes me. What would be so bad about taking a break from all this luxury? You could come along for the ride.'

She laughed hoarsely. 'You know how I *love* Beverly Hills. Little starlets showing everything they've got. *Dreadful* old men wearing gold chains and cracked suntans. Cheap people, Neil, darling. I *hate* cheap people!'

'Don't come then,' Neil said mildly. 'George could fly back here every Friday. We'll arrange a private plane.'

'I *have* a private plane,' Pamela laughed. 'Two in fact.'

'I know. But why use *your* plane when the production would supply whatever George requires?'

She raised an eyebrow. '*Whatever* he requires?'

'Name it.'

'Hmmm . . .' Pamela looked thoughtful.

Neil chalked up a small victory. The very rich loved the thought of getting something for nothing. 'Well?' he pressed.

'I'm thinking about it.'

'What'll it take for you to make up your mind?'

She indicated his glass of Perrier water. 'Why aren't you drinking?'

'Don't change the subject.'

'I hate a man who doesn't drink. It makes me uneasy.'

He summoned a hovering waiter. 'A double Jack Daniels on the rocks.' Then he turned back to Pamela. 'I wouldn't want you to feel uneasy.'

She grinned coquettishly. 'You *are* looking good, Neil. Maybe we *should* come to L.A. Do a bit of slumming.'

They were eating luncheon at the Palm Beach Country Club. An intimate luncheon for thirty guests, none of whom Neil knew, and most of them over the half century mark.

Suddenly he felt depressed surrounded by his contemporaries. He thought briefly of Montana and her exciting youth. He never felt the age difference when they were together. He felt it now surrounded by face lifts, expensive jewellery and liver-spotted hands. Then he remembered Gina Germaine waiting patiently at the hotel where they had checked into adjoining suites earlier in the day. She never made him feel old either. She made him feel young. Or at least she made his body feel young. His *cock* feel young.

'A cent for every dirty little thought that's clicking through your head,' Pamela said suddenly.

'What?' Neil was startled.

Pamela smiled. 'I always know when a man's thinking about sex.'

'Not me.'

She raised an eyebrow. 'No? What's different about you, Neil dear? Do you have cotton wool where you should have balls?'

He laughed. 'You're wasted here, Pamela. You should be writing steamy novelettes.'

'What makes you think I haven't tried it? I've tried almost everything else.' She leered at him. All the money in the world and her teeth were still yellow. 'Except you, Neil, dear. All these years and we've never taken a tumble together. You know we should make up for lost time.' She patted his knee intimately. 'And I always was a sucker for a British accent. So classy . . . so Richard Burton. In fact, I do believe you *look* a little like dear Richard. That same *ravaged* expression, that same—'

'Pamela.' He removed her hand. 'Stop making detours and let's get to the point. Do you, or do you not want George to make my film?'

* * *

'Goddamn!' screamed Ross, slamming down the phone. Agents. Fuck 'em and feed 'em to the fish. Goddamn parasites!

Hi, Ross . . . Yeah, Ross . . . Nothing doing, Ross.

What did they know? They knew nothing. They knew fuck all. They couldn't even wipe their ass without ripping off ten per cent of the toilet tissue.

All of his career he had brought everything to them. *Call Fox. Call Paramount. Call Wilder. Call Zanuck.* Jobs came to *him*. No agent had ever had to run his balls off on Ross Conti's behalf.

Now, after twenty-five years of dropping it in their laps, he wanted some action.

'What about the new Neil Gray film?' he had asked Zack Schaeffer. 'I hear it could be right for me.'

Don't know about it, Ross . . . I'll look into it, Ross . . . I'll call you back, Ross . . .

Screw him. *Why* didn't he know about it? It was his *job* to know about it. Sadie La Salle would know about it, and it was she who should be handling his career.

'Elaine!' he yelled.

Lina poked her head around the door. 'Meesus Conti go exercise class. You want coffee?'

He swore savagely under his breath. Elaine was never around when he needed her, only when he didn't.

'Yeah, coffee,' he growled.

Lina departed and he sat by the phone and sulked.

Sadie La Salle. She had started it all. Grudgingly he had to admit that without Sadie and her billboard it might never have happened for him.

So – how had he paid her back? He had run off with the first beautiful pair of tits that pointed in his direction, and signed with a big agency. No goodbye. No note. No phone call. Just a fast walk while she was out one day.

If all had gone according to plan Sadie La Salle should have just faded from his life never to be heard from again. And she did vanish – for a while. He didn't hear a thing about her as his career started to rise. And when he *did* start to hear her name mentioned it was nothing to get excited about. So she wanted to be an agent. Big deal. Without him she had no clients.

She found an unknown comic called Tom Brownie and built him into the biggest club act since Red Skelton. Then she nursed along a neurotic singer by the name of Melody Fame and turned *her* into the new Garland. Adam Sutton was struggling in B pictures when he joined the stable. Within two years his name was number one at the box office. George Lancaster defected from M.C.A. They all came running. Over the years she had built up the best client list in Hollywood.

Sadie La Salle. Short fat Sadie with the moustache.

Occasionally they ran into each other at parties and premieres. The moustache had gone, costly electrolysis had taken care of *that*. She had dropped thirty pounds and her clothes were expensive and well cut. A stylish bob replaced unruly black curls. She was no beauty but she was certainly an improvement.

He tried to be friendly. She gave him cold nods. He attempted conversations. She walked away.

In the early seventies he decided he needed her. Purely professionally of course. So he called her on the phone, got as far as her secretary, and suggested that Ms La Salle might care to drop by and see him.

She never returned his call. It burned the shit out of him. What kind of a grudge was she carrying?

He cornered her at the next party they both attended. She was with a gay dress designer – rumour had it she was a dyke. Ross knew better than *that*.

'Sadie,' he breezed. 'I think you just got lucky. Guess what?' He flashed the famous Conti smile. 'I'm on the market for a new agent and it might just be you.'

She glared at him coldly. 'I'm not looking for any more clients, Ross.'

Hurt. Surprise. Fix her with the famous baby blues. 'It's been fifteen years, sweetheart. This is business.'

'Screw business,' she said tightly. 'If making commission on you gave me my one hot meal of the week I'd starve to death. Do we understand each other, Ross?'

Bitch! Dyke! Slimmed down cunt! He had not exchanged a word with her since.

Maybe it was time to try again . . . now that he was married to Elaine . . . and another ten years had gone by . . . Maybe . . .

'Meester Conti.' Lina stood solidly in the doorway, her legs like tree trunks emerging from the white uniform Elaine insisted she wear.

He turned off the sulks and managed a smile. Mustn't let the fans down. 'Yes, Lina, what is it?'

'Miguel sick. Okay I bring boy in?'

Why the hell was she bothering him? Domestic matters were Elaine's province. God knows he shelled out enough money to see that everything ran smoothly. 'What boy?' he questioned, pissed off because he had wanted Miguel to wash the Corniche.

'A good boy. Very nice. Okay I let him do pool?'

'Can he drive?'

'Sure he drive.'

'Fine. Get him over here. Have him get the Corniche out, wash it, and I want it ready by one o'clock.'

Lina nodded and gave one of her rare smiles.

'Where's my coffee?' Ross asked.

She shook her head stupidly. 'I forget.'

'So bring it.'

'Yes, me do that.'

She backed from the room as the phone began to ring. Ross snatched the receiver to his ear and barked a sharp, 'Hello.'

'Welcome back, baby,' whispered a low husky voice.

'Who is this?'

'My, what a short memory you have. Was our afternoon at the beach such a forgettable experience? I know it was a few weeks ago, but really Ross . . .'

He laughed. 'Karen!'

'The very same.'

'When can I see you?'

'You name a time and a place and yours truly will be there.'

'Your beach house. Three-thirty.'

'I'll be waiting.'

'I'll be coming.'

'Oh I know, I know.'

They both laughed.

* * *

Elaine was late for her tennis lesson, and her coach – a swarthy New Yorker with teeth like dazzling snow and a grip like a Samurai warrior – was not pleased. 'Ten minutes late, Mrs C., is ten minutes lost.'

So what? she thought irritably. I'm the one that's paying. Or rather Ross is.

After three years of feebly hitting the ball over the net she had finally decided she must excel. It had nothing to do with the fact that Bibi Sutton had started to throw lavish tennis luncheons 'for the girls' at her Bel Air estate, and that Elaine had been invited once, performed like an amateur, and never been asked back.

She stood stiffly on one side of the court, her calf muscles killing her due to two days' hard work at Ron Gordino's exercise class. Going every day was just not on. Too punishing by far. She would cut it down to maybe three times a week. But what three days? That was the problem. What were the in days to go? When did Bibi Sutton attend? The ball wooshed past her racquet and she made a half-hearted swipe but missed it.

'Mrs C.!' her coach complained.

She wished he wouldn't call her Mrs C. It sounded altogether too familiar, and she was not one of those women who wished to be on intimate terms with her tennis coach. 'The name is Conti,' she said sharply.

'I know,' he replied, unabashed. 'Now, do you think you can concentrate, Mrs C.?'

She glared at him. He had hairy legs with rigid thigh muscles which disappeared into crisp white shorts. She wondered how his cock was. Probably hairy and rigid and . . . She shook her head sharply. What was she thinking about his cock for? She couldn't stand him. Quickly she adopted an athletic stance and returned the oncoming ball gracefully.

'That's better!' he said.

Encouraged, she indulged in a passable volley, darting nimbly around the court.

Three quarters of an hour later it was over, and sweating profusely she hurried to the changing rooms where she took her third shower of the day. Ridiculous! Her skin would dry up like a prune. Must remember not to do the exercise class on the same day as her tennis lesson. She took a small black leather Cartier pad from her purse and wrote a cryptic *Tennis Gym No!* Then thoughtfully she added *ask Karen.* Karen would most certainly know the right days to attend Ron Gordino's class.

She dressed slowly, feeling a little tired. And she wondered if all those vitamin pills her nutritionist had recommended were doing her any good. Ross had sneered when he had caught her swallowing a dozen pills a day. But when she told him they gave you energy, stopped colds, prevented cancer, improved your skin, sharpened your eyesight . . . Well he had soon changed his mind. And now he took them too. Plus Ginseng, which was said to jazz up your sex drive. But it didn't seem to have done *him* any good. After three weeks away he had not so much as glanced in her direction. Fallen asleep like a dead camel and snored the night away.

She hoped he had called Zack Schaeffer about the Neil Gray film, if it had been offered to George Lancaster it *had* to be good. Oh, what a triumph to be back on top again. When you were on every guest list and the phone never stopped ringing and new designers begged you to accept their clothes as a gift and chauffeurs and bodyguards monitored your every protected move.

She thought resentfully of Ross. Why had he allowed the slide to happen? When was the moment, the hour, the day, he had fallen from the heights?

He aged, that's what happened. He drank too much, developed a gut, bags under his eyes, and his skin was leathered like an old ranch hand. She had begged him to return to the loving care of her former husband, the plastic surgeon. 'Forget it,' Ross had snapped. 'I don't want my face looking like a goddamn mask.'

Every month he had to pay out various amounts of alimony to his two previous wives. When he was making big money it was hardly noticeable. When the big money stopped it was a shocking drain.

The cutting down process had been painful. First the chauffeur, then the live-in housekeeper and her staff of two, next the gardeners and poolman. Now it was just Lina, who came in daily, except weekends. And Miguel, who was a combination gardener, poolman and chauffeur.

Elaine snorted with anger as she dressed briskly in a thin knit T-shirt dress from Giorgio's, and strappy high heeled sandals from Charles Jourdan. One thing she had refused to cut down on was her clothes. My God! If you couldn't dress properly in Beverly Hills you might as well crawl under a stone and vanish altogether! She had weathered it well though. It was not as if they were broke by any means. It was just that they had to be a little bit careful now that – as Ross's business manager had put it – 'The big money days are behind you, Ross.' Stupid fool. What did *he* know? Elaine would get Ross back on top if she had to kill doing it.

* * *

'Get back on top, Ross,' Karen Lancaster requested huskily.

He raised his head from between her thighs. 'I don't do this for everyone,' he asserted in startled tones. 'In fact, I can't remember the last time.'

'What do you want – an award? Get back on top.'

He obliged, pumping away with quite a bit of vigour.

Karen was a groaner. Her *oohs* and *aahhs* and *go baby gos* got louder and louder.

The more noise she made, the faster Ross pumped, until they came together in a screechful climax.

He rolled off, said, 'Hot damn!' and waited for the praise.

Karen turned onto her stomach and played dead.

The sun slanted on the huge glass-walled room at an angle, playing across the enormous circular bed where they lay on top of a quilted satin bedspread.

Outside, the Pacific Ocean rolled lazily about its business, lapping the Malibu shoreline gently. It was a perfect clear day.

'Not bad,' he said at last, when it became obvious that she was not to be the first to speak. 'Not bad at all.' No reply. Lightly he patted her ass. No response. 'Are you asleep?' he asked incredulously.

'Gimme five mins,' she mumbled, rolling her body into a tight ball.

He rose from the bed and padded around the room.

Some room. A circular fantasy arranged around a central steaming Jacuzzi. On one side was the ocean, on the other a mass of greenery and a carport which now housed his gleaming gold Corniche and her sporty red Ferrari.

He found a space-age kitchen round the back, and extracted an ice cold can of Budweiser from the refrigerator.

Karen was definitely worth the trip to the beach. He had thought so the first time, but now he was sure. She had got him doing things he hadn't done in years.

Little Karen. Christ, he had known her since she was about six years old. George Lancaster had often brought her to the studio with him.

Little Karen. He had attended her first wedding to a real estate broker, read enough about her second to a spaced out composer, and spent many an evening in her company when she became one of Elaine's best friends.

Little Karen. A tiger in the sack.

They had bumped into each other outside Brentano's on Wilshire quite by accident the day before he left for location. 'You *must* come and see my new Ferrari Spyder,' she insisted. 'I only took delivery of it yesterday.'

She dragged him across the street to the American Savings carpark, where the attendant was taking special care of her latest acquisition.

'A present from daddy?' he asked casually, not taking much notice of the sleek red machine. He had never been a car buff.

'But of course! Come on Ross, take a ride with me. You're not in a hurry are you?'

Actually he was. He had a meeting with his accountant, but all of a sudden Karen was giving off signals, and he couldn't resist finding out if they meant what he thought they meant. He climbed into the low passenger seat and smelled fresh new leather.

'Nice, huh?' she said, settling herself on the driver's side. And then they were off, roaring down Wilshire at breakneck speed.

She was driving much too fast for the sedate three lane progression of Cadillacs, Mercedes, and Lincolns. But a delivery truck gave chase from a stoplight, and a kid drag raced her lane to lane. By the time they hit Westwood, Ross was enjoying every minute of the wild ride.

'You on for the beach?' she asked, fixing his eyes with a different unspoken question.

'Why not?' The meeting with his accountant could wait. Let his business manager take care of it. That's what he was paid to do wasn't it?

They made it to the door of her Malibu beach house in twenty minutes. Fifty-two seconds later they were rolling about on the thick pile rug groping at each other's clothes.

He mounted her like a stallion, ripping at her suede skirt and tearing through her brief panties.

She verbalized her enjoyment loudly.

They both had appointments in town to hurry back to, and the next day he had departed L.A. for the location.

He was glad she had called him upon his return. Karen was going to be more than just a passing diversion. Of that he was sure.

* * *

Gladrags resided in a penthouse apartment on Doheny Drive. He cohabited with a white interior designer by the name of Jason Swankle, and a hideous bulldog called Shag.

Buddy pressed the door buzzer impatiently. Now that he had decided to follow his former career he was hot to trot.

Jason answered the door. A plump dormouse of a man in a peacock blue jumpsuit festooned with gold jewellery. Shag accompanied him, took a perfunctory sniff at Buddy's leg, and mounted it as though it were the randiest bitch in the neighbourhood. 'Hey!' Buddy exclaimed, filled with horror. 'Get him off me!'

'Down boy. DOWN!' intoned Jason, tugging at Shag's diamante collar.

Buddy kicked out in disgust. 'Jeez!'

Shag dismounted and growled threateningly.

'And what can I do for you?' Jason inquired archly, placing one beringed plump hand on his waist, checking Buddy out, and liking what he saw.

'I'm looking for Gladra . . . uh . . . Mr Jackson.'

'He's dressing. We're going to a wedding. Can *I* help?' Jason beamed, then winked. 'I'd certainly *like* to.'

Why did fags love him? 'It's business,' Buddy said swiftly. 'Private. I'll only take a minute of his time.'

Jason pursed fleshy lips. 'Marvin doesn't like conducting business at home. Is it about the shop?'

Marvin! Buddy nodded and attempted to edge through the front door.

Shag bared his teeth, and Jason made a decision. 'Oh, all right. Wait here and I'll get him.'

He waddled off on short stumpy legs and Buddy reflected that he and Gladrags must sure make a bizarre looking couple. Gladrags so tall and skinny and black; and Jason so rounded plump and white. Oh well . . . Everyone to their own kick.

Buddy whistled softly between clenched teeth and hoped that Gladrags might have something for him right away. It would be nice to go home to Angel bearing gifts. A new sweater maybe or . . .

'Who in the fuck are you?' It was Gladrags himself, skinnier than Buddy remembered, his black hair cornrowed and decorated with multi-coloured beads. 'And what in the fuck you want?'

Nothing like a warm welcome. 'Hey – my man – G.R. It's me – Buddy Boy. You gotta remember me.' He stretched out a friendly hand which Gladrags slapped sharply away. 'Come on,' Buddy persisted. 'I used to work for you, man. Randy Felix brought me in. I was one of your best.'

Gladrags sniffed deeply. 'One of my best what?'

Buddy checked out the corridor. 'Can I come in? Can we talk?' He attempted to move through the door. Shag growled ferociously. 'I . . . uh . . . I wanna get back in action. See – I need some bucks like yesterday, an' you were always pretty good at arranging things.'

'I ain't in that business no more,' Gladrags spat, sniffing again and beginning to close the door. 'An' even if I was

– which I ain't – believe me, man, I sure *do* remember you. You was the weirdo could only get it up for the ladies. Right? *And* – if I remember correct, you dumped on me an' went inta business with that fat fucker Maxie Sholto. An' with *him* I understand if it moved ya screwed it. So if I *was* in that business still, which as I said repeatedly I *ain't* – then even if you farted stars an' stripes, an' sported a flag on your pecker every time ya got the bone – I *still* wouldn't be interested in puttin' you together with anythin' human. Now get lost.' He slammed the door sharply.

'Shit!' muttered Buddy sharply. 'Goddamn *shit*!'

Angrily he turned and strode towards the elevator. It was his own dumb fault.

Jason Swankle caught up with him just as he was driving out of the underground garage. 'So glad I found you,' he puffed, running up to the car, dragging a reluctant Shag behind him.

Buddy glared. 'Why?'

'Because I'd like to help you. I think I *can* help you.'

'You're not my type,' snapped Buddy sarcastically.

'Take my card,' Jason insisted. 'And call me on my business number. Tomorrow.' He thrust a small white card through the open window. It fluttered onto the floor of the car as Buddy put his foot down and roared off into the late morning sun.

Chapter Ten

The small Italian restaurant with its checked tablecloths, excellent pasta and potent house wine was busy. Saturday night always brought out the crowds. Millie Rosemont was enjoying herself, but Leon felt uncomfortable and ill at ease. He had promised Millie faithfully that the one thing he would never do was bring his problems home, and he had kept that promise up until the time of the Friendship Street murders . . . Up until the time he was faced with Joey Kravetz's mutilated body . . .

He remembered their second encounter. It was long before he met Millie . . . long before . . .

* * *

It wasn't just raining, it was pouring the proverbial cats and dogs. Driving home late, his windshield wipers fighting the rain, Leon decided he was hungry after all. Only an hour previously he had phoned to cancel a dinner date with an attractive divorcee he had been seeing. She was nice enough, but deep down he found her boring.

On impulse he made a left into a Howard Johnsons and parked his car in a side lot. Then he hurried through the rain to a corner booth where he ordered himself a toasted chicken sandwich and some good hot coffee. Opening up the paper he studied the sports page.

The waitress brought his sandwich and coffee, and he settled back to relax after a long and tiring day.

'You sonuvabitch!' a voice screeched.

Startled, Leon looked up from his newspaper and stared at the angry, short girl standing by his table, her arms crossed over a grubby T-shirt, her legs encased in army surplus trousers which seemed several sizes too big.

'Don't remember me, huh?' she glared.

'Should I?' he asked at last.

'Should ya? Ha! Should ya? You can bet your fat butt ya should!'

He put down his paper. 'Now wait a minute. Just who do you think you're talking to?'

'You – cop!' she spat.

'Do I know you?' he asked angrily.

'Ya got my ass locked up in some girl's prison for a fuckin' year. You should know me,' she crowed triumphantly.

It was then he noticed the cast in her eye, and suddenly it all came back. She was the baby-faced hooker who had propositioned him one night, then kicked him on the leg when questioned about her age, and fled. He had called Grace Mann over on Juvenile, given her a general location and description, and left it in her capable hands. Grace had obviously come through.

'I thought you said you were eighteen,' he accused.

'So I lied – big deal. An' 'cos of you they come trackin' me, an' locked me up on some crappy farm with a bunch of babies. Thanks a lot, cowboy.'

He tried not to smile, she was so desperately angry, and he had no wish to inflame her further. 'It was for your own good,' he said.

'Screw you!' she replied, and unexpectedly sat down. 'My date never showed, so y'can buy me a coffee. I reckon ya owe me more than that anyway.' She wiped the back of her hand across her nose, and hungrily eyed his chicken sandwich.

'You want something to eat?' he asked generously. She was such a ragged looking creature, he felt sorry for her.

'Awright,' she agreed, as if she were doing him an enormous favour. 'Gimme the same as you.'

He signalled the waitress and gave her the order. She filled his coffee cup and hurried off to get a cup for the girl.

'What's your name?' Leon asked.

'Joey,' she sniffed. 'What's it to you?'

'I'm buying you a sandwich. I may as well know who you are.'

She glared at him suspiciously, muttered, 'Lousy cop,' and set upon her sandwich with ravenous ferocity when it arrived.

Leon watched her eat, observing her short bitten nails, grubby neck and spiky dyed orange hair. She was a mess, yet there was still something appealing about her. She's bringing out the father instinct in me, he thought with a wry smile.

'I take it they let you out of the girls' farm,' he remarked. 'I'm not buying food for a runaway I hope.'

'They let me out,' she said between mouthfuls. 'They had to when my sister finally came t'get me. 'Sides, I'm sixteen now, I can look after myself.'

'I'm sure you can.'

'You bet I can!' She threw him a sly look. 'Thanks t'you really.'

'How's that?'

'Well . . . If I hadn't of hit on you, an' you hadn't of sent the kiddie patrol after me, I might never have got myself connected with all those boss chicks at the farm. Y'know something? I met 'em all, an' I learned me plenty.'

He didn't know what she was talking about and he didn't much care to find out. It suddenly occurred to him that he shouldn't be sitting down with her anyway. He gestured for the check.

'Where ya goin'?' she demanded.

'Home,' he replied, then added sarcastically, 'that's if you don't mind, of course.'

'I thought you'd at least give me a lift,' she whined pathetically. 'Just look at it out there.'

He turned to stare out of the large windows. The rain still pounded down. 'What makes you think I'm going your way?'

'Look – if it's too much trouble just drop me at the bus station.

I'm goin' to my sister, she lives outta the city an' I don't wanna miss my bus.'

He knew he should refuse her, but what the heck, he was off duty and she was only a kid.

'Get your coat,' he sighed.

'Don't have no coat.'

'In this weather?'

'Who knew it was goin' to piss?'

He paid the check, took his raincoat from the rack in the corner, was about to put it on, then changed his mind and threw it over her shoulders. 'Come on,' he said.

They ran for the car, Joey tagging behind, yelping as the full force of the torrential rain hit her.

'Come on,' Leon repeated, raising his voice as he opened the car door.

She hurled herself inside like an angry puppy. In spite of the protection of his raincoat she was soaked through.

He started the engine, and she found disco on the radio.

'Got a ciggie?' she asked.

'I gave it up,' he replied gruffly. 'And that's what you should do.'

'Sure,' she sneered. 'I mean I got so much goin' for me why should I need cigarettes?'

He glanced at her and turned the radio down. 'What time is your bus?'

She was silent for a moment, chewing on her thumb and wriggling on the seat.

'What time?' he repeated, slowing his speed as the rain increased.

'It don't matter what time,' she mumbled at last, ' 'cos there's no point in me catchin' it anyways.'

He frowned. 'I thought you wanted to be dropped at the bus station.'

'S'awright. I can sleep on one of them benches. I done it before.'

He was rapidly losing patience with her. Clicking off the radio he said, 'What are you talking about?'

'Well . . . Y'see my sister's gone off to Arizona to live on one of them communes. I was supposed to save some money an' go join her, but I had my money stolen.' She warmed to her story. 'These two black cats ripped me off, wanted to put me on the streets, pimp off me, but I got away from 'em, only thing is they got all the money I saved from workin'. Now I gotta start again.' She paused. 'You got any money to spare? I'll screw ya for ten bucks.'

Leon pulled the car over and stopped. 'Get out,' he said sharply.

'Waddya mean?' she whined.

'Out.'

'Why?'

'You know why.'

'I don't know what—'

'Get out. Or do you want me to run you over to Juvenile? They'll find a bed for you.'

'Pig bastard!' she spat, realizing he was serious.

He leaned across her and opened the passenger door. Heavy rain blew into the car.

Her voice quavered. 'You're throwin' me out in this? Why can't you take me to the bus station?'

'Because you're full of it, the bus station is out of my way, and you're a little liar. Now – out.'

Reluctantly she stepped from the car into the pounding rain. He slammed the door shut and drove off.

She had her nerve. Doing it to him again. Propositioning him like he was some john who had to pay for it. Dumb stupid little hooker. Maybe he should *have taken her to Juvenile, handed her in. Maybe that would have been kinder than dumping her on the street.*

Jesus Christ! Now he was feeling guilty!

Well she was only sixteen, and it was the sort of night you wouldn't leave a cat out in.

But then, he reasoned, she wouldn't thank him for handing her in, and she could look after herself. She was a toughie. A street kid. Besides, she wasn't his responsibility.

Angrily he drove home, parked underground, and took the elevator to his apartment.

It wasn't until he was standing under a hot shower that he realized she still had his raincoat.

* * *

Millie leaned across the table and said, very softly, 'Honey, if I left, would you miss me?'

'Huh?' Startled, Leon returned to his surroundings.

Millie patted his hand comfortingly. 'Welcome back.'

'I was just thinking—'

'Oh, really?' Her sarcasm was thick. 'I would never have guessed.'

'I was just thinking,' he repeated carefully, 'about where we should spend our vacation this year. Have you thought about where you would like to go?'

'California,' she replied, without hesitation. Then, anxiously, 'We can afford it, can't we?'

'Sure we can.'

'I've always wanted to go to California,' she said, her eyes sparkling. 'Haven't you?'

Leon frowned. He could honestly say that he had never had even the faintest desire to visit the West Coast. As far as he was concerned California was a land of sunshine, oranges and freaks. 'I'll talk to a travel agent next week,' he promised.

She beamed. 'We have plenty of time, but it sure would be nice to get it all planned.'

He smiled reassuringly and wondered if Deke Andrews had had it all planned. Had he *planned* to viciously hack three people to death? Had he *planned* to leave the small house looking like an abattoir? Had he *planned* to calmly wash up, walk out and vanish?

The waiter appeared with two steaming plates of spaghetti and clam sauce. Leon felt his juices rising. Millie grinned and murmured something about the only sure way of turning him on nowadays was with a good hot plate of food.

He didn't reply. He wasn't up to playful banter about the

growing infrequency of their sex life. It wasn't that he no longer desired Millie, it was just that he was so goddamn tired . . . And half the time when he got into bed and closed his eyes the images that he saw were not erotic, warm and sexual. They were of Deke Andrews. A photograph of him that had appeared in his senior class yearbook aged eighteen. 'He never changed much from that picture,' various witnesses had assured him. 'Just grew his hair some.'

The police artist had worked diligently on the photo, ageing it eight years and adding the longer hair. It had then been circulated across the country.

Leon knew the photo intimately. An ordinary boy with extraordinary eyes. Burning black deadly eyes. They haunted him. And so did the mutilated body of Joey Kravetz, her neck almost severed from her body so grotesque were her wounds . . .

'Eat up,' said Millie.

He stared at the plateful of spaghetti and felt distinctly nauseous. What was the matter with him? Had to get a hold of himself. Goddamn! He had lived through twenty years of gruesome murders and not one of them had ever affected him this way. He wound some spaghetti onto his fork and shoved it into his mouth.

'Good, huh?' questioned Millie.

Good, huh? mocked Deke Andrews in his head.

' 'Scuse me.' Leon pushed his chair away from the table and dropped his fork with a dull clatter. 'Call of nature, I'll be right back.'

Millie's eyebrows rose in surprise as he hurried from the room seeking refuge in the men's toilet. There, he rested his head against the cold tile wall and made a decision. He would open up the Andrews file. He would apply to the Captain for permission, and if he didn't get it, he would work on the case in his spare time.

Suddenly he felt better.

Chapter Eleven

Elaine Conti wore large tinted sunglasses, a wide brimmed hat, and a voluminous white linen coat. Casually she glanced around as she strolled through the make-up department of Bullocks, Westwood. Unobserved she pocketed a seventy dollar bottle of Opium perfume as she passed by a display table. Her eyes darted this way and that as she added a ceramic hand mirror and a lucite lipstick holder to the perfume already in her pocket.

By this time her heart was beating wildly, but her casual stroll never faltered. She drifted through to the sunglasses department and managed to pocket two sixty dollar pairs before taking the escalator down to the linens and notions. There she was accosted by a middle-aged saleslady in black and rhinestones who said, 'And what can I do for you today, madam?'

'Nothing, thank you,' Elaine replied. 'I'm just looking.'

'Do go ahead, please. I'll keep my eye on you should you find that you need me.'

Elaine swallowed aggravation, smiled, and beat a hasty retreat to men's casual clothes where she was able to add a silk Yves Saint Laurent tie to her collection of goodies.

She looked around and noted a male assistant checking her out. Her heart was really pounding now. It was enough. Slowly she sauntered towards the exit.

Leaving was always the moment of truth. What if a hand descended on her shoulder as she stepped outside? What if a voice said, 'Would you mind coming back inside for a moment?' What if she was *caught*?

Absolutely impossible. She was far too careful. She only took when she was sure no hidden eyes or cameras were watching. And she only took items priced at under a hundred dollars. Somehow she felt that she was safe.

Outside. On the street. No heavy hand on her shoulder.

She walked to the Mercedes which was parked at a meter on Westwood Boulevard, removed her linen coat, its pockets filled with ill-gotten gains, folded it carefully, and placed it in the trunk. Then she took off her hat and sunglasses and threw those in too.

She felt fantastic! What an incredible charge these illicit shopping sprees gave her. Better than an affair any day. Humming softly she climbed into the car.

Elaine had been successfully shoplifting for over a year. Once a week, regularly, she donned what she called 'her disguise' and hit a department store or a boutique. Department stores were safer, but the boutiques gave the biggest thrill of all. There you could *really* go to town, slipping a scarf, a silk knit sweater, or even a pair of shoes into your pocket right under some snappy little salesgirl's nose. Oh, the excitement! The kick! The shot of adrenaline that kept her vibrating for hours and hours. The greatest high of all!

It had started by accident really. She had been standing in Saks one day waiting for attention at the Clinique make-up counter. She needed face powder in a hurry, she was late for a lunch date, exhausted from a dance class (studying modern ballet had been the in thing to do then) and more than a little impatient and bad tempered. Suddenly, the easiest thing in the world had been to slip the box of powder – conveniently situated on the front of the counter – into her purse, and saunter quietly out of the store. She had quite expected to be stopped, and then coolly, calmly, she would just have explained that she was merely making a little protest, taking a stand against the gross rudeness of salesgirls who preferred conversation with each other to attending to a customer.

Would they have believed her?

She was Mrs Ross Conti. Of course they would.

But she wasn't stopped. Not then. Not the next time. Nor the time after that.

What had started out as a protest soon changed into a habit. An unbreakable one.

* * *

'Buddy,' Angel whispered softly. 'Can I meet your agent?'

'What?' He frowned. They lay side by side on the narrow bed in Randy Felix's borrowed apartment watching a game show on a badly functioning black and white television.

She sat up, long blonde hair falling around her perfect face, eyes shining with enthusiasm. 'I've been thinking,' she announced, 'it's silly – me sitting at home all day when I could be trying for a job too. If I met your agent he could send *me* up for things. Wouldn't it be terrific if *I* got something?'

He spaced his words carefully. 'It's not a good idea.'

Now it was her turn to frown. 'Why?' she demanded plaintively.

'Why yes?'

'Because,' she replied quickly, 'things don't seem to be coming easily for you and I'd like to help. Before I went to Hawaii I had made up my mind that I wanted to be an actress.'

He breathed deeply, evenly. It had not been a good day. 'Are you saying you don't think I can look after you?'

Her eyes widened. 'Of course not. I know you'll always look after me. But we do need money, don't we?'

He was suddenly angry. 'Who says?'

She gestured helplessly around the cramped room. 'Well . . . this isn't our apartment. The car we have is falling to pieces, and you're so jumpy lately. Honestly, Buddy, I'm not complaining. I just want to help out.'

'Fuck!' He exploded, jumping off the bed, pulling tight Levis over French Y-fronts, and grabbing a shirt.

She looked alarmed. 'What's the matter?'

He snatched his wallet and keys from the top of the television. 'You want to hassle me? Make me feel like nothing? Do it on your own time, lady.'

Before she could even reply he slammed his way out of the apartment.

Angel was shocked. She had not expected such a violent reaction. In fact, what she *had* expected was a tender scene between the two of them which would have resulted in Buddy stating deep love and gratefulness that she was such an understanding and helpful wife.

Tears filled her eyes. What had gone wrong? What had she said that was so unacceptable? Weren't married couples supposed to stick together, tell each other everything, and have no secrets?

As the days passed, and Buddy became more irritable and no starring role or even a bit part materialized, she had slowly begun to realize that things were not exactly as he had told her they would be. Not that she minded. She had read enough fan magazines in her life to know that Getting There and Making It were not always a fast jog up the yellow brick road. Sometimes there were Pitfalls and Hold Ups. Buddy had been away, and now it would just take him a little time to get back up where he belonged. But while he was waiting why couldn't she have a chance too? She only wanted to help.

Tearfully she climbed off the bed and straightened the covers. Their first fight. How she longed for him to come running back and hold her in his arms, tell her everything was all right, make slow gentle love to her. She shivered, and hugged her arms around her slender body.

Buddy. If he didn't want her to work she'd never mention it again.

Buddy. She loved him so much. He was all she had, and she planned to stay with him forever.

* * *

'Have you ever considered a red hot prick up the ass?' asked an agitated masculine voice.

'Do me a favour and go jerk off on your own time.'

Montana replaced the receiver briskly. Obscene phone calls. How did the cretins get hold of the numbers in the first place? Did they scour the phone books looking for single female listings? Or did they lurk around the supermarkets and stores checking out customers and their charge cards? Who knew? Who really cared?

Energetically she leaped out of bed. A wave of well publicized violence was spreading fear throughout the hills of Hollywood, Beverly, and Holmby. People were into security gates, guard dogs, electronic alarm systems, and guns. Montana bothered with none of the precautions. She refused to live a well guarded life. If something happened it happened. Fate. What would be would be. If an obscene phone caller hoped to upset her day he had the wrong number.

Humming tunelessly she launched into a few yoga positions out by the pool. It was only eight a.m. A clear smogless day – and she had an insane desire to trash everything and drive out to the beach.

Why not?

Many reasons.

Twenty actors with appointments scheduled exactly fifteen minutes apart.

A meeting with the young dress designer she wanted to hire for the film.

A trip to the airport to surprise Neil on his return from Palm Beach.

For the first time she felt really good about living in L.A. She was glad that Neil had talked her into letting him buy the house a few months back. They had leased their New York apartment, packed up forty cartons of books, records and assorted possessions, and finally made L.A. more than just a hotel suite.

Neil loved California. She had always been a city kid . . . But she could change couldn't she? For Neil she could do a lot of things.

Five years together and still she loved him, probably more than in the beginning, because in the beginning it had been lust. She grinned at the thought. She, who had only ever climbed into bed with body beautifuls and youth. Then along came Neil Gray with his middle-aged spread, greying hair, and bloodshot eyes.

She had wanted him then. And she wanted him now. Just as much. He had given her more than body beautiful and youth. He had given her knowledge, and in the long run that's what life was really all about.

Working together was a new phase in their relationship, and so far it seemed to be a definite bonus. He cared about the movie just as much as she did, in fact that's all they ever seemed to talk about. Not that she was complaining – what more could she want?

She wondered if he had landed George Lancaster.

Even bigger question. How would she feel if he had?

Disappointed. The more she thought about it the more she hated the idea. But as Oliver Easterne constantly said in his highly unoriginal way – 'A star is a star is a star.'

Oliver was turning out to be even more of a major asshole than she had first thought.

She dressed quickly in a Calvin Klein jacket, chain-store jeans, a six dollar T-shirt, and two hundred dollar cowboy boots. The mix suited her, especially when she pulled her luxuriant black hair tightly from her face, and twisted it into a long braid.

Skipping breakfast, she slipped behind the wheel of her somewhat battered Volkswagen. Neil was always nagging her to buy a new car, but the V.W. suited her. It wasn't flash, she could drive around the city virtually unnoticed, and that's the way she liked it.

Actors. Twenty more today. Maybe one she wanted – one that was right – one that would walk into her office and bring a character she had created to life.

God! Putting this movie together was exciting. More exciting than anything she had done in her life before.

Movie making. It got in your blood. And she and Neil together – what a team!

Grinning quietly to herself she started the V.W. and set off to her office.

* * *

'Why can't you get me a copy of the goddamn script?' screamed Ross down the phone. 'Christ almighty, Zack, I'm not asking for a table at the last supper. All I want is a lousy script. Ninety frigging pages bound together. Sounds like a simple task to me.' He tapped the glass table beside the pool with angry fingers as he listened to the answer. The answer was that *Street People* appeared to be under lock and key. Nobody had a copy – but nobody.

Only George Lancaster and Tony Curtis and Kirk Douglas and Sadie La Salle and Christ knows who else. Probably half of fucking Hollywood.

He slammed the phone down in disgust. Here he was – a major star – chasing a frigging part in some half-assed frigging movie written by a woman no less and *he hadn't even seen the script.* What the fuck was the matter with him? Was he losing his smarts along with his hair?

The very thought sent him running to the pool house in a panic. What made him think he was losing his hair? He wasn't. No way. Well, maybe a little . . . nothing noticeable . . . nothing that combing it a different way couldn't take care of.

He studied his reflection in the mirrored poolhouse.

Ross Conti. Movie star. Still a good-looking son of a bitch. Only he and Paul Newman had kept it all together. The others had fallen to pieces – got fat, bald, had disastrous face lifts, wore bad toupees. Sinatra still looked good enough with his sewn on thatch. Still had a set of pipes that kept them creaming their panties when they heard his world weary tones. Satisfied, Ross returned poolside.

Elaine was framed in the glass entrance to the living room. Elaine. His wife. She didn't look bad for an old broad. One thing about her – she kept herself in good shape, didn't drink, screw around or make a fool of him.

'Honey,' he said warmly, 'I want you to do something for me.'

She looked him up and down. He was definitely developing a gut. Quite noticeable in the madras shorts he had chosen to wear. 'I'll do anything you want Ross, dear,' she said sweetly, 'as long as you promise me you'll start going to the gym again.'

He feigned surprise and patted his stomach. 'You think I need it?'

'Everyone over twenty-five needs it.'

'What is this everyone over twenty-five crap?'

'A fact of life, my darling. The older one gets the harder one has to work at looking good.'

'Bullshit.'

'Truth.'

'Bullshit.'

She gave an aggravated sigh. 'What is it you want me to do?'

'Oh, yeah.' He scratched his chin and squinted the famous blues. 'Call Maralee Gray. Get hold of a copy of Neil's new script, the one we were talking about.'

'Couldn't Zack get it for you?'

'Zack frigging Schaeffer couldn't pull milk from a cow if you handed him the tit!'

Elaine nodded. He was finally coming around to her way of thinking.

'I need Sadie La Salle,' Ross suddenly blurted.

He was *definitely* coming around to her way of thinking. 'Do you want me to see if I can arrange it?' she asked slowly.

He looked enthusiastic. 'You think you can?'

She smiled. 'You've always said I can do anything I set my mind to.'

'So I'm giving you the word. Set your mind to getting me Sadie La Salle and a copy of that damn script.'

Her smile widened. There was nothing Elaine liked better than a challenge. 'Ross, sweetheart – you're on!'

He smiled back. 'Elaine, sweetheart – my money's on you.'

Marital bliss at last.

'I bought you a present,' she murmured, handing him the Saint Laurent silk tie she had stolen earlier.

He was pleased. 'Always thinking of the star, huh?' he said with a big grin.

She nodded. 'Always, Ross. Always.'

* * *

Mavericks was crowded, the bar six deep, disco music blasting eardrums.

Buddy hadn't been there in a long while – before Hawaii – before the days of fat little Maxie Sholto. He shuddered when he thought of Maxie. Fortunately he had woken up to reality before it was too late. No more drugs and orgies for Buddy Boy. That scene was purely for life's losers. Hitting on Gladrags for work was on thing. Maxie Sholto was a whole different ballgame.

'Buddy! Good t'see you. Where y'bin hiding?'

He waved at the barman. 'Around,' he replied. 'Here and there. What's happening?'

'Same old story. Business is good. Didja hear about me on "Hill Street Blues"? I had lines, man, *lines*.'

Yeah? So why was he still behind the bar at Mavericks?

'That's great,' Buddy said. 'Is Quince around?'

'In the back.'

'Thanks.'

He made his way to the end of the crowded bar, across a jammed dance floor and edged along a line of booths looking for Quince.

He found him surrounded by girls. Three of them.

Quince. Tall. Black. Good looking. A good actor too. They had worked together at Joy Byron's.

'Hey, man.' They spoke in unison, and slapped palms.

'Sit,' Quince said. 'Join the party.'

Buddy squeezed on the end of the leather banquette while Quince indicated the girls one by one. 'This is my lady – Luann. Her sister, Chickie. And a good friend, Shelly.'

Luann was a gorgeous chocolate blonde. Chickie was smaller, darker, with a set of teeth Farrah would kill for. Shelly was Shelly. The girl from the pool, looking good in a scant purple leotard and thin wrapover skirt.

'Hey—' he said. 'I know you.'

'Hey—' she replied. 'Buddy Hudson. Mister Married. Where's your old lady?'

'Buddy. Married. That'll be the day,' laughed Quince.

Shelly nodded. 'He's married.'

Quince raised an unbelieving eyebrow and grinned at Buddy. 'Tell 'em it ain't true, my man.'

Buddy scowled. His luck to run into Miss Bigmouth. It just wasn't his day. Or night. 'So I'm married, big deal,' he mumbled.

Quince began to laugh. 'I never thought the day would come when you would fall into *that* scene. What happened?' He hit his forehead with the palm of his hand. 'I know, I know. She's eighty-three, loaded, an' she has a *reaaal* bad heart. Am I hittin' it?'

Buddy's scowl deepened. He had run out on Angel to find a little relaxation. He didn't need this joke shit. 'Yeah, yeah, sure, you're right,' he said quickly. 'Only she's nearer ninety than eighty-three. More my speed, y'know?'

Quince guffawed loudly. 'That's my Buddy Boy! Always one eye on the main chance!'

'How about a little boogie?' requested Chickie, jigging about to the strains of a Donna Summer beat.

'Sorry,' Shelly intervened. 'I asked first.' She bumped against Buddy, forcing him to stand, then she slid from the booth, flung her arms around his neck and rotated her crotch against his on the edge of the packed dance floor.

'Eighty-three my ass,' she sneered. 'Twenty and goddamn spectacular. I've seen her out by the pool. Why you keepin' her a secret?'

He shrugged. 'No secret.'

'No shit? So where is she then?'

'What are you – a dyke?'

Shelly pushed her crotch sharply against his. 'If I *was* baby, I'd be scratchin' at your front door the moment you left with what *you* got stashed at home.'

He shoved her roughly away and went into his disco routine. He could give Travolta lessons – that's how smooth and sensuous and goddamn raunchy he was. *Allan Carr, walk in and see me now!*

Shelly matched him move for move, enjoying herself. She was good too.

He began to enjoy himself too. It was the first dancing he'd done in a long time, and when you had a partner who was with you all the way. Well . . . that was a real hot feeling.

They stopped when they'd had enough. When sweat coursed in little rivers down Shelly's bare arms and chest. 'Hmmm,' she said succinctly, 'you're good.'

'So are you,' he allowed.

They returned to the table. 'Should hope so. I'm a professional.'

'A professional what?'

She regarded him coolly. 'Dancer, asshole.' She turned to greet a new arrival who had moved in next to Chickie. 'Jer, babes, how'd it go tonight?'

Jer babes was a young good looking guy with nervous, shifty eyes. He shrugged. 'The same crap shoot. Y'know the scene.'

'Yeah,' she agreed sympathetically. 'Hey – have you two met?'

They shook heads negatively, summing each other up. 'Buddy Hudson – Jericho Crunch,' Shelly continued, the perfect hostess.

Buddy frowned. The loud music must be getting to him. Jericho Crunch! What kind of a name was that? Sounded like a religious Famous Amos!

Jericho's shifty eyes checked him over. 'You an actor?'

'What did you see me in?' Buddy asked quickly.

'Nothin'. I'm an actor too.'

'Yeah. What have you done?'

Jericho reeled off a few familiar television shows, then licked his lips and added, 'But I'm up for the big one. Think I'm gonna get it too.'

'What big one?' Buddy asked, immediately alert.

Jericho looked secretive. 'Nothin' I can talk about.'

'A television pilot?'

'Nope.'

'A commercial?'

'Nope.'

'So – what?'

'A movie. A real biggie.'

'A television film?'

'Nope. The real thing.'

'What's it called?'

Jericho narrowed his eyes. 'You think I'm gonna tell you so you can go runnin' after it too. No way. Besides, I'm almost set. I got the castin' bitch creamin' at the thought of usin' me,' he leered. 'Get the picture?'

Yes. Buddy got the picture. And the pisser was not about to give away a thing. He thought about Angel. She hadn't meant to nag. She had just caught him at a bad moment when all he had left in the world was forty-two bucks and no idea where to score. Unemployment was out. He had never wanted to get involved with forms and papers and all that crap. And he couldn't start now. 'Gotta split,' he said, rising from the table.

'Yeah,' laughed Quince. 'Time to run on home to old momma an' get out the bedpan, huh?'

'It's like this,' Buddy said patiently. 'If the Rolls ain't in the garage by two a.m. the Bentley gets lonely. You know what I'm sayin'?'

Quince hooted with laughter. Buddy pushed through the crowds, and took a deep breath as he hit the street.

Shelly followed him out. 'I need a lift home,' she stated.

He looked her over and decided she might be useful. 'Sure,' he said. 'My car's down the block.'

She walked beside him, smelling slightly of sweat and a heavy musk scent.

'What kind of dancing you do?' he asked.

'Artistic,' she replied.

'A stripper, huh?'

'One of the best.'

'Modest.'

'Screw you. I *am* one of the best and proud of it.'

They reached the car and he slid in the driver's seat springing the passenger lock for her.

'And you're an actor,' she stated, settling herself comfortably. 'I should have guessed.'

'One of the best,' he said quickly.

She laughed. 'Yeah. That's why you're driving this pile of crapola.'

'It gets me around. I'm not into image.'

'Can't afford to be, huh?'

'I'm gettin' by.'

She extracted a joint from her purse and lit up. 'I'll tell you somethin',' she said, offering him a toke which he declined because who needed to get stopped by the cops at this time of the morning? 'You'd make a terrific stripper. You got the body *an'* you got all the right moves.'

He laughed aloud. 'You have to be kidding.'

She was unamused. 'What's so funny? It pays good, an' just as many guys are doin' it today.'

'I'm an actor. I told you.'

'Doesn't mean you can't take off your clothes an' get paid for it.'

'I guess you think Sylvester Stallone did that kind of thing to get on?'

'Yeah. As a matter of fact he did – don't you read your gossip mags?'

'What about your friend – Brunch – Crunch – the great wall of Jericho. He take 'em off?'

'Undressed he's bad news. Sloped shoulders, knock knees, nothin' much in the bread bin. You dig?'

Silently Buddy nodded.

'He does a bit of waitering – Hollywood parties. Thinks he'll get discovered that way.'

The hell with it – Buddy reached for the joint and took a long satisfying pull, then casually he said, 'Maybe it worked for him. Like what's this movie he says he's all set for?'

'Oh, c'mon. You don't believe *that* do you? If Jer served a canape to Johnny Carson he'd tell everyone he was all set for The Tonight Show!'

'So there's no movie?'

'He went on an interview.'

'For what?'

She laughed softly. 'Wanna horn in on his action?'

Carefully he eased the car into a convenient parking space opposite their apartment house. 'It's a free country.'

'If you say so.'

'So what's the movie?'

'Come up for a snort. Coke always jogs my memory.'

He thought of Angel. Beautiful. Innocent. Waiting.

Then he thought of forty-two lousy bucks. 'Sure. Why not?'

* * *

Gina Germaine had an agent, a manager, a secretary, a make-up artist, a hairdresser, an accountant, a business counsellor, an acting coach, and two ex-husbands to support. Sort of. They all depended on her for *something*.

She was thirty-three years old – twenty-nine to the press. Blonde – dyed, not natural. Pretty, with round, slightly protruding blue eyes, a retroussé nose, and a maneater mouth filled with sharp white perfect teeth. There were thousands of girls on the West Coast of America who were just as pretty as Gina Germaine. But her body made her something special. Long skinny legs, small ass, tiny twenty inch waist, and an enormous bosom. Thirty-nine firm fruity inches with huge pale chocolate nipples.

* * *

Gina Germaine became a star because of her amazing breasts. Featured in Playboy *at the age of nineteen, she was immediately discovered by Hollywood. 'Send for her at once,' demanded two studio heads, three corporate executives, and four enthusiastic agents.*

She was already in town. Maxie Sholto, a canny hustler who knew a sensational pair of boobies when he saw them – had got there first. 'Let me represent you,' he said, his shifty smile going full force. 'Let me make you a star.'

The old-fashioned but meaningful words worked. Gina packed up a so-so modelling career in Houston, Texas, and flew with Maxie to Los Angeles, where he got her a few bit parts here and there. Nothing spectacular. Until one day she walked into a television executive's private office, sat on a high backed chair opposite him and casually spread her long skinny sexy legs just as Maxie had told her she should.

The executive's bloodshot eyes bulged with excitement. Gina Germaine was wearing a short white mini skirt with nothing underneath! No panty hose, no panties. Nothing!

She landed a role in a weekly television sitcom, and a weekly rendezvous with her television executive who expired two years later from a massive stroke. Gina was sorry to see him go. He was such a sweet old guy. But then again she really didn't need him any more. Television had made her a star, and Maxie had made her his wife.

Gina's television show lasted five years. Her marriage only a few months longer, but Maxie and she parted friends, and he was best man at her well publicized wedding to a macho actor whose main hobby was beating her up, so she divorced him too.

Her personal life was chaos, but her star continued to rise. A movie spinoff from her series had made big bucks at the box office. And she followed this with another money spinner. She was that rarity. A small screen star who could make it on the big screen. All at once she was hot. Every movie she did made money. She supported sagging superstars, playing straight lady to zany comedians, bubbled, wriggled and took her clothes off with monotonous regularity.

The public didn't think so. The public loved her. She was their Gina. A gorgeous package of golden flesh. A movie star whore with a heart of gold and tits to match. An old fashioned type movie star who evoked memories of Monroe and Mansfield.

'I want to be taken seriously,' she cooed on The Johnny Carson Show one night. 'Y'know John, I want to do different kinds of films – something with a social message.'

Johnny had just looked to camera, his face a study in restraint, his expression said it all. The audience had roared with laughter and Gina was smart enough to shut up and return to sticking out her tits and indulging in playful flirts. Inside she was seething with frustration. Why shouldn't she do serious movies?

Two weeks later she met Neil Gray at a party. He was with his wife, but a little obstacle like a wife had never bothered Gina. What she wanted – she had. One of the advantages of being a filmstar.

Neil Gray was serious with a capital S. He made important movies, meaningful movies. The kind of movies Gina knew that she should be doing.

She moved in quietly. Flattered him, hung onto his every word, made sure he got a good view of the amazing boobs when she leaned across him to reach for a cigarette, a drink, a scoop of dip. Three days later she called. 'I hope I'm not disturbing you,' she said in a throaty voice, knowing full well that if she was having her usual effect she was disturbing him a great deal. 'But I really do need some good advice, and you seem like just the person to help me.'

He was amused, intrigued. He knew 'some good advice' meant 'a good fuck'. They were both conversant with the language of Hollywood.

Lunch. Her house. A walled estate on San Ysidro Drive.

Salad Nicoise followed by solid fucking. Neither of them had the patience or the inclination to waste time.

A second rendezvous two weeks later. Same scenario.

They did not talk much, but Gina didn't mind. Once a man got lost in her beautiful boobs they always came back for more . . . and more and more . . . There would be plenty of time for talking.

She studied Montana at the dinner the Grays threw at the Bistro to announce their film. She was there with Chet Barnes. It sure startled the pants off Neil. But he needn't have worried, she was cool. She even chatted politely to Montana, told her about her own screenplay. Not that she had written it yet, but she was going to. So . . . Street People *was to be Neil's new film.*

The next day she called her agent, Sadie La Salle, and demanded a copy of the script.

'Nobody has seen it yet,' Sadie said briskly. 'Besides, I don't think it's your type of thing . . . From what I understand it's about two cops, an old one and a young one. And—'

'There must be women in it,' Gina interrupted tardily.

'Well . . . I expect so. But no star roles. I'm sure it's not a Gina Germaine vehicle.' She paused. 'Now tell me, dear, did you read And Baby Makes . . .*?'*

'No,' Gina snapped. 'I mean yes . . . and I hate it. Get me a

copy of Neil's film Sadie, let me *decide if it's a Gina Germaine vehicle or not.'*

* * *

When Neil Gray phoned and suggested a weekend in Palm Beach Gina said yes without a moment's hesitation.

'Separate everything,' he warned. 'Rooms, travel, everything.'

'Sure,' she agreed.

'You might get bored, I'll have to spend time with Pamela and George.'

'I'll bring a book.'

She brought a book, but she never got to read it. She filched a copy of *Street People* from Neil's suitcase the second he left their adjoining suites, and read it in fifty-five minutes flat. Then she read it through again, concentrating on the part of Nikki. A buzz of excitement, a jolt of adrenaline.

NIKKI – EARLY TWENTIES – UNSPOILED BEAUTY – FANTASTIC BODY ALTHOUGH NOT OVERSTATED – NATURAL BLONDE – CERTAIN INNOCENT QUALITY

I could play Nikki. I could. I could.

And it was a marvellous role. A catalyst between the two male parts. Daughter of one. Lover of the other.

I could play the crap out of a character like Nikki.

She was too old.

I've always looked younger than my age.

She was hardly unspoiled.

Good acting would take care of that.

Her fantastic body was more than a little overstated.

No shit? I'll diet. I'll bind the old boobies down. I'll fucking starve if necessary.

Innocent?

I can fake it.

She could hardly wait for Neil to get back. He looked tired and perplexed. She slid her arm around him and led him to bed.

'Pamela's a devious old bird,' he managed, as she started to unzip his pants.

'Really?' she questioned. 'Why?'

'Because—' he began, then groaned. She had him in her mouth and she was blowing him like her life depended on it – but then – in a way – it did.

Arriving back in Los Angeles Neil issued orders as they were leaving the plane. 'You'd better wait five minutes. I'll go ahead.'

Gina pouted. 'Ashamed of being seen with me?'

'Don't be ridiculous. We agreed to be . . . discreet.'

She sighed. 'Okay. But I will see you soon won't I?'

'Sooner than you think.'

He pecked her on the cheek and hurried on his way.

Most men were such bastards. But what did she care? She used *them.* No way did they use her. Her life was full of what she termed 'business fucks'. Men that could further her career, help her with her portfolio of shares (an impressive collection), assist her with real estate (three houses in Beverly Hills and an office block), and generally advise her on every matter from tax to abortion.

Gina always went to the best and never paid. Her current lovers included a Spanish real estate mogul. A Brazilian business whizz. A very rich Arab (he took care of her jewellery. That is he shopped 'Fred' and 'Tiffanys' every time he was in town). And the best lawyer, accountant and gynaecologist in Beverly Hills.

What she really wanted was a senator in her life, but she had yet to meet Teddy Kennedy whose fame attracted her the way plump skin attracts a hungry mosquito.

She looked upon Neil Gray as the next step in her career. He could treat her as badly as he wanted. For he would pay. One way or another. She would make sure of that.

* * *

Neil looked tired. Montana kissed him on both cheeks and said, 'Surprise! I thought we could talk on the way home.'

He glanced behind him. Thank God he had insisted on walking ahead of Gina. Quickly he grabbed Montana's arm and said, 'Wonderful, darling. You are just what I need after a weekend of Pamela and George.' Briskly he hurried her from the terminal.

'Well?' she questioned. 'I can't wait. Do we or do we not have the great George Lancaster?'

'You'll never believe this,' he said, hurriedly walking towards the open-doored limo where a chauffeur stood in uniformed attendance. 'But I still don't know.'

* * *

'Hey?' Buddy questioned. 'You really get off on that stuff?'

Shelly snorted a thin line of white powder from a mirrored table top through a folded banknote. 'Sure. Doesn't everybody?'

'Yeah. In Hollywood. I guess.' He prowled uneasily around her messy apartment. 'I used to be into it myself, but it got to be a drag.'

'A drag,' she repeated and grinned. 'You got broke and couldn't afford the habit. Right?'

'You know something?' He picked up a folder of photographs and flicked quickly through them. 'You have one smart mouth.'

She greedily snorted a touch more coke. 'So I've bin' told – *Mister* Married.'

'So?' he asked. 'Your memory got jogged yet?'

She stretched lazily. 'In a hurry?'

Yeah. He was in a hurry. He wanted to get back to Angel who he was sure was waiting up for him. 'No hurry.'

'Then relax! Take off your pants.' She yawned. 'If you like I'll give you a blow job that'll blow your mind.' She laughed. 'Get it?'

He sighed. 'Shelly, Shelly, who are you tryin' to turn on? There's only you an' me here, an' I think we got each other tagged.'

'You're right. But if ever you're in need . . . Like I give the best head in town. A hundred guys have told me. An' I'll tell you somethin' else, pal. I'm good because I enjoy it – *love* it.' She laughed again. 'Sure you don't want to give me a fast audition?'

'Quite sure, thank you.' There was something about her that reminded him of himself before he met Angel. A real smart ass. Master of the fast line and the quick come on.

'Well . . .' She rose, and pulled at the tie on her wrapover skirt. 'I guess if you're sure.' The skirt fell to the floor, and very slowly she hooked her fingers into the top of her leotard and peeled it down.

'Hey,' he said quickly. 'Enough. You sound like a hooker.'

'Takes one to know one,' she taunted, stepping out of her leotard altogether.

He frowned. 'We met before?'

'Ah ha! You remembered.' She walked towards him, all stiletto heels and tanned nakedness.

He backed away. 'I'm going home.'

'Don't you wanna know where we met?'

'I'm not losin' sleep over it.'

'Ah . . . Buddy . . . Let me give you head. C'mon, huh? I'm askin' nicely.'

He had backed himself all the way to the door. Slipping the latch he let himself out. 'See you by the pool, kid. Don't catch cold.'

She waved her tongue at him obscenely. '*Street People* is the name of the movie Jer is up for. Oliver Easterne's the producer. Give it a shot.'

'Hey – *al*right. I will.' He took the stairs two at a time. Thirty seconds later he was fitting his key into the front door and calling out softly, 'Angel, babe. I'm home.'

* * *

'I just don't believe the bastard wouldn't give you a yes or a no. I mean the whole object of your trip was to get an answer.'

'I'm well aware of that,' Neil replied caustically.

He and Montana lounged on the top of their king size bed. She wore huge reading glasses and a man's shirt, her long legs stretched out before her, while her heavy black hair hung in a straight curtain to her waist.

Neil, in his pyjamas, looked tired and haggard. Two solid days of Gina Germaine would make anyone exhausted. Even a Warren Beatty or a Ryan O'Neal might feel the pace. Gina liked to fuck. Correction. Neil couldn't make up his mind whether she liked to fuck or fucked to be liked. Interesting problem. Not his. He wanted her for one thing and one thing only.

'Stars!' Montana exclaimed scornfully. 'They're all a giant pain.' She reached for a Salem and lit up. 'The real reason George Lancaster won't commit is because he thinks if he says no you'll offer the part to someone else and his ego wouldn't like that.'

Neil scratched his chin. 'The problem is Pamela. She holds the balls in *that* household.'

'And is she squeezing them to say yes or no?'

'I don't think she's quite decided. She likes the idea of George doing a movie, but she doesn't like the idea of him running around Hollywood without her.'

'Ah,' Montana nodded knowingly. 'The lady is frightened of ambitious sixteen year old nymphets climbing on her old man's bones.'

Neil looked amused. 'You've never met Pamela, have you? The only thing that would frighten her is if the government threatened to take away her money.'

'Can't wait to meet her.'

'You'll like her.'

'Wanna bet?'

'I never risk my money with one of life's winners.'

A smile flickered across her face, and she pushed her reading glasses up into her hair. 'Such a charmer!'

'Of course.'

She reached out her arms. 'Come here, charmer.'

'I've got a headache.'

'Neil! That's supposed to be my excuse.'

'I really have,' he assured her.

She rose from the bed and padded towards the bathroom. 'I'll get you a painkiller,' she said sympathetically. A weekend in Palm Beach with George Lancaster and Pamela London can't have been all laughs. The poor bastard looked worn out. She hadn't really felt much like sex anyway – even though it had been a couple of weeks. Of course sex with Neil was still great, but they had been together long enough not to feel the need to do it every night, and right now work was the raging passion. Besides, getting a movie off the ground was never easy, and she sensed that he was more worried than he seemed.

She took two aspirin from a bottle, filled a glass with water and walked back into the bedroom. 'So,' she said, handing him the pills, 'we have to wait on his decision – is that it?'

He gulped the pills down quickly, not looking at her. There was no headache, but any more physical exertion after what he had been through with Gina was quite out of the question. 'George and Pamela will be here in two weeks' time. We'll get our answer then,' he said. Christ! He felt so goddamn guilty. He didn't need her sympathy to make him feel worse.

'Visiting royalty. What fun!' she said lightly.

'I promise, you'll like them both.'

She raised a cynical eyebrow. 'In a pig's ass I will.'

'Whatever you say, my dear, whatever you say.'

* * *

Angel was well aware of Buddy entering their apartment. Although it was almost three in the morning he made no effort to be quiet. He slammed the door, called out her name, and switched on all the lights.

She lay on her stomach in bed, silent and still. At first, when he had walked out on her, she had been anxious for him to return. But as the hours passed and he didn't even bother to call she had become hurt and angry. What was it about her that invited such behaviour? Why did she always end up being treated so badly? She had spent her life apologizing for just being around. With Buddy all that was supposed to change. He was her new beginning. The start of her own family.

Men. Hadn't her foster-mother always warned her?

'Angel?' he questioned softly.

Men. Never trust them.

'Are you awake, sweet stuff?' he asked more loudly.

Men. They have dirty habits and dirty minds.

He rubbed her back. 'Angel, babe?'

Men. They only want One Thing.

Slowly he slid his hands under the covers.

Men. If you give it to them they never respect you.

He pulled the covers off her immobile body. She was wearing her blue baby doll nightie with matching panties.

'You awake?' he whispered.

She remained silently on her stomach, her eyes squeezed tightly shut.

Buddy was underterred. He hooked his fingers into the elastic of her panties and pulled them off.

She said nothing. Why should she? She was mad at him wasn't she?

He parted her legs and bent his head, his tongue darting into her warm wetness like a lethal cold snake.

Why was his tongue so cold? Why was she suddenly shaking with ecstasy? Why couldn't she stay mad at him?

'Ohhh . . . Buddy . . .' The words fluttered from her mouth like summer blossoms falling from a tree.

He raised his head long enough to say, 'You're not mad at me, babe, are you?'

She sighed very very softly and murmured, 'Turn the light out, Buddy. Please . . .'

He ripped off his pants. 'Why? You got somethin' to hide?' God but she made him horny! He spread her legs wider and replaced his eager tongue with something he had been saving up for her all night long.

Chapter Twelve

Deke Andrews rode the subway out to Queens, and spent the morning checking out the used car lots along Queens Boulevard.

He finally found what he was looking for, a small brown van with tattered curtains on the back windows. It was five years old with plenty of mileage on the clock.

'How much?' he asked the shirt-sleeved dealer.

The dealer, a man with a bad case of B.O., summed his potential customer up. 'Price is on it,' he said finally.

'I know,' Deke replied, 'but you'll never get it.'

'Says who?'

'It's not worth it. Needs work.'

'How d'you know?'

'I can tell.'

'You ain't even driven it.'

'I can tell.'

The dealer spat a wad of chewing gum onto the ground. 'I can drop a hundred.'

'Three hundred.'

'That's my profit.'

'Cash.'

Curiosity got the better of the salesman. 'Don't you want to drive it?'

'I want to drive it out of here. Do we have a deal?'

The salesman nodded. He would have taken four hundred off if pushed. The engine was pure garbage.

Together they went into his office and did business.

Fifteen minutes later Deke drove away from the lot in the van.

He knew it was an inferior piece of machinery but he also knew that by the time he was finished with it the engine would sing. Deke had a way with cars.

* * *

Joey said, 'Do you have a car?'

Deke replied, 'No. I did have. I had a Mustang. It was—'

'Shee . . . it!'

'What?'

'I wanted to take a ride. Atlantic City maybe. Fun, huh? We could make out on the beach.'

'Make what?'

'Je . . . sus! Sometimes I don't believe you. We've bin seein' each other three weeks. Waddya think we're gonna make? Sand castles.'

'Sorry. I—'

'Don't say sorry. I hate it when you do that.'

'I could get a car.'

'How?'

'From the garage where I work.'

'When?'

'I don't know. I'd have to wait until one came in for repairs and was left overnight.'

'Shee . . . it!'

'What's the matter?'

'I wanna go for a drive tonight.'

'It's not possible.'

'Then I think I'll work. You'd better go home.'

'No! I'll get us a car.'

'Yeah? You sure, cowboy?'

'Yes. I'm sure.'

* * *

He drove the van slowly and carefully. Wouldn't do to get stopped. He drove out past Kennedy airport, turned off the main highway, and searched for a quiet side road. There, he parked and opened up the hood. The engine was no better and no worse than he had thought. A few days of hard work should do it.

Satisfied, he headed back for Queens, where he parked the van near the station and took the subway back to New York.

His room waited. A few impersonal square feet. A bed, a dresser, his scant possessions.

It took him only minutes to pack. And then, once more, he was on his way.

Chapter Thirteen

Lunch: The Bistro Gardens.

Cast: Elaine Conti. Maralee Gray. Karen Lancaster.

Menu: Salad, salad, salad. Nothing fattening. They were all on a permanent diet.

Subject: Gossip.

Karen to Maralee: 'You look absolutely sensational. Palm Springs must have agreed with you.'

Maralee, smiling: 'It certainly did. I met this very interesting man called Randy Felix.'

Elaine: 'Did he live up to his name?'

Maralee: 'How would *I* know. It wasn't *that* sort of relationship.'

Karen, cynically: 'There *are* no other kinds of relationships.'

Maralee: 'Randy is into preserving our environment.'

Karen, sarcastic: 'Really?'

Elaine, down to earth: 'How old is he? And does he have money?'

Maralee, laughing: 'I don't know and I don't much care. I'm not planning to *marry* him.'

Elaine: 'What *are* you planning?'

Karen: 'She's planning to get into the poor kid's pants. When does he get into town?'

Maralee, affronted: 'He's not a kid. He's at least twenty-six or seven. And as a matter of fact he will be in L.A. shortly, he has his own apartment here.'

Karen and Elaine in unison: 'Sure.'

Maralee: 'God! You are a couple of bitches.'

Karen: 'Nothing wrong with getting laid.'

Maralee: 'I never said there was. And if I do decide to investigate "the poor kid's" pants, I'll certainly be sure to let you know, Karen, dear.'

Karen: 'Details! I want details! Like is he hung and does he give good head?'

'Karen!'

'Sorry, sorry. I'll shut up.'

The three women were firm friends. They moved in the same circles and had the same interests – clothes, money and sex. Also none of them had children, which created a bond. Karen – because she didn't want any. Maralee – because she had miscarried twice when married to Neil and had then given up. And Elaine because she could not conceive – a fact which had never bothered her or Ross.

'Oh! Will you look who just came in,' Karen said.

Three sets of eyes guarded by three sets of different expensive optics studied the entrance. There, suitably clad in a white silk Ungaro dress and jacket, with Cartier daytime diamonds, stood Bibi Sutton.

Now Bibi was fifty years old if she was a day. But in the twenty years she had been one of the so-called social lionesses of the Beverly Hills elite she had not aged a jot. Her skin was smooth roman olive, her hair a rich burnished copper, her figure voluptuous, without one inch of fat.

It was said she had been a journalist in her native France and had been sent to interview the American movie star Adam Sutton at his hotel in Paris. It had also been said that she was a highly paid call girl who had visited him every night in his suite at the George V. For free.

Who cared? It had happened years before – and whatever she *had* been, she was now a lady to be reckoned with.

Bibi Sutton set trends. She could make or break a designer, a restaurant, an artist, a caterer. If Bibi put the seal of approval on something or someone – then that business or person was made. She had clout, style and a forceful personality. Plus a French accent which even after twenty years sounded like Bardot on a bad day. She cultivated broken English, it was part of her charisma.

In comparison, Adam Sutton was a tall, quietly spoken man. A fine actor with two Oscars to prove it. Still a star at sixty-two, and an upstanding member of the Los Angeles community.

They had two children. Jennifer, eighteen, studying at a college in Boston. Charles, nineteen, away at Harvard. Rumour had it that there was another child born to Bibi before her marriage – the result of a torrid affair with George Lancaster. But Bibi had always denied the fact. 'A filthy lie,' she told the one journalist brave (or stupid) enough to ask her about it. And the rumour was laid to rest.

Bibi and Adam Sutton were Hollywood royalty. The perfect couple. Rich. Socially acceptable. Powerful.

'Hmmm . . .' murmured Karen. 'How I'd *love* to catch our Bibi with her pantyhose around her ankles.' She had always been somewhat amused at the thought of her father and Bibi locked in hot combat all those years ago.

Maralee licked her lips. 'And how I'd love to catch our Adam in bed one dark night. Preferably with me.'

Karen looked amazed. 'Adam Sutton! You must be joking. He has to be the most boring fuck in Beverly Hills.'

'Who would know?' Maralee retorted tartly.

'*I* wouldn't for one,' Karen replied. 'In fact I can't think of anyone who would. The man does not screw around.'

'How unusual,' Maralee said.

Elaine ignored them both. She was on her feet and heading full speed in Bibi's direction.

'Darling!!' Both together. Kissy, kissy on each other's cheeks. Lips not touching skin. 'How *are* you?' Still together. 'You look *wonderful*.'

The ritual was finished. 'Bibi,' Elaine said quickly. 'I'm thinking of having a little soirée on the twenty-fourth of this month. It's a Friday. Nothing vast. But it's been such ages since I've had time to get anything together. Ross has been so busy. My God – I don't have to tell *you* what it's like. Can you and Adam come?'

'Sweetie!' Bibi looked quite shocked. 'Eh! How I know? You think I know *anything* without my book? You call me. We looove to come if we free. Okay sweetie?'

'Yes, fine, I'll call you later,' Elaine said obediently. It would be unthinkable to plan a party on a date the Suttons could not attend. Quickly she returned to her table in the fashionable sunlit garden.

'Any luck?' demanded Karen, who knew every move.

'I have to call her later,' Elaine replied sulkily. 'She doesn't know a thing without her book.'

'Horseshit,' said Karen succinctly. 'She never commits to *any*thing unless she's certain there is nothing better going on that night. Years ago my father had a birthday party for her, and she bowed out at the last minute to go to some half-assed dinner for Khruschev. Daddy was *furious.*'

'I bet,' agreed Maralee. '*My* father had Adam doing two movies for him, and she *still* wouldn't invite daddy to her house because he never turned up at one of her special dinners once.'

Elaine stared at her two friends. Sometimes she got an uncomfortable insecure feeling when she was around them. They were so sure of themselves. And so they should be. They had both grown up in Beverly Hills with rich famous fathers behind them, always had money, and whoever they were married to would always be accepted. It was their birthright. Little Etta Grodinski from the Bronx had had to struggle for everything. Marrying a movie star, landing up in a Beverly Hills mansion, and becoming attractive clever Elaine Conti had been no easy job. Moodily she sipped her white wine.

Think yourself lucky. These women are your friends. They accept you. They like you. They tell you about their lives and loves, their clothes and make-up, their plastic surgeons and gynaecologists. You're one of them now. You are. Don't ever forget it.

Etta. Elaine. How carefully she hid her background. Her parents, still alive, had long ago moved from the Bronx to a pleasant house on Long Island. To this day she had never invited them to visit her in Beverly Hills. To this day they had never met Ross. She phoned them once a week, and sent them a monthly cheque. They were nice simple people. They would never be comfortable in her world.

You're ashamed of them, Elaine.

I'm not, I'm not.

'Look who Bibi's with,' exclaimed Karen.

All eyes swivelled to inspect Bibi's companion who had arrived late and was now hurrying across the crowded restaurant to join Bibi.

'It's only Wolfie Schweicker,' Maralee said dismissively.

'My God! For a moment I thought it was a man!' exclaimed Karen. 'He looks different. What *has* he done?'

'Lost about thirty pounds,' said Elaine, joining in.

'So he has,' marvelled Karen. 'He's positively slimline.'

Wolfgang Schweicker. Professional walker. The term used for any affluent, well connected man who escorted married ladies when their husbands were not available to accompany them to the various openings and galleries and restaurants that they simply *had* to be seen at. Nancy Reagan had hers. Wolfie was Bibi's equivalent. Once grossly fat, he had managed to slim down to merely chubby. He was round of face, short of leg, and expensively clad in the best Gucci had to offer. He was in his early fifties, and owned a very successful chain of designer bathrooms with franchises across America. Everyone adored Wolfie. He was so witty. But he belonged to Bibi Sutton and never strayed.

'Do you know,' Maralee said, tapping her perfect fingernails on the table top, 'I once invited Wolfie to a brunch. Without taking a breath he asked if Bibi and Adam were coming. I was married to Neil at the time, he *loathed* Bibi, and didn't care who knew it. Called her a socially miscast French cunt!' Maralee giggled at the memory. 'Anyway, I said no, and *he* said no. Can you imagine! Wouldn't even come to a tiny little *brunch* without her.'

The lunch passed in a flurry of gossip, innuendo, and general bitchery. Reputations, love affairs, talent and looks were casually pulled to pieces. Elaine asked for the check and charged it to American Express. Karen hurried off to her analyst, and Elaine and Maralee strolled outside to get their respective cars from an attentive parking valet.

Maralee raised her sunglasses, peered conspiratorially at her friend, and said, 'What do you think?'

Elaine cast a professional eye on Maralee's recent surgery. She had not been married to a plastic surgeon without learning a thing or two. 'Excellent,' she declared, after a thorough inspection. 'Really a first class job.'

Maralee was thrilled. 'Honestly?'

'Would I lie?'

'Of course you wouldn't!'

The parking valet drove up with Maralee's brand new Porsche Turbo Carrera. She grabbed every cent of alimony she could from Neil, but actually didn't need a dime. Her father had settled two trusts on her, both of which she had gained possession of. When Tyrone Sanderson died she stood to inherit another fortune. 'I'm going to Neiman Marcus,' she announced. 'Why don't you come?'

Elaine shook her head. 'I have to get home. Now that Ross is back my time's not my own.'

Maralee nodded understandingly and headed for her car.

'By the way,' Elaine placed a restraining hand on her friend's arm. 'There's something I'd like you to do for me.'

'Yes?'

'Look . . . I know you're not on the greatest of terms with Neil—'

'That's the understatement of the year!'

'But could you . . . would you . . .'

Maralee was getting impatient. 'What, Elaine?'

'I need a copy of *Street People*,' she blurted quickly. 'It's important. I need it immediately.'

Maralee raised her eyebrows. 'That piece of garbage!'

'Have you read it?'

'Do I need to? Montana *supposedly* wrote it. Doesn't that tell you enough?'

Elaine felt a flush spreading across her face. How she hated having to ask anyone for anything. 'Can you get it for me?'

Maralee gazed at her friend shrewdly. 'Don't tell me Ross is interested?'

Elaine shrugged in what she hoped was a noncommittal fashion. 'He likes to see everything.'

'Can't his agent get him a copy?'

'Apparently it's under wraps.'

'Probably because it's so bad,' Maralee sniffed. 'Oh, well – if you want it – it's yours. There's nothing in this town that *I* can't get my hands on.'

'Thanks, Maralee.'

'It's nothing.'

Lips brushed cheeks, once on each side, and they parted. Maralee roared off in her new Porsche, and Elaine climbed disconsolately into her four year old Mercedes. Soon . . . It would all change soon. The Contis would be back on top and she would never have to ask anyone a favour again.

* * *

'I just left your wife,' Karen husked over the phone.

'So?'

'I told her everything.'

There was a long pause while Ross digested this information. 'You did what?' he said at last.

Karen's voice was filled with emotion. 'Everything, Ross.

About us. I think she'll probably kill you!' She could hold back her laughter no longer.

'Clever cunt.'

'You said it!'

'Where are you?'

'In my analyst's waiting room. I'm just about to tell him all about us.'

'Don't!'

'Why not? I'll tell you what he says. I promise.'

'Dammit, Karen, do not mention my name.'

'What's in it for me if I don't?'

'The biggest dick *you've* ever seen.'

She chuckled felicitously. 'I wouldn't be too sure of that.'

'I'll call you tomorrow.'

'Not good enough. When?'

He wanted her, but he wanted the script of *Street People* more, and he did not plan to leave the house until he had it.

'I said I'll call you tomorrow.'

She was not prepared to be dismissed so easily. 'I understand it's going to be party time in the Conti household soon.'

'Yup.'

'Elaine spent the entire lunch yearning after Bibi Sutton.'

'Did she get her?'

'She got a maybe. You know Bibi.'

Ross understood the social mores of Beverly Hills. If Elaine could not get Bibi Sutton to their party she may as well not bother giving it. Maybe he would give Adam a call, pull the old pals act.

'I have to go,' Karen said abruptly. She wanted to be sure to get off the phone before he did.

'Don't you *dare* mention my name to your goddamn analyst,' he warned.

She hung up without another word. Ross returned to the lounger where he was carefully taking the sun and imagined the scene at the Bistro Gardens. Bibi playing hard to get, Elaine chasing, and Karen enjoying every fawning minute.

Karen. For one wild second he had actually believed her when she said she had told Elaine. The broad had a wicked sense of humour. Maybe he should dump her.

But why? She would never open her mouth to Elaine, and he certainly wanted more of her horny body and wonderfully erotic nipples. Oh those nipples!

More . . . Not immediately. But soon . . . when he'd seen the script of *Street People* . . . When Sadie La Salle was his agent . . . When he felt more . . . settled.

* * *

It seemed to Buddy that he had hardly closed his eyes when the phone woke him. 'Whoozatt?' he mumbled.

A burst of static, then, 'Buddy? You awake?'

'Call me in the mornin',' he said sleepily.

'It *is* morning,' replied his caller testily. 'It's eleven o'clock and about time you moved it.'

'Randy!' Slowly he opened an eye. 'How're you doin'?'

'Doin' all right. Doin' more than all right. I found me a *real* hot rich one.'

'Hey – that's good.' Buddy opened the other eye and groped around the bed looking for Angel. She was not there.

'Too right it's good,' said Randy briskly. 'And no way do I aim to blow the opportunity. Like so far I am Mr Straight, an' she goes for me a lot – *and* with a great deal more input I think I can find myself *really* on the right track.'

'Good, good . . .' mumbled Buddy, hoping that the call had nothing to do with the apartment.

'I'm driving in tomorrow,' Randy said, 'and I'll need my apartment. I know it's short notice, but when I lent you the place we agreed it was only for a couple of weeks, an' well . . . you bin there a while. I'll be arriving around noon tomorrow.'

Buddy struggled for something to say. What *could* he say? *Hey, man. I got nowhere else to go. I got no money. I got a wife to support. I got* nothing. He couldn't say that. No way could he say that.

Pride. He had enough not to admit that in the time he'd been back he had not scored one lousy stinking job.

'We'll be long gone by then,' he said cheerfully. 'And thanks for the loan of the place, Rand. S'matter of fact we'll be movin' into Sunset Towers. Saw a place there only last week that's just right.'

'Sunset Towers, huh? Everything's goin' your way then?'

'It sure is.'

'Can't wait to meet your old lady.'

'We'll call you in the week an' get it together.'

He banged the phone down and leapt from the bed.

Shit! Shit! Shit!

He stormed the refrigerator, gulped orange juice from a carton, grabbed a handful of raisins, and bit into an apple.

Then he thought about what he could do.

Gladrags. No longer in business.

Maxie Sholto. Had to be a last resort.

Frances Cavendish. Call her at once about *Street People*.

Shelly. What did it take to become a male stripper?

He pulled on his shorts and automatically started in on some push-ups. Then he remembered Gladrags' roommate, the plump little fag with the horny dog. He had thrust his card at him and said, 'Call me.'

So why not? Find out the score.

Yeah. But where *was* the guy's card? What had he done with it? He tried to concentrate on his push-ups but it was useless. How could you concentrate on the body beautiful when you were about to find yourself out on the street?

Abruptly he jumped to his feet and punched out Frances Cavendish's number on the phone.

'Miz Cavendish is in a meeting. Can she call you back?' droned an unfamiliar voice.

'It's urgent,' Buddy snapped. 'Urgent business.'

'Oh. Well I'll see . . . Who shall I say is calling?'

'Robert Evans.'

Respect. 'Yes, Mr Evans.'

A thirty second wait, then, 'Bobby, how are you? And what can I do for you?'

'Frances, this is Buddy Hudson, and don't get mad at me, this *is* urgent.'

'Jesus Christ!'

He spoke rapidly. 'Frances. There's a movie called *Street People*. There's a part in it for me. You want to create another star? Then just send me for the part, okay?'

Frances was more than exasperated. 'Not okay.'

'Why?'

'Because, dear boy, there is indeed a movie being cast of that name. But whether there is a role in it suitable for you, I do not know, because I have not seen the script. Indeed – very few people *have* seen the script. It's under wraps.'

'That's crap, Frances. You see everything.'

She made a sound like an angry horse. 'Very true, Buddy, dear. However, on this occasion all casting is being taken care of by the writer,' her voice filled with scorn, 'who obviously knows better than all of us poor old casting experts. I mean I have only been in the business thirty years, that's all. What could *I* possibly know?'

'Who is the writer?'

'Montana Gray, the director's wife. Does that tell you enough? Now get off this line, Buddy, and don't *ever* use a phony name to get through to me again. Do you understand?'

'I need a job, Frances.'

She sighed. 'You always *need* a job, but you never get any of the ones I send you for.'

'You got something for me? Next time'll be my shot. I know it.' He could feel her thinking and he willed her to come up with an interview.

'Are you interested in work as an extra?' she said at last.

Anger flooded through him. Extra work. He'd sooner leave town than stoop to that. 'No,' he said coldly.

'Sorry. Then I can't help you right now.'

How he hated the phone. First Randy, then Frances. Always bad news, negative happenings.

The sound of Angel's key in the door and what was he going to tell her?

She looked particularly beautiful, shining with a very special innocence.

'I'm sorry I wasn't here to fix your breakfast,' she murmured softly, going to him and putting her arms around his waist. 'I had to visit the doctor.'

His mind was racing. Montana Gray, wife of Neil Gray the director. Casting the movie themselves. An Oliver Easterne production Shelly had said. He gave Angel a gentle shove. 'Call information for me, babes. I need the number of Easterne Productions.'

She stared at him with a hurt expression. 'I said I had to go see the doctor, don't you want to know why?'

'Yeah, sure, 'course I do.' And then as an afterthought, 'Why didn't you tell me you were going?'

'I . . . I wasn't sure you'd be pleased.' She gazed at him, the happiness in her eyes mixed with a small amount of uncertainty. 'But now that it's confirmed . . .'

The horror of what she was about to say struck him like a lead bullet. 'Christ, babe. You're not—' He couldn't bring himself to finish the sentence.

She nodded and whispered the missing word. 'Pregnant.'

'Oh, no!'

'Oh, yes! Isn't it wonderful, Buddy? Isn't it absolutely wonderful?'

He didn't know what to say. A choking feeling overtook him. He wanted to push her away, but controlled himself.

'Hey – I gotta swim, I'm runnin' late. I'll be back.' He rushed from the apartment like a thief.

'Buddy—' she called out after him, but he didn't stop.

She closed her eyes for a moment, squeezed them tightly shut and determined not to cry. Oh boy . . . It sure wasn't like it was in the movies, but she had to stop feeling sorry for herself. If Buddy wasn't happy about the baby that was just too bad. *She* was thrilled. And eventually he would be too. She was sure of it. After all, he loved her, didn't he? And this would make them into a real family.

Chapter Fourteen

Captain Lacoste said, 'You want it, take it.' He indicated the thick file on his desk. 'But you know we've done everything we can. His description is across the country, his photo, his fingerprints. The next move is his.'

Leon said, 'I know that. I just feel there's something we're missing, and I want to go over the file again. I need to take my time over it.' He picked it up. There was nothing in it he didn't already know. He left the Captain's office and went straight outside to his car. It was raining . . .

* * *

Leon was annoyed about losing his raincoat. It was the genuine English article, purchased by a good friend at Burberry's in London, and brought back as a special birthday present. The thought of Joey-the-hooker parading around town in it burned him up.

He thought about getting in his car and going out to look for her, but after a long hot shower the idea of venturing once more into the filthy night did not appeal to him. So instead he put on his pyjamas, poured himself a substantial glass of brandy and settled down to watch an old western on television.

He must have fallen asleep in front of the set, because an urgent hammering woke him with a start. Half asleep he groped his way to the front door, glancing at his watch on the way and wondering who the hell was bothering him at two in the morning.

He threw open the door and was confronted with a sorry sight. Joey Kravetz stood there soaked to the skin. Her T-shirt stuck transparently to her body, her baggy trousers clung damply, her orange hair was flattened to her scalp, and driblets of water dripped off the end of her crooked snub nose.

'I brought back your raincoat,' she said forlornly handing it to him.

He was pleased to see his raincoat, not too pleased to see her. 'How did you know where I lived?'

She fished a crumpled envelope from his raincoat pocket. 'Your electric bill,' she stated, then immediately began to sneeze.

'I guess you'd better come in,' he growled reluctantly.

'Gee, thanks,' she sneered. 'Thought you'd never ask.' And then a grin spread across her face. 'Nice pyjamas. Reaal sexy. I like the peephole!'

He was mortified to find his fly gaping open. 'Just a minute,' he said stiffly, and hurried to the bathroom where he threw on a bathrobe. When he returned to the living room she was standing by the television set dripping all over his carpet.

'Look,' he said testily. 'I'll give you something to put on while your clothes dry. Then I'll call you a cab.'

'I don't have nowhere to go,' she whined.

'There must be somewhere.'

'No,' she said stubbornly.

'So we're back to dropping you at Juvenile then.'

Her attitude quickly changed. 'Aw, shit!' she snarled. 'You gotta record playin' in your mouth. Juvenile! Juvenile! Is that all y'can say?' A few more sneezes rendered her speechless.

'Will you go into the bathroom and get those wet clothes off before you catch pneumonia.'

She nodded obediently. He directed her to the bathroom, and tried to figure out what to do with her.

'Can I take a shower?' she called out.

'I suppose so,' he replied ungraciously. 'And throw me out your clothes. I'll try and get them dry.'

He went in the kitchen and switched on the electric kettle, then he picked up her clothes from the floor and placed them on a radiator. After that he brought her a baggy sweater and some old trousers from his closet, and dropped them outside the bathroom ready for her to put on.

How had he, Leon Rosemont, landed up with a sixteen year old hooker showering in his bathroom? Jesus H. Christ. This would make him a laughing-stock if anyone down at the precinct ever found out.

She emerged dry and clean, ridiculously swamped by his clothes. The water was boiling, so he poured some in a cup, added a tea bag, two sugar cubes, and handed it to her.

She sat herself down at the kitchen table and sipped it gratefully.

'And what exactly am I supposed to do with you?' he said.

'Let me sleep on your couch an' I'll be outta here first thing in the mornin',' she replied, quick as a flash. 'Honest. I won't hassle ya or nothin', I'll be gone, man. Y'can lay bucks on it.'

'I can't do that.'

'Why not?'

He thought for a moment. What else was there to do with her? The only alternative was to turn her in to Juvenile, and that meant getting dressed and dragging over to the station. It was still pouring down, the poor kid would get locked in a cell until morning, and the paper work alone . . .

He made a quick decision. The hell with it. Let her sleep on his couch, and in the morning he would take her to her friend just to make sure she was telling the truth.

Somewhere in the back of his head a warning voice said, 'Wrong,' but he ignored it, got spare blankets and a pillow from the hall closet and left her to it.

He closed his bedroom door, got into bed, read two chapters of a Joseph Wambaugh novel, and fell asleep.

The storm hit around three-thirty. Wild forks of lightning and deep rumbles of thunder. Leon slept. Nothing disturbed him. Joey woke immediately, hugged the blanket around her nakedness, and began to shiver. The brilliant flashes of lightning and the heavy thunder petrified her. She had had a bad experience as a kid. Storms panicked her.

She leaped from the couch and rushed into Leon's bedroom. He slept on his back, snoring, oblivious to everything.

Quietly she lifted the cover and crawled in beside him. He didn't stir. She snuggled close, and his bulk comforted her. He moved in his sleep, groaned, muttered something under his breath.

'You awake?' she whispered, fitting herself spoon-like into the curve of his back, her hands moving around to his chest.

He was still, his breathing heavy.

She searched his chest – thick with curly hair, until she located his nipples. Experience told her that men could get just as turned on by nipple-play as women. She found one, then the other, and the tips of her stubby little fingers went to work. His nipples soon hardened beneath her touch. She moved her hands down, found the opening in his pyjama pants, slid her hands within and grasped his swollen penis. Very gently she began to manipulate it up and down. Slow rhythmic motions that caused a low moan of pleasure to escape his lips, although he remained asleep.

She grinned, the storm forgotten while she concentrated on bringing him to a climax without waking him. 'You got a beautiful johnnie there,' she whispered encouragingly in his ear. 'A real humdinger . . . Come on, cowboy, give me what you got . . . give it all to mama . . . Give me all that juicy jism . . .

Oh, she knew what they liked to hear alright. And it was so easy. He came quickly, his sperm pulsating in long throbbing spurts onto the sheets.

She snuggled closer to his back and drifted off to sleep. When she woke, dawn was breaking and the storm was long gone. Leon snored contentedly beside her. And why not? She had given him what he wanted. What all men wanted. He may have come on with that phoney fatherly concerned act . . . but he was only a man after all. He didn't really give a damn what happened to her.

Carefully she wriggled from the bed and with one eye on his inert form checked out his wallet lying on the dresser. Pay dirt. He was carrying three hundred and nineteen bucks. Impulsively she grabbed the money, collected her clothes from the kitchen, flung them on, and silently crept from the apartment.

* * *

Millie Rosemont cursed the day Captain Lacoste had given Leon permission to bring the Andrews file home. Every night, for two and a half weeks, he had shut himself away in his cramped study, the offending file laid out in sections on his desk. There he sat, for hours on end, scribbing nothing much on his precious legal pad (she checked the basket every morning and found page after page of cryptic *Why? Where is he now? When will he strike again?*).

Millie decided the time had come to have it out. She entered his study carrying a cup of coffee and a sandwich. 'Leon,' she said sharply. 'May I speak to you for a moment?'

He removed his heavy reading glasses, rubbed the bridge of his thick nose and looked up. 'If you can't I don't know who can.'

She placed his coffee and sandwich on the desk and stared at him gravely. 'This case is becoming an obsession with you, and I don't think I like it much.'

He regarded his wife sympathetically, and tried to see things her way. It would be better if he could explain things to her. Tell her *why* he felt so personally involved. But no . . . he couldn't do that . . . he was ashamed, embarrassed . . . He stretched, feeling the strain in his shoulders, the tightness around his neck. 'If you don't want me to continue . . .'

She made a helpless gesture with her hands. 'It's not what *I* want or don't want. It's what's best for you.'

'What's best for me,' he said slowly, 'is solving this case.'

'What do you mean – solving it?' she replied angrily. 'It's no secret who *did* the murders. You know the son did it. And you also know that he'll be picked up for something else. It always happens that way – you told me so yourself.'

He sipped the hot coffee. 'I want to know why, Millie. I *have* to know.'

'Didn't I tell you? It's an obsession with you. And not a very healthy one.' She looked at him for a long silent moment, then turned and left the room.

'Millie!' he called out after her. 'What did I *say*?'

No reply. She was mad at him.

He took another bite of sandwich, a sip of coffee, then picked up his pad. *Where was Deke Andrews born?* he wrote. *What hospital? What city? What date?*

It was probably unimportant. But still . . . Amongst the Andrews papers had been no documents that related to their lives before they had arrived in Philadelphia over twenty years before. No wedding licence, no birth certificates, no relatives' letters, no indication of *where* they had come from.

This bothered Leon. Why no record of their past? Were they running from something or someone? Had Deke found out something he shouldn't?

It was a thought.

In a neat script Leon wrote – *Get a computer check on Willis and Winifred Andrews.*

Why not? There was nothing to lose.

Chapter Fifteen

He looked the best he could – and that was something. The girl on reception double-taked and didn't even check out his name on the typed list she had before her. She directed him to the elevator with a glowing smile and a 'Lots of luck'.

Luck. He needed it.

Luck. His body craved it like a junkie craves drugs.

He pressed the elevator button. Floor twenty. Was twenty going to be the hot new number in his life?

There was a mirror on the side of the elevator and he monitored his appearance yet again.

You're lookin' good . . . you're lookin' good . . . you're lookin' good like a superstar should . . .

Keep thinking that way. Keep thinking up.

He stepped out of the elevator into a sea of people. They sat, they lounged against walls, they took up every inch of space, all sizes, shapes, and ages, and in the middle of the throng was a large lucite desk manned by a businesslike-looking blonde, and an elderly red-head. To Buddy, forty was elderly. Unless you were talking Jane Fonda or Raquel Welch.

He headed confidently towards the desk, and as he did so he quickly observed where the main action was. A panelled oak door. A small brass plaque. It read MONTANA GRAY.

Lady, you are in for a treat. Buddy Boy is here. Buddy Boy has come to star in your movie.

He went directly to the blonde. She had marvellous green eyes, a smooth skin, and a very bad nose job.

'Buddy Hudson,' he said confidently. 'Miz Gray's expecting me.'

The blonde smiled, popped on a pair of lavender reading glasses and consulted her list.

Knowing that she wasn't going to find his name on it, he added quickly, 'Bob Evans arranged my appointment personally.'

The blonde stopped reading. 'He did? With whom?'

'Uh, he spoke to Montana – Miz Gray. She said for me to come right over. I'm working on a special at NBC and I have,' he glanced at his watch, 'exactly forty-two minutes before my ass has to be back on the set.' Now for the smile that said *I think you are the most desirable female I have ever seen in the whole of my life and I would like to fuck your brains out because you are so totally and absolutely irresistibly gorgeous!* 'So,' he continued, 'I'd appreciate it if I could be next in. Not that I want to throw out your schedule or anything.'

The blonde had hardly led a sheltered life. She had been through many men and many scenes. She considered herself a tough nut to crack.

The smile never left her face. Buddy Hudson was something else! She knew instinctively that he desired her, and not just because she was the gateway to Montana Gray.

'I'll see what I can do,' she said, writing down his name.

His gaze was level, direct. 'I'd really appreciate that.'

* * *

The first thing that struck Buddy was that she wasn't his type. No way. Not at all.

She sat behind a big desk, cool and collected in a wide shouldered jacket and pinstripe shirt. Her jet hair was scraped back into a long braid and most of her face was obscured by huge, lightly tinted reading glasses. Her skin was olive toned and glowing. Her mouth wide and unrouged.

No sirree. She wasn't his type at all. Buddy Boy liked them soft and blonde, pretty and appealing. He liked them *girlish.*

She was busy writing something on a pad, and without looking up she indicated that he should sit. There was a leather chair opposite her desk for just such a purpose. He glared at it balefully. Who needed to sit? Where was the impact in that? First impressions were very important and when she looked up from her scribbling he wanted her to feel the full blast of his personality.

He hovered near the door ready for the walk towards the desk when he had her full concentration. The walk was important. It was part of him, the rolling thrusting strut. Jeez! He wasn't *nervous* was he? Buddy Boy was *never* nervous.

So what were the patches of damp under his arms? And why was his upper lip clouding with little beads of sweat?

Sonofabitch! Was she going to read all day? Up until now it had been a breeze. Who would have thought it would be that easy to lie his way in to see her? *And* get in ahead of a roomful of people who probably had appointments. He could thank the blonde with the bad nose job for that little piece of luck. *If all the blondes in Hollywood were laid end to end . . . Shit! They probably had been!*

He wished that he knew something about the role in the movie. Should he be aggressively sexual? Boyish? Charming? Dustin Hoffman with looks?

Goddamn it. All he knew was the title of the film and that she had written it and that her old man was going to direct it.

His stomach was knotting up. Tension. If he carried on this way he'd have ulcers before he was thirty.

Yeah. And why not? Randy was throwing them out of the apartment. He had no money, no job, and only hours before, Angel had calmly informed him she was pregnant.

Ulcers. Maybe they would kill him and do away with all the aggravation. He shuffled restlessly.

'I won't be a minute,' Montana said, without looking up.

I can wait. I mean why shouldn't I? I'm only another bum actor without a job. Why should anyone consider my feelings?

He had taken Angel's news calmly. She was so happy – somehow it had not seemed the right time to tell her that she'd have to get an abortion. No way could they afford a baby. He had acted like it was great news, the best. Then he had dressed in his one good outfit and moved ass. Fast.

Hitting on the Easterne offices had been a snap decision, and now he was here – and there *she* was – Miz Montana Gray. Not his type. No way. But quite a looker if you liked the strong ballsy type.

She stuck her pen in her mouth, pushed her reading glasses up into her hair, and hit him with laser beam tiger eyes. 'Buddy Hudson,' she said coolly. 'I don't remember Bob Evans calling me about you.'

She was no easy touch. He could see that. Try the honest approach and go for broke. He strutted toward her desk, and kind of threw himself into a chair, legs casually apart. 'He didn't.'

'He didn't,' she repeated patiently.

'Nope.'

'Then maybe you'd like to tell me why you're here?' Smoky ebony eyes met laser tigers and held.

'Because,' Buddy said slowly, with a touch of arrogance, 'you'd have been missing out if you hadn't seen me.' He favoured her with a long sexy stare.

She stifled impatience. 'I would?'

He was brimming with false confidence. 'Sure you would.'

She removed the tip of her pen from between her lips. 'Why don't we cut out the shit, Mr Hudson?'

'Huh?'

'Let's cut out the I-am-the-most-desirable-sex-machine-that-ever-walked and let me get a look at the real you.'

He frowned. 'Hey—'

She smiled agreeably. 'Can't win 'em all.'

'I—'

'Do you have pictures? A résumé?'

'I didn't bring anything with me.'

'Why don't you just tell me what you've done then?' She poised her pen above the notepad on her desk.

Jeez! She was interested in his acting experience. Really interested!

'I . . . uh . . . I've done a *Starsky and Hutch*. I was in *Smokey and the Bandit*. Well, like I mean I was in it, but by the time it hit the screen I wasn't—'

'I think I get the picture.'

'Not that I wasn't good in it,' he added hurriedly. 'I mean – shit – I was *very* good, *too* good. Like it was a scene with Burt Reynolds and—'

'Yes. I understand.'

He stood up and paced excitedly in front of her desk forgetting image and impact for the moment. 'I studied at Joy Byron's school of acting y'know. Like I was one of her best students. I played Stanley Kowalski in *Streetcar*. A special performance for talent scouts, agents, the whole schmeer. I was a smash, couple of studios wanted to sign me, but I had this singing gig in Hawaii I was already committed to – an' there was no way I would ever back out on a definite commitment.' He was speeding, his words tumbling out like an express train. 'I'm a professional all the way – you can bet on that.'

'I'm sure you are,' she murmured, watching him intently.

'Yeah . . . well . . . Like I came back from Hawaii straight into the recession. Ten thousand actors an' ten jobs, y'know?'

She nodded sympathetically. 'I think I've interviewed most of them.' The buzzer on her desk sounded and she said 'Yes' into the intercom.

'Mr Gray on the line,' said the receptionist.

'Find out where he is, I'll call him back.'

Buddy returned to his seat in front of her desk and wondered if he'd said too much. What did she care if he was cut out of a lousy Burt Reynolds movie? What did she care about ten thousand actors hunting ten jobs?

'Is the *Starsky and Hutch* worth seeing?' she inquired crisply.

Honesty had suddenly become his best policy. 'I got cut out of that too. Y'see – Paul Michael Glaser—'

She laughed. What a laugh. Very sexy.

'I know, I know. Paul Michael Glaser couldn't cut the competition, right?'

He grinned. 'You got it.'

'Then there's no film we can see you on?'

He pushed his hand through his hair nervously. 'Nothin' worth lookin' at.' Buddy Boy. Mister Cool. Where was all this leading?

'I understand.' She paused. 'So . . . Maybe you'd like to read for me, and if I like your work we can arrange for you to test.'

He could hardly speak. 'Test?'

'If the reading works out. Here.' She handed him a script from her desk. 'Take this outside. Study it for a while, then when you're ready tell my receptionist and I'll see you again.'

He stood and grabbed the script. 'Hey – you're not gonna regret this. I'll be great.'

She nodded. 'I hope so.'

He hesitated by the door. 'Uh – which part?'

She laughed aloud. 'I bet you don't even know what the film's about.'

He regained a little of his strut. 'Who does? Every casting director in town is pissed 'cos they can't get their hands on it. If I walked out with this copy now I could probably make myself a few bucks.'

'And maybe lose the part of Vinnie.'

'Vinnie. Right on!' He bolted from her office clutching the script.

She watched him go. He had a quality she liked – plus devastating good looks and a certain vulnerability.

Yes. Buddy Hudson certainly had it. Now . . . If he could only act.

* * *

Elaine lay on a sunbed, quite naked apart from small plastic eye covers. She had abandoned the Sony earphones in favour of pure undiluted thought. How to have the best party in town? How to make it fun and exciting – the kind of party that people were talking about for days after?

The mix. That was the most important ingredient. However great the food, the decor, the music, it all came down to the mix. If the people weren't right then you may as well not bother.

Bibi and Adam Sutton came first of course. If you had them you were guaranteed acceptance from most of the other guests. Since bumping into Bibi at the Bistro Gardens Elaine had called her twice. Both times she had been blocked by Bibi's officious secretary who faithfully promised Mrs Sutton would return her calls. So far she had not.

Elaine turned on her side and threw one arm up and back over her head. She had decided to obtain a light tan for her party, and the sun solarium was certainly better than sitting out in the real thing ruining your skin forever. She wished that Ross would stop baking himself to a deep mahogany, etching the lines even more deeply into his skin.

A sharp buzzing sound, and the full length machine automatically turned itself off. Thankfully she slipped from the clear plastic bed and studied herself in a full length wall mirror. Every inch of her gleamed radiantly. But there was no one to admire her gloriously glowing body, and Ross probably wouldn't even notice.

She frowned. Maybe it was about time she had some *fun*. But with whom? Her choice was limited if not downright nonexistent. After the dentist and the small time actor she had definitely decided affairs were not worth the bother. And the sex hadn't been up to much either.

You're spoiled, Elaine. After Ross, where would you turn? The Conti schlong is legendary.

She smiled at her reflection. Maybe if she got him the script, and Maralee *had* promised. And then maybe if she got Sadie La Salle to the party and she became his agent.

Good God! What kind of thinking was *that*? Did she have to get her husband in a good mood to lay her?

Well . . . it would certainly help.

* * *

Buddy bounced out of the Easterne production building on Sunset, and he was flying. The role of Vinnie was written for *him* – no doubt about it. He had given a dynamite reading, and the lady in the tinted glasses and cowboy boots – Montana Gray – she wasn't his type, but he had to admit that she was something else in the looks department – had said that he was impressive. Yeah – impressive had been the word she'd used. And then – more magic words – 'It looks like we're going to have to test you,' she had said calmly.

Hot shit! How could she stay so calm?

'Hey—' he had exclaimed, and then louder and wilder, 'Hey! Hey! Hey!' With a flourish he had grabbed her by the waist and whirled her round the room.

She extracted herself from his grasp and fled behind her desk, where, alarmed by his lack of control, she had started in on a whole speech about how it was only a test and she would be testing other actors and not to get too high on something that might only result in disappointment.

Didn't she know that testing for a major role in a major movie was the best thing that had ever happened to him in his whole goddamn life!

'Who is your agent?' she had asked.

Agent! Who had an agent?

'Uh, like I'm kinda between agents,' he had managed.

'I see. Let my secretary know where we can contact you, and you'll be hearing from us with a date.'

'When?'

'Maybe in a week or two.'

'Do I get to take a script with me so I can prepare?'

'My secretary will give you the pages I'd like you to work on.'

So he was walking tall. In spite of the fact that he still had no idea where he and Angel would be spending the night.

Goddamn Randy. Why couldn't he stay in Palm Springs with the mother and daughter act?

He needed a good agent. The fact that he was testing for Neil Gray's film should be enough to tempt *any* smart agent to sign him up – pronto. He would go to the biggies – William Morris, ICM, Sadie La Salle.

His old Pontiac sitting in a no-parking zone looked like a lump of rotting tin. The *first* thing he would do when he scored some big bucks would be to get himself proper wheels. A Caddy, a Merc, maybe even a Rolls. No, maybe not. A Rolls wasn't his image. Something sporty would suit him better. One of those Italian jobs or perhaps an imported Jaguar XJS. Now there was a car!

Jeez! He was finally on his way! He was going to be a star!

He opened up the door of the car, got in, and sat there silently buzzing with excitement.

Two hours later he was down again. Somehow he had gotten the idea that now that he was testing everything would change. His luck was on the rise and a good gambler always followed his luck. So, accordingly, he had presented himself at the William Morris Agency expecting action, and all he had got was a 'leave your name and number' from a secretary with about as much understanding as a slab of concrete. The same story at ICM. And at Sadie La Salle's office a mini-skirted monster had told him to send in a photo, a biography, and a list of his credits. Didn't the dumb idiot recognize a new star when she saw one?

He left the office on Canon in a fury, and slumped into his car which had now collected a parking ticket. It was then that he noticed the small white card on the floor and quickly he picked it up. JASON SWANKLE was printed in raised type neatly on the centre of the card, and down in the left hand corner it read INTERIOR DESIGN PERSONAL SERVICE, and there was an address and a phone number.

Buddy kicked the old car into action. Well . . . What did he have to lose?

Not a lot.

* * *

It was madness of course. He was exhausted from a weekend in her company, but when Gina Germaine called, Neil Gray came running. He had looked at the whole situation very logically, decided she had to be dropped from his life, and then decided to *hump* her out of his system.

They made love on her whorish pink quilted bed. Then she went down on him in her whorish pink padded bathroom with the heart shaped tub in the centre of the fur rug.

Two orgasms left him dripping with sweat, his heart beating like a sledge hammer. 'Enough,' he managed to gasp when she started to play with his limp organ yet again.

'You could never be enough for me,' breathed Gina, wondering how far she could go with the dialogue. Not too far, Neil was smarter than most men, although once you got their pants off part of their brain seemed to disintegrate and you could say whatever you liked and they would believe it.

'I've got to go,' Neil said weakly. 'Preproduction on a movie is the most important time of all, *and* my lovely lady, *you* are causing me to neglect my responsibilities.'

'I understand,' she murmured sympathetically. 'But we do seem to have something special together, don't we? We make sparks fly.'

Why did women always have to make such a big deal out of simple fucking?

'Of course we do,' he agreed, thinking of Montana and feeling more than a twinge of guilt.

The afternoon sunshine filtered through the bathroom blinds, and he suddenly felt totally ridiculous lounging on the fur covered floor of Gina's over decorated bathroom. The pounding of his heart was slackening somewhat. Christ! A session with Gina Germaine was probably equivalent to a week's workout at the health club.

He stood up. 'I'll have a shower if I may.'

She was mildly turned on by his Richard Burton accent, but the real appeal was his talent. 'You may *have* whatever you like.' She stretched provocatively.

It *was* one of the most beautiful bodies in Hollywood. And she knew it. He stepped into the shower, turning the control knob until the water that hit his body was bracingly cold. When he emerged, Gina had slipped a lacy bra and French knickers over her nakedness. She held a large bath towel ready for him to dry himself with. 'Neil,' she murmured softly. 'I have a confession.'

'What?' Briskly he dried himself, feeling refreshed and ready to get back to work.

'Well . . .' She hesitated as if reluctant to proceed.

'What?' he repeated, reaching for his shorts.

'When we were in Palm Beach I sneaked a copy of *Street People* from your suitcase and read it.'

He was surprised. Gina had never struck him as a reader. 'You did?'

'I did.' Her voice became crisp and businesslike, all trace of hesitant dumbness gone. 'And Neil, I *loved* it. And I'll tell you something else, the role of Nikki is perfect for me – *so so* perfect.'

He was speechless. Nikki! The innocent unspoiled beauty. The untouched-by-life sweet young girl. Nikki! Was Gina making some kind of obscure joke?

'You see, Neil,' she continued earnestly. 'The whole of my career I've been typecast. Cunty dumb blondes with hearts of gold – and let me tell you something, that kind of part is not the real me.' She paused for breath, then plunged on, her huge bosom heaving with emotion. 'Neil,' she stated dramatically. 'The real me *is* Nikki. Everyone sees Gina Germaine, the big sexy film star. Underneath the dazzle lurks a vulnerable girl. A child of *life*!'

Where, for fuck's sake, was she getting her dialogue?

'I want to do your film,' she continued, her round blue eyes protruding alarmingly. 'I *have* to do your film. I'm right for it, I don't care what anyone says. *I know*.'

'Gina . . . I don't know what to say . . .' he managed, while he tried to think of what he *could* say. If he wasn't bedding her it would be easy – enough actresses had pitched him for a part and he had always dealt with the situation in an honest fashion – sometimes a brutal one. 'I know that you're a good actress—'

'That's a load of garbage,' she interrupted fiercely. 'You've never seen me *do* anything decent.'

'Yes I have,' he lied.

'And you're just about to tell me that I'm not right for Nikki?'

He chose his words carefully. 'What I *am* about to tell you is that you are too big a star to even consider a role like that.'

She was silent for a moment, staring at him with eyes full of resentment.

He reached for the rest of his clothes and began to dress. The sooner he was out of this conversation and out of her house the better.

'I think I should tell you that I am prepared to do a test for this part,' she said slowly. 'And if that doesn't convince you . . .'

He imagined Montana's expression if he told her that Gina Germaine wanted to test for the part of Nikki. The whole thing was nonsensical.

'Why don't I think about it?' he said soothingly.

'Why don't you think about the fact that I have a hidden video camera in my bedroom?' She had not been married to street smart Maxie Sholto for nothing.

'You have *what*?' he groaned.

'All I want to do is test,' she said sweetly. 'Then it'll be entirely up to you whether I'm right or not.'

* * *

'We're moving, sweet stuff,' Buddy said, entering the apartment and swinging Angel off her feet.

'Moving? I don't understand.' She looked puzzled.

'Yup.' He kissed her on the lips. 'Buddy Boy's gonna be a star an' we're movin' on.'

'Oh, Buddy! You got the part!'

'Well . . . kind of . . . Like they want me to test. But y'know, that's only a formality. I mean *everyone* tests – even Brando had to test before he got *The Godfather*.'

'He did?'

He kissed her again. 'Sure. I told you – everyone does it.'

She smiled sweetly. 'I knew that something good would happen for us soon, and I was right.'

He patted her belly. 'Something good already happened, didn't it?'

She nodded happily. 'You're really pleased about the baby, aren't you?'

'Hey – of course I am.' And now that things were looking up – he was. Bye bye abortion. Hello baby. 'Why even ask?' he added, hugging her tightly.

She lowered her eyes. 'It's just that . . . well . . . this morning – when I told you . . . well . . .'

'I know. I kinda ran out of here. But I had a lot on my mind. You gotta understand me, babe, business first, then I can relax.'

'Oh, Buddy.' She snuggled close to him. 'I do love you.'

'Me too, sweet stuff, me too.'

'And we're going to be very happy, aren't we?'

'Happy. Rich. Famous. You name it.' He pushed her gently away. 'Hey – we really are moving. I forgot to tell you – Randy called and he needs the place.'

She was dismayed. 'When?'

'Would you believe tomorrow?'

'No—'

He held up an authoritative hand. 'Do not panic. I got us a place that is going to blow your little mind.'

'Where?'

'Questions, questions. We shall pack up, kiddo, and you will see for yourself.'

While Angel got their things together he decided to take a swim. It had been some day. A mixture of luck and shit. His adrenaline was racing full tilt. He needed to clear his head and relax. How one day could change your life. He was to be a father. He was to be a star. He had made contact with Jason Swankle and whether that was good or bad remained to be seen. But it had certainly turned out to be useful.

Jason Swankle's emporium was on Robertson Boulevard, an elegant glass fronted shop with spacious and luxurious offices in the back. Buddy had decided against calling first, a face to face confrontation was always best. Find out what he wanted, hopefully not his body. Buddy had never gone the gay route. Oh yeah – in his few wild months with Maxie Sholto he had been involved in plenty of far-out scenes, but always with females. Sometimes other men joined in with the girls, but they never went near Buddy. Oh no, he always made that clear up-front, however stoned he was. The closest had been the fat record producer on the night Buddy had freaked and smashed up a camera when he had discovered it filming the scene. He still shook with anger when he thought about it – which of course he tried not to – as with many other thoughts that slipped into his head – things he never wanted to think about again – but which refused to go away.

His friend Tony for example. Lying on a cold slab of concrete. Fourteen years old. Murdered by a bunch of fairies getting their rocks off.

Sometimes he saw the face of the man who had picked them up. A shifty face with small weasel eyes.

And the host of the party. Butterball. A plump babysoft man with a welcoming smile and the handshake of a dead fish.

Buddy saw them clearly every day – along with his mother. Naked. Smiling in triumph.

How he wished he could get rid of the images, just wash them away. But they were permanent, always with him. And he had no intention of adding any more nightmares.

'Can I do anything for you?' a sandy haired man in a light beige suit with matching moustache inquired as Buddy strode into Jason's shop. Only it wasn't a shop as such, it was more a showroom exhibiting exclusive Italian furniture and a few well placed antiques.

Buddy sprang Jason's card between thumb and forefinger, and waved it at the man. 'He wanted to see me,' he said.

'Mr Swankle?'

'Well I ain't here to see Ronnie Reagan.'

The sandy haired man looked down his nose in disgust. How he hated these flashy macho types who acted like they owned the world just because they were so butch. This one stunk of raw sex, *and* he knew it, *and* what was even worse he *flaunted* it. 'I'll see if Mr Swankle is available. Who shall I say wishes to see him?'

'Buddy Hudson. And *he* wants to see *me*.'

Sandy-hair retreated to the back of the store, while Buddy wandered around admiring the goods. There were leather couches, marble tables, carved lamps, and cut glass bowls filled with fresh roses. The place had class. Even he could see that.

Sandy-hair returned in minutes, his thin lips pursed disdainfully beneath his wispy moustache. 'Mr Swankle will see you now.'

Jason Swankle's office was a large white room filled with greenery, flowered couches, and a huge marble slab of a table covered in drawings and designs. On the walls were a series of framed David Hockney boy-in-swimming-pool drawings.

Jason himself stood centre stage. He wore a pink safari suit with a pale green silk shirt and a pink rose pinned to his jacket.

Shag, the randy bulldog, slumbered on the thick pile rug making asthmatic breathing sounds. As soon as Buddy entered the room the dog woke, growled, and hurled itself at Buddy's leg, intent on carrying on where it had left off at their last meeting.

'Jesus Christ!' snapped Buddy, kicking the growling dog off. 'Can't you control this fuckin' animal?'

'Shag!' shrieked Jason. 'Down boy. AT ONCE.'

Reluctantly the dog obeyed, and slouched back to its place on the rug.

'So sorry,' said Jason with a friendly chuckle. 'I don't know why he always picks on you.'

'Nor do I,' complained Buddy, sensing at once that he could ask Jason Swankle for anything he wanted and probably get it. Lovelight was shining out of the plump man's round blue eyes.

'Can I offer you a drink?' Jason fluttered, indicating a laden drinks trolley.

Buddy sat himself down on the edge of one of the flowered couches. 'Yeah. Why not. Vodka on ice. No mix.'

'Certainly. My pleasure.'

While Jason fixed his drink Buddy studied him carefully. He was a short, rounded man of about forty. He wore a bad hair piece, a fake tan, and the lavish jewelley that adorned his person was most definitely genuine. What was he doing with a freak like Gladrags? Silly question. What did he *think* they were doing – playing tennis?

As if reading his mind Jason said quickly, 'I do hope you have forgiven the way Marvin behaved to you the other day. He was *so* rude. It was inexcusable. I told him so, of course. He was very sorry.'

Oh sure! Marvin Gladrags Jackson sorry. That *would* be the day.

Buddy wondered how much Jason knew. Was he aware of the fact that his live-in friend had run a male call-boy service, and that he, Buddy, had been one of the boys?

Right on cue again Jason said, 'You see, you startled Marvin. His past is behind him now, he has *me* to look after him. I enlarged his premises,' delicate laugh at the double entendre, 'and now the clothes store is enough to keep him busy. He doesn't need to run that silly escort service any more, it's quite unnecessary.'

Escort service! Yeah!

'It's been a while, and you coming to our private residence and everything . . . It upset him.'

'I didn't mean to do that,' Buddy said, going along with the story. 'But I've been out of town an' I needed to score a fast buck, so I figured to look up old Gla – uh – Marvin, an' see if there was any action around. Y'know, tourist lady wanting to visit Disneyland – like that.'

'Believe me, I understand.' Jason handed him his drink in a mirrored glass and deliberately touched hands. Buddy snatched his away. 'That's why I came after you,' Jason added. 'I just hate to see Marvin behave that way. I thought that I might make it up to you.'

Here came the pitch. *Forget it. I don't need money that bad.* Buddy gulped his drink, the ice cold against his teeth.

'I wondered if you might be interested in doing me a favour,' Jason continued. 'For a fee, of course.'

'What favour?' Buddy asked guardedly.

Jason sat down on the flowered couch. 'I have these two ladies coming to town. Very wealthy, one is a widow and it appears her late husband left her a sizeable chunk of Texas.' He paused to allow that relevant information to sink in. Satisfied that it had, he continued, 'The other woman, a divorcee, has bought a mansion in Bel Air. On her last visit she handed it over to me to do with what I will.'

Buddy frowned. 'Huh?'

'Decorate, dear boy. Rebuild. Refurbish.'

'Oh . . . yeah.' So where was all this leading?

'Now you are probably wondering what this has to do with you, and how you can help me.'

The guy was telepathic. 'Yeah. I was wondering.' Buddy stood, drained the vodka, and moved across the room.

'Well you see,' continued Jason secretively. 'Two women, alone in a city where they have no friends, they need entertaining.'

'What kind of . . . entertaining?' Buddy asked suspiciously. He was going to be a star now. All thoughts of going back into business had vanished. The body was no longer for sale.

Jason let forth a maniacal giggle. 'Nothing . . . intimate. Nothing like that at all.' He rose from the couch and padded across the room so that he was once again in close proximity to Buddy. 'What I had in mind was for you to take the ladies out to dinner, the theatre, a club or two. For which, of course,' he added hastily, 'I will pay you handsomely.'

'How much?'

Jason threw his arms wide. '*You* tell me.'

Buddy thought quickly. Two old broads in town for a couple of days. No sex. Only taking them around a bit. It was a breeze. 'I don't come cheap,' he ventured.

'Nothing worth having is cheap,' sniffed Jason.

'I'd need a new suit . . .'

'Certainly.'

'And you'd take care of all expenses?'

'Naturally.'

'What about a car?'

'Would a chauffeured Cadillac be suitable?'

Does Streisand sing? This was turning out to be too good to be true. Where was the catch? He took a deep breath. 'Five hundred a day.'

Jason didn't even blink. 'Done.'

Shit! He'd sold himself too cheap. There had to be a catch. He couldn't help himself. 'So what's the scam?'

Jason beamed happily. 'No . . . scam. I just want these ladies to be happy, and if they are happy, then maybe the one who owns half of Texas will buy herself a simple three or four million dollar house to be near her friend, and *guess* who will get to fix it over? *Do* encourage her, Buddy, won't you, dear boy.'

Buddy grinned. Foxy little fucker.

'I'll tell them you are my nephew,' Jason decided, posturing around the room. 'And that you're an actor.'

'I am.'

Jason sniffed. 'Of *course* you are.'

'No, really. I am. Like I'm gonna be testing soon for Neil Gray's new movie.'

'How exciting!'

'Yeah, it would be, but I got problems . . .'

'Can I help?' Jason asked sympathetically, laying a friendly hand on his arm.

'I got a wife—'

'Oh dear! That's a *big* problem.'

'She's great,' Buddy said defensively, edging away so that the warm hand slipped from his arm. 'She's not the problem at all.' He stared thoughtfully at Jason while his mind was buzzing. 'You see, it's like this . . . We're staying in a friend's apartment, and he's comin' back tomorrow – unexpectedly. He only let me know a few hours ago, so what with everything I've had no chance to get another place together. I'd *like* to escort your two ladies . . .' he shrugged eloquently, 'but in the circumstances I guess I'll have to pass.'

Jason was not slow in catching a point. 'Because you have nowhere to live?'

Buddy nodded and helped himself to another drink. 'Right. I mean I'm gonna be too busy tryin' to find a place. You understand?'

'But what if I can assist you?' Jason asked quickly.

'Hey—' Buddy exclaimed. 'If you came up with something that'd solve my problem. I mean *you* help me . . . I help *you* . . . an' we're all happy. Right?'

'Just you and a wife?' Jason asked doubtfully, having second thoughts. 'No children or animals?'

'You gotta be puttin' me on.'

For a moment Jason remained undecided, but something about the handsome young man with the smoky black eyes and tousled hair had gotten to him. He wanted him in his life. Plus the fact that the two women were no story. They *were* coming to town. And they *would* appreciate an escort, especially an escort that looked like Buddy Hudson. It would mean another large mansion to decorate . . . more commissions on everything from the toilet seats to the onyx ashtrays.

Of course it meant taking a risk. What did he know about Buddy Hudson? And then there was a wife involved. Probably some Hollywood tramp . . . One of these days Buddy would wake up to the fact that boys have more fun . . . And wouldn't it be simply gorgeous if it was he, Jason Swankle, who could convince him of this?

Abruptly he cleared his throat. 'I've just finished work on a beach house,' he said. 'In the Malibu Colony. The owner is in Europe and won't be returning for three or four weeks. If you promise to be *very* careful . . . and I do mean *very*. No entertaining or parties or anything like that.'

Je . . . *sus*! It *was* his day. And what a day! A house on the beach for crissakes!

'Well . . .' Jason continued. 'I don't see any reason why you couldn't stay there, temporarily of course,' he added hastily.

Don't jump at it, Buddy. Cool it. Let *him* convince *you*.

'Jeez. Sounds good, but I don't know . . .'

'Oh, but you must. I insist!'

And that's how it had come down. Everything in position.

It was now six-thirty, and the pool was packed. No chance of doing his thirty lengths with the water crowded with tired bodies just back from a hard day's grind. Disgusted, he turned to go back inside and ran straight into Shelly. Her hair was piled high in tight gleaming curls and her muscular body wore only the smallest of bikinis. A beach towel was slung casually over her shoulders.

'Hey – Shelly! How y'doin'?'

She regarded him quizzically. 'Seems *you're* doin' okay. Where's the nervous wreck zoomed out my apartment last night?'

He laughed self-consciously. 'I guess I was uptight.'

'Uptight! Ha!'

'I'm glad I ran into you.'

She stretched a long leg in front of her and rotated her ankle. 'Whyssat?'

'Because I looked into that movie you told me about and I'm testing. Can you believe it?'

'Sure I believe it. Why not? Your Karma's on an up.'

He leaned forward and kissed her lightly on the cheek. 'Thanks, Shell, I'll say goodbye, we're movin' out of this dump.'

'When?'

'Right now.'

'Wow! One test an' you really take it to heart.'

'I'm gonna be a star, kid. I'll give you a part in one of my movies.'

She laughed lewdly. 'There's only one part of yours I want.'

He grinned. 'Cut it out, I'm a married man.'

'Yeah. Tell me that in six months.' She winked. 'Anyway, good luck, I'll see you around.' Without a backward glance she headed for the pool, dropped her towel, and executed a graceful dive between the mass of bodies.

In other circumstances . . . If there wasn't Angel . . .

What the hell was he thinking of? Angel was his life, his love. Abruptly he shook his head and took the stairs two at a time.

They were moving on. And things could only get better.

* * *

It took Neil several days before he could even bring himself to mention Gina Germaine in Montana's presence. The blonde bitch was *blackmailing* him. He was caught in her cheap little trap, and he was going to have to give her a test or suffer the consequences.

They were in Oliver Easterne's opulent office, amusingly decorated with framed telegrams from various directors and stars swearing they would never work with him again. Oliver, a sandy haired man in his late forties, was busy cleaning his desk with a chamois leather. He had a fetish about cleanliness that bordered on the ridiculous. If anyone so much as smoked a cigarette in his office he immediately washed out the ashtray.

Montana had been discussing several actors she wanted to test for the role of Vinnie, and then the conversation automatically led on to the girls for Nikki.

'If we get George Lancaster, they can both be unknowns. If we don't – then we gotta go with names,' insisted Oliver.

'You're repeating yourself,' said Montana coldly. 'Christ, Oliver, don't you think we know that by now? Neil can't put a fucking gun to George's head, we'll just have to wait.'

Oliver ignored her. 'Do you think you'll hear from George soon?' he asked Neil.

'I'm sure I will,' Neil replied. 'But while we're on the subject of stars I did have this rather interesting thought on the girl.'

'Who?' questioned Montana, lighting up a cigarette which put Oliver in a nervous sweat.

'Don't drop any ash,' he muttered. 'The carpet's new.'

Neil cleared his throat, then casually said, 'Gina Germaine wouldn't be bad.'

Montana snorted derisively. 'You *have* to be kidding!'

'Scrub off the make-up—'

'Cut off the tits—'

'She's big box office,' interrupted Oliver.

'Who gives a shit?' snapped Montana angrily. 'I don't believe we're even discussing her.'

'Big, big box office,' mused Oliver.

'All I had in mind was running a test on her,' Neil said quickly.

Montana raised a scornful eyebrow. 'Oh *did* you. How come we've never discussed it?'

'She'd never test,' Oliver interjected excitedly. 'Would she, Neil? Waddyathink?'

'I think she would,' Neil replied stiffly, well aware of his wife's angry stare. He walked over to the bar and topped up his glass with bourbon. 'And *I* like the idea.'

'Christ!' muttered Montana in disgust. 'I just don't know how you can even *think* of that bosomy freak playing Nikki.'

'Listen,' said Oliver quickly. 'If she'll do it what's to lose?'

Deliberately Montana allowed her ash to fall on his precious carpet.

'Watch the rug!' screamed Oliver in anguish.

'I'm going home,' she announced coldly. 'You have your car, don't you Neil?'

He nodded.

'Then I'll see you later.' She swept out in a fury. Gina Germaine! God almighty! Gina Germaine! When had Neil come up with *that* idea. And why hadn't he discussed it with her before mentioning it to Oliver?

She was furious. *Street People* was supposed to be their special project – but gradually she was being edged out. How dare Neil treat her like an assistant! Since getting back from Palm Beach he'd been a total pain. Surly, short tempered, and drinking like the old days. And as for sex – forget it. She was too busy to take much notice of his moodiness. She had put it down to the fact that he hadn't got a definite commitment from George Lancaster, and had made allowances because of that.

Fuck him! He surely knew the stupidity of mentioning Gina Germaine to Oliver before checking with her. *Fuck him!*

In the underground garage the attendant bid her good evening.

'I'll take my husband's car,' she said shortly. 'Give Mr Gray mine.'

'Yes ma'am.' He rushed to get the gleaming red Maserati, and Montana tipped him and climbed into Neil's favourite toy. He hated her little Volkswagen. Let him walk if he didn't like it.

Chapter Sixteen

'How about twenny for hot times?' the hooker drawled. She was a stockily built bleached blonde who had forgotten about the roots of her hair which sprouted black and coarse.

'Too much,' Deke muttered, glancing furtively up and down the dimly lit street.

'I'kin give ya a ten buck special blow job,' she announced proudly, as if offering a discount in the supermarket.

His teeth clenched. 'I don't want that,' he hissed.

She adjusted a torn bra strap beneath a sweat stained T-shirt. 'Take it or leave it. Twenny a screw. Ten a blow. What's it t'be?'

He wanted to slap her stupid sluttish face and walk away. But he couldn't. He needed her. There had been no one since Joey, and he needed to be close to someone.

'Where?' he asked gruffly.

'Hotel roun' the corner.'

She set off, tottering uncomfortably on six inch heels. She crossed the street and headed for a darkened alley positioned between a greasy diner and a porno magazine shop.

Deke followed closely behind her, sniffing at the trail of sweat and cheap scent she left in her wake. He had arrived in Pittsburgh only hours before after driving steadily all the way from New York. His newly acquired van had not let him down. Drove smooth and clean the whole way. And so it should. He had worked hard to get it exactly right. He'd had to spend a little money on new parts, but then he had expected to.

They entered the alley, and the hooker began to whistle a tuneless rendition of the Beatles song, 'Eleanor Rigby'.

The alley was dark and filled with the stench of rotting garbage. Deke followed the whistling girl as she clattered along.

Hookers. Whores. Prostitutes.

Women.

All the same. All there for just one thing.

Greedy grabbing hands. Slack lustful bodies.

Joey had been different. Joey had never regarded him as just another john. Joey had truly cared about him. Joey had—

The first blow caught him on the side of the head and knocked him to the ground where he was kicked in the stomach by a steel-toed boot. The pain surprised him.

Desperately he tried to roll himself into a tight ball as vomit came rushing from his mouth, and with it a fast rising rage as vicious as the kicks that were aimed at his crumpled body.

'C'mon, get the motherfucker's money an' let's get outta here,' he heard the hooker say.

Then hands were roughly tearing at his lumber jacket, searching for a wallet, a stack of bills, anything.

They had caught him off guard just like his two assailants on the streets of New York. Only he had shown *them*, hadn't he. And these two would get the same treatment.

With a sudden urgent scream he lunged out, grabbing at legs, pulling and throwing off balance.

A shape fell on top of him and he heard a sharp curse, then muffled laughter before something exploded on the side of his head and everything faded to blackness.

* * *

The car impressed Joey. She grinned with delight when he turned up with it an hour after her request.

It was a black Camaro, and getting into it and hot wiring the engine had given him no trouble at all. He only hoped that the owner was staying home and not planning any night trips. If that was the case, then, if Joey didn't want to stay too long in Atlantic City, he would have it back in the same parking place long before morning, and no one would be any the wiser. Especially if he gassed it up before returning it.

'Crazee!' exclaimed Joey, looking the car over before climbing in. 'Clever cowboy!'

She made him feel ten feet tall. Who had ever called him clever before? Certainly none of the sour-faced girls he had dated. He knew what they thought of him, a couple had even gone so far as to tell him. 'You're boring, Deke. Sorry to say, but you're too dull for me.'

Joey was prettier and brighter. She saw him as he really was. She didn't see dull, she saw a quiet intelligence. She didn't see boring, she saw a man who was prepared to go out and hot wire a car for her.

She was a terrific girl.

She was a prostitute.

The two facts didn't gel.

The drive to Atlantic City was wild, with Joey giggling and shrieking and urging him to go faster and faster. When they arrived they didn't go to the beach, but to the brightly lit casinos, where Joey played the slots, her cheeks red with excitement as she fed quarter after quarter to the hungry machines.

Later, she wanted to stay. 'Book us a room,' she whispered. 'I wanna screw you in Atlantic City.'

He was worried about getting the car back before morning. And he hadn't told his parents he would be out all night. He didn't dare tell Joey his reasons not to stay, she would only laugh at him, and that's the one thing he hated more than anything.

People laughing at him . . .

'I don't want to stay,' he said finally.

'Don't then, but I will. I like it here,' she replied cheerfully. 'I can hitch a ride back tomorra.'

He didn't want to leave her, but there was no choice, so he bid her goodbye on the boardwalk at three in the morning, and the last he saw of her was her hip swaying walk as she headed back into one of the casinos.

She did not return to Philadelphia for six weeks. He was frantic. Twice he stole cars and drove back to Atlantic City looking for her, but she was never around.

He lived his life waiting for her to return, and when she did, white faced, with bloodshot black circled eyes, he shook her by the shoulders and demanded to know where she'd been.

'Fuck you, man,' she muttered. 'You don't own me. I can do what I like.'

'Not if you're my wife you can't,' he replied vehemently, wild with burning jealousy. 'I want to marry you, Joey. I want to look after you. I want us to be together always.'

She had endured six weeks of being abused by men. In fact she had endured a life of being abused by men. She was tired and sick and zonked out from too many uppers and downers. She was disgusted with life, her own life in particular.

Deke Andrews was a real weirdo, but he seemed to care for her.

'Okay bigshot,' she sighed wearily. 'Name the day.'

* * *

Voices. Far off.

A sick feeling. A sick *smell.*

He opened his eyes and a flashlight beam hit him in the face. An involuntary groan escaped his lips.

'It's all right. We got an ambulance comin',' the large cop standing over him announced.

His own vomit stained his clothes. He knew without looking that the money he carried in his inside pocket was gone.

'How many were there?' the cop asked.

Automatically he tested his arms, then his legs. Nothing seemed to be broken, although everything hurt. 'What?' he mumbled. There was dried blood on his lips, and he could make out a few idle onlookers in the gloom of the alley where he lay on the ground.

'How many?' the cop repeated.

Shakily he stood. 'I wasn't mugged,' he said. 'I got drunk . . . must have fallen. Don't need an ambulance, I'm fine.'

'Don't give me that shit!' the cop blurted. 'You've been ripped off an' I want to know who did it.'

'No sir. Not me.' He began to shuffle away. 'Just fell down drunk.'

'Goddamn it!' exclaimed the cop in exasperated fury. 'Next time I'll let you lie there.'

Deke kept walking. The sooner he was away from the cop the better. The van was parked several blocks away, the keys down the side of his boot along with the bulk of his money. Lucky that he knew the wisdom of never walking the streets with money in the expected place. The bastard pigs had only found the fifty dollars he kept in the zipped inside pocket of his lumber jacket. They had missed the big haul. Five hundred bucks in fifty dollar bills. Every cent he had made in New York while working shifts at the hotel, less the money he had paid out for the van.

He was filled with rage. At himself for falling into such a stupid trap. At the grabbing hooker. At her accomplice who probably thought he was so clever.

Deke Andrews was clever. *He* was the one who was getting away with murder . . .

He reached the van and viciously kicked at a tyre.

They would pay for it. He had heard them laughing just before he had passed out . . . laughing at him . . . laughter . . .

They would pay. There was plenty of time to take care of them before continuing on his journey.

Chapter Seventeen

Three days after Elaine asked her, Maralee, good friend that she was, came through with the script. She phoned Elaine early in the morning to tell her that it had not been easy.

Elaine was thrilled. Twenty minutes later she arrived at Maralee's sweeping house on Rodeo Drive where several Mexican gardeners worked on the perfect front lawn, and another Mexican answered the door.

'You should put up a notice, illegal immigrants' working hostel!' Elaine joked.

Maralee smiled. 'None of them speaks a word of English. It's wonderful. So peaceful.'

'I can imagine!' murmured Elaine, following her friend into the huge living room where a genuine Picasso hung above the marble fireplace, and a potpourri of original art decorated the walls. They sat on an ivory couch while a maid served coffee and peach danish.

'How are the party plans progressing?' Maralee inquired. 'Do we have an answer from dear Bibi?'

'No. I've left three messages, and she has not yet felt it necessary to call me back.'

'Hmmm . . .' Maralee looked thoughtful. 'What you need is bait. The party should be for someone. Andy Warhol, Diana Vreeland, a visiting New Yorker is always useful – Bibi adores that sort of thing. Now let's see . . . anyone you can think of?'

Elaine shrugged helplessly.

Maralee suddenly clapped her hands together. 'I've got it! Perfect!'

'Who?'

'Pamela London and George Lancaster. Karen told me they're coming in at the end of the month.'

Elaine liked the idea immediately. She knew it would guarantee an excellent turnout if she threw the party for them, but Ross might not like the idea, and she had only met Pamela London once, and briefly at that.

Still . . . Karen could sound them out . . . Important people always liked having parties thrown for them. God! It would cost a fortune, she'd never get away with fifty people as she had originally planned. *Think of it as an investment, Elaine.* What a coup it would be. Everyone would want to come. Absolutely everyone. It could be the hottest party of the year.

She felt excitement creeping over her body like a rash. She could see the columns now:

Jody Jacobs:

ELAINE AND ROSS CONTI HOSTED THE BEST PARTY BEVERLY HILLS ELITE HAS SEEN IN A LONG TIME LAST NIGHT . . .

Army Archerd:

ELAINE CONTI THE HOSTESS WHO KNOWS HOW TO PACK THE STARS WALL TO WALL . . .

Hank Grant:

PARTY QUEEN ELAINE!!

'I'll call Karen as soon as I get home,' she said excitedly.

'Good.' Maralee picked up a large manila envelope and handed it to her. 'Here's the script. Now that's two favours I've done for you, and I want one in return.'

Elaine held the envelope happily. She couldn't wait to give the script to Ross, contact Karen, and get things moving on the party.

'Name it. It's yours.'

Maralee tried to appear casual as she spoke, but two red spots lit up her cheeks and Elaine noticed that her eyes seemed unusually bright.

'Remember I was telling you about that man I met in Palm Springs . . .'

'Andy something?'

'Randy Felix.'

Elaine nodded.

'He's here, in town, and I thought it would be nice if the four of us had dinner.'

'Fine. When?'

Maralee looked flustered. 'It's not fine . . . I mean it is, but I don't know if he has any money . . . and I can't *ask* him . . . and well . . . I'm sure he'd love to meet Ross, and you're so good with people . . .'

'Why don't you have him checked out?'

'I don't want to do that.'

Elaine was sympathetic. 'You like him, is that it?'

Maralee grinned. 'Yes.'

'Good. So we'll meet him, and I'll let you know what I think.'

'I don't want another bad experience,' Maralee sighed.

Since her divorce from Neil, her track record with men was disastrous. Invariably she attracted the fortune hunters and penniless studs, with an occasional drunk thrown in for good measure. They spent her money, roughed her up, and daddy had to send in the heavies to get rid of them. She was totally weak when it came to men.

'How about La Scala, Friday night?' Elaine suggested.

Maralee nodded thankfully. 'Perfect. I'll arrange to have the check taken care of before-hand so that Randy won't be embarrassed.'

'Wouldn't hear of it. It's our treat.' Elaine stood and aimed a kiss at her friend's cheek. 'Now I must run. Thanks for everything. La Scala, Friday. See you there at seven-thirty.'

* * *

Everything happened so quickly. It was like Jason Swankle had taken over his life. The trip to Malibu, and Jason there to greet them. 'He's an old friend.' Buddy had explained to Angel, 'who owes me a favour.' She had bought that. No reason why she shouldn't. And if she'd had any doubts about anything, they were all swept away when she feasted her eyes on the house. What a place! Small, but prime beachfront and decorated like a futuristic fantasy. All white, chrome, and electronic, with insane speakers everywhere and quadraphonic stereo equipment that could bring tears to your eyes it was so great.

The house was on two floors, the lower floor a glass fronted living room overlooking the ocean, and the upper floor one big bedroom dominated by a water bed.

'Please,' Jason insisted. 'Be most careful.'

'We will Mr Swankle,' Angel replied, wide-eyed and thrilled. 'I've always dreamed of a place like this and you can be sure we'll look after it as if it were our own.'

Jason was relieved. Buddy's wife was no Hollywood tramp as he had imagined. She was young and starry-eyed. Exceptionally pretty. But dull. He could accept her, she was no rival. He left, fully satisfied that lending them the house was not a rash move. And anyway, it was only for a few weeks.

Buddy and Angel settled in overnight. They spoke of Buddy's forthcoming test, read the few pages of script together, and later warmed frozen pizza in the microwave. Then they made long leisurely love on the waterbed.

'I love you, Buddy,' Angel told him many times. 'I love you *so so* much.'

He luxuriated in her adoration. He lay on the bed and imagined that the house was his, and that he was a star, and that no one, but no one, could take it away from him. Later he slept, and the nightmare faces came back to haunt him. But in the morning, when Jason's chauffeured car arrived, he was in good shape. He had jogged along the shoreline, swum in the icy surf, and eaten a solid breakfast of bacon and eggs.

He left Angel the keys of the Pontiac and fifty bucks. Jason had advanced him two hundred on his forthcoming date. The ladies were due in town in a couple of days, and Jason wanted to fit him out with some new threads before their arrival. He wasn't about to argue with *that.* He had thought that they would go to Gladrags' store, but this was not to be; when the car collected Jason, he instructed the driver to the most exclusive, expensive men's shop on Rodeo Drive, Bijan, where they spent three hours putting together two outfits.

Buddy could hardly believe his luck. All this for just taking out a couple of old broads?

'I get to keep the clothes, don't I?' he asked confidently.

'Of course,' Jason replied, beaming. 'Now. How about some lunch? Does Ma Maison appeal to you?'

Ma Maison appealed to him all right, but maybe being seen in such a restaurant with Jason Swankle was not the best idea in the world. The dude was an obvious queen, and everyone would think he was his boy . . . Shit! Not a good idea at all. He had seen the looks the salesmen had exchanged when he was trying on clothes and parading them for approval.

'No . . .' he hesitated. 'I really don't feel like heavy food. I'm into not eating too much.'

'But you could order something simple,' Jason insisted. 'The duck salad is quite divine!' He kissed his fingertips in fervent appreciation.

Buddy shook his head. 'I gotta get back to the beach, study my lines, y'know?'

Jason nodded understandingly. 'I'll send the driver for you at noon tomorrow, we'll have lunch then.'

'I don't think—'

'We simply must. I want to introduce you to Patrick, the owner of Ma Maison. When you take the ladies there for dinner I don't want you to walk in like a tourist.'

'Yeah, well—'

'Tomorrow,' Jason stated firmly.

There was no getting out of it.

* * *

Montana took Neil's Maserati, drove the hell out of it all the way to the beach, then zoomed along the Pacific Coast Highway, stopping only for a hamburger and a Coke. They were trying to edge her out. She knew it! She felt it! Bastards! *Street People* was her creation, and no way was she letting go.

George Lancaster . . . Gina Germaine . . . Did they want to make a piece of shit? The kind of movie Oliver was famous for. She had thought Neil had more style. She tuned the radio to a heavy rock station, smoked continually, and gradually calmed down.

What was she getting so excited about? So he wanted to test some busty dumb blonde. So what? Once he saw her on the screen playing Nikki he would know immediately how wrong she was for the part. So would Oliver.

Two major assholes. Men. Probably dazzled by Gina's outsize assets. She was making too big a deal over it. Getting pissed off because Neil hadn't mentioned it to her first. Well, she had four actors lined up to test for Vinnie, and she had no intention of asking his opinion until he viewed them up on the screen. Making movies meant taking risks. There was no way of knowing what would happen once an actor or actress got in front of the camera. It could be magic, it could be zilch. Maybe Gina – with the right clothes, hairstyle, direction . . . Unlikely, but maybe . . .

Let Neil and Oliver play their stupid Hollywood games. She was no idiot. She could play too if that's what they wanted.

She arrived home to find Neil asleep, with the television on. She didn't wake him.

The next morning they were scrupulously polite to each other, discussing locations over breakfast before departing for their day's activities.

'Oh, by the way,' Montana said casually, as she walked towards her car, 'If you *really* feel you have to test Gina Germaine – go ahead. Maybe she's got something that I haven't latched onto.'

'What do you mean by that?' he snapped defensively.

She frowned. 'Nothing earth shattering. But it would have been nice if you'd discussed it with me before telling Oliver.'

'I meant to,' he said weakly.

'By the way,' she continued, 'I've decided to direct the tests on the actors I've picked. You've no objections to that have you?'

He was relieved at the change of subject. 'I think it's an excellent idea.'

'Good. I want to set them up soon.'

'The sooner the better.'

She climbed into her car and drove off without another word.

Neil took a deep breath. It looked like everything was going to be all right. Test Gina. The test would stink. He would be off the hook.

Just who exactly did he think he was kidding?

* * *

Street People. What a property. What a *great part* for him.

Ross placed the script on the coffee table in the den. He shut his eyes and leaned back with a deep sigh. For a moment he sat silently. It was late and he was tired, but he was also exhilarated, his mind alive with ideas. It was one o'clock in the morning, and he had been reading solidly for two hours.

MAC. FIFTY YEARS OLD. A STREET COP FOR ALL OF HIS ADULT LIFE. CYNICAL AND TOUGH. BUT WITH A LOT OF COMPASSION AND HOPE FOR THE FUTURE. A WORLD WEARY MAN WITH OLD FASHIONED VALUES.

It was an Oscar nomination role, no doubt about that. Of

course, it was not the sort of part that he had ever played before. A man of fifty. Forget it.

What the fuck do you mean – forget it? You are no longer the boy wonder. You are fifty, or at least you will be this year.

Would his public accept him in such a role?

What frigging public? They gave up stampeding your movies a long time ago. Now half of 'em see you in some old movie on television and they think you're dead for crissake.

He rose from the couch and went to the bar where he fixed himself a scotch on the rocks. *Street People.* It was strange knowing a woman had written it. She got inside a man's head. She put down thoughts and feelings that he had imagined only men knew about.

You're a definite chauvinist pig, you know that? Your ideas are corny and out of date. You'd better start thinking today – or you'll find yourself in an elephant's graveyard for old-time movie stars.

Jesus! He wanted the part. He wanted it so badly he could taste it.

Twenty-five years of movies.

Twenty-five years of shit.

He sipped his scotch, rolled the booze across his tongue, allowed it to trickle slowly down his throat.

He was calm, excited, nervous, confident. Christ! He didn't know *what* he was. He only knew that whatever it took he *had* to have that part. *Had to.*

But how to convince everyone? How to convince Oliver Easterne, Neil and Montana Gray?

Oliver was a hustler, a money-man. He wouldn't see talent if it climaxed all over his deal-making face.

Neil Gray was an overblown English egotist. Talented but a total pain.

Montana Gray he didn't even know.

Sadie La Salle, you asshole. She could get you the part. She weaves magic in this town. She has the power.

Yes. Sadie. She would *know* he was right for it. She would *know* he was capable of playing the hell out of it.

Had Elaine invited her to the party yet? Had she got a yes or no? He hurried into their bedroom.

Elaine slept soundly, her hair held back from her face with a white alice band. Her face itself liberally smeared with some kind of Royal Jelly which Ross had unkindly christened 'bees come'. She hid her eyes beneath a black sleep mask, and snored softly.

Ross stared down at her, he had given her a tough day, and he felt sorry now. But sometimes she bugged him with all her nagging and Beverly Hills bullshit. She had come rushing back from Maralee Gray's clutching the script as if it were stock in IBM. Thrusting it at him she said triumphantly, 'There you are. How's *that* for service?'

Perversely he tossed the manuscript to one side.

'Aren't you going to read it?'

'Later,' he said, enjoying her look of annoyed frustration.

He kept it up all day long, dying to read the damn thing, but stubbornly refusing to pick it up while Elaine was around.

They had dinner, watched a movie on television, and then she swept off to bed. He had fixed himself a drink, made himself comfortable, and started to read.

'Honey, wake up.' He shook her roughly.

She shrieked. 'Who is it? What? God!' Frantically she pulled off her sleep mask, blinked twice, then said, 'What the hell is it, Ross? You frightened the life out of me.'

'It's frigging marvellous, that's what it is,' he said excitedly.

'Are you drunk?'

'No. I am not drunk. I am very sober.' He sat down on the side of the bed. 'Have you called Sadie La Salle?'

She struggled to consult her bedside clock. 'It's one fifteen in the morning. Is that what you woke me up to find out?'

'It's important . . .'

'Goddamn it! Surely it could have waited until morning?'

He reached out and playfully rubbed his finger over her cheek. 'You're covered in bees come again.'

'I do wish you wouldn't say that.'

'Why? Does it make you horny?' As he said it he could feel the sap rising. Automatically he reached for her breasts.

'Ross—' Elaine began to object, then thought better of it. Just because she wasn't prepared did not mean she shouldn't grab the opportunity when it arose.

They went through their familiar ritual. Marital sex was like a favourite meal. Good but predictable. She had given up wishing that Ross would do something different. He had his routine and he stuck to it religiously.

No more than ten minutes passed before they both climaxed. Her first. Him second. He might have the biggest dick in Hollywood but it still only took ten minutes.

After, he lit cigarettes for them both and said, 'Good, huh.' He always said, 'Good, huh.' It wasn't a question, it was a statement.

She remembered the early days. The first time they made love. The months they were secretly seeing each other. The beginning of their marriage. Oh, what a lover Ross Conti had been then!

Ross drew deeply on his cigarette and thought of Karen Lancaster. He really should call her. She was such a little wildcat in the sack. Not like Elaine who lay there like she was doing him a big favour. She quite obviously didn't enjoy sex like she used to. She always made him feel that he was pushing himself on her and that he should get it over with as quickly as possible. If the truth were known he could honestly say that sex with his wife was dull, and it certainly wasn't *his* fault.

'Very good,' Elaine murmured. 'I was beginning to think you'd forgotten how.'

He ignored the barb. Ha! She should only know!

'I read the script,' he began. 'And I don't know if Montana Gray wrote it – didn't write it, whatever. It's going to make one hell of a movie.'

Her interest was aroused. 'It is?'

'No doubt about it.'

'And . . .' she paused. 'How about the part for you?'

'Perfect.'

'Really?'

'Well, not perfect for *me*, Ross Conti, but perfect for *me* as an actor. Do you understand what I'm saying?'

Did she understand? Who did he think he was talking to?

'So we *have* to get Sadie La Salle,' she said excitedly.

'It's our best shot.'

They were on each other's wave length at last. Elaine smiled. 'I'm having lunch with Karen tomorrow, she'll have an answer for me on whether I can throw the party for George and Pamela. If I can – then nobody will dare not to come – even Sadie La Salle.'

* * *

Ma Maison. Friday lunch. The small garden restaurant was crowded, the umbrellaed tables in close proximity, the aproned waiters running this way and that.

Buddy had decided to test out the pale tan Armani jacket, beige slacks and matching collarless silk shirt. The look was right, expensively casual.

'You need just a touch of gold,' Jason said, fussily toying with a thick gold chain that hung around his own neck.

'No, I don't,' Buddy replied quickly. There was nothing worse than California casual ruined by great chunks of flash jewellery. Gold chains on men always reminded him of the ageing swingers who cruised around Beverly Hills in their Mercedes and Porsches, with hair combed concealingly forward, and fat guts held tightly in.

Settled at their table in the corner, just the two of them, Buddy felt free to cast an interested eye around the fashionable restaurant. There were a lot of women lunching together. Tables of them. Chic. Stylish. Beautiful.

Jason suddenly felt it his duty to give him a run-down on every famous face in the place. 'You see that group of women over there, well the beautiful one with the dark hair is Mrs

Johnny Carson – the devastating Joanna. And at the next table is Louisa Moore – wife of Roger – she's *such* fun. And the couple in the corner—'

'Stephanie Powers and Robert Wagner,' Buddy interrupted.

'And next to them—'

'Dudley Moore.'

'Very good,' said Jason crisply, 'but I bet you don't know who *that* is.' He pointed out an exquisite black haired beauty deep in conversation with a man.

'I give up.'

'Shakira Caine. Married to Michael Caine of course. She's with Bobby Zarem – he made the slogan "I love New York" famous – wonderful I.R. and so amusing.'

'Do you know all these people?' Buddy asked, impressed in spite of himself.

'Not intimately, but many of them come to the store.'

'Hey – maybe you know an agent I can meet . . . Like a real hot one.'

'Let me see . . . I'm sure amongst my connections . . . Oh, you see that woman sitting down over there – that's George Lancaster's daughter, and on the other side of the room is David Tebet – he's the vice president of Johnny Carson Productions, and I see Jack Lemmon and . . .'

Buddy glanced restlessly around not really listening as Jason carried on. He had eyes, he could spot the stars for himself. Clint Eastwood sprawled at a centre table, his long legs impeding the waiters' fast trips around the room. And Sidney Poitier, Tom Selleck . . . there were celebrities everywhere.

Buddy felt good. Not that anyone had so much as glanced in his direction, but he was still *there*, still part of it.

'Do you like it here?' Jason asked, well aware of the fact that indeed he did.

Buddy shrugged. 'I've been here before y'know.'

'I'm sure you have.' Jason couldn't help allowing his eyes to linger on Buddy's restless countenance. The boy had such looks . . . such beauty . . . Ah . . . now if he bided his time . . . was patient . . . Ah . . .

* * *

Karen's green eyes gleamed. 'I promise you, I spoke to daddy *and* Pamela. They would both be delighted to be guests of honour at your party.'

'You're sure?' Elaine asked for the second time.

'Elaine. If I say something, you can bet it will happen.' She smiled and waved at Dudley Moore. 'Pamela would like you to phone her at ten o'clock tonight – Palm Beach time.'

'She would?'

'Don't look so dumbstruck, it's what you wanted, isn't it?'

'Of course—'

'So thanks to me you've got it. The hottest party in town. Just watch Bibi jump now!'

Maralee joined in the conversation. 'Who's doing the catering?'

Elaine had imagined she could use Lina and two of her Mexican friends, but things were different now. 'I hadn't really thought—'

'Better start thinking!' warned Karen. 'That salmon mousse Tita Cahn served last week was to die! I think she's made a new discovery. Why not give her a call?'

'Mortons could do the whole thing for you,' Maralee suggested. 'Or La Scala. I always feel more secure when one uses professionals.'

'Yes, but that's so safe,' argued Karen. 'Daddy adores oriental food. How about a Chinese feast?'

'Madame Wu's?' ventured Elaine, thinking about how much it was all going to cost, and how loud Ross was going to scream.

'Marvellous food,' said Maralee.

'Marvellous,' echoed Karen.

* * *

Buddy sipped the hot black espresso and wondered how long he was expected to sit there. Jason seemed quite settled as he toyed with a small glass of Sambuca.

'Uh . . . I guess I should be gettin' back to the beach,' he said at last. 'I'm expecting a call about the test, an' I want to go over the script again.'

Jason nodded. 'Is everything all right for you at the house?'

'Couldn't be better, Angel loves it.'

It annoyed Jason that at every given opportunity Buddy mentioned his wife. It was almost as if he was screaming – *I'm straight! I'm straight! And don't you forget it!*

Jason clicked his fingers for the check. Some of his most memorable experiences had been with so-called straights. When they came out of the closet they came out with a vengeance. 'Yes,' he murmured. 'Angel seems such a sweet girl.'

'She is,' Buddy assured him.

'Quite so. But I do think it best if we don't mention the fact that you're married to Mrs Jaeger and her friend.'

'Sure.' Why bite the hand that was draping him in Armani?

'They'll be arriving tomorrow evening. Probably quite late,' Jason continued, squinting at the check. He withdrew a pigskin wallet from his jacket and extracted his trusty Master Charge card. 'I expect they'll be tired, so I'll have the driver meet them at the airport and deposit them at their hotel – the Beverly Hills of course – and I thought that on Sunday we'd all meet up for a perfectly wonderful brunch in the Polo Lounge. Won't that be fun?'

Buddy could have thought of another way to describe it. But he stayed silent and tried to look enthusiastic.

'Wear what you have on today,' Jason instructed. 'It suits you admirably.'

'Sure, thanks.' Impatiently Buddy glanced yet again at the tables around him. Clint Eastwood was long gone, but he spotted Allan Carr, Richard Gere and Rock Hudson. The famous producer and the two movie stars gave him a real buzz. Quickly he sneaked a look at his watch. Three o'clock in the afternoon. Shit! By the time he got back to the beach it would be four – too late to work on his tan. What a wasted day. Jason Swankle was a nice enough guy, but just who did he think he was kidding? Buddy *knew* the time would come when he would try to climb on his bones. Why else the beach house, the new clothes, and the money for dating two old women who any escort service could have taken care of for half the price?

The waiter returned the Master Charge card, and they rose to leave. Buddy strode quickly through the restaurant, leaving Jason to tag along behind. At the entrance he bumped straight into Randy Felix. They stared at each other in surprise, then delight.

'Hey—' Buddy exclaimed. 'What are *you* doin' here?'

'Meeting someone,' Randy grinned, and stepped back to look his friend over. 'And you're *lookin' good*!'

'Too right!'

They hugged quickly in an embarrassed masculine way, and parted just as Jason puffed up.

'Uh . . . this is a friend of mine – Randy Felix,' Buddy explained. 'Give me five minutes an' I'll see you out in the car.'

Jason pursed fleshy lips and nodded curtly at Randy. 'Just make sure you're not longer than five minutes,' he said possessively before leaving.

Randy stared quizzically at Jason's departing back. 'You changed sides, bro?'

'Come *on*. Who d'y'think you're talkin' to?'

'Just askin'. You never know nowadays.'

They both noticed the blonde waving. She had risen from her seat and was beckoning frantically. 'Over here, Randy,' she called, in case he missed her.

Randy waved back. 'The one I was telling you about,' he explained *sotto voce*. 'Maralee Gray, her father owns Sanderson Studios. Her ex is Neil Gray – the director. You like the set-up?'

'Like it – I want it!'

'Come meet her.'

Buddy was tempted. The mention of Neil Gray set bells ringing. But she was his ex-wife and probably had nothing to do with the movie. Besides, how would it look if Jason came waddling in to get him?

'Another time. Whyn't you buzz me later? I got plenty of news.'

They stopped a waiter for a pen and paper, and Buddy scribbled down his number at the beach. Then they slapped palms and went their separate ways.

* * *

'Who was that?' inquired Karen, when Randy was settled at their table and introduced to her and Elaine by a nervous Maralee.

'Who was what?' asked Randy, knowing immediately that Karen Lancaster was asking about Buddy. They *all* had the hots for Buddy. It was always the same.

'That gorgeous man you were talking to on your way in,' Karen persisted irritably.

'You mean Buddy.'

'Buddy?'

'Buddy Hudson. He's a friend of mine.'

'Gay?'

Randy licked his finger and exaggeratedly smoothed his eyebrow. 'If you say so, sweets!'

Maralee laughed nervously. 'Randy!' she admonished. 'Don't!'

Karen glared. She hated Maralee's new friend on sight. 'I have to go,' she drawled. 'Coming, Elaine?'

Actually Elaine was anxious to leave. She couldn't wait to get home and phone Bibi. But Maralee had begged her to meet Randy before their evening dinner date, and she could hardly say hello goodbye as soon as the poor man sat down.

'I'll stay a few minutes,' she explained apologetically.

'Suit yourself,' snapped Karen, and with an all-encompassing wave around the table she exited.

'You'll love Karen,' Maralee gushed, holding tightly on to Randy's hand, 'when you get to know her.'

He smiled and winked at Elaine. 'Can't wait!' he said cheerily.

She decided she couldn't stand him.

* * *

Angel spent the day dusting, polishing and vacuuming. The house at Malibu was really the most perfect place she had ever seen – straight out of a magazine, and she couldn't be more thrilled that they were lucky enough to be staying there.

She hummed softly as she went about her tasks, mopping the perfectly spotless kitchen floor, sponging the sparkling formica tops, pouring disinfectant down three unused toilets.

The beach was hazy all morning, but at twelve the sun broke through, and she slipped into a bikini and lay out on the patio deck overlooking the ocean. She took with her a pad and a pen, planning to write a letter to her foster family in Louisville. She had not heard from them at all, in spite of the fact that she had written several times. It was to be expected. They had never cared for her, her presence had merely been an extra source of income from the welfare people. But still . . . she wanted them to know about the baby. Maybe, just maybe, they would be pleased for her.

Dear Everyone,
Well I suppose you are wondering why I have not written for a while. Well you see—

She paused for thought and gazed at two joggers running through the surf. They were holding hands and laughing. A dog ran behind them. Buddy was so jumpy lately . . . Perhaps now they were at the beach, settled into a beautiful house . . .

But for how long? And who was Jason Swankle? And why was he part of their lives all of a sudden?

She sighed, then abruptly screwed up the writing paper and threw it across the sand. Buddy was her family now. Louisville was her past. Buddy was her future even if he did not confide in her, and fed her a bunch of lies when she would have been quite prepared to face the truth.

For instance – where did he come up with the money to buy new *expensive* clothes? Why were they installed in this beautiful house? Who was paying for the chauffeured car that kept on arriving to pick him up? When she asked him all of these questions he had laughed, ruffled her hair and said, 'Don't you worry about it, babe. My old pal Jason owes me. He's just settlin' a debt.'

Angel wondered, if there was a debt to be settled, why didn't *she* get any new clothes? Not that she begrudged Buddy his outfits, but surely it would have been nice if she could have gotten something too? He hadn't even asked her to accompany him on his shopping spree, and she was hurt. Soon she would *have* to get new clothes – maternity clothes.

The thought caused a secret smile to play across her lips. She couldn't wait for her stomach to swell – confirming the fact that a person she and Buddy had created was growing inside her. All thoughts of being a movie star had faded. *Buddy* would be the star of the family, and she would be his loving wife. The fan magazines would feature photo lay-outs of them at home. Buddy so macho and good looking, and she in flowing dresses with flowers in her hair and lots of beautiful children at her feet. Earth mother. The thought pleased her. She smiled broadly. How long would it take for him to become a superstar? Two years? Three? Whenever. She would be ready.

The surf looked inviting, so she slipped off her white sandals and hurried down the steps to the sand. Then she ran towards the ocean, her long blonde hair flying out behind her.

A man, sitting on the deck of a neighbouring house, watched her progress into the sea. He rose and walked to the edge of the deck, straining his eyes to get a better look at her as she plunged into the waves.

When she emerged he was still watching.

* * *

It took Bibi Sutton exactly eleven minutes to call back after Elaine had left a message with her secretary about the party being for George Lancaster and Pamela London.

'Sweetie!' she purred down the phone. 'I 'ave been so busy. You know 'ow it is.'

'Don't apologize,' Elaine said magnanimously. 'I know *exactly* what you mean.'

'Darling, you really 'ave party for Pamela and George?' Bibi always liked to check her facts before committing.

'I thought I told you it was for them,' Elaine replied innocently.

'No, no. Still. We come anyway, you know that.'

'Of course I do.' Elaine was enjoying herself. The worse star-fucks were the stars themselves.

' 'Ow many people you 'ave?' Bibi inquired.

'Nothing enormous. More an . . . intimate gathering. Close friends of George and Pamela's. Fifty, sixty. No more than that.'

'Ahhh . . .' Bibi sighed. 'This I like. An intimate gathering. Dressy I 'ope.'

'For the ladies, yes. I think the men are more comfortable casual,' Elaine replied firmly.

'So sensible, sweetie!' Bibi shrieked. 'I love it. *We* dress up. *They* wear boring sports clothes.'

Approval at last. Elaine glowed.

'Now,' Bibi continued, 'who do the food?'

Elaine hesitated for only a second. *Be positive. Don't let the bitch throw you.* 'I was thinking of using Madame Wu's.'

'No!'

'No?'

'I 'ave secret for you. A secret I tell only my good friends.'

Elaine waited.

Bibi paused dramatically. 'Sergio and Eugenio!' she announced triumphantly.

'I don't think I know them—'

'Sure you don't know them. Nobody knows them. They are *mine.* My *secret.*'

It was rumoured – though never proved – that Bibi got a kickback from every restaurant, caterer, store, etc., that she put her magic seal of approval on. Elaine wondered what Sergio and Eugenio would throw into the pot.

'Are they good?'

'Are they good! Ha!' Bibi laughed mirthlessly. 'Sweetie, would I recommend them if they not good?'

'Of course not, I—'

Bibi was in full flow. 'And I 'ave another secret for you. The Zancussi trio. Italian love songs straight from Roma. You tent the garden?'

'I hadn't really—'

'You must! Now, let me give you some advice—'

The conversation continued for another ten minutes while Bibi honoured Elaine with her suggestions. And all the time Elaine was mentally counting the cost. Tented garden. Trio of musicians. Sergio and Eugenio. Valet parking. Floral arrangements. Two special bartenders to mix the latest drinks. Waiters. Kitchen staff. A new outfit.

To do it properly would cost a fortune. But properly it had to be done.

Bibi ended the conversation on an encouraging note. She invited Elaine to a lunch she was having the following Monday at her house. 'I'ave the wonderful police come to speak about mace. We all get the permit,' Bibi explained brightly. 'What you think? Good idea, no?'

What did a woman like Bibi need a can of mace for? Her chauffeured Rolls never ventured out of Beverly Hills.

'Great idea,' gushed Elaine, hating herself for being such an ass licker.

Bibi Sutton calls – you run. I thought you hated her guts.

Shut up, Etta.

Later, dinner at La Scala with Maralee, and her new boyfriend, Randy, was a disaster. How did Maralee find them? How did she know just where to look for the sharp-eyed hustlers who homed right in on her money and position. Elaine had taken an instant dislike to Randy at lunchtime, and her first reaction was strengthened upon their second meeting.

Ross was annoyed that they had to go in the first place. He and Maralee had never really hit it off. He tolerated her because she was his wife's best friend, but he didn't see why he had to tolerate her boring dumb stud boyfriends, *and* pay for dinner on top of everything else.

They ordered drinks, and Elaine spoke to Maralee, while Randy attempted to communicate with Ross. He called him 'sir' which made Ross scowl, and he said things like – 'You were my mother's favourite' and 'I've seen all your old movies on television.'

An asshole of the first order. Ross summoned the waiter and proceeded to down a series of scotch on the rocks.

Halfway through the evening Karen Lancaster arrived with Chet Barnes. She swooped down on their table like a predatory bird, Chet trailing behind.

'He-*llo* everyone,' she greeted, her eyes bright from a snort of pre-dinner cocaine – the Hollywood equivalent of a pep up pill.

Ross sat up straight at the sight of her perky nipples straining the material of a thin silk tank top, and wondered why he hadn't bothered to call her. He decided to rectify the situation first thing in the morning.

'Have you eaten?' Elaine inquired, thankful for the diversion.

'We're just about to.'

'Why don't you join us?' Elaine said quickly, giving Ross a sharp kick under the table.

He took his cue, fascinated by Karen's nipples through the flimsy material. 'Yes, come on, join us,' he encouraged.

Karen looked him straight in the eye and smiled sweetly. 'No thank you. Chet and I are into a heavy discussion about multiple orgasms and whether having a big dick helps a guy to be a good lover. We wouldn't want to put anyone off their dinner.'

Elaine laughed. 'You are unbelievable!'

Karen shot Ross a deadly look. 'See you all later.'

'Come and have coffee with us,' Elaine begged desperately.

'Maybe.' Karen smiled around the table, her eyes flicking past Randy Felix as if he didn't exist. Then she grabbed Chet's hand, and a waiter directed them to an intimate booth in the back.

'I didn't know Karen and Chet were having a thing,' Maralee said excitedly. 'How long has she been seeing *him*?'

Elaine shrugged. 'I can never keep up with her affairs.'

And a good thing too, Ross thought. He looked across the room. Karen was snuggling up to Chet, whispering in his ear, or was it her tongue in his ear?

All of a sudden he wanted her badly. He wanted her on her knees in front of him sucking his—

'Are you all right, Ross?' Elaine asked sharply.

'What?'

'You look most peculiar.'

'You mean I look frigging bored,' he muttered angrily. 'Why do you have to stick me with these evenings?'

'Shhh . . .'

Elaine need not have been concerned. Maralee wasn't listening anyway, she was gazing into Randy Felix's eyes as he told her a whole lot of lies about his past.

* * *

Every day, around five, Buddy called the Easterne office and spoke to Montana Gray's secretary. She was the blonde with the bad nose job, and she and Buddy indulged in long intense conversations. He was anxious to know exactly what was happening. Was there a date set for his test? What other actors were testing? Who seemed to present the most competition?

The blonde, whose name was Inga, confided in Buddy absolutely, and fully expected him to invite her out on a date. When he didn't she finally said, 'Look, it's difficult for me to give out all this information on the phone. Why don't you come by my apartment?'

He knew what *that* meant. 'I'm stuck out at the beach an' my car's in the shop,' he lied.

She was not to be put off. She had read her *Cosmopolitan*, and she knew her rights; if she wanted to get laid she was perfectly entitled to do the chasing. '*I* can drive down to see *you*,' she said firmly.

'Not a good idea. I'm stayin' with this neurotic guy who jumps on anything that moves. It's a bad scene here, you wouldn't like it.'

'Try me,' she said boldly.

'One of these days, kid.'

'Just name it, Buddy.'

'Look. Why don't I call you same time tomorrow?'

He got off the phone and prowled nervously around the house. Angel was in the kitchen fixing tuna salad for their dinner.

'Hey – why don't we go out to eat?' He grabbed her from behind and gave her a hug.

'Everything's nearly ready,' she said primly, extracting herself and continuing to chop cucumber.

'So what? I feel like showing you off.'

'Not tonight, Buddy. My hair needs washing, I've prepared dinner, and there's a Richard Gere film on television.'

What did she need Richard Gere for when she had him? That really pissed him. 'Okay. Okay.'

Wide eyed and unbearably beautiful, 'You don't mind, do you?'

'Naw, 'course I don't.'

He wandered out on the deck. Shit! Angel was beginning to

sound like a wife. He would have thought she would have jumped at the chance of hitting the town with him. It wasn't like they had been living it up every night.

He felt uptight and restless. Jeez! You would think she would *understand* – what with the test coming up and everything.

They ate dinner with one eye on a space age television hanging from the ceiling. Then Angel yawned delicately and said, 'I'm sooo tired. Do you mind if I go to bed early?'

Yes. He minded. He needed to unwind, have a few blasts, relax.

'Sure babe, you go right ahead.'

She kissed him lightly and vanished upstairs.

He wished he had a joint to take the edge off.

He wished that he'd done the fucking test already.

He wished he was a star.

Chapter Eighteen

Joey Kravetz's sister was back in town. Louise Kravetz. Known as Lulu. Five years older than Joey. Arrested three times for prostitution, twice for drugs.

She arrived on a charter from Amsterdam on a Sunday morning, and Leon knew about it ten minutes after she cleared customs. He had his connections.

Ignoring Millie's objections, he jumped in his car and arrived at the run-down house where Lulu resided twenty minutes before she did. An angry black landlady let him into her room. It was a depressing array of musty clothes, dead plants, an old record player and stacks of worn rock albums. A thick film of dust covered everything.

In one corner stood an unmade bed. Over the other side there was a gas burner, with a few dirt encrusted dishes piled on top.

Leon positioned himself stiffly by the door ready to flash his I.D. and give the sister the bad news.

He wondered if she looked like Joey . . .

* * *

Leon awoke to the sound of an alarm ringing. Seven a.m. Without his alarm clock he could sleep forever.

He felt the dried stickiness around his crotch, and knew

immediately what it was. A wet dream. Jesus H. Christ, he hadn't had a wet dream since he was sixteen years old!

Wet dream, my ass. Joey Kravetz jerking you off in the middle of the night while you played possum.

Christ. Had he really done that?

Yes, you did it and you loved it, and you were never that much asleep that you couldn't have woken fully and stopped her.

Shame crept over him. He, Leon Rosemont, and sixteen year old hooker. It wasn't like he was desperate. He had regular sex – as much sex as he could use. Goddamn it! How could he have let her do it?

Shamefacedly he climbed out of bed, ripped off the offending pyjamas and covered himself with a bathrobe.

How could he face her?

How could he not?

He imagined the expression on her face. She would stare at him knowingly, triumphantly. You're just like all the rest.

But he wasn't. No way was he like the animals who prowled the streets. No damn way.

Angrily he marched into the living room. Get her up and out and give her twenty bucks to see her on her way.

That's right. Encourage her to keep on hooking. Pay her off and forget her. She's not your problem.

Oh yes she is. Sixteen years old and you should try and help her. Where's your sense of public duty?

Where had his goddamn sense of public duty been in the early hours of the morning?

The blanket and pillow he had given her were on the floor. The couch was empty.

He knew she had gone before he even checked out the kitchen and bathroom.

* * *

Lulu was taller than Joey, plump, like a stuffed chicken, her skin blotched red, and her eyes that sickly yellow colour that comes from too many drugs.

She was not alone. Accompanying her was a skinny nervous Chicano youth with matted wild hair and the same yellow eyes. They both had backpacks strapped to their shoulders, and the weight looked like it was just about to finish off the Chicano. Their landlady had obviously felt it best not to mention Leon's presence, because neither of them could have faked their looks of shocked surprise.

'Who the fuck are *you*?' Lulu shrieked. 'An' what you doin' in my room?'

Leon flashed his identification.

Lulu dropped her backpack, snatched his I.D. and studied it intently.

'Fuckin' pigs,' she finally muttered, throwing it back at him. 'I go away – they're hasslin' me. I come back – same thing.' She waved her fat arms in the air, revealing a tear in her Indian batik blouse. 'I'm clean, man. Search me.'

Lulu was an obvious charmer. However, the dialogue was getting her friend mighty nervous, and he began backing out the door without so much as a goodbye.

'Come back T.T.,' Lulu shrieked. 'You ain't runnin' out on me. Whatever they want, you're in it too.'

T.T. froze, sick yellow eyes darting around.

'I don't *want* anything,' Leon said quietly. 'I have something very distressing to tell you.'

'Distressing.' Lulu repeated the word blankly, as if she had never heard it before.

T.T. took his cue. 'Distressin', he mumbled.

'It's about your sister, Joey,' Leon intoned gravely.

'What's the little tramp done now?' demanded Lulu, vigorously scratching a denim thigh. 'Got herself finished off?' She laughed wildly at her own humour.

'Exactly,' said Leon.

'Don't fuck with me, mister,' she snapped. 'Cop or not I don't think that's very funny.'

'Your sister, Joey, has been murdered,' Leon said formally.

The blotched face crumpled. Her friend's head jerked nervously.

'I'm sorry,' Leon said gently.

'Sorry!' Lulu shrieked, recovering rapidly from her grief. 'You motherfucker. What *you* know about bein' sorry? You pigs killed my little sister.'

T. T. said quickly, 'Hold it, Lou. Remember, *he's a cop*.'

'Sure,' yelled Lulu, out of control and quivering with fury. 'An' I'll fuckin' remember the times she got hassled by the cops. All the time, man, *all the time*. A blow job in the back of the squad car. A screw in an alleyway. One even dragged her back to his stinkin' apartment when she was only fifteen years old an' did her. Cops!' she snorted in disgust. 'She had no chance – an' you pigs never helped her. You *leaned* on her, man, every step of the fuckin' way.'

Leon stared at her angry face. *One even dragged her back to his stinkin' apartment when she was only fifteen years old an' did her.*

He coughed and attempted to say something, but all the while his mind was churning. *Deke Andrews. Deke Andrews. Got to catch him. Got to catch him for Joey's sake . . . for my sake . . .*

The guilt was impossible to live with.

Chapter Nineteen

Mrs Norma Jaeger was not at all as Buddy had expected. Nor was Mrs Celeste McQueen. No doubt about it – they were no longer spring chickens, but life – as the saying goes – was not yet over. And the jewellery the two of them were wearing had to be seen to be believed.

Mrs Jaeger first. Hennaed red hair worn in a girlish frizz. The face hitting fifty if you looked close – but from a short distance – thirty-five – give or take a year or two. Subtle make-up, slightly too heavy on the amber eye-shadow. Figure very well preserved indeed, clad in a powder blue tracksuit. And round the neck a thick gold dog collar studded with several very large diamonds. A bracelet to match. And a gulls-egg diamond ring on her left hand which could lay a burglar out for a week and a half. No trouble.

Mrs Celeste McQueen, a year or two older – an inch or two fatter. Streaked short hair, light suntan, freckles. White tennis dress and really impressive legs. Lots of turquoise and silver Indian jewellery, and a heart shaped diamond ring that rivalled her friend's in size.

Sunday noon, and they both gazed at Buddy expectantly as Jason executed introductions in the dimly lit Polo Lounge.

'Hey—' Buddy sing-songed, all charm. 'Good to make your acquaintance, ladies.' He slid into the leather booth next to Mrs McQueen.

She patted him on the hand, fixed him with amused blue eyes, and said, 'Tell us that when we leave, sugar. Not when you just set your peepers on us.'

They all laughed.

'I've ordered for you,' Jason announced fussily. 'Champagne and orange juice. Smoked salmon with scrambled eggs.'

'Sounds good to me,' Buddy replied with an ingratiating smile.

What had he got himself into? What was he going to talk to them about? Light conversation had never been one of his smash acts.

'So, sugar,' Mrs McQueen said. 'Jason here tells us you're an aspiring movie-star. How exciting!'

Norma Jaeger leaned forward, green eyes glinting beneath the excess of amber shadow. 'I was reading an interview in *People* magazine,' she said excitedly, 'with this young actor from *Knots Landing* – or maybe it was *Dallas*, all those soaps seem the same to me. Anyway, it was *one* of those popular shows.'

'Get *on* with it,' Celeste McQueen said affectionately. 'It doesn't matter *what* show it was, just come to the point.'

'Shush, don't rush me,' smiled Norma, wagging a long manicured nail at her friend. 'You know I hate to be hurried along.'

'Oh, don't I just know it!' laughed Celeste.

Buddy did not miss the intimate looks they exchanged.

'Well, you see,' continued Norma, 'this actor who was being interviewed, *he* said that *he* thinks that nowadays actors get the casting couch treatment just like actresses used to.' She glanced wickedly at Celeste. 'Now what *I* want to know, Buddy, is – do you agree with that?'

'What she's *really* asking you, sugar,' grinned Celeste, 'is how far would *you* go to land a part?'

'No, no, what I'm *really* asking,' interjected Norma, 'is if you would . . . well, you know what I mean . . . I don't have to spell it out.'

'You just did,' laughed Celeste.

'I did not!' objected Norma.

They smiled warmly at each other, not at all interested in Buddy's reply.

He wanted to laugh aloud. They were a couple of dykes! He had been fixed up to escort a couple of lesbos! Oh boy! And he had been worried they would be after his body. They couldn't care less about the Buddy Body Beautiful!

* * *

Their relationship was shifting into another gear and Montana did not quite know how to handle it. But she was sure of one thing – no way was she ever going to become the little woman at home. Not that she thought for a moment Neil would want her to. But what *did* he want?

He was drinking again. It was his problem. He was a big boy, if he couldn't handle it she was not about to slap his wrist. He was spending more and more time at the office – leaving early in the morning, coming home late. She had never believed in the where were you? Who were you with? bit.

She knew he was worried about casting the main parts, so she concentrated all of her energies on getting the rest of the cast right.

One day she got in the Volkswagen and drove downtown to the streets where it had all begun. She sat in the little car and gazed at the passing faces. The hell with actors, why couldn't she use some of the real people?

One of the kids who had been in her short film swaggered by. He had grown in a year – a teenage macho with holes in his sneakers and a thatch of black hair. He didn't see her, he was busy blowing bubble-gum in the face of a blonde-haired child with advanced breast development.

She was reminded of Gina Germaine for a moment. Neil was actually going ahead with the test. She couldn't believe it, but the smart thing was to accept it – for now anyway.

Ah . . . the power of big boobs. Gina had built an entire career on her attributes.

Montana watched as two middle-aged men passed the teenage couple. She knew exactly what they would do, and their actions did not disappoint her. They checked out the girl's breasts, looked towards each other, licked their lips and sniggered out some lewd remark which caused them both to roar with laughter. Just your average man-in-the-street letting each other know that women were merely tits and ass. Because unconsciously that's what they had been trained to think all their lives. It was standard behaviour. She had seen it a thousand times before. Sometimes she felt she could climb into a man's thoughts and actions with no trouble at all. In a group they were so predictable. But it was the unpredictable ones that had always attracted her.

She thought of Neil when she first met him. A bum wasting his considerable talents by boozing himself half to death. But an unpredictable bum, brilliantly clever, witty, well worth the challenge.

A hooker wandered by in polyester hot pants and stiletto heels. A bespectacled man scurried along behind her, getting up his courage for the transaction. Street People.

Writing the movie had come so easily. She was an observer with an uncanny ability to figure out exactly how men thought. She understood them, had sympathy for them. And watching the interaction on the street she had been able to create a marvellous story of real people.

Now. What was Neil going to do with it?

Was he going to blow it because the pressures were on again and he had to deliver. Or, was he going to come through, and make the film she knew he had in him.

He was strong.

She hoped he was strong enough.

* * *

All Elaine seemed to want to talk about was her goddamn party, and Bibi-Hot-Shit-Sutton.

'Christ, Elaine!' Ross snorted. 'Don't you know she used to be a hundred-buck-a-night hooker on the Champs-Elysées? I had her – George had her – we *all* took a ride. In fact, when she first came to Hollywood there was some big scandal about her being knocked up by George.'

'Nonsense.'

'They were very hot and heavy until his wife found out. Story goes Bibi went off to Tijuana for an abortion.'

'I don't believe it,' Elaine said primly. 'It's just Hollywood folklore.'

'It's *not* frigging Hollywood folklore. It's the truth for cris-sake, so stop licking her saggy ass.'

'She's in very good shape, Ross,' Elaine said crisply. 'There's nothing saggy about Bibi's ass, it's *yours* that could do with a few sessions at the gym. *Especially* before the party.'

'You can never resist a dig can you?'

'And *you* can never accept the truth. Even when it's for your own good.'

'Don't be so frigging sanctimonious.' He stalked into his study and thought about phoning Karen. With Elaine in the house it was too dangerous by far.

He had taken the Corniche down to Nate 'n' Al's on Saturday morning, picked up lox, bagels and cream cheese, then he had stopped at a phone booth and dialled Karen's number. An answering service had picked up. He had no wish to reveal his name, so as a gag he said flippantly, 'Tell Miss Lancaster *Mr* Elaine called and would like her to contact him about making another appointment.'

She had obviously not received the message, for it was now Sunday night, and not a word. Of course, she could have called and Elaine picked up. Then again, maybe she figured phoning on a weekend was not the smartest move in the world, and Karen was nothing if not smart.

Elaine was in the kitchen complaining about placing two

frozen steaks on to broil. Lina did not come in on Sundays, even though she had tried to bribe her with double money. She really hated cooking, it played merry hell on her nails, and as for dish-washing – she left *that* to Lina, not even bothering to load the machine.

Ross wandered into the kitchen and began plucking radishes from the salad bowl. 'Who else is going to be at Bibi's kill and maim lunch tomorrow?' he asked casually.

'Learning to use mace is hardly kill and maim. It's a very useful and effective self-defence ploy.'

'Sure. Some cat with a magnum grabs you, and what do you do? Reach inside your purse, locate your cute little spray and say' – he affected a high squeaky female voice – 'Oh, do excuse me, sir. Would you just stand still for a tiny minute while I give you a quick whoosh of my mace. You don't mind, do you?'

Elaine was amused in spite of herself. 'I hope I never have to use it,' she said.

'Kick 'em in the balls an' run,' Ross advised. 'Forget about anything else.'

'What are you – an expert?'

'A man.'

She wanted to say – 'You could have fooled me.' But she didn't feel mean enough. Besides, as long as he didn't baulk too much at paying for the party – and costs were rising every minute. She peered at the steaks sizzling nicely. 'Garlic salt?' she questioned.

'No, I don't think so.'

'Going to get laid tomorrow?' she joked.

He tweaked her left breast. 'Tonight, if I'm lucky.'

Don't hold your breath, Elaine. Don't hold your breath.

* * *

Gina Germaine's voice was low and sexy on the phone. 'I didn't think my testing for your movie would end a beautiful relationship,' she purred.

Neil took a deep breath. He had arranged for her to test, which was what she had wanted. Now she wanted him to continue making it with her too?

'Gina, dear,' he said tersely. 'I'm trying to get a film off the ground. I hardly have time to go to the bathroom, let alone anything else.'

'All work and no play . . . I *miss* you Neil.'

God! But the blackmailing bitch had her nerve. 'I'm seeing you Wednesday, aren't I? You *are* going to turn up for the test you made such a fuss about?'

Injured actress. '*Of course* I am, Neil, sweets. And I'll be good, you'll be delighted with me, I—'

'I'll see you Wednesday.'

'Wait!' Her voice held a sharp command.

He sighed. 'What?'

'Come over later today,' she wheedled, changing tactics. 'I need to discuss the scene. I'd like you to help me.'

She was unbelievable. 'Gina,' he said shortly. 'I don't think you're listening to me. I am *very* busy. I—'

'We could watch our video,' she murmured. 'How does that grab you? Or would you prefer me to send a copy over to your house? I'm sure Montana would *love* seeing you on film. You look so virile and handsome and—'

What a first class *cunt.* 'I'll be there,' he snapped.

'I'll wear something sexy . . . Bye . . .'

He sat staring at the wall opposite his desk. Staring and seeing nothing. What was it they used to say in those old Laurel and Hardy movies . . . '*A fine mess you got us into Ollie. A fine mess.*'

* * *

Mrs Jaeger and Mrs McQueen wanted to play tennis after lunch, and since Buddy readily admitted he was no Connors or Borg, they did not ask him to join them.

Jason excused himself. 'I always spend Sundays with Marvin, otherwise he sulks.'

Marvin Gladrags Jackson a sulker? Never.

'However,' Jason continued, 'Mrs Jaeger wants to visit her house later, so why don't I meet you there around five-thirty? I've reserved a table at Matteo's for dinner.'

Buddy nodded, thinking of Angel at the beach with nothing to do but lie in the sun and swim in the surf. How he envied her. He waited until Jason left, then he excused himself from the tennis-playing ladies and headed for a phone-booth. Angel answered on the second buzz.

'Why aren't you outside?' he demanded.

'I'm cleaning,' she explained.

'Cleaning *what* for crissakes? The place looks like a hospital as it is.'

Her tone was frosty. 'I am cleaning out the kitchen cabinets. Did you know the builders left them full of wood shavings?'

'Really?'

His sarcasm was lost on her. 'They certainly did,' she said, full of righteous indignation.

'Uh, listen. I won't be back for a while, maybe not 'til tonight.'

'But I thought we were going for a drive.'

'We'll do it tomorrow.'

She sighed.

'Tell you what, kid. Forget about cleanin', an' move that beautiful body of yours outside. That's an order, I want to see you tanned.'

'Do you think it's good for the baby?'

'Yeah, yeah, the best.'

'I'll get changed right now.'

He blew kisses down the phone, hung up, searched for more coins, then tried Montana Gray's secretary, Inga.

'Anythin' happenin'?' he asked without so much as a hello.

'On a Sunday?'

'Just checkin' in.'

'You want to come over?'

'I would, but I got my two aunts in town. I'm playin' the good nephew.'

'As long as it's not the good fairy.'

What did she mean by *that* smart-ass remark? He ended the conversation and contemplated phoning Randy. Old pal Randy had been with some pretty heavy company at Ma Maison, maybe he should talk to him about Maralee Gray, see if she knew anything on *Street People.* He punched Randy's number, but there was no answer. Disappointed, he hung up.

Instead of heading straight for the tennis courts he detoured, checking out the activity, poolside. There were a lot of heavily tanned guys wearing mucho gold around their necks. And a lot of heavily tanned females wearing small bikinis, diamond stud earrings, and thin gold waist chains. They all looked the same.

He whistled softly as he strolled around. Quite a few of the women did a double-take. And one or two of the men. It didn't surprise him.

He recognized Josh Speed, an English rock star, and a couple of small-time-I'll-kiss-your-ass-if-you-kiss-mine actors.

Still whistling he returned to the tennis courts. Celeste and Norma were hard at it. Two ageing Chris Everts in full swing. They were good, and they obviously enjoyed the game. Buddy watched, following the ball as it zoomed back and forth. Jeez! He was hot. It was just the right kind of day to spend lazing around at the beach. But he had an assignment, and right now, Jason Swankle was the only crap-shoot in town.

'Game, set, and match!' crowed Norma triumphantly.

'Whew! You deserved it!' breathed Celeste.

They walked off the court, linking arms and smiling secretly at each other.

Buddy snapped to attention. 'What now, ladies?'

'A long icy shower,' said Norma.

'And a long cold drink,' added Celeste.

'Why don't I wait for you in the coffee shop?' he suggested. 'Then we can . . .' A shrug. 'Whatever . . .'

'How much is Jason paying you?' Norma asked, frizzy red hair glinting in the sun.

'Hey – it's a pleasure,' Buddy replied, surprised by her directness. 'I'm enjoying myself.'

Norma smiled. 'I thought you might want to enjoy yourself even more – for – shall we say double Jason's remuneration?'

He frowned. 'Come again?'

'And again and again and again. If we're lucky. And I'm sure we would all be very . . . compatible.' She paused, licked full lips and added, 'Don't you think?'

The message was beginning to seep through. A cosy little three-some.

'Uh . . . now much did you have in mind?' he questioned. May as well find out what they would be willing to pay. After all, it wasn't like he had never done it before.

Before Angel.

'I don't wish to bargain. You name it,' Norma said crisply.

Celeste nodded her agreement, and the two of them gazed at him expectantly.

He thought quickly. It wasn't like he was exactly rolling in the mighty dollar. This seemed like an opportunity not to be blown.

'Uh . . . I want a thousand bucks,' he mumbled, half expecting Norma to burst out laughing at what they both knew to be an exorbitant price.

She didn't. She grabbed his arm, linked up with Celeste on the other side, and drawled, 'What are we waiting for?'

* * *

Angel finished cleaning the kitchen before changing into a white swimsuit and heading outside. Truth was, she didn't enjoy lying in the sun that much. She found it boring.

She made her way carefully down the wooden steps at the side of the house, then over the sand towards the surf. The waves were gigantic, and further down the beach two bronzed teenagers played dangerous games with their surfboards. She watched them, fantasizing that it was she and Buddy frolicking in the great swell of the ocean. And then she remembered Hawaii, and Buddy so attentive and romantic and somehow . . . different. Hollywood seemed to have made him tense, unable to relax.

Slowly she wandered along the shoreline, the incoming surf tickling her bare feet. She gazed with awe at the luxurious beach houses, each one different from the next – but all in the two or three million dollar price range – or so the woman at the supermarket had confided.

'Excuse me,' a male voice said.

She turned around, startled. 'Yes?' Her aquamarine eyes caught the light from the sun and seemed enormous.

The man stared, struck by her innocent beauty. He cleared his throat. 'You don't know me,' he began hesitantly, 'but I've been watching you—'

* * *

They had a two bedroom bungalow. The air conditioning was going full blast, and the shades were pulled down. After the heat of the afternoon the place was freezing. Neither Norma Jaeger nor Celeste McQueen seemed to notice.

'Why don't you fix martinis,' Norma ordered, indicating a fully stocked bar, 'while we shower.'

'Right.' Buddy stood in the centre of the room and wondered why he felt nervous.

Nervous of banging two old broads? Buddy Hudson?

It had been a long time between professional engagements.

So what?

He set about fixing the drinks, poured himself a double vodka and gulped it down quickly. Too much alcohol slowed the action, but one fast blast always worked.

He wanted his thousand dollars first. Up front. On the table.

The sound of the shower filtered through the bedroom door. He picked up the two martinis and pushed the door open with his foot. The bed cover was folded neatly in half, and some money lay on the flowered pillowcases. Mrs Jaeger read minds.

He put the glasses down and swooped. Ten one hundred dollar bills in mint condition. Yeah. Cheap Mrs Jaeger was not. Quickly he stuffed the money in his jacket pocket.

So . . . what was the sequence of events? Mrs J. first, followed by Mrs M.? Or a double-header?

He threw off his jacket and unbuttoned his shirt to the waist. Unease rested over him like a shroud as he paced around the room.

What was Angel doing now? Probably cleaning out a closet or two. *That* brought a smile to his lips. My wife, the cleaner. Angel *had* changed. In Hawaii a free spirit – just like him. Now Miss Proper – scrubbing and making a big deal about every grain of sand he tracked into Jason's goddamn house.

'Ah-hah. I see you found the money.' Norma stood in the bathroom doorway, wrapped tightly in a terrycloth robe. 'Are you ready to shower now?'

Hey, hey. Didn't she think he was *clean*?

'Sure,' he replied. 'Why not?'

She walked into the bedroom, and he dodged past her into the bathroom, where he quickly stripped off his clothes.

A luke warm shower, scented soap, and then on with a thoughtfully supplied bathrobe. He glanced down at his dick. Softer than a well-cooked noodle. Psyche up time. Time to think sweet thoughts, flash onto erotic memories. *Time to get it on.* Confidently he swung into the bedroom.

Mrs McQueen and Mrs Jaeger were naked in each other's arms. A tangle of moaning flesh.

Was he supposed to join in? Watch? Wait?

The client always makes the choice. And for a thousand bucks these ladies could make any choice they wished.

He stood in the middle of the room awaiting instructions, feeling his hard-on deflate, feeling like a fool.

The women did not seem to be aware of his existence as they writhed and twisted on the large double bed, so he tried a subtle clearing of his throat, just to let them know he was around.

No reaction. Norma was intent on dive-bombing Celeste's muff, and heavy sighs and groans were signalling *somebody's* climax. Certainly not *his*. A climax was the last thing on his mind.

'Ahhhhh . . .'

'Come on, sweetie. Make it. Get there. *Come* on.'

They sounded like a drowning horse and a fast talking bookie. Buddy concealed a grin – not that they would have noticed if he had stripped right off and sung 'Jumpin' Jack Flash'.

At last their bodies separated, and while Celeste lay gasping, Norma sat up and said triumphantly, 'Well, Buddy? And what did you think of *that*?'

What did she want? A review?

Gee, the action was a little slow in places, and the dialogue unoriginal, but it wasn't a bad performance. Norma Jaeger shone as the aggressor, while Celeste McQueen was suitably hysterical as the second lead.

'Uh . . . nice.'

She hooted with laughter. 'Just nice?'

He thought he should show a little enthusiasm. 'Vereeee horny.'

'Why don't you come join in?' Norma invited. Celeste was obviously a silent partner.

'I was just thinking the same thing,' he said lamely. Maybe he could fake it.

Fake an erection? What an ace trick *that* would be. Wow! No more money problems. Patent the scam and *watch* the big bucks roll. He could see the book title now. HOW TO GET A HARD-ON WHEN YOU'RE NOT IN THE MOOD FOR SEX. A *sure* best seller.

'Take off your robe first. I want to look at you. I love looking at beautiful young men's bodies.'

Oh, shit! He wanted out.

'You're not shy, are you?' she teased. 'Jason doesn't usually send me the shy ones.'

So that was it. Jason knew the set-up all along. All that garbage about just taking out a couple of lonely ladies was just that. Jason must have seen him coming.

Celeste surfaced, her streaked hair in disarray. She had hanging breasts that looked like they had seen plenty of action. 'Ummm.' She stretched. 'What's happening?'

She reminded him of San Diego and a fourteen year old boy . . . his mother standing in the doorway . . . slipping off her robe . . . big hanging breasts and musky thighs . . .

'I gotta go,' he mumbled. 'I *really* gotta go.'

'What?' Norma and Celeste both echoed their surprise.

'I have this appointment I forgot about—' He stumbled into the bathroom, threw off the bathrobe, struggled quickly into his clothes. 'Like there's this test I'm doin', an' I gotta pick up the new pages—'

He was at the door. His hand touched freedom as he grasped the handle.

'My money, Buddy.' Norma Jaeger's voice was ice.

'Oh, yeah . . . sure.' He reached into his jacket pocket, fingered the stack of crisp new bills, silently wished them goodbye. 'Here you go.' He threw them on the bed. They landed on Celeste's stomach.

Then he was out of there, running, running, taking deep gulps of fresh air, putting time and distance between himself and his past.

* * *

Accustomed as she was to men approaching her, Angel had never quite figured out a way to repel them without getting involved in some way. Conversation led to familiarity, and suddenly you *knew* a total stranger – whether you wanted to or not.

The man on the beach was different. Angel sensed it

immediately. He didn't bother with the usual lines. He just came right out with – 'You don't know me, but I've been watching you. And let me tell you something – I could be the start of a whole new life for you.'

'Excuse me,' she said, backing away.

He pursued her. 'I don't want your body. I have no interest in anything personal.'

She backed away farther.

'Beautiful!' he exclaimed. 'Perfect!'

She looked around for someone to rescue her.

'We're neighbours,' he said, trying to calm her. 'I live in the house next to yours.'

'My husband is home,' she said nervously. 'He doesn't like me talking to men – he's very jealous – he's—'

'I don't give a damn about your husband!' he yelled, waving his arms in the air. '*Listen* to me, little girl, and listen carefully. I want to make you a movie star! If you can do to a camera what you do in person – then you're made. You understand me?' He paused dramatically. 'I want you in my movie.'

Her eyes widened. All her life she had dreamed of someone saying that to her. 'Who are you?' she gasped.

'Who am I?' He roared with laughter. 'Don't you read the trades? Didn't you see me on the cover of *Newsweek* last year?'

Silently she shook her head, awed by the frantic energy he gave off.

He narrowed his eyes and stared at her intently. 'You don't smoke do you? No, of course you don't.' He held his hands as if to frame her face. 'You, little lady, are going to be a star. I, Oliver Easterne, will make you one.'

Chapter Twenty

PITTSBURGH, THURSDAY:

THE BODIES OF A MAN AND A WOMAN WERE DISCOVERED IN A DESERTED ALLEYWAY EARLY TODAY. THE WOMAN, A TWENTY-YEAR-OLD CONVICTED PROSTITUTE, HAD BEEN BADLY MUTILATED AND SLASHED. HER THROAT WAS CUT.

THE MAN, A THIRTY-FOUR-YEAR-OLD CUBAN NATIONAL AND KNOWN PIMP, WAS ATTACKED IN A SIMILAR FASHION. THE BLOWS RAINED UPON HIM WERE SO FEROCIOUS THAT HIS RIGHT ARM WAS SEVERED ABOVE THE ELBOW. IT IS BELIEVED THAT HIS ATTACKER LEFT HIM TO BLEED TO DEATH. POLICE ARE SEEKING WITNESSES.

* * *

The old brown panel van roared along the highway, leaving Pittsburgh far behind. And the radio, which had not worked at all when Deke purchased the truck, now blared out from four hidden speakers. Rod Stewart. 'Passion'.

In the bars and the cafes – Passion
In the streets and the alleys – Passion
Lot of pretending – Passion

Everybody's searching – Passion.

How true the words were, Deke thought. Everyone was getting it. But where was the passion in *his* life?

Hear it on the radio – Passion

Read it in the paper – Passion

Hear it in the churches – Passion

See it in the schoolyard – Passion.

Joey. She had given him passion. The only one who ever had . . .

Can't live without passion

Even the President needs passion

Everybody I know needs some passion

Some people die and kill for passion.

Joey. He had loved her, even though she was a whore, even though she was a liar, even though she was a whoring lying bitch bitch bitch . . .

Some people die and kill for passion.

* * *

The fact that Joey accepted his proposal of marriage surprised Deke. She said, 'Okay, bigshot, name the day.' And then added, 'An' I want a ring – an' if ya want me t'give up hookin' then you're gonna hafta hand me some bucks every week.' She collapsed with a weary sigh onto her unmade bed. 'An' when we gonna do it? Soon?' She nodded, as if asking herself the question. 'Yeah, soon,' she decided.

He stared at her blankly. Asking was one thing. Doing was another.

There were all sorts of things to consider. His mother, for one. He had only brought a girl home on one occasion – and that had been when he was much younger. She had made the girl perfectly welcome, then later, when they were alone, she had smiled wistfully and said, 'Not for you, son, is she? Not good enough.'

But then of course nothing was ever good enough for his mother. School marks, his job, his hobbies.

'Cars!' She would screw up her nose distastefully. 'We paid for your education so that you could lie around under cars all day. Is that it, son? Is that what we struggled for?'

She had never accepted his job at the garage. She would never accept Joey.

'Alright, soon,' he mumbled.

'When?' Joey demanded.

'I'll make some plans . . .'

'Where'll we live?' she flashed.

He was almost sorry that he had asked her. He had not expected to have to make such immediate decisions. 'I'll find a place.'

'A house?'

The money he made at the garage wasn't that good. And then of course he had to give his mother a set amount. Before Joey, he had been able to put some away, but now he had only a few hundred dollars left in the bank.

'We'll see.'

She bounced off the bed, black circled eyes spiteful and menacing – the cast in her left eye emphasized by her tiredness. 'Listen, cowboy, don't do me no favours.'

'I'm not,' he assured her anxiously.

'You bet you're not.' She stretched her arms above her head and yawned. 'I coulda got hitched hundreds of times if I'd wanted to. I even hadda cop crazy about me. How d'ya like that?'

He didn't like it. Joey Kravetz was his. And anybody who tried to take her away from him was dead. Stone cold dead.

* * *

The van veered out of its lane, and an irate driver in a Cadillac gave Deke an obscene sign with his finger. Deke was incensed. Purposefully he changed lanes, came up real close behind the Cadillac, and began to beep his horn in short stacatto blasts.

Both vehicles were speeding, going way past the limit. But the Cadillac didn't give way, and Deke did not slow his pace.

Dangerously they raced along the two lane highway, the van only inches from the Cadillac's tail.

There were road works coming up, signals indicated that the two lane highway narrowed to one lane a mile ahead.

Deke pulled out and alongside the Cadillac. The driver, a middle-aged man, stared stonily ahead. He had decided that maybe he was dealing with a nut.

As they approached the road works the man slowed, ready to pull in behind the maniac in the van. But the maniac wouldn't let him, the maniac kept pace with his speed, blocking his entry onto the clear lane. Christ! The arrows indicated he must get over *now*. In a sudden burst of panic he put his foot down hard on the accelerator – there was no way a Cadillac couldn't outrun a faded old van. No way. Except that inexplicably it couldn't. The van stayed alongside him all the way, pulling ahead just before the Cadillac smashed full speed into a heavy concrete mixer.

The middle-aged driver knew agonizing pain for only seconds, and then – nothing.

Deke arrived in Cincinnati three hours later. He was tired and very very hungry. It took him no time at all to find a diner where he had two orders of steak. After that he slept for five hours in the back of the van, and then, refreshed, he continued his journey west.

California was waiting for him, he had to hurry.

Chapter Twenty-One

Bibi Sutton lived on a walled estate in Bel Air, with armed guards at the wrought iron gate; and specially trained German shepherd killer-dogs roaming the grounds. Nobody visited Bibi unannounced.

Elaine drove her Mercedes up to the gates and gave her name to a cowboy-hatted guard. He checked out a typewritten list. 'You know your way up to the main house, Ma'am?' he drawled.

'Yes, I do,' she replied, thinking how silly this whole rigmarole was. Everyone loved Adam Sutton. He was a legend – a John Wayne or a Gregory Peck. Who could possibly wish to do him harm?

Then she smiled. The security was for Bibi. Of course. Probably half of Beverly Hills wanted to slit her throat!

At one time the Sutton mansion had belonged to a silent movie star, Elaine could not quite remember which one. Maybe Barrymore or Valentino. It didn't matter, for Bibi had changed everything, and created a cool white roman villa with pillars, fountains, and marbled terraces. If she wasn't a professional movie star wife she could have taken a shot at interior design. She certainly knew what she was doing, even if it *had* cost a couple of million dollars.

A uniformed servant waited by the front steps to take

Elaine's car, and a maid escorted her through marbled hallways to a sunlit terrace overlooking an olympic sized pool. There, Bibi held court.

Elaine's eyes darted round the assemblage. The upper-echelon ladies of Beverly Hills, Bel Air, and other suitably monied locations were out in full force. Saint Laurent, Dior, Blass, and de la Renta, rustled expensively on perfect bodies. And if they weren't perfect they made a damn good try. Electrolysis, body firming, cellulite control, vein removing, fat removing. All these things had taken place on one or the other of the bodies milling around. Tit renovation, teeth capping, snatch tightening, eyelid lifting, nose bobbing, ass raising. All these things and more.

'Sweetie!' Bibi bore down on her, a vision in a white summery Galanos. Very simple. After all it *was* only a lunch-party. 'So nice you come. I like your suit. I see it before, no?'

'No.'

'Ah, yes. I see it in Saks last week.'

At least she was aware of the fact that it was new. 'You look lovely,' Elaine enthused.

Bibi laughed gaily. 'This old thing – I throw it on.'

Elaine looked around for a drink, and an attentive waiter appeared at her elbow. He carried a choice on a silver tray. Champagne or Perrier. She quickly reached for a glass of champagne. There was only one way to get through *this* lunch, and it certainly wasn't sober.

* * *

The moment Elaine left the house, Ross reached for the phone. Karen picked up on the second buzz. She sounded politely cold. 'I have to go, Ross. I was just leaving for Bibi's lunch and I'm running late.'

'What's the matter, baby? Don't I turn you on anymore?'

'Can we discuss this some other time?'

'What's wrong with right now? I'm sitting here with a hard-on that would bring tears to your eyes.'

'So jerk off.'

'It's not the same, Karen. Not when I could be with you.' He paused for effect, then continued. 'Jesus, but you looked horny on Friday night. What were you doing with a schmuck like Chet Barnes?'

'Fucking him.'

'That's nice.'

'It was.'

'Does he still come before he gets it all the way in?'

She gasped. 'How did you know that?'

'This here town ain't nothin' but a village, lady.'

'You bum!'

He had her, he could hear it in her voice. 'How about lunch with me instead of Bibi?' he suggested.

'You're such a bastard. Why didn't you call me when you said you would?'

'I didn't think a little thing like that would bother a liberated lady like you.'

'I'm not some make-up girl or hairdresser you're throwing on to one side, you know,' she complained.

'Where shall we meet?' he asked confidently.

She sighed. She never had been one to turn down a better offer. 'The beach I suppose.'

'It's a long ride.'

She laughed huskily. 'I sure hope so!'

* * *

Montana summoned her secretary into the office with a sharp buzz on the intercom. 'Inga, I want all the actors I'm testing for the part of Vinnie available on Thursday.'

Inga nodded, itching to dial the good news to Buddy Hudson.

'Have them arrive at the studio at hourly intervals from seven a.m. on. They are to wear their own clothes – casual, suggest Levis and a shirt. Make-up and hair will be taken care of.'

Inga nodded again, making cryptic shorthand notes on her pad.

'There's four of them, right?' Montana checked.

'Yes,' Inga confirmed. 'Do you want them to arrive in any special order?'

'It makes no difference. They'll all have the same chance.' She pushed her glasses up into her hair. 'God! I'll be glad when every last role is cast on this movie. I seem to have spent the last year of my life interviewing actors and actresses.'

Inga wondered if it was a good time to throw some questions at her boss. 'Um . . . Is George Lancaster definitely doing it?'

'I wish I knew!' snapped Montana. 'The whole goddamn movie is cast except for the three most important roles. Wonderful, huh?'

Inga smiled politely. 'I understand Mr Gray is testing Gina Germaine. Excuse me for saying so, but isn't she too *sexy* for the part?'

'Ha! Nice understatement, kid. Any coffee going around here?'

Inga retreated. Conversation with the boss over. She rushed to her desk and tried the number Buddy had given her at the beach. No reply. No service pick-up. Who had ever heard of an actor without an answering service? Somebody would have to get Buddy Hudson together. Maybe it would be her . . .

Oliver Easterne came bouncing into the office, interrupting her thoughts.

'Miz Gray around?' he asked, running a finger along the rim of her desk and inspecting it for dust.

'Yes she is. I'll tell her you're—'

Before she could even pick up the intercom he was past her and into the office.

Montana, looking through some photos at her desk, glanced up. 'Good morning, Oliver,' she said coolly. 'Don't bother to knock. Just come right in.'

He ignored her quiet sarcasm, polished off the seat of a leather chair with his pocket handkerchief and sat down. 'I have found us Nikki,' he announced.

'Oliver?' Montana questioned. 'Tell me, I'm curious. When you have sex do you disinfect your cock first?'

He stared at her, frowned, then laughed heartily. 'You got a cute sense of humour,' he allowed, 'for a woman.'

'Thank you,' she murmured mockingly. 'Your conversation never disappoints.'

He cracked his knuckles several times, then inspected his impeccable nails which were coated with clear nail polish. 'Don't you want to know who she is?'

'I do know. Gina Germaine. And the idea stinks.'

'No. I have found us a girl who makes Gina Germaine look like her fucking *mother*!'

She sighed, 'Have you told Neil this wonderful news?'

He leaned across the desk and lowered his voice. 'I wanted *you* to be the first to know.'

'Gee, thanks.'

'This girl I've found is sensational.'

'I thought you wanted Gina. I mean it was you who carried on about what a big star she was, and how great she would be for box office, wasn't it?'

'With George Lancaster who needs Gina Germaine?'

'George Lancaster is a maybe,' she reminded him wearily.

'He's a definite. I called him in Palm Beach last night and got a commitment. I'm having a meeting with Sadie La Salle this afternoon to firm up terms.'

'Does Neil know this?' she asked, feeling like a record stuck in the same old groove.

'Neil's the artistic side,' he said airily. 'I'm the business. *I* should have talked to George in the first place. Actors. *I* know how to treat 'em. Plus I'm paying him five mil and a piece of the action.'

Montana thought of the paltry sum she was receiving for the property. 'How nice,' she murmured drily. 'Don't you think you should tell Neil the good news?'

'He's out looking at locations. I'll see him when he gets back. In the meantime I came to tell *you* about this girl I've found.'

'Exactly where did you find her?'

'On the beach. She's my neighbour.'

Montana frowned. She was getting more and more disillusioned with the business side of making movies. First George Lancaster, news which didn't thrill her. Now a little nymphet Oliver had discovered roaming the beach. 'I've had it with the casting on this movie,' she said sharply. 'First Gina, then some bimbo you probably picked up. This is fucking amateur night, Oliver.'

He took no notice of her outburst. 'You'll see what I mean when you meet her. *She is Nikki.*' And with that he stood up, vigorously brushed the back of his pants, removed a dead flower from a vase on her desk, flicked it into the trash basket, and exited.

She took a long deep breath. Where was all this total control Neil had mentioned?

* * *

Late Sunday afternoon Buddy phoned the house at the beach. 'Pack up everything, get in the car, and come straight over to Randy's place. Leave the keys there, an' don't answer the phone. If Jason turns up don't talk to him about *anything*. Got it?'

'I don't unders—'

'Got it?'

'Yes.'

'Get moving. I want you out of there fast.'

Angel did as she was told, although her mind was alive with questions. She packed quickly. The phone rang once, but she ignored it. Jason did not turn up. Tearfully she realized it was goodbye to the house at the beach. Life with Buddy was certainly unpredictable.

He met her outside Randy Felix's apartment. She could smell liquor on his breath, and there was a wild excited look about him.

'I don't understand—' she began again.

He grabbed her in a hug. 'One day I'll explain it to you, babe.' And pulled her inside the apartment to meet Randy.

That was it as far as explanations went. Randy had a girl with him, Shelly. She seemed pleasant enough, although a little trampy to look at. They all sat around in the small apartment drinking cheap red wine and dragging on joints Shelly obligingly rolled. Angel did not indulge, and nobody seemed to mind, they were all too busy talking about themselves.

She sat in a corner, a slow steady anger building within. This was not the Buddy she had married. This was not the loving man she had met and fallen in love with – this jumpy, loud, stoned person.

Around twelve Shelly stood up and stretched. 'I gotta get me some sleep,' she yawned. 'I mean Sunday's my only day off, and I am *out-of-it*.'

Quick as a flash Buddy grabbed Angel by the hand and pulled her up too. 'You're sleepin' over at Shell's, sweet stuff,' he announced, like it was the most natural thing in the world. 'I'm gonna hit the sack on Randy's floor. Tomorrow I'll find us a place.'

She was dismayed. 'Buddy—' she began.

He squeezed her hand. 'Do it,' he muttered. 'It's the only game in town. She's a good kid, no hassles, she's not that way inclined.'

Angel stared at him coldly. His hair was tousled, his eyes blood-shot, sweat beaded his handsome features, and he smelled awful. 'What about my things?' she asked, feeling tired and disillusioned. 'Our suitcases are still out in the car.'

'Shell will set you up with anything you need, won't you, Shell?'

The curly headed girl nodded. 'And if you stop callin' me Shell, I'll even give her breakfast.'

Buddy grinned and swayed slightly. 'Thank *you*, Shelly,' he managed. 'I will remember you in my will.'

Shelly grinned back and patted his cheek affectionately. A move that did not go unnoticed by Angel.

'Let's go, Angel-face,' Shelly said. 'You'll love my apartment, it's even smaller than this dump.' She waved vaguely at Randy, who was slumped on the middle of his bed. 'Nice to meet you, thanks for the vino.'

He waved back in an uncoordinated fashion. 'Nice to meet *you* – neighbour. Good grass. Next time I'll buy if you got any to sell.'

'Grass. Coke. Quacks. Name it. I'm your man.'

'Some man!' slurred Buddy.

Shelly grinned. ' 'Night all.'

Silently Angel followed her from the apartment, two flights up the outside staircase, tears stinging her eyes, anger stinging her tongue. It wasn't often she lost her temper, but when she did it was a surprise. The Madonna turned into a tiger.

They stopped outside Shelly's apartment while she groped for her key. Then she flung the door open and said, 'Enter paradise, Angel-face. The worst little flop-house in Hollywood!'

* * *

'More champagne, Mrs Conti?' the young waiter inquired.

Elaine nodded, and vaguely wondered how he knew her name.

Why shouldn't he? I'm famous too. I am a movie star's wife. A soon-to-be-back-on-top-and-screw-everyone movie star.

Christ! She was drunk and she knew it. Not sloppy drunk, fortunately, but on the edge . . .

Surreptitiously she tipped her champagne glass so that a thin steady trickle of the finest Dom Perignon hit the grass.

She sat on a white canvas director's chair along with

thirty-six other women (she had done a head count after lunch). And along with the rest of them she was being bored to death by a muscular ex-detective who looked like a Kojak reject and spoke like an articulate boxer who had just found God. Only he had just found Mace, or so it seemed. And there was no detail too trivial for him to reveal about the goddamn stuff.

I want to pee, she decided, and shot a sideways glance at Maralee, whose expression was hidden behind tinted purple shades which matched her five hundred dollar Anne Klein jacket. Elaine knew it had cost exactly that for she had passed it by in her quest for the perfect outfit.

'I need to go to the bathroom,' she whispered.

'Who's stopping you?' Maralee whispered back.

She stood, caught Bibi's disapproving eye, mimed desperation, and hurried into the house.

A waitress, stuffing her mouth with expensive chocolates, jumped guiltily. Elaine swept past her to the pink and gold powder room. Idly she wondered about Karen. She had said she was coming to the lunch, so where was she?

Maybe a sudden flash of intuition had warned her that it was going to be the most boring luncheon of the year.

Elaine did what she had to do, checked out her appearance, and hurried back outside. Seated once again she reflected that by no means was the lunch a dead loss. The very fact that she had been invited in the first place was a plus. And a double plus was being able to say – ever so casually – to Sadie La Salle – 'I do hope you can come to the little party I'm putting together for George and Pamela Lancaster.'

Even Sadie La Salle could not afford to turn *that* invite down. She had nodded, said, 'Of course,' and even attempted a pleasant smile. Ross would be delighted. Once the woman was in his home she could hardly continue to ignore him.

Maralee gave a gentle snore. She had fallen asleep behind her shades. Quickly Elaine nudged her.

'Oh!' she started.

'And where were *you* last night?' Elaine whispered.

Maralee giggled. 'Recovering from Friday and Saturday night. Randy certainly lives up to his name!'

Elaine smiled and wondered if *she* should find herself a young boyfriend. Ironic really. Here she was married to the man with the biggest dick in Hollywood, and she was thinking about finding herself a young boyfriend. How on earth could anyone else measure up?

She almost laughed aloud.

* * *

'You ever thought about divorcing Elaine?' Karen inquired. She was astride him at the time, knees athletically gripping his hips, while tactile nipples rose and fell temptingly near his mouth.

He was so surprised that he failed to reply. As far as he was concerned, conversation while making it was a no no. He grunted.

'Well?' persisted Karen.

Her muscle tone was perfect. Why didn't she just keep her mouth shut? 'Divorce costs too much,' he gasped.

She manoeuvred her body on top of his and closed her legs.

He groaned in appreciation. This girl knew tricks even *he* hadn't tried. She was squeezing him with her muscles and driving him crazy.

'Would you divorce her if *I* wanted you to?'

He ignored the question. Gave himself up to the few precious moments before orgasm. 'Move,' he pleaded. 'I'm going to come.'

Her silent reply was to grip him even more firmly and rotate her body until she too was ready. As he exploded, so did she. Thrusting her extended nipples in his mouth, grabbing at his hair, squeezing her legs together so tightly that he felt the come was being suctioned out of him.

'Watch the hair!' he screamed desperately.

'Screw your goddamn hair!' she shrieked back.

They peaked together in a frenzy.

'Jesus H. Christ!' he gasped. 'You really are the best.'

Slowly she released him, leaned over to the bedside table and lit cigarettes for them both. 'You know how much money I have?' she asked.

He tingled all over. Hot damn, he felt about seventeen!

'How much?' he asked.

'Enough to pay Elaine off for a start. And when daddy goes, the sky's the limit!'

Wonderful talk. George Lancaster was only twelve years older than he was.

'What are you saying?'

She drew deeply on her cigarette. 'That you and I would make a good couple.'

He laughed half-heartedly, not at all impressed with the way the conversation was progressing. 'You and I are good together because we're *not* married.'

'You think so?'

'I know so.'

'We'll see . . .'

'We'll see what?' he asked alarmed.

'We'll just see, that's all,' she replied mysteriously. 'Why don't we swim?'

'In the ocean?'

'I don't see a pool around.'

'I haven't swum in the ocean for years.'

'Let's go then.' She jumped off the bed, rummaged in a drawer and came up with a pair of red shorts for him, and a one-piece cutaway suit for herself.

He slipped on the shorts, they were tight in the waist, even tighter between the legs. 'Ouch,' he complained.

'Never mind,' she crooned. 'Momma'll massage it all better in the Jacuzzi when we get back.'

'Why are you so good to me Karen?' he asked quizzically.

She grinned. ' 'Cos one good turn deserves another – and baby – your turns are *gooood*!'

They ran out of the house holding hands.

A lone photographer lying on his stomach under the wooden stilts of a nearby house adjusted his telephoto lens. Within five minutes he had shot two rolls of very interesting film indeed.

* * *

Angel hardly slept at all. The state of Shelly's rundown apartment shocked her. Clothes everywhere, dirty dishes, overflowing ashtrays, and cockroaches roaming the tiny kitchenette like it was their rightful home.

Shelly had indicated the unmade bed. 'Wanna share?' she questioned. 'I'm not fussy if you're not.'

Angel had already spotted a bulky armchair. 'I'll take that, if you don't mind,' she said quickly, memories of ex-landlady, Daphne, still fresh in her mind.

'Suit yourself, Angel-face,' shrugged Shelly, rummaging in a drawer. 'Want some coke?'

'I'm not thirsty, thank you.'

Shelly shot her a raised eyebrow look, which she ignored. Carefully she removed a scatter of clothes from the chair and placed them in a neat pile on the end of the bed. Sleep. Think. Work things out. She was upset and angry, there hadn't even been a chance to tell Buddy about her meeting with Oliver Easterne. A meeting that had left her breathless with excitement, his words ringing in her ears.

You, little lady, are going to be a star.

Naturally she had wanted to tell Buddy immediately, and he would have been as excited as she was. Now everything was spoiled. She would probably never get to see Oliver Easterne again.

Shelly threw over a grubby looking shawl as Angel settled into the chair. 'Sweet dreams, kiddo,' she said. 'If you should happen to be an early riser, move quietly. I don't like seeing daylight until at least eleven.'

Angel nodded. And then spent a miserable night trying to force her cramped body to sleep. By seven a.m. she was wide awake. Quietly she let herself out and went down to the pool.

As the morning progressed other residents appeared. Two girls in matching swimsuits who did a series of intricate gymnastics. An old bewigged lady leading a frazzled french poodle on a diaménta lead. A young schoolboy who had a secretive smoke under a palm tree.

Then came the serious sunbathers armed with towels and oils, nose covers and eye shields. Out of work actors all of them.

Angel sat quietly on a broken-down deck chair, her beautiful eyes tinged with worry and tiredness. She smoothed back her fine blonde hair and tried to stifle a sudden rumbling in her stomach. She was hungry, starving in fact. She glanced at her watch. Only ten minutes before eleven. She would have thought that Buddy would have come looking for her by now.

* * *

Buddy surfaced slowly, the heavy pounding in his head signaling life. Only just. He groaned loudly.

Randy, unshaven and bleary-eyed, shakily poured two cups of black instant coffee and silently handed him one.

'Didn't we just go to sleep?' Buddy complained, burning his tongue with the steaming liquid and letting forth a string of expletives.

'Seems like it,' agreed Randy, scratching a sweaty armpit and peering at his Patek-Philippe gold watch – a present from Maralee. 'However – it is now two o'clock in the afternoon.'

'What day?' groaned Buddy.

'Monday,' Randy replied, groping for the phone. He dialled a number and asked to speak to Mrs Maralee Gray.

Buddy staggered into the tiny bathroom. He knew he

should call Angel at once, she had not looked pleased when he stuck her with Shelly. But shit, it was only for the night, today he would get something together.

He splashed cold water on his face and peered in the mirror. Buddy Boy was not looking his best. He had really laid one on, drugs, booze – the first time since Angel. But he had felt so depressed and frustrated after running out on the two women at the Beverly Hills Hotel. He needed to let go for once.

Thank God for friends. Randy, who had understood when he turned up at his apartment, and Shelly, who had agreed to put Angel up for the night. No problem.

The cold water revived him somewhat. He began to feel almost human. Randy was still on the phone talking intimately. Snowing Maralee Gray with bullshit charm.

Buddy pulled on his pants and signalled that he was going up to Shelly's.

* * *

Two sharp raps. Three. Angel at the door, a cleaning cloth in her hands, the smell of Lysol in the air.

Buddy threw up his arms in exasperation. 'What are you doing?'

Her voice cold, hurt. 'Cleaning up.'

'Cleaning up *what* for crissake?'

'Your friend, Shelly, lives like a pig. I'm repaying her for any night's board. It's the least I can do.'

He grabbed her arm. 'Don't be a silly girl. It's not necessary It's—'

With venom she shook his hand away. Anger that had been building all night exploded. 'Don't silly girl *me*, Buddy Hudson. Just who do you think you are speaking to? A Barbie Doll?'

He was surprised by her outburst. 'Hey – baby – what's all this?'

Her eyes flashed dangerously. 'What is all *what*? Little Angel answering back? Little Angel showing feelings?' She threw the cloth angrily on the floor. 'I'm a *person*. I'm your *wife*. And I want to know just exactly what is going on, because if you don't care to tell me, I am packing up and getting out of here. You understand? Be truthful with me, Buddy, or I promise you, you'll never see me again.'

Chapter Twenty-Two

Lulu Kravetz did not even want to know where her sister was buried. Once she was informed of the murder and heard the details, she clammed up.

'I never knew no Deke Andrews,' she muttered. 'An' if you're so sure it's him, how come you don't catch the scum-bag?'

Logical enough. A simple statement. Why *didn't* they catch him?

Leon mumbled something about they were working on it, and Lulu threw him a look that needed no words.

'So, since you're not here to arrest me, or roust me for dope – can you split out of my life?' Restlessly she threw herself on top of the unmade bed and closed her eyes. 'I'm tired, man. I've been travellin' for fuckin' ever.'

He stared at the fat girl for a long silent moment. Did the murder of her sister mean that little to her?

Joey Kravetz. Nobody cared . . . Not one single person . . . Except maybe him . . .

'You going or not?' Lulu demanded.

'Yeah, man. You going or not?' repeated her Chicano friend, suddenly brave.

Slowly Leon nodded, and left. There was nothing to stay for.

Out on the street it was raining, a slow miserable drizzle. A bum slumped against the hood of his car. 'Move it!' Leon ordered fiercely, and the man staggered drunkenly off.

Why did he feel so depressed? Why did he feel like going to a bar and getting good and gloriously drunk. Hadn't done that in a long time.

Joey Kravetz . . . Joey Kravetz . . . Joey Kravetz . . .

Funny faced little hooker . . .

Relief was his first reaction. She had departed from his life without a murmur, and now he would not have to face her. He boiled water for a cup of coffee, and sat reflectively at the kitchen table. Should never have let her into his apartment in the first place. At his age he should have known better. She could have tried to blackmail him, screamed rape, anything . . .

He shuddered at his own stupidity, drained his coffee cup, and hurried to dress. It wasn't until he picked up his wallet that he realized his money was missing. Every last bill. He wasn't sure how much, but it was certainly more than three hundred dollars. Little Miss Kravetz had played him for a real sucker. She was probably still laughing.

He felt like the world's biggest fool. And then anger took over, and he thought about finding her and getting his money back. Just who exactly did she think she was ripping off?

His intentions were solid, but after a few days of cruising around streets where he thought she might hang out, a murder case came in, and his energies were otherwise engaged. Weeks turned into months, and the vision of the teenage hooker with three hundred plus of his hard-earned money faded. He had learned a valuable lesson, that was enough. Now all he wanted to do was forget the whole incident. Which he did. Until one night in Mackies Bar – a cop hang-out. He was there with several of his colleagues. They had cracked a big one. Arrested a forty-six year old man who had raped and murdered seven women over a two year period. The man had confessed after months of being their prime suspect. Celebrations were in full swing. Even Leon – not known for his partying – was feeling no pain.

He saw her before she glimpsed him. Who could miss the orange hair and squiffy eye? She was draped all over a young rookie, giggling and sticking her tongue in his bright pink ear.

Did she know she was in a cops' bar? Did she even care?

He waited until she went into the ladies room, a solitary door in the back, reached by walking along a dark deserted passageway. Ladies were not encouraged to frequent Mackies. Only the cop groupies survived.

Leon followed, positioned himself outside, waited until she emerged, then grabbed her and pinned her against the graffiti scarred wall, his breath heavy with too much alcohol. 'Remember me?'

'Oh. You,' she said cheerily, not at all surprised. 'How ya doin', cowboy?'

He wished he was sober and clear-headed. Drink had fogged his mind, even his tongue. 'You owe me money,' he slurred.

'Are you sure?' she questioned, blinking quickly while working out the best escape route.

'Yes, I'm sure,' he replied indignantly. 'Over three hundred bucks.'

'I think ya got the wrong girl, mister. Like I never hafta rip off anyone's bread. I make it – legit, y'know what I mean?' She grinned at him cheekily. 'For ten bucks I'll jerk y'off here. I just figured, in your apartment it's gotta cost ya more.'

His thoughts were tight but his mouth didn't follow through. 'Listen you—' he began slowly.

She ducked under his arms and was away. 'Fair's, fair,' she called out. 'Doncha think?'

By the time he got back to his friends she was gone.

He spent the rest of the evening trying to sober up, but two hours later when he got home, he was still in a bad way.

He must have slept for several hours before the need to relieve himself woke him. He felt like the bottom of a garbage can, and vowed immediately to give up drink forever.

He staggered to his feet, trying to ignore the shooting pains which attacked the back of his head like a thousand tiny needles. Then he saw her, curled on his couch, fast asleep, as comfortable and contented as a resident cat. Joey Kravetz.

For a moment he stared, too surprised to utter a word. Then he let out a sudden roar of rage – which did his head no good whatsoever. 'What are you *doing here?'*

She awoke quickly, rubbed her eyes, grinned. 'Glad t'see you're still alive.'

'What are you doing in my apartment?' he yelled. 'How did you get in?'

Like a cat she licked the tip of her index finger and cleaned under her eyes where shadow and mascara had mingled to give her the look of a forlorn clown. 'You left the key in the door. Some big-time cop!'

He quietened down. 'What do you want?'

She jumped off the couch, ridiculous in a fake leather white mini and over the knee boots. 'You'll never believe this, but I got me an attack of the guilts. You know – rippin' you off like I did when you was kind enough t'give me a place t'sleep an' all.' She peered at him intently. 'I got feelin's y'know, just like anyone else. An' I got to thinking—'

'After you saw me.'

'Yeah. After I saw you. I got t' thinkin' that even for a cop you're not so bad, an' like I should maybe say I'm sorry, an' pay ya back a few bucks.' She fumbled in a tattered purse and pulled out a ten dollar bill which she solemnly handed to him.

He stared at the money and at her, while his head throbbed and his eyes ached.

'You don't look so good,' she ventured. 'How about gettin' into bed an' discussin' this in the mornin'?'

'Christ!' he snapped. 'You're really full of it.'

She looked pained. 'I thought you'd be pleased . . .'

He pulled a disgusted face and marched into the bathroom.

Why was this run-down teenage hooker invading his life? What did she want from him?

He drank several glasses of tap water, and emerged to find that she had returned to her original place on his couch and appeared to be asleep again. It was four-fifteen in the morning, and he didn't have the strength or the heart to throw her out. Instead he double-locked the front door, then took his keys, wallet and gun to bed with him. He considered locking his bedroom door, but didn't.

Wearily he stripped off his clothes and climbed naked into bed. Deep down he knew that she would come to him. She was a kid, a hooker, a little nothing. Yet he knew that she would come – and worse – he wanted her to.

* * *

Mackies was crowded. It was at least a year since he'd been in. Nothing had changed.

He ordered a scotch and stood at the bar alone. Millie would be wondering what had happened to him. For once, let her wonder.

He downed the first shot and signalled for another. It was going to be a long hot weekend.

Chapter Twenty-Three

Thursday morning. At the studio. Washed and brushed. Nervous as an Arab in an Israeli bazaar. But looking good.

He gave his name to the guard on the gate and drove onto the lot like a star, even if he was only driving his old Pontiac.

His stomach felt queasy. He had *forced* hot coffee and a piece of burnt toast between his lips, then thrown up, dry empty heaves.

He had been a wreck ever since calling Inga, Tuesday afternoon, and getting a short sharp blast. 'Where have you been, Buddy Hudson? I have better things to do with my time than ruin my nails punching out a number that never answers.'

'What's up?' he had asked, adrenaline flooding his body because he knew what was up without her telling him.

'Your test. If you're still interested, that is. I never heard of a serious actor without an answering service. Honestly, I—'

'When?'

'Thursday.'

'Ohmigod!'

Now here he was. About to test for the chance of a lifetime. Jeez! No wonder he was nervous.

Buddy Hudson, this is your life. Can you hack it or can you not?

He parked his car, checked into reception, and was shown

to a dressing room adjacent to Stage Three by a butch-looking girl in jeans, a Dodgers baseball jacket, and sneakers.

'Do you know where the make-up room is?' she asked him.

He wasn't about to admit that he didn't. Cool. Stay cool. Don't let anyone glimpse the nerves. 'Sure. Unless they've moved it.'

'Same place. Ground floor, you can't miss it. Be there in fifteen minutes. Wardrobe'll come by to check you out. Okay?'

'What time will I be . . . uh . . . what time's my . . . uh . . . test?'

'I guess they'll want you on the set 'bout eleven. If you're lucky they'll have you out of here before lunch. The break's at one.'

Two hours. Was that all it would take? He had imagined a day of close-ups and long shots. Shit! They were probably only shooting one set-up.

'See you later,' the girl said, and left.

He had wanted to question her, find out about the other actors testing. Too late now to do anything except sweat it out.

He stared at his reflection in the dressing-table mirror. *Lookin' good. Lookin' good. Lookin' just the way a movie star should.* No thanks to Angel. His dear sweet wife. His dear sweet *departed* wife. The love of his life had split. Gone. Run off. Just like that.

True he had dragged her away from the beach house and back to Hollywood without so much as an explanation. But what was there to explain? 'Hey, Angel, babe, I was supposed to screw these two old lesbo broads, only I couldn't get it up – didn't want to get it up – on account of the fact that I love you. You see – Jason Swankle's a fag, an' he's after my body. So he hired me to keep these two ladies happy, and also to keep me in his life. That's why the beach house, the clothes, the chauffeured car . . .'

How could a girl like Angel ever understand a scene like that? She just wasn't into the trash and flash of life, and he didn't want her to be. Her innocence was one of the reasons he felt so strongly about her. There was no way he ever intended to tell her about his past. So . . . he had made a decision to keep her in the dark. It was the only way.

Somehow his decision had misfired. She wanted truth. He gave her lies. He had underestimated her anger. Placated her first outburst, soothed her with lies and kisses, and then collapsed out by the pool. By the time he felt human it was too late to start finding accommodation. 'Just one more night at Shell's, babe,' he pleaded. 'I'll get everything together tomorrow. Promise.'

She had gazed at him with those big eyes. Gazed at him long and hard. Only by that time he was into lighting up a little grass and getting high high high – because – goddamn it – since Sunday his mother was back to haunt him with a vengeance – and getting stoned seemed like some kind of an answer.

On Tuesday he slept late. It was almost three when he opened his eyes. Randy was long gone, and the small apartment was hot and stuffy. At least grass didn't give you a hangover, in fact it left you feeling quite mellow.

He knew that Angel was not going to be delighted with him, so he took his time showering and shaving. Then decided to check in with Inga, just in case. When he heard about the test he moved like a rocket. Couldn't wait to tell Angel. Only there was no one in at Shelly's, and he found himself pacing the sidewalk until five, when she came in alone.

'Where's Angel?' he demanded.

'I don't know,' Shelly shrugged. 'She was here when I came in last night, gone when I got up this morning.'

He knew at once she had walked. Even before he looked in the trunk of his car and found her suitcase gone. So here he was, ready to test, the most important day in his life. And where was Angel just when he needed her most?

* * *

'Why weren't you at Bibi's lunch, Karen?' Elaine asked, trying to avert her eyes from Ron Gordino's bunch-up – quite impressive in a Rudolf Nureyev way.

'I was laid up,' Karen gasped, stretching her left leg to its limit.

'What did you have?' puffed Elaine, desperately trying to emulate Karen's leg movement, but unable to complete the exercise.

'Some bug. I felt dreadful.'

'You look fine, now.'

'I'm known for my speedy recovery.'

'Need a little help here, Elaine?' Ron Gordino was bending to assist her, grabbing her ankle and *wheedling* the stretch out of her. He smelled of sweat and Brut after-shave.

'Ahhh . . .' gasped Elaine, enjoying the touch of his strong firm hands as they travelled from her ankle to her calf.

'Feel good?' he asked solicitously.

She nodded, flattered to be singled out for his personal attention. It was the first time it had happened to her, although she had often seen him bend to Bibi or Karen and *always* to the celebrities.

'Your muscles are real tight,' he drawled. 'Tense. Are you tense, Elaine?'

'Of course not.' She laughed nervously. 'Why on earth should I be tense?'

His hair was like dirty straw, long and coarse. She noticed a few stray hairs sprouting from his ears and wondered why he didn't do something about them.

His fingers dug into her calf muscles, causing her to wriggle uncomfortably. 'Come into my office after class, you need a massage.'

'I do?'

'Yup.' He raised his sinewy frame and ambled off.

'I think you just scored,' whispered Karen, hardly able to keep the amusement out of her voice.

'Not exactly my type,' replied Elaine crossly.

'Force yourself, darling. He's supposed to be an amazing lay.'

'I thought he was gay.'

'Bi.'

'How do you know?'

'*Never* ask me to reveal my source.'

The rest of the class passed quickly, and before she knew it, Elaine found herself lying face down on a massage table in Ron Gordino's office. His probing hands started at the base of her neck and worked their way down. She had experienced massages before, many times, but the way Ron Gordino operated was different. He sought out and found – with absolutely no trouble at all – every tight muscle in her body. His hands were so soothing that she nearly fell asleep under their touch. When he was finished he tapped her lightly on the ass. 'Better?' he drawled.

'Umm, yes.'

'Good. Next time I'll do it with oils. You'll love that.'

'I will?'

'For sure.'

She stood up and stretched. 'I feel so light, it's marvellous.'

He grinned. *My, what big teeth you have*, she thought.

'Understand you're having a party, Elaine.'

'Yes. For George Lancaster.'

'Nice.'

'I hope so. I think that's one of the reasons I'm so tense.'

'Could be. Pressure situation. You want to come by for a proper massage tomorrow?'

'What a good idea.' She wondered how much a personal massage with Ron Gordino cost. Probably a disgusting amount. Something else for Ross to complain about.

'Sure it is. We'll get you all lightened up in time for your party. In perfect shape.'

'Shall I settle with your receptionist or can it be added to my bill?'

He was affronted. 'I'm not going to *charge* you. Just invite me to your party and we'll call it quits.'

So that was it. He was not after her body – just her party. She didn't know whether to be flattered or insulted. At least it proved that her party was the hottest ticket in town! And that meant a lot more than any laid-back exercise instructor trying to get her in the sack.

'I'll put you on my list, Ron. You can count on that.'

'Thank you, Elaine.'

'Don't mention it.'

Oh, it was good to be hot again. So very very good.

* * *

Surprisingly enough Gina Germaine was not nearly as bad as Neil had thought she would be. Certainly no Fonda, but passable – if one ignored the monstrous bosom – which in spite of copious wrapping refused to lie down.

Viewing the test alone in the screening room he was quite pleased. At least it proved that he was not totally mad. Now he could show it to Montana and Oliver without embarrassment. Gina Germaine was not Nikki, but he had brought something out in her, a quality unseen before now. With him directing her in the right role . . .

He sat quietly in the screening room as the lights came up. Maybe it wouldn't be such a bad idea to have Gina in the movie he planned to do after *Street People.* He had bought a property over two years previously, and two young writers were working on it. With a few changes here and there it could be just the vehicle to launch a new Gina Germaine on an unsuspecting public . . .

Of course, the woman was a blackmailing bitch, and he was furious about the way she had behaved to get herself tested. But if he put her in the new movie he would have her in his power, and that should provide ample opportunity for getting his own back.

Childish but satisfying. He liked the idea.

* * *

Angel had absolutely no intention of returning to Louisville. How could she possibly go back a failure, and pregnant as well?

When she crept from Shelly's apartment early in the morning she had no idea where she would go or what she would do. She only knew that she had to get away from Buddy for a while, let him see that she meant business. He needed to be taught a lesson, day by day it was becoming increasingly obvious that he was interested only in himself. He *said* he loved her. But if he loved her how could he treat her in such a casual way?

Conversations with Shelly had not helped. 'You gotta understand a guy like Buddy, Angel-face. Basically he's a loner. Doesn't need anything or anyone. Gets off on just being himself.'

Advice from a girl like Shelly she could do without.

'I'm having a baby,' Angel informed her stiffly. 'So he'll just have to learn to be a family man.'

Shelly had snorted with laughter. 'Buddy? A family man? Angel-face, you are so way off track it's a joke. You'd better get yourself an abortion – and quick.'

Angel did not appreciate Shelly's snide amusement and unwelcome advice. She huddled in the chair that night and brooded about what to do. Then at seven-thirty in the morning she collected her suitcase from the car and trudged resolutely up the hill towards Sunset. Fifty-two dollars was all the money she had, but unlike Buddy she had no fear of taking an ordinary job.

After a while she passed a hairdressing salon with a card in the window advertising for a receptionist. There was a coffee-shop nearby, and she decided to wait until the salon opened and try for the job. She bought a couple of movie magazines, settled herself at a corner table, and for two hours absorbed herself in stories of the stars.

At ten o'clock she put away the magazine, paid her cheque, and retraced her steps to the salon.

A wild redhead with black ringed eyes and back-combed hair informed her the owner never appeared before twelve.

'Can I wait?' Angel asked.

Pencilled eyebrows shot up. 'You wanna wait two hours?'

'If that's all right.'

'Take a seat, it's your time.'

Angel did just that, leafing through various magazines and observing her surroundings. The entire place was white, with lots of plants. Loud rock music blared out of carefully placed speakers, and the hair stylists wore a unisex uniform of tight white jeans and tropical T-shirts.

Everything was quiet until eleven-thirty, when a stream of clients began to arrive. Women *and* men. Angel reflected that back in Louisville, men and women would not be caught dead in the same hairdressing establishment.

Around twelve-thirty an extremely tall, exceptionally thin man in his late thirties appeared. He wore a check shirt, faded pink boiler suit, and white tennis shoes. His hair was a rich halo of Shirley Temple yellow curls which surrounded an aquiline face. 'Morning darlings!' he sang out to all and sundry. 'Everyone happy?'

A plump woman, emerging from the dressing-room in a fern print robe, threw her arms around him and squealed with joy. 'Koko! That boy you gave me last week is a genius. He made me look positively Candy Bergen!'

'*Of* course he did, dreamheart. That's what we're here for – to please. That's what we're *all* here for. Isn't that right, Darlene?'

Darlene, the back-combed receptionist, did not crack a smile. She jabbed a three inch scarlet lacquered nail in Angel's direction. '*She's* been here since we opened. It's about the job. Give it to her for God's sake, because I'm warning you, Koko – I am *not* taking any more shit from Raymondo.'

Koko removed himself from the plump woman's grasp and

scowled. 'I *know* your stance on this matter, Darlene. Not now, *please.*' He turned to Angel and gave her a sweeping glance. 'Well now, aren't we a pretty one. Just come along with me, dear, and let's talk experience.'

All she had to offer was a year's work in a small Louisville salon, but it was enough. Koko was obviously just as anxious for Darlene to leave as she was herself.

'I don't suppose you could start today?' he asked hopefully.

'I have to find an apartment,' Angel said.

'One room, cheap, close by?'

'Why, yes . . .'

'Your *lucky* day, dreamheart. I know of just the place. Darlene!' he screamed, his piercing voice rising above a raunchy James Brown.

'What?' she screamed back from her position behind the front desk.

'Such a lady!' tisked Koko. 'What a definite *joy* to see her go!'

'About that apartment—' Angel began tentatively.

'Ah, yes. One of my girls got married last week – poor fool. She wants to sub-let her place.'

'Where is it?'

'On Fountain. Are you interested?'

Within an hour she had viewed the apartment and taken it, talked Koko into giving her an advance on her salary, and started work.

Darlene gathered together her bits and pieces, shoved them in an army surplus bag, and departed the world of hairdressing with a pitying snort in Angel's direction.

'Lovely girl!' sang Koko. 'Never got along with a soul.'

Angel wasn't really listening. She was marveling at the fact that in such a short period of time she had found a job, money, and an apartment. It just proved it *could* be done.

So why hadn't Buddy done it?

She wondered if he was missing her yet. Her decision was

not to contact him for at least a week. By that time he might just be ready to talk truth, and if he was – *then* they could start getting their lives back together. Not before. Angel had made up her mind.

* * *

Ross decided a work-out was not going to kill him. Elaine nagging on about his gut was beginning to have some effect. He had always been in great shape, never had to worry about a thing. Maybe now he *was* getting just a touch heavy around the middle.

So what? After all I'm nearly fifty for crissake. Can't stay frigging perfect for ever.

Besides, at his age they should want him for his acting ability, not his pristine pectorals.

Age. Fifty. Coming up fast. Racing towards him like an out of control groupie.

He thought about his life as he drove the Corniche along Santa Monica to the private health club he had once attended regularly. That had been in the days when he couldn't afford an inch of surplus flesh anywhere. The days when he had really been on top. King of the whole frigging heap. And willing to work at it.

A bitter smile twisted his lips. Where had all the gofers gone? The yes-men. His asshole buddies.

Oh, yeah. When he was king they were his best friends. The real estate moguls, bankers, rich men who handed out hospitality like peanut-butter cups because they wanted to be friends with a star. When the star faded so did the friendships. No more offers of private jets to fly him wherever he wanted to go, or parties in his honour. No more yachts and houses and islands to borrow whenever he wished. No more hot rich wives begging for his body. Or fanatic fans driving him crazy.

Fuck 'em. Ross Conti had learned a thing or two about people and the way they used each other. When he hit the magic circle again they could *all* go take a flying fart, unless *he* wanted otherwise, unless *he* cared to use *them*.

If the party was a success . . . If he got back with Sadie . . . If *Street People* became his . . .

The traffic on Santa Monica was heavy, and the stares were hitting him from all sides as he drove his Corniche slowly along the street. He was still a famous face in a city of famous faces – thanks to television which ran his old movies at least once a week. But what good was fame without the perks? Without the money to go along with it? *Fuck 'em all.*

He pulled up at a red light and considered the action on the street. Santa Monica had been taken over by the gay community. There were gay discos, open-pavement cafés, clothing stores, all catering more or less exclusively for gays. Personally Ross had never had any inclination in that direction, he had always been too fond of women. He thought of Karen and grinned. An oiled and muscled youth lounging by a bus stop took a tentative step towards the car. 'You going my way, mister?' he sing-songed through the open passenger window, one hand already reaching for the door.

Ross's grin turned quickly to a scowl. 'No, I'm not!' he snapped. 'And get away from my car.'

'Don't get excited.' The boy stepped back. 'If I'm not your style then that's cool.'

That's cool, is it? Angrily Ross gunned the car away from the light. Did he look like a closet cruiser? A fine thing – getting hustled by a hustler in broad daylight. Didn't the stupid kid know who he was?

He made a sharp left turn and pulled into the parking lot. What he needed was some vigorous activity. The only vigorous activity he got nowadays was screwing Karen Lancaster. His countenance brightened again. Some broad! Maybe her talent was inherited. Old George had always had quite a reputation with the ladies. Like father . . . like daughter . . .

His grin firmly restored, Ross entered the health club.

* * *

'Cut!' Montana said sharply, turning to the first assistant. 'Let's take a ten minute break. I want a little rap with Buddy.'

She had already spoken to him six times. There had been six takes. He wasn't getting any better – in fact he was getting worse. But he was the best of the bunch. He had the look, and that's what really mattered. Where would Nicholson be without the sneer? Eastwood without the ice-cool stare? It was the look, and *then* came the acting ability. She could bring it out in him, she knew she could. She approached him warily. He was nervously muttering lines under his breath.

'Hey,' she murmured softly. 'You're not listening to me, are you? You're not taking in one single word I say.'

'I sure am,' he answered, wishing he were somewhere else.

'Just loosen up,' she crooned softly. 'It's a very simple piece of action if you relax, slow down, and take your time.'

'I can't get the words right. I can't—'

'Forget the words,' she soothed. 'I want you to give me the *essence* of the man . . . just go real real easy and give me Vinnie.'

He was shocked. 'Forget the words? You've got to be puttin' me on. I was up all night. I know every bit of dialogue. I mean I *really* know it.'

So why do you keep on blowing it? she wanted to ask. But she didn't, she put her arm around his shoulder and led him away from the set. 'Buddy,' she said softly, 'I know you can do this scene. I wouldn't have asked you to test if I wasn't sure you could do it.'

'Yeah?' He relaxed slightly.

'I don't need to waste your time, or mine. You're good. I can sense it. You're *very* good if you forget about the lines and just let yourself become Vinnie. If the words go – no big deal. Just stay in character and say anything you want. Don't blow the take. Let's get something in the can other than you saying oh shit!'

He nodded sheepishly. *Buddy Hudson gets his chance and oh shits himself out of a job!*

'I know what you want,' he assured her, taking a deep breath. 'Believe me, I got it now, really, you'll see.'

She smiled encouragingly and fixed him with her tiger eyes. 'We'll do another take, and this time you're going to be dynamite. Right?'

He licked dry lips and nodded. 'You got it.'

She kissed him lightly on the cheek before striding back behind the camera.

A make-up girl darted forward and powdered him down. 'Good luck,' she whispered.

A little luck in his life was *just* what he needed.

'You ready, Buddy?' Montana asked.

He nodded, bile rising in his throat, tenseness knotting his stomach.

'Remember. You *are* Vinnie. Okay. Action!'

Action. Walk into the scene from off camera. Glance in a mirror – instinctively he ruffled his hair. Phone cue. Pick up. Words. What were the fucking words? He wasn't going to screw up again was he?

The first line came out all right. Pause. Light a cigarette. *What came next*? Couldn't remember. Took her advice. Said his *own* words, made up the fucking dialogue, pretended he had Angel on the line and was sweet-talking her the way it used to be.

All of a sudden he forgot about the camera, the crew, blowing it. He made out like he was at home, confident, charming, good old Buddy Boy.

Montana watched him intently. He had taken her advice – at last. The lines went out the window and he was ad-libbing like a professional. He was doing his thing – and the magnetism was coming off him in waves. Christ! If the qualities he projected translated themselves onto film, he had it made.

'Cut!' she said jubilantly.

He almost didn't stop he was so into it.

'That's a print,' she said, walking over to him. 'Thank you, Buddy. You were great.'

'I was?'

'Exactly like I said you would be.'

'Hey—' His confidence was returning. 'I'm just gettin' started. How about once more?'

She shook her head. 'Two more actors waiting their turn and no more time. You wouldn't want them to miss their chance, would you?'

He grinned, full of adrenaline. 'Why not?'

She smiled and for a second they locked eyes, then she pulled her tinted reading glasses down from her hair and very business-like extended her hand for a firm shake. 'You came through and I couldn't be happier. Goodbye Buddy, and good luck.'

Goodbye!! Was she out of her mind. 'Hey—' he gulped. 'When will I know?'

'We'll be in touch with your agent.'

He didn't *have* an agent, but it wouldn't look good to admit that sad fact. He'd just have to keep in constant touch with Inga.

'Yeah,' he said lamely. 'Like when?'

'When we decide,' she said firmly, conversation over. She turned and walked away humming to herself. She felt almost as high as he did. The charge of working with an actor and having it pan out was a kick indeed. She couldn't wait to see his test on screen and find out if she was right.

No wonder Neil became so immersed when he was shooting a movie. It was all in the director's hands – he or she created the magic. Oh, the satisfaction!

Buddy watched her retreat. It was fine for her, she had it made. But what about him?

The make-up girl approached. 'That last take was sensational,' she enthused. 'I wouldn't be a bit surprised if you got the part. You knocked *me* out.'

Now *that* was the kind of talk he liked to hear. Confidence flooded his veins. 'What makes you think that?' he asked.

'I just got a feeling.'

'You saw the other tests?'

'They weren't you.'

'You bet they weren't, but tell me about 'em anyway.' He took her by the arm. 'Let's go get some coffee.'

No harm in finding out about the competition . . . No harm at all.

Chapter Twenty-Four

How alike the outskirts of each city seemed. Huge giant freeways spewing off exits where squatted identical gas stations, motels, coffee shops.

To keep driving was all that mattered to Deke. Ohio, Indiana, Missouri, Oklahoma, slipped by almost unnoticed. The road became a mesmerizing force, beckoning him on, leading him mile by mile to his final destination.

Joey had led him on.

Joey had laughed at him.

He saw her often.

Bitch.

She was dead.

It was her own fault.

* * *

'I wanna meet your family an' make plans. I'm sick of bein' shoved around.' She stared at him hatefully. 'You hear what I'm sayin'?'

He heard her clearly. She had been saying the same thing for weeks now, and he had been countering with a variety of feeble excuses.

'Ya think I'm not good 'nuff to meet them. Is that it? 'Cos if it

is, y'can take your freakin' ring an' shove it where the sun don't shine.' She pulled the cheap garnet ring from her finger and flung it at him. 'I'm gonna meet 'em this week or we're through, buster.'

He wanted to marry her. He hadn't changed his mind. But wouldn't it be better if they snuck off and did it? And then *he could take her home, and they would be forced to accept her.*

He had made this suggestion to her, but she would not hear of it. She wanted everything 'nice an' proper' as she had put it. 'Just like normal folks.' She had even gone so far as to buy a copy of Brides *magazine and cut out a picture of a wedding dress.*

'Don't they want *to meet me?' she demanded sullenly. 'Aren't they waitin' to meet the girl their precious son is gonna marry?'*

He did not dare to tell her that he had never so much as mentioned her name to them. They would never approve of any girl he brought home. And they especially would not approve of Joey with her flashy clothes, heavy make-up, and spiky orange hair.

'Next week,' he promised lamely. He did love her. She satisfied his flesh if that's what love was about.

'You'd better mean it, buster,' she snarled like a wild alley cat.

He meant it. But why did the thought of introducing her to his parents create such a throbbing in his head? WHY WAS HE SO AFRAID OF THEM?

Memories came flooding back.

He was six years old and playing mud-pies with a friend. His mother appeared, face of darkness, voice an uncontrolled screech. 'You filthy dirty boy! Those clothes were fresh on today. Get inside at once.'

She beat him until the sweat stood out in tiny beads all over her face, and blood ran down the back of his legs. His father said nothing.

That was the first time, but there were many more occasions and always for some minor matter like food uneaten, or a wash-cloth left on the bathroom floor. When he was sixteen the beatings ceased as unexpectedly as they had begun. Instead, the tongue lashed him. A stream of verbal abuse more devastating than the physical damage.

He grew to believe her destroying words. After all, she was his mother, as she never tired of telling him. She had given birth to him. Painfully. 'You nearly killed me,' she often cried. 'I nearly died *bringing* you *into the world.' Guilt hung heavy. He had nearly killed his mother, and that's why she punished him, and that's why he had to accept it. She told him he was weak, dirty, useless, a parasite, a fool. What girl would ever look at him? What employer would ever give him work?*

Yet she was full of contradictions. When he brought a girl home she wasn't good enough for him. *When he got a job it was never the right job.*

Knock him down, build him up. Which was he to believe?

Confusion and guilt were the two emotions he grew up with. Along with a dark lingering fear which woke him most nights . . . And sometimes sent him out on the street to do things . . . things he was supposed *to do.*

He raped women. They were the enemy, and deserved to be punished just as he *deserved to be punished.*

He was always careful, picking elderly victims who were too frightened to fight back.

When he met Joey things changed. If his parents would only accept her, everything would be all right . . .

* * *

It was nearing dusk just outside of Amarillo, Texas, and Deke had stopped to fill up with gas. As he rejoined the freeway he noticed a girl hitching a ride. She was tanned, and carried a backpack. Her outfit consisted of brief khaki shorts and a T-shirt emblazoned with the words – JOGGERS DO IT IN THEIR SHOES.

He stopped. Didn't know why. Realized as soon as she was sitting next to him that he had made a mistake.

She wanted to talk. 'What's your name, hon?' 'Where are you heading?' 'What do you do?' 'How long you bin on the road?'

His surly grunts did not silence her. Ignoring the fact that he did not answer, she chatted on about herself. She was a Southern girl, she told him, married at sixteen, divorced at seventeen. A waitress for two years, until one day she just decided to hit the road and travel the country. 'Ah've had a real good time evah since,' she confided. 'No stinkin' time clock to punch. Just free an' out for fun.' She edged across the front seat. 'For a ten spot ah'll give you real sweet relief. I'll even share a joint with you. How's that grab you?'

It didn't grab him. It infuriated him. They were all whores.

She took his silence as acceptance and patted him lovingly on the knee. 'For an extra ten I'll relieve you with mah mouth, an' for five more ah'll swallow it all down just like a good lil' old gal. Whaddya think of *that*?'

He thought he would kill her. It was so easy to dispose of the slime. Rid the world of bad people. Clear out all the whores and pimps and PEOPLE WHO LAUGHED AT HIM.

But she hasn't laughed at you.

She will.

'Pull over at the next rest stop,' she said matter-of-factly. 'And hon', you sure as sugar gonna *looove* mah southern comfort.' She laughed.

There, you see.

He was satisfied. It was a sign that he should do what he had to do. He would dispose of the whore. She had been sent to him for just such a reason.

More and more he was beginning to realize that things didn't just happen, they were worked out ahead of time, and certain human beings were put on earth to keep order. He liked the phrase 'to keep order'. The words were clean and precise.

'I am a Keeper Of The Order,' he said resolutely.

'Sorry?'

Mustn't let her *know*. Must not *warn* her ahead of time.

'Nothing,' he mumbled.

'C'mon, hon, find us a spot an' pull on ovah,' she said,

wriggling close to him. 'Ah'm a lil' lady who *enjoys* her work. Hot damn! You an' I are in for some wild time!'

Hot damnation.

Another sign.

He put his foot down hard on the accelerator. The sooner it was done . . . The sooner he could get on with his real mission . . . The Keeper Of The Order had work to do in California.

He was getting closer all the time.

Chapter Twenty-Five

For three weeks Elaine had been having an affair. Her first one in two years. She had not meant to start anything as unsettling and time consuming – especially with her party plans progressing so well, and a great deal of organizing still left to do.

The party meant so much to Ross and herself, she really should not have allowed anything to distract her. But the best affairs are never planned, they just slide into your life like potent after dinner drinks, one leads to another, and before you know it you are deliciously tipsy.

Elaine's had started exactly like that. A private massage with Ron Gordino. 'Put on a towel,' he had drawled, 'and settle yourself on the table.' Casually he indicated his private bathroom, and she had slipped out of her leotard and wrapped the pink towel he had so thoughtfully supplied tightly around herself.

An affair? The farthest thing from her mind as she lay face down on his massage table and gave herself up to his strong probing hands.

He used scented oils, just as he had promised, and he worked her shoulders, her back, the base of her spine, firmly and sensuously. And as he worked he moved the towel lower and lower, until quite naturally he had whisked it away, revealing the lace panties she had prudently kept on.

'Elaine,' he complained. 'You're not supposed to wear anything for this kind of massage. These oils get real messy, an' I wouldn't want to ruin your fifty dollar panties.'

She was startled. How did he know they cost fifty dollars?

'That's all right,' she said quickly.

'No it's not, take 'em off. You're not shy are you?'

She hesitated for only a moment, and then decided she didn't want to seem unsophisticated. Little Etta from the Bronx.

'So let's go,' he said.

She nearly objected, but it seemed so silly, because he was only going to see her ass, and she had a very nice one, even Ross had confirmed that fact. Gingerly she reached back and wriggled awkwardly out of the offending garment.

He helped her, pulling them off with an easy authority. 'That's better,' he said, squeezing oil from a plastic bottle on to her now bare bottom.

She squirmed slightly – wondered if this was the service he gave Bibi Sutton – then surrendered to the deep circular motion of his kneading fingers. What a sensation! Instant turn on. Especially as the oil began to dribble down the division and Ron Gordino's fingers found a spot at the base of her spine that made her let forth an involuntary gasp of pleasure.

'Good, huh?' he drawled confidently.

'Very,' she replied, hardly daring to trust her voice.

'Turn over.'

Turn over? She was naked, vulnerable, tuned to a sexual pitch. Turn over, and what then? Sex? With an exercise instructor? Didn't she deserve better than that, even if he *was* the flavour of the month?

You had your dentist, Elaine. You had a two-bit actor. What are you, suddenly choosy?

She turned over. And so it all began.

Three or four times a week they met in his private office and he relieved her tensions along with his own. Conversation was limited, sexual acrobatics were not. Ron Gordino believed in stretching the body to its limit. Elaine was a willing pupil. For two years she had been sexually neglected, and suddenly she was like a desert survivor who craved as much water as she could get.

'You're a crazy lady, Elaine,' drawled Ron.

How right he was. Crazy to be involved with him, but enjoying every clandestine lustful moment.

Of course Karen noticed almost at once. 'What's going on with you and the Sheik of the exercise biz?' she inquired playfully. 'You spend more time in his office than he does.'

Karen was one of her best friends but a rule of survival in Hollywood was – 'Never trust anyone – *especially* best friends.'

'He gives great massage,' Elaine replied innocently. 'Remember my old back problem? I swear he's almost got it cured.'

'*What* old back problem?'

'I had a slipped disc – years ago. I've suffered with back aches ever since.'

Karen looked at her sceptically. 'Hmmm . . .'

The acceptance list for the party was shaping up nicely. Right at the top there was a definite yes from Sadie La Salle – for whom – although she did not know it – the party was being given. Elaine could not have been more delighted. If all went according to plan, life could be good again.

Things were already looking up.

* * *

Angel departing from his life without a trace did not thrill Buddy one little bit. In fact, it frightened the hell out of him. She might be twenty years old, but she was still a baby, and the streets of Hollywood were alive with pimps and hustlers who would be only too happy to get their slimy hands on a girl like Angel.

He shuddered at the thought and tried to believe that she had jumped a plane home. Although he knew it would be the last thing she'd do. He had Shelly phone Louisville anyway.

'Some woman says she's in Hollywood,' she stated, hanging up.

'Maybe she took a train, hasn't arrived yet,' he reasoned.

'Yeah. And maybe she's still here. Let's face it, kid, there *is* life in this town after Buddy Hudson.'

He ignored her. What did she know?

In his mind he played out a scenario. Angel, in Louisville, back with her foster family. Buddy, in Hollywood, signing a major deal to star in *Street People.* Then flying – first class of course – to Louisville. Being met by a limo – the kind that stretched for sixteen feet with television and a bar in the back. Driving to Angel's house where the chauffeur would open the door of the car, he would climb out, and Angel would come running to meet him . . . Beautiful Angel pregnant with his child . . . And let them all eat their hearts out . . .

'Any word on your test yet?' Shelly questioned.

Change of thought. Change of mood. He picked up the phone and dialled Inga's number. 'What's happening?' he asked anxiously.

'Buddy! This is the third time you've called me today. You only tested four days ago, and I've told you – I'll buzz you as soon as I know anything.'

Not good enough. Was Inga telling him everything she knew?

'How about dinner tonight?' he asked abruptly, deciding that a little personal attention might help.

Inga was startled, for weeks she had been trying to lure him into a date. 'You're on,' she said quickly, before he changed his mind. 'When and where?'

'I'll pick you up at your office. What time are you through?'

She wanted to say, 'No – make it later. I have to go home and get myself together.' But Buddy was mercurial and she didn't want him backing out. 'Five,' she said.

'Five,' he repeated. 'I'll be there,' with an eye to maybe bumping into Montana Gray, getting the true scam on what was happening.

He had forgotten Shelly was in the room. 'Goin' out on dates already?' she asked sassily. 'How quickly you guys forget.'

'Lend me fifty bucks?' he asked.

Shelly was outraged. 'I lent you fifty two days ago. Borrow from Randy – he's the one with the bread. I'm just a working girl who wants to get paid for your liberal use of my telephone as well as gettin' my fifty back.'

Buddy headed for the door. 'Don't worry about it.'

'Easy for you to talk – big man.'

* * *

'I think Elaine's playing doctor,' Karen Lancaster announced.

'What?' questioned Ross, lazily squeezing one of her incredible nipples between thumb and forefinger.

'Ouch!' she exclaimed mildly, rolling across her large circular bed to escape his touch.

'Come here, woman!' he demanded.

'Come get it, man!' she replied.

He crawled across the tangled sheets growling like a tiger, and fell on top of her, his tongue out and in action, his penis erect.

She laughed, loving every minute. 'You're becoming insatiable, Ross!'

'You're not exactly the Virgin Mary yourself.'

They made love noisily, knowing that their grunts and groans would disturb no one at the isolated beach house. And afterwards Karen said again, 'I think Elaine's playing doctor.'

And Ross repeated, 'What?'

And Karen said, 'She's screwing the hired help. She's got herself a lover-boy. She's having an *affair*.'

Ross snorted with amusement. 'You're nuts!' he exclaimed. 'Elaine doesn't even like sex at home, she's the last person who would go out looking for it.'

'Wanna bet?'

'You're way off base.'

'What's the matter, baby? Don't you like the thought of wifey getting it on with somebody else?'

Irritation crept into his voice. 'And who do you have picked out for Elaine's so-called lover?'

'Ron Gordino!' she announced triumphantly.

'Who the frig is Ron Gordino?'

'Ron Gordino is a twenty-eight year old, six feet two inch ex-lifeguard – now *the* body man in Beverly Hills. *Personally* recommended by Bibi Sutton.'

Ross began to laugh. 'Shit! That fairy!'

'Bi, darling. There's a big difference between gay and swinging both ways. Our Ron *definitely* swings every which way – *in*cluding loose – *I* can assure you of that. And right now he's giving Elaine everything you probably think she doesn't want at home. She's getting royally laid, Ross. Just take a look at her if you doubt it. She's positively glowing.'

'Elaine doesn't screw around,' he said shortly, racking his brains to remember when he'd last taken a good look at his wife.

Karen rose gracefully from the bed. 'Suit yourself,' she murmured sweetly. 'I've never met a man who truly believes his wife would cheat on him. Even though *he* may be jumping on anything that breathes.'

Elaine? Cheating?

Ridiculous.

Elaine was into the house, clothes, entertaining, doing the right thing. She didn't even *like* sex.

'Listen,' he said confidently. 'I *know* Elaine wouldn't do that to me.'

'*You're* doing it to *her*.'

'That's different.'

Karen pursed her lips and blew a short sharp raspberry. 'Chauvinist!'

'Cow!'

She selected a joint from a silver box, jumped back on the bed, and sat cross-legged while she lit up.

Ross watched her, his fingers aching to get back to work on her erotic nipples.

'Would you mind?' she inquired artlessly, dragging deeply, then passing the joint to him.

He took a satisfying long pull. 'Yes. I'd mind,' he said. And why shouldn't he? He paid the bills. He paid for her nails, her hair, her clothes, her *exercise* class. She was Mrs Ross Conti. And if she *was* screwing around (although he sincerely doubted it) then wasn't that a direct attack on his masculinity?

'Why?' Karen demanded.

'Can we cut out the questions? Who gives a frig?'

'You. Obviously.'

He would have liked to have shut her up by turning her on her back and giving her a touch more action. But nearly fifty was nearly fifty, he'd need a crane to get it up again.

'How about making a bacon sandwich?' he suggested.

'Changing the subject?'

His patience snapped. 'You want to fix me a frigging sandwich or not?'

She bit back a sharp retort. The seed had been planted, it was enough.

* * *

It did not take long for Angel to become the darling of Koko's hairdressing salon. She sat behind the reception desk all wide eyes, smooth skin and soft blonde hair falling loosely around her shoulders. What a change from the fiercely lacquered Darlene, high priestess of the bitchy comment.

'Who *is* she?' everyone asked Koko. 'And where did you find her? She's so sweet, and so polite.'

'Don't I know it,' Koko tisked, watching over her like an overpossessive pimp, terrified that she would be stolen from him by some marauding talent scout. It was the first time he could remember calm in the salon. No screaming hysterical women or bitter fights about over-booked appointments. Even

Raymondo, the best stylist in the place, was calmed by Angel's presence. He kept a respectful distance, which for him meant not pinching her on the ass every time she passed.

Her beauty struck everyone, but up front she announced that she was happily married and that her husband was out of the country for a while. Politely she declined all offers of social engagements – whether they be from staff or clients. She was friendly but aloof, revealing nothing about herself, but being quite prepared to listen to other people's problems for hours at a time.

Several times daily someone or other told her she should be a model or an actress, and she smiled and explained that she just wasn't interested. And with Buddy's baby growing inside her she honestly wasn't. Oliver Easterne and his wild promises were forgotten. Straightening out her life was more important.

She thought about Buddy a lot. He had let her down badly. Instinctively she knew that she must give him time if only to make him realize how important their relationship was.

In a way she felt very strong and proud of herself for what she was doing. Being alone wasn't easy, but it was better than being with Buddy and watching him destroy himself.

'You wanna go dancin' tonight?' Raymondo leered, passing by the reception desk for the tenth time that day.

Demurely she shook her head.

'No she doesn't,' snapped Koko, materializing from a private cubicle. 'Do you, dreamheart?'

She smiled softly. Koko's concern touched her. He fussed around her all the time. She turned to greet a fat woman in a voluminous caftan with frazzled yellow locks. 'Good morning, Mrs Liderman, and how are you today?'

Mrs Liderman beamed. 'Feeling the heat, and so is Frowie.' She scooped a miniature poodle from the floor and thrust it across the desk at Angel. 'Give baby a drinkie, there's a good girl.' Diamonds flashed on her fat hands.

'They'll cut off your fingers for those one day,' Koko sighed. 'I do wish you would be more careful, Mrs L.'

The woman giggled coyly. 'I'd feel naked without my little sparklers.'

Koko mock sighed. 'Then for God's sake keep them on – do!'

Mrs Liderman giggled even louder. Angel smiled politely, and the fat woman waddled off to be dealt with by Raymondo's capable hands.

'One of the richest old bags in L.A.,' Koko confided sotto voce. 'And she *still* looks like she buys off the rack at the May Company.'

'I like the May Company,' Angel protested.

'You would.' He sighed. 'Dreamheart, one of these days I shall simply *have* to educate you. With your looks, you too could end up being one of the richest ladies in this town. But there is *so much* for you to learn.'

'What?'

'Everything.'

* * *

Gina Germaine padded barefoot across her thick white carpet and threw her arms tightly around Neil Gray's neck. 'You *really* liked my test, didn't you?'

He extracted himself from her grip. 'Yes.'

She was hungry for praise. 'Just yes?'

'You were very good.'

'What did Oliver and Montana say?' she asked anxiously. 'Am I Nikki, Neil? *Goddammit, am I Nikki*?'

He shook his head, said, 'No.' Held up a hand to silence her sudden anger, and explained his future plans for her.

She listened intently, twisting a lock of platinum blonde hair between her fingers, biting her full lower lip, staring at him with protruding blue eyes.

The way he explained things it sounded good. No, she wasn't Nikki. He had far greater plans for her. A new movie. A showcase that would really establish her as a serious actress.

'Have you got a script?' she demanded excitedly when he had finished.

He smiled to himself. She had taken the bait. 'Enough of one to know that any actress in this town would mutilate to play the role.'

She licked her voluptuous lips, attempted to remain cool, but the need was in her voice as she asked, 'When will it start?'

'When *Street People* wraps.'

She stared at him even harder. Was he fooling her? Throwing out promises to escape from her trap? 'Why can't I do *Street People* first?' she demanded.

'Don't you understand a word I'm saying? That would ruin everything.'

A petulance crept into her voice. 'You're offering me pie in the sky.'

'I am offering you, my dear, the chance to stop playing dumb cunt of the year – to become a serious actress.' She looked thoughtful, so he took the opportunity to add, 'And I want the video tapes of us together. I have no intention of letting *you* run the show. You'll be putting yourself in my hands. I'm going to make you the hottest *actress* in town. When I've finished with you they'll all come running.'

'What guarantee do I have that you mean any of this?' she asked quickly. 'It all sounds good, but I'm no fool.'

'I never said you were. You see, my dear, I am prepared to sign a contract with you. Oliver Easterne will negotiate the deal with your agent, but don't be greedy, you need this film a lot more than I do.' He paused. 'And no press announcements. Nothing until I say so. Do you understand?'

She chewed on her lower lip and nodded.

'I want the tapes back the same day you sign the contract. No games, Gina. No copies. Because once we embark on this venture, I can make you . . . and then again . . . I can break you . . .'

'Let's go to bed, Neil,' she purred, his sudden forcefulness exciting her.

'Let's not,' he replied harshly. 'From now on our relationship is strictly business. You do understand that, Gina dear, don't you?'

* * *

Montana slipped off her cowboy boots and buzzed the projection booth. 'Run those tests through for me again, Jeff.'

'Comin' up Miz Gray.'

She settled back to watch the four actors she had directed one more time. Four actors. All different. All with something to offer. But it was Buddy Hudson who grabbed her attention and held her riveted. He was not the best actor by any means, but he had that special screen presence she had suspected all along, and *she* had brought it out in him.

Reflectively she sat in the dark and lit up a cigarette. What she really wanted to do was share her discovery with Neil. They should be together at a time like this, but when she had asked him to come and see the tests with her he had made some excuse about a meeting he had to attend. What meeting? She wasn't about to question him, and he had not bothered to elaborate.

A frown creased her forehead. Something was happening to their marriage. Something that she could not control, and did not like. Neil was drinking heavily again. They had no sex life. But the thing that *really* disturbed her was that they had always been so close, and now, suddenly, there seemed to be a huge void bridged only by the movie.

Her frown deepened. She wondered if it was just the pressure of working together for the first time, and decided yes, that was it. Pre-production was draining most of her energy, and Neil probably felt the same way. But somehow she knew there was more to it than that. Working together should be bringing them closer, not further apart. Angrily she ground out her cigarette. Maybe it was time for a long talk.

Buddy Hudson's image played on the screen. He really had

it. Electric magnetism. Just as she had thought the day he bluffed his way into her office.

She wanted him for Vinnie. Her mind was made up. Now all she had to do was convince Oliver and Neil.

Chapter Twenty-Six

The computer check on the Andrews family finally came in. Leon Rosemont studied it intently. There was not a lot of information, but one discovery was the date of their marriage. 1946, Barstow, California. There was no information relating to Deke Andrews at all.

Leon wired off immediately for a copy of the wedding certificate. If he was to find any clues at all, then he might as well start at the beginning.

In the meantime it was Millie's birthday and she had planned a family party. She went wild in the kitchen making spare ribs, fried chicken, curried rice and her special black-eyed pea salad. For dessert he surprised her with a huge strawberry cake, and just in case he had forgotten she made chocolate fudge brownies which almost brought tears to his eyes.

He gorged himself, while her many nieces and nephews played The Jacksons on the stereo, and the grown ups kept pushing for James Brown. There was dancing and laughter and more good natured fun than he could remember in a long time.

One o'clock in the morning and they were alone, surrounded by stacks of dirty dishes.

'I'll wash – you dry,' Millie suggested.

'Why don't you wash *and* dry,' he countered.

'You lazy sonofagun!' she exclaimed, affection lighting her features. 'Just get that big fat butt in the kitchen right now!'

* * *

'Who does the dishes, an' your washin' an' all that garbage?' Joey demanded.

'I have a cleaning woman.'

'Yeah?' Reflectively she chewed on her thumb. 'I could do it if y'wanted. And *wash your shirts. That oughtta save y'a buck or two.'*

He did not want to save a buck or two. He wanted out of an unfortunate situation. They had been seeing each other – if that was the right phrase – for two months. And he had helped her a lot. Got her a job selling ice-cream at a movie theatre. Moved her into a decent rooming house. Given her a feeling of self-worth. And in return she had given him her youth, and a mighty fine hard-on. She made him feel twenty-two, and for a while that was nice. Now she was talking about doing his cleaning and washing, and he knew the time had come to close the chapter. It was only fair for both their sakes.

'Joey,' he said gently, deciding that now was as good a time as ever. 'Don't you sometimes think about having friends your own age?'

'Nope,' she replied blithely. 'After all, you're not exactly a granpop are you. You're about the same age as Paul Newman.' She had just seen Butch Cassidy and the Sundance Kid *twenty-eight times on account of the fact that it was playing at the cinema where she worked. And now every conversation was peppered with remarks about Paul Newman, whatever the subject.*

'I think,' he said measuredly, 'now that we've got you back on the right track—'

'Right track, what am I? A fuckin' train?'

'You know what I mean,' he said evenly. 'And don't swear.'

'Okay then,' she announced, desperately trying to change the subject. 'I'll be cleanin' up for you – its a favour. Like I don't

wanna get paid – I was just kiddin' 'bout that part. Maybe you'd better give me a key.'

'Let's face facts, Joey, we've gone about as far as we can go. Now you have to start making a life for yourself which doesn't include me.'

'Why?' she demanded aggressively.

'Because it will work out better that way,' he explained patiently. 'You've got your life ahead of you. There's plenty of exciting things for you to do out there. A lot of new people for you to meet. And somewhere there's a nice young man—'

'Aw shee . . . it!' she exclaimed, disgust curling her lip. 'Exciting things to do, nice young man . . . what kinda dumbo d'ya think you're talking to here?' She glared at him, then added, 'I bin around y'know.'

'It's not right,' he continued stubbornly. 'It never has been, and I think you're smart enough to accept that. What do you want with an old man like me anyway?'

'Found yourself another little chickie y'kin get off on?' she jeered. 'Y'know, a real young one. Like I'm sixteen . . . Gettin' past it, huh?'

'Don't be so stupid.'

They argued back and forth for more than an hour. Joey did not want to leave. She screamed and yelled. Tried being sweet. Hurled insults. Even cried.

The more of an act she put on the more he realized that he was making the right decision. Finally at two o'clock in the morning, she left.

The following week was not easy. She phoned him constantly, begging and crying for them to get back together or shouting more insults. He couldn't take it, so he requested a six week vacation that was due to him, locked up his apartment, and took off for Florida. On his way to the airport, he dropped by the rooming house where Joey lived and paid her landlady six months' rent in advance.

Guilt money?

No. Just a parting gift to help her out.

He never saw her again.

Not until he saw her dead body lying slashed and mutilated on the floor of the house on Friendship Street.

* * *

Methodically Leon finished stacking the dishes, helped himself to a dish of ice cream and followed Millie upstairs.

She was at the dressing-table removing her make-up.

He wanted to confide in her, tell her about Joey . . . But he was so ashamed. He did not want to see the disgust in her eyes.

'Some party, huh?' Millie enthused.

He forced a smile, said, 'Sure was,' and wondered what would have happened if he had agreed to meet Joey one week before her death. She had called him right out of the blue. A three year silence, and then there she was on the phone, like they had only spoken yesterday.

'I gotta see ya, it's real important. I need your help.'

He did not respond. He changed his voice and stated that she had a wrong number. Millie was sitting across the room at the time.

Before he replaced the receiver he heard Joey say, 'Aw, shee . . . it, Leon. I know it's you.' But she hadn't called back.

One week later she was dead.

Chapter Twenty-Seven

On the morning of the party Elaine awoke at seven. She left Ross snoring on his side of their bed and went into her bathroom. There, she inspected her face closely in a magnifying mirror, tweezed a few hairs below her eyebrows, carefully squeezed a minute whitehead, and marvelled at how clear and blemish-free her skin was. Some would say she had Aida Thibiant to thank. Aida gave facials to many stars – including Candice Bergen and Jacqueline Bisset – both of whom were coming to the party. But Elaine knew better. She knew who she should *really* thank. Ron Gordino. Lithe, athletic Ron, whom she had really grown quite fond of in spite of herself.

Never get too familiar with the hired help, Elaine. Even if they are wonderful in bed.

Not that they had ever been to bed as such. Just massage table, couch and floor! Elaine allowed herself a fleeting smile before slipping off her silk nightgown and stepping beneath the icy needles of a cold shower.

Carefully she ticked off details of the party in her head. Everything was taken care of, from table decoration to valet parking. She could not think of one thing she had forgotten. And soon an army of workers would be arriving to make it all perfect.

She towelled herself dry, and quickly applied a light

make-up before slipping into a brown silk shirt and beige cotton pants. Then she walked over to the window and gazed out. It was going to be a perfect California day, the sun already high in the sky without a cloud in sight.

Ross snored loudly. Impatiently she shook him awake.

'What time is it?' he groaned.

'Early,' she replied. 'But I want you up.'

'I'm up all right,' he leered, indicating a healthy erection. 'What about a little head?'

'Don't be silly,' she said briskly. 'Have you forgotten it's party day?'

He groaned again. 'How could I forget? You've breathed and lived this frigging party for more weeks than I care to remember.'

'Get up,' she said firmly. 'Go to the gym or out to lunch or something, but please *do not* get in anyone's way today.'

'Whose way? It's my house,' he stated indignantly.

'Don't be difficult, Ross. This party *is* for you.'

'No, it's not,' he replied truculently. 'It's for George frigging Lancaster and Pamela frigging London. And it's costing me a fucking fortune which we can't afford.'

'It's for Sadie La Salle. Let's not lose sight of the *real* reason we're having it. Why don't we call it an investment in our future?'

He yawned loudly. 'It better be.'

'I'm going out,' she said, not prepared to put up with his complaints.

'Where to?' he asked, consulting his watch. 'It's not even eight o'clock yet.'

'I thought I told you last night. I'm having an early breakfast with Bibi at her house.'

'What for?'

'Do stop questioning me. We're going over the final list if you must know.'

'Why doesn't she come here?'

Elaine decided such a stupid question did not even deserve a reply. 'See you later,' she said. 'And don't forget to go to the bank and pick up some cash, we'll need a lot of twenties for tips.'

'Where are you going after Bibi's?'

Elaine swallowed her aggravation. Since when did Ross have to know every move she made? 'The hairdressers,' she snapped. 'Can I go now?'

'Feel free.'

She hurried into the kitchen. Lina had just arrived with two helpers. The three women were chattering excitedly in Spanish. It was the first time Elaine had seen Lina employ an expression other than surly resignation.

'*Buenos dias*, Señora Conti,' said the maid cheerfully.

'Good morning, Lina.'

'Theees my two amigos. Conceptia an' Maria.'

The other two women nodded and grinned. Probably wetbacks, Elaine decided, only too delighted to be working in such a beautiful house. Well, it *would* be beautiful when they had finished scrubbing it from top to bottom.

'Do they speak English?' she demanded.

'Leetle,' said Lina. 'I 'splains everythings.'

'Good. I want this place spotless. The tent people will be here at eight o'clock. The flowers at nine. And there'll be other deliveries. I've left a list in the hall.'

Lina nodded encouragingly. 'No worry, Señora.'

'*You* answer the phone, Lina, and *take messages*. Write them down.' Hesitantly she used her only words of Spanish. '*Entiende ud*?'

'Sure. I understand good,' replied Lina, grinning proudly at her friends. 'You go. Everythin' fine.'

'I'll be back by twelve-thirty.'

Outside, safely in her Mercedes, she took a deep breath. The day had begun smoothly enough. Now if only everything went according to plan . . .

She started the car and set off. Thirty seconds later it occurred to her that she had not told Lina about the two ex-rock musicians arriving at twelve to set up their discotheque equipment. Ron Gordino had recommended them. 'You want the funkiest party of the year, then go with Ric and Phil,' he had stated. So it was the Zancussi Trio for the early part of the evening, and Ric and Phil for later on. God! Lina would never let them in with their wild long hair.

She spun the Mercedes into a U-turn and headed quickly back home.

* * *

Ross heard the front door slam and the rev of Elaine's Mercedes. For a moment he wondered if there was any truth in the things Karen had said about her having an affair. The very idea was laughable. She was Mrs Ross Conti. She wouldn't dare screw around. He rolled lazily over and punched out Karen's number on the phone.

'What?' she mumbled sleepily.

'This is a dirty phone call.'

'Ross?'

'Who else do you get dirty phone calls from at this time in the morning?'

'You've woken me.'

He lightened his voice and did a passable imitation of Elaine. 'Have you forgotten it's party day!'

She laughed huskily.

'What are you wearing?' he asked.

'A red satin shortie nightie from Frederick's.'

'With crotchless panties?'

'And nippleless bra.'

'Jesus, Karen, you've just given me a giant hard-on.'

'I would hate to see it go to waste. Why don't you come on over?'

'I can't.'

'Why not? You know you want to suck on my tits.'

The thought of her erotic nipples in his mouth strengthened his desire. 'You're tempting me.'

'I know what turns you on. So why don't you climb into your jockeys, stick on some dark shades and let's chance it. I'll leave the name Edward Brown at the desk.'

He had never visited her at the fashionable Century City apartment where she lived. They had both decided it was too risky and stuck to the isolated beach house. But what was a risk or two between friends?

'I'm coming right over,' he decided.

'No. Wait till you get here.'

'Fun . . . eee.' He replaced the receiver and hurled himself under an ice cold shower. Then he was sorry, because without an erection he wasn't sure if he *did* want to visit Karen. He felt anxious. The thought of Sadie La Salle in his house was unnerving. What if she refused him as a client again?

Unthinkable. He'd turn the Conti charm on full force – dazzle her with it. She'd have no chance.

Quickly he dressed.

* * *

Elaine swept into the kitchen and was about to tell Lina about the two disco men when she spotted a light on the phone. Thinking it was for her she picked it up, and heard Ross say, 'Jesus, Karen, you've just given me a giant hard-on.' She listened silently to the rest of the conversation, hung up at the same time as Ross and hurried out the back door.

Once in her car she coasted down the driveway, started the engine and ripped off down the street barely screeching to a halt at the first stop sign.

She was being royally screwed by her best friend.

No. Correction. *Ross* was being royally screwed by her best friend.

Etta Grodinski from the Bronx.

Karen Lancaster from Beverly Hills.

A scream rose in her throat which she stifled, although many a therapist had told her to let it all out.

'That . . . that . . . cunt!' she hissed.

That cunt with those awful nipples.

'That cheating, stealing bitch!' she yelled out loud. 'Just who does she think she is?'

A man in the car beside her stared.

'What are you looking at?' she raged, and sent the Mercedes rocketing off down Sunset heading for Bel Air and Bibi. Because, whatever else, she wouldn't dream of letting Bibi Sutton down. A royal audience was a royal audience. And nothing would make her blow that.

* * *

Angel's silence had unnerved Buddy to such a degree that he hardly even cared anymore.

Not strictly true. He cared so much that to even think about it sent him into a total panic. So he blanked out on the subject of *Street People* and the role of Vinnie. He even stopped calling Inga seventeen times a day. He settled for once – in the morning at precisely eleven o'clock. Then he would inquire tersely, 'Any news?' and she would try to keep him on the phone because since their date she loved him madly – even though nothing had happened – no fault of hers. Once he heard the doom words – 'No news, but you're still being considered' – he just hung up. All he wanted to do was run.

And run he did. Literally. He bought himself a good pair of sneakers and covered Sunset from Doheny to Fairfax and back. Every morning.

It felt good channelling his excess energy that way. Stripped to a brief pair of white shorts he had never looked better. He was lean and tanned, his body like a sleek oiled machine.

Only Angel wasn't around to see it. She had dumped him like a sack of old garbage.

After two weeks of silence Shelly told him that Angel had called with a message. 'She doesn't want to see you again, she's had an abortion, met some guy, and you, Buddy Boy, are out of her life forever. She wanted me to be sure to tell you *forever.*'

He was shocked. He did not believe that Angel could be that harsh. 'Didn't you get her phone number? Or at least find out where she's living?' he demanded angrily.

'What am I – a message service?' Shelly retorted. 'I'm tellin' you, man. She just wanted out. O – U – T.'

He almost slept with Shelly that night. He was stoned. She was there, coming on to him strong as usual. She took off her clothes to the throb of Donna Summer and danced around in front of him. She did have a great body, but that's all it was – just another great body.

She sank to her knees in front of him, fiddled with the belt on his jeans.

She couldn't even excite him. The hurt of Angel running out and getting rid of his baby penetrated the grass and the coke. He just felt empty.

He didn't want anyone except Angel.

'You're crazy,' Shelly stormed. 'What are you – gay or something?'

Turn downs were not a great feature of her life.

He stayed at Randy's, hoping for the big break, and missing Angel.

Shelly did not hold a grudge for long. 'I'll get you one of these days,' she joked. 'Guess I've just gotta keep hangin' in, huh?'

Money he borrowed from them equally. Shelly was reasonably good natured about it, but Randy finally blew when he tried to hit him for yet another fifty.

'Come *on* man. I'm not a freakin' bank. I need every buck I got to keep this thing with Maralee going. If she thinks I don't have shit she'll run.'

He nodded, understanding only too well. Maralee Sanderson was Randy's shot at the big time, and after a lifetime of hustling maybe old Rand deserved a taste of the good life.

Reluctantly he could see he was going to have to get himself some sort of a job until he heard about the test. Having made that decision he put on his only clean silk shirt, persuaded Shelly to press his black gabardine pants, and finished off the outfit with his white Armani silk jacket – courtesy of Jason Swankle.

Once dressed he took himself off to see Frances Cavendish in the hope she would have something for him.

'Hey, Francie,' he breezed, walking into her office like he had only seen her the day before.

She leaned back in her brown leather chair and surveyed him carefully from head to toe. 'Well, well . . .' she said slowly. 'Look what the Santa Anas blew in off the street. I thought you were *dead*.'

He frowned. 'Huh?'

'An unseen actor is a *dead* actor in my book.'

'You're seein' me now.'

She squinted over her glasses. 'And looking quite fit I'm glad to say.'

'I bin running a lot.'

'It suits you.'

There was a long silence which she didn't seem inclined to break.

He cleared his throat. 'So what's happening, Francie?'

'For God's sake do *not* call me Francie.'

She had changed her rhinestone trimmed glasses for heavy hornrims, and now she looked more mannish than ever with her close cropped grey hair and masculine style suit – too heavy for California by far, but one of her famous trademarks. She unlocked a side drawer in her desk and produced her other famous trademark – a somewhat battered roach-holder into which she fitted a joint. She lit up, dragged, then offered it across the desk. 'Still married?' she inquired brusquely.

Instinct gave him the right answer as he drew deeply on the cigarette. 'Nope.'

'Good. Marriage didn't suit you. I've got a job for you. A low budget horror epic for which you will be just right. Two weeks. Scale. You want it?'

He nodded, afraid to mention *Street People* in case he jinxed himself. 'When?' he asked.

'Universal. Next Monday.'

'Sounds good to me.'

'So it should.' She retrieved the roach and hung on to it. One drag was apparently all he was going to get. But one drag was better than none at all.

'Are you available tonight?' she asked abruptly.

In the past he had escorted Frances to a couple of boring award dinners, and an evening on the town with her eighty-six year old mother visiting from White Plains. He had no plans to do any more escort duty. On the other hand the picture at Universal probably hinged on whether he was free or not. 'Yeah, I'm available,' he decided.

'Good,' said Frances crisply. 'Ross Conti is having a party for George Lancaster and Pamela London. Pick me up at seven-fifteen promptly. You remember my address, don't you.'

It wasn't a question, more a statement. He nodded, delighted to be going to a big party – even if it was with Frances.

'Oh, and dear,' she added, 'wear something decent. Right now you look like one of those male hookers cruising the Polo Lounge.'

He tried not to scowl. What did she know anyway? If it was descriptions she wanted he could truthfully say she reminded him of a female Rodney Dangerfield.

Cheered by that thought he said, 'Seven-fifteen, then.' And made his exit.

* * *

Oliver Easterne absentmindedly emptied out the ashtray in which Montana's cigarette lay smouldering.

'Oliver!' she complained sharply. 'I was still smoking that.'

'What?'

'My cigarette!' She turned to Neil and made an expression of disbelief.

Neil was more interested in the glass of bourbon he was nursing.

Oliver scrabbled in the basket to put the offending cigarette out.

The three of them sat in Oliver's spotless office. It was eleven in the morning, and they were awaiting the arrival of George Lancaster. He was already an hour late.

Oliver and Neil both knew him well, but Montana had never met him. She was excited in a funny sort of a way – after all she had grown up with George Lancaster. He had always been there, a familiar face on the big screen and in the fan magazines. George Lancaster, John Wayne, Kirk Douglas. At thirteen she had nurtured a crush on all of them. Now things were somewhat different. She had written a movie, and George was all set to star in it. Unfortunately she did not consider him to be a very good actor, and the role of Mac in the film was so very important. But George Lancaster equalled big box office. And who could fight that fact of life?

Besides, with George starring, as Oliver said, they could use who they liked for the two other leading roles. And she liked Buddy Hudson. And so did Neil and Oliver after they saw the reaction of several secretaries she invited into the screening room when they ran his test.

'He may not be the greatest actor in the world – but he comes across like instant sex. He's pure Vinnie,' she explained.

Neil said, 'You don't have to convince me. I like him.'

Oliver agreed, while still fretting about the fact that he could not find the girl on the beach who he wanted for Nikki. She appeared to have vanished, and so after abandoning the idea of Gina, they had tested several other actresses for the role, and a couple of them were excellent. It was now a question of convincing Oliver to forget about his beach nymphet and make a decision.

The fact that George Lancaster had been signed was an extremely well kept secret. 'We want maximum press coverage,' Oliver kept on saying. 'When George hits town it's going to be an event. And when we call a press conference to make the announcement, it's worldwide headlines.'

George had hit town late the previous evening. And Oliver was delighted. George Lancaster starring in his first movie for seven years. *Street People* – an Oliver Easterne Production. The suckers would be lining up to invest in his future projects.

A buzzer sounded on Oliver's desk and the flustered voice of his secretary announced, 'Mr Lancaster is here.'

Before she could finish saying 'here' the door was flung open and George Lancaster made his entrance.

He was larger than life. Tall, bronzed, rugged. A true old-fashioned film star.

Oliver rushed into a welcoming speech. Neil didn't bother to get up. Montana stood, and waited for Oliver to stop crawling and introduce her. Naturally Oliver was too busy doing his Big Producer number to bother with introductions.

No slouch in the height stakes, standing near George Lancaster made Montana feel positively small. She waited until Oliver paused for breath, then she stuck her hand out and said, 'Hello. I'm Montana Gray.'

He almost ignored her, not quite. She got a fleeting handshake and a brief, 'I'm gasping for a cup of coffee, little lady.'

He thought she was an assistant, a secretary, just some female there to see to his every need! Oliver did nothing to correct this impression, he just kept right on talking.

'I'm Montana Gray,' she repeated. 'I wrote *Street People.*'

George favoured her with another quick look. 'You did? My, my, things are sure changing around here. I could still use that coffee, little lady.'

She did not believe it. No way. Who the fuck did this ageing macho man think he was?

'Then I suggest,' she said icily, 'that you have Oliver's secretary get it for you.'

Her iciness had absolutely no effect. He greeted Neil, told a few off-colour jokes, strode around the office with Oliver nervously dogging his every step.

The secretary, when she brought his coffee, was rewarded with a pat on the ass. 'Pretty lady,' he remarked to no one in particular.

Oliver outlined the plans for the following morning's press reception at the Beverly Hills Hotel.

'Yes, yes,' George sighed, bored with his own celebrity. 'We'll make every front page from here to Jipip.' He rose to leave. 'You're all coming to my party tonight?'

'Wouldn't miss it,' Oliver enthused.

'We'll be there,' Neil said.

George turned and gave Montana the benefit of his attention. 'And you too, little lady. You're coming, aren't you?'

'Every time I look at your picture, Mr Lancaster,' she murmured sarcastically.

His eyes froze for a moment. 'I don't like women that talk dirty,' he said, and then he was off, undeterred. George Lancaster was a superstar. And superstars didn't have to take crap from anyone.

There was a moment of silence after he left the room. Then Montana said, 'Thank you, gentlemen, for your support.'

'What?' Oliver said vaguely.

Neil swigged his bourbon.

She stared at them coldly. 'I'm going shopping,' she said. 'If you need any coffee why not give George a call.'

She swept out.

* * *

The salon was busy. In fact it was the busiest day Angel had seen. 'This is nothing, dreamheart,' confided Koko. 'Try Oscar night. Chaos! Pandemonium! Wonder . . . ful! I looove it. All the little dears out-bitching each other. And if you're not invited to Swifty's party you're dead!'

'Swifty?'

'Forget it, dreamheart. He'd *adore* you.'

'Why *are* we so busy today?'

'Ross Conti is throwing a big party for George Lancaster. You *have* heard of George Lancaster, haven't you?'

She nodded.

'Thank God for small mercies!'

Raymondo slid up to the desk, his jet hair slicked into a fifties swirl. 'Wanna go dancin' tonight, blondie?'

She shook her head.

'Wanna eat the best tacos in town?'

'Raymondo!' Koko screamed. 'Back to work if you please.'

Raymondo scowled. 'Bet you are a *natural* blonde,' he muttered. 'Huh? Are you, pretty Angel?'

'Raymondo!' Koko's shriek forced him to move on, making way at the desk for a harassed Mrs Liderman minus her precious dog.

'Where's Frowie?' Angel inquired solicitously.

Mrs Liderman leaned confidentially across the desk, her eyes puffed and swollen. 'Dognapped!' she revealed tearfully. 'They took him two days ago and I'm waiting for the demand.'

'Who are "they"?' Angel asked, concern flooding her voice.

'I don't know,' quavered Mrs Liderman, twisting a huge diamond solitaire ring on her finger. 'This town is full of crazies. It could be anyone.'

'Perhaps it's not dognapping,' Angel said reassuringly. 'Maybe Frowie's just wandered off. I wouldn't worry, Mrs Liderman. I'm sure it will be all right.'

'Do you really think so, dear?'

'Oh, yes. I'm positive. Frowie will be back, you'll see.'

'You're such a lovely girl!' the fat woman sighed. 'A real comfort.'

'Thank you,' Angel replied modestly. 'Raymondo will be with you in a minute. If you'd like to take a seat . . .'

Koko waltzed over. 'What was *that* all about?' he asked, sotto voce.

She told him, then added, 'Nobody would kidnap her dog, would they?'

'Why not? This *is* Hollywood, dreamheart.'

The morning passed quickly, and by noon Angel was starving. She seemed to have developed a huge appetite and wondered if it had anything to do with being pregnant. Fortunately the swell of her stomach did not notice yet – not when she was dressed anyway. Eventually her secret would have to be revealed, but she was not in a hurry to tell anyone.

She thought about the baby all the time. And she tried not to think of Buddy at all. She had kept her promise to herself and not contacted him for two weeks. Then she had called Randy's apartment where there was no reply. She replaced the receiver and phoned Shelly. After all, it was only fair that she let Buddy know she was all right. Stoned or not he was probably concerned.

'Hi, this is Angel Hudson,' she announced when the phone was answered.

'Good for you,' slurred Shelly, still half asleep.

'Pardon?'

'Whaddya *want*?'

'I wondered if you would be kind enough to pass on a message to Buddy for me.'

'Spit it out, Angel-face.'

Hesitantly she began. 'I'd like you to tell him that I'm fine. I'm working at an interesting job, and I'll phone him at Randy's tomorrow, the same time.'

'Hmmm . . .' Shelly groped for a cigarette and tried to wake up properly. 'Still pregnant?'

'Yes I am,' Angel replied defiantly.

'You dumb bunny. Get rid of it, take my advice and el aborto.'

'I don't need your advice, thank you. The baby is Buddy's and my concern.'

'Oh, sure. But Buddy's bin' sleepin' in *my* bed lately, so that gives me some sort of a say.'

Angel could not keep the shock from her voice. 'What?'

'You heard. So why don't you grow up and face facts. Stop playing Daisy Mae an' get your shit together. Buddy doesn't care about you, he just cares about number one – himself, and I can dig that because it takes one to know one. So get rid of the kid, find yourself some real straight dude, an' hike your ass home. 'Cos Angel-pie, I'm tellin' you – Buddy's through with you. Capishe?'

Without uttering a word, Angel had replaced the receiver, her eyes filled with tears.

That had been weeks previously, and since that time she still hadn't decided what she should do. Divorce Buddy? She had no idea how to begin. He was no good, but she was still finding it hard to accept that sad fact of life.

Raymondo cruised by the desk as she was preparing to leave for lunch. 'Change your mind? Wanna hot date with me?'

'Leave the girl alone,' Koko scolded. 'Pick on someone your own size.'

'Nobody is *my* size!' Raymondo leered.

'Don't you wish,' retorted Koko tartly. 'Come dreamheart, I'll buy you a hero sandwich – everybody needs a hero in their life.'

* * *

Bibi Sutton was not getting the full focus of Elaine's attention and she knew it.

'Darling,' she said. 'Sweetie. Everything all right?'

Elaine nodded, forcing a bright smile to her lips. 'Of course it is. I'm just concerned about the party running smoothly.'

'How's Ross?' Bibi asked shrewdly.

Ross is a no-good cheating son of a bitch. 'He's fine,' she said flatly.

'You sure, sweetie?'

For a moment she nearly crumbled. How nice it would be to confide in someone, but she curbed herself just in time. To confide in Bibi would be like taking out a full page ad in the *Hollywood Reporter*.

'Of course I'm sure. Why?'

Bibi shrugged expensively clad shoulders. 'Nothing. People in this town so vicious. I take no notice . . .'

'What have you heard?' Elaine demanded, suddenly realizing that maybe the whole town already knew.

'You know sweetie, just nasty gossip . . .'

'What?' she insisted.

'That the movie Ross just finish not so good . . . I hear this from two or three people . . . Of course I no believe. This town, darling . . .'

Elaine almost gave a sigh of relief. So what if the movie stank? When he got *Street People* it would be a different story.

'Nobody's even *seen* the film,' she said calmly. 'It's still being edited. Who told you this?'

'It no important, darling.'

'Hmmm . . . I know what you mean about this town. Why, I heard the same thing about *Adam's* new movie. People are just *so* bitchy.'

Bibi was not used to being answered back. She wasn't quite sure how to handle Elaine this morning, she certainly wasn't her usual subservient self.

'Let me see the final list, sweetie. Then I must rush,' she said briskly.

Not to be outdone, Elaine replied, 'So must I. I had to squeeze you in this morning.'

'What you give up? Your exercise class?' Bibi inquired sweetly.

French cunt. She probably knew about Ron Gordino. And in view of what she had heard on the phone that morning Elaine didn't much care if the whole of Beverly Hills knew.

An exercise instructor, Elaine? Couldn't you at least have picked Robert Redford?

Shut up, Etta. What's wrong with an exercise instructor?

She handed over the final party list and Bibi checked it through like a computer expert. It *was* a great list, apart from the odd name here and there Pamela London had personally requested. Elaine could see that even Bibi was impressed.

She rose before she was dismissed. 'I have to rush. There's just so much to get organized.'

Bibi rose also. 'Sweetie. Tonight will be a night to remember.'

Elaine smiled vacantly. Was her erstwhile husband even now humping Karen Judas Lancaster's horrible body?

'I hope so, Bibi. I certainly hope so.'

* * *

Gaining entry to Karen Lancaster's high security apartment in the area known as Century City was no mean feat. Ross could remember when Century City was Twentieth Century-Fox Studios, and a sad day it was indeed when they sold off a goodly portion of their land and the real estate developers created Century City – a sea of concrete, glass and high-rises. He decided he wouldn't like to be around *this* section of town when the earthquake struck. No thank you very much.

'Who're you visiting?' the female guard at the gate demanded. She wore a permanent scowl and a tough looking uniform.

'Miss Lancaster. She's expecting me.' He wondered if the guard recognized him. He had taken the precaution of covering the famous Conti blues with a pair of Ray Charles shades. But there was always the famous dirty blond hair to contend with.

'What's your name?' the guard asked with an accusing stare. Obviously she was not a fan.

'Ross—' he began, before quickly remembering he was supposed to be incognito, and that Karen had left another name at the desk which for the life of him he could not remember.

'Er . . .'

'Yes?' snapped the guard.

'Mr Ross.'

'Okay Mr Ross. Please wait a minute.'

I've already waited more than a minute. What is this place anyway? Colditz?

The guard produced a pencil and pad, and walked around to the front of the Corniche where she took note of the licence plate. Then she slowly made her way around the back of the car and did the same thing.

Ross was not a patient man. He would have driven through, but a wooden barrier blocked his entry. '*Come* on,' he muttered.

Deliberately moving as slowly as possible, she returned to her glass booth and dialled a number. After a long mutter on the phone she came back to the car. 'Do you know which way to go?'

'No,' he snapped.

'Proceed straight ahead. Stop at courtesy parking and a valet will take you to Miz Lancaster's apartment.'

She returned to her booth and raised the mechanical barrier. The Corniche shot through, narrowly missing an exiting Porsche.

'Ross!' screamed a blonde female waving from the Porsche's window. 'See you tonight.'

He had no idea who she was, but whoever she was he would now have to think of an excuse for being there. Damn! He didn't even feel horny anymore.

The two Mexicans stationed at valet parking were fighting in Spanish. They ignored Ross, the Corniche, the baby blues and the dirty blond trademark hair.

Ross alighted from the car. 'This place is a frigging prison,' he screamed. 'Give me some attention.'

They forgot their fight and stared at him with looks of 'Who is this American fool?' Then one of them gestured to an open motorized buggy, while the other handed him a ticket and zoomed the Corniche away.

Ross indicated the buggy which resembled an open golf cart. '*I'm* supposed to get in *that*?'

'Si, Señor. Door to door service.'

'Shit!'

* * *

Elaine decided that she had to confide in *somebody*, otherwise she was just going to crack with fury. Outside the gates of the Sutton estate she slowed the Mercedes and tried to decide whether she should call Maralee, or just turn up at her front door. Since the country style sidewalks of Bel Air were hardly littered with phone booths she decided to take a chance and go right over. There was still half an hour of grace before she had to appear at the hairdressers where her stylist was waiting to create something sensational for the hostess of the week. That was the trouble with giving a big party in Beverly Hills – there was always someone around the corner waiting to top you. Why, only ten minutes earlier Bibi had murmured that she must throw a little soirée soon. Bibi's 'little soirées' made Oscar night seem like an evening at McDonalds.

Make the most of it, Elaine. Hostess of the week is better than a kick up the ass.

Fuck you, Etta. What do you know anyway?

What do I know? Ha! I know that I wouldn't sit back and let Karen Lancaster get away with screwing my husband. I'd bust her ass, and damn the party. Have you forgotten New York Elaine? You're a street kid, not some laid back Californian cooze.

Three cars were parked in Maralee's driveway. And two gardeners worked on the front lawn aimlessly hosing fallen leaves from one area to another. Elaine parked behind a silver Jaguar, alighted from her car, and rang the doorbell.

One of Maralee's army of Mexicans opened the door a crack and stared at Elaine, the security chain firmly in place.

'*Buenos dias*,' said Elaine pleasantly, although she didn't feel pleasant, she felt like screaming long and loud. 'Is Señora Gray up?'

'Que, cual?'

'Señora Gray,' Elaine repeated. 'Is she up?' Why couldn't Maralee hire Mexicans who at least spoke English?

'No.'

Before Elaine could object the door was slammed shut. She was speechless. Maralee definitely needed a talking to about the way her help conducted themselves. The stupid woman hadn't even asked who she was. She could have been someone important. She *was* someone important.

Frustrated and angry she returned to the comfort of her pale blue Mercedes and sat behind the wheel.

Where to now, Elaine? The hairdressers where you get to put on a wife of the star act? Or maybe Ron Gordino's for a decent fuck? Or how about confronting Karen and Ross?

Shut up, Etta. I'll do what I want.

What *did* she want?

She wanted to cry.

She wanted to yell and scream.

She wanted to kick out.

She wanted to have never picked up the phone and heard her betrayal.

It was the most perfect day for a party. All around her immaculate green lawns received attention, maids walked children to school, and dogs did their duty beneath the palm trees. A police car cruised slowly by, and a Sparkletts truck stopped two houses down.

Beverly Hills.

How she loved it. When you were up it was the greatest.

How she hated it. When you were down it was the worst.

At the hairdressers she was unusually quiet. When she was finished she contemplated phoning Maralee, but then she thought no, I don't need to tell anyone. I can handle it. I'm Elaine Conti. Not big-mouthed Etta Grodinski from the Bronx.

Screw Etta Grodinski.

Screw Ross Conti.

Screw Karen Lancaster.

Calmly she reclaimed her car from the parking lot and once more sat behind the wheel contemplating her next move. She *should* go home, time was pressing, yet she felt so safe and secure behind the wheel of the Mercedes, it was the only place she really wanted to be.

A man in a Cadillac bleeped his horn impatiently, and she found herself heading towards Wilshire. *I want to spend money, she thought. I want to spend every red cent that bastard hasn't got.*

She drew into the parking lot of Saks and entered the department store like a gladiator entering the arena. Within an hour she had charged eight thousand dollars worth of merchandise to be sent.

She left the store with a smile on her lips, and strolled down Wilshire to yet another large department store. Immediately she spotted an enamel bracelet she had to have. 'Charge it,' she told the salesgirl imperiously.

The girl took her charge card and since the amount was over a hundred dollars, went to the phone to check.

She returned full of apologies. 'I'm so sorry, but there appears to be a problem . . . If you would care to go up to our credit department I'm sure that it can be settled . . .'

'But I want this bracelet,' Elaine announced firmly.

The girl was embarrassed. 'I'm sorry . . .'

'You will be,' said Elaine, her voice rising sharply. 'Don't you know who I am?'

The girl gazed at her blankly. She saw a passably attractive woman with an elaborate hair-do. She certainly did not see a Goldie Hawn or a Faye Dunaway. Fortunately, another customer claimed her attention, and she moved quickly away from Elaine.

'Bitch!' Elaine said out loud. And then she felt sorry for calling the girl names. It wasn't her fault. It was Ross's fault. The bastard hadn't paid their last account.

For a moment she was uncertain what to do. Then, quite calmly, she realized there was only one thing *to* do. She glanced around her. The salesgirl was busy, other shoppers were going about their business. She was unobserved, free to do anything. Quick as a flash she scooped the bracelet from the counter where in her haste to get away the salesgirl had left it. Then, humming softly to herself, she headed for the exit.

Once outside she took a deep breath. And the adrenaline started to flow. *Now* she was ready to go home and look Ross in the eye without so much as a flicker to reveal she knew he was a no-good unfaithful *bum*.

What did she care anyway? *She* was Mrs Ross Conti, not spoiled rich bitch Karen Lancaster whose only claim to fame was a famous daddy.

A firm hand on her arm stopped her progress along Wilshire. 'Excuse me, madam,' said a tall bespectacled woman. 'Would you mind returning to the store with me? The manager would like a word with you.'

* * *

Karen greeted him not clad in the red satin nightie, crotchless panties, and nippleless bra she had promised. Instead she wore a yellow track suit and a nasty scowl. She flung open the door and started to harangue him about the amount of time it had taken him to get there.

He marched inside the tribute to *Architectural Digest* and flung himself on a white leather couch. 'Will you shut up? It has just taken me twenty frigging minutes to get from the front entrance of this jail house to your front door.'

'Don't be ridiculous,' she stormed. 'You probably went back to sleep while I've been standing around waiting for you like some . . . some little groupie!'

He started to laugh. The thought of Karen Lancaster as a groupie was too absurd.

'Don't laugh!' she yelled. 'I could have had an extra hour's sleep!'

He stretched his arms above his head and groaned loudly. 'Nagging I can get at home. I came here for a fucking not an ear bashing.'

Her scowl deepened. 'I don't feel like it now.'

He got up and headed for the door. 'Take your bad mood out on someone else. *I* don't feel like it either.' He slammed the door behind him and buzzed for the elevator. Karen Lancaster in a track suit and a bad mood was not the way he wished to spend the morning. Impatiently he buzzed for the elevator again, letting forth a sneaky fart.

A middle-aged woman emerged from the apartment opposite and gave him a dirty look. She was clad in a multi-coloured robe, her hair full of shocking pink curlers.

'Yaes?' she said in a European accent, staring at him suspiciously.

'Yes what?' he snapped.

'Vat are you doing in my hallvay?' the woman said icily, sniffing the air with a look of disdain.

Ross raised his all concealing dark shades and glared. '*Your* hallway?'

She glared back. 'Yaes. *My* hallvay.'

'*And* Miss Lancaster's I presume.'

'Miss Lancaster did not give you key to the elevator. Since you do not have one I can only say you are trespassing in *my* hallvay, and therefore I call security. At once.' She stepped smartly back into her apartment, slamming the door firmly behind her.

Ross did not believe it. You needed a key to get *out* of the place! This was better than San Quentin!

He hammered on Karen's front door.

She opened it on the chain. 'What?' she asked in a bored tone.

'Give me the key for the elevator. Let me out of this prison.'

'Why should I? You've ruined my morning.'

'I've ruined *your* morning.'

'I don't think I like screwing a married man. Your hours don't suit me.'

Through the crack in the door he couldn't help noticing that she had finally come through with the nippleless bra. An erotic nipple temptingly emerged from black and red lace.

'Hmmm . . .' he said, changing his mind about leaving. 'Aren't you even going to offer me a cup of coffee?'

Karen licked her index finger and lasciviously brought it down to her nipple. 'Maybe . . .' she said, making no move to release the chain.

He felt the return of his early morning hard-on. 'Come on, sweetheart,' he pleaded, enjoying her little game. 'I've got something for breakfast that you are going to *love*!'

'Something soft?'

'Not any more!'

'Something hot?'

'You bet your—'

Before he could finish his sentence a baby-faced security guard nervously wielding a pistol emerged from the elevator. 'Okay you—' he commanded Ross in a high-pitched voice. 'Up against the wall an' spread 'em.'

'What?' asked an outraged Ross, drowning out Karen's hysterical giggle.

'Don't think I won't use this thing,' twitched the guard. 'Do as I say or I'll shoot.'

The European woman in the pink hair curlers and the multi-coloured robe opened up the door of her apartment. 'Yaes,' she said firmly. 'That iss the intruder.'

'Holy shit!' exclaimed Ross.

'Spread 'em,' said the guard.

'What's the matter with all of you,' said Karen, releasing her security chain and stepping out into the hallway. 'Don't any of you recognize Ross Conti when you see him?

Three pair of eyes turned to stare at her simultaneously.

Karen Lancaster wore nothing but a nippleless bra and an amused smile.

Chapter Twenty-Eight

It was early morning when Deke drove the van slowly into the small town of Barstow, California.

He was tired and unshaven, having driven non-stop from New Mexico. The very thought of being near his destination had sent him speeding along the arid desert roads, radio blaring, thoughts alive with the inspiring words – KEEPER OF THE ORDER.

He saw Joey often. Sitting in a passing car – her skirt hiked high above her thighs. Thumbing a lift roadside. Posing provocatively on billboards along the way.

He was not tempted to stop though. Oh, no. Not tempted one little bit. He knew better. Now.

California was not how he had imagined it would be. He had expected white palaces, blue seas, wide streets lined with palm trees. Instead he found dusty sidewalks and the same old gas stations and motels. The heat was acrid. It enveloped like a blanket and tried to suffocate.

Still. He had arrived.

Barstow, California.

He took a crumpled piece of paper with an address scribbled on it from the hiding place down the side of his boot and studied it intently.

For a moment the image of the girl's face in Amarillo danced before his eyes 'Why?' she had screamed in terror. 'Why me?'

The moment of her death was ecstasy. Her screaming stopped, and her body became slack and peaceful. He had felt so close to her then, because he alone had helped her . . . The knife was an instrument of God sent to do His work . . .

Upon her death she became Joey, and he was able to relieve himself of the passion that had been building in his body for so many months . . . The relief was glorious.

PASSION. EVEN THE PRESIDENT NEEDS PASSION.

A broken neon sign offered coffee and doughnuts. He steered the truck into an unkempt parking lot and alighted.

The place was deserted except for a lone counterman picking his nose and studying a sex magazine.

'Coffee,' Deke said, taking a faded plastic seat at the counter.

The man barely raised his eyes from the magazine, he merely yelled 'Coffee' to someone in back.

'And a doughnut,' Deke added.

'Doughnut,' yelled the man, not moving.

A line of ants had taken up residence around a grimy sugar container. Deke reached for a paper napkin and methodically squashed them.

'You ever see a naked broad with no legs?' the counterman asked, removing his finger from his nose and thrusting the open magazine across the counter.

Silently Deke regarded the pictures.

'Hot, huh?'

The girl in the pictures looked like Joey. The pictures were grossly obscene. Yes. He had done the right thing removing Joey from temptation. She was safe now. The Keeper Of The Order had performed his duty well.

'Waddya think?' asked the counterman, hoping for a discussion on the merits of sex with a legless woman.

Deke raised his cold black eyes from the magazine and stared. It wasn't right that Joey had posed for such pictures and that strange men could feast their eyes on her naked body. If he had time he would remove the scum, squash him dead, just as he had squashed the ants.

'They're all whores,' he said at last, realizing that the Keeper Of The Order did not have time to deal with every stinking pervert who crossed his path.

The counterman laughed derisively. 'You're so right, pal. I couldn't've said it better myself. Hookers – every damn one!'

Damnation is closer than you know, Deke thought.

A fat girl emerged from the back, coffee in one hand, doughnut on a plate in the other. The counterman winked lewdly at Deke who ignored him. He drank the steaming coffee, wolfed down the greasy doughnut, then slammed some money down and left.

He was in California now, and nothing was going to stop him doing what he had to do.

Chapter Twenty-Nine

A psychiatrist would say that it was a scream in the dark. An attention-getting act performed by a person who desperately needed help. Elaine knew all the psychological garbage. She had not sat on an analyst's couch for a year without learning a thing or two. She had learned that seeing a shrink was expensive, time consuming, and ego boosting. Who wouldn't enjoy talking about themselves non-stop, an hour at a time, three times a week? It was one little luxury she had finally decided to do without.

These thoughts ran through her head as she sat in the manager's office and said – yet again – 'I am *outraged* that you could even have thought for one moment that I intended to . . . to *steal* that *tacky* bracelet. My husband is Ross Conti. If he so desired he could buy this whole store for me!'

'Yes. I understand that,' said the manager, not understanding at all. 'But you must see *our* point of view. You left here with the bracelet in your possession, and it was unpaid for.'

'A mistake,' she said haughtily. 'I misunderstood your salesperson. I thought she had charged it to my account.'

The store detective hovered by the door.

'I really must go,' Elaine said quickly. 'This whole incident is a gross error on your part.'

'I'm sorry, but we cannot allow you to go yet.'

Why had she been so *careless*? How *could* she have risked everything on the day of her party? What if it got in the *newspapers*?

'Why?' she demanded imperiously.

'Because,' said the manager, 'our policy is to prosecute.'

She leapt up in a panic, thinking of the publicity. 'Please!' she implored. 'You can't do that! I've told you who I am. Why can't we just forget it?'

He frowned. 'You've *told* us who you are. But that doesn't *prove* who you are.'

'I've shown you all my credit cards. Surely that's good enough?'

'No driving licence, no picture—'

'I never carry my licence,' she interrupted quickly.

'That's a shame . . .' He pursed his lips. If the woman was who she said she was, then the publicity would help neither of them. On the other hand, he couldn't just let her stroll casually out of the store merely because she claimed to be the wife of a film star. An idea came to him. 'If we could perhaps contact *Mr* Conti, and he came to collect you then maybe we could forget about prosecuting. I'm sure, as you say, it was a genuine mistake.'

The female detective's lip curled in disgust.

'Yes,' said Elaine quickly, filled with relief. 'I know exactly where I can find him.'

* * *

Eventually they made love, because that had been the purpose of Ross's visit in the first place.

Karen kept laughing as he pumped solidly away. 'Did you *see* that woman's face?' she gasped. 'I mean *did you see it*?'

'I could hardly *help* seeing it,' he huffed.

'Ummm . . . let's change positions.' Skillfully she rolled around – keeping him firmly inside her – until she was on top.

He had noticed that Karen was not too thrilled by the missionary position. He liked it himself, it gave him somewhere to rest his bones when he needed a break.

'And that security creep!' she giggled. 'Can you imagine! If you had been a burglar he would've wet his pants!' She angled an erect nipple into his mouth and he sucked greedily. 'Niiiiice . . .' she sighed.

He felt the beginning of the rush. Not bad. He had given her ten minutes of solid action, she couldn't complain about *that*.

'Christ!' he groaned. 'Jesus H!'

The phone rang just before he hit. Valiantly they tried to continue, but the ringing was too intrusive.

Disengaging her nipple from his mouth Ross said, 'Well *answer* the frigging thing.'

She grabbed the receiver. 'Yes?'

Ross could not hear who it was, but from the way she pulled herself off him he knew it must be George Lancaster.

'Daddy!' she cooed in confirmation. 'Sorry . . . I mean George. How are you today?'

Ross watched his erection deflate. He felt like a horse blocked at the gate. Ten more seconds and he would have been a winner. Now he would just have to run the whole goddamn race again. If he had the strength. He looked pointedly at his watch. 'I've got to go to the bank,' he mouthed.

She nodded, covered the mouthpiece for a second. 'Okay. Go, and come back after,' and then she went back to her riveting conversation.

Enough was enough. Karen had given him more crap than he cared to handle for one day. He dressed, found the elevator key, and let himself out.

The morning had hardly been perfect. He hoped the day would improve as it progressed.

* * *

Karen spoke to her father for twenty-five minutes, and at the end of the conversation he invited her to a late lunch in the Polo Lounge.

'I'll be there,' she said breathlessly, conveniently forgetting that she had told Ross to return.

She ran a bubblebath, pinned her long hair up, and slid into the warm water. Daddy was back in town. And if he wanted her to she would spend every second with him. She might be thirty-two years old but she had her priorities straight.

The phone rang again and she picked up the bathroom extension. 'George?' she questioned hopefully. He didn't like her calling him daddy – said it made him feel too old.

'No. This is Elaine,' said the voice of her friend sounding uptight.

'Oh, hi.' She could hardly conceal her lack of enthusiasm. 'All set for the big night?'

'Yes,' said Elaine in a strained voice. 'Can I have a word with Ross?'

'*Ross*?' Surprise filled her voice.

'I know he's there, and I need to speak to him urgently.'

Karen laughed hollowly. 'Why would *Ross* be *here*?'

'This is urgent. Put him on.'

'I don't understand,' Karen said in a concerned tone. 'Are you all right?'

'He's not with you then?'

'*Of course* he's not here. I don't—'

Elaine hung up.

Karen was stunned. She stood up in the bath, bubbles sticking everywhere. How had Elaine known? Had Ross *told* her?

No. He wanted it kept a secret more than she did. Come to think of it she couldn't care less whether it was kept a secret or not. Having Ross Conti was the next best thing to having daddy. And since having daddy was a definite no-no . . .

She felt a brief feeling of remorse about Elaine, but that soon passed. Karen always got what she wanted, it had been that way since she was a little girl. And if someone got hurt along the way . . . Well . . . That's show biz – as daddy always said.

* * *

Elaine hung up the phone tight-lipped. 'It may take me a few minutes to locate my husband,' she said, wondering if perhaps she was having a nightmare and would wake up at any minute.

Then she called Lina, their bank, Ross's health club, Ma Maison, their business manager, Lina, the Polo Lounge, the suntanning salon, the Bistro, Lina, and finally Karen Lancaster again. Her phone did not answer, which convinced Elaine that even now they were rolling around on Karen's king size custom built bed having wild sex and laughing at poor Elaine.

'I'm having a big party tonight,' she said desperately to the manager. 'Is this really necessary?'

'Was it really necessary for you to take the bracelet?'

Suddenly she snapped. 'I hope you know what you're doing,' she screamed hysterically. 'I have important friends in *very* high places, and you are making a nasty mistake keeping me here.'

He had been on the verge of letting her go. After her series of phone calls there was no doubt that she was who she claimed to be. But he had never liked to be threatened, and just who did she think she was anyway?

'I'm sorry,' he said smoothly. 'You have a choice. The police or your husband. Whichever you prefer.'

* * *

As the Corniche glided away from Karen Lancaster's Century City apartment, so a shabby brown Datsun slid into the lane behind it. The Datsun was driven by a man named Little S. Shitz. A name he had never been happy with, but one he had become used to over the years. The kids at school had dubbed him 'Little Shit'. His ex-wife had called him 'Big Shit'. And the people he came in contact with during the course of his work invariably ended up calling him every other name you could think of.

Little S. Shitz was a private detective – the kind you could hire for a hundred bucks a day as long as you paid in cash. And the sort of people who hired him *always* paid in cash. He was a weedy looking man in his late thirties, stoop shouldered, sharp nosed, with ferret-like eyes that continually darted this way and that. His thinning brown hair was plastered close to his scalp, and dandruff scattered on the collar of his scruffy brown shirt. He was not a class act. But he knew how to play dirty, and he specialized in divorce cases – the seamier the better. He was an expert at catching a cheating husband or wife. Many a motel door had felt the force of his shoulder as he burst in – flash camera in hand.

Little S. Shitz felt that he had lucked into the big-time with the Glynis Barnes divorce case. 'I want to know every move my husband makes,' she told him on her first visit to his one-roomed Hollywood office. 'I want times, dates, and *most-important* – photographs of every woman he sees.'

He went to work at once. Following Chet Barnes was a pleasure and he soon settled into a daily routine which hardly ever took him out of Beverly Hills. He sat outside some of the best restaurants taking the occasional shot of Chet Barnes emerging with various women. Once a week Glynis Barnes arrived at his office bearing cash. She collected the photographic evidence, then departed with the words – 'Let's give it another week.'

One day a particular picture grabbed her attention. 'Do you know who this is?' she asked sharply, thrusting it at him.

He glanced briefly at a photo of Chet Barnes emerging from La Scala, his arm around a copper-haired woman in a tight dress. He shook his head while Glynis Barnes paced his small office muttering to herself.

'Have you seen him with her before?' she demanded. 'Did he spend the night at her place? What happened?'

Frankly he had no idea. Immediately after taking that picture he had quit and gone home. So he lied. 'Yeah, he spent the night. I thought you'd want me to stay until morning, so I did. Anything after twelve is double rate you know.'

'That doesn't matter,' she said. 'Now, this is what I want you to do . . .'

She told him the woman was Karen Lancaster. The name didn't mean anything to him until he put it together with George Lancaster and found out it was his daughter!

Glynis had suspected all along that her estranged husband had the hots for Karen. Now that she was sure, she wanted to prove to him what a tramp Karen was. 'I want her followed,' she said. 'And get me some *good* photos. Explicit. Watch her twenty-four hours a day. I don't care what it costs.'

He followed her to the beach house just a couple of days later. The photos he managed to get were hot. First he risked a roll of film through the glass front of her house while she rolled around on the bed with a man. Then he captured her and the boyfriend in the ocean.

It wasn't until later when he developed the photos that he realized the man was Ross Conti. And he had stills of him the like of which his fans had *never* seen!

He decided that handing the photos to Glynis Barnes would be crazy. Why settle for a few hundred when it could mean thousands?

He waited a week, then withdrew from the case much to Glynis Barnes's annoyance.

He waited a while longer, then enlarged some of his favourite shots and set about finding Ross Conti. It was easy. All he had to do was buy a cheapo map of the movie stars' homes, and the Contis were listed right there along with Tony Curtis and Johnny Carson.

Early one morning he parked opposite the Conti house and waited for the moment to be right.

Three maids arrived, giggling and chattering away in Spanish.

The milkman delivered twelve quarts of orange juice and six cartons of milk.

A woman left the house, climbed into a pale blue Mercedes, zipped out the drive, changed her mind, drove back to the house, then re-emerged and shot off again.

He bided his time until eventually he was rewarded with the sight of Ross Conti in his Corniche a mere twenty minutes later. He followed the car all the way to Karen Lancaster's apartment in Century City, and was delighted to think that the affair was still going strong.

Later, when Ross Conti drove out in the distinctive gold Corniche, Little S. Shitz was right there behind him.

* * *

Randy's apartment stank of Au Sauvage aftershave, Yves Saint Laurent deodorant and Jean Naté body splash.

'I hate all that crap,' Buddy said, busily doing one-armed press-ups.

Randy emerged from the bathroom clad only in brief jockeys. 'What crap?' he demanded.

'All that shit you're spraying yourself with. Doncha know that stuff can give you cancer?' He released his weight and lay flat on his stomach. 'Jeez, y'know I don't feel so good. I think it's breathin' in all these poison fumes.'

'You don't like it you know what you can do.'

Buddy got up off the floor and leaned weakly against the wall. 'I didn't sleep so good last night. I had a real bad dream – like it was vivid. I was—'

Randy held up a commanding hand. 'Don't tell me your dream. My own don't thrill me, so why should I want to know yours?'

Buddy went to the refrigerator. 'You've never got any food here,' he complained.

'Christ! You're worse than a wife! Why don't you go over to Shelly's an' excite her with your belly-aching?'

'That's the trouble. I excite her with more than my belly-aching. I'm not into another relationship. What Angel did to me was—'

'Cut it out,' said Randy sharply. 'I got a lot on my mind and I don't need your problems too. You wanted to sleep on my floor – I lent you my floor. You wanted to borrow some bucks – I lent you bucks. Now for this I don't need a running commentary on your lousy life.'

'Thanks. It's good to have friends.'

Randy had been in a bad mood ever since Buddy had mentioned that he too was going to the George Lancaster party. 'Stay away from me and Maralee,' Randy had warned, nervous of his past.

What did the schmuck think he was going to say. 'Hey – Maralee. Nice to meet you. Did you know that your boyfriend and I used to do a little hustling together?' Jeez! He wanted to forget about it just as much as Randy.

He had made his daily phone call to Inga, and got the usual – 'They're interested. They like you a lot. You're really a hot favourite.' How hot could he be when weeks were passing and nothing was happening? Maybe Inga was giving him sweet-bullshit. Maybe the role was already cast. Maybe he didn't have a hope . . .

'Angel!' He muttered her name under his breath. 'Why did you have to run out on me?'

* * *

Montana drove into Beverly Hills, but the thought of shopping for a new outfit to wear at George Lancaster's party failed to excite her. She was outraged by his arrogant and rude attitude. Just who exactly did he think he was? An over-the-hill ageing superstar, that's who. And as for Oliver and Neil, they had really let her down. Oliver, crawling like a modern day

Uriah Heep, and Neil, nursing his bourbon like it was mother's milk.

She had tried to talk to Neil several times in the past few days, but he had dismissed her attempts at meaningful conversation with disruptive comments about the script, sidetracking her into heated discussions. All of a sudden she was fighting for scenes he wanted to cut. Scenes he had never objected to before. Important scenes.

She felt frustrated and out of control. What the hell was going on? Why was everything turning sour? *Street People* – her baby – was slowly being taken away. She had written the script and now it was as if the words no longer belonged to her. Okay so she had practically cast the film except for the leading roles – but so what? From now on it would be a George Lancaster movie and he was the kind of man she had always hated. Self-important, tough, assured in his mistaken knowledge that men are superior beings to women.

She decided not to go back to the office. The beach seemed like a much better idea, so she drove along Wilshire all the way to the ocean, where she parked the car and strode along the seashore, trying to calm down.

The waves were high enough to surf, and plenty of kids were indulging, their bronzed bodies flying over the water with speed and grace. She wished she had a swimsuit and a board – for that's just what she felt like doing. And why shouldn't she? On impulse she hurried back to the car and drove to a sports shop on Santa Monica. There, she purchased what she needed.

She hadn't surfed in years – certainly not since she had known Neil. Entering the swell of the ocean, at first she felt awkward and stupid – even – at twenty-nine – too old. But soon she was back in the swing of it, riding the waves just like the good old days – having a marvellous time.

She forgot about George, Oliver, the movie, and most of all Neil. Excitement swamped her as skills she had forgotten came into play.

How good it was to feel young again and to have nothing on your mind but the next wave.

How good it was to be in control.

* * *

'Can I talk to you a minute?' Little S. Shitz sidled up to Ross Conti outside Bijan on Rodeo Drive.

'Sure,' said Ross magnanimously, thinking the seedy looking man was a fan. 'What do you want to know? Did I *really* jump off the clifftop in *Prowler* myself or was it a stand-in? Don't worry, everyone asks me that, and I can tell you it was me. If you lend me a pen I'll sign your envelope. Who's it for – your sister?'

Little was speechless. You don't go up to a man to blackmail him and have him offer to autograph the envelope with the *blackmail* pictures inside it.

'You don't understand,' he stuttered. 'I have photographs.'

'Oh, you want me to sign your photos,' said Ross easily. He had always believed in being nice to his fans. Treat 'em good and they'll never stop flocking to your movies.

They stopped years ago, putz.

'Photographs you wouldn't want published,' he continued rapidly before this big-time movie star could confuse him further. 'Or your wife to see, or your mother, or your daughter, or your granddaughter.'

Granddaughter! Ross was incensed. How old did this scurvy prick think he was anyway?

'My mother is deceased. I do not have a daughter. I *certainly* do not have a granddaughter – so why don't you take whatever you have in that envelope and stick it up your ass.' Ross spoke with dignity, then headed abruptly for his car parked in a red zone.

Little hurried after him. 'How would you – in bed with Karen Lancaster – look on the cover of the *National Inquirer*?' he asked, twitching nervously.

For one brief moment Ross's stride faltered, but then he thought – come on, what am I getting worried about? Who could possibly have photos of me and Karen?

Little S. Shitz fumbled in his envelope.

He produced an eight by ten black and white glossy of Karen and Ross in bed together.

Little S. Shitz had the goods.

'How much?' Ross asked wearily.

* * *

Karen entered the Polo Lounge with confidence, waved to Nino, the maître d'hôtel, and headed for the table George Lancaster always had when he was in town.

To her disappointment he was not yet there, so she sat herself down, ordered a Bloody Mary, then took an exquisite Fabergé compact from her purse and studied her chiselled features. Fortunately she had inherited her father's looks *and* his spirit – which she was pleased about because to her way of thinking her mother had been a weak woman, too weak by far to handle a daughter like Karen – *or* a husband like George, which was probably the reason he had sought out other women so consistently during the course of his marriage. When her mother died Karen got to spend a lot of time with George. For a dizzy six months they were inseparable. Then some ice-blonde starlet stepped into the picture and blew everything. George, like a fool, married her. It lasted nine months and cost him plenty. In the meantime Karen married the first man she could – a real estate broker who had just sold her a house. Her marriage broke up two days after George's. But instead of moving back together as Karen had hoped, George went off to Palm Beach with some friends, met Pamela London, and as soon as his divorce was final, married her. Their wedding was *the* social event of the year. Karen got stoned and gave head to her date under a table. Two months later she married a spaced-out composer who spooned so much coke his nose gave way. When she realized George didn't care *who* she was married to she got a divorce, and since that time had been a single lady living alone in Beverly Hills. A single lady with a huge trust fund, a great apartment, a terrific house at the beach, three cars, four furs, and anything else her little heart desired.

George Lancaster made a rowdy entrance. People jumped to attention as he passed their tables, conversations stopped, flunkeys jumped to their feet and paid homage.

Karen stood as he approached. She wished she was a little girl again and could leap into his arms. Instead she settled for a quick hug.

'How's my girlie?' he boomed.

'You look wonderful da . . . um . . . George. Honestly, you look really *great*.'

'Naw . . . I'm gettin' old.'

'Come on. You – ne-ever.'

He grinned boyishly. 'Me and Reagan, kiddo. We're holdin' up pretty good for two old broncos.'

'Better not let *him* hear you say that.'

'Who, Ronnie? He wouldn't mind.'

'I love you, daddy,' she said, all of a sudden the little girl she wished she still was.

'Cut out the daddy, will ya? You know I can't stand it.'

She took a hurried gulp of her Bloody Mary, then brightly asked, 'How's Pamela?'

'For an' old broad she's not bad.' He laughed loudly. 'Did you hear the one about the Eskimo and the ice cubes?'

For fifteen minutes he told jokes, stopping only to josh with assorted staff and patrons who stopped by the table in a steady stream.

Karen munched her way through a delicious Neil McCarthy salad, downed two more Bloody Marys, wondered why the *hell* Elaine Conti had phoned *her* looking for Ross, and listened patiently to all of George's sexist jokes.

He didn't like women. Even Karen had to admit that.

Finally, he imparted the news of his commitment to *Street People*.

Karen had heard rumours – but she had dismissed them as just that. After all, how many times had George told her that there was no way he would ever do another film.

Her reactions were mixed. It would be glorious having George back in town. But what about Ross? *He* wanted *Street People*. He *needed* it.

'Oh, shit,' she mumbled under her breath.

'What?' boomed George.

'Nothing da . . . George. I was just wondering if you're sure it's the right part for you.'

'What's right? *I* don't become the role, the role becomes *me*. *That's* the secret of being a star in this town, and don't you ever forget it.'

* * *

By late afternoon Angel was exhausted. All she wanted to do was go home and collapse. The salon had been a madhouse all day, and everybody's tempers were frayed. The phone on the desk rang for about the hundredth time. Wearily she picked it up. 'Koko's. Can I help you?'

'Angel, dear?' gushed Mrs Liderman.

'Yes.'

'I'm so glad I caught you. You'll *never* guess what. Frowie came home! And it's *all* thanks to you, dear, and your positive vibes.'

'I only said—'

'It doesn't matter *what* you said,' interrupted Mrs Liderman. 'You sent out positive thought waves and that was enough to persuade my baby to come home to me. I'm *so* grateful.'

'What *is* going on?' hissed Koko.

Angel covered the mouthpiece and whispered, 'Mrs L's dog came home, she seems to think I had something to do with it.'

'Good. Maybe she'll give you five hundred dollars.'

As if on cue Mrs Liderman said, 'I have to reward you.'

And Angel said, 'Don't be silly.'

And Mrs Liderman said, 'I'm sending my car to collect you. I'm taking you to a party tonight, you'll have a marvellous time. It's a very special party being thrown for my dear friend, Pamela London.'

Koko – who was now listening in, nodded enthusiastically, while Angel said, 'That's very kind of you Mrs Liderman, but I don't think I can go.'

Koko snatched the phone from her grasp. 'Mrs Liderman,' he cooed, 'Angel would *love* to go. Could your driver pick her up at her apartment? I'll give you the address.'

Angel shook her head helplessly while Koko arranged her life, and when he hung up she said, 'I'm not going. There is *no way* I'm going.'

'Dreamheart!' he exclaimed. 'Trust me. You *have* to go, there is no question about it. You simply have to learn that in life we do not always do what we want to do. Sometimes fate pushes us in other directions, and fate has said that tonight you *will* go to the ball.'

'What ball?'

'Haven't you ever heard of Cinderella? Oh, God! Must I teach you *every*thing?'

* * *

It was four o'clock in the afternoon. Elaine was calm. Her thoughts were clear and concise. After fourteen phone calls she had failed to locate Ross, and it was becoming increasingly obvious that she would be arrested.

She stared dreamily off into space.

Headlines.

WIFE OF STAR ARRESTED IN SHOPLIFTING BUST.

BEVERLY HILLS BABE BACK TO THE BRONX.

GEORGE LANCASTER SAYS, 'ELAINE WHO?'

Well, everyone would have a big laugh at her expense. She would be forced to leave town. The disgrace, the humiliation, the *embarrassment*.

Where was Ross Conti?

Where *was* the biggest lying, cheating shitheel in the world?

Chapter Thirty

Leon Rosemont's investigation of the Andrews family yielded very little. There appeared to be no living relatives, and of the two witnesses listed on their marriage certificate, one was untraceable and the other dead.

It occurred to Leon that the only way he was going to find out any more about them was to go to Barstow and dig around. Millie had *said* she wanted to vacation in California. Somehow he didn't think she had Barstow in mind . . . But still . . . he could always make a side trip on a day when she was busy.

On impulse he went out and purchased two plane tickets to California and presented them to Millie with a flourish.

'We're going to take a month off,' he told her. 'The time is due me, and I figured we should do it properly. We'll hire a car and just drive around.'

'San Francisco?' she asked, her eyes gleaming.

He nodded.

'The Napa Valley? Arizona? *Hollywood*?'

He nodded again.

She threw her arms around his neck and hugged him. 'Honey,' she crooned, 'you are somethin' else.'

A week before they were due to leave he handed her four hundred dollars and told her to go buy some vacation clothes.

She rushed off to the shopping mall as happy as if he had given her four thousand.

While she was gone he took the opportunity to secrete the Andrews file at the bottom of his suitcase. It wasn't strictly legal, but he had photo-copied all of the official documents, including the pictures . . .

There were fifteen still shots taken that morning in Friendship Street.

Fifteen photos of . . . murder.

Chapter Thirty-One

At approximately four-fifteen Ross Conti strode angrily through the front door of his house. Chaos reigned. Strange people were everywhere.

'What in the hell is going on here?' he roared at Lina, who stood weeping in the doorway to the kitchen.

'Señor Conti,' she sobbed. 'Is impossible. I no take it. I quit.'

She clung to his arm and he shook her off while demanding, 'Where is Mrs Conti?'

A wild-haired youth in tight jeans and a Hells-Angel studded jacket intervened. 'Hey-hey, man, you the boss man 'round here? I gotta get me more power – my amps just gonna blow I don't get me more juice.'

A middle-aged woman in a flowered pant suit thrust herself forward. 'Mr Conti. *Please*. Your wife assured me that she had twenty matching vases which I need *des*perately if the miniature daisy arrangements are to be ready in time.'

A courtly Italian man carrying a violin case inquired in pained tones. 'Where is our room? The Zancussi Trio *always* has a room.'

'Christ!' exclaimed Ross. 'Lina. Where *is* my wife?'

Lina wiped her tears on the corner of her apron. 'She no come back. She leave everything to me. I quit.' She marched into the kitchen where her two friends stood in a huddle by the back door.

Ross followed her. The wild haired youth following him. The woman in the flowered pant suit and the pained Italian trailed behind.

Already in residence in the kitchen were two gays preparing raw vegetables at the sink. Two bartenders emptying out cardboard boxes of liquor. Another sad-eyed Italian, this one with an accordion. And a blonde teeny-bopper in shorts and a cut-off top, Sony headphones clamped firmly to her ears.

Ross pursued Lina to the door, wondering bitterly if Little S. Shitz had shafted him, and already shown the pictures to Elaine. What else would explain her not being home on the day of their party?

'Did Mrs Conti phone? Leave a message? Anything?' he asked desperately.

'She phone five times,' Lina said sourly. 'But she no come home.'

'Hey-hey-man. About my power?' sing-songed the wild haired youth.

'And my vases?' shrilled the pant suited woman.

'And a room for the Zancussi Trio?' sighed the melancholy Italian, determined not to be left out.

'Fuck off!' Ross screamed, losing control.

'Hey-hey-man, back down,' said the youth, holding up a steadying hand.

'Really!!' huffed the woman.

'Mama mia! Americanos!' The Italian shook his head sadly.

At that point the phone rang. Ross picked it up. 'Yes?' he yelled. And then listened in disgusted silence. A few moments later he slammed the phone down and without so much as a glance at any of the assorted injustice collectors stalked out of the house.

* * *

Oliver Easterne combed his sparse sandy hair first this way and then the other, but no amount of primping could conceal the fact that he was most definitely going bald. He had recently showered, but the effort of trying to organize his hair had caused pools of sweat to form under his arms.

The phone began to ring, but he did not bother to grab for it as he usually did. Let the staff get it. They could do *something* for the thousand bucks he shelled out every week.

Should he take another shower?

It might screw up his hair.

He could put on a hair net.

A sharp spasm across his stomach made him wince with pain. Bleeding ulcers, as if having thinning hair was not enough. And on top of everything else – haemorrhoids. At least they weren't bleeding. But they soon might be if he had any more aggravation with *Street People*.

Neil Gray was a pain in the neck – but then what director wasn't?

Montana Gray was a pain in the neck – but then what writer wasn't?

George Lancaster was a pain in the neck – but then what actor wasn't?

Oliver hated talent. But Oliver needed talent. Because all he was capable of doing was The Deal.

As a producer he was a legend in his own lifetime. Not as a great producer – but as a sensational dealmaker. Oh, the deals he had made! The scams he had pulled! The flops he had put up there on the silver screen.

Not that flops affected Oliver. Before the movie was even in production he had stashed away what he considered was rightfully his. The budget on an Oliver Easterne film always had that little extra bit – or a large bit – depending on what schmucks were putting up the money. And if the original budget didn't suit – well getting out two budgets wasn't against the law – not if you weren't caught it wasn't. And Oliver Easterne knew every trick there was to know.

He sniffed cautiously under one arm, and decided another shower was definitely going to be necessary.

On with the hairnet, off with the bathrobe.

Tonight, at the Contis' party, he would kiss ass. He would brown-nose his way from room to room. Montana, Neil, George, they would all feel the warmth of his sincerity. And he would enjoy doing it, because eventually he knew who would be top of the heap. Once the movie was made, it was his – and he could tell them all to go fuck themselves.

Total control for Neil and Montana my ass, he thought. They could whistle for it. He had tricks Houdini never knew!

Now, if he could only track down the girl from the beach . . . make her a star . . . sign her to a personal contract . . .

He spotted a dirty mark on the mirrored wall. Diligently he began to rub at it with a Kleenex. His stomach twinged again. Being a movie mogul was not all laughs.

* * *

They were in Angel's tiny apartment which smelled of Lysol and was impeccably clean and neat.

'I have nothing to wear,' she said stubbornly.

'Something simple . . .' Koko mused, rifling through her closet. 'Simple yet tasteful. Every bitch in town will be done up like Zsa Zsa at Christmas. I want you to stand out like a single rose at a bar mitzvah.'

'What's a bar mitzvah?'

He shot her a disbelieving look. 'Sometimes you go too far.' Then he pulled a black cotton ruffled skirt off a hanger, held it against her and said, 'Hmmmm . . . I like. What can we find to go with it?'

She shook her head. 'Koko . . . please . . . I don't even *know* Mrs Liderman . . .'

'Dreamheart, don't expect to spend the evening with her. Every stud in Hollywood will take one look at you and—'

Angel was not conceited, yet she knew the effect she had on

men. 'That's just it,' she wailed, 'they'll all be coming on to me with their phony lines. I'm *married*, Koko, I—'

Now it was his turn to interrupt. 'I never pry, Angel, dear. But I do know that married or not your husband has done something to you that has hurt you a great deal. You just want to shut yourself away and be miserable. Well, being miserable never helped anyone. I'm not telling you to go out and jump into bed with every would-be Warren Beatty that approaches you. All I'm saying is get out and enjoy the attention. You'll feel much better for it.'

She wondered how he knew so much. In just a few words he had managed to sum up her situation exactly. And he was probably right, getting out *would* be good for her. After all, it wasn't every day she got invited to a big Hollywood party.

'I'll go,' she said softly.

He was busy inspecting her blouses. 'What?' he asked vaguely.

'I said I'll go,' she repeated firmly.

A pleased smile spread across his aquiline features. 'Of course you will, dreamheart. There was never any doubt.'

* * *

Buddy had the apartment to himself while he prepared for the party. It was a bummer – having to escort Frances Cavendish. On the other hand it was a definite plus to be going at all.

He didn't know what to wear. Frances Cavendish's remark about his clothes had pissed him off. What did she know anyway? She'd probably never even heard of Armani. And wearing Armani was chic – any fool knew that.

With Randy safely out of the apartment he checked out his closet, found a shirt he liked, and tried it on. It was too narrow across the chest, so he discarded it.

He wondered if Montana Gray would be at the party, and if she was how should he come on? 'Hey – uh – listen, if I don't hear anything by Monday I'm gonna have to sign for a movie over at Universal.' Sounded good to him.

A sharp buzz at the door interrupted his train of thought.

Shelly stood on the threshold. 'Where have you been?' she demanded. 'I thought you were coming right back after seeing Frances Cavendish?' She walked uninvited into the apartment and threw herself down on the bed.

He could see she was stoned. Why had he ever gotten involved? He didn't want to go back to the kind of life he had lived before Hawaii, before Angel . . .

'I've got a job,' he said quietly. 'I'll be able to pay you back the money I owe you.'

'When?' she yelled.

'Soon.'

'Screw soon. I want it now. Why don't you go out an' score a few tricks? You don't remember *me*, Buddy, but I knew *you* when you were one of Gladrags' studs. We even worked together one time. How does it feel fucking old ladies for a living?'

He hit her across the face.

She laughed.

He grabbed her and half-pushed half-carried her to the door.

'Hustler!' she screamed. 'Hooker! *Pimp*!'

He gave her a final shove and shut the door on her hysterical yelling.

A sour feeling spread across his gut.

Stoned little tramp.

Stoned little tramp telling the truth.

Jesus. When was it going to happen for him? When was something in his life going to go right?

* * *

By the time Montana got back from the beach it was late afternoon. She felt exhilarated, like a kid who's played hooky from school. She didn't bother going to the office, instead she drove straight home, washed her long black hair and showered the sand and sea from her body. Then, wrapped in a white bathrobe, she called Inga to see what she had missed.

'Nothing much,' said her secretary. 'Mr Gray called around three and said to tell you something came up and he'd meet you at the party tonight.'

'Where is he?'

'He didn't say.'

Now Neil didn't even bother coming home any more. She was tempted not to go to the party. But then she figured George Lancaster would think he'd scared her off, and if she was to make her presence felt it had to be right from the beginning. She didn't want him to feel that he could do what he wanted with her script. She intended to be on the location every single day. Mr. Lancaster was just going to have to accept the fact that every woman did not fall at his feet in a faint.

She put an Al Green tape on the stereo and decided that her look for the party should be strong and noticeable. Something George Macho-Man Lancaster wouldn't forget in a hurry.

* * *

Ensconced in Bungalow Nine at the Beverly Hills Hotel, Pamela London lay on a folding massage table and enjoyed the firm masculine fingers manipulating her flesh.

'I heard you were good,' she said languidly. 'But you're *very* good.'

'Um . . . thanks, Mrs Lancaster,' drawled Ron Gordino. 'I usually send one of my boys, but when Karen told me it was . . . um . . . for you, I decided to come myself.'

'Never send a boy to do a man's job!' said Pamela coyly.

'I wouldn't . . . um . . . dream of it, Mrs Lancaster.'

'Don't call me that. Miz London will do.'

How about Pamela? he thought. I'm sure as heck not

calling you Mrs Lancaster *or* Miz London at the party tonight. Elaine had come through with her promise and invited him.

She groaned as he dug his fingers into the spare tyre around her waist. She wasn't doing too badly for an old broad, she had to be at least fifty-five. But then, when you are the third richest woman in America you can afford to keep in shape.

He wondered what would happen if he gave her his 'special'. Would she, like all the other Beverly Hills matrons, fall for his special? Most of them were so easy . . . Get them on the table . . . out of their jewellery and clothes . . . take away the labels . . . A little pressure here – a little pressure there – and they were his.

Just as he was deciding whether to make a move or not George Lancaster breezed noisily in.

He ignored Ron, slapped Pamela resoundingly on her almost bare ass, and said, 'How's it going you old bat?'

She laughed hoarsely. 'Not so bad frog-face.'

'Getting all dolled up for the party.'

'I suppose we *do* have to go. I don't even know these Conti people.'

'So what? As long as they're paying. If we don't like it we can take a group on to Chasens.'

'Good idea.'

'Hey, you,' said George, acknowledging Ron Gordino at last. 'When you've finished with the heifer you can do me.'

* * *

Gina Germaine was perfumed, powdered and coiffeured to perfection. She was, however, not yet dressed for the party. She wore a flimsy negligee with black undergarments – a plunge bra, bikini panties, and sheer black stockings attached to a lacy garter belt.

Gina Germaine employed three live-in maids, but when the doorbell rang she answered it herself, having dismissed all three for the night.

'Hello, Neil,' she murmured softly. 'You look very elegant.'

He had changed at the office into a plum coloured smoking jacket, black silk turtle neck and black pants. He was all set for the party.

'Thank you,' he said curtly trying to ignore the fact that she was half naked. 'Do you have the tape?'

'I most certainly do,' she replied, all injured innocence. 'A deal is a deal is a deal, isn't it?'

She turned and led the way into an overdecorated pink living room.

'I can't stay, Gina. I don't want to be late. Just give me the tape.'

'How about a drinkie?' She handed him a bourbon mixed with ice in a crystal glass. 'Isn't this your pleasure?'

He accepted the drink automatically, forgetting the three or was it four he had already consumed since five o'clock.

'I'm so excited we've signed the contract,' she cooed. 'How long before we can – you know – let it slip out?'

He frowned. 'We cannot let it slip out. Not at all. To anyone. You do understand that, don't you?'

'It turns me on when you're forceful,' she purred.

'From now on my dear, we are just actor and director.'

'Actress,' she corrected.

'Actress,' he conceded. 'Where's the tape?'

'Come.' She took him by the hand, enveloping him in clouds of Tatyiana.

He hoped the sweet perfume wouldn't cling to his clothes.

'This is my games room,' she announced, leading him into a large room where every inch of wall space was covered with framed magazine covers of herself. The rest of the room housed everything from a pin-ball machine to the latest in video games. 'I love to play,' she added, somewhat unnecessarily.

'The tape, Gina.'

'Coming up.' She pressed a switch and before he could object there he was in living colour on her giant video screen.

Bare assed and humping the second most popular blonde in America. 'I figured you'd want to *see* it,' she explained sweetly. 'After all, you'd hardly want to take it home and run it for Montana, would you?'

Indeed he would not. He took a gulp of bourbon, sat down and considered the action on the screen from a professional point of view. Bad camera angle, you couldn't see her – Oh God, yes you could, she had moved around until those two great upstanding globes of flesh were filling the screen.

He felt the erection in his pants and silently cursed the inevitable.

On screen she heaved and panted while he slavered over her.

Off screen she threw off her negligee, stepped out of her panties and sat astride him.

One more time.

The last time.

He didn't know how right he was.

* * *

Sadie La Salle left her office two hours earlier than she usually did. Miko, her Japanese chauffeur, held open the door of her black Rolls Royce, and she sank gratefully into the luxurious leather seat and adjusted the air-conditioning to its highest point.

'Home, madam?' Miko inquired.

'Yes please.'

Home was in the exclusive Hills of Beverly. Home had a long winding driveway. Home was a mansion to rival those of the stars she represented. Home was never home without Ross Conti.

Damn! Damn! Damn! Twenty-six years since they were together, and still she thought about him.

Unseeingly she gazed out of the black tinted windows as the Rolls sped majestically along Rodeo Drive. Tonight she was going to his house. *The bastard.* Tonight she would see where he lived. She would make polite conversation with his wife. *Oh, how I hate you Ross Conti.* She would even talk to him.

Twenty-six years. She was a different person. Important, respected, some said even feared. She wore designer clothes, spent a full day a week at Elizabeth Arden, and wore jewellery from Cartier.

Oh sure she had seen him over the years. Hollywood. Such a small community. It was inevitable that they would be invited to the same parties and events. Once he had even suggested she handle him again. *Who did the son of a bitch think he was?* Did he imagine he could walk back into her life as a client and that she would just forget about the past? She had given him cold words and ignored him ever since.

The good times were always in her memory. She remembered every detail.

The first time she ever set eyes on Ross in Schwab's. Ohhh gorgeous, she had thought, and then when he had ambled over like a blond bronzed God and bummed a coffee she could not believe her luck.

The first time they made love. His hands on her breasts . . . His hardness deep inside her . . . His tongue buried between her legs . . .

The trip to New York to show him off on *The Tonight Show.* And the thrill when it all worked. Riding through Central Park in an open buggy. Admiring his billboard in Times Square. Eating hotdogs on Fifth Avenue.

And sex, sex, sex. Under the shower. In his dressing room at NBC. On the back seat of a cab. Pressed up against the wall of the hotel elevator. Ross was insatiable, and she loved it.

Twenty-six years later she could still feel his hands on her breasts. 'I'm a tit man,' he used to say. 'And baby, you've got the best.'

Until something better came along. Something that was packaged a lot more prettily than she was. And he just walked out of her life without a care in the world and not so much as a thank you.

The pain was still with her. The loss. The humiliating rage.

She stared sightlessly from the car as it glided across Sunset.

There had only been one other man since Ross and he didn't count. It wasn't for lack of opportunity. She was a star in her own way, and many a man had tried to pitch his way into her bed. She wasn't beautiful, not even pretty, but once she began to climb towards the pinnacle of success – Oh boy! Did they come running.

Very occasionally she went to bed with a woman. Sex with another female was not a threat, more a diversion. And Sadie called the shots. She liked that.

Her work became her passion. It was almost enough. Success can be very rewarding.

But now enough time had passed . . . too long in fact, and she wanted revenge for twenty-six years. And tonight she would have it.

* * *

At approximately four fifty-five Ross arrived at the department store.

At approximately ten minutes past five he left with Elaine by his side.

They both got into the Corniche tight-lipped and silent. Without a word being exchanged they endured the ride home.

Outside the house Elaine said coldly, 'It was all a mistake you know.' *You bastard, you think I stole the bracelet.*

Ross nodded. 'Anyone can make a mistake,' he said reasonably. *Stupid dumb broad. Do it if you must – but don't get caught.*

They entered the house. The wild-haired youth had blown a fuse. The pant suited woman was having hysterics. The sad-eyed Italians were trying to flirt with the pubescent teeny bopper who was dancing across the living room – oblivious to everything – earphones clamped firmly in place. The two gays were making faces as they prepared a gaucomole dip while observing the action. The two bartenders were lolling on a couch smoking grass; and Lina and her friends were stationed by the kitchen door ready to make a fast exit.

'Elaine, sweetheart,' said Ross. 'I'm going to take a shower. You wanted this party, and now it's all yours.'

Chapter Thirty-Two

Barstow, California, was hot. An oppressive heat with no cooling breeze to bring relief.

Deke checked into a cheap motel. He lay on a hard mattress in a small dusty room and gazed at the ceiling. A noisy fan whirred monotonously, while several flies buzzed around searching for escape. In the room next door a television blared, hardly drowning the sounds of a woman yelling in anger.

He had removed his boots, pants and shirt. On the table beside the bed he had placed his money, the hunting knife he always carried, and the piece of paper with the name and address written on it. The same paper that had been handed to him in Philadelphia while the three of them laughed . . . three pigs . . . laughing at him . . . laughing at The Keeper Of The Order.

Only he hadn't been The Keeper Of The Order then . . . No . . . Before striking out he was just plain Deke Andrews . . . A nobody . . . And their laughter had been a sign . . . Yes, a signal to control the vermin.

A shudder shook his body, and he drew his knees up to his stomach and hugged himself tightly. It would have been nice if Joey could have shared some of his triumphs . . .

* * *

Joey was wearing a red mini skirt, white plastic boots, a cheap pink blouse, and her usual alarming amount of smeared make-up.

Deke stared at her. To him she was beautiful, but he knew what his parents would think. They watched television constantly and called all women whores.

'Every one of those Hollywood starlets is a prostitute,' his mother would say.

'They sleep their way up the ladder,' his father would agree. But neither of them ever made any attempt to switch channels or turn off the set.

Deke never watched television with them. He preferred to be in his own room where he could lie on the bed and think about Joey and how he could safely bring her home.

There was much to consider. He wanted to marry her, but he didn't want to upset his mother.

All the time he tried to show her that he cared, but whatever he did was never good enough. 'One day you'll run off and leave your poor mother who went through such pain to have you,' she often told him. 'It'll kill me, you know.'

He always denied that he would.

'Maybe, maybe not,' she would say, adding craftily, 'If you stay, one day everything we have will be yours. Not much I know, the house, the car, your father has a nest-egg . . .' She always trailed off at that point, as if the nest-egg was too exciting to discuss.

He wondered how much there was. His father worked hard. Neither of them smoked or drank. Their only luxury was the colour television set.

Sometimes he lay in bed and fantasized about the two of them being killed in a car crash or a fire. Then everything would be his. The house, the car, the nest-egg . . . And nobody to nag him . . . make him feel small and unimportant and guilty . . .

Then Joey came into his life. For months he had kept her a secret. But eventually he had got up the courage to tell his mother. Or rather Joey forced his hand.

'I want to bring a . . . a . . . girl h . . . home,' he stammered one day.

Now he stared at Joey in her colourful outfit with her orange spiked hair. And he knew his mother would never approve.

'We ready, big boy?' she asked, cocking her head to one side.

He nodded.

She winked happily. 'Well then, it's up an' at 'em – ain't it?'

* * *

'You dirty stinkin' piece a crap!' screamed the woman in the room next door.

There was the sound of flesh being struck, and a child began to wail.

Were they calling for him? Was he being summoned?

He sat up abruptly, reached for his knife, fingered the sharp blade.

Before he could decide what to do the noise ceased. The Keeper Of The Order could rest. He was not needed. Not for now, anyway . .

Chapter Thirty-Three

A line of cars snaked their way up the Contis' circular driveway where female and male valets wearing white T-shirts emblazoned with 'Superjock' waited to take control of the parade of Cadillacs, Lincolns, De Loreans, Rolls Royces, Porsches, Ferraris, Bentleys, Mercedes and Excaliburs.

Clustered at the bottom of the drive were six or seven paparazzi, cameras at the ready, eyes alert for the real celebrities – not the producers, money-men, super-agents and society flash. They wanted the real thing, the International Celebrity with the face that was recognizable from China to Chile.

They were rewarded by a smiling Burt Reynolds, followed closely by Rod Stewart and his striking wife, Alana. The paparazzi snapped happily away.

Inside the house all was under control. Elaine, fortified by two Valium and her new seventeen hundred dollar Galanos dress, greeted her guests as though she did not have a care in the world. She smiled, she hugged, she exchanged kisses and 'Don't you look wonderfuls' with everyone. She introduced people who had not met, she summoned waiters with a mere flick of her wrist, she was charming, witty, gracious, in command. Who would have ever dreamt that only a short time before the first guest arrived she had been a raving screaming wreck?

Ross – the unfaithful swine – had vanished into the shower while she alone had attempted to create calm and organization from total chaos. She had done it. Etta from the Bronx had sprung into action. And now Elaine from Beverly Hills was taking the bows.

It had not been easy dealing with three recalcitrant maids, two stoned bartenders, a hysterical flower arranger, two temperamental members of the Zancussi Trio, and a hyped up ex-member of a rock group who gave great live disco, plus his zonked little girlfriend.

Elaine had sorted that lot out just in time – for more people had begun to arrive. The caterers. Security. Parking valets. The third member of the Zancussi Trio. The second member of the live disco twosome – another freak.

Finally, with only fifteen minutes to go before the party officially commenced, she had locked herself in her dressing room and forced herself to get ready in a hurry. She would have liked the luxury of more time – but it was amazing what one could do when one had to. She had emerged triumphant, ready to greet the first guest – Sammy Cahn who had promised to sing one of his famous parodies – this time on George Lancaster.

Now time had passed and the guests of honour had not yet arrived, nor had Sadie La Salle. But Bibi and Adam Sutton were making a spectacular entrance, trailed by the ever present Wolfie Schweicker. Bibi looked stunning in a black silk Adolfo dress, and breathtaking Cartier emeralds. Adam was handsome and dignified as usual. Elaine hurried forward to welcome them.

* * *

Koko had a way with make-up that enhanced even Angel's beauty.

'I didn't know you were so clever!' she exclaimed, gazing at her reflection in the mirror.

'With you – dreamheart – it's easy.'

She looked exquisite. He had pulled the front of her hair up and away from her face, leaving the rest to fall softly past her shoulders. He had flattered her with touches of gold scattered over her flawless skin. There was gold on her cheekbones, eyelids, even a touch on her lips. Her eyes he had emphasized with thick brown mascara on her long lashes, and pink and bronze shadow blended round the brow-bone. The effect was startling yet subtle.

She wore the black skirt he had chosen with a simple white off-the-shoulder blouse, and a white lace choker he had found.

'Hmmm . . .' He stood back to survey her. 'Divine!'

The buzzer rang. It was Mrs Liderman's chauffeur.

'I'm so nervous,' she fluttered. 'Are you sure I should be going?'

He kissed her warmly on both cheeks. 'Have a wonderful time, dreamheart. Have a ball for *both* of us.'

* * *

'The hors d'oeuvres, Lina,' Elaine hissed through the kitchen door. 'They must come out faster. See to it.'

Lina nodded. She had not, as threatened, walked. Instead she and her friends had changed into clean black dresses and frilled white aprons, and were happily helping out. When Mrs Conti was home things ran smoothly and Lina did not have to take responsibility for anything. That was the way she liked it. Besides, rumour had it that Erik Estrada was an expected guest, and the very sound of his name brought tears to her eyes.

Elaine kissed Bridget and David Hedison, waved at Dyan Cannon, squeezed Ryan O'Neal's hand, and moved in the direction of Sadie La Salle who had just walked through the door. Ross was nowhere in sight. Last seen talking to Adam Sutton and Roger Moore, he had now vanished.

'Damn!' she muttered. He was never around at the right moment. 'Hello, Sadie,' she gushed. 'Don't you look lovely. Do come in, I'm sure you must know absolutely everyone.'

* * *

'You're late, Buddy,' Frances Cavendish said crisply, answering the door of her Spanish hacienda, then slamming it shut behind her. 'Good grief! Is that your car?' She glanced at his ancient Pontiac parked in the street. 'We can't possibly arrive in *that*.'

'Why not?' he asked truculently.

'My God, dear. Isn't it obvious?'

'It's good enough for me, Francie.'

'Don't call me Francie,' she snapped. 'We'll take *my* car. Wait here, I'll get the keys.'

She marched back inside her house while he moodily marked time on the sidewalk.

She emerged shortly. She was wearing a wide-shouldered velvet pant suit that smelled faintly of mothballs, and for the occasion she had dug out her diamanté trimmed glasses.

He wondered if she had ever been married. Rumour had her listed as a dyke, but no little nymphet starlet had ever complained of her demanding a free pass to pussy-land.

She handed him the keys to what turned out to be a very large, very old Mercedes, and they set off.

* * *

'This is Angel,' announced Mrs Liderman to anyone who would listen. 'She psyched my Frowie into coming back to me. Isn't that clever of her?'

'Your what?' inquired a tall thin man who looked like he had a perpetual bad smell under his nose.

'My Frowie. My poodle.'

Mrs Liderman in purple taffeta was positively rattling with huge diamonds. They made Bibi Sutton's emeralds look ordinary.

'Who that woman?' Bibi demanded jealously.

'I don't know,' replied Elaine. 'She must be from Pamela's list.'

'And where *are* George and Pamela?' Bibi shook her head disparagingly. 'They come too late, sweetie. The guests of honour should arrive first.'

How well Elaine knew it, she did not need Bibi to tell her. 'They're on their way,' she said testily, hoping desperately that indeed they were.

* * *

Montana zoomed her Volkswagen up the driveway and waited while the silver stretch Cadillac limo in front of her disgorged its passengers. She couldn't have timed it better – or worse. George Lancaster and Pamela London were alighting from the Cadillac.

Well, she certainly wasn't going to skulk in her car waiting for them to get inside. Quickly she got out of the VW and walked over to Macho-man and Richo-wife.

'How's it going, George?' she asked heartily. 'I'm parched. Think you can get me a drink?'

* * *

The Zancussi Trio began to play tasteful background music at precisely eight o'clock. Ross, who had been doing a pretty good job of circulating, took the opportunity to sneak into the busy kitchen and stuff his mouth with canapes.

Elaine was not far behind. 'Where have you been?' she hissed. 'Pamela and George just arrived, and Sadie La Salle has been here twenty minutes. Is it too much trouble for you to put yourself out? Or do you just intend to stay in the kitchen all night?'

'I've been talking to the de Cordovas, the Lazars, and the Wilders. What do you want from me – blood?' he said defensively.

'I want you to greet the guests of honour – if it's not too much trouble of course.'

They glared at each other. Both trying to concentrate on the party. Both seething with their own personal thoughts.

'Right,' said Ross at last. 'I'll go kiss ass. If you cruise the room, Elaine, maybe you can rip off a purse or two.'

* * *

'And this is Angel,' said Mrs Liderman to Pamela London. 'She saved Frowie.'

'Christ, Essie,' sighed Pamela. 'You still got that god-awful canine – the one that peed all over my apartment in New York?'

'Frowie is thirteen years old,' Mrs Liderman said proudly. 'In human years that's ninety-one. For ninety-one years of age she's like a young pup.'

Pamela inspected Angel. The girl was far too beautiful, although she didn't look like the usual predatory starlet. 'And how did you save Frowie?' she asked mildly. 'Because I don't know, dear, whether you should be rewarded or shot. That dog is a spoiled little pest who *ruined* one of my Persian rugs.'

'Pamela!' exclaimed Mrs Liderman affectionately.

The two women hugged. They had known each other since college days, and since Essie Liderman was almost as rich as Pamela, their friendship had survived. The very rich are only really comfortable with the very rich. A fact of life that both ladies had learned, although Essie enjoyed spreading it around more than Pamela.

Angel was dazzled. By the house. The people. The atmosphere. *She*, Angel Hudson, was at a REAL HOLLYWOOD PARTY. And there were stars there. She spotted James Caan, and Elliott Gould, and Liza Minnelli, and Richard Gere. RICHARD GERE!! She could die now and feel perfectly satisfied.

If only Buddy were here to share it with her.

Buddy.

She frowned. He was not the man she had thought he was, nor the man she had married, and now she must forget him.

Essie and Pamela were reminiscing, oblivious to her presence. She looked around in awe.

'He-llo,' said an impressed male voice. 'And where have *I* been hiding all your life?'

* * *

'I should never have turned down *Raging Bull*,' said the actor in the lizard skin boots. 'It was a key career mistake.'

'He pays me, I think it turns him on,' said the redhead in the mink-trimmed cape.

'I buy them dresses, take them to Acapulco – I have to give them head too?' asked an outraged stud.

Snatches of conversation as Montana made her way across the room to the bar. She looked incredibly striking. Six feet tall in white silk jodhpurs tucked into knee-high boots. A white silk blouse unbuttoned to the waist, and a long white leather vest fringed with Indian beads. Her jet hair was braided and decorated with beads and fringes. Around her neck she wore a solid silver choker studded with turquoise and thin silver hoops hung from her ears.

Neil was not yet at the party to appreciate her look. But Oliver Easterne looked twice when he saw her, and actually complimented her original style. Coming from Oliver she wasn't sure whether to be flattered or upset.

What a bunch of phonies, she thought, looking around. I had more fun at the beach today than they'll have in a lifetime.

She wasn't sure, but she thought she spotted Neil's ex-wife. Pretty, and blonde. Groomed, and plasticized. The perfect Beverly Hills look.

Maralee must have felt Montana staring, for she turned and for a moment their eyes met.

* * *

'Sadie, I'm so glad you could come, it means a lot to me . . .' Direct stare. 'You know that, don't you?'

Sadie felt her stomach knot as it did whenever she saw him. 'Ross,' she said carefully. 'It's nice to be here.'

He pushed for a reaction. 'Just nice?'

She met his gaze steadily. 'I like your house.'

'Not bad, is it.' He leaned close. 'You know – *you* are looking sensational.'

'Thank you,' she said, edging away. She needed another drink before dealing with him.

'My little Sadie, you really made it didn't you?'

Oh God! He was as corny as ever. She backed away further, and with relief saw a friend approaching. 'Do you know Emile Riley?' she asked quickly.

'Yes, sure. Emile, nice to see you.'

'You too, Ross,' replied Emile. 'What a magnificent turn out. *Love* the flower arrangements. I must congratulate Elaine, where is she?'

Sadie quickly took his arm. 'Let's go and find her. We'll see you later, Ross.'

Famous eyes still projecting. 'You can bet on that.'

He watched her cross the room. Powerful Sadie La Salle, the hottest agent in town. She had been his for a moment – he was sure of it. And the evening was only just beginning.

Karen appeared at his side. 'I want to talk to *you*.'

She wore gold lamé harem pyjamas which did nothing to conceal her amazing nipples through the thin silky material. He had a strong impulse to touch them, but controlled himself.

'Welcome to the house of Conti,' he said.

'Welcome my ass. Did you know Elaine phoned me today looking for *you*?'

'Me?'

'Yes, you.'

'Why me?'

'If I knew would I be asking?'

He frowned. 'Something's going on. Some asshole came up

to me on Rodeo Drive today and thrust some pictures in my face.'

'What pictures?'

'Pictures of us. In bed.'

'Whaaaat?'

'Sweetie. Why you and Karen so close together? Naughty, naughty. I tell Elaine!' Bibi Sutton was joking of course, but they leapt apart like scalded cats.

Wolfie Schweicker was not far behind, resplendent in a velvet suit, ruffled shirt, and embroidered evening slippers. His hair, recently permed, framed a round face with small bitter eyes, a snub nose, fleshy lips and ferret-like teeth. Some said he resembled a feisty goldfish.

'It's a *very* good party, Ross. Bibi and I were just saying.'

'Thanks, Wolfie.'

'Not at all. Bibi and I always give praise where praise is due.'

'That's nice.' Ross couldn't stand the man. He wondered how mild mannered Adam Sutton even allowed him in the house.

Karen joined in the conversation. 'Great dress, Bibi.'

'Yes? You think? It nothing darling.'

'Nothing – my ass,' said Karen. 'It has to have set old Adam back at least two grand. If you got it, Bibi, flaunt it.'

'Darling, you so vulgar.'

'I'm my father's daughter – and I don't have to tell *you* what he's like, huh, Bibi?'

* * *

What was the quickest way to dump Frances Cavendish?

Good question.

Buddy pondered the problem as he checked out the party. Talk about hitting the action. He was moving with the stars, man. The place was jammed.

'If you're thinking of cruising the room, forget it,' said Frances acidly, as if reading his mind.

'Cruising. Who's cruising?' he said indignantly.

'Just a warning.'

'Am I allowed to go to the bathroom?'

'Now? We just got here.'

'What d'you want me to do – piss on my shoes?'

'Make it fast. I didn't bring you with me so that I could stand around on my own.'

He clicked his heels together. 'Yes, *ma'am.*'

* * *

'Hello, Elaine.'

'Hello, Ron.'

Why had she ever invited him. He looked quite out of place dressed.

'This is some . . . um . . . gathering,' he drawled.

'Thank you.'

'I'd sure like to meet Clint Eastwood.'

Who wouldn't? Only *she* wasn't going to take him by the hand and introduce him.

'Excuse me, Ron. I have a million things to do.'

'Stay loose, Elaine. Don't let the tension get to you. Did you take those vitamins I recommended?'

She nodded brusquely. He reminded her of a large shaggy dog. How come in the privacy of his office she had never noticed the moles all over his face, and the coarse straw coloured hair growing out of his ears and nose?

How could you have, Elaine?

Any cock in a storm!

* * *

'. . . she's like a Barbie doll – you wind her up and she buys new clothes . . .'

'. . . he'd fuck a bush if he thought it would invest . . .'

Buddy weaved his way through the room. He felt higher

than he had in a long time. This was where he belonged, and this is where he would be – permanently – if only he got the part in *Street People.*

He smiled at Ann-Margret and she smiled back. He said, 'How 'r'you doin'?' to Michael Caine and got a friendly reply. Shit! Was he flying!

And then he saw her. Angel. *His* Angel. And he couldn't believe it, but she was there.

* * *

Oliver Easterne engaged in a stilted conversation with Montana. Their dislike of each other was mutual but the movie bound them together.

'Where's Neil?' Oliver asked, glancing at his watch.

'I thought *you* might know,' replied Montana. 'He had a meeting. He's supposed to see me here.'

Oliver was sweating, and he had a horrible feeling that he could smell it – in spite of two very thorough showers. 'Excuse me,' he said. 'I have to go to the men's room.'

He shut himself in the guest bathroom and ripped off his jacket and shirt. A quick sniff revealed the fact that he did indeed stink. Hastily he grabbed the cake of soap lying in a silver soap dish and lathered his offending armpits. Then he lowered his pants and swooped a soapy hand under his jockeys – just in case. He had not bothered to check the closed toilet and when Pamela London emerged they stared at each other in shock.

'What *are* you doing?' inquired Pamela in piercing tones. She had no idea who he was.

He failed to recognize the wife of the soon-to-be star of his movie. 'Fucking a goat,' he said swiftly. 'Why don't you mind your own business?'

* * *

'Angel?'

'Buddy?'

For one moment they nearly fell into each other's arms. Then Angel's face clouded over, remembering her phone conversation with Shelly. And Buddy scowled, remembering Angel's message via Shelly.

'What are you doing here?' they said in unison.

And the half-assed star of a television sit-com who had spent the previous half hour coming on to Angel put a proprietary hand on her arm and said, 'Everything all right, my lovely?'

My lovely!! Buddy wanted to smash his capped teeth right through the back of his obvious hairpiece.

'Fine, thank you,' she said politely.

'Uh, listen . . . maybe we can talk,' said Buddy quickly.

'I don't know . . .'

'What d'you mean – you don't know?'

'Well, I—'

'The lady means she doesn't know,' said Mr Sit-com. 'So, why don't you check back later, sport?'

'Why don't *you* butt out, sport?'

'Now look here—'

They were interrupted by a half-naked Oliver Easterne pursued by a madder than hell Pamela London emerging from the guest bathroom.

'Don't you *dare* talk to me like that – you dirty little man!' yelled Pamela, wielding a hair brush.

'What's the matter with you – you menopausal old bag. Get away from me – you're fucking nuts!'

'What's going on?' boomed George Lancaster, breaking away from a group of sycophants.

'This pathetic man was jerking off while I was in the toilet,' announced Pamela in ringing tones.

'This *cunt* is crazy,' screamed Oliver in a fury.

'This *cunt* is my wife,' announced George Lancaster. 'Darling, have you met Oliver Easterne, my producer?'

Chapter Thirty-Four

There's no fool like an old fool . . .

Or a young fool . . .

Or a middle aged fool . . .

Clichés.

Gina Germaine was a cliché. She was also a hot, blonde, sexy, big breasted WONDERFUL LAY.

I am lost in her juices, thought Neil Gray. I have no defence to this case.

What kind of fool am I?

Who can I turn to?

Why think of Newly/Bricusse songs at a time like this? A time when America's blonde of the year is sitting on my stiff organ, her private parts churning out an international message of lust.

Lustful thought.

The first woman I ever bedded was wearing black stockings and a suspender belt. Her name was Ethel and she hailed from Scotland. I was fifteen at the time and she was twenty-three. She had hairy legs and a predilection for cunnilingus.

Montana would never wear a garter belt as the Americans so charmingly called it. She would laugh in his face if he ever mentioned that it excited him.

Milky white thighs, enclosed, encased. A thick bush in the centre of the frame.

Oh God!

Gina shifted her weight, withdrew.

'I'm not ready,' he objected.

'I know,' she soothed. 'But I've got a surprise for you.'

'Not another hidden camera?' he groaned.

'Don't worry. This is our celebration, and I want to make it a night to remember.'

'The party—' he said thickly, watching Gina walk towards the door. He wanted her to come back and finish off what she had started. It was either that or someone would have to douse his ardour with a bucket of cold water.

'We'll go to the party,' she crooned. 'Eventually.'

He lay back in the chair and waited.

There's no fool like an old fool . . . a young fool . . . a middle aged fool . . .

The second woman he bedded was a Piccadilly prostitute. She charged him five pounds and gave him the clap. He was sixteen. She did not wear a suspender belt.

Suddenly there were two of them.

Gina. Voluptuous. Wanton. The all American sex goddess.

And beside her a slightly built Eurasian female. Dark olive skin, black hair that fell like a curtain to the top of her thighs, small breasts, and a tiny waist. She was quite naked apart from a white lace garter belt which emphasized her silky tangle of pubic hair. 'This is Thiou-Ling,' said Gina. 'My present for us. She speaks no English, but she understands. She has been trained in the art of making love since childhood. We shall celebrate our contract, Neil . . . And *then* we shall go to the party . . .'

Chapter Thirty-Five

'Your *what*?' said Oliver in horror, seeing his brilliant casting fade before his very eyes.

'Your *what*?' screamed Pamela. And then she started to laugh, great guffaws which shook her entire body. '*This* is Oliver Easterne,' she gasped between spasms of mirth. 'This . . . this . . . angry little man.'

George started to laugh too. 'Yes, you silly sow. Mustn't insult the producer, he's the one who pays us.'

She was choking with mirth. 'Oh, *he*'s the one!'

Oliver turned his fury and embarrassment into a sickly smile as he attempted to pull his pants up with a vestige of dignity. He knew when to eat shit. And how. 'Mrs Lancaster,' he grovelled. 'Please forgive me. I had no idea . . . Mrs Lancaster, it's such a pleasure to meet you at last. Mrs Lancaster—'

'For God's sake call me Pamela. I think we know each other intimately enough, don't you?'

And with that she collapsed in a further paroxysm of uncontrollable laughter.

* * *

The furor with Pamela London and Oliver Easterne was over, but the sit-com star had not budged from Angel's side.

Buddy tried to ignore him. 'We have to talk,' he said urgently, putting his hand on her arm.

She shied from his touch. 'I . . . I don't think there is anything to say.'

'There's plenty to say.'

'Why don't you just back off, man,' said the sit-com star.

Angel saw the anger building in Buddy, and she quickly said, 'Please, don't cause trouble . . . Maybe we can talk later.'

What was she *doing* to him? What kind of a dumb game was she playing? She was his *wife*. He was her *husband*. 'Now,' he said flatly. He had things to say that couldn't wait.

The sit-com star said, 'Who *is* this creep?'

Before Angel could intervene Buddy swung a wild punch that glanced off the sit-com star's chin who, being a former stunt man, rolled with it and came back with a short tight poke to Buddy's stomach that pulverized him. He bent double with pain, and by the time he could stand straight, Angel and her gallant escort had vanished into another room.

* * *

Maralee Sanderson flicked her paged blonde hair with annoyance. Elaine had warned her she would be inviting Neil and his wife. So where was Neil? And why was Montana strutting all over the place like a deranged Indian? The woman looked ridiculous in all her fringes and braids. How old was she anyway?

It beat Maralee how Neil could ever have married her. She was a freak. Too tall. Too wild-looking. Too everything.

Randy's hand crept up her thigh. She slapped it away like an aggravating fly. Randy was okay in bed – great in fact. But at a party like this he faded into the background. Didn't he *know* anyone? He lacked what her father called 'social strut'. It had never bothered her before, but tonight the way he refused to leave her side bugged her. Maybe Karen and Elaine were right . . . neither of them had said anything . . . but she could tell they didn't approve. You don't marry a man like Neil Gray one day, and go with a man like Randy Felix the next . . . Besides which, she was beginning to suspect that he had no money, and nobody was getting one red cent of her inheritance. No mistake about *that.*

* * *

'The biggest prick I ever knew had the smallest!' exclaimed a soignée middle aged woman in a chic black dress.

'If it cost him a nickel to shit he'd vomit,' said a fast-talking producer.

'Every day she comes to my office, locks the door, gets under the desk and sucks my cock,' said the head of a studio.

Hollywood conversation. Ross had heard it all before. His mind was racing with thoughts of his own. Why had Elaine called Karen looking for him? Had she perhaps seen the pictures? Little S. Shitz wanted ten thousand dollars. If Elaine *had* seen the pictures then the prick could go whistle for it – which he'd probably have to do anyway. There was no way he could come up with ten thousand, he was over extended in every direction as it was. His business manager called him daily demanding a meeting. His business manager would shit himself when the bills for the party started pouring in.

He just had to hope that Sadie La Salle would save his ass and bring him back to the top where he belonged. She had done it once . . .

* * *

Oliver Easterne skirted the room looking for someone to talk to who had not witnessed his humiliation at the hands of George's drag queen wife. What a witch! Even *he* would find it hard sleeping with that, in spite of her millions. Although of course it was a well known fact that Oliver would do anything for money.

He had laughed with the red-headed cooze even though inside he was seething, his ulcer burning, and his haemorrhoids giving him trouble. He would get his own back though. When the movie was finished and there was more money in *his* pocket than in any of theirs.

Oliver had not been in the business as long as he had for nothing.

* * *

Dinner is served. And who sits where? For in Beverly Hills the placement is almost as important as the party itself.

Elaine had spent hours poring over the guest list deciding where to seat everyone. Twenty tables. Twelve people per table. Baccarat crystal. English bone china. Porthault napkins. Daisies, anemones, and freesia arranged in fine Waterford glass holders as a centrepiece to each table. The place cards were engraved – Elaine and Ross Conti at the top, and in fine calligraphy script the name of each guest underneath.

She had seated herself between George Lancaster and Adam Sutton. Ross, she had placed between Sadie La Salle and Pamela London.

After the Pamela/Oliver incident she had raced upstairs and gulped another Valium. By the time she came back down all was at peace. Oliver had apologized. And Pamela and George seemed to find the whole incident uproariously funny. And naturally – when George laughed, the whole world joined in. Elaine sighed with relief.

* * *

Ross watched Sadie approach his table, she certainly looked better in her fifties than she had in her twenties. She was almost slim, almost attractive. He wondered if she still cooked. What a cook! What a fuck! What tits! But she hadn't been right for his image . . .

She sat down.

'It's been a long time,' he said warmly. 'Too long, and you're looking sensational.'

She fixed him with soulful black eyes – her eyes always had been one of her best features. 'You told me that already, Ross.'

'So you look good enough to tell twice – big deal. After all, you and I – we go back forever, don't we?' He leaned confidentially towards her. 'Remember poor old Bernie Leftcovitz? And that night I turned up at your apartment when you were cooking him dinner?'

How could she ever forget? 'Bernie who?'

'Bernie Leftcovitz. You can't have forgotten schmucky Bernie. He was all set to hit you with a proposal. Come on, Sadie, it was the night you and I . . . the first time we . . .' He trailed off and grinned. 'Don't tell me you've forgotten *that.*'

She smiled thinly. 'You know this town – easy come, easy go.'

A waiter hovered with the wine.

'At last!' Pamela London said loudly, as if she had been sitting parched for hours instead of only five minutes. 'Show me the label, waiter, and if it's not a decent Cabernet Sauvignon you can take it back!'

* * *

'Aw – go sleep with your ego!' said a tall redhead to a cruising movie star. She turned to her friend. 'That guy's so out of it he needs a map to find his way home!'

'Don't tell me,' replied her friend. 'He's cheap too. Took me to the ball game and wouldn't even buy me a candy bar 'cos he didn't want to break a large bill!'

Oliver Easterne moved past them and bumped straight into Karen Lancaster. At the same moment he thought he spotted the girl from the beach on her way out to the tented patio with an older woman.

'Excuse me,' he said quickly.

'What's the matter?' Karen asked with a throaty chuckle. 'Got to go to the bathroom again?'

He ignored her and walked outside. The girl was sitting down at a table that included Pamela London. Much as he wanted to grab hold of her and make her a star he was not about to go over with that woman there.

* * *

Montana had no desire to join the other guests. She wasn't hungry, and she had already checked the place cards and found herself stuck between two people she didn't know. On top of that Neil had not yet put in an appearance which really infuriated her. What am I doing here? she thought. I may as well split because this is just not my ball game.

Then she saw Buddy Hudson hovering by the bar. He looked about as pissed off as she felt. Maybe she could bring a smile to his face. She went over and touched him lightly on the arm. 'Surprise. Are you having as much fun as I am?'

Buddy turned around and faced the wild looking female, all braided fringes and jet hair.

'Montana Gray,' she announced, noting his confusion. 'I look a little different out of working hours.'

He whistled softly, relieved that Frances hadn't tracked him down, and delighted to see Montana. 'You can say that again.'

'Friend of the bride or groom?'

'Huh?'

'I figure the Contis are the bride, because they're going to end up getting fucked – not to mention the check for all of this. And the Lancasters are the groom, because they don't give a good goddamn about anyone except themselves.'

He laughed, ready to forget the dull ache in his gut. 'I came with someone. I don't know any of them.'

'It's the best way.' She took a sip of the Pernod and water she was holding, grimaced and said, 'Hate the taste, love the effect.'

He was torn. Continue talking to Montana or try to find Angel. Instinct told him to stay with Montana – while heart told him to follow Angel.

'What's happenin'?' he asked automatically, expecting another bullshit 'we're still interested'.

'I was going to call you tomorrow, after George Lancaster's press conference.' She grinned. 'But since you're here . . .'

Oh shit! Was she going to say what he *thought* she was going to say? All of a sudden his throat was dry. 'Yes?'

'You're Vinnie, kiddo.'

For one wild moment he thought he might piss in his pants. 'Sweet Mick Jagger! Holy shit! I don't believe it!'

He was yelling, but what did it matter?

'Shhh . . .' Montana laughed, enjoying his excitement. 'I haven't appointed you President.'

He was flying high. 'As good as!'

'I'm glad you're pleased.'

'Give me a break – I'm out of my head!' He hugged her. 'You're *sure*? You're not jivin' me?'

'Would I lie?'

'Jeez! I can't believe it.'

'Believe it.'

'I . . . I gotta be dreaming.'

'Buddy! I never had you figured for a farm boy. Calm down. It's only a movie.'

'To you it's a movie. To me – it's my life.'

* * *

Oliver Easterne stories were buzzing from table to table amid much mirth. Angel did not understand the ones she heard – to her way of thinking he sounded sick. She recognized him as the man from the beach. She hoped he did not remember her.

All she could think about was Buddy. *I love you* – she wanted to say. But he had spoiled everything and there was no going back.

Only he looked so handsome tonight . . . And she was carrying his child . . . Perhaps they *should* talk in spite of everything. She felt bad about the sit-com star hitting him. But it was his own fault, he had struck out first.

She sighed, filled with confusion. She wanted Buddy. She didn't want him. Yet she still loved him . . .

'Are you all right?' Kindly Mrs Liderman leaned across the table. 'You look a little pale.'

'I'm fine,' she replied politely. She should, in fact, be having a wonderful time, but Buddy had ruined everything.

A curly haired man in an immaculate white suit sitting on her left leaned across and said in a stoned voice, 'I gotta go work the room – you think it's easy bein' me? Who *are* you, dear?'

He was good looking. But not as good looking as Buddy.

* * *

'. . . use my apartment? Honey, I wouldn't let you use my Kleenex!'

'. . . You know what the bum says to me? He says – don't fuck on my property – you want to screw around do it on a bed someone else paid for . . .'

Elaine gazed around the room at her guests and smiled glassily at George Lancaster. 'Everyone seems to be having a good time, don't they?'

'They sure do. But why have I got an empty seat beside me?' he complained.

Elaine snapped to attention. 'I'm so sorry! Gina was supposed to be sitting there. Have you seen her?'

George leered. 'If I'd seen her I wouldn't forget it. She's the one with the big—'

'Quite,' Elaine said crisply, pushing her chair away from the table. 'Let me see if I can find her. She's probably still inside. I won't be a moment.'

'No problem, little lady.'

She hurried into the house where a straggle of guests were still sitting around. She spotted Montana Gray and some man she didn't know chatting at the bar. Next to them were the Sean Connerys and the Roger Moores deep in conversation. Karen Lancaster and Sharon Richman emerged from the guest bathroom giggling and laughing.

Oh, Karen. I'm not finished with you. In fact, bitch, I haven't even started.

She went to the front door and checked with security. Gina Germaine had not yet arrived.

* * *

'Where *is* Neil?' asked Pamela London in a loud voice. 'I haven't seen him all night.'

Ross, who was trying to concentrate on Sadie La Salle, turned to the real guest of honour. She looked like she was wearing a bright red fright wig – why didn't someone tell her about her hair?

'He's around, isn't he?'

'I haven't seen him, and he's supposed to be sitting next to me.'

Christ, Ross thought. What kind of organization is this? Both guests of honour with an empty seat beside them. Can't Elaine get anything right?

* * *

As soon as Elaine left the table, Bibi slid into action and moved next to George.

'George, sweetie,' she sighed. 'This party nice – but no exclusive. I 'ave very special dinner for you and Pamela. Just a few friends. What you think?'

'I think you're holding up pretty good for an old broad.' He pinched her thigh. 'You're still a sexy piece.'

'George!' She pushed his hand away and tried to act insulted, but it didn't work. George Lancaster had known her since she was sixteen and walking the Champs-Elysées – something she hoped he had long since forgotten.

* * *

Montana put her finger to her lips and said, 'Not a word to anyone, Buddy. I shouldn't have told you until after the Lancaster story breaks.'

'I'm starring in your movie an' you're gonna tell me I can't mention it? *Come on* – I don't have that kind of control.'

'Learn it.'

'If I had a wife could I tell her?'

'Do you?'

He hesitated for a second, then realized now was not the time to start revealing truths. 'Do I look like the marryin' kind?'

She laughed. 'So why are you asking dumb questions?'

'I'm confused.'

'Un-confuse yourself. You've got to realize it's in your own best interest not to say a word. Hollywood law, kiddo – don't jinx yourself.'

'What happens next?'

'We call your agent.'

'I don't have one.'

'So get one.'

'How do I get an agent if I'm not supposed to say anything?'

'Agents are like priests – you can confide in them. I'll tell you what. *I'll* talk to Sadie La Salle, maybe set up an appointment for you tomorrow. How's that?'

'I think I love you.'

They both laughed.

In the distance he saw Frances Cavendish approaching, a furious expression on her face.

'Like I gotta split,' he said hastily. 'This . . . uh . . . person I'm supposed to be escorting tonight is comin' my way, an' I don't want to expose you to the language.'

Montana nodded gravely. 'I understand.' She liked him – instinctively she knew where he was coming from and that it hadn't been easy. She was pleased that he was going to get his chance.

He took her hand and squeezed it tightly. 'Thank you,' he said warmly. 'I think you saved my life.'

'Come on. Don't get dramatic on me – keep it for the cameras.'

* * *

Karen was burning. How come she was stuck at the shittiest table in the room with all the nothings and nobodies? How *dare* Elaine do that to her?

The final insult was Ron Gordino who just casually strolled over and sat himself down. *She was seated next to Ron Gordino – a fucking exercise instructor. What had she done to deserve this?*

I will kill Elaine Conti, she thought. No way is she going to humiliate me like this and get away with it. Better still, I will steal her husband away from her once and for all, and I'll have parties that *she* won't even be invited to.

Fat-ass Etta Grodinski. Oh yeah. I know all about your crappy beginnings. Your dear sweet unfaithful husband told me.

'Um . . . this is a great party,' drawled Ron Gordino.

'Tell me,' Karen said, smiling sweetly. 'How many times have you laid our hostess?'

Chapter Thirty-Six

Legs, arms, breasts. The whisper of mouths, the teasing of tongues, hot breath, saliva, taste and touch and tactile sensuality.

It was years since he'd been with two women. Maybe ten years. Paris. And they were sisters who fiercely resembled each other.

This was different. Two women from two separate cultures and they were transporting him to a plateau of ecstasy that he had thought was no longer his to visit.

Thiou-Ling was indeed an artist. Only she did not work with a palette of paints, instead she worked with scented oils and her feathery child-like fingers. She tended both Gina and Neil at once, touching first Gina's ripe nipples, then Neil's rampant penis which threatened to burst, the skin was stretched so tight.

She fussed and fretted over each of them, her long hair trailing on their skin like strands of fine silken thread.

After a while it was torture.

Exquisite torture.

He shoved the Eurasian girl away and mounted Gina, who wanted him as much as he wanted her. She was so wet and ready that he almost slipped out, but Thiou-Ling had not deserted them, she was there to help him enter the moist warmth of the second most popular blonde in America. She guided him into paradise. And he knew without a doubt that this was to be the most exciting sexual experience of his life.

Montana was long forgotten.

Street People was long forgotten.

The party was long forgotten.

He was entering Heaven.

Chapter Thirty-Seven

At eleven o'clock precisely the Zancussi Trio faded out with a soulful rendition of the theme from *The Godfather*. Ric and Phil, their speakers in place, their long wild hair freaked out, moved into action. Kool and the Gang imploring everyone to 'Get Down On It' blasted out from seven hidden speakers.

'Shit!' Ross shot out of his chair. 'What a noise!'

A space had been cleared for dancing and Pamela thought he was offering. She leapt up too. 'Yes, Ross, let's show 'em how it's done!'

Six-foot, red-headed Pamela London dragged him onto the dance floor.

Sadie was only too pleased to have a short respite from the pressure of his charm. He had been coming on strong to her all night, and although she knew it was all a game, she couldn't help being affected. She felt uncomfortably aroused. He still had the power to excite her with words alone. How different it all could have been if he hadn't deserted her . . .

* * *

'Wanna dance?' Karen Lancaster demanded of Buddy Hudson.

He was sitting between her and Frances Cavendish, feeling confused. He *should* be feeling great. Instead he had one eye on Angel at a table across the room, and a nervous stomach that told him to keep a hold on himself until the contracts were signed.

Jeez! This was the best night of his life. It was also the worst. Who the fuck was Angel with?

He decided to go over and ask her to dance. Then he would get her in a quiet corner and say – 'Why did you get rid of our baby? Why did you leave me? Why can't we try again?'

'I said let's dance,' slurred Karen. She was high, her pupils huge. She and Shelly would make a great pair.

He wanted to say no, but with George Lancaster being her father and all he thought it might be better to say yes, so he turned to Frances, who had just returned from smoking a joint in the guest toilet. 'Do you mind if I dance?' he asked.

'Do what you like,' Frances replied irritably. She was not pleased. He had hardly turned out to be the attentive escort she had envisaged. He could whistle for the Universal job. She would tell him when he took her home.

'Yeah, sure, let's go,' he told Karen, and they joined the third richest woman in the world – who couldn't dance – and Ross Conti – who couldn't dance – for a whirl around the floor.

Karen could Get Down On It with the best of them. She moved in such a fashion that her body went one way, and her bra-less breasts with their exotic nipples another.

'Hey—' exclaimed Buddy. He loved to dance, and among this group it was a pleasure.

Angel, baby, understand that this is purely business.

Karen moved nearer to Ross. 'Pamela, you old dog,' she slurred. 'Dint' know you were such a swinger. Here, Buddy, you dance with Pammy – I'm taking Ross.' Skilfully she moved between them, and Buddy found himself dancing opposite Pamela London which really blew his mind.

He grinned politely. She exhibited yellow horse teeth in response.

'Come on, Elaine, if they can do it so can we, old girl,' boomed George Lancaster, pulling her up.

Elaine forced a smile. She wasn't too fond of the 'old girl'. Karen had grabbed a vice-like hold on Ross, and was pushing her disgusting body up against his leg like a bitch on heat. The entire party was watching.

Put on a happy face, Elaine.

Screw you, Etta.

'I think I'm having an orgasm from your knee,' Karen husked drunkenly into his ear.

'Pull yourself together, everybody's watching,' he said tersely, keeping an alert eye on Sadie who was deep in conversation with Shakira and Michael Caine.

'So what?' slurred Karen.

'So cool it.'

'Cool it . . . cool it . . .' She raised her arms above her head and shimmied like a stripper.

'That's my girl!' shouted George, and he abandoned Elaine and moved over in front of his daughter.

Reluctantly Ross found himself partnering Elaine. At that particular moment the blonde in the Porsche who had waved to him that morning boogied on by. Now he recognized her as Sharon Richmond.

'And who were you visiting this morning?' she giggled. 'Caught you – didn't I?' she giggled again. 'Only joking, Elaine. I know for a fact that there are three practising dentists who live in *my* complex alone.'

Her date, sensing Ross's fury, yanked her away.

Elaine narrowed her eyes. 'You *bastard*!' she hissed.

In unison they left the dance floor.

* * *

'Jogging sucks!' said the curly-haired girl with an unlady-like hiccough.

'You know what I want?' mused her friend, a tastefully

dressed brunette with a body like Bo Derek. 'I want a big star who'll do windows!'

Scintillating conversation, thought Montana.

Since Ric and Phil had taken over the music scene, and three hours of liquor had taken care of everyone's inhibitions, it was all happening. Only not for her. She might have been able to have a good time if Neil had put in an appearance. But his absence was beginning to worry her. Oliver didn't know where he was. She had tracked his secretary down and she didn't know either. All of a sudden thoughts were creeping into her mind about the way he drove his Maserati. Fast. Much too fast. Maybe he had had an accident.

* * *

As soon as Pamela left the table Oliver jumped to his feet and hurried over to Angel. 'It is you, isn't it?' he said, leaning over her chair.

She started. 'Sorry?'

'You're the girl from the beach. Don't tell me I'm mistaken, I know it's you.'

'Oh . . . yes . . .'

'I've had people trying to find you. Aren't you interested in becoming a star?'

'I . . . I . . .' She thought about Buddy's baby growing inside her, far more important than any quick shot at stardom. 'No,' she said.

'No?' he echoed in disbelief.

'No,' she repeated firmly.

'What's the matter? There something wrong with you? Nobody says *no* to becoming a movie star.'

'I do,' she said in a small voice.

* * *

'Sadie, we had such a great thing going between us. Where did we go wrong?'

We. He had the nerve to say *we*. What a selfish, self-obsessed egotist Ross Conti was.

So what else was new?

She waved at Warren Beatty and Jack Nicholson who were making a late entrance.

'Sometimes I wake in the middle of the night,' he continued, 'and I think to myself – why isn't Sadie lying here with me? Why isn't she next to me? With her soft warm body and her big fantastic tits . . .'

The man was actually still calling them tits. To her face. And he expected her to be flattered. Hadn't he heard of the women's movement and the sexual revolution? He was coming on to her as though she were a piece of ass that he could sweet-talk into the sack.

Poor Ross. He had learned nothing over the years.

He was going all the way. 'I want you, Sadie,' he whispered. 'I want you so badly that if you put your hand under the table you can feel just how much.'

* * *

'I wish to be escorted home,' said Frances Cavendish coldly.

'Now?'

'No. Tomorrow morning will do nicely.' She narrowed her flinty eyes. '*Now*, Buddy.'

'But the party is just gettin' going.'

'For us it's just ending.'

For one wild moment he contemplated telling her to get stuffed. After all, he had *Street People*. Who needed Frances Cavendish? But common sense prevailed, and he decided to drive her home, return to the party, corner Angel, and really talk things out.

'Let's go,' he said, pleased with his decision.

'I must say goodbye to the Contis.'

That's what he was counting on. While Frances thanked Elaine he skipped over to Angel's table, bent over her shoulder and said, 'I have to go somewhere, but I'll be back in twenty minutes, and I want us to talk – without any schmucks butting in. You at least owe me that, don't you?'

She frowned. 'I don't owe you anything. After what Shelly told me—'

'What did Shelly tell you?'

'That you and she . . .' She hesitated, unable to repeat what she had heard. 'Is it true?'

Goddamn Shelly. Had she been in contact with Angel again and not told him?

'What's going on, dear?' questioned the curly-haired man on her left, not so immaculate now, rather dishevelled and wild-looking. Angel ignored him, and pushed her chair away from the table. 'Okay, let's talk. Let's go somewhere quiet and—'

'Buddy. I'm waiting.' Frances Cavendish's commanding tone as she approached.

Shit. 'Twenty minutes,' he said desperately in a hoarse whisper. 'Just gotta run this old broad home. Like it's business, y'know?'

Sadly she nodded. He hadn't changed. What good would talking do?

* * *

'I'm telling you, Montana. She's right for it. Better than anyone we've tested,' Oliver said excitedly. 'I want *you* to talk to her. Maybe she'll listen to you. When—'

'What do you think can have happened to Neil? Should I call the police?' Montana interrupted anxiously.

'Are you nuts? I'm telling you about the perfect Nikki and you're talking police.'

'I'm worried about Neil.'

'He's a big boy.'

'Really?' Her sarcasm brushed off him like dandruff.

'Come on, forget about Neil – he can look after himself. I want you to talk some sense into this girl. Her name's Angel. Can you believe it? I think we should call her Angel Angeli – the press'll eat it up. Let's go, Montana, you can talk some *brains* into the kid. *Everyone* wants to be in the movies.'

Chapter Thirty-Eight

He was climaxing. Thick salty spurts of life's essence.

And Thiou-Ling was breaking a small glass phial of Amyl Nitrate under his nose.

And he was coming and coming and coming . . .

Life's sweet wish. The never ending orgasm . . . Nirvana . . . Paradise . . . Bliss . . .

And then the pain. So sudden. So unexpected. A thunderbolt of agony that gripped him across the chest and down one side with an intensity that was killing.

'Oh good Christ,' he said. At least he thought he said it, but he didn't hear the words come out.

His cock was still hard, still pulsating, but the pleasure was no longer his, and no words would emerge to tell the world that he was slipping . . .

The two women did not realize that anything was the matter. His weight did not bother Gina, it merely enhanced her own moment of ecstasy. And then . . . when her moment was over . . .

'Neil?' she murmured. 'Neil, please move, you're crushing me.' Her voice rose. '*Neil.*' She tried to push him off her. 'Stop fooling around – it's not funny.'

He groaned. 'I . . . don't . . . feel . . . good . . .'

Oh, no. The English prick wasn't having a heart attack. Not on top of her. Not in her house. Oh, no!

She panicked and tried to throw him off, her vagina contracting in a most peculiar way. '*Get off me*!' she screeched.

The pain around his chest subsided and he attempted to withdraw from her clinging wetness.

Strangest sensation in the world. He couldn't pull out. His penis felt like it was caught in a vice.

'Gina, there's something wrong,' he mumbled weakly.

'Cut it out, Neil,' she snapped angrily.

Ah, but if only he could . . .

Chapter Thirty-Nine

'One thing I'll always remember, and baby, *never* will I forget it. There has never been anyone else who did it for me the way you did. You feel the same, don't you?'

In a way Sadie wished he would stop. But then in another way she was enjoying every phony minute.

'Haven't you always felt that what we had was the best?' Ross persisted, wishing that Phil and Ric would turn their goddamn speakers down. Loud rock music was hardly conducive to stirring up a romance. And yet he felt he was doing pretty well. He hadn't got her to place her hand on his dick yet, but she was attentive all right. Lapping up every line of dialogue he came out with. 'Well?' He was determined to get an answer out of her. 'Has there been anyone better for you?'

She knew what he wanted. She decided to put him out of his misery. 'Do you want me to be your agent?'

'What?' He pretended to be shocked.

'I said how would you feel about me representing you again?'

'Sadie . . . I never really thought about it . . .'

'You thought about it a few years ago. Remember, at the Fox party?'

He laughed casually. He was not above getting in a dig.

'Yeah. I remember. You told me to take a hike – or something like that.'

'Actually I said if making commission on you gave me my one hot meal of the week I'd starve to death.' As if he didn't remember.

'You did?'

'I've mellowed since then.'

'I should hope so!'

'Well? Do you want to be my client or not?'

He pretended reluctance. 'I'm happy with the agent I have . . .'

'That's a shame. In that case—'

'No, no. I'm not *that* happy, and there *is* something I think you might be able to pull off for me.'

'Really?'

'Yes. It's—'

'Not now, Ross. Why don't you come to my office tomorrow. Does five o'clock suit you?'

It suited him. But was it right that he should have to go to her office like an aspiring client? Shouldn't it be lunch at Ma Maison or the Bistro Gardens? Shouldn't *she*, the agent, be pursuing *him*?

Cut it out. Who do you think you're kidding? The game is getting her back in your corner. Not playing footsie over chicken salad, and jerking off because a roomful of assholes can see that you're with Sadie La Salle.

'That'll be fine,' he said.

'Good,' she replied, getting up. 'Now you must excuse me, I have to spend some time with George.'

He watched her walk away.

It wasn't all that difficult getting you back, Sadie. You may be a toughie, but with me you're still cream cheese.

The heavy throb of disco turned slow, and the dancing space packed up with couples clinging closely together. A lone paparazzi had managed to break in and climb a tree where he perched precariously, desperately trying to get pictures before security yanked him down and out.

For a moment Ross thought about Little S. Shitz and the incriminating photos. Karen had plenty of money, maybe she would feel like buying the negatives . . .

He looked around. Everyone seemed to be having a terrific time. It was past twelve and no one was making any moves to go home. Hollywood was basically an early town, and past twelve was late. Elaine's party was a big success.

His thoughts rested on her for a moment. What had she been thinking of stealing a bracelet? Was she crazy? Hadn't she considered the consequences? It was back to the shrink time for Elaine. No doubt about that.

Where was she anyway? His eyes sought her out and found her dancing close with some superman clone. The throbbing beat of Donna Summer caressed them. Ross leaned across the table to Maralee. 'Who's Elaine dancing with?'

Maralee glanced over. 'Oh, that's Ron Gordino, our exercise instructor.'

Karen's words flashed across his brain. *I think Elaine's playing doctor.*

He peered intently at the entwined couple. Was it a trick of light or was the creep nibbling her ear?

Impossible. Elaine was his wife. She wouldn't dare screw around.

Or would she?

* * *

'I think we should be going,' Mrs Liderman said. 'Poor little Frowie will be wondering what's happened to his momma.'

Angel glanced helplessly around. Buddy had said he would be back in twenty minutes, but an hour had passed. It was quite obvious that he no longer cared . . . just as Shelly had said . . .

Her eyes clouded over, and she realized that once and for all she must forget him and be strong. 'I'm ready whenever you are,' she said resolutely.

'I don't have to ask if you've had a good time,' Mrs Liderman said happily. 'I've been watching you, the centre of attention.'

Angel smiled wanly. She was being asked to appear in a movie, and the more she said no the more they seemed to want her. Oliver Easterne had even gone so far as to bring the woman over who *wrote* the film. 'Isn't she Nikki,' he had insisted. And the woman had narrowed her eyes and said, 'Maybe . . . If she can act.'

'But I'm not interested,' Angel had protested.

Interested or not Oliver Easterne had insisted that she call him the next day. She had finally agreed, although she had no intention of doing so.

Mrs Liderman said, 'We won't say goodbye. I hate goodbyes. Besides I'm having lunch with Pamela tomorrow.'

Outside, Mrs Liderman's chauffeur waited at attention by the door of her cream coloured Rolls Royce.

Angel sank back into luxury as the car glided smoothly down the driveway.

Had she been looking out the window she would have observed a harassed looking Buddy paying off a cab at the curb-side. He had just enough to cover the fare, although not enough to make it back to Randy's apartment. What a night! The new movie star in town was busted out. He raced back into the thick of the party anxious to find Angel. Methodically he went from room to room, checked the guest bathroom, the dancing throng, the outside tables. And he couldn't find her. His luck that the Pontiac had picked tonight to finally expire. Fortunately *after* he had dropped off an uptight Frances who had told him on her doorstep that she did not think he was right for the picture at Universal after all. 'I made a mistake,' she said, expecting him to crumble.

'That's the way it goes,' he had replied cheerfully.

She was furious. Robbed of her spiteful moment of triumph.

He searched in vain for his beautiful Angel. The least she could have done was waited. He didn't even have an address or a phone number for her. How could he have let her get away again? What kind of a jerk was he?

And yet . . . She had got rid of his baby . . . She had done that without even speaking to him about it . . . *She* had walked on *him* . . .

He went to the bar and gulped down a Perrier water.

'Ah . . .' Karen Lancaster staggered over. 'There you are – the dancer. Let's go, killer. Let's show 'em steps'll make their eyes bulge!'

* * *

Montana felt foolish phoning the police. But she shut herself away in the Contis' bedroom and phoned the Beverly Hills station anyway. They had nothing to tell her, so she tried home again – but there was no reply, just as there had been no reply for the past two hours.

Neil's a big boy, he can look after himself, Oliver had said. Did Oliver perhaps know where he was?

She sat silently for a moment collecting her thoughts.

Yes. Oliver knew. He *had* to know. That's why he wasn't at all worried.

She sought him out.

'Okay, cut out the bullshit. Where is he?'

'What is it with you? I don't know.'

'You *know*. And if you don't tell me I'll cause one hell of a scene. You want that? Here? Tonight? In front of dear old George and your new good friend Pamela?'

'I never had you figured as the jealous wife.'

'Jealous wife. Ha! I just want to make sure that my old man's not lying in some hospital. Then I can split from this crummy party and get some sleep.' She paused and glared at him. 'I'm not like you, Oliver. I don't have to ass kiss my way around the room. *I* can go home. Now where is he?'

Oliver was suffering. His ulcer was sending out spasms of pain. His piles were pure anguish. And the scene with George

Lancaster's vulgar rich wife was an intolerable embarrassment which would haunt him for at least two days.

On top of that he couldn't stand dealing with Montana. They had the screenplay. They no longer needed her. And why was he protecting Neil anyway? The schmuck couldn't even be bothered to put in an appearance at a party for the star of their movie.

'He had a meeting with Gina Germaine,' he said, savouring the moment. 'Who knows? Maybe it's still going on.'

She stared at him, tiger eyes cold as Siberia. 'Thank you,' she said icily.

He tried to meet her gaze, but he couldn't. 'My pleasure.'

'You know something, Oliver?' she said very loudly. 'You're a prick. And on top of that you stink – literally.' She strode angrily away while he surreptitiously tried to check out his armpits.

Pamela London, on her way to the powder room, caught him at it.

'Well!' she exclaimed, her strident voice carrying across the room. 'I've heard of kinky – but *you* are ridiculous!'

* * *

Dancing with Karen Lancaster was a kick he didn't need. She was drunk, *and* stoned. And she was using him to make Ross Conti jealous. He didn't want to be rude. After all – before Angel he would have loved meeting Karen. But now – so what? He wasn't Randy Felix, looking to hitch up with a rich one. He was his own man – and he had made himself a promise, whether things worked out with Angel or not he would never sell himself again. Self-respect and truth were the name of the game from now on.

Karen moved in close – her gyrations were being ignored by Ross and she didn't like that.

'Wass your name 'gain?' she slurred, pressing her sweaty body against his white Armani jacket.

'Buddy Hudson,' he said, pushing her gently away.

'Buddy, huh?' She fell against him, grabbing at his lapels for balance. 'Wanna be my buddy, Buddy?'

This flash of humour broke her up, and while she was laughing he spotted Randy and Maralee sitting at a half-empty table talking intently. He steered her over and deposited her on a chair.

'Karen,' Maralee exclaimed, pleased by the interruption. 'You look like a strong black coffee wouldn't do you any harm.'

'The hell with coffee,' slurred Karen. 'I know what *I* need.' She turned to Buddy. 'Sit down.'

He did so, studiously avoiding Randy's glare.

'Now . . . lemme see . . .' she continued. 'This is Maralee . . . an' her *friend* – I forgot his name . . .'

'Randy Felix,' said Maralee, toying nervously with a spoon.

'Now how could I forget a name like Randy.' She giggled. 'What-tayado sweetie-pie?'

Maralee frowned. 'Karen—' she began.

'So-rry. Mustn't ask what Randy does.' She grabbed a hovering waiter by the sleeve. 'Vodka. On the rocks. Now.' Absent-mindedly she did not let go of the waiter's jacket and Buddy painstakingly pried her fingers loose.

She looked at him gravely. 'This is Bud,' she announced. 'He's a dancer.'

'Hello,' said Maralee politely.

'Nice to meet you,' said Randy coldly.

Karen looked first at Buddy, then at Randy. 'Thought you two knew each other. Didn't I see you together at Ma Maison?'

'No,' snapped Randy.

Buddy did not want any hassles. He jumped up. 'You'll have to excuse me,' he said. 'I have a date here somewhere, and she's probably looking for me.'

'Sure,' said Karen vaguely. 'Better run find her. Give me a call sometime, Bud.'

'I'll do that.'

He made his escape with a sigh of relief.

* * *

George Lancaster was getting ready to make a speech. Montana decided it was definitely time to leave. Her mind was churning. Neil . . . with Gina . . .

Neil . . . screwing around . . .

Damn him.

Maybe it wasn't true.

Buddy Hudson caught up with her at the door. 'You going?'

'Uh-huh.'

'Can I bum a ride?'

'Where's your car?'

'It died on Sunset.'

'Where do you live?'

'Just off the Strip.'

'Come on.'

He was about to follow her as she strode out the front door, when the sight of Wolfie Schweicker emerging from the guest bathroom pulled him up sharply.

Slimmer by far . . . hair different . . . But there was no mistaking those small mean eyes, that round face, the ferret-like teeth emerging from fleshy lips.

Butterball . . . the fat man at the party . . . twelve years ago . . . Tony's battered body lying on a slab in the morgue . . .

He shuddered, the memory too painful to contemplate.

Wolfie must have felt him staring because he glanced over, and, misjudging the intent stare for sexual interest, said, 'Hello.'

'Do you want a ride or not?' Montana reappeared at the door, her voice edgy.

Buddy dragged his eyes away from Butterball. He must be mistaken. It couldn't be the same man.

Why not?

He followed Montana outside. 'Who was that guy?' he asked urgently.

'What guy?'

'The one in the hall.'

She frowned, her thoughts elsewhere. 'Wolfie something – Schwartz or Schweiss – No, Schweicker. He hangs around Bibi Sutton all the time.'

'Wolfie Schweicker . . .' Buddy repeated the name slowly. He never intended to forget it.

* * *

George Lancaster stood up, tapped the side of his champagne glass with a fork, and boomed, 'Let's have a little quiet for the star.'

The assorted gathering obliged.

'I'm going to make a speech here,' he announced.

There were a few good-natured groans and catcalls.

'Bo-ring!' Pamela cried loudly. Laughter filled the tented patio.

'Ignore the old sow,' George thundered. 'I should have put her out to pasture long ago!'

More laughter.

'Seriously though, folks,' George continued, 'it's a real pleasure to see all my old friends here tonight . . . some of them a little older than I remember . . .' Riotous laughter. 'But that's all right . . . What's a rug an' a set of false teeth between friends?'

Everyone fell about.

'You're probably all wondering what the Captain is doing back in town. Why isn't he sitting on his ass in Palm Beach with his rich broad wife, huh? You really want to know that, don't you?'

'Get on with it,' shrilled Pamela, loving every minute.

'I'm making a comeback,' roared George. 'You know what that is – it's the thing Frank does once every year!'

'Right on!' someone yelled.

'I'm doing a movie for my friends Oliver Easterne and Neil Gray because Neil talked Pamela into what a swinging time she'd have here, and Oliver gave me an offer even *I* couldn't refuse. Also they couldn't get Burt—'

He droned on, but neither Elaine nor Ross were listening. They were exchanging shocked glances. George Lancaster doing *Street People? George Lancaster*, who – according to his loving daughter Karen – had turned it down months ago. And *they* were hosting a *party* for him. Spending a fortune they could ill afford – for what?

Elaine could not believe it. She wanted to just give up and crawl into bed.

Ross was even more stunned. He had *known* the part was his. Convinced himself that only he could truly play the role as it should be played. And with Sadie La Salle on his side . . . He could almost taste the bitter disappointment that flooded his body.

Chapter Forty

The American Airlines plane was crowded, but Millie didn't mind. It was the first time she had ever flown and her excitement was catching.

Leon was excited too. But for other reasons.

Timing was so strange. You waited and waited for something to happen, and nothing ever did. Then you went ahead and made your plans – and bingo . . .

Two reports had come up on the computer. The first a double murder in Pittsburgh. A whore and her pimp slashed to death. And the second a hitchhiker in Texas, stabbed twenty-eight times.

In both cases Deke Andrews had left his mark – his fingerprints.

Leon had wanted to cancel his vacation plans and investigate the new developments. But he couldn't do that to Millie. It would have been cruel.

A young detective by the name of Ernie Thompson was assigned to both Pittsburgh and Texas to check out the new findings. He would report in to Leon, wherever he was. It wasn't the most satisfactory of arrangements – obviously Leon would have preferred to make the trips himself – but in the circumstances it would just have to do.

'I can hardly believe we're on our way!' Millie squeezed his arm and kissed him on the cheek.

He responded to her affection. They were on their way all right. And they seemed to be heading in the same direction as Deke Andrews.

Chapter Forty-One

They were locked together. Gina Germaine, the second most popular blonde in America, and Neil Gray, respected and revered film director.

Gina, impaled like a fish, whimpered non-stop.

Neil merely groaned. Trapped by the object of his desire like a fly in the web of a praying mantis, he felt strangely unreal and weak. The pain that had gripped him before had subsided, but he was frightened by the intensity of it, and terrified of the situation he was now in. He was feverish and exhausted. Too tired to do anything but slump on top of Gina and wait for her to release him from her deadly female trap.

Thiou-Ling, no longer a sweet and docile Eurasian sex object, had done everything in her power to separate them – everything had included throwing cold water over their lower anatomy, wild tugs at Neil's nether regions, and vaseline liberally applied down there. Nothing had worked.

'Goddamn it, Gina,' snapped Thiou-Ling, who had suddenly developed a fierce New York street accent. 'Cut the fuckin' hysterics an' tell me what you want me to do.'

'Oh God,' Gina whimpered. 'What have I done to deserve this?' She wriggled around uncomfortably. Neil was hardly light. She felt like someone had jammed a cold cucumber inside of her and just left it there. She knew she would go mad if something wasn't done soon.

'Maybe I should call the paramedics,' Thiou-Ling suggested.

'Oh, for crissakes,' Gina groaned. 'We'd be the laughing stock of Hollywood. Try some more cold water. God! *Do something*!'

* * *

The small Volkswagen hit the road like a rocket. When it reached Sunset and Montana crossed over to Benedict Canyon instead of going towards Hollywood, Buddy said, 'Hey, uh, I think you forgot to turn.'

'No I didn't,' she said tonelessly. 'I just want to check something out. You don't mind do you?'

Who was he to mind? She was the one with the wheels.

The car zoomed up Benedict, swung right to Tower Road, an even sharper right on San Ysidro Drive, and finally slowed to a stop across the street from heavy iron gates.

Montana killed the ignition, shook a cigarette from a full pack, lit up, inhaled deeply, and said, 'I could do with a favour.'

He nodded obligingly. 'For you – anything.'

'Look – I feel kind of stupid asking you,' she said hesitantly.

He had no idea what she wanted and hoped it was nothing sexual. She was a beautiful woman . . . but he had to be needed for his talent not the action he could supply.

'What do you want me to do?'

She dragged on her cigarette and stared sightlessly out of the car window. 'Get past those gates, check out the driveway and garage of that house, and see if there's a red Maserati parked anywhere.'

He digested her request. How was he supposed to get past the gates? Climb them? And if he did, what if the owner mistook him for a burglar (highly likely at one in the morning) and *shot* him? After all, it was a well known fact that most of the residents of Beverly Hills were armed to the teeth ready for the revolution.

'Hey, listen—' he began.

'You don't have to,' she said flatly.

'Whose house is it anyway?' he asked, playing for time while he thought things out.

'Gina Germaine's.'

His luck. A movie star's house. She probably had armed guards sleeping on her doorstep.

'I'll do it,' he said reluctantly. After all, she had given him Vinnie, he had to give her *something* in return.

* * *

Oliver Easterne drove a gleaming English Bentley – vintage 1969 – a very good year for Bentleys. The car was immaculate, as it should be, for when not in use it was kept under pristine cloth wraps in the four car garage of the Bel Air house Oliver rented – three mansions to the right of Bibi and Adam Sutton's estate. The Bentley had been with him since birth. Straight from the factory to Oliver Easterne. An immaculate car for an immaculate man.

He reflected on his day. Pamela London had ruined it for him. And, of course, Montana. They were both too smart for their own good. If Montana and Neil broke up because of the information he had let slip – then fine. He for one would be delighted. She had her nerve talking to him the way she did. Calling him an ass-licker for all to hear. Didn't she know that it went with the job?

You produce. You ass-lick. There wasn't a producer in town who hadn't licked his share.

The early part of his day hadn't been bad. Signing Gina Germaine for Neil's new project was a plus. He looked forward to seeing Montana's face when she heard the news on *that* one.

Once home he showered, took a thick milky liquid for his ulcer, applied Preparation H to take care of the other end. He then put on fresh silk pyjamas, a hair net over his thinning locks, and climbed into bed thinking of Angel. Her unspoiled beauty and freshness were so right for Nikki. He had to convince her to do the role. She was just so perfect . . .

He fell asleep still thinking of golden haired Angel.

* * *

Buddy contemplated the heavy iron gates. They were spiked at the top, and at least ten feet high. 'Shit,' he mumbled, removing his white jacket, folding it, and placing it on the ground. He studied the gates again. They were surrounded on each side by an impenetrable sixteen foot hedge, and controlled electrically. The only way past was to climb.

He then noticed the signs, one on each side. The first read DANGER GUARD DOGS. The second WESTEC SECURITY ARMED RESPONSE.

'Oh, no,' he muttered. 'What am I *doin*' here?'

He visualized the scene. Buddy Hudson gets his chance and ends up being chewed by a Great Dane or – even worse – shot.

He hurried back to the car where Montana sat alone in the darkness.

'There's dogs and armed guards,' he stated indignantly.

'Don't take any notice of the signs. Everyone has them.'

Great. Thanks, Montana. It's not your ass out here.

He returned reluctantly to the front line and gingerly began to climb the gates. Fortunately the Art Deco design made them climbable, although going over the spikes at the top was a problem and he felt his pants tear which really pissed him. He muttered curses and made it over.

There was a steep driveway the other side, lit by evenly spaced green lights. He sprinted up it, keeping to the side, holding his breath, hoping to Christ that he didn't come face to face with an alert German Shepherd.

* * *

It came to her in a rush that Oliver was the only person who could help. If *he* couldn't keep his mouth shut, who could? The director of his movie. The star of his next production. Christ, it was *his* responsibility. What were producers for if not to get you out of a jam?

'Call Oliver Easterne,' she groaned to Thiou-Ling, who was now dressed and ready to make a fast exit.

'Who?' Thiou-Ling asked insolently.

'Do it!' screamed Gina. 'Don't question me!' She pushed at Neil's heavy body, she beat on his chest, she groaned again. His breathing was laboured. He had passed out which really infuriated her. *She* was the one stuck underneath him. He had been no help at all slumped on top of her like a massive hulk. 'Get a doctor,' he had gasped before losing consciousness. English fool. Did he honestly expect her to let a doctor see them like this? 'Oliver Easterne's number is in my book on the desk – try it – please. Hand me the phone when you get him. I think I'm going to die!'

'Save it for the screen, sister,' muttered Thiou-Ling.

'What?' gasped Gina.

'Forget it,' said Thiou-Ling, locating Oliver's number. 'I hope this dude is home because *I* have to split.'

'You have to what?' gasped Gina, outraged. 'You're in this with me all the way, you Chinese cunt.'

'I am not Chinese, I am Asian,' Thiou-Ling smiled inscrutably, and knew for a fact that the moment Oliver Easterne arrived she would leave. This kind of thing had a way of being bad for business, and with Thiou-Ling business always came first.

* * *

The phone shattered his pleasant dreams.

'Oliver!' gasped a hysterical Gina Germaine. 'I need you! Come quickly!'

Oliver Easterne dressed hurriedly, putting on a dark blue cashmere sweater, jeans with perfect creases, and Italian loafers. His hair was a little mussy though – he needed time for that.

Gina Germaine's hysterical phone call had unnerved him. Calls in the middle of the night were especially ominous, and this one would inevitably be no different from the rest. Unfortunately.

He drove quickly through the deserted Beverly Hills streets, gulping Maalox as he went, cursing and wondering – what now?

* * *

The Spanish style house at the end of the driveway was set in a square courtyard, and lights blazed from almost every window. Buddy didn't have to go searching for the red Maserati, it was parked right outside the front door for all to see. Keeping to the shadows he prepared to retreat.

One day he would own a house with guard dogs and an armed security guard. One day. Soon. Although he would make sure his dogs were on the loose ready to grab any poor slob that came climbing over *his* gates.

He skirted down the driveway, feeling for the damage in his pants – a ten inch tear at least. He mouthed a few more curses.

The whir of the electric gates opening startled the hell out of him and he stood stock still. Then the headlights of a car travelling full speed came roaring down the drive. Just in time he flung himself into the bushes landing on his right arm which sent out messages of serious agony. He groaned. The ground was wet from the constant attention of sprinklers, and he was rolling in mud.

He heard a dog bark and froze.

* * *

A petite gentle Asian girl answered the front door.

Oliver liked Orientals, they knew their place. 'Oliver Easterne,' he said respectfully. 'Ms Germaine called me.'

'Where the fuck you been?' the not so gentle Asian girl said rudely. 'Follow me.'

Put out by this greeting he trailed her upstairs to the bedroom. There, the sight that met him was startling to say the least. Gina Germaine – American sex symbol supreme – spread-eagled like a beached great white. And lolling on top of her, his naked hairy ass on display, was Neil Gray.

'Holy shit!' exclaimed Oliver. 'You got me out of bed just to watch you two fuck? I seen it before you know – only with a better class of actor.'

'You *prick*!' screeched Gina, summoning all of her strength. '*Do* something, goddammit! You're the producer around here.'

Chapter Forty-Two

'I'm looking for a woman,' Deke said tonelessly.

The plump female in the purple sweater and short black skirt, a small child straddling her hip, laughed and said, 'Ain't everyone?'

She stood in the doorway of her run-down house and waited expectantly for him to say something else.

'Mrs Carrolle,' he said, fumbling for his piece of paper although he knew what was written on it only too well. 'C-A-R-R-O-L-L-E,' he repeated slowly, spelling it out.

The woman shook her head vaguely. 'Dunno.' The child's nose started to run, and she wiped it absentmindedly with the back of her hand. 'Dunno,' she said again.

'Who is it?' came a masculine voice, and a short squat man joined her at the door. 'Yes?' he barked. 'What do you want?'

Deke blocked the door with his foot. 'Who lived here before you?' he asked coldly.

Something about his eyes – so blank and steely – stopped the man from objecting. 'Some old witch.'

'Was her name Carrolle?'

'I don't know.' He tried to push the door closed, but Deke's foot held firm.

The woman said in a loud whisper, 'What's he want? Why don't he go away?'

'How can I find out who lived here before?' Deke asked, his black eyes burning with frustration.

'I guess y'could try the bum we lease this place from,' the man said, anxious to get Deke out of his doorway. 'He'll be able to tell ya. We don't know nuttin'.'

'Naw,' the woman agreed. 'We keep ourselves private.'

The man went inside and returned with a scribbled name and address on a torn off piece of newspaper. 'Y'kin tell the money-grabber he's bin' promisin' us a new roof for five years.'

Deke took the paper, removed his foot from the door, and set off down the street without another word.

'Fuckin' weirdo,' snapped the man, slamming his front door.

Deke walked quickly, staring straight ahead. Paper. Bits of paper. And all leading somewhere . . .

* * *

They sat side by side in a neighbourhood bar. Deke sipping plain Coca Cola, while Joey downed three rum and cokes in a row.

'It's gettin' late,' she said, crinkling her face. 'What time didja tell your folks we'd be there?'

'Anytime,' he replied. 'It doesn't matter.'

'Why?' she demanded. 'Ain't they all' cited 'bout meetin' me?'

'Sure they are,' he said dully, remembering his mother's words. She had stared at him as if sensing that this one was different. 'Bring her home if you must, and I'll tell you what I think of her.'

'Shall we come for dinner?' he had ventured.

'After dinner. I'm not cooking for some cheap tramp that I don't even know.'

'She's not a cheap tramp,' he had protested.

His mother had smiled thinly. 'If you picked her she's a tramp.'

'Let's go,' whined Joey. 'I'm tellin' ya cowboy, one more drink an' I'm gonna puke all over 'em.'

Deke looked at his watch. It was nine-thirty. 'I don't feel well,' he mumbled.

'Don'tcha go tryin' t'back out again. This is it.*'*

'I wasn't trying to back out,' he said indignantly.

'Sure,' she muttered. 'An' pigeons don't shit.'

He took a deep breath. 'We'll go now. Are you ready?'

From her purse she whipped out a grubby tin mirror and stared at her face. Then she foraged for a lipstick and applied even more. 'Wanna look nice for your ma,' she explained. 'Women notice things like make-up an' stuff. Didja tell her I was a model like I said?'

'I forgot.'

'Aw, shee . . . it. She would've thought that was real classy. Sometimes you're so stupid.'

He gripped her wrist tightly. 'Don't say that.'

She pulled free. 'Okay, okay. You know I didn't mean it.' Her voice became babyish. 'Gimme a smile, cowboy. I'm your little girlie.' Playfully she tweaked his ear. 'Girlie luvs big boy lots.'

He relaxed.

She was relieved. Didn't want another delay in getting to mom and dad. She knew they would like her once they met her, it would all be so easy if they did. She needed a family, somewhere she belonged. Eighteen years old and burnt out. She had been on the streets since she was thirteen. It hadn't been easy but she had made out. She had hoped things would work with the cop. He was the first man who treated her kindly, and she would have done anything for him. She had phoned him to give him one last chance. He had pretended not to know who she was and hung up. Pig!

Leon, the cop. Like all the rest in the end. Fuck'n run.

Then along came Deke, and she knew he was a screwball from the beginning. But she handled him carefully, quickly learning what knobs to push to make him work for her.

The possibility of family life thrilled her. Mrs Deke Andrews with a mommy and daddy – his *mommy and daddy, but they would grow to love her just like she was their own.*

She sighed. Deke was better than nothing. Not bad looking if he would only cut his spooky shoulder length hair. His mother hated his hair, she had learned that much. Together they would make him cut it off. When they were married she would do a lot of things.

'Okey-doke, cowboy', she winked cheerily. 'This little girl is ready.'

* * *

He could not remember such heat. It was desert heat – all encompassing, suffocating.

He visited a barber shop and requested that they shave his scalp.

'You want I should take it all off?' asked the old man who owned the place.

Deke nodded.

'You got an infection? They got lotions take care of that.'

'Can you shave my head or not?'

'What are you? One of them religious persons?'

He nodded. It seemed the easiest way.

The old man performed his task, babbling on about this and that.

Deke ignored him.

He liked his shaven scalp when it was done. It looked clean and fine. It looked like a beginning. Very fitting for The Keeper Of The Order.

He got directions for the new address he had written down. It was a one-storey office building on a quiet street. A secretary sat alone in reception picking at some carrot strips. Propped up on her desk was a copy of *Us* magazine which she read intently. 'Everyone's out to lunch,' she told him, returning to an article on Tom Selleck.

Deke said, 'Maybe *you* can help me.'

Without looking up she said, 'Sorry. I'm only a temp.'

'You know where the files are, don't you? I want the file on Nita Carrolle. I need her new address.'

She glanced up briefly, didn't like the look of him. 'Whyn't you come back in an hour?'

He had no time to waste. 'Are you alone here?' he asked.

She was alone but she had no intention of telling this creep that. 'No, I'm not. So why don't you just go?'

He moved swiftly, knocking the magazine to the floor, pinioning her arms behind her.

'Show me the filing systems and I won't hurt you.' His voice was a lethal whisper.

She began to shake. He was a crazy, she should have known it immediately just from the look of him. 'You bald headed bastard,' she hissed, still shaking but determined not to break. 'I've been raped once and I'm not letting it happen again.' Her voice rose. 'You touch me and I'll *kill* you – you damned bastard.'

He was surprised at her reaction, but also strangely pleased.

He hadn't intended to do anything to her, but the message she put out was so strong and clear. She was *asking* for it.

Damnation.

Bastard.

Rape.

His knife was in his hand before he knew it. Her throat was so ready. After all . . . he was The Keeper Of The Order . . . There were certain things he *had* to do.

Chapter Forty-Three

The last guests departed at five past two precisely. Ross's grin stayed in place until the front door shut behind them, and then he marched through the empty rooms to the bar where he sat morosely amidst the debris nursing a double scotch, waiting for Elaine to come and beg his forgiveness and offer her condolences.

He waited twenty minutes, and when she didn't show he sought her out, and found her in his dressing-room furiously throwing clothes into an open suitcase.

For a moment he stood watching, filled with confusion. Then the reality hit him and he roared. 'What the fuck are you doing?' Although it was quite obvious that she was preparing to throw him out.

'I . . . have . . . had . . . enough . . . Ross,' she said tightly, her face contorted with fury. 'How . . . dare . . . you. HOW . . . DARE . . . YOU. With . . . my . . . best . . . friend. You *bastard.*'

He had learned – at an early age – that whenever in doubt – deny it.

'I don't know *what* you are talking about,' he said, trying to sound outraged.

'Don't . . . give . . . me . . . that,' she spat, throwing silk shirts in on top of hand-lasted shoes. 'Save . . . your . . . acting . . . for . . . the movies.'

He had learned – at an early age – that the best form of defence was offence.

'*You* can talk. What about you and that overgrown surfer?'

She paused mid-throw, on an Yves Saint Laurent sweater. 'Don't you *dare* accuse *me* of anything. I have been a wonderful wife to you. An asset – as if you ever appreciated it.' She threw the sweater in his face and blazed, 'Karen Lancaster indeed. I thought you had more taste.'

He blew it. 'How could you think that? I married *you* didn't I?'

She slammed the suitcase shut, thrust it at him. 'Get out,' she hissed.

He wasn't thinking rationally otherwise he would never have gone.

'OUT!' she repeated.

'Don't worry, I'm going. I've had just about all I can take of your friggin' nagging.'

She escorted him to the door. 'Tomorrow I am phoning Marvin Mitchelson,' she announced grandly. 'By the time I am finished with you the only milk you'll be able to afford is from Karen Lancaster's tits!'

'Fuck you – you moaning bitch. At least she doesn't *steal* it!'

'OUT!' she screamed, and suddenly he was standing in his own driveway at two-thirty in the morning with nowhere to go.

* * *

By the time Buddy picked himself up and sprinted for the gates they were closed. In the distance he could still hear a dog barking, but the noise wasn't coming his way which was a relief. That's all he needed, some mad dog at his throat.

His arm throbbed painfully from the fall. Maybe it was broken. Who could he sue? Certainly not Gina Germaine.

Another thought. Could he play Vinnie with a broken arm?

Even more important. Could he get over the gates with a

broken arm? He made an attempt, but failed dismally, managing only to rip his silk shirt.

'Montana,' he called urgently into the darkness.

She hurried across the street. 'What are you waiting for?'

'I've hurt my arm. I don't think I can make it back over.'

They stared at each other through the heavy gates.

'You'd better try,' she said at last. 'We can't hang around here much longer. Patrol cars cruise this area all the time.'

'Thanks,' he said bitterly.

'Come on,' she coaxed. 'You're in good shape. Scale it with one arm and *throw* yourself over.'

Since there seemed to be no other way he did as she suggested, landing on the cement with a thud and a grunt of pain. Two dogs began to bark in the house next door.

'Let's get out of here,' she said, hurrying over to the Volkswagen.

By the time he followed she had already started the little car and was raring to go. He hurled himself into the passenger seat and they took off.

Neither of them spoke for a minute, then she asked in a matter-of-fact voice, 'Was the Maserati there?'

'Yeah – it was there. Hey, listen, I'm not kiddin', I think I broke my arm.' He paused expecting words of sympathy, but she was silent. '*Shit*!' he exclaimed. 'I left my jacket on the ground outside. We'll have to go back.'

'I'm not going back.'

'C'*mon*, it's my best jacket. It's Armani. Besides, all my money's in the pocket.'

'I'll buy you a new jacket, and refund your money. How much?'

A dollar fifty. He was straightening out but need was need, and he could always pay her back when he was flush.

'Six hundred dollars,' he said, being careful to strike a balance between too much and too little.

Abruptly she stopped the Volkswagen just as they were about to hit Sunset. Oh Christ, she's going back, he thought.

She spun the car around and headed up Benedict again, making a sharp right on Lexington.

'I'm taking you to my house,' she said decisively. 'I can look at your arm and give you some money. All right?'

Who was he to object?

* * *

Sadie La Salle had a little ritual at bedtime. First she took a long scented bath. It relaxed her. Then she selected one of the many Sony Betamax video tapes that she kept neatly lined up on a shelf. She put the tape into her video, switched on the television and went to sleep every night with an old Ross Conti movie playing.

Tonight she chose one of her favourites. A big smash in 1958. Ross at the beginning of his career – young and careless – the baby blues and the blond locks and the sleek hard body. Not an ounce of excess then. Tonight she had noticed the beginning of a gut, and the eyes were not as bright, the hair not as blond, the skin leathery from too much living.

She wondered about the rest of him and shuddered with anticipation, although she hated herself for doing so.

Soon she would have him again. And she would use him as he had used her.

And this time *she* would do the walking.

No phone call. No letter. No explanation.

Nothing.

Ross Conti had *ruined* her life, and now, finally, she wanted him to pay for it. When *she* finished with him he would regret the day he met her.

On the television screen Ross smiled. Mister Irresistible.

Sadie settled back to watch the movie. She had seen it hundreds of times before.

* * *

Buddy prowled around the sparsely modern living room. The throb in his arm was easing, maybe it wasn't broken after all.

'Where's . . . uh . . . your old man?' he asked casually, a question which had been bugging him all night.

Montana was fiddling with the combination of a wall safe concealed behind a painting, and didn't look up.

'I mean . . . well like . . . shouldn't I meet him? Did he like my test? What did he say?'

She opened the safe, selected a bundle of notes from inside and began counting off hundred dollar bills. Then she handed him a wad. 'Twelve hundred dollars. That should cover your lost cash *and* the damage to your clothes.'

He could kiss her. Guilt overcame him all the same.

'And incidentally,' she added, 'I spoke to Sadie La Salle. She said for you to stop by her office at eleven o'clock tomorrow morning.'

His luck was getting better all the time. 'Hey, that's great.'

She reached for a cigarette on the table and lit up. 'It's nothing. Now – let's take a look at your arm.'

'I think I just fell on it the wrong way,' he said, flexing it out in front of him.

She insisted on looking anyway, feeling for broken bones with her long tapered fingers. 'You'll live,' she pronounced crisply.

Now he was feeling really bad. How could he possibly con money from her? He had more style than that. 'Uh . . . listen,' he began apologetically. 'I didn't really have six hundred bucks in my jacket. I was just kind of . . . uh . . . joking.'

She stared at him gravely. 'Do you need the money?'

He nodded.

She drew deeply on her cigarette. 'Call it a loan then. When you get your first paycheque I'll expect it back with interest.'

'*You* are one terrific lady.'

'Thanks,' she said drily. 'But don't tell me how great I am because right now I feel mean and vicious and not terrific at all.' She seemed immediately sorry to have revealed herself to him – even with so few words. 'Help yourself to a drink,' she said brusquely. 'I'll just go change, then I'll drop you home.'

'You don't have to bother. I can call a cab.'

'I promised you a ride home, and that's what you'll get. Anyway I feel like driving.'

She left the room and he looked around. The decor was comfortable and modern. The view of Hollywood spectacular. A silver framed picture of Neil Gray stood on a coffee table. On it was inscribed – TO MY DARLING M – WHO TAUGHT ME HOW TO LIVE AGAIN.

Montana breezed back into the room wearing skin tight faded Levis tucked into well worn cowboy boots and a plain white T-shirt. 'Come on, star,' she said, slamming the safe shut. 'Let's get you home – I don't want you appearing at Sadie's tomorrow with bags under your eyes. I gave you a build up as the best looking actor since Marlon in *Streetcar*.'

One thing about Montana. She certainly knew how to say the right thing.

* * *

Valium had calmed her. She knew she was taking too many, but so what? It wasn't every day you were almost arrested, threw the hottest party in town, and threw your husband out on the same night.

Elaine nodded grimly. The bastard deserved it. If he wanted to walk a tight rope he had to be prepared to take a fall.

Come off it, Elaine. You would never have shoved him out if you thought there was a chance of him getting the movie.

Shut your fat face, Etta. You know from nothing.

I know that you've turned into a miserable Beverly Hills bitch. So he screwed Karen. Well you screwed Ron, didn't you?

It's not the same!

Says who?

Her past and her present. She wished the past would just

vanish. Why did she have to be reminded of dumpy Etta Grodinski all the time?

Ross needed you tonight.

Ross doesn't know what the word means.

She thought she might cry. But then she thought about red swollen eyes on top of everything else and abandoned the idea.

Elaine Conti. Separated wife. What would she do? Who would she see? How would she manage?

Women's liberation had never interested her. Woman was there to look good and play hostess. Man was there to provide.

Bullshit.

I'm entitled to my opinion.

She prowled around the empty house, double checked the burglar alarm, wished that she had a cat – a dog – anything.

She didn't like being alone. Throwing Ross out had been a big mistake. He might be a son of a bitch, but at least he was *her* son of a bitch. Tomorrow she would get him back.

* * *

Montana felt sad as she drove Buddy down the hill. She was sad for herself, even more so for Neil. She had expected so much more of him. That he had decided to risk their life together for a fling with someone like Gina . . . What a waste. Because for a while they had had something really good . . .

How could he be so goddamn stupid? Five terrific years down the drain. For what? Some big-bosomed movie queen.

For a moment she was angry. How could he do it? How *could* he betray her trust?

Anger wouldn't help. He *had* done it. No inquests. Now her decision was whether to stay in Los Angeles until the film was complete, or make it easy on everyone and get out of town.

Hey – wait a minute, why should *I* go? She thought furiously. Why should *I* abandon a movie that has taken so much out of me, and leave it in the hands of Neil, and Oliver, and George to probably fuck up beyond recognition?

She made her plans. First thing was to move out – Neil could have the house, she didn't want one red cent of his money. She would take her clothes and records and books, *and* her car which she had paid for anyway. There was enough money in her bank account to last until she decided what she wanted to do next. Instinctively she knew that Neil would not let her go without a fight. He would make every excuse he could think of . . . Poor Neil . . . She was almost sorry for him.

Buddy's voice intruded. 'You're going the wrong way.'

'I am?' she said vaguely. 'I guess I've got a lot on my mind.'

He laughed. 'I'm glad my presence is really felt.'

She flashed tiger eyes at him and he thought how incredibly beautiful she was in a wild and sensual way. She was also troubled, and he had been so busy thinking about himself that he had not realized she had her problems too.

She slowed the car, looking for a place to turn.

'Uh . . . if you want to take a drive I'll come along,' he ventured.

She welcomed the thought of company. Without saying anything she put her foot down – sending the small car careening around the curves and twists of Sunset. 'Now's the time I wish I had a Ferrari,' she said softly.

He nodded, taking the time to figure out what was going on. Neil Gray. Not at the party. Gina Germaine not at the party. A red Maserati parked outside the blonde movie star's house. You didn't have to be Kojak to get the picture.

He leaned forward and pressed a tape into the cassette player. Stevie Wonder. *That Girl.* Good music all the way to the beach and the two of them wrapped in companionable silence.

Montana thought about being free again. She would miss Neil, but how surprisingly sweet the thought of freedom was . . .

Buddy thought about Angel, and getting the part in the movie, and being seen by the legendary Sadie La Salle . . . Then his face clouded over as he remembered the man at the party . . . Wolfie Schweicker . . . And the memories he could never shake . . .

She drove the car far along the Pacific Coast Highway, finally pulling onto a bluff overlooking the roaring dark ocean.

'You want to take a walk?' she asked.

'Why not?'

They left the car and made their way down a slope towards the beach. The tide was high, and they stopped while she pulled off her boots and he removed his shoes and socks.

'I used to live at the beach when I first came to L.A.,' he said. 'This is the best time. No one around.' He took a deep breath. 'You know what I miss? The smell.'

She smiled in the darkness. 'Up front you come on like stud of the year – and really you're not like that at all, are you? You're very caring and nice, and the combination comes across on the screen. It's a great mixture. Don't ever lose it.'

Nobody had ever called him caring and nice in his life. And yet . . . why not?

'Hey . . .' he mumbled, not knowing what to say.

She laughed softly. 'Let's walk, Buddy.'

* * *

The gold Corniche went first in the direction of Karen's Century City apartment, made an abrupt U-turn and came back towards Sadie La Salle's Bel Air house, then finally settled on the Beverly Hills Hotel – home of the stars.

Ross checked in with no difficulty although they were – as usual – booked to capacity.

'I'm a friend of the owner, Mrs Slatkin,' he informed the night clerk, lest there was trouble with his reservation.

'No problem, Mr Conti. For you there is always a room,' said the eager clerk.

'Good.' If Elaine wanted him out, that's where he would stay – out. She had proved herself to him tonight. Revealed herself as an unfeeling heartless bitch. She, above all people, had known what *Street People* meant to him. And she should have been there for him.

* * *

Never before had Buddy felt so at ease with a woman. Subconsciously women were the enemy. You either fought, outsmarted or conquered. But there was something different about Montana. He could actually talk to her, and talk he did, forgetting about her problems as for the first time in his life he unburdened himself. Walking along the dark seashore with the sound of the pounding surf, he found it almost easy. And once he started it was hard to stop. She seemed genuinely interested in his life story – crummy as it was.

He began by telling her about his childhood – and once he started talking about San Diego it all came pouring out. Although he didn't tell her everything. He left out the two most important things. Tony's murder, and the night his mother came to his room . . .

He told her about arriving in L.A. young and broke and eager. His days at the beach, and Joy Byron's acting classes. Then about his Hollywood nights, the tricks he turned, the drugs, the disappointments, and the promises that never materialized. He got as far as Hawaii, and stopped. For some reason he didn't want to mention Angel. She was his secret. 'So I came back,' he finished off. 'And I heard about your movie . . . and . . . uh . . . here we are.'

She liked the way he called it her movie. He was about the only one who did. She knew that Neil would try to intimidate him, George Lancaster would walk all over him, and she wanted so much for him to succeed with the only chance he was likely to get.

It was almost sunrise by the time they got back to the car, and lone joggers were beginning to appear on the horizon.

She felt better having listened to his story. Listening meant not having to think about her own problems.

They sat in the car for a while silently watching the sun rise, then she said, 'How's your arm?'

'Hey – you know something? I forgot all about it.' He flexed it tentatively. 'Nothin'. How about that?'

'You know what I want to do,' she said huskily. 'I want to make love with you – because I like you and I think you like me – and it's something I need right now. No heavy relationships – just . . . togetherness.' She stared at him expectantly – wild tiger-eyes.

He hadn't really thought about sex with her.

It had been at the back of his mind since they left her house.

* * *

Oliver had a doctor who was expensive and discreet. One look at the unhappy couple and he summoned him instantly. For a fleeting moment it occurred to him that the paramedics would be faster. But, oh, the headlines. In that respect he and Gina thought along the same lines. On very rare occasions no press at all was the name of the game.

'I feel terrible,' she moaned. 'I'm sick, Oliver. You'd better help me.'

She didn't look sick to him. All giant tits and ass. Voluptuous women had never appealed to him. He liked them understated, neat and very very clean.

He averted his eyes from Gina's rolling mammaries and concentrated on Neil. Now *he* looked sick. His complexion was greenish and his breathing laboured.

Oliver was not versed in first aid. He had no idea what to do. He certainly didn't want to *touch* them, the very thought digusted him. So, while he waited for the doctor to arrive he did what came naturally. He picked up the nearest ashtray and began to clean it.

* * *

They lay together on a water bed in an oceanside motel naked and relaxed. They had made love urgently and fast, and now it was Montana's turn to talk. She was giving him fragments of her life. Thoughts, opinions, ideas. She never once mentioned Neil.

Later they made love a second time, slowly and leisurely like two key athletes at play.

She was long limbed, sensual, and also aggressive – a trait which excited Buddy because he wasn't used to it and found he liked it.

She had a marvellous body, sleek and feline, with wide shoulders, high breasts, a narrow waist, and long legs. Her skin had the sheen and texture of dark olive oil and she was a wonderful lover. Skilfully she sought out the pressure points which really turned him on, massaging his neck, his chest, and slowly . . . slowly . . . further down until she was enclosing his hardness in her hands and bringing her lips down to caress him with her tongue.

He put his hands into her long jet hair and held her head steady as she teased him. He wanted to come in her mouth, but he also wanted to taste her. He withdrew and changed positions, burying his head between her legs.

Their pleasure was intense, the two of them expert and caring participants in a game they both enjoyed.

For Montana it was the release she needed. Five years . . . just Neil . . . She had almost forgotten the sharp thrill of a new body.

Silently they played out the scene.

Luxuriously they approached their climaxes.

Buddy had thought he was unique in that he never made a sound. But in Montana he had found a soul-mate. Just a long drawn-out sigh as she shuddered to a halt. And as he felt her vibrations so he came too.

It was nearly four in the morning. They fell asleep in each other's arms.

The sound of children playing on the beach woke them

hours later. Sun streamed into the room, and for a moment Buddy could not remember where he was. Then it all came back to him, and automatically he groped for his watch.

Eight forty-nine, and Sadie La Salle at eleven. Time to get moving. Lightly he touched Montana on the shoulder.

She mumbled something and stretched like a leopard.

'It's nearly nine o'clock,' he said quickly. 'And I've got to get back and change my clothes before I go see Sadie La Salle at eleven. Can we make it in time?'

'Wow! You're a real romantic in the morning, aren't you?'

He grinned. 'Hey – what do you want from me? Business is business. I need an agent, don't I?'

She wrapped a sheet around her nakedness and said crisply, '*You're* telling *me*? I arranged the appointment. You use the bathroom first while I order us some coffee. Don't worry, I'll have you back at your apartment before ten.'

'You got it.' He hurried into the bathroom.

Montana picked up the bedside phone. 'Two coffees. Ditto orange juice,' she said, feeling surprisingly good. The sex had been excellent therapy. Maybe it was silly, but in a way she felt that she had evened up the score between her and Neil just a little.

She switched on the television, changed channels until the reassuring face of David Hartman greeted her. 'Good morning America,' she murmured softly. Several commercials dominated the screen. She wondered what Neil would have to say. He would lie of course. How depressing to have to go through it with him.

'*This is Angela Black with the news*,' said the beautiful newscaster on the screen.

Probably a former actress, Montana decided, not really listening as Ms Black proceeded with the news. All bad. As if there was anything different about that.

'*Film director Neil Gray was rushed to hospital early today suffering from a massive coronary attack. A spokesman for Cedars of Lebanon Hospital said that he is in intensive care and in stable condition. In New York, Senator—*'

Blankly Montana clicked the set off. She could hardly think . . . Neil . . . a heart attack . . . massive coronary . . . intensive care . . .

Numbly she shook her head. Then, galvanized into action, she began to dress while calling out urgently for Buddy.

'What's the matter?' He came bounding in from the bathroom dripping water.

'There's an emergency,' she said tightly. 'We've got to leave. Now.'

Chapter Forty-Four

Ernie Thompson phoned Leon just when Millie was by his side, instamatic camera in hand, summery dress and white sandals complementing her deep bronze skin. They were about to set off on a bus tour around San Diego. How he longed to tell her to go without him, but she was having too good a time for him to burst her bubble.

'Give me your number, I'll have to call you back,' he told Ernie reluctantly.

'Who was that, hon?' Millie inquired, after he hung up.

'Nothing. Business.'

She arched an eyebrow but remained silent. When Leon was ready to tell her he would do so. She did not believe in prying.

They spent the day on and off the tour bus enjoying the sights of San Diego. Or at least Millie enjoyed. Leon merely plodded along behind her, wondering what news Ernie had, and planning how to get some time on his own.

From San Diego they were renting a car and driving to Los Angeles, stopping off at Catalina and Long Beach on the way. It was their last night in San Diego, and another couple they had met on the bus wanted them all to go to La Jolla for dinner. He resisted. She insisted. In Tijuana he had picked up a stomach bug, and he used this as an excuse, urging her to go without him.

'Leave you alone?' she protested. 'Never.'

'If you promise to be back before eleven I think I'll survive.'

She was tempted. La Jolla, or so she had been told, was a quaint little beach resort only twenty minutes away. Picturesque open air restaurants and little shops. Marvellous sea food. A place not to be missed.

'Well . . .' she hesitated. 'If you're sure that you don't mind my going without you . . .'

The moment she left he phoned Ernie. They spoke for twenty minutes, Leon questioning, repeating, absorbing every bit of information that came his way. He made notes on a scratch pad and requested that the typed up reports be sent on to him at the Holiday Inn in Los Angeles where he would be arriving in three days.

So, Deke Andrews had finally surfaced. In Pittsburgh and Texas. The bastard was out there somewhere . . . Leaving a trail . . .

Eventually he would be caught. When he was, Leon had every intention of being there.

Chapter Forty-Five

Beverly Hills buzzed with the news of Neil Gray's heart attack. Coronaries were a hot subject around town. Everyone had their own opinion on how not to have one.

Gotta keep fit.

Gotta cut the cholesterol.

Gotta pop vitamins.

Gotta give up doing drugs.

Gotta jog, run, skip, jump, pump iron . . . Gotta EXERCISE!!

Oh, yes, and . . . Gotta fuck a lot (this from a twenty-three year old studio executive who didn't even know what a heart was!).

Juicy secrets have a hard time getting kept anywhere – especially in Hollywood – mecca of gossip.

'Did you hear he was with Gina Germaine?'

'Did you know they were taken into the hospital *joined* like a couple of mating dogs?'

'Did you hear they were snorting coke?'

'. . . smoking grass . . .'

'. . . popping ammis . . .'

'. . . gulping quacks . . .'

'. . . shooting speed . . .'

'He's a fag of course.'

'She's a dyke.'

'They were having an orgy.'

Oh gossip! Oh Hollywood!

What fun everyone had with rumour and insinuation and downright dirt.

Montana rushed straight to the hospital in her jeans and T-shirt, her long black hair flying wildly behind her. The photographers were lined up and waiting, along with the press, television, and radio.

'Why weren't you with him?'

'Who was he with?'

'Where were you?'

'How come he wasn't at George Lancaster's party?'

'Any comment?'

'Can you say something for our viewers?'

She rushed past them and into the arms of one of Oliver Easterne's gofers, who escorted her upstairs to the great man himself.

'Where have you been?' were Oliver's first words. He stopped pacing the hospital corridor to stare at her accusingly. 'What do you think it looks like to the press? A man has a heart attack and his wife is on the missing list.'

She controlled her fiery reply. 'How is he?'

'Christ! How is he she asks. He's in intensive care, *that*'s how he is. He's been fighting to stay alive since he was brought in.'

She endeavoured to remain calm. 'What happened?'

He didn't know whether to tell her the truth or to lie. Montana was smart. She wouldn't be so easy to fool, and he himself had told her that Neil was with Gina earlier.

'Er . . .' He grabbed her by the arm. 'I got the use of a private room. Let's go talk.'

'I want to see Neil,' she said stubbornly.

'I don't think they're letting anyone in,' he muttered.

'I'm not anyone, Oliver,' she reminded him coldly. 'I'm his wife.'

'Why don't you talk to his doctor. It's not my decision.'

'I should bloody well hope not. If it was, we'd be in deep trouble.'

* * *

Elaine's phone rang early. She reached for it in her sleep, ready to receive the stream of compliments from people thanking her for a sensational party. Her groping hand sent a glass crashing to the ground and she opened her eyes with a start. She was not in her comfortable bed as imagined, but instead on a sofa in the living room surrounded by the aftermath of the party.

'Ross,' she said aloud, and then she groaned.

You threw him out you dumb bunny.

Don't remind me, thank you very much.

The phone was still ringing. She got up and approached it with caution. If it was Ross she had to be sure to say the right thing. He was a difficult bastard, it would take honey and coaxing to get him back. She lifted the receiver, not thrilled when she noticed it was only seven-thirty in the morning.

'Hello,' she said sweetly, in case it *was* Ross.

'Elaine!' sobbed Maralee. 'Something terrible has happened.'

Yes. To me. How did you know?

'What?' she snapped. It better be really terrible for Maralee to wake her at this hour of the morning.

'It's . . . it's Neil.'

'What's Neil?'

'He's had a heart attack. He's been rushed to the hospital. I must go to him. Will you come with me?'

Elaine was too shocked to reply for a moment. Anyone getting sick always shocked her. Somehow she expected everyone to stay healthy and live forever.

'Gosh . . . I'm sorry . . . it's awful . . .'

'Can you come with me?' Maralee pleaded tearfully.

'Not right now I can't. I've got . . . er . . . problems here.'

A very small disappointed, 'Oh.'

'But I'll tell you what,' Elaine rallied. 'I'll meet you later.'

'I'd appreciate it. I don't want to be alone at a time like this.'

You're never alone with your millions. Where's Randy? How is he taking this sudden ex-husband-love?

'Of course. I understand. What hospital?'

'Cedars.'

'I'll be there.'

She replaced the receiver, caught sight of her reflection in a mirror, and gasped with horror. Stale make-up ran riot over her face. She looked like a hag. How could she have possibly fallen asleep with her make-up on? God, she really must have been upset.

* * *

'And who *else* was there, dreamheart?' asked Koko. 'Was it divine? Did you have a fabulous time? Aren't you just *full* of the joys of spring today?'

Angel smiled wanly.

'Was Mrs L. wearing lashings of diamonds?' Koko continued excitedly. 'Did she out-sparkle Pamela London? Is George Lancaster *gorgeous*? How about Richard Gere? Did he look divine? Who was *there*, darling one? Tell me all.'

Buddy was there, she wanted to say. I know I have to forget him, but I love him so much that it hurts. And he doesn't even care for me anymore. He made that obvious enough by not coming back . . .

'It was fantastic, Koko,' she said, summoning enthusiasm, because she knew how disappointed he would be if she didn't give a glowing report. 'Absolutely amazing. . . .'

* * *

After dropping Montana at the hospital Buddy raced back to Randy's. Montana had loaned him the Volkswagen which at least made him mobile again. He was worried about the movie. With Neil Gray in hospital it had to mean a delay. Just his luck.

He burst into the small apartment and was surprised to find Randy home – sprawled across the bed asleep. All he needed to do was change and get out of there fast. It wouldn't do to keep Sadie La Salle waiting. Problem. What to wear? Best jacket, pants, and shirt ruined. He opened the crowded closet, couldn't see a thing, raised the window shade.

Randy growled restlessly, 'Pull the goddamn shade down and get lost. I'm sleeping.'

A fine greeting. Quickly he shuffled through his things crushed at one end of the closet. He grabbed at his other Armani jacket. It was wrinkled and needed a trip to the dry cleaners, but it would have to do. The pants and shirt he chose were in the same condition. He swore softly and began to change.

Randy sat up and glared. 'Get your own fucking place, Buddy. I'm no charity, and man, I've had it with you.'

'Things didn't work out with Maralee, huh?' Buddy asked sympathetically.

Randy was not amused. 'Piss off and don't come back. Leave the key. And send me the fucking money you owe me.'

Buddy got his things and put them in a suitcase. He couldn't fault Randy. There *was* such a thing as overstaying your welcome.

* * *

A face to face confrontation with Neil's ex-wife was not exactly what Montana had expected. But she stayed cool, introduced herself with a brief handshake, and was humiliated to have to ask, 'Have you seen him?'

Maralee, stationed outside intensive care, shook blonde curls negatively. 'No visitors,' she explained.

I'm his wife, Montana thought. I'll visit him whether they like it or not.

The doctor appeared. He was good-looking, fortyish, and groomed to within an inch of his life. Montana did not trust him on sight. Gucci shoes and thick gold chains beneath a starched white coat had a way of making her uneasy.

'Mrs Gray?' he questioned smoothly, heading straight for Maralee.

'Yes,' gasped Maralee. She was one of those women who on stressful occasions adopt a breathy little-girl voice.

'I'm Mrs Gray,' Montana said forcefully, stepping between them.

The doctor gave her a confused look. He plucked his eyebrows she noticed, and hid the dark circles under his eyes with just the tiniest dab of pancake.

Confusion gave way to a smile when he remembered that this was indeed Hollywood. 'Ah . . .' he sighed knowingly. 'You're *both* Mrs Gray.'

'Top marks, doc,' snapped Montana. 'Is there somewhere we can talk privately?'

'You're the current Mrs Gray?'

She withheld a sarcastic reply.

He led her into a private office. Maralee tried to follow, but she stopped her with a look.

'Mrs Gray,' said the doctor, pressing his fingers together and gazing at her sincerely. 'Your husband is a very sick man.'

'I think I realize that, doctor. I would like to know exactly what happened.'

He picked up some papers from the desk and studied them intently. 'Have you spoken to Mr Easterne yet?'

'Er . . . yes . . . I mean to . . . He hasn't told me anything. Did Oliver Easterne bring him in?'

The doctor hesitated a moment. 'Mr Easterne called me . . . it was fortunate that he was with your husband at the time.'

But Oliver was at the party. Why would he leave the party and go and visit Neil? She frowned. Neil's Maserati parked outside Gina Germaine's house . . . and while she was waiting outside the gates for Buddy a car had arrived . . . travelling fast . . . on reflection it could well have been Oliver.

Neil must have had the heart attack while he was with Gina . . . *she* had summoned Oliver . . . and Oliver had sent for the doctor who was quite obviously supposed to keep the whole thing quiet.

'What brought his attack on?' she asked coldly.

He shrugged. 'Who knows, Mrs Gray. Overwork, rich foods, stress—'

'Sex?'

He was no actor. Guilt clouded his handsome features. 'Maybe sex. Anything can trigger these—'

'With Gina Germaine?' she interrupted.

Now it was the doctor's turn to frown. Damn Oliver Easterne with his cover-up plans. The wife knew. And probably the whole hospital knew. It wasn't every day that emergency admitted a couple locked together who had to be surgically parted. Especially when one half of the couple was a movie star.

He sighed. 'You're obviously aware of the circumstances, Mrs Gray. Unfortunate, but then we are all human, and I am sure that your main desire is to see Mr Gray up and out of here.' He changed voices from understanding friend to businesslike doctor. 'He has suffered two attacks. The first before we brought him in, and the second after he and Miss Germaine were . . . er . . . separated.'

She wasn't sure that she had heard correctly.

'What?' she asked, feeling shivery and cold.

Carefully the doctor explained the procedure. 'Vaginismus. A severe contraction of the vagina causing Mr Gray to be . . . er . . .'

She stopped listening. She felt sick. For Neil to have had a heart attack was bad enough . . . But the circumstances . . .

Vaguely she heard the doctor droning on.

'. . . dehabilitated and weak . . . unconscious . . . pulse and blood pressure nil . . . resuscitation brought good results . . .

Intensive care . . . condition now stable . . . everything possible being done.'

She felt a weakness creeping over her body. A clammy feeling. Suddenly, with no warning, she slumped into a deep faint.

* * *

The faraway rustle of room service woke Ross Conti. Discreet sounds in the corridor outside his room, trays rattling, whispered Spanish. He stretched, cleared his throat, and reflected on the pleasures of sleeping alone. Then he reflected on George Lancaster's announcement, and scowled grimly. What a way to ruin a movie. George Lancaster couldn't act himself out of a French letter. Everyone knew that.

His scowl deepened, and he picked up the phone and ordered a large breakfast.

So Elaine wanted out did she? Well, if that's what she wanted she could damn well have it.

Elaine the nag. Elaine the ballbreaker. Elaine the *shop*lifter.

He was fed up with being told to do this – do that – go on a diet – get to the gym. You're fat. You're old. You're losing your hair.

He was *not* losing his hair. If anything *she* was losing *hers*. It came out in handfuls in her brush – he had seen it. Gleefully he reminded himself to tell her.

When? You won't be seeing her, schmuck.

He got up and emptied out his jumbled Vuitton suitcase. At least she had sent him on his way with decent luggage. Not that he gave a dog's turd. Labels didn't interest him, they never had. She was the one that lived her life by labels.

He yawned loudly. 'Don't *do* that,' Elaine would say. He farted – a trumpeter's salute. 'God, Ross! You are utterly disgusting,' she would complain. Like she never farted. Come to think of it she probably never did. Now if only someone would come up with designer farts . . .

He laughed aloud. He would survive. Leaving home means never having to see the early morning bills . . .

Room service arrived with a cart laden with goodies. Freshly squeezed orange juice, hot coffee, corned beef hash with two eggs sunny-side up, buckwheat toast and a side order of hash browns. He fell upon it ravenously.

Should call Karen.

Didn't feel like it. Hadn't enjoyed her flashy behaviour at the party. She had no claim on him. Besides, if he was going to be free may as well enjoy it and play the field. Now that he was on the loose he could think of several women he would like to meet – Gina Germaine for one. She had boobs on her that would support an army of drowning soldiers for a week.

He smiled to himself and tried to forget the disappointment of losing the part and being thrown out of his house. At least he was seeing Sadie La Salle later in the day, and if anyone could save a sagging career she could.

* * *

It seemed that Neil had done the unthinkable. Montana had never thought he would fall into the obvious trap of an attention grabbing big breasted movie star – but he had turned out to be just another man. His betrayal stung, because she had expected so much more of him. It hurt that he was weak . . . so weak he had almost killed himself.

She didn't hate him. Yet she didn't love him. She was numbed by his behaviour, and she knew for sure that whatever they'd had together was no longer there.

She made her plans. While he was in the hospital she would stay by him. But when he came out . . . well . . . As far as she was concerned there was no going back.

* * *

Eleven o'clock. Punctuality is next to stardom. Buddy felt confident in spite of his wrinkled clothes.

'Miz La Salle,' he said to the receptionist who was busy filing her nails.

'Who?' she staccatoed.

'Miz La Salle.'

This exasperated her. She was a girl of few words. 'Who *you*?' she snapped.

'Uh . . . Buddy Hudson.'

She consulted an appointment book, indicated a chair, said, 'Wait,' and relayed his name through an intercom.

Five minutes grew to ten. He checked out *Time* magazine, *Dramalogue* and the trades.

Ten grew to twenty. He thought briefly of Angel, reviewed his evening with Montana. She was a fantastic woman and he hoped that they would remain friends. The sex had been great, but it was just something they had both needed at that particular moment – nothing permanent. He knew she felt the same way.

The intercom buzzed.

'Go,' said the girl, pointing an eight inch lacquered nail in the direction of a corridor filled with offices.

He took a deep breath. Lately he was moving into the big time, and it was making him very nervous indeed. Buddy Boy could hold his own with the best of 'em. But suddenly it was all happening so fast . . .

A secretary in a red mini-skirt headed towards him. 'Buddy, welcome,' she smiled. 'Please come this way.'

She guided him to the end of the corridor, and flung open the door of an outer office where a man sat typing. He looked up and made a quick visual assessment of Buddy's assets.

'Hello,' he said. 'Sadie won't be a moment. Do take a seat.'

'This is Ferdie Cartright,' the secretary explained. 'Miz La Salle's personal assistant.' She smiled and departed.

Buddy sat down. Sweat was staining the underarms of his shirt. He hoped it wouldn't seep through to his jacket.

Ferdie finished typing with a flourish and pulled the paper from the machine. 'Done!' he exclaimed. 'Just a personal note from Sadie to Barbra.'

Buddy stared straight ahead and silently rehearsed his opening line. *'Miss La Salle.' Correction. 'Miz La Salle. I have been dreaming of this day ever since I first set foot in Hollywood.'*

Corny bullshit!

'Sadie. You and I . . . we're meant to be together.'

Even worse.

'Sadie La Salle,' said with reverence. 'A legend in her own town.'

Oh shit!

'Miz La Salle will see you now,' said Ferdie in response to three sharp buzzes.

Buddy leapt up. Cool blown in all directions. He followed Ferdie who led him through the door of the fabled inner office.

'Miz La Salle, may I present Buddy Hudson,' Ferdie said formally.

She sat behind a large antique desk stacked with scripts. A dark haired woman of middle age, with bobbed black hair and a non-descript face apart from huge liquid black eyes. Not attractive . . . not unattractive . . . There was something familiar about her which he couldn't quite place.

She was smoking a thin brown cigarillo which she waved at him to indicate he should sit.

Immediately Sadie saw what Montana meant. The boy didn't walk into her office, he sauntered with a special hip-swaying thrust which would be hard to miss. He had a great body – easy to see in the clothes he wore, and although he was dark she was reminded of the first time she ever saw Ross. Same walk. Same thrust. A direct sensuality that could leave you breathless. She had used it to propel Ross to stardom. What a challenge to do it again . . . Oh, she had created plenty of stars . . . But never in the same way . . .

How would Buddy look on billboards from coast to coast? The exact campaign all these years later. Faded Levi cut-offs and WHO IS BUDDY HUDSON?

The thought intrigued her.

He perched nervously on the edge of a chair, all opening

gambits long forgotten. She was looking him over like he was prime beef and it was making him uncomfortable.

Finally she said, 'I'm glad you could come, Buddy. Montana Gray gave you glowing notices. I ran your test this morning and I agree with her.'

'You do?' He felt a buzz. His luck was on an up. Everything was falling into place. 'I'm glad,' he mumbled.

'You'll be more than glad by the time I've finished with you. You'd like to be a star, wouldn't you? And I think I'm the person that can do it for you.'

He could hardly believe what he was hearing, but then again he had been expecting it all his life.

Black eyes met black eyes.

'I'm ready,' he said.

'I know you are,' she replied.

Chapter Forty-Six

Deke knew he had the living force of power flowing through his body. He had felt it growing within him for a long time . . . Now that his head was shaved the force was set free and he knew that he could do anything he wanted for the aura of power would protect him. He was invincible. He walked by himself in a world of scum. And he alone could give people liberty if he so wished.

Cutting a throat and watching the blood flow was an act of salvation. The Keeper Of The Order did not have to be careful anymore. He was untouchable.

Proof positive.

He had released the receptionist from her miserable existence. Cut her until the blood flowed and life vanished. Then he had washed in a nearby toilet, removed his stained shirt, squeezed the sticky blood out under the cold tap, put the wet shirt back on his body, and searched for the filing cabinet.

He did not hurry as he did all of this. He felt perfectly calm and secure.

He found what he was looking for, and tipped all the rest of the files from the steel cabinet to the floor. Then he set a match to the papers and watched the flames.

He walked unhurriedly to his van parked a block away. Joey would be proud of him.

Now he sat on the hard bed in his dreary motel room and flipped through the file searching for the information he required.

* * *

His mother said, ‘So nice to meet you,’ thin lips a prism of disapproval.

Joey enclosed the surprised woman in a clumsy hug, and deposited a jammy kiss on her cheek. ‘Mama!’ she blurted. ‘That’s what I’m gonna call you – I’cided that first moment Dekey told me ’bout you.’

Winifred Andrews shoved the girl away with a certain amount of force and tried to recover her composure. She hated being touched. ‘Don’t call me that,’ she said, her bony features a passionless mask. ‘It is not correct for you to do so.’

‘Yet!’ added Joey, with a saucy wink.

Deke stood in the doorway to the tidy living room, every piece of furniture, every ornament polished and in its proper place. He didn’t want to enter. He knew that things weren’t going to work out, and that he was going to lose the one person who had ever meant anything to him.

‘Wow!’ Joey exclaimed. ‘What a neat place ya got here. It’s so . . . wow . . . like it’s so homy. I love it!’

A nerve twitched beneath Winifred Andrews’ left eye. She was an austere looking woman with grey hair and a pious expression. Her husband, Willis, was so drab and downtrodden it was possible to be in the same room and not even realize that he was present.

Joey had done exactly that. She had concentrated all of her energies on Mrs Andrews, determined to be liked. ‘Where’s Mr A?’ she asked coyly. ‘Is he as good lookin’ as my Dekey?’

Winifred turned and glared at Deke, still hovering in the doorway. ‘Introduce your . . . friend . . . to father.’

Reluctantly he entered the room and awkwardly performed the introduction.

‘Ooooh, Mr A. I never saw ya sittin’ there,’ Joey oozed pertness. ‘Wow! You’re a looker too! Can I lay a kiss on ya?’

She didn't wait for an answer, but bussed the colourless little man on both cheeks.

Willis shot a nervous look at his wife.

'Sit down,' Winifred said, her voice freezing 'It's Josephine, isn't it?'

'Yeah,' Joey replied. 'But my pals call me Joey. Like it's a nick-name, y'know?' She plumped herself down on a narrow brown sofa and beckoned Deke to sit next to her.

He did so reluctantly.

Silence.

Winifred broke it. 'You are very late, Deke. Why is that?'

'I told him we was late,' scolded Joey. 'I kept on telling the dumbo but he wouldn't listen to me.'

Deke was listening now. How dare she call him names in front of his mother. How dare she.

Winifred said, 'It's no good telling Deke anything. He never listens, just goes his own way, the wrong way, without a thought or feeling for anyone else.'

Joey nodded understandingly.

Winifred gave a long-suffering sigh. 'We've done everything for him. Sacrificed ourselves beyond reproach. Did he tell you that I nearly died giving birth to him?'

Joey shook spiky locks.

'Of course he didn't tell you,' Winifred continued. 'Why should he consider it important? It was I who almost died, not he.'

'Gee, that's a bummer,' interjected Joey, delighted at the way Mrs Andrews was confiding in her.

'You might think that after what I went through I would have borne a considerate son, a boy who cared about his mother. But no. Deke has caused me nothing but pain and worry. He has . . .'

Deke could hear his mother's harsh accusing words pouring from her thin tight lips. He had heard them so many times before . . . All of his life . . .

Useless . . . good-for-nothing . . . weak . . . uncaring . . .

Joey was hanging on to every morsel, jammy lips parted, squiffy *eye darting this way and that. She was nodding in agreement. SHE WAS SIDING WITH HIS MOTHER.*

He felt horribly betrayed. They were making him nothing. Only, with Joey, he had been a big man. Her Cowboy, her Lover . . . HAD THE WHORE BEEN LYING TO HIM?

Very slowly rage began to envelop him. He would not allow his mother to destroy what he and Joey had.

Abruptly he stood up. 'We're going to be married,' he said.

Willis Andrews scuttled over to the television and switched it on as if his very action would avert the argument to come.

Winifred looked at Deke as one would regard a putrefying body.

Joey clapped her hands together like a child with a new toy. Then she said the wrong thing. 'Y'see Mrs A. When we're married I'll straighten Dekey out. You an' I – we'll get him together.' She giggled inanely. 'We'll have him cut off that gross hair, an' buy some decent clothes.' Her eyes were shining. 'Mrs A. I promise I'll make you a terrific daughter. You'll love me.' Hope oozed from every pore. 'Really y'will.'

Winifred Andrews gazed first at Joey then at Deke.

'Is this *what you want, son?' she asked in disbelief. 'This . . . this . . .* tramp?'

Joey's face clouded over.

Willis Andrews stared at the television.

'Yes,' said Deke.

Her thin lip curled. 'Did I hear you say yes?'

'She loves me and I want her.'

'Loves you. *How could anyone love* you?'

His head began to throb. 'She does.'

'Have you ever looked *at her. She's trash.'*

'Hey—' Joey began, but neither of them took any notice.

'She's kind to me . . . nice . . .'

'She's poor street trash. And still she's too good for you. Any woman is too good for you – you know that, don't you?'

Joey shrank into the old brown sofa, somewhere she must have overplayed her hand. Best to shut up until she could steer things back onto the right track.

Winifred continued to debase her son, her voice rigid and unbending as she heaped abuse upon him.

All of his life he had taken it. And never once defended himself or answered back. Even when they made him sell his car – his pride and joy. But with Joey sitting there, listening . . .

'I hate you,' he suddenly screamed. 'I wish you had died when you had me. I wish you'd fucking DIED. You've ruined *my life.'*

Winifred was stunned into only a brief moment of silence.

'You ungrateful parasite,' she seethed. 'Gutter language from gutter filth. We took you from nothing. Gave you a home and food and clothing. Even though you were not of our flesh. Your mother did not want you—"

'Winifred,' objected Willis.

'Be quiet,' she blazed. 'It's time he knew the truth.'

Deke shook his head. What was she talking about . . . he was confused . . .

'We bought you,' she said, her dull eyes almost alive. 'Like you would buy a dog. We chose you – the pick of the litter. Ha! Some pick.'

'What are you talking about—' he whined pitifully.

'One hundred and fifty dollars. A lot of money then.' Her face glowed triumphantly as though she had experienced some glorious relief. 'What do you have to say about that?'

He trembled. 'You're lying.'

'I am not.'

He yelled, 'Liar!'

'I am not,' she repeated stubbornly. She crossed the room to the desk she always kept locked and opened it. The only noise in the room came from the television set. Willis Andrews placed his head in his hands and mumbled incoherently.

Joey sat transfixed. What a bad trip this *had turned out to be. Some loving family to welcome her with open arms.*

Winifred produced a piece of paper and thrust it at him.

'Here,' she said. 'This is the name and address of the woman we bought you from in Barstow, California. A baby broker. God knows where she found the likes of you . . .'

He thought he was dying. His life flashed before him like a film. The beatings, the humiliations, the constant torture of being told he was no good . . .

And the guilt . . .

I NEARLY DIED HAVING YOU. YOU COULD'VE KILLED ME WHEN YOU WERE BORN.

All of his life the guilt.

For nothing?

She wasn't his real mother. Oh Lord no she wasn't . . .

The throbbing in his head, the haze around his eyes. He felt choked with frustration and fury.

Winifred Andrews. Stranger. Began to laugh mirthlessly.

IT'S NOT SO BAD . . . IT'S NOT SO BAD . . .

Joey joined in. A nervous reaction.

YES. IT IS BAD. YES. I MUST DO SOMETHING.

Willis laughed too. Or was he crying? No matter.

Three pigs. Three laughing faces. Teeth and eyes and hair. Three pigs.

The information was there in the file among the yellowed letters of complaint. Dry rot. Damp. Mice infestation. Mrs Nita Carrolle had lived in the house from 1956 to 1973 whereupon she had moved to Las Vegas. Her forwarding address was typed neatly on a tattered white card.

Mrs Nita Carrolle.

He hoped she was still alive. He desired the pleasure of killing her after he had found out the information he needed to survive.

Chapter Forty-Seven

Friday lunch at Ma Maison. Enter Gina Germaine. Every eye in the restaurant turned to stare. Silence. Only for a second. Then normal business resumed.

Gina joined Oliver Easterne at his regular table and spat venom. 'What *the fuck* are they looking at?'

'You, of course,' replied Oliver, dabbing at a mark on the tablecloth. 'You should be used to it by now. How many years have you been in the movies?'

'Long enough to know that in this restaurant – on a Friday – at lunchtime, *no*body stares. Racquel Welch could walk in naked and they wouldn't bat an eyelid.' Her eyes popped alarmingly. 'Everyone knows, Oliver, don't they? The word is out.'

He patted her hand reassuringly, and wondered how she could possibly think that she and Neil being rushed to the hospital – locked in combat so to speak – could be kept a secret. Everyone *was* talking. Big deal. If she was smart she would just brazen it out and enjoy the notoriety.

A week had passed. Neil Gray still languished in the hospital. The prognosis was not good. Oliver had not been idle. He wasn't about to let the film go down the drain just because Neil was out of action. Conveniently he had forgotten about the girl at the beach and reconsidered using Gina. A few discreet meetings had shown him the viability of the film starring George Lancaster *and* Gina Germaine. The two of them together spelled money in the bank. He had been offered a record breaking cable deal if he could deliver the goods. And that's just what he intended to do.

If Neil and Montana didn't like it – fuck 'em. They were hardly in a position to fight.

Gina summoned a waiter and ordered a Bloody Mary. She wore a white strapless dress which emphasized her magnificent breasts. Oliver did not find them magnificent at all, he found them disgusting. But as a showman he knew that you must give the public what they wanted, and one thing about Gina – the unwashed masses loved her and she was big big box office.

'Why the lunch, Oliver?' she asked pointedly.

'I'm reconsidering on you playing Nikki.'

'Oh!' She gave a little gasp. 'You are?'

'I always liked the idea, but Neil and Montana didn't think you were right. Frankly, I think you could do it.'

She purred softly. 'I always said you were a smart son of a bitch. Whenever anyone put you down I *always* stood up for you.' She fluttered long false eyelashes, and squeezed his hand. 'I'm very fond of you, Oliver.'

He quickly removed his hand. 'Thank you.'

'I mean it.'

'I'm sure you do.'

She fluffed out candy-floss white hair and lowered cornflower blue eyes. 'I'm really embarrassed about the other night. The whole thing was so . . . degrading.'

'Don't worry about it,' he consoled. 'Just think of your future.'

'Yes. I must.' She looked determined. 'The thing is I'm always so concerned about *other* people. For once in my life I must think about myself.' Deep sincerity entered her voice. 'I want to do *Street People* very much, but when will it start shooting? With Neil in the hospital and all . . .' she trailed off. 'What are your plans?'

He cleared his throat, waved at a few people. 'Well, Gina,' he began. 'Business is business, and as bad as I feel about Neil's . . . er . . . unfortunate illness . . . the show must go on as someone once said. I've got . . . ideas. Another director, maybe. Don't worry, just imagine the marquee.'

'Gina Germaine and George Lancaster,' she giggled.

Silently Oliver said it his way.

AN OLIVER EASTERNE FILM
AN OLIVER EASTERNE PRODUCTION
GEORGE LANCASTER AND GINA GERMAINE
IN STREET PEOPLE

'Right,' he said. 'I'll call Sadie after lunch.'

'What are you doing later? Why don't you come by my house for a drinkie?'

He shuddered. The very thought of going to bed with Gina gave him the horrors. 'I'll take you up on that invitation another time,' he said smoothly.

'Bet on it,' she flirted.

'I certainly will.'

* * *

Elaine's attempts to get Ross back under the marital roof were fruitless. First it took her two days to find him, and when she did track him down to the Beverly Hills Hotel he refused to return her calls.

She could not believe her stupidity in throwing him out. The big question was how to get him back without causing a public scene. That was the trouble with Beverly Hills, everyone knew your business.

The house looked like a flower shop. Yellow roses from Pamela and George – somewhat faded now. Orchids from Bibi and Adam. Tulips, lilies, palms and yucca plants . . . A never ending delivery of exotic blooms with short notes thanking the *wonderful* Contis for a *wonderful* party. Flower Fashions must have had a field day. Normally Elaine would have been thrilled. But without Ross she felt disoriented and empty. She had no one to talk to. Only Maralee, who was more interested in keeping her ridiculous vigil at the hospital.

'You're divorced from Neil,' Elaine had pointed out firmly.

'It makes no difference now,' Maralee had replied tearfully. 'I still love him and I want him to know that.'

Randy had been cast by the wayside and Maralee refused to talk about him. Occasionally Elaine stopped by the hospital to keep her company. But she didn't feel comfortable, especially when Montana appeared and strode around like she owned the place.

The bills were piling up. She stacked them by the front door ready to send on to Ross's business manager. Cash was running low, and she wondered what she was supposed to do about *that*. Not that she needed much, everything went on Visa or American Express. But Lina required cash, and it would be too embarrassing to admit to the maid that she had no money.

Oh, Ross. Why did you do it?

He didn't. You did.

A week after Ross's departure Ron Gordino turned up at her front door carrying a large hanging plant.

'Thought you might find a place for this,' he drawled.

Her eyes were drawn to the crotch of his jogging pants where his maleness made an impossible lump.

'Thank you,' she murmured. He looked better during the day than at night.

He hovered on her doorstep reluctant to leave, until finally she invited him in for a glass of iced tea. It was midday and Lina glared suspiciously as they sat out by the pool.

'Why haven't you . . . um . . . been in to see me?' Ron asked. 'You gotta keep in shape, Elaine. The body goes . . . everything else follows. Are you taking your vitamins?'

She nodded, quite touched by his concern. At least he *cared*.

'There's a rumour goin' around that you and . . . um . . . Ross have taken the road to splitsville.'

'Who told you that?'

'It's talk.'

'We're just taking a breathing space.'

'You look tense.'

'I'm fine.'

'You look like you need an . . . um . . . massage.'

'Not today, Ron.'

'Why not?'

'I'm not in the mood.'

He leaned across and lazily dug his thumbs into the base of her neck. 'One tense lady,' he drawled. 'You'll get facial lines.'

She sighed wearily. 'I've got facial lines.'

'Lie down.'

'I can't.'

'Why?'

She thought of Lina inside the house. 'It's impossible.'

'No sex, Elaine,' Ron drawled. 'I just want to . . . um . . . help you. You need it.'

Was she going to run her life for some Mexican maid. She *did* need it.

She led him into her bedroom and locked the door. Then she stripped down to her bra and panties and lay face down on the bed.

He went to work immediately – unkinking, smoothing, talented fingers relaxing her body.

'Turn over,' he instructed.

'No sex,' she protested weakly.

'Wouldn't . . . um . . . think of it, Elaine.'

He began to massage her feet, a sensation she particularly liked. Then slowly he started up her leg – the ankle, the calf, the thigh. The inside of her thigh. Firm fingers kneading, massaging . . . Firm fingers pulling away the crotch of her panties and entering her with an authority she did not care to fight.

Oh, Ross. Come home now, all is forgiven.
Ohhhhh . . .

* * *

For one week Ross did not screw around. The Neil Gray-Gina Germaine incident had scared the shit out of him. Yes, sure, all macho men boasted about how they wouldn't mind going in the saddle. But the reality. Jesus H. Christ. Forget it. He couldn't imagine anything worse. And what kind of a snatch did Gina Germaine have anyway? A honeyed trap that no right thinking man would ever go near again. How fortunate that he had never met her. With *his* schlong it would have been trouble all the way.

Getting laid, for the moment, was out. Getting Sadie became a much more important item on his agenda.

He met with her at her office. She was ruthlessly businesslike. She kept her gay assistant in the room at all times, and went over his career with an acid tongue.

'You've made plenty of mistakes,' she said coolly.

Tell me about 'em.

Their meeting lasted an hour, and then she dismissed him with a brisk, 'I'm going to think about what we can do for you. No point in taking you on if we don't feel we can give you our best.'

He felt like a struggling starlet. Not that starlets struggled, they merely lay back, opened their legs, and welcomed America.

Hotel life was okay. Television. Room service. Monitored calls. No one to bug you. An occasional stroll around the pool. A random lunch in the coffee shop. A pre-dinner drink in the Polo Lounge.

He ignored Elaine's calls, deciding to let her suffer a little. Elaine was no fool. She knew the score. Married to him she was a somebody – however much he had slipped. Without him she was a nobody. Beverly Hills law, whether she liked it or not. Now, if she had a lot of money – which she didn't. Or maybe power – which she didn't – things might have been different. All she had was him, and she wouldn't be slow to realize it.

When Sadie didn't call he phoned her. 'Miz La Salle will get back to you as soon as possible,' was the response.

Miz La Salle took her time. In fact, four days later he called again and Miz La Salle finally saw fit to come to the phone.

'Sorry, Ross,' she said in that same businesslike tone as if the night of the party had never happened. 'It's been one of those weeks.'

'I've left Elaine,' he announced.

She didn't take a beat. 'I hope you have a good lawyer. Your alimony payments must be murder.'

He was aggravated by her lack of concern. 'I thought you were going to call.'

'I just told you – it's been one bitch of a week.'

'Yes I know. But it's important that you tell me. Are we a team again or not?'

Deliberately she paused far too long. Then she said, 'I'm going to Palm Springs this weekend. Maybe you'd like to meet me there and we can discuss it.'

He was perplexed. He knew a game when he saw one – he had played enough in his time. 'What about dinner tonight?' he countered.

'Love to, but I've got a screening.'

'Tomorrow night?'

'I'm afraid it's this weekend or nothing.' She paused, savouring the moment. 'What's the matter? Don't you *want* to spend the weekend with me?'

He had planned the seduction of Sadie. But on *his* terms. Now *she* was calling the shots.

'There's nothing I'd like better,' he said, attempting to change the course of things. 'In fact I'll pick you up and drive you there.'

'I'd love that,' she sighed wistfully. 'But I have other

arrangements. I'll give you the address and why don't you just turn up around five on Saturday.'

He accepted her terms. Once he got her into the sack things would be different.

* * *

Guilt twisted Montana. And yet she knew that she had no reason to feel guilty. She stared at Neil in his hospital bed, still in intensive care, and she wanted to scream – 'It's your own fault.' But of course she didn't.

She passed the week in a daze, moving into a nearby room to be as close to him as possible. He lay like a stone, pale and wasted, as though the life had already drained from his body. There were tubes and drips and monitors to keep him alive. He couldn't speak, but she sensed that he knew exactly what was going on.

The doctor – whom she had christened Mister Gucci on account of his label mania – said he was pleased with Neil's progress.

What progress? She wanted to get another opinion, but on checking out Mr Gucci she found he had an excellent reputation.

Maralee was always there, blonde and tearful. Montana decided that she wasn't the bitch Neil had portrayed her as.

Oliver Easterne put in an occasional appearance, usually accompanied by several gofers. Speculation in the trades was rife about *Street People*, but Montana didn't even bother to read them.

One day Oliver cornered her and said, 'We should talk about the film.'

She couldn't believe that he wanted to discuss business at a time like this and she told him so.

'Don't be naive,' he snapped. 'I got commitments to fulfil. The delay is costing.'

'What do you intend to do?' she asked sarcastically. 'Make the movie without Neil?'

'Yes,' he snapped. 'And I got a lawyer says I have every right to do so – check out the sickness clause in his contract.'

She was outraged. 'You wouldn't do it.'

'Watch me. When it comes to a buck I'll do anything.'

* * *

Sadie La Salle issued orders. 'I am arranging a photo session for you, Buddy, with one of the best photographers on the coast, and I want you to look your absolute best. So, until you hear from me – plenty of early nights and sun. Can you manage that?'

He could manage a naked flash down Sunset Boulevard if that's what she wanted.

'Are you into drugs?' she asked crisply. 'Have you ever done porno? Nude photos? *Anything* I should know about before we get started? I don't want your past suddenly catching up with you – so please be truthful.'

He wasn't truthful. Didn't want to blow it before he had even begun. So he became Mister Clean and admitted to nothing except a few puffs of grass on occasion.

'What about family?' she asked. 'Any Billy Carters in the closet?'

He thought about his mother for one bitter moment, then shook his head.

'Are you married? Divorced? Gay? Bi?'

He admitted to being very straight with no marital attachments past or present. Angel would be a surprise. A pleasant one.

They discussed *Street People*, his test, and the fact that Montana Gray had assured him the part was his.

'There are no sure things in this business,' Sadie said. 'Learn that and remember it – however big you become.' She paused. 'Of course I'll talk to Oliver Easterne about you immediately. Although with Neil Gray still in hospital I expect he has other things on his mind. The film will probably be delayed, so let's not narrow our horizons.'

'I'm in your hands,' he shrugged. 'Whatever you think is best for me . . .'

'That's a smart attitude. Try and keep it.'

He left their first meeting truly believing for once that he *could* make it. If Sadie La Salle saw stardom then he hadn't been kidding himself all those years.

First priority was finding somewhere to live. He had money in his pocket – enough at least to settle on something decent for a change. He bought *The Hollywood Reporter* and checked out the real estate section.

After looking at a few places he settled on a furnished apartment on Wilshire near Westwood. No dump. It was costing, but there was a fully equipped gym in the basement, a large *clean* rooftop pool, and maid service.

He moved in and handed the maid twenty-five bucks to go through all his clothes, wash, mend and take to the cleaners. Twelve hundred bucks, courtesy of Montana Gray, had saved his life, and he resolved to pay it back with his first pay cheque.

A car was not an immediate problem, for Montana had said he could borrow the Volkswagen until she needed it. He tried to phone her at the hospital to tell her how sorry he was to hear about her old man, but she wasn't taking any calls. He left his new number so that she could claim her car when she was ready.

Angel, of course, was in his thoughts constantly. But maybe she would be more of a liability than an asset at this particular time, so he put her to the back of his mind for the moment. Sadie La Salle had said plenty of early nights and sun, so that's what he did, concentrating only on the body beautiful. By the time he presented himself for the photo session he wanted to be in even more sensational shape than ever.

Sadie did not leave him hanging. She called him as soon as she had spoken to Oliver Easterne and said it was as she had thought – no decisions were being made. He felt a twinge of anxiety. Why the hell did Neil Gray have to go and have a heart attack? What kind of timing was that?

'Your photo session is arranged for tomorrow,' she continued, seemingly unconcerned about the delay. 'A limo will collect you at nine o'clock in the morning. Be prepared to work hard.'

She wasn't kidding. At nine o'clock the limo arrived, and sitting in the back was Sadie herself.

He had been concentrating on his tan and his body. He looked in peak condition – like a runner just about to start the race.

'I'm pleased with you,' she said. 'You know how to take direction.'

He grinned. He could do with all the praise he could get. Then he wondered if she was going to come on to him. And hoped desperately that she wasn't.

She would. It was always that way when someone did something for you.

The session went well. Nine solid hours with just a short break for lunch. Seven people totally concentrating on him. A hairdresser, make-up artist, clothes stylist. The photographer, with his two assistants. And Sadie.

She had her say in everything. She conferred with all of them on every set-up. She knew what she wanted, and she didn't care to quit until she felt that they had captured it.

By the end of the day he was burnt out, but exhilarated all the same. If this was a taste of things to come he wanted more.

'When can I see the proofs?' he asked anxiously when Sadie dropped him off.

'Soon. I'll call you,' she promised.

The next day he was summoned to her office. When he entered the inner sanctum she was on the phone and waved for him to sit down.

He could hear a male voice shouting on the other end of the line. Sadie seemed unperturbed, she held the receiver away from her ear and listened patiently.

He glanced around the office. Framed photographs of

superstars lined the walls . . . Where would she put *his* photo? Jeez! He could hardly believe all the good things that were happening for him.

'Don't worry, George,' she said soothingly into the phone. 'I'm meeting with Oliver again this evening. I'll have a start date for you without fail.'

More yelling echoed round the office.

'Later, George,' she said firmly. 'Trust me.' She hung up, reached into a silver box and lit up a long thin cigarillo.

'Can I see my photos?' he asked expectantly.

'They're not ready yet.'

'Oh.' He was becoming jittery. Why had she sent for him? Was it good news or bad?

She gazed at him speculatively. 'Well, Buddy, *Street People* is definitely yours. Fifteen thousand a week on a ten week schedule, and best of all your billing will be "introducing Buddy Hudson as Vinnie" on one line. The contracts are being typed now.'

He didn't say a word. He just sat there stunned.

'Is that all right with you?'

'Fifteen thousand dollars a week?' he managed.

'Would you prefer roubles?'

'Je . . . sus.'

'I'm glad you're pleased. It's nice to have one satisfied client.'

He didn't know what to say.

'Any other agent would have got you a quarter of that money,' she said bluntly. 'I want you to remember that in the future.'

'I'll never forget it,' he gulped.

'You'd be surprised how quickly you can,' she said succinctly. 'Within a year we'll be talking big bucks for your services and *that*'s the time you're likely to forget who started you off.'

She hadn't exactly started him off – he had Montana to thank for that. But he had no reason to doubt that it was she who had gotten him the big money – and for that he would be forever grateful.

Suddenly questions were falling from his lips. 'When can I get a script? Is Neil Gray directing? When do we start shooting?'

She answered briskly. 'No set date yet. But soon. I have a script being messengered over. Wardrobe will be contacting you later. The P.R. department want a current bio and photos – *don't* mention our photo session, that's very important – it's nothing to do with the movie – let's see it stays that way.' She had not yet told him of her plans to plaster him across America.

'I'm gonna be dynamite,' he said, gathering together his ego. 'I won't let anyone down.'

'I should hope not.'

'I really 'preciate the billing.'

'So you should.'

He stood up and prowled around the office wondering if now was the time to mention Angel.

No. Find her first. Start the movie. *Then* bring her onto the scene.

'I'm going to Palm Springs this weekend,' Sadie said casually. 'I have a house down there.'

He had known it would come.

'Do you know the Springs at all?' she asked.

Why was there always a price?

'Never been,' he mumbled warily.

'I'd like you to come on Sunday. It's only a short drive. You have a car, don't you?'

He saw an escape route. 'It's kind of broken down on me.'

'Sounds like you need a new one. Why don't I arrange an advance for you. I have a very good business manager who will take excellent care of you.' She jotted down a name and number and handed it to him. 'Call him later today. I'll see that he knows who you are.'

'About Palm Springs—' he began.

'It's important that you come, Buddy. I have a surprise for you. Arrive sometime between ten and eleven on Sunday morning.'

He nodded reluctantly, and wondered how much of a star you had to be before you could quit putting out.

Oh shit. He hated the whole deal.

Chapter Forty-Eight

Millie had hordes of cousins in Los Angeles. She was happy to see them, and they were delighted by her presence, so when Leon said that he had to go to Barstow for the day on business, she did not object too strenuously.

He set off early in his Hertz rented car, hitting the Hollywood freeway before the early morning traffic.

Millie was enthralled by Hollywood. She loved everything – from sleazy Hollywood Boulevard with its star imprinted sidewalks – to the palm-tree lined streets of Beverly Hills.

Leon hated the place. It was too hot and unsettled. He felt it was a town in which anything could happen and usually did.

Driving along Sunset Boulevard one afternoon they observed a teenage hooker discussing terms with the driver of a sleek silver Mercedes. The girl looked barely fourteen. A baby face and pubescent body in black leather hot pants and a cut-away top. She reminded Leon of Joey and he looked quickly away.

'Did you see that?' Millie had demanded. 'My oh my – little girls soliciting in the streets. Why isn't anybody doing anything about it?'

He knew then that there would never come a time when he could confess about Joey. 'So how come you didn't help her?' Millie would cry indignantly. He would have no reply, just his shame.

Barstow was hot and dusty. He spent the day gathering information about Winifred and Willis Andrews – who came together in holy matrimony and then faded into the woodwork. The only lead was a retired doctor who Leon found from tracking an old medical record at Willis' place of work where *nobody* at all recalled him.

He phoned the doctor who sounded old and bad tempered.

'I don't know if I can help you, I've been retired twenty years.'

'Would you have a case history on Willis Andrews?' Leon asked hopefully.

The old doctor muttered something about having a basement filled with case histories of hundreds of patients.

'Can I come and look through them?' Leon requested. A grunt gave him permission.

The doctor lived an hour out of town, and as Leon drove through the arid desert he thought to himself – What am I doing out here in the middle of nowhere? What has any of this detective crap got to do with Joey Kravetz?

It was dark by the time he found the house. He was sweating and hungry but anxious for any information – however trivial.

A washed out looking woman answered the door.

'Excuse the mess,' she said, bringing him into a comfortable living room. 'But it's not often we get visitors. Da,' she called out, leading him to a basement door. 'That policeman's here.'

'Send him down,' yelled the old man.

Leon descended into the basement, a damp musty room stacked to the ceiling with rusting furniture, cardboard boxes, old bikes, and general junk. In the middle of it all sat the doctor. A gnarled nut of a man with a shock of wild silver hair and piercing grey eyes. Leon reckoned him to be a well preserved eighty at least. He was surrounded by old record books and scattered papers. More than a dozen boxes spilled documents and information onto the cold stone floor. At a glance Leon could see that it would take at least a week to sort through. He held out his hand and introduced himself.

The doctor gave him a bone crusher in return.

'How're we doing?' Leon asked.

'Now that's a good question,' said the old man, indicating the confusion.

Leon sighed. 'I don't suppose you remember anything about Willis Andrews?'

The old man chortled. 'Ah that my memory could tell me what I had for breakfast today.'

Three hours later he was riding the freeway back to Los Angeles with a promise from the doctor that he would telephone if he ever located the Andrews file. Not that it was important. He was chasing straws and knew it.

It was four in the morning by the time he got back to the hotel. Millie slept soundly. He climbed into bed beside her and she mumbled but did not surface.

He lay awake for an hour before sleep finally came.

Chapter Forty-Nine

Palm Springs and the temperature hitting one hundred and three degrees.

Sadie arrived Saturday at noon with her assistant, Ferdie Cartright. Ferdie had been with her for seven and a half years. He was forty years old, nattily dressed, sharp-tongued and extremely efficient.

The house she owned was on Sand Dunes Road in exclusive Rancho Mirage. Nothing fancy, just somewhere to get away to from time to time, or so Sadie liked to say.

Ferdie was delighted to accompany her, although she had made it quite clear that he was not to stay.

'Your house is divine,' he enthused, darting from room to room wishing he was there as an invited guest rather than just to help Sadie out setting up some surprise for Buddy Hudson. Frankly, Ferdie was somewhat taken aback by Sadie's sudden and all consuming interest in Mr Hudson. Surely she liked ladies?

At her age wasn't it rather odd to switch?

In her position wasn't it rather crass to pick a young out-of-work actor?

Granted Buddy Hudson *was* gorgeous. But Hollywood was crammed with gorgeous.

He wondered if they had done the dirty deed yet – or if this weekend was to be the consummation. 'Ferdie,' Sadie called sharply. 'I appreciate the fact that you love my house. But do you think you can unload the car?'

He obliged. She was certainly going to a lot of trouble for Buddy Hudson. He sniffed disapprovingly, and hoped that she found him worth it. Although in his humble opinion the pretty ones were always a *vast* disappointment between the sheets.

* * *

Montana had always allowed Neil to take care of business. They shared a New York lawyer who was excellent at what he did, getting Neil top dollar and taking care of her interests adequately. She didn't know him well – a few business meetings, one dinner. After her conversation with Oliver she rushed straight to the phone. He was suitably sympathetic, made all the right noises, but then said something which stunned her. 'Of course, you must realize that Oliver Easterne owns the script of *Street People*. If Neil is unable to keep to the terms of the contract . . . well . . .'

She hung up the phone, furious. Paced around the room she was camping out in at the hospital and seethed. There had to be an answer . . . Oliver couldn't be allowed to do what he liked with her property. Correction. *His* property. She had sold it to the jerk.

Yes. But what about total control? What about the overall deal?

There was an answer, and it occurred to her slowly. Why couldn't *she* direct the film? Take over until Neil regained his health.

She shivered with anticipation. It was a far better idea than bringing in a new director, and if Oliver wanted to stick to the original schedule, she was ready. Nobody knew the property better than she did.

But could she do it?

Sure she could. It was something she'd been working

towards all along. It wasn't her fault that Neil had suffered a heart attack and presented her with this perfect opportunity. Besides, she wouldn't be stabbing him in the back. When he recovered he would be able to just walk in and take over. Fired with enthusiasm she called Oliver and demanded a meeting. He agreed to lunch the next day in the Polo Lounge.

That evening Neil took a turn for the better and she knew immediately that she had made the right decision.

* * *

Surrounded by an abundance of greenery Elaine felt nothing but lonely. She had not realized quite how much her day to day existence depended on Ross. Oh sure she nagged and screamed at him, but he was the very centre of her life – like a spoiled only child. Everything she did was in some way connected to him. Excluding Ron Gordino of course. Whom she hated. With his hometown drawl. And sneaky fingers. And long thin cock.

She had been separated from Ross only three times during ten years of marriage. And they were enforced separations because he was on location and she had spent the entire time he was away doing things for him. Everything she did was for him – whether it was buying a new dress or having her legs waxed.

Realization hit hard. She actually loved the lazy, two-timing thoughtless son of a bitch.

She went to her shrink and told him.

'I know, Elaine,' he said smugly. 'That's what I've always tried to tell you.'

The phone stopped ringing as soon as the Beverly Hills grapevine went into action. Single women were not welcome at screenings and dinners and parties – not unless they were rich and famous in their own right. Elaine, on her own, posed a threat. One of the husbands might get itchy balls – and Elaine, in her position, was hardly likely to say no.

She discovered that she had no friends. Only fair weather acquaintances.

There was Maralee of course. Saint Maralee as the show biz community had bitchily named her since her vigil at Neil's bedside.

Then there was Karen.

Screw Karen and her outsize nipples. Elaine *hated* her with a passion. She only hoped, indeed prayed, that Ross was no longer seeing the bitch.

During the week Ron Gordino appeared at her front door again – this time with a loaf of whole grain bread and some farm fresh brown eggs.

She hid in her bedroom and told Lina to say she was out.

He gazed at her blue Mercedes parked in the drive, then finally ambled off and climbed into the ridiculous jeep he drove.

She began to drink. Never before noon. But white wine at lunchtime helped, and then maybe a tiny shot of vodka to see her through the afternoon. After six o'clock, with Lina safely out of the way, she consumed more wine, a vodka or two, and several rich liqueurs before sleep saved her.

Sometimes she forgot to eat. Soon she was a wreck.

* * *

On Saturday Ross had the Corniche washed and waxed. While this was being done he settled himself on a chaise out by the hotel pool and watched the world and the tourists go by. Several acquaintances waved in his direction, but nobody bothered him.

Understandable. He wasn't hot enough to be bothered. He wasn't even luke warm.

Idly he observed a blonde hooker doing her number on an out of town schmuck dripping with sweat and gold chains.

The blonde teetered past the man's cabana several times until he could not help but notice her. She was wearing a string bikini and spindle-heeled white sandals, with every inch of her skinny body lubricated by a rich dark oil.

'Hello,' she cooed eventually. 'Do you mind if I glance at your copy of *Variety*?'

'Get lost, girlie,' the man said, not such an out of town schmuck after all.

'Excuse *me*,' snapped the hooker, and looked around for other prospects. She spied Ross watching her and threw him a tentative smile. He turned onto his stomach and pretended not to notice.

He must have fallen asleep in the hot sun, for the next thing he knew someone was dripping cold water on his back, and the unmistakable husky tones of Karen Lancaster were saying – 'You lousy bum. Walk out on your wife and I have to read about it in the trades. Charming!'

He groaned and turned over. 'What are you doing here?'

'I'm having lunch with daddy and Pamela. More to the point – what are *you* doing here?'

'I'm living here.'

'Nice of you to tell me.'

'I'm telling you now.'

'Big fucking deal,' she pouted. 'The least you could have done is call me. I mean correct me if I'm wrong, but I thought we had something special going.'

'You told Elaine about us.'

'I did not,' she objected strenuously. 'How can you even *think* that?'

'*Somebody* told her.'

'It wasn't me. She called looking for you the day of your party and I just acted amazed.'

'Maybe your acting's not so hot.'

'What's the big deal anyway? You were all set to leave her – so don't make her finding out about me an excuse.' She removed her mirrored shades and glared at him. 'Why did you move in here when you could have come straight to me?'

He could not think of a suitable reply. Karen Lancaster had no claims on him.

He was saved by the appearance of George Lancaster, Pamela London, and assorted entourage making their way to the Lancaster cabana where tables were set up for lunch.

'Ross!' boomed George.

'Ross!' echoed Pamela.

He should have known better. The pool at the Beverly Hills Hotel was hardly the place to come for a quiet sunbathe.

'Join us for lunch,' trilled Pamela, her angular body alive in an animal print muu-muu.

'Yes,' insisted George, resplendent in a white safari suit.

'I'd like that too,' husked Karen, replacing her mirrored shades.

It was just past twelve-thirty and he didn't have to be in Palm Springs until five. If he left by two it would give him more than enough time to make the drive. 'Why not?' he said, getting up and putting on his shirt.

Pamela linked her arm through his. 'I'm *so* sorry about you and Elaine,' she gushed warmly. 'But these things do happen.' She laughed hoarsely. 'I should know, I've had enough husbands!'

* * *

Saturday was always the busiest day. Koko rushed around like a madman organizing 'his ladies' as he liked to refer to the various females who frequented the salon. Raymondo leered and flirted as usual. Angel answered the phone, juggled appointments, phoned out for snacks, and generally organized everything.

'I don't know how I ever managed without you,' sighed Koko. 'Darlene was such a witch, getting her to order a tuna sandwich was like persuading Nancy Reagan to wear off the rack!'

Angel smiled wanly. Since the party she had not been feeling her best. She was not sleeping properly, and every morning she felt exhausted and sick.

Koko looked at her shrewdly. 'Are you feeling all right?'

Her beautiful eyes filled with tears. 'I'm fine.'

'Fine!' he scoffed. 'With a face on you like the end of the world.'

She dissolved into tears. 'I'm just so mixed up.'

The telephone rang. A frantic woman, hair in rollers, rushed up to the desk and yelled. 'Order me a taxi, I'm already ten minutes late.'

Raymondo screamed from the back of the salon, 'Next bitch pleeeaze!'

Koko enveloped Angel in a comforting hug. 'Your timing is off, lovely. Why don't we save the breakdown for this evening. Dinner at my house, and we'll play the truth game. Yes?'

'Yes,' she sobbed gratefully, realizing how much she needed to confide in someone. 'I'd like that very much.'

* * *

While Ross lunched out by the pool with the Lancasters, Oliver Easterne and Montana Gray respectively picked at their food in the Polo Lounge.

Oliver toyed with an omelette. Montana took random stabs at a spinach salad.

Both were busy with their own thoughts while trying to carry on a civilized conversation. Both hated each other. Both needed each other. Montana had realized it the day before. Oliver was only just beginning to accept the fact – thanks to Montana's persuasive dialogue. Relentlessly she carried on about how she was the only possible choice to direct the film until Neil was well enough to take over.

At first he had laughed in her face. What did she think he was – a crazy man? But as she set forth her case so she made sense.

She knew the property better than anyone.

She knew Neil's hand-picked crew better than anyone.

She had cast the picture with the exception of George and Gina (he hadn't told her about Gina yet. He was saving that little morsel for dessert). She had discovered Buddy Hudson – who according to Sadie was going to be hotter than shit.

She had directed a movie before – true it was only a low-budget short – but she *had* won an award for it.

Best of all – she wanted it so much she would probably work for nothing. And of the three directors Oliver had already approached, two of them were asking for an arm and a leg – and the third his balls.

Montana directing the movie was not such a bad idea at all.

Of course he hadn't told her that. He was enjoying the fact that she was actually treating him with a little respect for a change. He would like to think that she was crawling – but she wasn't – not yet.

'I don't know . . .' he stalled. 'You're inexperienced. I doubt if George would accept you. My investors would probably laugh me out the door if I even suggested you.' He played his trump card. 'If *you* call me an asshole I can imagine what *they* would call me.'

She regarded him coolly through black tinted reading glasses. 'I apologize, Oliver. Sometimes I say things I should only think.'

* * *

'What's in Palm Springs that we should know about?' thundered George.

'It's just business,' Ross said, excusing himself from a dull lunch.

'I bet!' muttered Karen furiously.

'The only business *I* ever did in Palm Springs was with a golf ball or a tootsie,' leered George.

Ross smiled politely.

'You must visit us,' Pamela said loudly. 'If George's stupid movie doesn't start soon we're going home and good riddance to lotus land. This place is an absolute bore. Your party was the most fun.'

Ross felt a tingle, and it wasn't Karen's hand which had been grabbing at his balls under the table throughout lunch. 'Really?'

'Yes. I should call your wife. Nice woman.' She laughed, horse teeth flashing. 'Although I'm sure *you* don't think so.'

'When *does* the movie go?' he asked casually, standing up from the table.

'God knows. That peculiar Easterne man keeps on telling us yesterday. He's muttering about having to find a suitable director. I've told George, if it's not soon we're off.'

'When will you be back, Ross?' Karen asked tightly.

He wondered what Sadie had planned. Two days in bed, perhaps three. 'Tuesday or Wednesday.'

'Where are you staying?'

'My God, Karen, dear – you sound like the poor man's wife,' trilled Pamela.

Karen glared at her, while Ross exited fast. He strode briskly towards the hotel almost missing Oliver Easterne on his way out to the pool.

'Oliver!' he exclaimed, just in time. 'How are you?'

Can't the dumb schmuck see I'm the only actor for his lousy movie?

'Hi, Ross. How's it going?'

God save me from has-been movie stars in madras shorts.

'Great. Never felt better.'

Look at me. I look sensational. All I need is your frigging movie and I'm a star again.

'Good, good. See you around.'

They went their separate ways. Ross to prepare himself for Palm Springs and Sadie. Oliver to seek out his star and placate him.

* * *

Sadie dressed carefully, finally deciding that a white satin peignoir was perfectly suitable for what she had in mind.

It was a quarter to five, and she hoped that Ross would arrive on time. It was unlikely. Ross Conti had never been punctual in his life.

She peered at herself in the mirror and as usual was disappointed with what she saw. She had done her best, but nothing could ever change the fact that she was a plain looking woman, although she did have lovely eyes and thick glossy hair.

She switched on the stereo, placing a record on the turntable that had always been one of Ross's favourites. Stan Getz. Bossa Nova. Oh, the times they had danced around the room, laughing, joking, planning their future together . . .

Ross. She was going to have him again after twenty-six years. She felt the excitement between her legs and leaned her forehead against the coolness of the mirror.

What if she couldn't carry through her plan? What if she got caught up in the heat of the man . . . And Ross had so much heat . . .

She turned the music louder, checked the champagne chilling in a silver ice bucket, and waited for him to arrive.

* * *

Koko had never invited Angel to his house before. Sometimes after work he dropped her home, and occasionally he came in and chatted for a while, but she really didn't know that much about him.

She was surprised to discover that he did not live alone in the small stylish house he took her to in the Hollywood Hills. He introduced her to his friend, Adrian – a handsome man in his early thirties. Adrian did not rise to greet her, and for a moment she thought that he might be mad at Koko for bringing her there. But he seemed quite friendly and made polite conversation while Koko busied himself in the kitchen fixing *linguini al pesto*. It was not until dinner was ready, and Koko matter-of-factly transferred Adrian into a wheelchair, that she realized he was a paraplegic.

Adrian felt her stare and said, 'Vietnam,' without elaborating.

The *linguini* was delicious. So was the lemon mousse which followed.

'Koko's a whizz in the kitchen,' Adrian said, looking at his friend warmly.

'You're hardly in a position to object,' Koko retorted.

The two men's eyes met for a moment and Angel felt the love that flowed between them. She immediately thought of Buddy and how it had once been. Her eyes filled with tears.

'Now, now dreamheart,' Koko soothed. 'Don't go getting maudlin on us. I'll clear away the dishes and then we'll talk.'

Adrian discreetly vanished into the bedroom after dinner.

'He gets tired,' Koko explained.

'It's so awful . . .' she whispered.

'It's not awful at all,' he said sharply. 'It's life. And if Adrian can accept it then I don't know why the rest of us can't. Being paralysed is not a disease you know.' He shook his head angrily.

'I'm sorry,' she said.

He sighed. 'Don't be. It's just that it is . . . awful. But I can't allow myself to think that way.' He took a deep breath. 'Now, let's talk about you. That *is* why you're here, isn't it?'

She felt such a need to confide in Koko. He was warm, and kind, and somehow she knew her secrets would be safe with him. For a moment she hesitated.

'Come along, sweet girl, begin at the beginning,' he encouraged.

She started off tentatively, telling him about Louisville, her foster home, the way her surrogate family had treated her. Then winning the contest in the magazine, coming to Hollywood and all her hopes and dreams.

He listened without interruption as she told him about Daphne, Hawaii, and finally Buddy. Her face became alive and her eyes sparkled as she spoke of him.

'He's so marvellous, Koko.' Quickly she corrected herself. 'I mean he *was* so marvellous . . .'

She told him about the borrowed apartment, getting pregnant, shortage of money, then of Jason Swankle and the beach house.

He raised a cynical eyebrow when he heard of Buddy's shopping spree with Jason.

'When we left the beach nothing was right anymore,' she continued sadly. 'Randy and Shelly and the drugs . . . Buddy seemed like a different person . . . so one morning I just left . . . that was the day I came into the salon and met you.'

'And you haven't been in touch with him since?'

'Only sort of . . .' She mentioned the phone call with Shelly and the awful things Shelly had said. Then she finished off with the Contis' party and shrugged helplessly. 'I just don't know what to do anymore. Should I forget about Buddy? I mean it's silly to think about him all the time if he doesn't even care . . .' She began to cry.

Koko reached for her and rocked her back and forth in his arms. 'My poor baby,' he soothed. 'A regular modern day Cinders – and for God's sake don't say who!'

She loved the warmth of his arms, the softness of his sweater. Just the feeling of being held was so . . . comforting. He touched her eyes with a Kleenex. 'When you saw Buddy at the party did he *mention* the baby? Ask how you were or anything?'

Miserably she shook her head.

'Legally he has to support you and the child. What we need in the picture is a sharp lawyer.'

'Buddy doesn't have any money.'

'Then he will just have to go out and get himself a job like us ordinary folk,' Koko said matter-of-factly. 'It won't kill him you know.'

Stubbornly she shook her head. 'I don't want anything from him.'

'Now don't be so foolish . . .'

'I mean it.'

He looked perplexed. 'Shall we sleep on it? Tomorrow you might look at things differently.'

'I would *never* take his money.'

'Hmmm . . . In that case we'll just have to find you a rich husband won't we?'

'Koko!'

He put a finger to his lips. 'Don't worry, only joking.'

She managed a small smile. 'I should hope so.'

He gave her a hug. 'There, you're feeling better already, aren't you?'

She nodded. It was true. Somehow she was not alone anymore.

* * *

Ross made the drive in record time, flying down the freeway in his golden Corniche like frigging Charlton Heston in 'Ben Hur'. The news that George Lancaster might drop out spurred him on. Sadie was George's agent, she had her finger on the pulse. If George walked she would be the first to know and Ross Conti would be right there – ready and waiting.

He hummed to himself as he searched the parched streets for her address. Palm Springs was hot, and when he stopped at a gas station to ask directions the heat seeped in through the open window of the car like sticky molasses.

'You're Ross Conti,' said the old crone in the gas station as though she was telling him something he didn't already know.

'Yes,' he agreed amiably. 'I am.'

'Didn't like you in that film.'

'What film?'

'*Some Like It Hot*.'

'I wasn't in *Some Like It Hot*.'

She wagged an accusing finger at him. 'Oh yes you were.' She leaned closer to the window, all rotten teeth and knowing eyes. 'What was Marilyn Monroe *really* like?'

He drove off without replying. Being mistaken for Jack Lemmon or Tony Curtis was a first.

By the time he located Sadie's house it was five-thirty. He pulled into the curved driveway, parked outside the front door and honked the horn a couple of times just to let her know the star had arrived. Then he jumped out, opened up the trunk, and took out his suitcase.

By this time Sadie was at the door.

'Welcome,' she said, holding out a chilled glass of champagne.

He double-taked. She was wearing a night-dress. Talk about pushing the season.

He walked towards her, dumped the suitcase, took the proffered glass, and went to kiss her on the cheek.

She grabbed him in a vice-like embrace and stuck her tongue firmly down his throat nearly choking him.

He came up for air quite shocked. *He* was the one that was supposed to be making the moves.

'Let's go to bed,' she said throatily. 'I've waited long enough.' She clutched his hand and pulled him into the house, kicking the door shut behind him.

This wasn't the Sadie he remembered. She of the huge tits and reticent bed manners. Never once had she come on to him in all the time they were living together. But years had passed . . . and everyone had to grow up . . .

She dragged him into a cool bedroom. The drapes were closed and the hum from the air conditioner was drowned out by Stan Getz on the stereo. He took a quick gulp of champagne – which was fortunate – because she took the glass away from him and set it down on a night stand.

'I want you now,' she said urgently, ripping at his clothes.

'Hang on a minute . . . wait . . . let me shower at least,' he protested.

'Now,' she said insistently, unbuttoning his shirt, dragging it from his shoulders, and going for his fly.

He knew he was not hard. In fact he knew that his schlong was probably curled up like a frightened rabbit.

'Just a minute,' he complained loudly. 'I can't perform on command.'

She stopped immediately. 'I thought it was what we both wanted,' she said coldly.

'Of course it is. But I just got here. It was a long drive . . . I feel dirty and tired. I don't want it to be like this.'

Christ! He sounded like a woman!

She managed to look disgusted and hurt all at the same time. 'I'm sorry,' she said. 'Perhaps I misunderstood.'

He was sorely confused. At the party she had been reasonably cool. In her office efficiently businesslike. Now this. He just hadn't been expecting her to come on so strong. She had thrown him completely off balance. He felt like a fool.

'Nice house,' he said lamely.

'The bathroom's through there.' She indicated a doorway. 'There's soap and towels, everything you need. Be my guest.'

He slunk into the bathroom feeling like he had done something wrong, but not sure what. He stayed under the shower for a safe ten minutes, hoping that by the time he emerged she would have cooled down.

No such luck. She waited for him on the bed, leaning against the padded headboard smoking a thin black cigarillo and sipping champagne.

He had dressed in his pants and shirt but that did not faze her.

'Come,' she patted the space beside her. 'It's been a long time. I can't help my impatience.'

He approached the bed warily. What did she want from him? He was prepared to give her his body, but couldn't she wait?

'Aren't you going to take your clothes off?' she inquired. Amused man talking to shy virgin.

Again he felt like a fool. He removed his shirt, stepped out of his pants, but kept his jockeys firmly in place covering the Conti jewels.

'That's better,' she said, holding out her arms in welcome.

He thought of her fantastic tits . . . they should get him going.

Close your eyes and think of Karen.

Why Karen? The thrill has gone.

Close your eyes anyway, schmuck.

Again she attacked him with her tongue, exploring his teeth, his gums, licking the roof of his mouth with sharp little stabs.

'Remember what you said at your party,' she whispered. 'About how great it was with us? And how it's never been that good for you with anyone else? Remember, Ross?'

Did he really say that?

Her tongue slid into his ear and for the first time he felt a stirring. The smell of her was bringing back warm sticky memories. Musky, womanly . . . Sadie's smell. He breathed deeply. Every woman gave off her own special aroma, and that's what was making him hot.

He reached for her breasts and disappointment flooded his body. They were gone! The best pair in Hollywood were now two hard little mounds, barely a handful.

'What happened to your tits?' he gasped.

'I had them fixed.'

'There was nothing wrong with them!'

'Yes there was.'

'I *loved* your tits.'

'I'm sorry. If I'd known you were coming back twenty-six years later I'd have hung onto them.'

He pressed her nipples, they felt like rubber. 'You made a big mistake,' he groaned.

'For God's sake!' she snapped angrily. 'Are we going to fuck or are we going to hold a funeral service for my tits?' She paused for a moment, then added, 'And I think you should know, Ross, that any man who doesn't wish to be labelled a dumb male chauvenist does not call them tits anymore.'

'Sadie, you've changed.'

'Goddammit! I should hope so.'

* * *

Buddy met with the business manager Sadie recommended. The man treated him like a somebody – and why not? If he was going to be making fifteen thousand a week he was hardly a nothing anymore. It never occurred to him that this man looked after people who made millions and that he was merely doing Sadie a favour by agreeing to handle his affairs.

'Sadie tells me you need a car,' he said. 'I can get you an excellent deal on a brand new Mustang G.T. Are you interested?'

'I don't have the money . . . yet.'

'That's all right. It's all taken care of. When your cheques start coming through it'll be deducted. Tell me, what do you need in the way of cash for now?'

Sometimes Buddy felt that if he pinched himself he would wake up. It just didn't seem possible that everything was going right for a change. *Everything except Angel . . .*

He picked up the car Saturday afternoon. It was black with leather upholstery, and best of all four speakers and a tape deck. He drove straight to Tower Records where he purchased two hundred dollars worth of tapes. The Stones mostly. A lot of their early stuff. Then he drove around listening to 'Satisfaction', 'Jumpin' Jack Flash' and all the other golden oldies.

He thought about how he was going to find Angel. Obviously she had not run on home as he had hoped.

He frowned. Maybe he should take out an ad in the trades and hope that someone would show it to her. Only trouble was that Sadie would see it.

On Sunday morning he set off for Palm Springs earlier than necessary. The little car went like a pistol, and he arrived in the Springs at nine, an hour too early.

He stopped for breakfast and found that he had lost his appetite. Morosely he stared out of the window. He just wanted the whole scene over and done with.

* * *

Sunday morning Sadie awoke before Ross and hurried to the bathroom to repair the damage of the previous night's activity. She looked a mess. Black hair unruly and kinked. Every trace of clever make-up ground into her skin. Circles under her eyes, and the sharp cruel lines of age etched deep.

Her hand shook slightly as she applied fresh eyeshadow. The evening had gone as she had planned – up to a point. She had confused the hell out of Ross with her 'get your pants off' approach. He had been disconcerted and she had enjoyed every minute of his discomfort.

But then . . . eventually . . . he had her. In every way. And things were different. For a while.

She hated herself for being weak. She loathed the fact that he had been able to get to her with his unbeatable sexual prowess.

She shivered and wondered if she should still go ahead with her plan. It would be so easy to accept him back into her life. But then she knew what would happen. He would use her for as long as it suited him. And then he would leave her for some vacuous nothing with big boobs and a pretty face.

Ross Conti was not to be trusted. He had to be taught a lesson.

She dressed and returned to the bedroom. He was sprawled across the bed sleeping.

Staring at his slumbering form she realized with a furious pang that she still loved him – whatever love was. There had certainly never been anyone else in her life who made her feel the way he did. *Damn* the power of sex.

Angrily she marched into the kitchen. He was a selfish egotistical bastard. Nothing about him had changed except that he had gotten older.

* * *

A final snore. A quick start. And he was awake.

For a moment he was disoriented. Where was he? At home?

Karen's? The Beverly Hills Hotel? Then it all came back to him. Sadie. Not so tough after all. A hard exterior. A sharp tongue. But once he gave her a little of his secret recipe . . .

He yawned, and grinned. She may have lost the tits, but she certainly had not lost the enthusiasm. He'd had her moaning and screaming – begging for it just like the old days.

He had always enjoyed getting Sadie into a frenzy. Once, he had taught her the words to use . . . made her say things which caused her to flush beet red all those years ago. She knew the words now – probably better than he did – but last night he had made her repeat every one of them ten times – and the game had made her gasp with long lost pleasure.

He was back in her life. And now they could both concentrate on his career.

A luxurious stretch and he looked forward to the day ahead.

* * *

Buddy paid his check and set off.

Maybe he wouldn't do it. Maybe he'd tell her the truth. Maybe she'd cancel out his contract, take back his car, whistle in the advance . . .

Shit! What's a fuck between friends?

Plenty.

Shit!

* * *

Ross grabbed her from behind, full of early morning confidence. 'Good morning, baby,' he crooned, grinding against her while reaching a hand inside her silk shirt.

She spun around fast, throwing him off. 'For God's sake get dressed. There's nothing that puts me off my breakfast more than a man with no clothes on. You look ridiculous.'

He was stunned. Where was the moaning, gasping, pleading lady of the night?

'Remember me? This is Ross baby.' He went to grab a tit. She slapped his hand away.

'May I suggest that Ross baby goes and gets dressed.'

He was semi-hard, ready to spring into action if necessary.

'I thought an early morning trip down memory lane . . .'

'You thought wrong.'

He hadn't quite figured her out yet. She was certainly doing a Jekyll and Hyde. But he could play games too, and tonight he'd *really* make her beg. He threw up his hands in a gesture of defeat. 'Okay, okay. I never forced a lady yet.' He aimed a kiss at her cheek, but she turned quickly away and he found himself kissing air. Somewhat puzzled he returned to the bedroom and put on his swimming shorts.

Today he wanted to straighten out a few things. One – *Street People*. Two – their relationship.

A little breakfast, a few hours' sun. Perhaps she would be in a better mood later. Right now she was probably feeling guilty because she had enjoyed the sex so much. Some women were like that, especially the older ones.

* * *

At exactly ten o'clock Buddy rang the bell of Sadie La Salle's Palm Springs house. He cracked his knuckles impatiently as he waited.

Sadie was in the kitchen. She called out to Ross who was still in the bedroom, 'Can you get the door for me?'

He emerged in a pair of striped madras shorts. 'Are you expecting anyone?'

'Can you get it or not?' she snapped impatiently.

He walked to the front door, threw it open, and came face to face with Buddy.

The two men stared at each other. Buddy recognized Ross Conti immediately and wondered if he had got the wrong house.

Ross recognized Buddy also, although he didn't know his

name, he merely remembered him as one of Karen's partners when she was doing her drunken show-off dance at his party. 'Yes?' he said coldly. He was never particularly friendly towards young good-looking studs – they reminded him with a vengeance of his lost youth.

'Uh . . . Is this Sadie La Salle's house?'

'Yes.'

'Is she . . . uh . . . home?'

'Why?'

Sadie came up behind Ross, a welcoming smile lighting her features. 'Buddy! I'm so glad you could make it.' She peered past him. 'And I see you got your car. Are you pleased?'

'You gotta be kiddin'. It's great.'

'Come on in. Do you know Ross Conti?'

'Uh . . . Mr Conti, sir. It's a pleasure.' He proffered his hand, which Ross ignored.

'Ross. This is my new star to be,' Sadie said, savouring the moment. 'Buddy Hudson. Remember the name, he's going to be big. He's already been signed for one of the lead roles in *Street People*,' She grabbed Buddy by the arm and led him inside. 'I have a surprise for you which I know you're going to love. Ross, come with us. I think this will also interest you.'

Ross wondered why she hadn't told him she was expecting company. And what was all this – 'my new star to be' crap? And 'Buddy Hudson. Remember the name, he's going to be big.'

Once she had said the very same words about him. She had always introduced him that way in the beginning – 'Ross Conti. Remember the name, he's going to be big.'

He trailed them through the house, not pleased by this latest turn of events.

She held on to Buddy's arm, a proprietary air about her that really infuriated Ross. Something was wrong somewhere. It was *him* she should be hanging on to after last night. He was surprised she could even *walk* after last night.

They passed a glistening blue swimming pool and arrived outside the guest house. With a flourish Sadie unlocked the door, sprang the lights and the three of them entered a large white room, empty apart from a billboard size poster covering one entire wall. Buddy was there in living colour. Buddy with his curly black hair, smoky dark eyes and little else except faded Levi shorts and a bronzed and perfect body.

It was a sensational photograph. It was the same photograph Ross had posed for all those years ago with his ruffled blonde hair, deep blue eyes, and bronzed and perfect body.

Scrawled across the poster in bold red handwriting were the magic words – WHO IS BUDDY HUDSON?

'Je . . . sus!' exclaimed Buddy. 'It's sensational, but what's it for?'

'It's a surefire way to make you a star,' Sadie said. 'That poster will be on billboards from coast to coast.' She turned and looked Ross straight in the eye. 'I did it once before and I can do it again. All it takes is a little manipulation and an appreciative client.' She locked eyes with Ross until she was sure that he had received the message, then she linked arms with Buddy and said, 'Let's drive back to L.A. Palm Springs turned out to be a great big disappointment this weekend – one that I'll never repeat.'

Chapter Fifty

Las Vegas welcomed Deke like the eye of the tiger. He drove at night through the black desert, and there suddenly – blazing in the distance – a million sparkling lights. Las Vegas. He had never seen anything like it in his life.

He drove into the city slowly, staring at the casinos, the flashing neon signs, and the people. Like ants they scurried all over the place. In and out, laughing, drunk, some clutching paper cups spilling quarters and silver dollars.

He remembered Atlantic City with Joey. She had loved to gamble, loved to stuff the silver shiny machines as though feeding an army of ravenous sharks.

He should have stopped her. The machines were evil. They ate money. Money was evil. People who played with money were cannibals. Blood sucking evil cannibals. Those people had taken Joey and devoured her.

He cruised around for a while getting the feel of the place, and all the time watching – with cold black expressionless eyes – the ants run in and out of their places of worship. Cannibal ants. Their God was money. They worshipped in the casinos. They had taken Joey as their sacrifice.

He was tired and needed sleep, food, and cold water to cleanse the dirt of living from his body.

A hundred cheap motels beckoned. They offered swimming

pools, water beds, closed circuit porno movies, slot machines, and free breakfasts. Joey would have loved Las Vegas.

Sweet Joey. Where was she now? He missed her.

He frowned, unsure for a moment. Then he remembered. She was home with mother. She was safe.

He checked into a motel, but as tired as he was sleep eluded him.

Perhaps there was something he had to do before he was allowed the luxury of rest. After all, he was no ordinary man. He was The Keeper Of The Order. He had certain responsibilities . . . Perhaps there was something . . .

At three in the morning he prowled the downtown streets on foot. He needed sleep. His eyes were raw with the effort of keeping them open. But there *was* something for him to do . . . and he must wait for a sign . . .

The hooker spotted him long before he saw her. He was a weirdo all right with his shaven head and staring eyes, but business was way off and she had to score. Besides, what was weird nowadays? As long as she walked away with the money and he didn't beat up on her what did she care?

She followed him for a while before tapping his shoulder. 'Hiya, Cowboy. Lookin' for a good time?'

He spun around, red ringed eyes wild, and for a split second the hooker contemplated backing off. But then she figured – what the hell – he's only another dumb john.

'Joey?' he questioned.

'Who, me? You gotta be kiddin', I'm *all* woman. Wanna take a walk an' find out? Twenty greens'll buy plenny.'

Deke knew that he must go with her because she was Joey, and she was reaching out for his help. She had called him Cowboy. That was the signal.

He fumbled in the pocket of his shirt for money and counted out sixteen dollars in single bills.

'That all y'got?' she asked in disgust. Then she grabbed his arm in case he changed his mind. 'It'll do, I suppose,' she said as she hurried him down the street.

He went with her willingly.

A five minute walk took them away from the bright lights and into deserted dimly lit streets. She pulled him into a doorway and fiddled with the belt of her skirt. The material parted. She was naked underneath. Casually she leaned back against the wall and spread her legs.

'Seein' as ya can't quite reach twenny it's gonna have to be standin' up.'

She reached for his zipper.

He reached for his knife.

She was quicker than he was. She had him out of his pants before he knew it, and began to fondle him expertly.

He froze, the knife in his hand unmoving.

After a few seconds she said, 'Come on,' her voice an impatient complaint.

He did not move. Somewhere in the night a woman yelled drunken insults.

More manipulation. Then her voice again, 'Wassa*matter* with you? Got problems?'

He used his knife then, his real weapon, and release was sweet.

She screamed like an animal, while in the distance the drunken woman continued to yell.

When she slumped to the ground he was covered in blood. He took off his shirt and threw it on top of her.

'You can rest now, Joey,' he said in a low voice. 'When I've done what I have to do I will join you.'

Chapter Fifty-One

The speed at which things were happening for him had Buddy dazzled. One moment he was just another actor hustling a break, the next he was Sadie La Salle's new discovery, and one of the stars of a hot new movie.

Thank Christ he was only Sadie's discovery. She hadn't come on to him at all – much to his relief. He had been sure that Palm Springs was to be the pitch, but no, she had shown him his poster, and then they drove back to L.A., he dropped her at her house, and that was that.

Sadie La Salle and Ross Conti. Kind of a mind-blowing combination. But on asking around he discovered that it wasn't so unlikely after all. According to Hollywood gossip Sadie had discovered Ross, made him into a star – whereupon he had promptly dumped her.

'I hope you liked your poster,' Ferdie sniffed archly, when Buddy stopped by the office on Monday. 'I had to drag it all the way down there, and now I've got to drag it all the way back.'

'I wish I looked like that!' Buddy joked.

Ferdie cracked a smile. 'And how was your weekend?' he couldn't help himself from asking.

'Hey – some weekend. Like no sooner did I get there than Sadie wanted me to drive her back to L.A. I never even got to sit in the sun.'

'You mean you didn't stay the night?' Ferdie asked.

'Nope.'

He was clearly astonished. 'Er, Sadie will be with you in a moment. She's on the phone to Oliver Easterne.'

'No problem.' Buddy prowled around the office, checking out the signed pictures of famous stars which decorated the walls. His eyes came to rest on a photo of the sit-com star who had been hanging around Angel at George Lancaster's party. 'You know this creep?' he demanded.

'I hardly hang pictures of *strangers*,' Ferdie replied crisply. 'He's with the agency. Sadie doesn't handle him personally of course. We have a television department.'

'Can you do me a favour?'

'It depends what it is. I do a lot for madam's favourite clients. But I do not supply drugs or members of the opposite sex.'

'Shit!' Buddy burst out laughing. 'If I needed *that* kind of a favour you'd be the last person I'd ask!'

'Thank you very much,' said Ferdie huffily.

'No offence. You see there's this girl I'm tryin' to find. She was at the Lancaster party – maybe with schmucko.' He pointed at the picture.

'What's her name?'

He could hardly say Angel Hudson could he?

'I never got her name. It might have been Angel. She's a very pretty blonde – beautiful in fact.'

'I'll see what I can do. Let's face it, there can't be many Angels in Hollywood!'

* * *

The day it was announced that Montana Gray was going to direct *Street People* George Lancaster walked. He didn't even stay around to fight. He and Pamela boarded her private plane and jetted off to Palm Beach with hardly a backward glance.

George Christy in the Hollywood Reporter quoted Pamela

as saying, 'Hollywood sucks,' but then Pamela had never been noted for her tact.

At first Oliver was furious. He saw his cable deal going right down the toilet. Then he started doing a touch of fast thinking, figured out the money he would save by *not* having George Lancaster, and decided it wasn't such a disaster after all. Gina's name alone would carry the film. And he'd gotten *her* for half her normal price – much to Sadie's disgust. Plus Buddy Hudson was getting monkey piss – and the amount he was paying Montana was a joke.

He had decided to build up the Buddy Hudson part – go for the young market. Much as he hated to give her credit, Montana had really produced a winner – the kid had potential.

Now all he had to do was come up with a stroke of creative casting for the newly vacated role of Mac – which he planned to have rewritten anyway – cut down and made less important.

Who needed another George Lancaster? Not Oliver. He wanted a reasonable actor with a half-assed name who would not ask for the moon.

Ross Conti sounded good to him when his agent, Zack Schaeffer, called with the suggestion. Not that he was the only game in town. A lot of anxious agents were calling offering clients, but Oliver liked the *smell* of Ross Conti. It was offbeat casting. Pretty Boy Conti playing a beat-up old cop, his first decent acting job ever – the magazines would love it. He could see the cover of *People* now. Plus Ross was divorcing again, which would mean more good coverage. And the chemistry between Ross and Gina should be something . . . It was common knowledge that Ross was a tit man.

Put 'em together and what did you have?

A lot more good headlines that's what.

Yes. Oliver liked the aroma. He loved putting the final package together. Especially when everything was going his way.

* * *

Neil Gray was allowed to go home from the hospital three weeks after his heart attack. Only it wasn't home he went to – it was a rented house at the beach with a private nurse as his companion.

Montana arranged the whole thing. 'It'll be for the best,' she said.

'What about you?' he asked, feeling like a man dragged back from the brink of death – which in fact he was.

'I'll try and get down on weekends,' she said vaguely.

They had not talked about the cause of his heart attack. There had been no screaming fights, no accusations. But Neil knew that she was aware of the circumstances, and he was desperate to keep her.

'Promise?' he asked, hating the begging tone he heard creeping into his voice.

'I'll try. But with the movie and all . . .' she trailed off.

'Montana—' he began.

'I don't want to talk about it,' she said fiercely. 'Not until I'm ready.'

So he was banished to the beach with instructions to rest, and regain his health, while his wife took over his movie – starring Gina Germaine – which made the whole thing *really* bizarre.

He wanted to ask her why she had agreed to have Gina in the film, but he could not bring himself to mention the woman's name.

If he had she would have told him that the choice was not hers, and that if she wanted to direct the movie she had to go along with everything Oliver Easterne desired or he would hire another director.

'Take it or leave it,' Oliver had said, enjoying every minute. 'But remember – if you take it I don't expect any trouble from you. I'm in charge – the asshole rules – Okay?'

The *dumb* asshole. Because once shooting began she would

be in control – everyone knew the director had the producer by the balls once they were rolling.

It was difficult to believe that Oliver had signed Gina. But it was done, and there was no other alternative but to go with it, so she summoned her to the studio for a meeting. Somehow or other she had decided to try and wring a creditable performance out of her.

'I was so upset to hear about Neil,' Gina gushed, all pop eyes, white hair, and impossible boobs.

Montana killed her with a look that said it all. Then she killed her with words. 'I want you to lose twenty pounds. Your hair is not natural enough, it'll have to be changed. And no specially made clothes. Off the rack. As for your make-up – no false lashes, lipgloss, or shading.'

Gina glared.

'I don't want to see Gina Germaine, movie star, up on the screen. You have to try and capture the simplicity of Nikki.'

Gina looked bored.

'Let's not kid each other,' Montana continued, determined to get things straight up front. 'I didn't want you for the part – you probably hate the fact that I'm directing. But basically we're both after the same thing – a good movie. So let's cut out the crap and work for the film. Can we shake on that?'

Gina looked surprised. 'Why not?' she decided, and the two women shook hands.

* * *

'He wants lunch with you today. Ma Maison,' said Zack Schaeffer. 'I think we might have a deal. Short money but it's something you should grab.'

The schmuck was telling *him* he should grab it. Who the hell had he been bugging about *Street People* for months? The moment he heard George Lancaster had defected Ross had contacted Zack and insisted that he call Oliver Easterne at once.

'I've called him, a million times,' complained Zack – who was more interested in chasing coke and girls than in getting his clients jobs.

'So call him again. Immediately.'

The timing was right. George's quitting hadn't even hit the newspapers yet. Karen had given him advance warning. She had finally come up with a call that interested him. Usually it was – 'Why haven't I seen you?' 'What's *wrong* with you?'

He did not know what was wrong with him. Since the episode in Palm Springs with Sadie he had been in a bad way. She had treated him like some kind of a sex object. She had *used* him to make her new stud jealous. And for once in his life he had been made to feel rejected and a fool. It wasn't a good feeling, damn her.

He shut himself in his room at the hotel and watched television day and night, calling for room service and not even bothering to shave.

His depression lasted several days and he didn't like it one little bit. It made him feel old and vulnerable, and to top everything off when his beard grew in it was grey. Christ! What with that and his tan fading he looked frigging ancient.

That was when he pulled himself together, just in time for Karen's call about George's imminent departure.

Elaine's messages mounted up daily. At first she had just left her name with a request that he call. Then the message slips that were put under his door became more personal – embarrassingly so. Did she want the world to know what was going on?

He had to do something about her. Go to his lawyer and talk about divorce. But when it came right down to it he wasn't sure if that was what he really wanted.

She should never have thrown him out. Let her suffer a while longer, then maybe he'd see . . .

* * *

Buddy had never been busier in his life. But he loved it. There were hair, make-up and clothes tests. Stills sessions. Meetings with the publicity people to get together a suitable biography. Came the evening he fell into bed exhausted. Friday was his first free day, and he decided to drop by and see both Shelly and Randy just in case they had heard from Angel. He also wanted to repay the money he had borrowed.

It was noon by the time he got to Randy's place. He pressed the bell for several minutes until eventually Shelly staggered to the door, clad only in an outsize T-shirt, red curls a tangled mess, sleep clouding her stoned eyes.

'Yeah?' she mumbled, not even registering that it was him.

'Hey – it's great to be remembered.'

She stared blankly until recognition dawned. 'Bud,' she slurred. 'S'nice t'see you, Bud.'

He followed her into the small apartment. Randy was sprawled naked and asleep across the bed. The place was more of a mess than usual – clothes and records everywhere, empty wine bottles, half-eaten pizzas, and on a table next to the bed a spilled bottle of quaaludes, a syringe and needle, and a tin box containing a small amount of cocaine.

Buddy took the scene in at a glance. 'I see you two found each other,' he said restlessly.

'Why not?' countered Shelly, yawning and running her hands through her tangled hair. 'Beats sleepin' alone.' She picked up a pair of jeans and swiped them at Randy's inert body. 'Wake up, we got us a visit from Bud.'

Randy mumbled, 'Piss off.'

'We had a heavy night,' she explained, gesturing vaguely towards the drug paraphernalia. 'In fact, we've had a heavy week. Don't time *fly* when you're havin' fun. Wanna blow?'

Buddy shook his head. Had he really been a part of this? No wonder Angel had run off.

'Look,' he said quickly. 'I just stopped by to pay you both the money I borrowed.' He reached for his bankroll.

She giggled hysterically. 'Whatcha do? Hold up Safeways? Randy! Wake up. Bud's here. An' he's got money.'

Randy sat up abruptly, wild-eyed. 'Goddamn it. Don't ever yell like that again. I hate it.'

'Toooo bad.' She turned her back on him, bent over, and waved her naked ass in his face.

He slapped it, hard.

Buddy felt claustrophobic. The whole scene was getting him down. He really didn't want to hang around.

'Where did you score?' Randy demanded. He looked like he was falling apart. Wild glassy eyes in a white drawn face.

'What's going on with you?' Buddy asked, indicating the syringe. 'Since when did you go that route?'

'Aw, cut out the phony concern. Just give us the bucks an' get outta here.'

For a moment Buddy felt that maybe he should get involved, at least try and talk to them. But then he thought – what am I? Crazy? They can both look after themselves.

'Here.' He peeled off some bills and handed them over. 'I guess this covers it.'

'Got yourself a job, Bud?' slurred Shelly.

'Yeah,' he replied. No way was he telling these two stoned zombies his news. 'Uh . . . listen. I've moved into a new place. If Angel calls I want you to be sure and give her my number.' He wrote it on a pad by the phone. 'And please – try and get her to tell you where she is. I've really gotta reach her.'

'She's ice cream, man,' mumbled Shelly, rubbing red ringed eyes. 'Melts under pressure.'

'So – I guess I'll see you two around,' Buddy said, backing towards the door.

'You sellin' it again?' demanded Shelly.

He didn't reply. He was out of there, running down the steps, jumping into his car, putting space between himself and the way things used to be.

* * *

'Adrian and I have discussed it, and we both agree that you should move in with us,' Koko said.

Angel began to protest.

'No objections,' he said firmly. 'Besides, I heard from the girl whose apartment you're leasing and she's coming back. So you see, it's all arranged.'

She wanted to put up a fight, assert her newfound independence. But the thought of moving in with Koko and Adrian was just too tempting to resist. They could be her family. Temporarily. Was that such a bad thing to want?

A few days later they loaded her possessions into his car and she moved into the little house in the hills.

At first she felt awkward and out of place, but Adrian was so cordial towards her, and Koko so kind, that she soon felt quite at home.

The baby was just beginning to show.

'Ah-ha!' Raymondo sneered one morning. 'You no wanna play han' ball wit the King. But you sure been playin' *some*where.'

'Go stuff a client,' said Koko tartly, hovering as usual.

'Sure glad *one* of us can,' snapped Raymondo in reply. 'That good for beezzness, y'know, man?'

'God save us from horny Puerto Ricans,' Koko muttered. He turned to Angel. 'I've found you a doctor. He'll look after you until the baby is born – in fact he'll even deliver the little monster.' He mock sighed. 'How we are going to deal with a baby in the house beats me.' He hugged her protectively. 'But not to worry – we'll manage. I'll probably adore every squealing minute!'

She squeezed his hand. 'I do love you, Koko. I'll always be grateful for everything you've done for me.'

He blushed beneath his halo of outlandish curls. '*Please* dreamheart – no mushy stuff. I can't take the emotional pressure. It's bad for my hormone level!'

* * *

Oliver liked playing with a hungry actor. Especially a famous one. Usually they had *him* by the balls, and usually they squeezed tighter than an angry dyke. With Ross Conti, Oliver held all the cards, and he loved it. In fact he double loved it, because he had insisted that Montana join them, and the very coupling of the names Gina Germaine and Ross Conti may well have caused her permanent damage.

'Christ, Oliver,' she said angrily when she heard. 'I can maybe understand why George Lancaster was so important to you – but why Ross Conti when there are so many really good actors around?'

Sitting at his usual table at Ma Maison, Oliver was in his element. Even his haemorrhoids had vanished – which only proved that aggravation did not agree with him – having it all his own way did.

Montana was edgy, not her usual cool together self.

Ross was on his best behaviour, and Oliver played with him like a spiteful cat.

'I think it's one of the best scripts I've ever read.' Ross said eagerly. 'It's got great pace and realism, and it's a terrific part for me.'

At least he likes it, Montana thought. An improvement on George who probably never even read it.

'Sadie called me this morning,' Oliver said, vigorously polishing his fork with a napkin. 'She seems to think Adam Sutton might be interested . . .'

Ross swallowed bile and said nothing. He knew what Oliver was doing and all he could do in return was sit it out.

'Of course, Adam's price is ridiculous,' Oliver continued, waving at Dani and Hal Needham. 'And Bibi on the set is enough to guarantee the poor bastard never works again. However . . . he *is* very popular, especially in Europe.' He finished polishing the fork and admired his handiwork. 'You know Ross, Zack is being very difficult. I'm aware that you have your price . . .' He shrugged. 'But I think I should tell you that this movie is over budget before we even begin.'

Ross began to sweat. He had talked to Zack before lunch, and what Oliver was offering was an insult. Did he expect to go even lower?

'Frankly,' Oliver said magnanimously, 'if we can meet on price the part is yours. If not . . .' He shrugged again. 'I must have a decision by four o'clock today.'

Montana rose. 'I know you'll excuse me,' she said. 'But I can't afford the luxury of long lunches these days. We start shooting in a week and I have a hundred things to do.'

'A week?' gulped Ross.

'Exactly,' she said, feeling sorry for him, liking him, thinking that perhaps he wasn't so wrong for the part after all. She waved briefly at Oliver. 'See you later,' she said, much to his annoyance, and was gone.

'I think she'll make a hell of a movie,' Oliver said grudgingly, 'even if she is a woman.'

'She wrote a marvellous script.'

'Yes. It's good,' Oliver was forced to admit. 'Of course I've had to make a few changes, nothing major.' He sipped a glass of Perrier and glanced around the restaurant. 'Isn't that your wife?'

Ross turned around in time to observe Elaine walking in with Maralee.

Christ! That's all he needed. He quickly straightened his chair and looked away in the hope that she would not spot him.

No such luck. She saw him the moment she entered, and once Maralee was settled at a table she came sailing over.

'Hello, Oliver,' she said, managing an ingratiating smile. 'Hello, Ross.' Hurt accusing eyes.

They both returned her greeting.

Awkward silence.

'Will you join me for coffee later, Ross? There's something I want to discuss.'

At least she had the good sense not to do a number in front of Oliver. 'Why not?' he said graciously, having no intention of doing so.

She gave a little nod. Quite humble for Elaine. 'Thank you.' She returned to Maralee without another word.

'I hear you two are separated,' Oliver said, as if it wasn't common knowledge.

'It's only a temporary thing,' Ross said airily. 'Nothing we can't work out.'

'Good. Wouldn't like to think you were on the loose around Gina . . .'

The way Oliver was talking it sounded like he already had the part. But then Oliver was about as trustworthy as a hungry piranha.

'How much truth is there in the Neil-Gina story?' Ross asked, mildly interested.

'Take what you've heard and treble it.'

'Really?'

'You've heard the phrase "grabbing cunt" – well that's what Gina is – literally.'

Both men guffawed – all guys together – relieved that Neil Gray was the schmuck that got caught and not them.

'I have a feeling we're goin' to work something out on this deal,' Oliver said. 'Only talk to your agent – I can't pull money out of my left sock. Be reasonable, and I think we can do business.'

Prick, Ross thought. What happened to all the money you no longer have to pay George Lancaster? Now, if Sadie was his agent . . .

But she wasn't. And to even think about her caused him extreme humiliation – an emotion he was not used to – and one he had no plans to encourage.

* * *

'He looks terrible,' Elaine fretted.

'He looks exactly the same to me,' Maralee replied. And she wanted to add – it's you who look terrible.

'His hair is too long, he's got bags under his eyes, and he's put on weight,' Elaine stated. 'He's neglecting himself.'

So are you, Maralee wanted to say. She had never – but never – seen Elaine with chipped nail polish before. And talk about adding a pound or two – her friend looked positively jowly. As for her hair – was that a grey strand right at the front for all to see?

Maralee patted her own immaculate blonde locks and reflected that whatever personal crisis she might be going through there was always time for grooming. Elaine was making a grave mistake letting herself go this way.

'I wonder what Ross is doing with Oliver,' Elaine mused.

'There's a rumour that he might replace George Lancaster,' Maralee said.

'Thanks so much for telling me,' Elaine snapped frostily.

'I only just heard, and I knew I was seeing you for lunch.' She paused, determined to get on to the subject *she* wished to discuss. 'Neil told me. I talk to him every day. He's making great progress you know.'

'Correct me if I'm wrong,' Elaine said irritably, one eye observing her errant husband's every move. 'But he *is* still with Montana, isn't he?'

'I suppose so . . . in a way . . . But I don't see it lasting much longer.'

Elaine could hardly conceal her surprise. 'And you want him back? After the way he dumped you?'

Maralee tossed her blonde curls imperiously. '*You're* hardly in a position to talk about being dumped. Would *you* take Ross back?'

Elaine choked in anger. 'Ross *did not* dump me. I threw him out because of his affair with our dear friend, Karen. And while we are on the subject, *you* must have known what was going on. Why didn't you tell me?'

Maralee widened blue eyes, beautifully nipped and tucked so that you couldn't even tell they'd been fixed. '*I* didn't know.'

'Probably not. Too busy screwing Randy whatshiscock. Whatever happened to *him*? Didn't his bank balance match his hard-on?'

Maralee quickly put on a pair of wrapover white sunglasses. 'I just don't know what's the matter with you. You certainly say things no *friend* should say.'

'If your friends don't say 'em, who will?' stated Elaine logically, grabbing at a passing waiter. 'Another Vodkatini,' she said. 'Make it two. I hate the pause between drinks.'

* * *

Ferdie caught Buddy in the middle of a push-up.

'You *must* get an answering service,' Ferdie scolded on the phone. 'Shall I arrange it?'

'Why not,' Buddy decided. If he was going to be a star, may as well start with the trimmings.

'I have a number on that girl you were looking for,' Ferdie said matter-of-factly. 'Her name *is* Angel. And she works at a hair-dressing salon on the Strip.' He proceeded to give Buddy the number, and then he gave advice. 'You have to be careful who you date now, you know. Soon everything you do will be photographed and written about . . . Usually it's best to stick to dating actresses who know how to handle that sort of thing.'

Buddy grinned. Sometimes Ferdie sounded like a pale imitation of Sadie. She had already given him the same speech.

'Thanks, I'll remember that. Gotta split. I have Linda Evans waitin' in the hot tub!'

'Smart ass,' sassed Ferdie.

'Don't you know it!'

Buddy hung up and took a deep breath.

Angel. You are comin' back to me today!

He dialled the number Ferdie had given him and waited impatiently while it rang.

A male voice answered. 'Koko's.'

'Yeah . . . uh . . . I'd like to speak to Angel.'

A pause. 'Who is calling?'

'Tell her a friend.'

'I'm sure you are, but Angel is not available right now, so

perhaps you would be kind enough to give me your name and number and I'll see she gets back to you.'

Fuck! Uptight creep.

'I'll call back later,' Buddy said, not pleased.

'Thank you,' Koko sing-songed.

Buddy put down the receiver and gazed into space. He should have gotten the address, climbed into his car and just driven over.

Then he could have grabbed Angel back into his life with no arguments.

But maybe she wouldn't come . . . The thought frightened him more than he cared to admit.

* * *

'Somebody telephoned you,' Koko said, when Angel returned from a visit to the doctor.

'Who?'

'He wouldn't leave a name.'

Buddy, she thought. Oh, please God, let it be Buddy.

'Will he call back?' she asked anxiously.

'If he doesn't it's his loss, isn't it dreamheart?'

* * *

One moment he was there, the next – gone. Elaine stared in helpless fury at Ross's empty table. She had only been in the ladies' room for a minute, and the bastard had taken that minute and made his escape.

'Did you see Ross go?' she snapped at Maralee.

'No.'

Elaine slumped into her chair. 'I *hate* this goddamn place,' she said. 'Full of fucking phonies – worried about this party and that one. And if you're not invited you stay in with the lights off so everyone thinks you're out of town.'

Maralee blinked. 'What?'

'Nothing,' Elaine said, her voice brittle. 'I'm beginning to sound like Ross.' She sighed. 'Let's have another drink.'

'I don't think so,' said Maralee disapprovingly. 'I have ballet class this afternoon.'

'Shit!' exclaimed Elaine belligerently. 'This place is full of it.'

* * *

At five to four exactly Ross Conti instructed Zack Schaeffer to call Oliver Easterne and accept his terms – whatever they were.

'If we drop your price it's going to be common knowledge this time tomorrow. It'll be a bitch bringing it up again.' Zack lowered his voice. 'You know, Ross, an actor is like a whore. She either fucks for fifty or five. You know what I'm saying?'

'I want this movie, Zack. And I'm the whore who'll do anything to get it. Call Oliver. Now.'

Chapter Fifty-Two

The doctor caught Leon early in the morning while he still slept.

'I wondered if you'd like to drop by and see me,' the old man said, as if he lived next door. 'I have the Andrews case history, and it's interesting stuff.'

'I can't do that,' Leon replied regretfully, edging away from Millie's inert body. 'Can you hold on a minute?'

He hurried into the bathroom and closed the door. Then he sat on the toilet and listened. It *was* interesting stuff. Once the doctor had found his file, he seemed to develop absolute recall.

'Willis Andrews was a quiet little man,' he remembered. 'Came to see me first because of migraine headaches. Wasn't migraine at all – it was his wife. Sexual problems . . . this didn't come out until he had visited me three or four times. You know, back then it wasn't like it is today, with sex discussed openly.'

'Quite,' agreed Leon.

'The problem with Mr Andrews was that he could not maintain an erection,' continued the doctor. 'And this was causing friction at home. Mrs Andrews, it seems, was most anxious to become pregnant.'

'Yes?'

'I counselled with the man. We talked of vitamins, diet,

technique.' He paused, then added proudly, 'I was way ahead of my time you know.'

'I'm sure you were.'

'Yes indeed,' the old man chuckled. 'Sex was always one of my favourite subjects. I liked to help people with problems in that direction. It was a challenge.'

'Did you help Willis Andrews?'

'Alas, no. He was eager to be helped, but I remember thinking at the time after several consultations that maybe the problem did not lie with him. Maybe Mrs Andrews was at fault . . .'

'Did you see her?'

'Unfortunately not. I suggested that it would be a good idea, but he became very agitated. In view of what happened later I wish that I had insisted.'

'What happened later?' Leon asked curiously.

'I clipped the piece from the newspaper and put it in his file.'

Leon persisted. 'What piece?'

'The Andrews couple adopted a child. A girl. There was an accident . . . the child was killed. They said that she fell down the stairs. The neighbours claimed the child was beaten to death . . . They were arrested, but somewhere along the line the charges were dropped. Not enough evidence, something like that. They left town of course. I could never understand the whole thing. Willis Andrews was not a violent man at all.'

Leon's mind was racing. Why did they adopt a child in the first place?

Could it be that because of Willis's problem they were unable to have a child of their own? In all of his checking Leon had been unable to come up with any information about Deke's birth. *Could it be that he was adopted too?*

Adrenaline coursed through his veins. He needed more information. Much more.

He needed to know who Deke Andrews really was.

Chapter Fifty-Three

The cast was set.

An Oliver Easterne Production; *Street People*; Starring Gina Germaine, Ross Conti, and introducing Buddy Hudson as Vinnie.

Produced by Oliver Easterne. Directed by Montana Gray.

Two weeks of interiors in the studio. Followed by eight weeks out on location.

A press party at the Westwood Marquis Hotel three days before shooting to introduce the cast to the media.

Montana could have strangled Gina Germaine. Blonde hair puffed and backcombed to breaking point. A white dress that oozed over her curves, barely making it across the famous boobs.

'The idea,' Montana told her acidly, 'was to let the press know that this role is a big departure for you. How do you expect them to take you seriously when you look ready to open your act in Vegas?'

'Don't get touchy, sweetheart,' cooed Gina. 'I'm afraid you will find that I am *always* the centre of attention – what*ever* I wear.'

Obviously the woman was a total idiot who hadn't understood a word of their previous meeting.

'Listen,' Montana said quickly. 'I think we should talk.'

'Not now, sweetie,' Gina cooed dismissively, gesturing

towards the waiting press and running her tongue over glistening lips.

'How about tomorrow morning?' Montana insisted.

'When I'm not working I *never* get up before twelve,' Gina scolded, as if everyone should know that.

'Lunch then.'

A reluctant sigh. 'Oh, alright.'

Montana then spotted Ross Conti. He looked positively handsome. Whatever happened to the ageing actor she had lunched with at Ma Maison?

Three solid hours under a tanning lamp. Subtle bleach to cover the grey in the hair. A facial. A massage. A two day fast. Special eye drops to take the red out.

'Oh, no!' she muttered. What she had here was a couple of Hollywood movie stars determined to look their best and screw the movie. But they were going to have to deal with her, and she wasn't going to take it.

Only Buddy looked right. Nothing he did could conceal his animal sexuality. There was no mistaking the fact that he was going to walk right off with the film whether she managed to coax a performance out of him or not.

Gina did a long double-take when she met him. She appraised him the way an expert appraises fine gems.

While Gina was checking out Buddy, Ross zeroed in on her. She had a pair – the like of which he had not seen in a long time. Why couldn't he find a woman with Gina's tits, Karen's nipples, Sadie's business acumen, and Elaine's knack of looking after him??

He avoided Sadie at the party. He would never forgive her for treating him the way she had.

Still . . . the last laugh was his. He was staring in *Street People*, although he had been extremely pissed off when he saw the new script. His part was slashed to hell.

'Don't worry,' Montana had assured him. 'Ignore the cut version. We're shooting the original – only don't mention it to Oliver just yet.'

Sadie observed Ross with a mixture of regret and satisfaction. She knew she had hurt him – at least wounded his pride.

Her revenge was *nothing* compared to the way he had treated her. She should have demanded more.

Too late now – he was avoiding her. Shame. She could have gotten him twice the amount of money he had settled for.

Buddy sparkled. He was born to be in the limelight. A shining star. Well maybe not a star yet, but he was in orbit wasn't he? All set to soar.

A pretty black girl with a snub nose said, 'Hi, I'm Virgie from *Teen Topics.*' She fumbled with a tape recorder. 'Can I ask you a few questions?'

He smiled. 'I'd love it.' Talking about himself was becoming a habit. Twenty-three pre-movie interviews in five days. Hardly time to go to the bathroom, let alone track down Angel. He had called her just the once. Time and space were needed to win her back.

Virgie's tape recorder clicked into action. 'Where were you born?' she asked.

Breathy little voice. Sweat beading her upper lip. Was she nervous? Talking to *him*?

'New York,' he lied. 'Hell's Kitchen. It was tough, but I made out.'

'When did you come to Hollywood?'

'Last year. I hitched my way from New York. When I got here I tried several jobs. Lifeguard, sports counsellor with kids, taxi driver. Things like that.' He paused. Dramatic effect. 'Sadie La Salle climbed into my cab one day and whammo! "Are you an actor?" she says. "Yes," I reply. "Then I want you to see Oliver Easterne at once," she says.'

Virgie's eyes widened. 'Gosh!'

'Hey – it was unreal. The next week I'm testing. Can you believe it?'

She faithfully recorded every word.

'Everything okay, Buddy?' asked Pusskins Malone, the chief P.R. man who had helped him make up his new biography.

Buddy made an affirmative circle with his thumb and forefinger.

'They want pictures of you with Gina. Excuse us, dear.'

The girl nodded. 'Thank you,' she said gratefully. 'I'll be watching for your film. Maybe we can do another piece when it comes out.'

'Sure. Why not?' Gracious star to the hilt. He *loved* it.

'Did you get a press kit, dear?' Pusskins asked. 'Pictures, bios – they're by the door. If you need anything else just give me a buzz.'

'I will.'

'Cute little thing,' he said, hurrying Buddy in the direction of Gina who was surrounded by a heavy throng of enthusiastic photographers. 'You met supercunt yet?'

'Haven't had the pleasure.'

Pusskins laughed cynically. 'Attila the Hun with tits!'

'Not my type.'

'Doesn't matter. Are you *her* type? 'Cos if you are – run for the hills!'

'Thanks, but I already heard the Neil Gray story.'

'He was lucky. Some guys have dived between those thighs and haven't been seen for a week!'

Gina greeted him with hungry eyes, a manufactured smile, and a great thrusting of boobs.

'Isn't he sexy, darlings?' she cooed to the photographers.

'Kiss him, Gina.'

'Hug him, Gina.'

'A little more cleavage, Gina.'

She grabbed Buddy in all the right poses.

He noticed that beneath the make-up and hair and flirtatious banter she was cold as an ice-chip.

The photographers clicked non-stop while she threw a few instructions his way. 'Smile.' 'Look sexy.' 'For chrissakes move, you're in my shadow.' 'What are you doing later?'

He thought of the old joke.

I wouldn't go near you with a ten foot pole.

Show me a pole with ten foot and who needs you.

Oliver strode over, beaming. 'What a couple! Inspired casting.'

Montana, conducting an interview with Vernon Scott of UPI, viewed the scene from afar and cringed. A fine send off for her movie.

Ross had been discovered by Virgie, and her anxious tape recorder was thrust in his face.

Sadie watched Gina and Buddy as they posed for the photographers. Now, if Ross was her client there would be no way he was not up there with them. Tomorrow these pictures would run nationwide and it would be *Street People*, Gina Germaine, and Buddy Hudson who were mentioned. Poor old Ross was left at the post. Again.

She felt sorry for him. Then she remembered and her expression hardened. The hell with Ross Conti. He was getting everything he deserved.

She turned away just as Pusskins grabbed Ross and hustled him over to the photographic throng.

* * *

'You owe me two weeks' money. Four hundred an' sixty dollars, Señora.' Lina stood stoically by the back door.

'Four hundred and sixty dollars,' Elaine repeated blankly.

'Two weeks. An' Miguel two hundred on Saturday.'

'You will be paid,' she said grandly.

How come when Lina talks money her English is perfect?

'When?' demanded Lina.

'Soon.'

'When soon?'

'Oh, leave me alone you stupid woman!'

She ran into her bedroom and slammed the door. Loyalty. That was a laugh. Lina had worked for her eight years. She had paid her regularly – through sickness and vacation. And now you would think she would be prepared to wait an extra day or two. Goddamn help. If Lina wasn't careful she would fire her and do the house herself.

You should have had children, Elaine. That way he could never have left you without money.

Leave me alone, Etta. Don't you think I know it?

She was lonely, rattling around the big house all by herself. Screw the money. Maybe it would have been nice to have children around. Grown ones preferably. She wouldn't go so far as to welcome diapers and toys and all that nursery stuff. But it had not been possible, so why was she even thinking about it? And Ross hadn't minded. In fact he was quite pleased. Typical actor. Didn't relish competition.

Pulling herself together she ventured out of the bedroom. Better make the peace with Lina. A stupid maid was better than no maid at all.

* * *

Little S. Shitz drove past the Conti house three times. He was hesitant about going in. He had never met Mrs Conti, and wives could be very prickly when approached with pictures of their husbands in bed with other women. But after Ross Conti failed to turn up for their meeting, he decided she was his best bet.

A police car cruised slowly past, and the cop gave him a brief once-over. Little turned quickly into the Conti driveway and parked. He had read in the newspapers about the Contis separating. If Mrs C. wanted evidence for her divorce he had it – in spades. And if she could pay – it was hers.

He got out of his car and approached the front door, observing that some people certainly knew how to live.

He rang the bell while chewing hungrily on his thumb-nail.

A surly Spanish maid answered the door, her face a thundercloud. '*Si*?' she spat rudely.

He pulled himself up to his full height, all five feet five inches, and handed her a battered business card.

'Give this to Mrs Conti,' he said with all the authority he could muster. 'Tell her I have come regarding her husband.'

'Meester Conti no here. He go away – you come back 'nother time.' She began to close the door on him.

He used the foot ploy. Something he had learned from overdosing on Mickey Spillane books.

'Mover your goddamn foots,' yelled Lina.

'I want to see Mrs Conti. *Mrs* Conti,' he insisted. 'Give her my card.'

Lina glared at him suspiciously. 'Why you no *say* Meesus in place first?'

'I did.'

'You wait.'

She slammed the door with maniacal force, dislodging his foot and nearly crippling him for life. He jumped up and down filled with pain and rage. Whatever Elaine Conti was like she had to be better than her maid.

* * *

'Ah, Lina, there you are,' Elaine said sweetly. 'I wanted to apologize for my rudeness earlier.'

Lina scowled darkly and thrust the card in her face.

'What's this?'

'Man at door,' she muttered, and marched into the kitchen mumbling.

Elaine squinted at the card. She didn't have her contacts in, and the printing on the card was obscured by several dirty marks. She followed Lina into the kitchen. 'What does this man want?'

Lina shrugged disinterestedly. 'Don' know.' She busied herself at the sink.

Oh, God, it's a creditor. Ross has stopped paying the bills.

'Lina,' she wheedled. 'Would you please tell him I'm not at home.'

Lina banged a few dishes around and ignored her.

'Lina, dear. Please.'

The maid turned and glared at her. 'Man very rude. I no deal weeth him.'

Elaine stamped her foot. 'I *pay* you to deal with him.'

'You pay me nothing,' Lina crowed triumphantly.

Elaine stalked out of the kitchen. God! She could certainly deal with one lousy creditor herself, she didn't have to plead with the goddamn maid. How *dare* Lina behave in this fashion.

She marched to the front door and flung it open. 'Yes?' she shrieked. 'What do you want?'

Little took one look at Elaine Conti, wild-eyed in a peach negligee, and took two steps backwards, promptly tripping and nearly breaking his neck.

Elaine helped him to his feet, ever mindful of the fact that he was on her property and if he broke anything he could sue.

'I'm Little S. Shitz,' he gasped. 'Private investigator. And I have some photos that I think might be of interest to you.'

* * *

'What *are* you doing later?' Gina whispered in Buddy's ear.

The press reception was coming to an end. The bar had just been declared closed, and that usually meant a mass exodus.

'I don't know about you, but I'm studying my script,' he said.

She licked full glossed lips and smiled invitingly. 'Wanna go over lines together? Wanna screw a movie star?'

He feigned surprise. 'Hey – do you really think Ross Conti would let me?'

She frowned. 'If *you're* gay, sweetheart, then *I'm* Sadie La Salle's mother!'

'You said it.' He backed away, making a swift escape while there were still people around. Who would have thought that the day would come when he turned down a real life honest to goodness movie star. Hey-hey-hey – with age he was definitely getting smarter. He had *her* number the moment he set eyes on her, and he didn't even have the hots for her. What was the famous Paul Newman quote? Why have hamburger when you got steak at home.

Only he didn't have anything at home. And he should have Angel waiting for him.

He had to make a move. The longer he waited the more difficult it would be. Resolutely he searched out a phone booth. It was past six, but maybe she would still be there.

The same male voice answered. 'Koko's.'

'I want Angel,' Buddy said.

'Don't they all,' sing-songed the voice.

Buddy began a slow burn. 'Is she there or not?'

'Sorry, not. Can I give her a message?'

'Where can I reach her?'

'You can't.'

'But I need to talk to her.'

'Sorry. Any message or not?'

Reluctantly he left his name and number. 'See she gets it. It's urgent.'

Koko wrote the information down, and debated whether to give her the message. She was so settled and happy now. Did she really need the husband back in her life?

He thought perhaps not, so he folded the piece of paper and put it in his shirt pocket. He would discuss it with Adrian later, see what *he* thought. Adrian always made the right decisions.

* * *

Gina Germaine, miffed by Buddy's disinterest, switched her attentions to Oliver, much to his consternation.

'Your star is available for dinner at Chasen's,' she purred. 'Unless you'd prefer something cosier. We could always go back to my place and send out for Chinese.'

'Chasen's,' he said hastily. 'I've asked Ross.' Which was a lie, but one he would quickly amend. 'I was just about to invite you.'

Ross already had a dinner date with Pusskins Malone. The two men went back quite a way and enjoyed swapping stories of lurid pasts.

'You can bring Pusskins,' Oliver said reluctantly. Never one to spring for a large check.

Ross wanted to say no. But a rule of the game was be nice to the producer, so he said, 'Sure, we'll come.'

He did not know that Oliver planned to invite Sadie La Salle. Had he known that, wild buffalos wouldn't have dragged a yes out of him.

Oliver also decided to ask Montana and Buddy. Didn't want anyone feeling slighted. Besides, if he was going for a check, may as well go all the way. It would come off the budget anyway.

Somewhere between the lobby of the Westwood Marquis and the waiting limos the venue was changed from Chasen's to Morton's. A mistake as far as Ross was concerned, because the moment he entered the cool casualness of Morton's restaurant, Karen materialized in front of him.

'Why haven't I seen you?' she hissed, nipples on prominent display through a white silk shirt. 'If you're worried about Elaine I don't *mind* being named in the divorce.'

Without thinking he automatically reached out and touched an erect nipple. She let forth an animal groan. Several interested diners turned to stare. He realized what he was doing and dropped his hand quickly.

Pusskins came up behind. 'Karen, lovely. How are you?'

'Fine, thank you, Puss.' Her green eyes swivelled to take in Gina Germaine's entrance. 'Jesus!' she snorted, glaring at Ross. 'Are *you* with *that*?'

'It's a dinner laid on by Oliver,' he explained. 'Who are *you* with?'

'Some bore. I'll get rid of him and meet you in the parking lot as soon as you can shake your group. Give me a signal. Are we on?'

He dropped his eyes to her nipples. 'We're on.'

She walked off, wearing nothing beneath skin tight white silk pants.

'And she's loaded too,' groaned Pusskins. 'Some guys have all the luck.'

Gina shoved between the two of them and linked arms. 'Hi, everybody,' she giggled, aware of the fact that the entire restaurant was observing her entrance. 'This girl is *starving*. Anyone for dindin?'

* * *

The table was round. The seating thus.

Oliver. Gina on one side, Sadie the other. Beside Gina a truculent Ross, with Pusskins on his other side, and then Montana. Buddy was placed between Sadie and Montana, with Gina eyeing him hungrily across the table.

Conversation was stilted to say the least. Pusskins was the only one with anything to say. He regaled the somewhat uptight group with hilarious stories about the Cannes Film Festival, a celebrated actor and his even more celebrated toupee, and a few Monroe anecdotes.

Gina thrust out her formidable bosom determined to dominate the conversation. 'When I was in Vietnam entertaining the troops, some of the guys kept twelve year old hookers as *pets.* Can you imagine.' She paused, then added hurriedly, 'Of course, I was only a teenager myself.'

Ross shot a quick look at Sadie. Her strong dark eyes met his and did not waver. He tried to stare her out but could not make it. Bitch.

Buddy glanced around the restaurant restlessly. Much as he enjoyed being in such illustrious company he would sooner be home waiting for Angel's phone call. He excused himself from the table with a muttered, 'I gotta make a call.' Then he checked with his newly acquired answering service. 'Any messages?'

'One moment, Mr Hudson.'

Angel had called him back! And he wasn't even home! He hoped she had left her number.

'Shelly phoned you,' said the message service lady. 'She wants you to return her call immediately. She said it was extremely urgent.' He took down the number and slumped with disappointment. He would have ignored Shelly's call but for the fact that maybe it had something to do with Angel, so he sprung another dime.

Shelly answered on the second ring, her voice flat, stoned, and frightened. 'You gotta get over here quick, Bud,' she mumbled. 'I think Randy's dead.'

Chapter Fifty-Four

'Mrs Nita Carrolle?' Deke asked politely.

'Who wants her?' crowed the old woman suspiciously, glaring at Deke who stood on her doorstep, shaven head gleaming in the early morning sun.

'A friend in Barstow suggested that I stop by and see her.'

'Barstow!' she cackled. 'I never had no friends in Barstow, sonnyboy.'

'Are you Mrs Carrolle, then?'

'I sure as fanny ain't Ava Gardner!' She placed one fat hand coyly on her hip. 'Who sent you? Charlie Nation I bet. He was hardly a friend – more of a son of a bitchin' louse.' She roared with laughter.

'I'm Charlie's son,' Deke lied.

'Charlie's son!' she screamed. 'Goddamn! C'mon in sonnyboy, tell me all about the bum. He still spend half his life at the track?'

It was that easy to enter Nita Carrolle's house where she lived with two yapping poodles, and a plethora of frills and flounces.

Nita Carrolle was fat. Her arms were fat. Her legs were fat. Her chins wobbled dangerously. And beneath a voluminous kaftan lurked more fat.

She was also old. Seventy or eighty, it was hard to tell.

Grotesque make-up covered her leathery skin, a slash of vermilion lipstick, beads of sticky mascara, green eyeshadow that lay like leaded paint in the cracks of her eyelids. Dyed yellow hair swirled around her head. There were pearls at her throat, diamonds in her ears, jangling bracelets on each fat wrist, and an assortment of fancy rings.

She steered him towards a stuffed velvet love-seat, inquiring warmly, 'How is the little worm? I ain't seen Charlie in years.'

'He passed away,' Deke said tonelessly.

She visibly sagged. 'Passed away,' she repeated blankly. 'Old Charlie? Sonnyboy, they'll never be a better louse on this earth.' She plucked a lace handkerchief from the folds of her kaftan and blew her nose. 'The old biddy is still going strong though, I bet,' she said, when she'd recovered.

'Yes,' he replied.

'Givin' you a hard time, huh?' she asked sympathetically, blowing her nose again.

He nodded.

She pulled herself together. 'So – what you got for me? He always promised me his diamond pinky when he went. You bring it with you? Is that why you're here?'

'Do you live alone?' he asked politely.

'Just me an' the doggies. Why?'

'Because I want to stay for a while.'

'Y'can stay as long as y'like.' She shook her head sadly. 'Your daddy used to talk about you all the time. And your sister – what was her name?'

'I don't know.'

'Huh?'

He stared at her. Expressionless eyes in a pale face. His shaven head adding a sinister starkness.

She made a soft noise in her throat. A very small noise for such a fat person. 'You're not Charlie's son, are you?'

'No,' he replied calmly.

She gathered her strength and courage. 'Then who in hell are you?'

He reached for his knife in one easy motion, and tested the blade on the tip of his finger. A spot of blood appeared.

'That's what *you* are going to tell *me*,' he said calmly.

Chapter Fifty-Five

'I gotta split,' Buddy whispered in Sadie's ear.

'What are you talking about?' she demanded in a low voice. 'This may be a boring dinner but it is also an important one.'

'I know that,' he continued sotto voice. 'But this friend of mine is in trouble an' I have to help out.'

'In this business the only friend you have is yourself.'

He shrugged. 'They're not gonna throw me off the movie 'cos I didn't stay for dinner.'

He made his excuses and strode quickly from the restaurant.

Sadie frowned. His career hadn't even started yet, and already he was being difficult.

Gina pouted. She was not used to turn-downs. Buddy intrigued her.

Ross was pissed off. With Buddy's early exit it meant that he would have to stick around longer than he wanted.

Montana just wished that it was she making the early getaway.

Pusskins didn't care either way. As long as the booze flowed he was happy.

* * *

Elaine clicked the television remote control and stared at Merv Griffin. She adored Merv. He was so comforting and warm. Full of gossip and fun. Sometimes she felt closer to Merv than anyone in the whole world. He was always there, the same time every night. Reliable, dependable, and friendly.

Much as she loved Merv, tonight he could not hold her attention. The smell of Little S. Shitz was in her nostrils. Cheap aftershave, stale sweat, and sour hunger. The horrible little man's image danced before her eyes, and she leaned across the bed and reached for the large tumbler of vodka.

Ah! The clear sharp taste. So bittersweet and refreshing. She allowed a piece of ice to slip into her mouth, and sucked on it for a moment, enjoying the cold shock.

Little S. Shitz had certainly produced the goods. Pictures of darling Ross that would never grace the covers of 'Life' or 'Ladies Home Journal'. Even 'Playgirl' would baulk at using them. 'Too much cock,' they would say. Hmmm, Elaine thought with a wicked drunken smile, was there ever such a thing . . .

She hiccupped in a most unladylike manner. One thing about living alone, you didn't have to look your best. You could cover yourself in bee's come from head to toe and there was no one around to complain. She slavered on some more of the face cream that Ross hated.

Little S. Shitz wanted ten thousand dollars.

She didn't even have enough cash to pay the maid.

'I must have an answer by the weekend,' he had said. 'I'll be back.'

It occurred to Elaine that she could summon the police, blackmail was an offence. They could lock the revolting little man away.

Only she was smart enough to realize that it didn't quite work that way. Some grubby lawyer would bail him out, the photos would become a *cause célèbre*, and everyone would know about Ross Conti and Karen Lancaster. She would become the laughing stock of Beverly Hills, not to mention the rest of the world.

With a rush of determination she picked up the phone.

'Maralee Gray here,' said her friend's dulcet tones.

Elaine took a deep breath. 'Maralee darling,' she said unevenly. 'Can you lend me ten thousand dollars?'

* * *

Shelly answered Buddy's insistent buzz by opening the door an inch and peering through the crack.

He pushed past her into the stuffy apartment.

'Am I glad you're here,' she said excitedly. 'I'm gettin' out.'

'Hey—' He grabbed her by the arm. '*You* are not going anywhere.' He took in Randy's inert body spread across the bed, and twisted her arm until she faced him. 'What *you* are going to do is sit right down and shut up.'

She did not argue, just slumped to the floor cradling her head in her hands. 'I told him it was too much,' she mumbled. 'I warned the crazy fuck – but he wouldn't listen to me. And I *know* about drugs, man. Jesus. I know. My old lady was a junkie.'

He ignored her and approached Randy's unclothed body. One arm dangled limply off the bed. Gingerly he lifted the wrist and felt for a pulse. There was none. He rolled Randy onto his back and stared at death.

For a moment he was in San Diego. The morgue. Tony. The smell of formaldehyde.

Vomit rose in his throat. He wanted to run.

Shelly began to snivel. 'Wasn't *my* fault. He wanted it. If he wanted it he shoulda bin able to handle it. Right?'

'What did you give him?'

She threw her arms up in despair. 'We were doin' a little of everything – goofing around – havin' good times.'

'Some good times,' he said grimly.

'Rand was depressed,' she said defensively. 'Since that rich bitch dumped him. When you blew in with the money we just went wild. I scored some ace coke, and Randy wanted to speedball . . .' she trailed off. 'It just all got to be too much.'

'Have you called a doctor?'

'Are you kiddin'. I'm gettin' *out*, man. I don't need no hassles with the cops.'

Buddy suddenly realized that he didn't either. He could just imagine Sadie's face if he was involved in a drug bust. There was nothing he could do for Randy now.

'Let's go,' he decided. 'We'll call the paramedics from a phone booth.'

'Can I come with you?' she pleaded.

'Look – I don't—'

'Please, Bud. Please,' she begged. 'I can't be alone now. I'm really freaked by this whole scene. Just for tonight, that's all.'

He remembered the money she had loaned him. The bed that was always available whenever he had needed it.

'Come on,' he said reluctantly.

She clutched onto his arm. 'You're a pal,' she said thankfully.

'Yeah,' he replied cynically. 'A real prince.'

* * *

'Give her his number,' Adrian said.

'It's not that simple,' Koko argued. 'She's such a babe in the woods. This Buddy person is a user. In her condition, I don't think it's wise to put her in contact with him.'

Adrian spun his wheelchair around the kitchen. 'She can handle it. She's not as naive as you think.'

'She's vulnerable.'

Adrian laughed bitterly. 'Aren't we all?'

'Oh dear!' Koko exclaimed. 'You do still *like* her don't you? You're not upset about me bringing her to live with us?'

Adrian shook his head. 'I love her. You know that.'

'Good,' sighed Koko, relieved.

'But give her his number,' Adrian added. 'She's got her own life to lead.'

After dinner Koko did just that. 'I'm sorry, dreamheart. I forgot all about it,' he explained.

Angel tried to hide her delight, but she found it a hard job.

Koko wanted to ply her with warnings, but Adrian was watching him so he kept quiet.

A few minutes later she asked if she could make a call.

'Use our bedroom,' Adrian said. 'You'll be more private there.'

She glowed. 'Thank you.'

Koko gave a deep worried sigh.

'Cut it out,' scolded Adrian. 'You're like an old mother hen.'

'Just call me the mother, darling,' Koko retorted tartly. 'The old and the hen I can do without.'

* * *

They stopped at a call box and summoned the paramedics, then against his better judgement Buddy took Shelly to his new apartment. She was impressed. 'Je . . . sus!' she exclaimed. 'And what big mama is payin' *your* rent?'

He was too down to even bother to answer. Nobody had ever said Randy was the greatest guy in the world, but he had been a good friend, and Buddy felt a deep sadness, not only at Randy's death, but at the *way* he had died. Maybe it could have been him . . . Buddy Boy . . . If fate and Montana Gray hadn't taken a hand in his future.

He threw a blanket and a pillow on the couch in the living room. 'You can sleep here,' he said.

'I'd sooner sleep with you.'

'Let's get something straight up front. I don't want you in that way.'

He noticed that her pupils were dilated, her movements nervy and fast. She was still high on whatever cocktail had sent Randy over the edge.

'Why don't you sleep it off,' he said.

'Are you kiddin'. It's ten o'clock at night – I won't be able to sleep for hours. Not unless you give me somethin'.'

'What?'

'A few 'ludes will do it.'

'I'm fresh out.'

'You really became Mister Super-Straight didn't you?'

'I'm trying.'

She fished in her purse. 'I got a prescription – you want to run it by a pharmacy for me?'

'Is it forged?'

'The genuine article, man.'

He took the prescription from her, figuring it was the only way that either of them would get any sleep.

'I'll be fast,' he said. 'And don't answer the phone, let the service get it.'

As soon as he left she reached in her purse for a joint and lit up, letting the lazy smoke fill her lungs. She felt better immediately and started to look around the apartment, figuring that Buddy must have found himself a rich woman who had set him up for her convenience.

The telephone rang, and ignoring his instructions she reached for it.

A casual, 'Yeah?'

Angel's voice, breathy and sweet. 'Can I speak to Buddy Hudson please.'

She took a quick drag on her joint. 'Who wants him?'

'Angel.'

'He-*llo* Angel. This is your old friend, Shelly. How're you makin' out?'

Angel's voice faltered. 'Fine, thank you.' Why was Shelly there?

'Haven't run on back to the sweet old backwoods of Kentucky yet?' Shelly questioned.

'Is Buddy around?' Angel demanded, sounding stronger than she felt.

'Buddy is out. O.U.T. When he returns I shall tell him you

phoned. And if you want my advice don't call again.' She paused to let her advice sink in. 'When it's over, Angel pie, it's over. And I can get real mad about sharing. Get my drift?'

Helplessness and anger engulfed Angel. She could not understand why Buddy was playing these cruel games. First, at the party, telling her he would be right back, and then not appearing at all. Now, asking her to call him, and having Shelly answer the phone. If he wanted Shelly he could damn well have her, because she had had enough. She slammed the receiver down with surprising force.

In the other room Koko and Adrian exchanged glances.

'Maybe you were right,' Adrian murmured. 'Perhaps she *shouldn't* have called him.'

Koko nodded wisely. 'I would say it is time to suggest a lawyer.'

* * *

Montana left the restaurant shortly after Buddy. She had to work with these people, she certainly didn't have to eat with them.

She drove home in Neil's Maserati. Somehow a fast car suited her mood. The Volkswagen was old times. The Maserati was her future. Speedy and sleek, capable of leaving everything in its wake. She felt really good. Apprehensive, but in control at last. She couldn't wait for the movie to start, although Gina was going to be trouble all the way if her behaviour tonight was any indication. Whatever had Neil been thinking of taking *that* to bed?

Gina Germaine. A golden cow. She hated Neil for his lack of taste. She could hardly bring herself to call him at the beach. The awful truth was she couldn't care less anymore. When the movie wrapped so would their marriage.

Secretly she hoped he would not be well enough to take over directing the movie. It was her baby now. She loved the power and thrust of being in control. Momentarily Oliver was holding her back . . . But once they started shooting – watch out asshole! Run for the hills, dope!

She thought of Buddy and their one night of passion, scrupulously never mentioned by either of them. He had arranged for the Volkswagen to be left outside her house, washed, the tank full, and the keys in the mailbox. She was glad that he had turned out to be the sort of man who understood that beautiful nights sometimes happened between friends. And after that, they could still be good friends with no inquests about how or why. She was looking forward to working with him.

Gina was another matter. She was going to have to clear up a thing or two at lunch. The woman might think she had got away with screwing her husband, but she certainly wasn't going to screw her movie too.

Once home she stripped off her clothes, threw on an old shirt, searched for her tinted reading glasses, and sat down with the shooting script. Right now the movie was all she cared about.

* * *

Watching a relationship develop between Gina and Ross was giving Sadie heartburn or heartache. One of the two. She made her excuses and left.

Pusskins Malone departed immediately after her. He had a date with a cabaret singer who crooned the blues and gave great head. Not at the same time, but near enough.

So then there were three. And Oliver was anxious to make tracks. But at long last Gina and Ross seemed to have found each other, and neither was interested in leaving.

Ross said, 'I think I'd like another Irish coffee.'

Gina said, 'And I'd like another Brandy Alexander.'

Oliver said, 'I know you two kids'll excuse me if I go home. I've taken care of the check.'

As if either of them cared. Ross was staring down her

neckline, and she was wondering if the famous Conti dick was as large as rumour had it.

Oliver rose. 'Good night.'

They barely glanced in his direction. He hurried out to the parking lot and gave his ticket to an attendant. While he was waiting for his car Karen materialized from the shadows.

'Where the hell is that scurvy prick?' she demanded.

Oliver could think of many who fitted that description.

'Who?' he asked mildly.

'Forget it.' She stomped off to her Ferrari and exited amid a cloud of angry exhaust fumes.

Inside the restaurant Gina husked, 'My place or yours?'

Ross could hardly imagine smuggling the very visible Ms Germaine into the Beverly Hills Hotel. One look at her and the late night tourists would probably riot!

'Yours,' he said.

'Good,' she said.

* * *

Buddy handed the bottle of prescription quaaludes to Shelly, and asked, 'What kind of a doctor supplies you with these?'

'They started life as prescription drugs, man. Like for depression or relaxation – anti-stress – that kinda shit.'

She stretched, and the short tank top she was wearing pulled up and revealed inches of hard tanned stomach. 'I got one doctor thinks I'm *real* depressed. Another that'd hand me a slip for the big H if he thought I'd drop my pants for him.' She shrugged nonchalantly. 'And the third guy just likes the bread.' She nodded wisely. 'Always gotta keep a good supply of friendly doctors. Makes life a lot easier.'

He thought of Randy. Had it been easy for him? When the drugs hit . . . when the coke and grass and heroin all combined to blow him straight to heaven – or hell. Whatever.

The phone rang and he sprang for it, catching it on the second ring. 'Angel?' he blurted, so sure it was her.

'Who is Angel?' came Sadie's acid tones.

'Just a guy I know,' he answered, without taking a beat.

'I'm very mad,' she said angrily. 'And when I am mad I do not sleep – so rather than ruin my night's rest I decided to let you know what's on my mind.'

'Hey – Sadie. If it—'

'Just be quiet and listen. You came to me for representation. You arrived with your sexy strut and some half-cocked promise of a role in a movie.'

'Hey—'

'I took you on. Got you the film, special billing, excellent money. *I* am financing your billboard. *I* choose *you*, Buddy. And believe me there are plenty of other actors I could do exactly the same for.'

'Are you sayin' I don't appreciate it?' he interjected heatedly.

'I am saying that I do not like the way you behaved tonight. How *dare* you walk out in the middle of dinner. You *do not* treat people that way. Especially not me, any producer you are working for, or your director. When you are Al Pacino do it if you must. But let me tell you this – if you're going to be difficult I'll drop you now and cancel the billboard campaign. Do you want that? Better tell me now before it's too late.'

'I'm sorry, Sadie,' he said, suitably humble. 'It *was* an emergency. It won't happen again.'

'Just so long as we both know exactly where we stand,' she said crisply, and hung up.

'Tell me more about Sadie,' giggled Shelly. 'Is she Sadie Sadie married lady? Is she the one that set you up here?'

'Do me a favour, drop some more pills and go to sleep.' He headed towards the bedroom.

She was not anxious to see him go. 'Sure you don't feel like stoppin' by Mavericks? I feel so low.'

'*Sleep*, Shelly.'

He closed the door. Then he sat on the end of the bed and thought things out. If Sadie was pissed at him for running out on some dumb dinner how would she feel about him suddenly coming up with a wife?

Worse still. What if his *mother* materialized?

He never ever thought of her. Only in his nightmares did she come to him uninvited and unannounced.

Incest.

A filthy word.

His skin crawled every time he was forced to remember. His whole past was a mess. Names danced in front of his eyes. Maxie Sholto, Joy Byron, Gladrags, Jason Swankle, and a hundred faceless women who might see him on the screen and say – 'Wasn't that the stud I paid money to?'

The whole thing could blow up in his face if he wasn't careful. Yet how could he be careful now? What was done was done.

He hated living a lie. Wasn't truth supposed to be the name of the new game he was playing? How about coming clean with Angel for a start. If they were going to make a life together he owed her that at least. The more he thought about it the more he realized it was right.

A new beginning.

An unwelcome thought occurred to him. He should make the peace with his mother first. It had to be done before she came screaming recognition back into his life. Which could happen when all the publicity he was doing hit. As soon as his schedule allowed he would take a day and go to San Diego.

With that decided he felt better. Then he checked with his service to see if Angel had called. She hadn't.

Immediately he was depressed again. Why was he feeling so bad when finally everything was going so well?

He did press-ups until he was exhausted.

Then he slept.

* * *

On very rare occasions two people meet in bed who are totally compatible in every way – or so they both fondly imagine.

Gina Germaine and Ross Conti were just such a couple. She, all white-blonde hair, sensual mouth and voluptuous breasts.

He, all leathery tan, blue blue eyes and enormous cock.

'Where have you been all my life?' he gasped, near orgasm, his rigid member clamped firmly between her heaving bosoms.

'I don't know,' she gasped, also on the point of divine release. 'But wherever it was, honey, I ain't going back.'

They exploded in a cacophony of moans, grunts, sighs and screams.

'Hot damn!' exclaimed Ross.

'Oh boy!' exclaimed Gina.

They had found each other with a vengeance.

Chapter Fifty-Six

Emmy-Lou Josus had been a maid for sixty of her eighty-two years. She had seen a thing or two in her time. Worked in a whorehouse in New Orleans, a cathouse in St. Louis, a bordello in San Francisco. She had observed fights, and stabbings, abortions and suicides. She had acted as a confidante to the girls, adviser to the johns. By the time she came to Las Vegas she figured she had more or less seen it all.

Emmy-Lou Josus was a tough little lady, nutcracker brown, with a few tufts of peroxide hair ribboned about her scalp. She muttered to herself most of the time. Incoherent ramblings of a past life filled with adventure. The ladies she worked for didn't seem to mind. Why should they mind as long as she vacuumed and dusted and walked the dogs and let the cats in or out and peeled the potatoes and took care of life's grand shit?

She mumbled happily as she let herself into Nita Carrolle's bijou house with her own key. Mrs Carrolle was one of her favourites. She trusted Emmy-Lou. No locking up the booze when she was in *her* place.

The house smelled. Emmy-Lou sniffed and looked for the dogs to come running to greet her as they usually did. 'Doggie fellas,' she called out. 'Stinky fellas.'

She scratched her armpit and removed a faded wool jacked liberally decorated with moth-holes. Mrs Carrolle had promised her something new. Maybe for Christmas. Or perhaps her birthday. She frowned. Couldn't remember when her birthday was. Couldn't remember much of anything nowadays.

She scratched under her arm again, sniffed the strange odour which filled the small house, and went into the kitchen. The dogs were on the table in the middle of the room, their throats slit.

For a moment Emmy-Lou stared. The white formica was covered in blood and she knew she was going to have to clean it. She didn't like blood. It got on your clothes and hands and the smell lingered and . . .

Silently she crossed herself. Mrs Carrolle shouldn't have done it. It was a cruel thing to do. Emmy-Lou could not abide cruelty. Resolutely she set about cleaning up the mess.

She placed the dogs in black plastic garbage bags, scrubbed the heavily stained formica, mopped the floor, all the while muttering ferociously to herself.

When this was done she made a cup of hot sweet tea, sat down at the table and drank it broodingly.

Eventually she went into the living room armed with duster, mop, and vacuum. Maybe it wasn't such a bad thing Mrs Carrolle had done. Maybe not so terrible. 'No more doggie shitty,' she giggled.

The words froze on her lips, and she knew for sure that she would never get the wool jacket Mrs Carrolle had promised her.

Chapter Fifty-Seven

Neil Gray stomped restlessly around his rented beach house. Nurse Miller sat in her usual place knitting. She was a thin, tight-lipped Scottish woman, and Neil was sick and tired of her dull company.

The doctor had given him a list of instructions: No drinking. No excessive exercise. No smoking. No fatty foods. No stress. No sex. In fact none of the things he enjoyed in life. He felt fine, wonderful in fact. Why should he continue to live his life like an invalid? The horror of the heart attack was behind him. He took his pills every day, and quite frankly believed he was fitter and stronger than he had been in years.

'How about a big juicy steak tonight, and a bottle of wine?' he suggested to Nurse Miller, who had abandoned her knitting, ready for her daily trip to the market.

'Now, now Mr Gray,' she said, as if addressing a naughty child. 'We'll have none of that talk.'

'Ah, but we will Nurse Miller. I *fancy* steak and wine. Maybe even a cigar if they have anything smokable.'

'Quite out of the question. The doctor would never allow it.'

'The bloody doctor's not here, is he?'

She pursed her lips. 'I have been hired to look after you. And that is exactly what I intend to do to the best of my ability.'

She left for the market in her car, the only means of transport at the house. He had been delivered there by a chauffeur and Montana. The one and only time she had visited. Not that he blamed her. He had been caught in a situation that nightmares are made of. The question was – what to do now? He wasn't prepared to sit quietly at the beach while he lost his wife, his movie, and his sanity.

Impatiently he paced the room and glared out at the ocean. He hated the bloody sea. The noise alone was enough to drive him mad.

In due course Nurse Miller returned. She brought him the newspapers and the trades which he greedily devoured.

Inside the Herald Examiner there was a large photo of Gina Germaine and Buddy Hudson, accompanied by a short piece on the film. The picture was of Gina and Buddy, but the story was all Montana. He got a line or two. It seemed that he had graduated from being the celebrity in the family to just the sick husband.

He read the story through twice. It irritated him.

Then he stared at the photo of Gina – chief cause of all his troubles.

'Nurse Miller,' he shouted abruptly. 'Give me the keys to your car. I am going into town for an hour or two. Don't worry. I will not smoke, drink or have carnal knowledge of any female. You may rest assured that I shall behave perfectly.'

She confronted him immediately, her thin lips tight with disapproval. 'I cannot allow you to do that, Mr Gray.'

He strode into the kitchen and plucked the keys from her purse. 'The choice, my dear woman, is mine, not yours.'

Her voice rose. 'Mr Gray. If you insist on behaving like this I shall be forced to summon the doctor.' She hurried in front of him and blocked the doorway with her formidable self.

He shoved past her in a most ungentlemanly fashion. 'Frankly, Nurse Miller, I don't give a shit.'

* * *

Shelly was not easy to get rid of. She refused to wake with all of Buddy's pushing and shoving, so he was forced to leave her in his apartment while he went off to a business lunch with Pusskins Malone. He left large pieces of paper with 'DO NOT ANSWER' taped to both phones.

In the lobby of the Beverly Hills Hotel, Pusskins thrust two newspapers under his nose.

GINA GERMAINE AND NEW STAR BUDDY HUDSON.

They called him a star, and he hadn't done a thing!

'Can I get six copies of each?' he asked anxiously.

'You can get cancer if you want it bad enough,' replied Pusskins obscurely.

Lunch was in the Polo Lounge. A beautiful. Mexican journalist with shiny black hair and a Miss Universe figure waited to interview him.

He had it down pat. Same questions. Same answers. Smile. Exert plenty of charm. He had yet to meet a heavyweight, although Pusskins assured him they existed.

The girl made shorthand notes while he gave her the same old replies and let his mind drift. He wondered if there was anything in the paper about Randy. Probably not.

Sin. To die in Hollywood and be a nobody.

How about funeral arrangements? Who would take care of everything?

Second sin of the day. To die broke.

Pusskins snapped his fingers. 'Junior. Get with it,' he commanded. 'Michelle just asked you the same question twice. You got an answer for her or not?'

Buddy sprang to attention. Yeah. He had an answer for her. He had an answer for everything.

* * *

A piece of human garbage suitably nicknamed Rats Sorenson had started his long and non-illustrious career peddling nude pictures of his sister for twenty cents a throw. That was in the forties, when nude photos of females were something to get excited about. Realizing he had a talent for promoting, Rats soon progressed to selling photos of himself *and* his sister. By the time the fifties bloomed he was publishing, printing and distributing (under the counter of course) a crude attempt at a magazine subtly titled 'Twats That'. He made his fortune and swiftly produced a series of blue movies which also made money. In the sixties he decided to go legitimate. And he produced a glossy magazine about gardens which lasted for three issues and took every penny he possessed. By this time he was married to a sixteen year old nymphet who waited until the money went, then followed it. He caught her in a motel with a seventy year old married man and shot the old guy right between the eyes. For this he got a twenty-five year sentence. And with time off for good behaviour (he soon became the warden's favourite for reasons known only to himself and his cellmate – a blackmailer by the name of Little S. Shitz) he was set free on an unsuspecting world after fifteen years. Rats soon returned to the business he knew best, and made his second fortune. 'Twats That' reappeared – this time *on* the news stands and retitled 'Hard Pussy'. A waiting public embraced the magazine fondly.

But, of course, Rats wanted more. He married a seventeen year old go-go dancer, and accompanied her on weekly trips to the supermarket where he noticed a certain type of newspaper gain great prominence at the check-out stands. It started with the 'National Enquirer' which was swiftly followed by all kinds of imitators.

Rats wanted in. He decided to launch a newspaper which followed the same formula – but with an added ingredient. Hot, compromising *pictures* of celebrities – as hot as he could get 'em. Of course the supermarkets wouldn't carry *his* magazine, but that didn't worry him. People could buy it at their news stands.

Running into his old pal Little S. Shitz, turned out to be a fortunate coincidence for both of them. They collided outside Tony Romas restaurant deep in the heart of Beverly Hills.

Conversation revealed the fact that the new hot newsrag 'Truth & Fact' was owned, published and edited by none other than Rats himself.

'Have I got some pictures for you . . .' Little boasted. 'Not cheap, but worth every fat buck.'

The very next day business was done. Rats bought the entire Karen Lancaster-Ross Conti set of negatives and chose a rather tasteful shot of Ross just about to chew on a nipple for the cover. The real low-down dirty stuff he saved for the centre spread.

'I'm rushing it through for the next issue,' Rats said.

'Maybe I could have photo credit,' Little suggested tentatively. He never had been particularly smart.

* * *

Maralee turned down Elaine's request to loan her ten thousand dollars. In fact she was quite shocked that Elaine had summoned the nerve to ask her. She phoned Karen to complain, but Karen was most unfriendly, accusing her of siding with Elaine, and not calling her.

'I've been too concerned about Neil to contact anyone,' Maralee explained.

'But you hate the louse,' Karen said, perplexed.

'Hate is a word that is no longer a part of my vocabulary,' Maralee replied piously. 'Neil has changed. I think he's ready to get rid of whatshername and come back to me.'

'You can't be serious?'

'Absolutely.'

There was a short silence while they both digested Maralee's new personality. Then Karen remembered a small item she had read buried somewhere in the L.A. Times.

'What was your friend Randy's surname?'

'Felix. I introduced you to him enough times, the least you can do is remember his name. I know he's not famous, but—'

'He's dead,' Karen interrupted.

'What?'

'There's a piece in the paper. Someone called the police and they found him overdosed in some shitty one-room apartment in Hollywood. I thought you said he had money.'

Maralee was devastated. She had broken up with Randy, but still . . . How could such a thing happen? And what was he doing in a dump? According to him he had lived in a very nice apartment – 'It's only three bedrooms, but I find it comfortable,' he had told her. Of course she had never been there . . . Perhaps it was just as well . . .

'I must go to him,' she decided.

'What are you *talking* about? He's dead,' snorted Karen. 'The *police* are involved. They seem to think a woman was with him when he died, and they want to interview her.' A thought occurred to her. '*You* weren't doing drugs with him were you?'

'Don't be so ridiculous,' snapped Maralee. 'I don't even smoke marijuana.'

'Hmmm,' Karen sighed. 'You've no idea *what* you're missing.'

Maralee concluded the conversation and went into her bathroom to gaze at her blonde prettiness in the mirror.

Why did she always pick losers? What was it about her that attracted the fortune hunters and the burns?

She thought of Neil. An older man. English, respected, a fine director.

Once he had been her husband and she had let him go. The time had come to win him back.

* * *

Neil hit the Pacific Coast Highway in Nurse Miller's pristine white Chevrolet. Now that he was out he had changed his mind about storming Oliver's offices and regaining control of his film. He wanted Montana more than he wanted the bloody movie, and she would certainly not appreciate him barging in and taking over. He decided to stop off, have a drink, return to the beach and call her. If he requested a meeting she could hardly turn him down, and then they could thrash everything out. A confrontation was long overdue.

He found a bar he knew and pulled into the parking lot.

A couple of decent brandies couldn't possibly hurt, they would probably do him more good than harm. Everyone knew brandy was a medicinal aid.

The first one was like nectar. And the second merely a complement to the first. His capacity was huge. In Paris he had thought nothing of killing a bottle a night. Of course that was years previously, but you never forget how to handle your liquor. Or your women.

He laughed hollowly at that, and ordered another drink.

* * *

'Move in,' suggested Gina, the morning after their night of passion. She was rushing to get ready for her lunch appointment with Montana.

Ross lay in bed watching her. He grinned lazily. One thing was for sure, he certainly didn't need asking twice. Her house was fabulous, her tits perfection – besides – the Beverly Hills Hotel was costing him an arm and a leg.

* * *

Montana arrived for lunch at El Padrino in the Beverly Wilshire Hotel on time. She looked around, ordered a pernod on ice, and sat back to wait. She knew for sure that Gina would make her wait.

True to form Gina made a typical movie star entrance thirty-five minutes later. She wore yellow silk slacks, a diaphanous blouse, huge white sunglasses, and a fluffy red fox jacket although it was seventy-five degrees out.

'Goddamn!' she exclaimed, flopping onto the banquet seat. 'Did I have a night! Ross Conti is everything they say – and more.' She giggled. 'Several inches more! Best lay I've had in a year!' She grabbed a passing waiter. 'Vodkatini. On the rocks. Lots of 'em.' She lifted her sunglasses and peered at Montana. 'So what's with the meeting? I coulda slept another two hours.'

Montana shook her head trying to hide deep aggravation. 'Gina,' she said slowly, as if talking to a recalcitrant child. 'I told you to lose twenty pounds, get your hair fixed, play down the sexy image. Didn't you understand me?'

Gina retreated behind her sunglasses and glanced restlessly around the dimly lit restaurant.

'Montana. Dear. You must realize I have a certain image to project. My public expects me to look . . . glamorous.'

'I don't give a good goddamn what your public expects. I, as your director, expect a hell of a lot more. And if I don't get it, you're out.'

'*I'm* out!' she laughed disbelievingly. 'Dear. Let us not forget who the *star* of this movie is.'

The waiter brought her drink and she almost downed it in one gulp.

Montana sipped her pernod and considered how best to deal with the situation. She felt surprisingly calm, because she knew she was going to win. Gina *would* toe the line. She didn't know how she was going to manage it, she just knew that she was.

She regarded the blonde woman coolly. 'O.K.,' she said. 'Fine. Have it your way. I guess I'll be busy enough taking care of Buddy, and I know Ross is going to be great. I think he may surprise everyone.'

Gina had not expected retreat so quickly, and it knocked her off balance. She shrugged her fox jacket off her shoulders – causing several nearby males to choke on their drinks. '*I'm* going to surprise a lot of people too,' she said petulantly.

'Sure you are,' agreed Montana. 'Voluptuous Gina Germaine does it again. Tits and ass wins the prize for non-performance of the year.'

'I resent that remark,' Gina snapped. 'Just because I screwed your husband don't think you can talk to me any way you like.'

Montana's eyes flashed dangerously, but she kept her temper.

Oh, Neil! With this? She was never worthy of you.

'Whatever you did with Neil is his affair, and your affair too. I never believed in putting on the shackles,' she said quietly.

Gina took off her sunglasses and narrowed her protruding blue eyes. 'You're really strange, you know that?'

Montana shrugged. 'I believe everybody has their freedom. Neil wanted you. He had you. Big deal. Look where he ended up.'

'God! That's not a very nice thing to say.'

'Why not? It's true.' She signalled for the waiter. 'Check please.'

'We haven't had lunch yet,' Gina objected.

'No point to it,' Montana said crisply. 'I wanted to talk to you about the role, try to help you with it. But I can see I'm wasting my time. You just want to play power games, and that's not my trip. I'm a working woman, Gina, not a Hollywood wife.'

'You're really a pistol.' A grudging admiration entered Gina's tone.

'Nope. Just a professional who wants to make the best movie I can. I told you that at our first meeting – I thought we had the same goal in mind, but obviously I was mistaken.' She accepted the check from the waiter and fished in her purse for a credit card. 'If you don't want to cooperate, I'm certainly not going to force you. I'll just concentrate on Buddy and Ross. They'll be so good that nobody'll notice *Miz* Germaine. And it's a shame because you could have been dynamite. It's all there, Gina. Hidden beneath the hair and the boobs and the make up.' She paused for a moment. 'You just need someone to work with you – someone who *cares* about what you're doing. I could bring it out in you, and you know it.'

'I don't work well with women.'

'Bullshit. When have you ever tried? You might find you enjoy the experience.'

A slow smile spread across Gina's face. 'Y'know something? You remind me of me!'

God forbid! Montana thought.

'Yeah,' enthused Gina. 'Fast with the mouth – and you got balls, kiddo. You can make it happen – I *bet* you can.'

'Does this mean you're going to listen to me?'

'Why not?' Gina said decisively. 'Yeah. Why not indeed? I've been listening to schmucks who wanted to get their rocks off all my life – so who knows? Working with you might make a change.' She leaned forward confidentially. 'I'll tell you something, Montana. Neil and me – it didn't mean a thing – just sort of a business arrangement.'

'I'm sure.'

'And you would be right to be sure because I am here to tell you that all men are unfaithful bums. *All* of them, honey. Never trust 'em as far as you can spit.' She nodded wisely. 'I *know*. I have been out on my own since I was fifteen years old, and let me tell you – it has not all been a pot of honey. How would you like to hear about some of the things I had to do to get where I am today?'

When Gina talked, she talked. Two hours later she was *still* talking. And Montana listened. Quietly.

Actors. Actresses. They were all the same. Give them a little sympathy, a little understanding, and they were yours.

When the movie rolled, Gina would be putty in her hands. And she would get a performance out of her the like of which her horny public had *never* seen before.

If Neil could do it so could she.

Chapter Fifty-Eight

Leon went immediately to work. He made some vague excuse to Millie and returned to Barstow. There, he checked out police files, newspaper reports, and adoption agencies.

A day was not enough to do everything, so he took a room at the Desert Inn Hotel and called Millie. She was not happy. 'This is our vacation,' she reminded him flatly. 'You're not supposed to be working.'

'I know. But it's important. And I'll make it up to you – I promise.'

'Captain Lacoste phoned. He wants you to contact him.'

He was too caught up to notice the sullenness in her voice. 'Thanks. I'll probably be back tomorrow.'

'Don't rush,' she muttered coldly. But he had already broken the connection.

The captain had news that made Leon's skin crawl. Deke Andrews had struck again. This time in Las Vegas. The victim was an old hooker who cruised the downtown bars and casinos. 'He left enough signs to let us know it was him. Prints, saliva, semen. The same distinctive knife wounds. And his shirt. The police in Vegas have a couple of witnesses who may or may not have spotted him leaving the scene. We're sending his photo over the wire. Are you prepared to go there?'

Leon didn't hesitate. 'Of course. I want to be taken off vacation and declared officially on the case.'

'That's what I hoped you'd say. I'll contact Vegas and let them know you're on your way. They've promised full cooperation.'

Leon's mind was already racing. Why Las Vegas? Somehow he had thought that Deke was heading for Barstow. Just a hunch . . . Something . . . someone in Barstow . . . But what if Deke had *already* visited Barstow.

As soon as he got off the phone he decided to check out all local homicides over the last four weeks. And then he would head for Vegas – fast.

Chapter Fifty-Nine

'Where is he?' demanded Maralee, blue eyes anxious and concerned.

'He *stole* my car,' stated Nurse Miller dourly. 'Assaulted me, and used foul language. I wish to tender my immediate notice.'

'Don't be so silly,' Maralee said vaguely. 'He's not allowed to drive.'

'I know that, Mrs Gray. But I couldn't stop him. He was like a madman.'

Maralee could not control her disappointment. She almost stamped her foot. 'I wanted him to be here. It's important. How *could* you let him go?'

'I expect two weeks' severance pay. And you are most fortunate that I am not planning to sue for bodily harm. If my car is not back here within the hour I am reporting it as a stolen vehicle to the police.'

* * *

Before long two or three drinks turned to four or five, and his heart began to thunder in his chest, but it didn't bother him. Nothing bothered him.

He was going to have it out with Montana. Tell her the

whole story. Lay it on the line – as the Americans so charmingly put it. Come clean. Confess. Beg her forgiveness.

Only Montana wouldn't buy it. Montana, so clear-headed and cool. 'Fuck off, Neil,' she would say. 'I don't need your jerk-off excuses.' And she was so right, for that's all it would be . . . stupid excuses explaining several acts of lust for which he *had* no excuse.

He was going to order another drink, thought better of it, and walked unsteadily outside.

* * *

Shelly was still in residence when Buddy returned. She was stretched out on his couch painting her toenails bright scarlet.

'Hiya, star.' She picked up the Los Angeles Times and waved it at him. 'Why didn't you *tell* me?'

He shrugged, irritated that she hadn't made a nice quiet exit in his absence. 'We had other things on our mind. I was going to.'

'You and Gina Germaine. Wowee! Like it's big time, man.'

'Hey – listen. I got a lot of work to take care of. Why don't I drive you back to your place?' Before you move in, he wanted to add, but controlled himself.

'I don't have to go,' she said. 'I quit my job last week, and with Randy gone . . .' She held her leg in the air and admired her newly painted toes. 'Besides, I can help you. Read through your script with you. Then maybe we can drop by Mavericks and knock 'em all out. Just looove to see those green faces, wouldn't you?'

'It'll be better if I take you home,' he said bluntly.

'For you it'll be better –' she said glaring at him balefully. 'Why can't I stay?'

'Because I'm expecting Angel.'

'Like hell you are.'

'What makes you think I'm not?'

She jumped off the couch. 'Okay. Take me home big-shot. I can live without you.'

'What makes you think I'm not expecting Angel?' he repeated.

'Forget it,' she muttered.

'I don't want to forget it.'

'Well I suggest you do.' She grabbed her purse and slung it roughly over her shoulder. 'I'll get a cab – star. Wouldn't want to put you out.'

'Did Angel call? Did you answer my phone?' he asked furiously.

She reached the front door and turned, one hand on her hip, a sneer on her lips. 'That's for me to know and you to find out.'

She slammed the door on her way out.

He was already reaching for the phone.

* * *

When Maralee refused to loan Elaine ten thousand dollars it was just as well because Little S. Shitz failed to turn up for their second meeting which was okay because Elaine would never file for divorce anyway. If Ross wanted out, let *him* make all the moves.

Lina quit, but Elaine was able to cash a cheque at Ron Gordino's establishment (it would bounce – but so what?) and she bribed Lina back with a bonus.

A television actor in shorts and a UCLA T-shirt picked her up at the check-out counter of Hughes Market on Beverly, and she rather rashly invited him back to the house. Once he got a sniff of luxury he pounced.

She fought him off and sent him on his way.

He did not go quietly.

Lina quit again. She was a Catholic, and there was only so much she could take.

Elaine consumed four straight vodkas and passed out in front of her beloved Merv.

She missed the news flash which informed Los Angeles that Neil Gray had suffered another massive heart attack, collapsed and died in the parking lot of a Santa Monica drinking establishment.

Chapter Sixty

Las Vegas behind him now, the glittering city in the desert fading into the distance as he spurred the van towards Los Angeles. He wanted to fly – to take off along the deserted road as he knew the van was capable of. But he did not do that. He kept within the speed limit. Had to be careful.

His mind was full of ugly images. Hate flowed through his veins. Yet he knew that Joey was watching over him. Kind, sweet Joey . . .

Where is the whore?

For a moment he couldn't remember and fury engulfed him.

The harlot was with another man.

The van screamed to a stop. He couldn't see anything, red flames engulfed him. Red . . . blood . . . Nita Carrolle's blood . . . Joey's blood . . .

It was alright. She was safe. He had saved her from sin . . .

He had stopped at one of the big hotels before leaving Vegas, and purchased black wraparound sunglasses – so dark that his eyes were not visible through the protective lenses.

He liked them. They were windows to the world outside, while he remained safely behind them, hidden and anonymous.

Joey would say he looked fine. She often complimented him. She was the only one who knew the true person behind Deke Andrews.

The thought of his name infuriated him.

'I am *not* Deke Andrews,' he screamed aloud.

Then he alighted from his truck and pissed across the empty highway.

He knew who his mother was.

He was going to Los Angeles to kill her.

Chapter Sixty-One

Neil Gray's death was a shock. But Buddy felt sure that it would have no adverse effect on *Street People*. Everyone knew that Montana had taken over. The word was that the start date would be postponed by a week.

He realized that now was the time to make the San Diego trip and square things with his mother. But first he wanted Angel back. He had waited long enough. Reaching her, however, was no easy task. He called. She was never there. He called back. She was still not there. He requested her home phone number and was refused the information. Eventually he got in his car and cruised slowly past the salon hoping to spot her. Some guy with a halo of wild curls sat at the glass fronted reception desk.

Buddy parked the Mustang and sauntered in. 'Hey—' he said casually. 'Is Angel around?'

Koko knew without a doubt that this must be Buddy. The looks were dazzling. 'She no longer works here,' he said, playing with the zipper on his orange jumpsuit. It was no lie. He had decided that she should stay home until after the baby was born. She had protested of course, but he had finally convinced her that Adrian needed the company.

'Where can I find her?'

'I don't know.' Koko had never been the best of liars. He cracked his knuckles nervously.

Buddy slid his hand over the desk, a folded twenty conveniently placed. 'Where?'

Koko shoved the money away from him. 'Really!' he snorted. 'You've been seeing too many movies!'

Raymondo chose that moment to appear. His flashing brown eyes took in the scene. 'Koko! You is *bad* momma. You is sellin' it! On the premises, man!'

'Piss off,' iced Koko.

Whistling and cat-calling Raymondo did just that. But first a parting shot – 'Wait until I tell pretty Angel,' he sang. 'She no like!'

'Cut out the shit,' said Buddy angrily, leaning across the desk. 'I'm her husband. Where is she?'

'She wants a divorce.'

Buddy reached for the zipper on Koko's jumpsuit and pulled it up sharply until it dug into the flesh beneath his neck. 'Where . . . is . . . she?'

Brave was not one of Koko's attributes. He squealed in pain. 'She doesn't want to see you,' he gasped. 'Why don't you leave the poor girl alone?'

'And why don't *you* just butt on out?'

'Angel is my friend. And God knows she needs friends after the way *you've* treated her.' He wrenched himself free. 'If you don't leave the premises at once I shall call the police.'

Buddy picked up the phone and smashed it down on the desk. 'Go ahead. I have every right to look for my wife. And another thing – I'm gonna be here every day until you tell me where she is. You understand what I'm sayin'?'

Koko understood all right. But he wasn't prepared to reveal her whereabouts until he had checked with her. 'Very well,' he said tightly. 'I'll contact Angel and see what she says. If she refuses to see you will you stay away?'

'If she tells me so herself.'

'Tomorrow. The same time.'

'Six o'clock tonight, my friend. I'll be back.' He stalked out.

Koko agonized for a few minutes, then phoned Angel and

told her the story. 'What do you want me to do?' he asked anxiously.

'I'll speak to him and tell him that I don't want to see him again,' she said firmly.

'*And* about the divorce,' Koko prompted.

'Yes,' she said, and at the time she meant it. But came six o'clock and Buddy on the phone and she was weakened by just the sound of his voice.

'Things are different,' he told her. 'It's all happening for me an' I want us to be together – y'know – like some kind of a new start. What d'you say?'

She hesitated. 'Buddy. It could never be the same between us. I've changed. I don't want to go back to the life we had.'

'Hey – aren't you listening to me? The past is behind us. We both did things we shouldn't have. Let's give it a fresh shot, babe.' He was huddled over the phone, his voice a low husk, while Koko stood across from the desk with folded arms, pretending not to listen.

'Why don't you stay with Shelly?' Angel said desperately. 'She's your kind of girl. I'm not like her.'

He laughed. 'If you were like her I'd shoot myself!'

'You've been living with her since I left,' she accused. 'Twice she's told me to leave you alone. I just don't understand. What do you *want* from me?'

'Shelly told you to leave me alone?' he asked incredulously. 'She told you *that*?'

'I don't lie.'

'She's full of shit. I've been searching for you ever since you walked.'

'You moved in with her.'

'No way.'

Angel gave a little sigh. She wanted to believe him, but then again she was not fresh off the plane from Louisville anymore.

'I have to see you,' he urged. 'We've got to discuss this.' He huddled closer to the phone. 'I love you, babe. Only you. You gotta know that by now.'

'I'm confused, Buddy.'

'I'll un-confuse you.'

'I need time to think things out.'

'Think *what* out? I got a great apartment, a new car, I'm starring in a movie.'

'I know. I saw your picture in the paper. I'm very happy for you, Buddy.'

'Be happy for *us*. So much has happened, but I need *you* to share it. Without you it doesn't mean anything. Can you understand that?'

He realized as he spoke that it was the truth. Everything was going his way, but he had to have Angel to make it complete. When she came back to him he did not intend to keep it secret. He would tell the world, and if Sadie didn't like it – too bad. Angel was his wife, and he was proud of it. Together they would make a new start, and this time it would work.

'Give me a few days,' she said at last.

'What do you need a few days for?'

'I have to be sure that you mean what you say and that tomorrow you won't change your mind.'

Are you *kidding*?'

'I'm very serious,' she said gravely, and added, 'Are you still involved with drugs?'

'I'm so clean I don't even do grass.' He paused. 'Can I at least know where you are?'

'I'm staying with friends.'

'Where?'

'It doesn't matter. Why don't we speak tomorrow at this time.'

'You got it.'

'But please, *promise* me that you won't try and see me until I say so.'

'Scout's honour.'

She laughed softly. 'You were *never* a scout, Buddy.'

'I am now.'

She gave him her phone number which he committed to memory before they said their goodbyes.

Koko glared at him, bad vibes filling the air.

Buddy did not say a word. He walked from the salon without a backward glance.

As far as he was concerned it was just a matter of time before he had Angel back.

* * *

'*Street People* is cancelled,' Oliver said bluntly. 'Over. Finished. Kaput.'

Montana stared at him, not quite registering what he was saying. They were in his office, everything gleaming, polished, and meticulously clean. Neil Gray had been buried an hour before. A stately funeral, with a respectable turnout.

Montana had conducted herself with dignity.

Maralee had thrown herself across the coffin in screaming hysterics.

'What?' she said at last, unable to believe what she was hearing.

'The party's over.' He was quite enjoying the moment, even though she was a recently bereaved widow. 'This film has cost me a fortune with delays and everything. Now, with Neil's er . . . untimely death . . . I can pick up on insurance and cover my losses.'

'You can *what*?'

'Don't worry, you'll get paid.'

Her voice was controlled, but inside she was shaking. 'Let me get this straight. You're cancelling the film so you can collect the *insurance*?'

'Business smarts. Gotta have them if you expect to survive in this town.'

All the emotions she had been bottling up came spilling out in a diatribe of fury. 'You no-talent ass-licking crawling little *turd*. How can you *do* this?'

'You gotta stop holding back your thoughts, Montana. Get 'em out. Say what's on your mind.' He sniggered, enjoying himself. He had total power, and he revelled in it.

She recovered her composure quickly, determined not to give him the satisfaction of seeing her crumble. 'Oliver,' she said sensibly. 'Surely you must know what this film means to me? It's an important *good* film. It'll make money. A lot more than your goddamn insurance.'

'Every movie is a risk,' he said patiently. 'It can star Redford and Jane Fonda and nobody knows if the public'll go see it. This way I come out on top – it's a no risk situation.'

'You're really serious?'

'The movie is cancelled.'

She was too tired to fight him further. 'Is that all that interests you – making money?' she asked wearily.

'Let's put it this way – I am not in this business to get my cock sucked.'

'You're a real charmer.'

'I love you too.'

She left his office head held high, but spirit defeated. There were moments when she needed Neil desperately, and this was one of them. She marched into her office and slammed the door. Then she took a deep breath and tried to control the tears which threatened.

She did not need Neil. She had learned to get along without him. No good crying out in moments of stress. She had to be strong and deal with things herself.

Neil is dead, she thought, and it's his own damn fault. For a moment anger engulfed her. Once their love had been all consuming . . . then time passed and things changed.

He had deserted her.

But she was a survivor.

Finally she let the tears flow.

It felt good.

* * *

Sadie accepted the news calmly. It wasn't the first time and it would not be the last. The movie business was unpredictable to say the least.

Oliver told her over drinks in the Beverly Wilshire Hotel. He also informed her that he had found a director for the other project Neil had been working on – the one with Gina Germaine.

'We can start on pre-production immediately,' he said. 'Gina'll be happy. It's a much better part for her.'

'I didn't even know there was a completed script,' Sadie replied in surprise.

'There wasn't a few weeks ago. But ever since we signed the deal I've been behind it. Got a *great* script now – of course it needs a little work . . .'

'I'll have to read it,' she said shortly. 'The deal we signed was for Neil to direct. This is a different ballgame.'

'But one we can work out, huh Sadie?'

She refused to commit. 'We'll see,' she said, thoughtfully sipping Perrier water. 'Is there anything for Buddy Hudson in it? He's going to be a big star. You may as well get in at the beginning.'

'I think we can find something.'

'Something won't do. It's got to be right.'

'Read the material and see.'

'I'll do that.'

'Fast, please.'

'What a hustler you are, Oliver.'

'Just like you, Sadie.'

She couldn't argue with that.

* * *

Koko swept into the house later than usual. Angel was in the kitchen fixing southern fried chicken, while Adrian sat in front of the television watching male go-go dancers.

'Ah . . . sweet domesticity,' he snapped. 'While I work my buns off.'

Adrian clicked the remote and blanked the screen. 'What's eating you?'

'Nothing. I was only physically abused by dear Angel's macho husband today. Where *is* madame?'

'In the kitchen.'

'Ha! Hasn't she run off into his waiting arms yet?'

'What happened?' asked Adrian carefully.

'*You* should know. *You* were sitting here with her.'

'We can't hold on to her forever,' said Adrian mildly.

'For God's sake. Don't *you* go giving me lectures. I know. She's old enough to look after herself. But Adrian,' his eyes misted over. 'How can I explain this. She's such a *sweet* person. I want her to stay with us so that we can protect her.'

He had not heard Angel walk into the room. She stood quietly by the door. 'Thank you, Koko,' she murmured softly. 'But don't worry, whatever happens we'll still see each other, and we'll *always* be friends. I'll never forget how you've helped me.'

'You *are* going back to him then?'

Her hands fluttered towards the swell of the baby. 'I've got to give him another chance.'

'Ha!' he snorted. 'You'll regret it.'

* * *

Lying out by Gina's Italian tiled swimming pool watching two Japanese gardeners tend the exotic trees and blooms, while a maid served him iced tea, Ross decided that this was the life for him. All this luxury and activity, and he hadn't paid one goddamn red cent. Why hadn't he thought of it before? Find yourself a working woman, sit back and enjoy the advantages. After all – women had taken enough from him over the years – he deserved a little something in return.

Today was his birthday. He had finally reached the big five-o and it was not half as painful as he had thought it would be. Upon waking he had told Gina – he hadn't meant to – but what the hell – it wasn't every day you hit a milestone. And he could hardly hide his age – the film reference books had him coming and going. Fifty was hardly senile. Guys like Newman and Bronson had made passing the half-way mark a mere trifle.

'Why didn't you tell me before?' she exclaimed. 'We could have had a *huge* party.'

He did not want a 'huge party'. He had just suffered through one, although maybe it wouldn't be so bad with someone else footing the bills.

Gina gave him several birthday presents of the physical kind, leaving him exhausted but content. Then she dressed and left for lunch with Sadie.

He sat up, took a sip of iced tea and reached for the script. His lines were underlined in thick red pencil. He knew every one of them. A first – usually he just sauntered on the set and played it by ear. Things were different now. He had a great opportunity, and he did not intend to blow it.

* * *

Sentiment had never been one of Gina Germaine's attributes. She breezed through life caring only about what was good for her public image. When Neil Gray died she did not think – 'Poor Neil – what a terrible thing.' She thought – 'Thank Christ it didn't happen while he was in bed with me – I'd never have lived *that* down.'

She attended his funeral, a vision in black lace, and posed happily for photographers, Ross Conti by her side. The chemistry that she and Ross created together seemed to arouse great public interest.

Ah! And the chemistry in the privacy of her bedroom was more than right too. For a guy his age he sure had what it takes.

When Sadie told her that *Street People* was cancelled over lunch in the Bistro Gardens, she opened her mouth to yell.

Sadie silenced her immediately with the news that the other

movie she and Neil had planned was an immediate go situation with a finished script, a new director, and Oliver Easterne in charge.

'I read it last night,' Sadie said briskly. 'It's a much better role for you. Trust me, dear.'

Gina always had trusted Sadie, her judgement was the best. She chewed on a lettuce leaf, then said something so totally out of character that Sadie almost spilled her glass of Perrier.

'I'll do it if there's a part for Ross.'

'What?' gasped Sadie.

'We're good together,' Gina explained nonchalantly. 'The press love us. We'll be dynamite on the screen. Fix it, you got the clout.'

'There's nothing for Ross in it,' said Sadie tightly.

'Have them write him in.'

Sadie stared at her lettuce munching client. Why had Ross moved in with this calculating blonde bombshell? She had wanted him for herself and now Gina had him. And worse . . . Gina – who wouldn't give a wooden leg to a cripple – wanted to help him. 'Do you know what you are suggesting?' she said.

'Sure I do.'

'You'd better think about it carefully. Writing Ross in could take weeks or even months. The film would be delayed and you should work at once. I'm sure you realize that.'

Gina gazed reflectively at her agent. One thing about Sadie, she always made sense – maybe it wasn't such a good idea. 'You're right. I guess I shouldn't wait. Send me over the script.'

Sadie patted her large Vuitton purse. 'I have it with me.'

'By the way,' Gina said. 'It's Ross's birthday – and I'm putting together a surprise party at the Bistro tonight. You'll come, oh, and tell Buddy.'

The last thing Sadie wanted to do was celebrate Ross's birthday, but business was business and Gina was a valued client.

'Wouldn't miss it, dear.'

* * *

Gina returned home at four o'clock laden with presents. A photographer from an Italian magazine accompanied her, and while she plied Ross with half of Gucci, the photographer captured every sentimental moment.

Ross was not aware of the fact that in exchange for exclusive photos the magazine had paid for all the expensive gifts.

He loved everything, although the photographer didn't thrill him – a stoned lounge lizard in tight white pants who kept on touching Gina's ass.

'Tonight we are dining at the Bistro,' she announced. 'With a couple of friends.'

'Who?'

She giggled mysteriously. 'Just you wait and see. I adore surprises, don't you?'

* * *

'Huh?' A look of stunned disbelief crossed Buddy's face.

Sadie said, 'There is no such thing as a sure thing in the film business.'

'But I got the part,' he said blankly.

'You certainly did.'

'They can't do this to me!' he yelled.

'Producers play God. They can do what they like.'

'Fuck 'em!' he screamed.

Ferdie popped his head around the door. 'Everything alright in here?'

'Perfectly fine, thank you,' Sadie replied.

Buddy was unaware of the interruption. He slumped into a chair, mumbling to himself.

Sadie picked up a gold pen and tapped it impatiently on her desk. 'Get a hold of yourself. This is but a small setback. You'll get fully paid, and you've had the benefit of quite a bit of publicity. Something *better* will come along.' She did not wish to reveal the fact that something already had. Timing was everything when dealing with a client.

'Jesus!' he moaned. 'Does Montana know?'

'Of course. It will be in the trades tomorrow. And Buddy – I was going to surprise you. Monday your billboard goes up across America, so pull yourself together and start feeling great again. This evening Gina is having a surprise birthday party for Ross – I want you there. You never know, by tonight, I might have good news for you. I am not known as the fastest agent in the west for nothing!'

He nodded with as much enthusiasm as he could muster – and wondered why every time he passed GO some smartass kicked him right in the balls with a cement foot.

* * *

Gina did not create her night-time appearance without a little help here and there. A professional South American make-up artist arrived at the mansion every evening promptly at six. He was preceded by a Hungarian masseuse, and followed by a French hairdresser.

What with the Japanese gardeners, the Philippine maids, and Gina's English secretary, the place was like a regular United Nations. Seven magnificent bedrooms, seven matching bathrooms, six enormous living rooms, staff quarters, and a hotel-size kitchen, yet Ross still had trouble finding a quiet spot for himself.

They did not treat him in the manner to which he was accustomed. This pissed him off. They treated him like 'the star's' boyfriend, blissfully unaware that he too was a star.

Gina appeared between make-up and hair. 'Did you call your agent today?' she asked crisply.

'Should I have?'

'Honey, everyone should speak to their agent at least twice a day.'

'Why?'

'Because you gotta keep a finger on the pulse.' Damn! she thought, he doesn't know the movie's been cancelled, and *I'm* not telling him. Why hasn't his schmucky agent called him?

'How about a finger on my pulse?' he leered.

'For an old guy you *suuure aaare* horny. But catch me before the make-up next time, huh?' She hurried from the room with an offhand, 'Call your agent.'

He was speechless. *Old guy.* She had to be kidding. She was no nubile nineteen year old herself.

He fixed himself a scotch on the rocks and admired himself in the mirrored bar. Old or not – he could still knock 'em dead. Ross Conti had a long way to go before they counted *him* out.

* * *

Elaine and Maralee resumed friendship. It was better to bore each other than not to bore at all.

Neither lady was looking her best, so they avoided Ma Maison, the Bistro Gardens, Jimmy's, and other fashionable places for lunch. Instead they stayed at each other's pools, taking ruinous for the skin sunbaths, and large glasses of various exotic alcoholic beverages. The ten thousand dollars Elaine had wished to borrow from her friend was discreetly forgotten.

Elaine talked of nothing but Ross.

Maralee talked of nothing but Neil.

Ron Gordino and Randy Felix were never mentioned. But in a town dedicated to who you were and how much money you had this was only to be expected.

* * *

Montana raged. She paced her house on the hill with the wonderful view and called Oliver Easterne every name she could think of – and a few more besides. She felt helpless, a feeling she was not used to and did not like.

The movie business.

You could shove it.

She had contacted her attorney in New York and demanded that he get the rights back to *Street People*. When he returned her call an hour later he informed her it was impossible.

'Nothing's impossible,' she stormed.

'I'll work on it. But what are you worried about anyway? You've been paid.'

She had always sensed that beneath the Savile Row suits lurked an insensitive fool. What did *money* matter?

Mental note. Change attorneys.

She tried to calm herself by sorting through Neil's desk. In a drawer she found a first draft of *Street People* – her handwriting scrawled across the title page. *To my darling husband from your darling wife – together we shall rise above the bullshit.*

Oh yeah? Where was Neil when she really needed him?

An idea formed in her mind, and for the first time in ages she managed a small smile. She would show Oliver Easterne something he wouldn't forget in a hurry. Something the whole fucking town wouldn't forget in a hurry.

Oh yeah.

Her smile widened as she remembered a little saying Neil had taught her. *Don't get angry – get even.*

She had a plan. It was crazy. But oh . . . the satisfaction! Neil would have loved it.

Chapter Sixty-Two

Once things started to happen they happened fast. Over the years Leon had discovered it was always that way. One break set the course. A hunch had told him that now Deke Andrews had resurfaced it would be hard for him to vanish again. Pittsburgh, Texas, and now Las Vegas. A trail of death. Two hookers, a pimp, a rootless hitchhiker. A pattern was beginning to emerge. Deke went after the low life . . . women were the enemy . . . women who sold their bodies . . .

These thoughts crossed Leon's mind as he raced his rented car across the desert towards Las Vegas. And another thought. Did Deke Andrews have anything to do with the murder and arson case that had taken place in Barstow only two days previously? No definite signs that he was there. The building had gone up like a tinder-box destroying all evidence. But an autopsy on the charred body of the secretary revealed she had been stabbed repeatedly – there was nothing to tie Deke Andrews to the case, but Leon just had a gut feeling, and over the years his gut feelings had been proved right more times than not.

As his car sped down the highway towards his destination he was unaware of the oncoming traffic headed west. Even if he had been he would have taken no notice of the shabby brown van speeding resolutely towards Los Angeles. The driver was

Deke Andrews, his face a mask, black sunglasses concealing eyes of death.

Leon felt a chill for no particular reason. He reached forward and turned the air conditioning unit down.

The lights of Las Vegas twinkled a false welcome in the distance.

Chapter Sixty-Three

Normally last minute invitations were ignored by one and all. But Gina's secretary was a persuasive English girl with a honeyed voice and a smart brain. It also helped that nothing else was going on the night of Ross's birthday. No premieres, private screenings, parties or special events. So a perfectly respectable group arrived to celebrate in the upstairs room of the Bistro on Canon Drive.

Gina and Ross naturally made a late entrance. On the street outside lurked a group of paparazzi. Gina posed for them prettily, clinging on to Ross's arm.

Gently he tried to loosen her grip. She was wrinkling his jacket.

They entered the restaurant and proceeded upstairs where the group waited. Ross was really surprised by the turnout. He had expected maybe a dozen people but there were at least sixty.

Gina turned to him with a wide smile, her perfect teeth dazzling. 'Not bad, huh? And all arranged at the last minute.'

He surveyed the room and boasted, 'I'm a star again. I can lure 'em out anytime I want.'

'Sure you can. Only a little phone call from me helps you know.'

She hoped his agent had told him about *Street People* being cancelled. She had a horrible feeling the putz hadn't. If Ross knew he would be bitching and beefing from here to the beach.

Oh, well. It was not her problem. She refused to be the bearer of bad news. Let Oliver or someone give him the word. Then, when he came to her with the inevitable – 'Why didn't you tell me?' she would shrug and casually say, 'I *told* you to speak to your agent.' Then she would add, just so he could see how concerned and thoughtful she was, 'Besides, I didn't want to spoil your birthday.'

* * *

Buddy stood in the doorway and checked out the action. He saw fame, power, and money mingling easily together. And for a moment he felt that he belonged.

Not yet, Buddy Boy, not yet. Don't get carried away. Keep your cool.

He had offered to pick Sadie up and go with her, but she had declined. Now he searched for a familiar face.

Karen Lancaster sat at a table with a spiky-haired English rock star, Josh Speed, a caustic television comedian, and three assorted groupies.

Josh, the comedian, and Karen conversed excitedly, while the three groupies – all shaggy hair, skinny bodies, and eager eyes – listened hopefully.

Buddy wandered over. He didn't see anyone else he knew.

'Hey – Karen, how're you doin?'

She gazed up at him, total non-recognition.

'Buddy,' he reminded her, slightly miffed. 'Buddy Hudson.'

Josh Speed and the comedian looked at each other, took a beat of three, and chorused, 'Buddy . . . Buddy Hudson.' Then they fell about laughing.

Karen, as stoned as they, joined in the laughter, followed quickly by the groupies.

The amusement slid from the comedian's face. 'What the fock you laughin' at?' he demanded of the youngest girl.

Her face froze. 'Nothing,' she whispered.

Buddy backed away. He wasn't sure why he was here. Sadie had said she might have some good news for him, and he trusted her to save him from falling back into obscurity.

He edged over to the bar and scored an orange juice. Earlier he had spoken to Angel. 'My movie's been cancelled,' he told her regretfully. 'But I got me this agent – Sadie La Salle – who is the best. And she says she'll find me something else. I still got paid – we're rich, babe.'

He was proud of the fact that he was being honest with her. And she seemed to appreciate it, for her voice filled with warmth, and he knew that any day now she would agree to come back.

* * *

Across the room, chatting to a talk show producer and his doll-like wife, Sadie noted Buddy's arrival. She watched him carefully. He handled himself well, and as he moved towards the bar she noticed the eyes of several women following him.

'What do you think of my new client?' she asked the wife, pointing out Buddy.

The woman – at least thirty years younger than her jovial husband – stared longingly. 'Handsome,' she said at last, fingering a ruby and diamond necklace which swamped her pale swan neck.

'Yes,' agreed Sadie. 'He's going to be a big star.'

'Should we have him on the show?' questioned the producer.

'I'm sorry,' Sadie said regretfully. 'I've promised him to Carson first. But I'll give you second shot.'

'C'*mon*, Sadie. Don't give me that. We want him. First. Name a day.'

'Why don't we speak tomorrow?' she said, excusing herself and hurrying over to Buddy.

How easy it was to play the game – and win. When you knew all the rules.

She patted him on the shoulder. 'On time. Looking good. Drinking orange juice. You see – I told you it wasn't the end of the world.'

He grinned ruefully and shrugged. 'Guess I've learned to roll with the punches.'

'Well roll with this. There's a *very* strong chance that you are going to get the leading role in Gina's new film.'

He perked up. 'You're kidding.'

'Sadie La Salle does not kid.'

Jeez! Why hadn't he been nicer to Gina. Maybe she would bad-mouth him.

'When will I know? What kind of a part is it? Can I see the script?'

'The script is being rewritten. When it's ready you'll do a test with Gina, and if the sparks fly . . .'

He had known it was too good to be true. 'I've got to test again?' he groaned.

'Of course you do. But I have every confidence that you'll be wonderful. Don't you?'

Glumly he nodded.

'Smile, dear. Produce the charm. Tonight you are going to be exceptionally polite to Oliver Easterne – who – need I tell you – is the producer of the new vehicle. And even nicer to your fellow client, Gina Germaine.'

'I'll do my best.'

'I want better than that.'

'I don't think Gina likes me.'

'Make her like you. That shouldn't be too difficult for you.'

'You want me to fuck her?' he snapped angrily. ' 'Cos I don't fuck to work.'

'I never said you did. And don't speak to me like that.'

He glowered. 'Sorry.'

'Come. Let's start with Oliver.'

* * *

'Sweetie. So sorry to hear your film no more. They offer it Adam but he turn it down. No right for him. Perfect for you. Darling, I *so* sorry.'

Ross stared at Bibi Sutton blankly. He never understood a word she said.

'Sweetie. Elaine? She fine now? I hear she drinkie too much. She fine now though, yes?'

'You're looking magnificent as usual, Bibi,' he leaned forward and whispered in her ear. 'One of these days I'll catch you in the sack and screw the life out of you.'

She offered a coy smile. 'Naughty boy!'

Adam Sutton appeared at her elbow, nodded curtly at Ross, and said, 'The Lazers and the Wilders want us to sit with them.'

'Yes?' She glanced around to see if she could spot a better offer. 'In a minute, I come soon.'

Adam retreated. Ross leaned forward again. 'If you were between the sheets with me you would!'

'Ross! You bad boy!'

'Who's a bad boy?' Karen Lancaster thrust herself between them, all beige satin and erect nipples. She was accompanied by the rock star. 'This is Josh Speed,' she announced formally. 'He's in the middle of his American tour. This is his first Hollywood party and he's bored out of his skull, aren't you baby?'

He spoke perfect cockney. ' 'Ere, leave it out, gel. I'm lovin' every bleedin' minute.'

'He sounds like Mick Jagger,' Karen said knowledgeably. 'Only Mick fakes it. Josh is the real thing.'

'How George, sweetie?' asked Bibi.

Karen did not answer. She glared balefully at Ross. 'I'm glad your movie bottomed out,' she said spitefully.

'I wouldn't mind 'aving a bash in a fillum,' remarked Josh.

Karen grabbed his arm. 'How old are you?'

'Twenty-two.'

Bibi became bored with the conversation and moved away.

'Really? Ross is fifty you know. Today.' She laughed. 'Practically old enough to be your grandfather.'

They both sniggered.

Ross was unamused. Grandfather indeed. She was being ridiculous. And what did she mean about his movie bottoming out?

Before he had a chance to ask her she launched into an elaborate necking session with Josh. He was hardly going to stand there watching them exchange tongues. He looked around for Gina, and came eyeball to eyeball with Sadie on her way to the ladies room. They greeted each other stiffly and both moved quickly on.

Gina was deep in conversation with Oliver. Ross strolled over.

'Having fun?' she beamed.

His eyes dipped to her considerable cleavage. She certainly gave Dolly Parton a run for her money. 'I think I'll have more fun later,' he said, pinching her behind.

'You don't know how sorry I am,' Oliver said insincerely. 'But these things happen. I don't have to tell you that, Ross.'

'Excuse me,' Gina said hurriedly. 'I must say hello to Wolfie.'

'Sorry about what?' demanded Ross.

'You've been in the film business long enough to understand the way things are,' Oliver continued expansively. 'As long as you can take the money and run. Right?'

Three thoughts hit him.

Call your agent.

Sweetie. So sorry to hear your film no more.

I'm glad your movie bottomed out.

Christ. He didn't have to be a genius to figure things out.

'Oliver,' he said sharply. 'What the *frig* is going on?'

* * *

Buddy learned fast. Being nice to people usually meant listening to what they had to say, and not interrupting. He hung on to every word, tried to look interested, and watched their eyes constantly flick around the room. Twice he was deserted in mid-sentence when a better prospect came into view.

Adam Sutton granted him a few moments of his valuable time.

'I think you've got a great future ahead of you,' Adam said. 'With Sadie as your agent and—'

He never finished the sentence. Bibi beckoned and he ran.

Buddy saw Gina, took a deep breath and went over.

She greeted him coolly.

He exerted all the charm he could muster.

She thawed. 'Changed your mind about screwing a movie star?' she purred sexily.

He was saved from answering by her personal P.R. man who strode over, threw him a dismissive look, took her arm in a proprietary fashion, and said, 'Army Archerd wants to talk to you.'

Buddy cruised around the room again, smelling the money, anxious to be a part of it all, wanting to be recognized. Then he saw Wolfie Schweicker and stopped dead. The plump man was entertaining a small group with an obviously hilarious anecdote, for they were all falling about laughing.

Butterball. That's what Buddy had called him in his head. Butterball . . .

On second sight he was sure it was the man who had fed Tony cocaine the night of the fateful party.

He continued to stare. His black eyes chips of ice.

Wolfie felt the power of his stare and glanced over. His stomach tightened with sexual anticipation. 'Who *is* that?' he asked Bibi.

She threw a casual glance in Buddy's direction. 'Sadie's new discovery. Nobody important, darling. Why?'

'I saw him at George's party. I just wondered who he was.'

'Sweetie. Gina's dress. You think she make it herself?'

Wolfie tore his eyes away from Buddy and applied himself to keeping Bibi happy. He inspected Gina's outfit, a red dress which plunged to the waist. 'Hmm . . .' he said archly. 'Zody's with a touch of Frederick's of Hollywood, don't you think?'

* * *

And out of the giant cake sprang a nubile redheaded girl in a fluffy white bikini. She leapt on Ross's knee while everyone yelled and cheered and catcalled. Business conversations were suspended while the men inspected the near naked girl who began to sing 'Happy Birthday' as she wriggled around on Ross's lap. She was stacked, but not stacked enough to allow business discussions to be suspended for long.

Ross acted out his role. He was no slouch when it came to putting on the right face for the right occasion. He grinned, made all the correct noises. Blew out fifty candles while trying to dislodge the stoned ding-a-ling from his lap. And all the while he seethed.

Goddamn Gina Germaine. How dare she put him through this charade. How *dare* she do it to him when she knew – *had* to know – that the film was a no go situation.

Why hadn't the dumb broad told him? He could not wait to get her alone. Oh, how he seethed. But the easy-going smile remained in place. The blue eyes – a little crinkly around the edges but still knock-out – flirted their way around the room.

He was humiliated. Sadie would never have let something like this happen to him.

'I can score you some ace coke,' the girl on his knee whispered.

'Get lost.' He dislodged her by getting up.

'Speech,' someone yelled, and the request echoed round the room.

In a pig's ass they'd get a speech.

* * *

Seeing Butterball soured the evening for Buddy.

He wanted out.

He wanted Angel.

'Is it all right for me to split?' he checked with Sadie.

'Yes,' she said. 'We'll speak on Monday. I'm going to Palm Springs tomorrow, but I'll be back in time to get something definite out of Oliver early in the week. Don't worry, everything's going to be fine.'

'I hope so.'

He drove home fast and dialled Angel's number.

'Yes?' answered a male voice.

She had told him she was living with two gay guys. 'Angel,' he demanded.

'She's asleep.'

He controlled the edginess in his voice. 'Do me a favour and wake her. This is important.'

'May I ask who's calling?'

'Buddy.'

An unfriendly, 'Just a minute.'

A long wait and then at last she was there. 'I can't go on like this,' he blurted urgently. 'I need you to be with me.'

'Are you high?' she asked accusingly.

'Stone cold straight, babes.'

'We made an agreement. Why are you calling me in the middle of the night?'

'Because we decided to be honest with each other. And if I'm honest then you have to know that I can't go another day without you.'

'Buddy—'

'I love you. We *should* be together.'

'I don't know—' she began hesitantly.

'Yes you *do* know, an' I'll tell you what's goin' on.' He took a deep breath. 'Like I have a mother I never mentioned—'

'You told me your parents died in a car accident', she interrupted accusingly.

'I *know* what I told you. But from now on it's the truth, right?'

'Yes.'

'My mother lives in San Diego. I haven't spoken to her in ten years.' He was silent a moment. 'I want to settle things, so

I'm going to drive to see her early in the morning, and when I get back I need you to be waiting in my – our apartment. Will you do this for me, baby? Because you mean everything to me – and I don't want there to be any more lies between us.' He paused, willing her to say yes. 'C'mon, Angel. You know the time is right.'

Somebody up there liked him. For a change.

'Alright,' she whispered.

The love he had for her burned hot. From now on she came first. Without her everything else was nothing. Including the career he still wanted but refused to lie for.

'I'll arrange a limo to pick you up at five o'clock tomorrow afternoon, the maid'll let you in, and I'll be back around six or seven. If I'm going to be late I'll call.'

She gave him her address.

'Tomorrow,' he said. 'You won't ever regret it.'

* * *

'Bullfriggingshit!' screamed Ross.

'Smile, there's photographers outside the house gates,' an unfazed Gina replied.

'Who gives a flying fuck about frigging photographers?' he yelled, the veins in his neck standing out like telephone cords.

'*I* do.'

'Well FUCK YOU!'

'Maybe later. If you stop behaving like a horse's ass.'

'Up yours, lady!'

They had been screaming at each other ever since leaving the party.

'Did you know the film was down the tubes?' he had asked the moment they were alone.

'Yes, I knew. But it's not *my* job to tell you. I *said* for you to call your agent.'

'Too much trouble for you to mention it?'

'Is it *my* fault you have a dumb agent?'

The fight had started with name-calling and progressed to open warfare. Ross could not remember ever having been so angry.

Their limo was slowly approaching the gates of Gina's house. The photographers pressed forward. She had forgotten to mention to Ross that her personal public relations representative had alerted the wire services only half an hour before they left the Bistro, that Ms Germaine was likely to announce her engagement to Ross Conti before the end of the evening. The press waited anxiously.

Gina realized that she might have picked the wrong moment for this particular publicity stunt.

'Oh, Jesus!' she exclaimed, pressing a button which operated the wall of glass between her and the chauffeur. 'Don't stop,' she instructed tersely.

'I'm afraid we have to Ms Germaine. The remote control for the gate is not in the car.'

'*Why not*!' she hissed angrily.

He shrugged a 'how should I know, I was only hired for the evening' reply, and pulled the white stretch Cadillac limousine to an abrupt halt.

The photographers surged. Ross glowered.

Gina manufactured a quick smile and opened her window. 'Hi boys,' she said genially, trusting that her personality and Ross's sense of survival would get them past the gate. 'And to what do I owe this pleasure?'

They all spoke at once, asking the same question. Were she and Ross Conti planning a wedding?

'A wedding!' Ross screamed, his fury out of control. 'Number One – I am a married man. And Number Two – take note – ladies and gentlemen of the press. I wouldn't marry Gina Germaine if she were the last friggin' cunt in Hollywood!'

Chapter Sixty-Four

Night time on Hollywood Boulevard and the prostitutes and the pimps and pushers and the junkies and the muggers on parade.

Deke drove down the street slowly, his cold eyes taking in the scene.

At a red light two bored hookers sauntered over to the van.

'Interested in a threesome?' they asked in unison. 'Round the world, golden shower, name it.'

He shook his head negatively and rubbed the front of his dark glasses. Whores. The world was full of them.

'Come on,' one of them encouraged, putting a bony hand with six inch false nails on his arm.

'The sins of the flesh will kill you,' he warned, shaking her hand from him with such force that three of her false nails came off and fell on the floor of the van.

'Mothafucker!' she screeched in a fury, attempting to wrench his door open so that she could retrieve her precious nails.

He gunned the van into motion, and she fell back screaming obscenities.

Hollywood Boulevard. Gateway to the City of the Angels. Alive with vermin. Alive with the dregs of the earth. As The Keeper Of The Order it was his job to deal with this seething mass. He was sent to do such things . . . But first . . . A woman he must find. A whore mother . . . Joey would want him to deal with her first . . . She had told him so . . . Joey never left his side . . . She was a good girl . . . a sweet girl . . .

Los Angeles. City of the Angels.

Whoretown, U.S.A.

'Mother,' he said aloud. 'I know who you are. I will find you soon. I promise.'

'Good, cowboy,' said Joey. She sat beside him so bright and pretty, her skirt pulled demurely over her knees.

Familiar lights flashing 'MOTEL' attracted him.

'Are you tired, Joey?' he asked solicitously. 'Shall we stop?'

She had gone.

The whore had vanished.

He fingered the knife down the side of his boot. Next time he saw her he would slash the bitch to pieces.

Chapter Sixty-Five

Buddy could not sleep. After speaking to Angel he paced around his apartment excitedly. He had made a commitment and now he had to follow through. The thought of facing his mother was unwelcome . . . but the sooner it was over and done with . . .

No more lies.

Everything clean.

What about Sadie? The idea was to tell her before Monday when his billboard hit America.

He lay on his bed, fell asleep thinking about what to do, and woke early with an answer.

He did not have the nerve to wake Sadie with his outpourings of honesty at seven a.m. on Saturday morning, but he had no such qualms about stopping by Ferdie's before leaving for San Diego.

Ferdie was up and dressed – natty in a red cutaway T-shirt with matching shorts. He was suntanned, oiled and muscled, unlike the soberly suited man of office days. He seemed quite embarrassed to be caught out of character. Even more so when a tousle-haired youth of fourteen or fifteen appeared behind him at the front door demanding. 'Who *is* it?'

The boy wore a towel around his waist and nothing else.

'Get back in the kitchen,' Ferdie commanded, the tone of his voice brooking no argument.

'Glad you're up,' Buddy said breezily.

'Would it make any difference if I wasn't?'

'I had a choice – wake you or Sadie – I figured you were my best bet.'

'And how did you find out where I lived?'

'Looked you up in the phone book.'

'This *is* an emergency I presume?'

'Most definitely.'

Ferdie sighed with annoyance. 'You'd better come in I suppose.'

'Hey – don't make me feel so welcome.'

'What do you expect at seven in the morning? Flowers and a band?'

Buddy followed him into a spacious white apartment. A lone Andy Warhol silk screen of Marilyn Monroe took pride of place above the old fashioned mantle. Two burned out candles were placed beneath it.

He sat down without being invited and said, 'I can't stay long.'

Ferdie replied with crisp sarcasm, 'What a shame.'

The juvenile, now lurking in the kitchen, put on loud punk music just to let everyone know he was still around.

'God!' exclaimed Ferdie, then in a louder voice, 'Use the *head*phones, Rocky.' He turned to Buddy. 'Well? Do tell. I'm dying to know what couldn't wait until Monday morning in the office.'

'I'm going to San Diego.'

'A short trip, or will you be taking up residence?'

'I have to be straight with Sadie.'

'Ahhh . . . I know.' Ferdie smirked knowingly. 'You're really a transvestite, and you couldn't bear to keep it a secret a *moment* longer. Is that your exciting news?'

'Cut the smart ass cracks. This is serious.' Buddy stood up and walked to the window. The view offered a swimming pool with two girls doing lengths while another one skipped rope by the side. 'Uh . . . there's a few things I never told Sadie about.'

'Like what?' asked Ferdie, intrigued at last.

'Like I'm married. I have a beautiful wife – and I don't want to hide the fact anymore.'

'Oh dear.'

'Is she gonna freak?'

'Let's put it this way – she is hardly going to dance on table-tops wild with delight.'

Buddy shrugged. 'That's the way it is.' He gazed at the view. 'I . . . uh . . . want you to tell her for me.'

'*Thank you*. You're *so* kind. But I must decline your generous offer. Tell her yourself on Monday.'

'I can't do that.'

'Why not?'

'Because she has to know today. The billboards will be up on Monday. I don't want to let it go any longer. It's just something that has to be done.'

Ferdie looked exasperated.

'Listen,' Buddy said persuasively, turning away from the window. 'You do this for me an' I gotta owe you one big favor. Right?'

'Maybe.'

'So *you* know an' *I* know that there's nothing like havin' stored favours in this town. Right again?'

Ferdie nodded reluctantly.

'Hey – who knows what's gonna happen to me,' Buddy continued expansively. 'I could become a big star or I could end up on the shit heap. It's all a role of the dice, huh?' He patted Ferdie firmly on the shoulder. 'But hey – if I make it big, a favour from me should be worth *somethin'*. Am I right?'

Ferdie sighed. He could never resist the lethal combination of pressure and charm. Besides, he wanted Buddy out of his apartment. 'Alright, alright, I'll do it. I don't mind *ruining* my day. Now what exactly am I to tell madame?'

'Tell her I got me this wife. Her name is Angel. And she's beautiful.'

'Oh, wonderful. Is that the one *I* found for you?'

'Don't worry – we were already married.'

'Then why did—' He stopped abruptly, as the juvenile wandered into the room, headphones clamped over ears, fingers snapping to the beat.

'Ferdie,' the boy whined. 'When we goin' to the picnic?'

'When you get dressed.'

The boy flicked the knot on his towel with studied insolence.

'For God's sake—' Ferdie began, and stopped when it was revealed that the juvenile wore a scant white bikini underneath.

Buddy was already at the door. 'Tell Sadie I'll be in the office first thing Monday.'

Ferdie followed him out. 'Don't worry, she'll be waiting.' He lowered his voice. 'Kindly do not discuss my personal life with anyone. *Especially* Sadie.'

Buddy winked. 'You got it. Hey – you know what, Ferd? Telling the truth is the best thing that's happened to me in years!'

'Yes,' said Ferdie drily. 'Especially when I get to do it for you.'

Chapter Sixty-Six

A letter. Special delivery. To Leon Rosemont in Las Vegas.

Dearest Leon,
We had a good time together.
Sometimes good times don't last.
This is sad . . .
But it is so . . .
Our vacation is over and I am going home – alone.
I shall always remember the good times.

Millie

He had received the letter earlier, read it through quickly, then stuffed it in his pocket. No time to deal with it . . . Everything happening fast . . .

Arriving in Las Vegas to investigate the murder of a hooker only to be summoned to a house where Deke Andrews had most certainly spent time.

Killing time.

Leon felt his stomach turn as they photographed the body of the old woman – her face a morbid grimace of fear and death.

Carnage . . . blood . . . mutilation . . .

Deke Andrews' fingerprints everywhere. He had made no attempt to cover his tracks.

Scrawled across the bathroom mirror in smeared lipstick were the words – I AM THE KEEPER OF THE ORDER. WHORE MOTHER – I WILL FIND YOU. It was as if he felt he didn't have to be careful . . .

Leon spoke to the maid who found the body. She was hysterical. Hadn't seen anyone or anything, just kept on mumbling incoherently about a wool jacket.

Who was Nita Carrolle? Why had Deke broken his pattern, entered her house, and murdered her?

WHAT WAS THE CONNECTION?

Leon went to work, sifting through the remnants of a life.

He persevered through the night, and at seven-thirty on Saturday morning hit pay dirt. Hidden beneath piles of clothes in the basement he came across an old ledger. He studied the yellowing torn pages – some of which were missing. His original hunch was correct. Deke Andrews *was* adopted, but not by legitimate means. Nita Carrolle and her sister Noreen had run a babies for sale operation.

At last the puzzle began to make sense. Leon had the scent of Deke in his nostrils. There was much to do.

Chapter Sixty-Seven

Elaine awoke to blinding sunlight. She had forgotten to close the drapes again and the early morning sun spilled into her bedroom. For a few moments she lay perfectly still, knowing full well that as soon as she moved her head would begin to throb as it did every morning lately.

She moved. Her head throbbed. She swore off drink forever. And knew for sure that the only way to get through the day was to add a slug of vodka to her breakfast orange juice.

Elaine Conti, you're a drunk.

Absolutely not, Etta. I can quit any time I want.

Who are you kidding? You need the booze. It kills the pain.

I'll stop tomorrow. Damn you, Etta. Just leave me alone.

She walked unsteadily into the bathroom and tried to recall what she had done the previous evening. She could not remember one single thing, even though she thought hard.

Maralee. Were they together?

No. Maralee had left for Europe with her father two days ago. Or was it longer? She honestly could not remember.

Better get your act together, Elaine.

Better leave me the fuck alone, Etta.

She wandered into the kitchen without even a passing glance in the mirror.

Elaine Conti. Tangled hair, streaked by the sun instead of

from a bottle. Perfect white skin tanned for the first time in ten years. Figure slightly voluptuous – she had gained at least ten pounds. Instead of a lace nightgown – derigueur bedtime dress for ladies in Beverly Hills – she wore Ross's old pyjama top, the sleeves rolled high. For someone who should be looking lousy she looked pretty good. A little puffy around the eyes, but more attractive than the usual groomed to within an inch of her life Elaine Conti.

She was naturally unaware of this fact. She knew for sure that she looked terrible. But since she was seeing no one and no one was seeing her – what did it matter? Even Lina had deserted her.

The orange juice in the refrigerator appeared to have seen better days, but she poured half a glass anyway, and added a healthy blast of vodka – just to chase away the blues. Then she sat down and wondered how she was going to pass yet another long and lonely weekend.

* * *

Ross awoke shortly after Elaine. Only he had not had the luxury of a bed to spend the night in. The back seat of his yellow Corniche had done duty – and it was not the most comfortable place in the world, although better than sharing Gina Germaine's California Eastern King. Jesus Christ! Anything was better than that.

He kicked open the back door of the car, uncramped his body, painfully climbed out, and stretched long and hard.

A rat scampered across the garage floor. Beverly Hills was full of them. The four legged *and* the two legged kind.

Ross Conti. Movie star. Sleeping rough.

Not exactly planned, but since leaving Elaine nothing much had gone his way. Which was one of the reasons he had returned to the roost. Unfortunately too late at night to gain entry. The previous evening he had rung the doorbell for ten minutes and nobody had answered. His key was somewhere among his things at Gina's place. Too bad, but he wasn't going back.

When every dog in the neighborhood started to bark he had abandoned his attempt to get into his own home and driven the Corniche to the alley behind the house. There, he had used the remote control to gain entry to the garage, parked, and taken up his sleeping position on the back seat.

Christ! His back was now killing him, and at that particular moment in time taking a piss was the most important thing in his life.

He hoped that Lina was around to let him in. Didn't want to disturb Elaine's beauty sleep. He wanted her in a good mood for the return of her hero.

Chapter Sixty-Eight

Deke had more information than he desired. It filled his brain like maggots swarming over the carcass of a dead cow. Eating at his sanity. Driving him mad.

Nita Carrolle.

Silent at first.

Until he punctured that fat flesh . . . And the words came spilling out like rich red blood . . .

She knew plenty. She was old, but her memory was sharp as an ice-pick. When he mentioned the names Winifred and Willis Andrews she faltered for a moment . . . but then she remembered. And she found papers to prove it.

He knew who his mother was.

He knew where she was.

Immediately he thought of Joey. At last they would be able to meet. Joey . . . so lovely . . . she could be a movie star . . . So much prettier than the trash that paraded the boulevards.

Next time he saw her he would tell her. She would love him for it. She would kiss him and hug him and call him cowboy again . . .

He missed her so badly.

If he took care of everything would she come back? He resolved to ask her.

Of course, The Keeper Of The Order could not beg.

Or pay.

Had he paid her? He frowned, unsure.

Maybe once.

SHE WAS NOTHING BUT A DIRTY WHORE.

Fury filled his head already bursting with the name of the woman who had brought him into this filthy world.

Nita Carrolle's words shattered like a zillion fragments.

'. . . always knew who the mother was . . . my babies special . . . followed their lives if I could . . . never sold them cheap . . . nice girls who got in trouble . . . your mother's done so well . . . your mother . . . your mother.

DAMN HIS MOTHER.

She left him. She gave him away. She abandoned him like garbage.

THE BITCH HAD NEVER EVEN WANTED HIM.

She would pay for every year of his life.

In blood.

Slowly.

Chapter Sixty-Nine

'I'm leaving today,' Angel said quietly.

'I expect you are,' Koko replied crossly, spooning all-bran and raisins into his mouth while attempting to fix a cup of coffee.

Gently she took the cup from his hand.

He snatched it back. 'I'm quite capable of making my own coffee, thank you very much.'

She sighed. 'Why are you mad at me?'

'Mad? Who's mad? *I'm* certainly not.'

'Please don't be angry.' Tentatively she touched his arm. 'You're the one who has taught me to stand up for myself. Without you I would never have had the strength to give Buddy another chance.'

'Hah!' he snorted. 'I just hope you realize what you are doing.'

'I'm going back to my husband in the hope that things are going to work out and that my baby will have a father.'

'Adrian and I would have been perfectly wonderful fathers,' he sniffed.

'Will you settle for godfathers?'

'The Mario Puzo kind?'

'Who?'

'Oh goodness! You still don't know much do you?'

'I know enough, thanks to you. I'm not the same stupid girl who came crying into your salon looking for a job.'

'You were *never* stupid. Just unbearably sweet!'

They both giggled and embraced.

'I hate goodbyes,' he said gruffly.

'I'm not being picked up until five.'

'You know Saturday's our busiest day. I won't be back by then.'

'Can I bring Buddy over next week?'

'God! Do you have to?'

'Please.'

'We'll see.'

They hugged again, and he stroked her silken blonde hair and held her to him very tightly. 'Be happy, dreamheart,' he whispered.

'I will,' she whispered back. 'I know I will.'

* * *

Montana refused to mourn for Neil. During the course of their marriage he had lost two good friends and both times he said the same thing. 'Never look back. Face whatever's coming to you head-on and let the bastards know that you know.' And then he had gotten uproariously drunk.

She knew that he would not want her to sit around and mope, so she didn't. Instead she set her plan to get her own back on Oliver in motion. It took a lot of organizing, but now it was all set and every time she thought about it a wide grin broke across her face. Monday morning was Oliver Easterne day and she could hardly wait!

In the meantime she packed up the rest of Neil's things, and then started on her own possessions.

Saturday morning she called Stephen Shapiro, a realtor she knew, and he came up to look at the house.

'Put it on the market at once,' she instructed. 'I'll leave it in your hands. I shall be flying to New York on Monday.'

Stephen seemed to think a price of two million dollars was not unrealistic. 'If we find the right buyer,' he added.

She deliberated over whether to call anybody and say goodbye. But then it occurred to her that all her real friends lived in New York. She only had acquaintances in Los Angeles. Would they care if she stayed or departed? Probably not.

She tried to reach Buddy Hudson, but his service picked up. She would try him again before she left, he deserved a proper explanation about the demise of the film, not the crap he was no doubt being fed.

Goodbye California . . . She would miss it in her own way. The ocean and the beach. The mountains and the parks. The very seduction of living in the sun. And of course, the view from the top of their hill. That very special spread of lights laid out like fairytale land.

Yes. She knew she would miss L.A., but as Neil would say . . . 'Never look back . . .'

* * *

Buddy had driven by his old home three times. The street and the house looked exactly the same. What had he expected? That everything would have been replaced with multiple skyscrapers, and freeways, and that there was no way he could ever trace his mother again.

Nothing like that had happened. He had no excuse.

Maybe she didn't live there anymore.

Maybe she was dead.

He hoped.

And hated himself for hoping such a thing.

He did not feel well at all. Why couldn't he just walk over, ring the doorbell and get it over and done with?

Determinedly he started to leave the car, but as he did so the front door of his former home opened and a boy of about six emerged. Buddy paused while the boy ran over to a maroon station wagon, flung open the back door, and climbed inside.

The front door of the house remained open, and Buddy waited, knowing for sure she would appear at any moment.

And so she did.

He ducked back into his car as guilty as the day he had left. He felt sixteen again. *She looked exactly the same.*

This really freaked him. Somehow he had expected – hoped – that ten years would have taken their toll. But even from a distance he could see that she had hardly changed. Her hairstyle was different, but that was it. Instead of hanging to her waist in rich curls, her auburn locks were trimmed to shoulder length, which made her look even younger than he remembered.

How old *was* she? He recalled asking her when he was about eight and she had replied primly, 'A lady never reveals her age. Always bear that in mind if you please.'

Eight years old and his own mother didn't even want to tell him how old she was.

She got into the station wagon and drove off in the opposite direction, leaving him in a hopeless state of deep frustration.

He decided hanging around outside the house waiting for her and the kid to come back was stupid. He had other things to do in San Diego, and the sooner he did everything and headed back for L.A. and Angel the better.

Wolfie Schweicker.

Wasn't it about time he told the police?

* * *

They confronted each other warily.

Elaine thought – My God – what do I look like?

Ross thought – My God – what does she look like?

They always had had a lot in common.

'Where's Lina?' he asked.

'She quit,' replied Elaine, aware for the first time in ages that her nails were chipped, her hair undone, her outfit unsuitable.

'That's my pyjama top,' he said accusingly.

'I know,' she replied. For some strange reason she felt quite lightheaded.

'Am I coming in?'

'Are you?'

'It's my home isn't it?'

She nodded. He was an unfaithful lying cheating bastard. She *should* tell him to go take a hike.

He was *her* unfaithful lying cheating husband. And he was back.

'Come in,' she said.

The famous blues twinkled. 'I thought you'd never ask.'

* * *

There wasn't much to pack. One suitcase and a carryall bag with all her bits and pieces in. Never again would she be able to travel so light. Soon there would be the baby to consider.

She looked in the bathroom mirror, turned sideways and regarded her bulge. What was Buddy going to say when he saw her? He hadn't even asked about the baby . . . not so much as a 'How are you feeling?'

Suppose Koko was right and going back to him was a big mistake?

She shook her head resolutely. He deserved a final chance. He sounded so different on the phone, so positive and sure about their future together. It was all going to work out, she just knew it.

Adrian knocked on the door of her room. 'Do you need any help?' he inquired solicitously.

'I'm all set,' she replied. 'By this time tomorrow you'll have forgotten I was ever here.'

He wheeled himself into the small spare room. 'I hope not.'

'I want to thank you for everything,' she blurted. 'Without you and Koko I don't know what I would—'

'Remember to keep in touch. Koko's very broody about you – don't disappoint him.'

They both laughed.

She brushed a strand of pale hair from her forehead and shivered with the anticipation of seeing Buddy again. He had said he was sending a car for her at five o'clock, but who could wait? She was ready to leave now.

* * *

'Hey – listen, man, I didn't *have* to come here,' Buddy said restlessly. 'I just figured – hey – y'know – like I'd be doin' you guys a favour.'

'A ten years later favour,' snapped the big detective. There were two of them in the interview room. The big man, and his partner – a silent black who stoically chewed gum and cleaned his nails with a toothpick.

'So what are you going to do about it?' Buddy asked impatiently. He had given them the information. Willingly. Nobody had dragged him in off the street.

'Just what do you expect us to do?' questioned the big cop. 'Put out a warrant on Wolfie whatever his name is because you walk in here an' tell us he killed your boyfriend ten years ago?'

'Why don't you look up the case?' Buddy persisted. 'Pull out your files. Understand what the hell I'm talkin' about.'

'You want the case re-opened?' asked the black cop wearily, speaking for the first time.

'Hey – listen, I'm not here to get a manicure,' Buddy snapped, outraged by their indifference.

'Means a lot of paperwork,' mused the black.

'Tough,' muttered Buddy sarcastically.

The big cop sighed. 'Leave your name an' address. We'll put it to the Captain. We need authority.'

Buddy shook his head in amazement. Being a good citizen was no easy job. Then he thought about the implications if the case *was* opened up. Publicity of that kind was not what he needed right now. Naively he had just assumed he could walk into the precinct, tell them about Wolfie Schweicker, and split. How dumb could you get?

Pretty dumb, Buddy Boy, pretty fucking dumb.

'I've changed my mind,' he said abruptly. 'I'll come back tomorrow.'

The detectives exchanged bored glances. Another weirdo with nothing better to do than waste their time.

'Yeah, you do that,' said the big cop with a liberal yawn. 'An' don't forget – we already caught the freeway strangler an' the joggin' killer, so think of something new to waste our time with, huh?'

Buddy left in disgust, got in his car, and headed back to his mother's house.

* * *

Sadie had planned to spend the weekend in Palm Springs, but when she awoke – late – she found she could not summon the energy to move. Seeing Ross with Gina had depressed her. Did he have no taste at all? Gina Germaine was a movie star, but she was also a tramp – sleeping with any man who might – in some way or another – further her career or her life. What she wanted from Ross was hard to guess at.

Sadie guessed anyway. And knew immediately she was right.

The legendary Conti schlong. What woman wouldn't be thrilled to wake up with *that* beside her?

Frustratedly she buzzed for her maid, and then remembered that she had given the maid and her husband the weekend off as she had expected to be in Palm Springs. No matter. She would enjoy being on her own for a change. No parties, screenings or business meetings. Just uninterrupted peace – something she did not manage to get very much of.

Ross.

She kept on thinking of him.

Ross.

She still loved him.

In spite of . . .

She reached for the phone and dialled Gina's private number.

The disgruntled voice of an American sex goddess answered. 'Shit, Sadie,' Gina complained. 'Have you *seen* the papers?'

Sadie, as it happened, had not. 'What, dear?' she inquired soothingly, knowing full well that Gina always had some complaint or another regarding the items which were written about her.

'You can take Ross Conti and shove him up your ass,' Gina fumed.

'What did he do?'

'Ha!' snorted Gina, incensed, even after a night to mull things over. 'Read all about it. I threw the bum out.'

'You did?'

'I sure did.'

'Where did he go?'

'Who gives a fast fuck?'

'I'm leaving for Palm Springs now,' Sadie said hurriedly. 'I'll call you on Monday.' She could not wait to get off the phone.

'That's a pity,' said Gina, her voice a disappointed whine. 'I thought you could come over, there's things I wanna discuss.'

'You wouldn't want me to forgo my one weekend of peace and quiet, would you?'

'Why not? You can go to the Springs any time.'

Selfish as always. 'I'm afraid I *have* to go. As I said, we'll talk on Monday.'

She put the phone down before Gina could bitch further.

So Ross had dumped the big movie star . . . And not a second too soon . . .

She thought for a minute, then called the Beverly Hills Hotel, the Beverly Wilshire, and the Bel Air. Ross was not registered at any of them. Could he perhaps have gone home? Back to the waiting arms of his wife? Sadie had no doubt that Elaine *was* waiting. In Hollywood, stars were *always* welcomed home, whatever they might have been up to. Hollywood wives were a breed unto themselves. Perfect, pretty women with a ticket to ride. That ticket being the famous husband.

She hesitated only a moment before trying his home number.

* * *

The phone interrupted their reunion. And what a reunion it was. Elaine spread-eagled on the thick pile rug while Ross pumped away above her like a shore hungry sailor.

He had taken her by surprise, strode into the house a conquering hero returned from battle.

'You look a mess,' he had said. 'And the house looks even worse.' Then he roared with laughter. 'What's been happening around here anyway?'

The embarrassment at being caught! He might at least have warned her he was coming home. She could have spent a day at Elizabeth Arden, had professional cleaners in to deal with the house, bought fresh flowers . . .

Oh, why bother. He would just have to take her as he found her. He wasn't looking too sensational himself, plus he smelled like a sweaty horse.

They circled each other warily, then Ross blurted, 'I'll tell you something – you look damn sexy.' And he had pounced, surprising both of them. Silently they began to consummate their reunion on the living room floor.

Then the phone rang and automatically Elaine's arm reached for it while Ross growled, 'Forget it.'

Too late. Whoever was on the line was in the room with them. A disembodied voice echoing, 'Hello, hello . . .'

'Yes?' said Elaine impatiently.

'Ross Conti please.'

'Who's calling?'

'Sadie La Salle.'

'Sadie! How are *you*? This is Elaine.'

Ross's erection deflated. He grabbed the phone, spoke briefly, hung up and turned to Elaine with a satisfied smile.

'I think we're back in business,' he said. 'Miz La Salle requests the pleasure of my company at her house.'

'When?'

'Now.'

'You'd better get dressed.'

He fell back on top of her. 'Not until I've finished what we started.'

'Ross!'

'Let her wait . . .'

Chapter Seventy

How long was he going to hang around? All day if necessary. He was not returning to L.A. without straightening things out. Laying ghosts they called it. Some ghost. His own mother.

Buddy chain smoked half an hour away, and at last the maroon station wagon reappeared.

No more sitting around waiting for the moment to be right. He stubbed out his cigarette and hurried from the car.

By the time he walked up the driveway the station wagon was parked with the back open and the kid was unloading brown supermarket bags. He looked up. 'Can I help you?'

'Sure,' Buddy replied. 'I want to see the lady of the house.'

'What about?' asked the boy, too precocious for his years.

'About none of your business.'

'Mommy,' he yelled. 'There's a man here being rude.'

Buddy double-taked on the kid just as his mother rushed from the house. Was this his *brother*?

She glanced from one to the other, not recognizing Buddy at first. But on second look she knew and a small gasp escaped her lips. 'Buddy,' she whispered. 'My God!'

She made no attempt to come towards him. Just stared as if she had seen a ghost.

'Who's Buddy?' demanded the boy.

'Go in the house, Brian,' she commanded.

'Don't want to,' he whined.

'Go!' Her skin was still olive smooth. Her hair burnished bronze. She had put on a few extra pounds, but other than that she had not changed. Brian dragged reluctantly indoors.

Buddy threw his arms wide, an expansive gesture, but not one that she responded to. 'Hey—' he said. 'I figured the time had come to make the peace.'

* * *

It was a hot clear day in Los Angeles. By ten-thirty in the morning the heat was already blistering and there was a general rush of cars heading for the beach.

The high temperature bothered Deke. He cut the sleeves from the black workshirt he wore, and hacked his jeans off at the knee. With his bald head, wraparound black sunglasses, boots and ragged outfit he looked bizarre. But in California anything goes, and when he strolled down Hollywood Boulevard muttering to himself nobody so much as second glanced him.

His head was filled with snakes. They enveloped him. They were round his neck, on his arms, legs, body, even in his mouth.

He spat on the sidewalk and watched the reptiles slither away.

A seedy doorway offered tattooes and he walked in. MOTHER took only a scant half hour to become a part of his life forever.

He was ready.

He walked to his old brown van parked on a side street and set off to do the necessary deed.

* * *

When the bell rang Sadie hurried to answer it. She didn't even bother checking who it was for she knew that it had to be Ross, and this time she wanted him for keeps.

She flung open the massive oak door in anticipation.

'Hello mother,' said the sinister figure in black. 'I'm home.'

Book Two

Chapter Seventy-One

Sadie La Salle was twenty years old when she first came to Hollywood from Chicago in the fifties. It seemed the most unlikely place in the world for a girl who looked like Sadie to choose. Usually it was the beauties who flocked to tinsel town – long haired lovelies with smooth skin, and lissome bodies. Sadie was short, plump, ferociously dark, her hair a frizzy mass which grew not only on her head but everywhere else as well. Fortunately she had no desire to be an actress. She just wanted to get away from a stifling mother and live a life of her own. Hollywood seemed like a good idea at the time.

She arrived by Greyhound bus on a Monday morning, and by Tuesday afternoon she had an apartment and a job. Having worked for two years as a secretary in Chicago her references were glowing. Goldman, Forrest and Mead, a Beverly Hills law firm, took her on immediately. She started in the typing pool, but soon progressed to being Jeremy Mead's personal secretary. He was a tall gawky married man, tanned from golf, fit from tennis; with small brown eyes, an eagle's nose and thinning brown hair. It did not take Sadie long to become indispensable to him.

Work was fine. Her personal life was not. The only time men ever second glanced her was when they spied her extremely large breasts, and for a moment interest gleamed. If she was lucky enough to get asked out on a date it was always the same old story. A fast dinner in some secluded restaurant and then the great pounce. The third time this happened to her she decided that the dinner was not worth the struggle, and she gave up dating and took up going to the movies and reading. Both infinitely more exciting.

She developed a passion for books about Hollywood and the movie industry – storing every bit of information for future use. Eventually she wanted to do something concerned with films – although she didn't quite know what. While she waited to find out, she worked hard and absorbed all the knowledge that came her way. Jeremy Mead had an interesting client list which included producers, directors and several famous actors. She studied their various contracts, finding out about percentages, the difference between gross and net profits, the intricacies of billing. She also learned to go over the small print with an eagle eye, and on several occasions she pointed out things to Mr Mead that he had missed.

He was pleased enough to invite her out to lunch, and since it was business she accepted.

Three glasses of wine was over her limit. A motel in Brentwood was certainly not a colleague's office – which is where he had said they had to go. He pounced. Of course. It was her overabundance of bosom that did it every time.

She allowed him certain liberties. After all, a girl couldn't stay a virgin forever.

He paid ten minutes faithful homage to her breasts, then with no further preliminaries, attempted to mount her. She stared at his small eyes, his hook nose, his thinning brown hair and decided that her virginity was far too precious a commodity to be surrendered to a man like Jeremy Mead. Besides, he was married.

She pushed him off. No easy job as by this time he was in full flight.

He complained hotly, but somehow his hardness became buried between her mammoth breasts, and a sudden orgasm left him red-faced and satisfied. He collapsed with a happy sigh while she locked herself in the bathroom and cried.

They drove back to the office in stony silence. Passion was over, and an uneasy business relationship took its place.

Two days later in Schwab's drugstore she spotted Ross Conti. And she knew for sure that if she was going to lose her virginity to anyone this blond bronzed Adonis, with eyes the colour of sapphires, and a smile to melt any girl's heart, would be the man.

She did not know how she did it, but she willed him to her side, and soon they were sipping coffee and chatting. Apart from his incredible looks he had an easy charm which was quite irresistible. He invited her to dinner (she paid, but it didn't matter) and when he made the inevitable pass she summoned every bit of will power she possessed and turned him down. She wanted Ross Conti, but she also wanted it to be more than just a quick one-nighter.

They became friends.

She cooked for him, listened to his problems, did his washing.

He confided in her, asked her advice, discussed his various girlfriends.

She bided her time while continuing to work for Jeremy Mead, who suggested two more lunches, both of which she declined.

One day she met a sad-eyed accountant by the name of Bernard Leftcovitz, and while Ross was out laying every female from the valley to the ocean, she began to date him.

Since Ross had a habit of telling her everything, she knew all about his latest passion – a married woman who wore Arpège perfume (and probably Frederick's of Hollywood underclothes). The woman's husband was a musician who travelled a lot, and one night when he was in San Diego, and Ross was spending the evening with his wife, Sadie decided to take action. It was simple for her to find out where the husband was playing, and whisper an anonymous phone message in his ear.

The stage was set. All she had to do was sit tight.

Bernard Leftcovitz ate dinner by candle light in her apartment when an outraged Ross burst in. He behaved badly, bitching about nearly being caught, talking about himself non-stop, glaring at Bernie just as Sadie had hoped. He outsat the unfortunate Mr. Leftcovitz, and then in a fit of possessiveness claimed his prize.

Oh yes. Ross Conti was certainly worth waiting for. Their love-making was all that she had ever dreamed of. She gave up her virginity thankfully.

And so began the most wonderful months of her life. She loved him. She would have done anything for him. And did.

Their relationship was one-sided, but it suited them both.

'I'll make you a star,' she told Ross when he despaired of his career ever taking off. 'I'll be your agent.'

He laughed, but she meant it, and what's more she knew she could do it. Suddenly everything she had been working towards made sense. She left her job, borrowed money, and with her brilliant billboard campaign forced Ross into orbit. The rest was easy.

They were halcyon days. New York. The Carson Show. *A triumphant return to Los Angeles. Offers pouring in.*

Negotiations. She had been born to make deals.

Sadie felt complete satisfaction for the first time in her life.

Ross left her on the day she planned to tell him she was pregnant. The doctor confirmed her suspicions at four o'clock in the afternoon, and she rushed straight from his office to buy champagne.

All the way home she rehearsed what she would say. 'I'm pregnant. It won't change anything. I'll work right up until the birth. You'll be number one, Ross, always. Isn't it fantastic?'

She knew he might not be pleased. At first. After all it would mean marriage of course.

She parked the car, and hurried up to their apartment.

His closet was bare. His Sinatra records were missing. His bottles of 'Man-Tan' and 'Old Spice' and his toothbrush had vanished from the bathroom shelves.

The emptiness in the pit of her stomach was like a dull throbbing ache. Ross was gone.

She sat in a chair by the window and waited for him to contact her. She sat through the night, and half of the next day without moving.

Eventually the phone rang and a business-like female voice informed her that Mr Conti had requested that all of his contracts and business papers were to be forwarded to the Lamont Lisle Agency who would be handling his affairs from now on.

Numbly she travelled to her office and gathered together all of his photos, contracts, press clippings and correspondence. It did not occur to her to fight. Never crossed her mind to hire a sharp lawyer and establish the rights she most definitely had over his career.

Ross Conti walked. And she allowed him to.

For a few weeks she did nothing at all except stare at the television like a zombie and eat. Then the bills started to come in, and a visit to the bank made her aware that Ross had cleared their mutual account of everything except a thousand dollars. She accepted this fact also. And thought about killing herself because as far as she was concerned there was nothing left to live for.

Jeremy Mead unwittingly saved her. He had lent her the money (albeit reluctantly) to launch Ross Conti's billboard campaign, and although she had since paid him back it irked him that she had never consummated their relationship. So when news of Ross's marriage to Wendy Warren hit the papers, he called immediately and invited himself over.

When he arrived he found her contemplating an overdose of sleeping pills which he talked her out of. An hour later they were in bed.

She felt nothing except the weight of his bony elbows, and when he left she sobbed long into the night, breaking the numbness that had enveloped her since Ross's departure.

In the morning she took a deep breath and decided to get on with her life. No man was going to destroy Sadie La Salle. She would show Ross Conti a thing or two by becoming rich, powerful, and successful without him. She did not know how – but somehow she would do it.

The first thing was to get an abortion. She was already four months pregnant, but because of her natural bulk it was hardly noticeable. She waited four weeks – then telephoned Jeremy Mead and requested a meeting. He came to her apartment thinking she could no longer resist his charms.

'I'm pregnant,' she said simply. 'It's yours.'

'Mine?' he spluttered. 'How do you know?'

'Because there hasn't been anyone else since you.'

He stared at dark fiery fat Sadie, and cursed the fact that he had not stuck to calm competent prepared blondes.

'Goddamn it,' he said angrily. 'Why weren't you careful?'

'Why weren't you?' she retorted, hating him almost as much as she hated Ross.

'You'll have to get an abortion,' he stated callously.

'I don't have the money.'

'I'll pay.'

'Thank you so much.'

Two days later he sent her round an envelope with the name and number of a doctor and an amount of money to take care of everything. The doctor was in Tijuana, Mexico.

She took a tourist bus there the next day, booked into a cheap hotel, then called the doctor who agreed to see her at his clinic at five-thirty.

His clinic turned out to be a small room in back of a souvenir shop. The only furniture being an old rattan desk and worn leather bench. He was a man of about fifty, with red rimmed eyes and a bad stutter. At least he was American.

'I'm pregnant,' she said quietly. 'I was told you could help me.'

'How p. .p. .pregnant?'

'Three months,' she lied.

He nodded, told her the price, and requested that she remove her clothes and lie on the bench.

She thought he was going to examine her and tell her to come back the next day to his hospital or wherever he took care of such matters, so she disrobed and lay down, prudently keeping on her bra.

'Take that o. .o. .off,' he commanded.

The small room was hot and dusty. A fly buzzed incessantly. Gritting her teeth she unclipped her bra.

The doctor's red rimmed eyes bulged. He licked his lips as he approached her. 'Open your legs.'

She shut her eyes and did as he bade.

His fingers were inside her immediately, roughly probing and searching. As she cried out he said sharply, 'Be quiet. I'm not hurting you.'

She wanted to get up, dress and leave. But what was the point? Ross's child was growing inside her and it had to be removed.

He finished his examination, pressed each breast roughly, and said, 'I can take care of it.'

'When?' she asked, sitting up.

'Now,' he said. 'If you've g. . g. .got the money with you.'

She was aghast. 'Here?'

He snorted. 'You g. .g. .girls are all the same. You get yourselves pregnant, want it terminated, then expect f. .f. .first class service. May I remind you that an abortion is illegal.'

'I know. But . . . here . . .' She gestured hopelessly around the dusty room.

'I've taken care of five hundred girls here,' he said dismissively. 'You w. .w. .want it or not?'

She was frightened, but want overcame fear. She lay back. 'Go ahead,' she said dully.

'The money first.'

She rose naked to get the money from her purse, and his red rimmed eyes followed her across the room.

'You need to lose some w. .w. .weight,' he said, when she lay down again. His hands passed lingeringly across her breasts. 'These m. .m. .must be heavy to carry around.'

'Let's just get on with it,' she muttered furiously.

An hour later she stumbled out to the street barely able to walk. He had probed and pierced and stabbed. But nothing had happened. Nothing except agonizing contractions and a steady flow of blood.

As time passed he had begun to sweat. His hands started to shake. His stutter became worse. Abruptly he threw down the steel instrument he was using. 'Go home,' he said. 'It's g. .g. .going to take more t. .t. .time with you. I've s. .s. .started it o. .o. .off. It'll h. .h. .happen spontaneously. There's n. .n. .nothing else I c. . c. .can do.'

'I don't understand,' she screamed weakly. 'I've paid you.'

He thrust a wad of cotton between her legs and quickly brought over her clothes, helping her to dress. 'It'll h. .h. .happen,' he assured her, pushing her out to the street. 'G. .g. .go h. .h. .home. It'll happen s. .s. .soon.'

Somehow she staggered back to the hotel, her contractions becoming worse all the time. There she lay on the bed and watched the blood seep through the cotton pad bunched between her legs.

The pain was excruciating. When blood began to soak through to the bed, she realized hazily that she needed help. The doctor had not given her an abortion, the bastard had butchered her.

She attempted to get up and for one brief moment Ross's image danced in front of her eyes. Then she lost consciousness and slumped to the floor.

She drifted back to the real world days later, remembering nothing of the events following her collapse. Her eyes fluttered open and took in her surroundings. She was in a bed, a rubber tube attached to her arm. Her mouth was dry and parched, and she longed for a drink. A white screen enclosed the bed and the brightness hurt her eyes. She tried to gather her thoughts. Where was she? What had happened?

She must have drifted some more, for when she next awoke there was a face peering down at her. A middle-aged woman who gently said, 'Feeling better?'

'Can I have a drink,' she whispered.

'Certainly, dear.'

Vaguely she wondered why the woman was not in nurse's uniform. Surely she was in some sort of hospital? Then she remembered and when the woman returned with a paper cup of water she gasped, 'The baby? Am I still pregnant?'

The woman gazed at her silently for a moment, then nodded.

'Oh, no,' she groaned.

'It's God's way of telling you there are other ways . . .' the woman said mysteriously. 'Rest, dear. We will talk later.'

And later they did talk. Sadie found out that the woman's name was Noreen Carrolle. She was a former nurse. One day she had travelled to Tijuana with a girlfriend who needed an abortion. 'I did not approve nor disapprove,' Noreen said. 'It seemed a sensible decision. But my friend was treated like an animal, and later that night she died.'

Sadie listened carefully as Noreen told of how from that moment on she got what she claimed to be 'the calling'.

'I knew I could save other girls from the same fate,' she said simply. 'And that is what I have been doing ever since.'

'How did you find me?' Sadie asked curiously.

'The hotels know me. When a girl checks in alone they alert me. You acted so fast that I didn't have time to reach you before. But fortunately I found you in time, and even more fortunate your baby is safe.'

She shut her eyes, thought of Ross's baby safe inside her, and wanted to scream aloud with fury.

'Don't worry,' Noreen said quietly. 'I have an alternative plan. A happy solution for everyone concerned. Of course,' she added, 'I could have taken you to a hospital. The police would have been alerted, your family and the prospective father would certainly have been dragged into it. There might have been a prosecution.' She paused, watching for Sadie's reaction. 'Usually the girls like to keep this sort of thing to themselves, and I don't blame them.' She nodded knowingly. 'You see, I understand what happens. One night of passion . . . things get out of hand . . . no time to think about the consequences . . .'

She had Sadie's rapt attention. Carefully she outlined her plan. 'You'll have your baby, dear. You're too far gone to attempt another abortion anyway. I'll send you to my sister's place in Barstow where you can rest and regain your strength. When you give birth you'll be fitter than you've ever been and we'll take the baby off your hands. There are couples who long for a child . . . We arrange it without the fuss and bother of adoption. All those papers to fill out . . . it's dehumanizing. One simple document is all you have to sign . . .' Noreen smiled reassuringly. 'And my sister, Nita, and I will take care of everything.'

Chapter Seventy-Two

'I beg your pardon.' Sadie spaced her words carefully and spoke slowly.

Deke stared at her, his eyes glowing coals.

His eyes. Her eyes. Disturbingly familiar.

She felt a shiver run down her spine, and automatically began to close the door.

'Don't do that.' He blocked it with his foot. 'I'm home . . . Mother. Nita Carrolle sent me. It's been a long journey, but I'm here.'

The name Nita Carrolle made Sadie hesitate. 'I . . . I don't understand . . .' she said falteringly.

But she understood. Twenty-six years earlier she had given birth, and now part of her past stood before her.

'Push dear, push.'

'I am pushing. I am. I am.'

Tears streaked her face. A pause between contractions. Then the pain again, and her screams of agony. Long animal screams, while her hands tore at the roots of her hair. 'Help me, someone. Please help me.'

'Shut her up for God's sake.'

The mask descending over her face. The gas. Deep gulps. Relief. Drifting. Away from her body. Away from the pain.

Dully she stared at the familiar stranger. 'You'd better come in.'

Already she was thinking fast. Why was he here? What did he want? If he expected her to fall on him crying with pleasure he had another think coming. She had no maternal feelings. None whatsoever. Oh God! If it ever got out . . .

Maybe he wanted money. He looked like a freak. Do not admit anything. See what he knows.

How can he know anything? They promised me – those two women – they promised me nobody would ever know.

He followed her into the house. She led him through to the kitchen, glad that the servants were away for the weekend. At least she could deal with him alone.

'Sit down,' she said, recovering her composure. Purposefully she tried to sound casual. 'You know, I think you've made a mistake. Maybe you'd like to tell me who put you up to this?'

'I had a whore named Joey,' he said, covering his eyes with oblique wraparound sunglasses. 'She's not here now, but I loved her. You'll love her too.'

A shiver of fear. 'What?'

'Whores belong together.'

Her patience snapped. 'Who are you? What do you want?'

'I'm your son,' he replied calmly. 'You know that.'

'Oh, come on. Please. What makes you think such a ridiculous thing?'

'Nita Carrolle told me.'

'I don't know anyone of that name.'

He turned unexpectedly and struck her full force across the face. 'You lie, whoring bitch!' he screamed. 'I know the truth and you will tell me more.'

The force of his blow threw her to the floor and she lay there stunned, suddenly realizing her peril.

This was no long lost son. This was some sort of maniac. AND SHE HAD LET HIM INTO HER HOUSE.

* * *

Elaine brushed her hair vigorously. She could feel the tingle all the way down to her toes. There was nobody like Ross . . . nobody. He was the greatest lover in the world when he wanted to be.

She lined up her programme for the following week. The hairdressers, the nail clinic, the gym – no more Ron Gordino – who needed Ron Gordino? Maybe she would try Jane Fonda's Workout or Richard Simmons' Body Asylum. She hummed softly to herself. She would call Bibi and suggest lunch. Bibi would spread the news of Ross's return faster than The Hollywood Reporter.

And what about Ross's career? Sadie La Salle calling was an excellent sign, even if she had interrupted the best sex they had shared in years. The phone call had not fazed Ross. He could screw and talk at the same time, a feat not every actor could manage.

She felt so good. Ross had brought her to a majestic climax, then showered, and left for Sadie's house with a grin on his face. He was happy to be home. She was happy to have him. Together they would make it to the top again.

* * *

Angel took a cab and arrived at Buddy's apartment in the morning. She was sure he wouldn't mind.

'I ain't got no word to let anyone in,' grumbled the maid. Buddy's regular girl was out sick and she had omitted to inform her replacement of his message.

'But I'm Mrs Hudson,' Angel protested. 'And Bud – er Mr Hudson assured me he had left word with you.'

The maid sneered, ever so slightly. 'If'n you're his missus how come you ain't livin' here permanent?'

'I don't think that's any of your business.' Angel flushed, but stood her ground.

The maid's glance took in her swollen stomach. 'Okay,' she said grudgingly. 'You'd better come in. Ain't no skin off *my* ass if you rob the place.'

Angel re-entered Buddy's life. Not quite the way she had expected to, but she was back, and the anticipation of seeing him again made her breathless.

* * *

Ferdie knew that Sadie was going to Palm Springs for the weekend. He also knew that she wasn't planning on leaving until ten-thirty or eleven. He took pride in being aware of every move she made. Buddy's news *could* be given to her on the telephone, but *should* be given to her in person.

He vacillated for only a moment. It meant changing out of his beach clothes into a more suitable outfit. It meant explaining to Rocky that the picnic would have to be delayed, and Rocky would no doubt sulk . . .

Ferdie stamped his foot. A moment of unbridled aggravation. What was so important about Sadie knowing immediately anyway? God! If he had the news and she ever found out that he saved it for Monday. It *was* important, what with the billboard and everything . . .

Madame La Salle was *not* going to be pleased.

He stripped off his red T-shirt and shorts and hurried into the bedroom to change.

* * *

Ross felt surprisingly up. Things had a way of turning out for the best. An interlude away from Elaine had done them both good, and now he felt a togetherness that he thought had gone forever. Elaine was a fighter. She was no Beverly Hills bimbo. Sure she liked to spend money and live it up, but something he knew for sure – she would always be there when he needed her.

Sadie phoning – causing temporary coitus interruptus – had delighted both of them.

'She's changed her mind,' Elaine enthused. 'She must want to handle you.'

Ross had to agree. Why else the summons to her mansion on a Saturday morning?

He drove happily along Sunset, fit, tanned and fifty. Every career has its ups and downs. His was headed for an up, he could feel the good vibrations.

* * *

'Mother whore!' spat Deke. 'Harlot. Filth.'

He had tied her up, the threat of his knife ever present. Bound her tightly to a chair.

The fear of being cut prevented her from struggling. Ever since Tijuana, the doctor, and the unsuccessful abortion, she had been fearful of blood. In a way it was his fault . . . If he was her son . . . as he claimed to be . . .

The mask was pulled roughly away. The pain returned. And maybe death would have been more welcome as she felt herself torn. Screaming was her only release. Different voices were everywhere.

'Shut her up.'

'You want every neighbour in the area to hear her.'

'What's taking so long?'

'It's a breech birth, goddamn it.'

The mask again. The sweet thunder in her ears and nose and throat like death inviting her to stay.

Drifting . . . drifting . . .

Sharp reality . . .

'It's a boy.'

'He's not breathing.'

'Christ!'

'Do something before it's too late.'

Smack.

Nothing.

'He won't make it.'

'Like hell he won't. We need the money.'

Smack.

'C'mon you little bastard!'

And crying.

Brief respite.

The surprise of another contraction. She knew it was the afterbirth, soon it would be over.

She sucked in her breath, let it all out in one long piercing yell that seemed to last forever.

Rough hands clamped the mask over her face again and she faded once more to welcome unconsciousness.

When she awoke it was over. She lay in bed clean and washed, only the dull throbbing ache between her legs reminded her of the ordeal. Noreen Carrolle stood next to her sister Nita. They both smiled. Two faces . . . one plain and kindly, the other over-made up and coarse.

'Your worries are behind you dear,' said Noreen.

'Yeah, no more screwin' around an' you're in good shape,' laughed Nita.

She drifted back to sleep.

She tried to keep her voice calm. Somewhere she had read when dealing with a psychotic that it was important to try and remain in control. Besides, she was no shrinking violet, she was Sadie La Salle. Grown men had been known to shiver in her presence.

She thought of her elaborate alarm system. Unfortunately it was turned off. But if she could only reach the panic button by the kitchen door a distress signal would go straight through to the police.

Deke stalked around the kitchen muttering to himself.

She wondered if she should try to get him talking. Personal contact. Another way of getting through.

If she *was* his mother, what could be more personal than that? And if she *was* that meant that Ross was his father. And even now Ross was on his way up to her house.

Deke stopped marching up and down and slumped to

the floor in a sitting position, his back against the refrigerator.

'This is a big house,' he remarked.

In a strange way he reminded her of someone. She couldn't think who. He had her eyes. Oh God! He reminded her of herself, this bizarre disgusting stranger.

'I said you have a big house,' he repeated.

'Yes,' she agreed quickly.

'Joey would've liked it here.'

'Who is Joey?'

'My fiancée.'

She forced herself to sound as natural and friendly as possible. 'Where is she? Shall we call her and invite her over?'

He stood up. 'She's fucking men. That's what the whore does. She's like you, opens her legs for the world.' He said the words blankly, as if they meant nothing.

Sadie tried to change the subject, although her throat was so dry she could hardly talk. 'What's your name?'

He was pacing again. 'It doesn't matter.'

'Yes it does. What does Joey call you?'

'Joey?' He stopped and looked surprised. 'How do *you* know Joey?'

'Why don't you untie me and we can talk about her?'

'Talk about who?'

'Joey.'

'The whore bitch is dead.'

'I'm sorry.'

Deke resumed his pacing, lost in thought.

She eyed the panic button by the kitchen door, and wondered if there was any way she could get near enough to press it.

'This is a big house,' he said, repeating himself for the third time. 'I think I'll look around.'

'Yes, why don't you do that,' she said quickly.

He didn't hear her as he walked from the kitchen.

Laboriously she attempted to edge the chair towards the back door. It was no easy task. He had bound her with electrical cord, and it was cutting into her wrists and ankles. Nevertheless, painstakingly, she began to inch forward.

Chapter Seventy-Three

Leon Rosemont flew out from Las Vegas early Saturday morning. He felt a sense of urgency, but at the same time he knew that Deke Andrews was within his grasp . . . Maybe . . .

* * *

Ferdie drove his zippy white E-type Jaguar faster than the speed limit allowed. Next year a Mercedes. For sure. And the year after that – well maybe in two years – a Rolls.

Ferdie had goals. He aimed to attain every one of them. In the meantime he enjoyed the fast English sports car. It was a luxury he felt he deserved. Besides, his young boyfriends *loved* it.

He pushed one of Rocky's Rod Stewart cassettes into the tape machine and reflected on the boy's stupid behaviour. What a pain! Sulking and complaining all over the place. That was the trouble with the young ones, they acted like children.

'I wanna come with you,' Rocky had griped. 'I wanna meet the great Sadie La Salle.'

'Another time,' Ferdie replied firmly.

Another time. Another century. Never mix pleasure with business. A cliché. But a true one.

Then Rocky had burst into his 'You don't love me anymore' number and 'I'm splittin'.'

Ferdie had been forced to abandon everything and placate the boy. They ended up in bed. An exciting interlude that lasted far too long.

Anxiously he looked at his black Porsche watch. A Christmas present from Madame.

It was nearly eleven. He hoped that she hadn't left for Palm Springs yet.

* * *

The Rolls stalled at the corner of Canon Drive and Sunset, refusing to restart. Ross was furious.

When he had successfully worn the battery down to a mere click, he alighted from the car and gave it a resounding kick. A group of Mexican maids and children at the bus stop outside the Beverly Hills Hotel stamped and cheered. He gave them a mock bow and jogged across the street and up the driveway to the hotel.

'Car trouble,' he explained, handing the keys to the doorman. 'You buy a frigging Rolls you just don't expect it. It's on the corner of Canon.'

'I'll take care of it, Mr Conti. Will you be in the Polo Lounge?'

A cup of coffee and a cigarette was tempting before meeting Sadie. 'The coffee shop,' he decided. 'It's nothing much, I think I just flooded the engine.'

'Don't worry, Mr Conti. I'll have you paged when it's fixed.'

Ross entered the hotel.

* * *

The luxury of the house did not affect Deke as he walked from room to room. He stared blankly at expensive paintings and fine objets d'art. They meant nothing to him.

In her bedroom he stood before the four poster bed and

slowly, deliberately, unzipped his jeans. He shut his eyes, thought of Joey, and did what he had to do.

In the corner there was a giant Panasonic television set. He stabbed the screen with his knife, methodically ripping it to pieces.

Joey would certainly love the place. He planned to send for her as soon as possible.

* * *

In the kitchen Sadie made slow progress. The cord around her ankles cut into her flesh, and every time she edged forward another inch it was all she could do to stop from crying out. She wanted to close her eyes and wake up from the horrifying nightmare.

Where was Ross? What a strange twist of fate that the intruder in her house might be their son. *Their love child.* Bitterness enveloped her. Their love child indeed. The hateful reminder of Ross's disinterest and desertion.

Why hadn't the baby aborted as it should have done?

She moved too fast and the chair hit the side of the kitchen table, teetered and fell – taking her down with it.

She cried out, then bit down hard on her lower lip hoping he hadn't heard.

She was trapped now. Tethered like some thing. Bile rose in her throat and she felt more alone and frightened than she had ever done in her entire life.

* * *

Deke continued his tour of the house. In her bathroom he emptied all the bottles of make-up and perfume and bath oils down the sink. Joey didn't need any of that artificial trash.

He removed his sunglasses and gazed at himself in the triple mirror over the vanity unit. The reflection he saw surprised him. He leaned closer to the mirror and rubbed his bald scalp – slowly at first – then faster . . . faster . . . faster . . .

He felt another erection grow in his pants, but he ignored it, didn't touch himself, couldn't touch himself. Must wait for . . .

'Joey,' he said. Then he began screaming wildly. 'JOEY. WHERE ARE YOU, WHORE? COME OUT WHEREVER YOU'RE HIDING, BITCH. I'M GOING TO KILL YOU, SLUT.'

He picked up a bronze figure and hurled it at the mirror.

The glass shattered into a thousand or more fragments.

* * *

Ferdie pulled into the driveway of Sadie's house. When was the woman going to put in security gates? Hers was practically the only house on the street without them.

He tut-tutted to himself. When he had enough money he would lock himself in a gilded cage immediately. Los Angeles was full of creeps and perverts and God knows what. Couldn't be too careful.

He hurried from his car and rang the front doorbell hoping that he hadn't missed her.

* * *

Trapped on the floor Sadie heard the buzz and relief flooded over her. Ross was here. At least she wasn't alone anymore.

* * *

Upstairs, Deke heard the bell ring too and reality intruded on his thoughts.

He remembered where he was.

He remembered his mother, his *real* mother.

He didn't want to lose her. Not after all he had gone through to find her.

He put down the thick black eye crayon he was playing with, loped quickly down the stairs, and rushed into the kitchen. For one blank moment he thought she had gone and he was filled with red hot fury. Then he saw her on the floor, tied and helpless.

'Who did this to you?' he demanded.

She stared at him in horror. He had blackened around his eyes as though drawing a cosmetic mask. High on his forehead he had written in smudgy letters WHORES DIE.

'Untie me,' she said rapidly. 'I'll see who's at the door. I can send them away. Hurry.'

He bent to do as she said. She held her breath, weak with the anticipation of escape. Ross would save her. Thank God he was here! Maybe if they could get to his car, lock the doors, drive quickly off . . .

He had unbound one ankle when the door buzzer sounded again. He stopped what he was doing and cocked his head to one side.

'Hurry!' she urged.

A look of disgust swept across his face. 'You think I'm stupid, don't you?'

'No . . . no . . . I—'

'If you laugh at me I'll kill you.'

'I'm not laughing at you.'

He slapped her across the face, snapping her head back hard. 'Don't ever laugh at me, whore.'

She could taste blood in her mouth. 'No,' she whispered. 'I wouldn't ever do that.'

'Stay here and be quiet,' he commanded.

Silently she nodded.

* * *

Ferdie's immediate instinct was to step sharply back at the sight of Deke. 'Who are *you*?' he questioned, shocked.

Before Deke could reply, Sadie began to scream.

Ferdie's reaction was unfortunately slow. He did nothing.

In one smooth action Deke stepped forward, knife in hand. He plunged it into the startled man, puncturing him through the heart. Ferdie's eyes bulged with a mixture of sorrow and surprise as Deke dragged him through the doorway and threw him down on the hall floor. He was dead before his head hit the tiles.

Deke kicked the door shut and went back into the kitchen.

Sadie's screams turned to a whimper when she saw him. His clothes were soaked in blood.

'Please,' she moaned. 'Don't hurt me.'

'You made a lot of noise,' he said mildly. 'You shouldn't have done that.'

She began to shriek wildly. 'What did you do to Ross? What did you *do* to him?'

'And the Lord giveth. And the Lord taketh away . . . Mother. You must realize, I am The Keeper Of The Order. A man of honour.'

Her voice rose even more hysterically. 'You killed him, didn't you? You goddman *bastard*.'

'Am I a bastard . . . Mother?'

'If I'm your mother,' she screamed, 'then you just killed your own father.' Wild laughter fell from her lips. 'How do you feel about that . . . you . . . you fucking stupid moron.'

His eyes were insane with black anger as he walked towards her.

* * *

'Hi, Ross.' Montana slid onto the stool next to him in the coffee shop.

He glanced up from reading about himself and Gina in the morning paper. 'How are you?'

She shrugged. 'Okay I guess.'

He put the paper down. 'I was really distressed about Neil. I didn't get a chance to speak to you at the funeral.'

'Thank you.' She touched his arm lightly. 'I'm sorry about the movie.'

'Yes, well I'm sorrier than you are. That was one hell of a part you wrote. I really could have made an impact with a role like that.'

'I'm sure you could.'

He shrugged. 'Of course, with Oliver producing who knows what would have happened . . .'

She nodded her agreement.

'What'll you do now?' he asked.

'I'm going back to New York on Monday.' She sighed. 'I guess I'll miss the sunshine, but really I'm a city person. I figured a last breakfast in the coffee shop of the Beverly Hills Hotel was a fitting goodbye.' She glanced along the curved counter and laughed. 'I've gotten some of my best dialogue in this very room!'

He laughed with her.

'And how about you?' she inquired. 'What next?'

He smiled a crooked smile and projected with the famous blues. 'Something between Love Boat and death.'

'Huh?'

'An actor's joke.'

'Oh.' She ordered a double chocolate milkshake and an apple danish.

'Some breakfast,' he said admiringly.

'I've always been an eccentric eater.'

I bet she gives great head, he thought, and then scolded himself for having such a thought. Wasn't it possible to sit with a woman and not think about sex?

No.

Elaine did not like dipping her head to him. Maybe it was because he never returned the courtesy. He thought they might experiment. Together. It was never too late.

'I'm back with my wife,' he remarked.

'Good,' she replied with enthusiasm. 'I never did see you as just another of Gina's consorts.'

A bell boy arrived to inform him that his car was fixed. He tipped a couple of bucks and decided to stay for more coffee. Talking to Montana was no hardship. Besides – let Sadie wait. He didn't have to jump the moment she called, did he? He was still a star, wasn't he?

* * *

The voices in his head told him he had done the right thing. But he wasn't sure . . . Doubt crept over him like a dark hood as he moved from room to room in the big house. Restlessly he walked around muttering to himself. All rules of logic, time, and reason were suspended. He had travelled towards a goal and achieved it . . . But now what?

His head hurt. He felt disoriented. There was a throbbing in his temples, and the stroke of death surrounded him.

Where was Joey?

Out whoring of course. WHORE . . . WHORE . . . WHORE . . .

She thought he was ugly. She thought he was a nobody.

She didn't want him anymore.

He screamed with anger and kicked open the door to Sadie's study.

The scream died in his throat and he stood stock still, transfixed.

Oh, if Joey could see what he could see . . . Oh, yes . . . Oh, yes . . .

Tentatively he entered the room and approached the giant cardboard poster propped against the wall.

He reached forward to touch, to marvel.

It was him.

The picture was of him.

Chapter Seventy-Four

Buddy's mother gazed at him levelly. 'I thought you were dead,' she said, 'like your friend Tony.'

He laughed hollowly. For the first time he began to see things from her point of view, and whatever she had done to him he knew that he must have hurt her terribly. 'Still breathing,' he said, trying to make a joke out of it.

She nodded.

He shuffled his feet uncomfortably feeling like some young jerk. 'Can I come in?'

'No,' she replied flatly.

'Look,' he said, 'I've come back to make my peace with you. We both did things we shouldn't have – but what's that old saying – blood is thicker than water. Right?'

She glanced anxiously around, noted one neighbour watering her garden, another conversing with the postman. 'I suppose you *had* better come in,' she said reluctantly. 'But don't you say anything in front of Brian. Do you understand?'

He followed her inside the house and took a deep breath. It smelled the same – faint minglings of garlic, musky perfume and clean linen. Nostalgia enveloped him. He was prepared to forgive and forget if she was. One day he might even bring Angel here.

She led him into the formal living room, the one reserved for guests, and said, 'Sit down.'

On the black piano stood her collection of old silver photo frames. Grandma and Grandpa in sepia tinted Italy. Their beautiful daughter dressed in white, her hair braided to her waist. A wedding picture. The man in the photo not his father. Brian, at a younger age. No photos of him. No Buddy Boy once the light of her life.

She noticed him looking and said, 'I married again.'

He was shocked. Yet why should he be? She had her life to live too. 'Hey – that's great.' Sincerity was not in his tone. 'So I guess I got me a brother . . . I mean like a half brother. That's . . . uh . . . terrific.'

'No,' she said coldly. 'Brian is nothing whatsoever to do with you.'

He needed a family and a background again. 'I know you're mad. I should've contacted you – but I had to work things out my way. You've got to admit that what happened between us wasn't normal.' He paused, then continued insistently, 'Hey – you've got to accept *some* of the blame.'

Her eyes were ice chips. 'For what?'

His voice rose. 'Don't do this to me. You *know* what.'

'I wouldn't worry about it if I were you.'

'Look – I've worried about it for ten years. Now I just want to forget it.'

'Incest. Is that what you thought?'

Her callous way of saying that forbidden word shocked him. He'd had enough. He wanted out. Inexplicably he felt like crying – a sentiment he hadn't experienced in years. 'Why?' he managed.

'Because you are not my son, Buddy. You were adopted by us when you were four days old.'

He could not believe what he was hearing.

'It wasn't a legal adoption,' she continued calmly. 'We . . . bought you for a sum of money because we desperately wanted a son. I was told I could never have children . . .' She paused.

'But I gave birth to Brian, so you see – the doctors were wrong.'

He didn't know what to do or say. So many thoughts, such a mixed-up bag of emotions. And in a way – although it was a tremendous shock – relief almost. 'Who am I?' he asked at last.

'I was never told,' she said coldly, then added, 'I don't feel responsible for you, Buddy. You saw fit to leave me ten years ago. Let's just make believe you never came back.'

* * *

Elaine showered, then made an appointment at the hairdressers. She had tried tidying the house, but cleaning had never been her forte – so she phoned Lina and graciously requested her return.

'I have 'nother job, señora,' Lina said stoically.

'But I *need* you,' Elaine insisted as though there were some special bond between them. 'Mr Conti is back, and you know how upset he'll be if you're not here.'

'Mebee I find you someone else.'

'Not good enough, Lina. He'll want you here, first thing Monday. Please don't let him down.'

She replaced the receiver firmly and made herself a cup of coffee. Fleetingly she was tempted to add a little shot of something, but the temptation passed as soon as she considered her new situation. Ross was back. She had standards to maintain.

She phoned Bibi. 'Guess what?' she announced dramatically, ignoring the fact that they hadn't spoken in weeks.

'What, sweetie?' inquired Bibi, barely disguising her aggravation at being caught.

'Ross and I are back together. I wanted you to be the first to know.'

'How you together?' Surprise spilled from her voice. 'Last night he together with Gina. I sorry, darling, you make a mistake.'

'Bibi,' said Elaine assertively, 'I am not a fool. Last night he may well have been with Gina, but this morning he came back to me. To stay.'

'You *sure*, sweetie?'

'Of course I'm sure.'

Bibi's voice warmed up. She thrived on exclusive gossip. 'So what happened with Gina?'

'How about lunch on Monday and I'll tell you all about it?'

'I busy Monday, but I think I change it. Yes, sweetie, for you I change it.'

'Wonderful. Jimmy's, one o'clock?'

'Jimmy's so boring, darling. I find new place, very nice. Chinese. My secretary call you early Monday with the address.'

'Perfect.' Elaine put the phone down and smiled. Lunch with Bibi. A fitting re-entry into the swing of things.

* * *

Angel waited until the maid left the premises, then she launched into action. Out came the Lysol, Ajax, and cleaning equipment. She tied her long blonde hair away from her face and earnestly set about cleaning Buddy's apartment the way it *should* be cleaned. Thoroughly. Not a lick and a spit. When he came back she wanted everything perfect. And it would be.

Humming softly to herself she started in the bathroom.

* * *

Leon Rosemont arrived at the house in San Diego just as Buddy was leaving. Sometimes perfect timing occurs, and although Leon did not know it he was in exactly the right place at the right time. Five minutes later and he might have missed Buddy altogether.

They passed on the front steps.

'Excuse me,' said Leon sharply. 'Are you Buddy Hudson?'

Buddy was in no mood for conversation. The guy had cop written all over him. Shit! They had pulled the file and now they wanted to investigate the case. 'Yeah. But listen – I made a mistake this morning. I was blowin' steam, y'know?'

Leon looked at him strangely. 'What?'

'I got bombed last night,' he insisted. 'You can put the file away. *I* don't even know what I was talkin' about.'

Leon frowned. 'What *were* you talking about?'

'Hey – you *are* a cop?'

Ponderously Leon produced his identification. Buddy looked at it quickly. All he wanted to do was get back to Angel and let a little love into his life.

'Can we go inside and talk?' Leon asked.

Buddy indicated the house. 'In there? You gotta be kiddin'. I'm about as welcome in there as the clap.'

'It's urgent we talk. And I want your mother to hear what I have to say.'

'She's not my mother, man.'

'That's one of the things I want to talk about.'

* * *

And he took off his blood-soaked clothes and ran them through the washing machine.

And he removed the inky writing from his forehead and the blackness from around his eyes.

And naked, he knelt before his poster and touched the hardness he felt.

And climaxed, throbbing with ecstasy.

And wondered why the words WHO IS BUDDY HUDSON? defaced *his* poster.

* * *

'I've got to go,' Ross announced.

'I'm glad we had a chance to talk,' Montana said. 'Who knows . . . if I ever get the rights to *Street People* back . . . raise the finance . . .'

'You'll think of me.'

'Naturally.'

He alighted from his stool and kissed her on the cheek. 'You're one hell of a lady.'

She smiled ruefully. 'That's what Neil used to say.'

* * *

And it became clear. An impostor had taken his face, his image, his countenance, and PRETENDED TO BE HIM.

Rage swept over him.

WHO IS BUDDY HUDSON?

He went to her desk and picked up the leather bound address book.

WHO IS BUDDY HUDSON?

He flicked through the neatly typewritten pages searching for the letter H.

WHO IS BUDDY HUDSON?

There were many names listed under various cities. He ran his finger down the page marked Los Angeles.

WHO IS BUDDY HUDSON?

He snapped the book shut.

He knew where to find him.

* * *

'Nothing much wrong with it, Mr Conti. As you said – the engine just flooded up a bit.'

Ross climbed into his Rolls and transferred a twenty into the doorman's palm. A middle-aged tourist recognized him and nudged her husband. The two of them stared.

Ross started the Rolls and moved out of the hotel driveway. After all these years it still pleased him to be recognized. In his rearview mirror he observed Karen Lancaster and her English rock star zoom up in Karen's bright red Ferrari. He figured he had had a lucky escape from *that* one. *And* from Gina Germaine.

He had hardly been circumspect in his choice of women. Still . . . he had enjoyed himself, for a while anyway.

He wondered what Sadie wanted. Was she going to apologize for the way she had treated him? Or was she going to try and grab him back in the sack and then attempt to humiliate him all over again?

He did not wish to speculate. All he required from her were her business services, and if she had anything else in mind she would just have to forget it.

* * *

Clothes still damp, but they would do.

Outside a white Jaguar with the keys in.

He put on his black shades and slid behind the wheel.

Oh, mother.

Oh, Joey.

If you could see me now.

He turned the ignition, revving the engine until it roared like a tiger raring to pounce. Music blasted out from all four speakers. Rod Stewart. A fitting growl.

He steered the car down the long and winding driveway and stopped when he got to the street. His van was parked beside a ditch, partially concealed by a clump of trees. He reached inside for his carryall bag, then returned to the Jaguar. He took out a map of Los Angeles and studied it until he was satisfied he knew exactly where he was going.

The Jaguar had the power he desired. Together they ripped off down Angelo Drive fusing together in a blur of speed.

* * *

'Wolfie, are you up?'

'Always for you, Bibi. Although it is a trifle early for a Saturday morning . . .'

'Darling, it nearly twelve. What you do?'

'I'm in bed. Where is Adam?'

'Oh, Adam. He so boring. One day I leave him.'

'You're always saying that.'

'So what? I mean it.'

But they both knew she didn't. Who else would put up with Bibi and her deliciously bitchy tongue?

'Sweetie, guess that?'

'Tell me. Put me out of my misery.'

'Ross Conti, he leave Gina, he go back Elaine.'

'How do you know *that*?'

'I know everything first, darling.'

* * *

Ross was not a *bad* driver. But his attention wandered, he hogged the middle of the road, and drove too fast. He especially drove too fast as he and the Rolls progressed up winding Angelo Drive, a twisting street which meandered its way up into the hills, narrowing as it advanced.

Sadie's house was near the top. Normally two drivers heading towards each other would be aware of the fact that the street was dangerous, reduce speed, and keep a foot prudently near the brake.

Ross, racing up the treacherous road, did not do this.

Deke, speeding down, did not do it either.

By the time they saw each other coming it was too late.

Chapter Seventy-Five

Buddy drove back to Los Angeles in a daze. So much had happened in a very short period of time. He had gone to San Diego with one purpose in mind. To find his mother and make the peace.

So he found her, *and* the truth. That was soul destroying enough – but what happened next was so bizarre and quirky that he was still in shock.

Leon Rosemont. A cop. But not come about the Wolfie Schweicker identification as he had thought.

The two of them returned to the house and his mother (no, not his mother. Estelle . . . that's how he must think of her from now on) allowed them in only after Leon produced his identification and mentioned the name Nita Carrolle.

He thought of the words which once again changed his life. '*. . . brother . . . twin . . . murderer . . . will strike again . . . searching for mother . . . calls himself The Keeper Of The Order . . .*'

What an odd twist of fate. *Searching for mother.* Hell, it could become a national pastime.

He had asked questions. 'Who is my real mother? Where is she? Is she still alive?'

Detective Rosemont had shaken his head blankly and produced a yellowing piece of paper with the date marked on the top. The page was divided into two columns. One side listed Mr and Mrs Willis Andrews and a Barstow address. The other listed Estelle and Richard Hudson, and their San Diego address. Written beneath this in thick red pen across both columns was a notation – TWIN BOYS – one to each family – and on the appropriate sides were the prices paid. It seemed – at the time – that the Andrews family got themselves a bargain. The Hudsons had shelled out two thousand dollars – over fifteen hundred dollars more.

A scribbled notation on the bottom read 'see page sixty'.

'Page sixty was ripped out,' Leon explained. 'So the only connection was you, Mrs Hudson. I tried to phone you – when I got no reply I thought it important enough to get on a plane and come here.' He paused. 'Who is the real mother?'

'I don't know,' she said coldly. 'It never interested me. Everything was taken care of – even a birth certificate with our names on was supplied.'

Buddy put his foot down hard and zoomed along the freeway. How could he lay this whole trip on Angel?

Hey – kid. You'll never guess. I got me this weirdo brother. Like he's . . . uh . . . my twin. And you know what? He goes around killin' people.

Angel would widen those big beautiful eyes and think he was taking drugs again. Shit! Talk about being in the wrong place at the wrong time. If he hadn't been there when Leon Rosemont turned up on her doorstep they never would have found him, and he wouldn't have had to hear all that garbage about some maniac twin out there somewhere.

But they would have found him because he had never bothered to change his name, and all at once he knew why. He had *wanted* to be found. *Wanted* his mother to care enough to come looking for him.

She never had.

Now he understood why.

Detective Rosemont said he would arrange a police guard for him back in Los Angeles. Buddy had said no, and quickly explained his situation. 'I'm just not connected to this whole story,' he ended flatly. 'An' I don't intend to be. There's no way this Deke character could ever track me.'

'Look at this,' Detective Rosemont said, and handed him a photograph.

Some long-haired jerk with staring eyes.

Some long-haired jerk with his features.

Different in a way . . . But chillingly the same. That's how the detective had recognised him.

It gave him real bad vibes. He had shoved the photo back at Leon abruptly. 'Looks nothin' like me,' he said roughly. 'I gotta head back for L.A. now.'

He had departed shortly after, reluctantly handing over his address and accepting a number to contact the detective should he need to.

Goodbye San Diego.

He drove down the highway, towards a fresh start, towards Angel . . .

Somewhere he had a mother . . .

It didn't matter. He was free now.

* * *

Sitting in a cab on his way to the airport Leon felt depressed. He had hoped that the Hudson family would be the key. But Richard Hudson was dead, and Estelle Hudson didn't know and didn't care. What kind of a woman adopted a baby and didn't even want to know who the natural mother was? The same kind of woman who *bought* a baby in the first place. He shook his head in disgust.

Questions . . . questions . . .

But where were the answers?

He desperately needed to know the identity of Deke's real mother . . . That's where Deke would go . . . If she was still alive . . . and a hunch told Leon that she was.

At the airport he went straight to a phone booth and called

Captain Lacoste in Philadelphia. 'I'm on my way back to Vegas,' he said. 'There's nothing here.'

'Wait!' shouted the Captain. 'I just heard from Los Angeles. They think they got him. Get on the next plane.'

Chapter Seventy-Six

The moment of impact was so unexpected. A flash of white car, a staring face. Too late to do anything but jam on the brakes and wrench the wheel of the Rolls to the right.

The two cars collided. The crunch of bodywork crumbling, the shatter of glass, the unearthly noise.

Then silence except for the raspy raunch of Rod Stewart coming from the tape machine still functioning in the Jaguar.

In the bars and the cafes – Passion
In the streets and the alleys – Passion
Lots of pretending – Passion
Everybody searching – Passion

* * *

Angel finished cleaning the apartment around one o'clock. She walked from room to room admiring her work. Everything was gleaming and sparkling, just the way it should be. She felt the baby kick and stopped for a moment placing both hands on her stomach. It was a magical feeling. She wanted a boy, a miniature Buddy. Excitement swept over her at the very thought. They would call him Buddy Junior and he would grow up to be just like his father. Well . . . maybe not exactly the same . . .

She smiled softly, entered the bathroom, removed her clothes, and stepped under the shower.

* * *

Deke Andrews crawled from the wreck unhurt except for a cut on his forehead and a pain in his right leg. He should not have taken the white car. To steal was a sin. He was being punished.

But surely The Keeper Of The Order was above punishment?

He could hear Joey's laughter.

Oh whore of whores shut your painted mouth before I shut it for you.

'I thought ya could drive, *cow*boy,' she jeered.

He hated her with a

Passion
Even the President needs passion
Everybody I know needs some passion
Some people die and kill for passion

He realized he must move on. Get away from the two smashed cars. Dragging his leg behind him he started up the hill.

Not once did he even glance in the other car.

* * *

She put on a simple white shift, plain sandals, and fluffed her hair – allowing it to dry naturally. Koko had wanted to cut it all off, or at least style it. But she hadn't allowed him to. She knew that Buddy loved it exactly the way it was.

She applied scent behind her ears, on her arms, and between her breasts. Youth Dew by Estée Lauder. Koko had presented it to her. 'Better on you' dreamheart, than on some of the old bags who come in the salon. My God! If they saw a youth the only dew they'd get would be on their foreheads!'

She wanted Buddy and Koko to meet. Properly. Not as

adversaries. And Adrian too, of course. Maybe she would throw a small dinner party. There was a nice little dining nook, space to seat everyone comfortably, and she could make all of Buddy's favourite foods.

So deep was she in thought that she did not hear the doorbell the first time it rang. It was only on the second ring that she responded, and hoping that it was Buddy home early she ran to answer it.

* * *

'You're all right, gel,' said Josh Speed.

'I should be. I've been perfecting my act since I was thirteen,' replied Karen Lancaster drily.

'Thirteen, eh?'

They resumed athletic making out in a closed cabana located in a prime position beside the Beverly Hills Hotel pool. Courtesy of Josh's record company. The cabana not the fucking.

'Cor blimey!' screamed Josh suddenly. 'I'm comin' so fast it's like a bleedin' express train runnin' through me cock!'

'You're so poetic,' husked Karen, reaching her own peak.

He squeezed her nipples, always the main attraction. 'You ain't heard nothin' yet, gel. Later on I'll play yer some of me songs – that'll *really* get y'goin'.'

She rolled across the floor reaching for her abandoned swimsuit. 'Sounds good to me.'

He was not Ross Conti. But he would do.

* * *

'I won't be long,' Ferdie had said.

'I won't be long . . . I won't be long . . .' Rocky mimicked furiously three hours later as he stormed around the apartment. He had been looking forward to the beach picnic – sun, surf and new connections. He had not skipped off to Hollywood to spend his time waiting around for the likes of Ferdie. This little prince did a lot of things but he did not wait. Screw waiting.

He gathered together his things, stuffed them in a bag, then headed for the door.

* * *

For a moment Angel just stared, eyes huge and alarmed. 'Buddy?' she questioned unsurely as she backed into the apartment, shock etched across her face. 'Your hair . . . and you look so pale . . . My God! Buddy, what *happened*?'

* * *

WHO IS BUDDY HUDSON? *She* knew who he was. This Madonna with corn silk hair and the face of an angel.

Deke stepped inside, closing the door behind him.

She was Joey, of course. He had known all along he would find her.

And she was pregnant. With his child.

Chapter Seventy-Seven

The freeway allowed Buddy time to think, and the more he thought the more confused he became. In the end he put on the radio and lost himself in weather reports, rock music, commercials, and newscasts.

We can expect a beautiful high of eighty-five degrees today so get out those boogie boards and head for the beach . . .

Yeah. That's what he would like to do.

Stevie Wonder. 'Ribbon in the Sky'. Hot Chocolate. 'Chances'. Randy Crawford. 'Rio de Janeiro'. Music soothed him. Maybe he'd have to see a shrink, get his head together.

Shit! You ain't a movie star yet kid. Let's not go getting big ideas.

If being with Angel couldn't straighten him out nothing could. He'd be alright. He was a survivor . . .

Only he felt so alone . . .

Time on the freeway didn't mean anything. Like an endless conveyor belt cars proceeded to unknown destinations. A black Porsche zoomed by, doubling the speed limit.

He wondered what Monday would bring. Would Sadie have good news for him?

Sure she would. Think positive. Stardom was inevitable, he'd waited long enough. Especially with his billboard hitting America.

He hoped that Ferdie had kept his promise and told her

about Angel. No more lies or false beginnings. He was going to make it on the truth – all the way to the top.

* * *

Santa Monica was too crowded for the likes of Rocky, the competition too fierce. He hung around for an hour but there was no action at all, and he did not like struggling to be noticed. Screw that game. At seventeen years of age he looked like an angelic fourteen year old and thought like a shrewd thirty-five year old. After only a brief six weeks in Los Angeles he felt that he knew his way around, and Santa Monica Boulevard was not the only game in town.

He put on his T-shirt, picked up his carry-bag, and headed up Doheny towards Sunset.

* * *

Gina Germaine swept into the Polo Lounge half an hour late for a luncheon appointment with a female journalist from a weekly news magazine. The way she looked at it the reporter was lucky to be getting her at all. How many other stars gave up their Saturdays to further the course of publicity? Not too many. And that is why *she* was at the top and others got stuck halfway up the ladder.

They treated her like royalty in the Polo Lounge. But then, of course, she *was* royalty – the Hollywood kind.

Gina was not in a good mood. She felt rejected. First by Ross Conti – who was a no-good has-been son-of-a-bitch anyway. And second by Sadie La Salle. Her friend. Her agent. And a woman who was too selfish to give up Palm Springs and spend the day with her.

Disloyal was a word that hovered in Gina's mind as she beamed a greeting at the woman journalist and launched straight into a '. . . I'm a simple person really. All I want is a little cottage, a bunch of kids, and the right man in my life.'

'What about Ross Conti?'

Ice cold. *'Who?'*

* * *

Josh Speed wore bikini swimming briefs that left nothing to the imagination.

'Hmmm . . .' observed Karen, sharing a joint with him before emerging from the cabana. 'You certainly believe in letting it all hang out.'

'If yer got it, let 'em see it. I can make a groupie come from twenty yards!' He roared with laughter.

She smiled. Josh would be a riot with Pamela and George and their bunch of dinosaur friends.

They walked out of the cabana hand in hand. Instinctively they paused, aware of the fact that the tourists needed to feast their eyes. Then Josh yelled, 'First one in's a sissy,' and with arms and legs flailing wildly leapt into the pool.

Karen smiled indulgently. What a pleasant change to be with someone who knew how to have fun. She made her way more sedately to the deep end of the pool and executed a graceful dive.

'C'mere, sexy,' yelled Josh, scissoring her round the waist with his bony legs. ' 'Ere,' he whispered. 'Let me stick me big toe in yer drawers.'

'Not here, Josh,' she giggled huskily.

'Why not?' he demanded. 'Yer think this group a toffee noses never seen a big toe before?'

* * *

Elaine arrived at the Beverly Hills Hotel in good time for her two o'clock appointment at the beauty shop. She wore a pale blue silk shirt, white linen slacks and sunglasses.

'Mrs Conti,' exclaimed the girl who usually did her hair. 'You look terrific! Have you been on vacation?'

She nodded vaguely. 'Sort of.'

'Hawaii?'

'Not exactly.'

'Wherever it was it's certainly done you the world of good. A tan really suits you.'

'It'll suit me even better when you do something with my hair.'

* * *

Oliver Easterne left a lunch meeting at Nate 'n' Al's, and hurried to a *late* lunch meeting at the Beverly Hills Hotel.

There was just not enough time in the day. But Oliver had developed his own philosophy. Never let a potential investor off the hook. Even if it meant choking to death.

* * *

Wolfie Schweicker was not in the habit of picking up boys. He had no need of doing so. His sexual appetite was not vast, and the once a month special parties that he and a select group of friends arranged were more than enough to take care of his every need. So when he spotted Rocky lounging against an RTD stop on Sunset the *last* thing he had in mind was to stop.

His silver Mercedes took the decision right out of his hands. The car slowed, the blond baby loped over, and before you could say Disneyland he was in the car.

Wolfie looked anxiously around to see if anyone had noticed. Apparently not. He drove quickly off.

How can I take the boy home? he thought. What will the servants think? He had *never* committed indiscretions under his own roof.

But what was the alternative? A motel? A baths? None of them the kind of places he frequented.

'Where we goin'?' the boy asked, as the Mercedes turned off Sunset and headed for the hills.

'My home,' Wolfie said crisply.

To hell with the servants.

* * *

News travelled like bush fire. Bad news faster than good.

The Beverly Hills Hotel was the perfect breeding ground for a rumour to get going. An accident on Angelo Drive was no big deal. But an accident involving Ross Conti in his Rolls was.

'He's hurt badly.'

'He's crippled for life.'

'He's dead.'

The story had its variations as the news passed from one mouth to another. How easy it was to embellish, distort and twist.

Gina Germaine was told by a red-faced publicist who hovered by her table like a nervous flamingo. She received the 'in serious condition' story.

'How terrible!' she fluttered, casting her eyes down, and allowing her lower lip to quiver appealingly.

'Shall we forget about the interview?' the journalist asked sympathetically.

Gina made a rapid recovery. Up came the eyes, and a wan smile took over the lips. 'No,' she said bravely. 'Ross would want me to keep going. I know that. He's a wonderful man.' Short pause. 'Now, what was I saying?'

Karen heard from a producer friend of her father's who took her to one side when she emerged from the pool and discreetly whispered in her ear that Ross Conti had been killed in a car smash. 'I think you should call George,' he said solemnly. 'He and Ross were always very close.'

Yes, but Ross and I were closer, Karen wanted to say, and she started to shiver uncontrollably.

Oliver heard the whisper in the Polo Lounge. Ross Conti was in intensive care. They didn't give him long to live. Thank

Christ, Oliver thought, that I cancelled the movie. And then he had second thoughts. Maybe it wasn't such a smart move . . . look at the insurance he could have picked up!

Montana was still in the coffee shop when the news travelled from ear to ear. She had run into a journalist friend from New York, and they were catching up on old times. Badly injured was the story she got. 'Poor Ross . . .' she murmured. 'I just can't believe it . . .'

Elaine was not told at all. At first, anyway. A group huddled by the entrance to the beauty shop trying to decide who should impart the bad news. Finally her stylist volunteered and gingerly approached her as she sat reading *Vogue* under a heat machine, her hair wrapped in a hundred tinfoil corkscrews.

'Mrs Conti,' she whispered. 'Apparently there's been some sort of awful car accident up on Angelo.'

'Why are you telling *me*?' snapped Elaine.

But she knew why the girl was telling her, and she pushed the hood from above her and shakily stood up. Beneath her suntan she paled. 'It's Ross, isn't it?' she gasped. 'Oh no! It's Ross.'

Chapter Seventy-Eight

When he touched her she knew. He held his hand – cold and clammy, to her cheek. She shrank away from him, her eyes wide with fear.

THIS MAN WAS NOT BUDDY.

In some horrible strange way he looked like a paler, thinner, ugly Buddy . . . but of course he wasn't, and how could she have ever thought that he was?

'Who are you?' she whispered.

'Who is Buddy Hudson?' he retorted calmly.

'My . . . my husband,' she said quickly. 'He'll . . . he'll be home . . . in a minute. He really will be. I promise you.'

Deke's black eyes grew angry. 'Joey. I do not want you to play your stupid mind games with me anymore. It upsets me.'

'I'm . . . I'm not Joey. I'm Angel.'

'I know that. I've always known that.' He reached forward to touch her face again.

'Don't!' she cried sharply, pushing his hand away.

He gripped her wrist. 'I have killed to reach here. I have done it once and I can do it again.'

Her hand flew to her mouth. 'Please. What do you want?'

'You, of course. I've always wanted you, Joey.'

'I'm not Joey,' she screamed.

But he was not listening.

* * *

Halfway to Los Angeles Buddy observed the black Porsche which had roared past him earlier pulled over to the side, a police car in evidence – lights flashing. Instinctively he reduced his speed. The last thing he needed in his life was more hassles with the police.

He checked out the time. It was two-thirty. Another hour and a half and he would be back at his apartment. At five, the limo would pick Angel up and bring her to him. He couldn't wait. They would talk . . . and make love . . . and talk some more . . . and make love . . .

He put his foot down hard, to hell with the cops.

* * *

The stewardess passed by with a cheery smile and a 'Can I get you a drink, sir?'.

Leon knew that he probably looked like he needed one. He was bleary eyed and unshaven, with wrinkled clothes, and the faint aroma of stale sweat. If Millie caught a glimpse of him she would have a fit.

He thought of Millie and dredged up a rueful smile. When she got mad she *really* went all the way.

'A drink, sir?' repeated the stewardess, slightly impatient.

'A club soda,' he replied.

He had not replied to her letter, and had no intention of doing so. What was the use of trying to explain? She would never understand. When it was over he would go home and she would take him back. It was as simple as that.

And maybe it would be over . . . soon.

He fell asleep before his club soda arrived and woke just as they were landing in Los Angeles.

* * *

She looked different, but that was as it should be. He had disposed of the old Joey, slashed away the squiffy eye, the jammy mouth and the brazen body. Now she was perfect. A Golden Angel Of Hope. True consort for The Keeper of The Order.

But she was being difficult, and he could not allow that.

Trapped beneath him she struggled tearfully, so he decided to tie her just as he had tied his mother. This he did quickly, and marvelled at how calm they became when the cord restrained them. How quiet and beautiful.

He left her trussed on the floor while he examined the rest of the apartment. In the bedroom his image awaited him, covering an entire wall. He was not surprised.

WHO IS BUDDY HUDSON?

Was *he* Buddy Hudson? Or was Buddy Hudson Deke Andrews?

Confusion and anger mixed with the fury that welled up inside him. He took his knife from the side of his boot and ripped at the offending poster. Joey had done this.

ONCE A WHORE ALWAYS A WHORE.

'Are you still whoring?' he demanded, striding back to where Angel lay. 'Are you, Joey? *Are you*?' His eyes glared blackness as he leaned over her. He felt the swell of her stomach on his chest, and wondered if he should cut the baby free. Soon he would have to . . . But not now . . . Later . . .

'I've never been . . . a whore,' she whispered.

'You were *my* whore,' he replied slyly. 'You did things to me that only a whore would do.'

He touched her breasts and she began to cry.

Why was she crying? Wasn't she happy to see him? He had been through so much for her . . .

Marriage.

The thought struck him.

Joey wanted marriage.

They had discussed it so many times . . .

I wanna meet your mother. Whatsamatta, cowboy, ain't I good enough t'meet ya mother?

Abruptly he stopped touching her and rose to his feet. 'Alright,' he said. 'I agree with you. We've been together long enough. You shall meet my mother, Joey.'

'I'm not Joey,' she whimpered.

He ignored her denial, left her crying, and went back in the bedroom. There, he picked up a thick red marker and wrote a message across the tattered poster. Then he stood back, surveyed his work, and returned to his captive.

He bent over her and held the tip of his knife lightly against her stomach. 'I'm going to untie you now,' he said quietly. 'Do not cause me any trouble. If you make me angry you *will not meet my mother*. Do you understand me, Joey?' He put his knife away and began to loosen her bonds.

She was sobbing uncontrollably. 'Oh please God, somebody help me.'

'And God shall help The Keeper Of The Order,' he said piously. 'And I am he.'

Chapter Seventy-Nine

Somehow Elaine got from the beauty shop to the front of the hotel – a ridiculous sight with tinfoil sprouting out all over her head.

Her stylist followed her. 'Mrs Conti,' she implored. 'You can't drive. You mustn't.'

Elaine screamed for her car ignoring the concerned girl. She did not care what kind of a spectacle she made of herself. The only thing that mattered was getting to Ross.

'But you don't even know where they've taken him,' the girl wailed. 'Please wait. We'll phone the police. Mrs Conti, you *can't* just rush off like this. You're too upset.'

Mrs Conti could do what she liked. And did.

* * *

Disappointment. Frustration. Every negative emotion and more.

Leon stood in the noontime heat and watched the breakdown trucks remove the Rolls and the Jaguar – or what was left of them.

He gave a heavy disgusted sigh and spat on the sidewalk. He had hoped it was all going to be over. It wasn't.

The chase was getting him down. Especially when the

message 'they've got him' turned out to be just Deke's carryall bag on the floor of the Jaguar – with his driver's licence to identify it. The bag was better than nothing, although it contained no leads. Leon had already gone through it thoroughly. The only items of interest were the newspaper clippings of the Philadelphia murders carefully preserved between the pages of a racing car magazine.

He was tired, rushing from city to city, not eating or sleeping.

But he wasn't too tired to go on. The chase was only just beginning.

* * *

Elaine turned left on Hartford Way and realized that she had no idea where they had taken Ross, so she drove home with the thought of getting on the phone and finding out.

A police car stood ominously in the driveway.

She felt the blood drain from her face and the heat vanish from the day. If Ross was dead she couldn't stand it. She loved him too much to lose him again just when she had him back.

What if he's crippled, Elaine?

I'd sooner that than death.

Suppose he can never work again? No more charge accounts, fancy restaurants or parties. No more Beverly Hills.

Get off my back, Etta. I love Ross. Nothing else matters.

'Mrs Conti?' A cop jumped from the car as she pulled into the driveway.

Her heart stopped. 'Yes?'

'Mr Conti's inside.'

She ran into the house.

Ross propped up the bar, a large tumbler of brandy in one hand. There was a small bandage across his forehead, and his left arm reclined in a sling. A second cop stood beside him jotting notes on a pad.

'Ross!' she yelled ecstatically.

'Sweetheart!' His famous blues crinkled with pleasure, then he started to laugh. 'What are *you* doing? Auditioning for *Star Wars*?'

Her hands flew to her tinfoil encased head. She looked dismayed.

'What the hell kind of a Hollywood wife are you?' he teased. 'If Bibi saw you running around like that she'd boot you out of the club!'

A slow grin spread over her face. 'Quite frankly – to quote my wonderful husband – who gives a flying fart!'

Chapter Eighty

Heat. Smog. Sweat. Tiredness. Muscle cramps. A bad day. One Buddy wanted to forget as soon as possible. Wearily he parked in the underground space reserved for him, got out of the car, stretched and yawned. He'd had it. Physically. Emotionally. In every way.

It was four-fifteen exactly. In ten hours he had managed to totally fuck up his life – or straighten it out. He'd have to think about which. At least he'd gotten rid of the incest nightmare.

He paused in the coolness of the garage for a moment and decided that maybe he was lucky after all. No past. No shit. No nothing. Was that such a bad thing considering former events?

He rode the freight elevator up as the passenger one was busy. Seductive scent lingered in the air, it made a change from smelling garbage. Not that the building was kept in bad shape – there was a resident janitor on duty twenty-four hours a day. Some of the female tenants did not think that was enough. He had been asked to sign a residents' petition demanding a security guard in the basement parking area too. He sighed. What the hell. He wouldn't want Angel down there alone.

Angel. He ached to see her. Maybe he would cancel the limo and go and pick her up himself now that he was back early.

The scent stayed with him all the way to his apartment and when he opened up the door it was still there. His first thought was that the maid had been wearing it. But then he felt instinctively that Angel was there, and his heart quickened pace like some thirteen year old.

'Angel?' he called out. 'Hey – baby, where are you?'

He threw open the door to the bedroom and knew at once that something was horribly wrong.

* * *

Angel could hardly breathe, the back of the van was so filthy and stuffy, the heat unbearable, and the windows blacked out.

She clung to the side as the vehicle raced and jolted along, fearful for her baby as random pains stabbed at her insides.

She closed her eyes tightly and thought of Buddy, repeating his name to herself over and over like a mantra.

* * *

His poster hung in tattered shreds. But the eyes were intact – and written across them in heavy marker pen were the words:

THE FACE IS MINE
THE ANGEL IS MINE
WHO IS BUDDY HUDSON?
HE CEASES TO EXIST
THE KEEPER OF THE ORDER

Chillingly snatches of Detective Rosemont's conversation returned to him – *. . . brother . . . twin . . . murderer . . . calls himself The Keeper Of The Order . . .*

And Buddy could remember thinking – what bullshit – who cares – and it's nothing to do with me.

With a feeling of dread he had only to look around the apartment to know for sure that Angel had been there. On a table beside the bed was her alarm clock, next to it a small group of photo frames containing pictures of the two of them together. He wrenched open the closet and sure enough her clothes hung tidily beside his. In the bathroom her toothbrush, comb, assorted make-up . . .

There was no doubt she had been there. And if so . . . where was she now?

'Oh Jesus!' he groaned. 'Oh, no!'

* * *

Leon went to work, with the help of the Beverly Hills Police, the Department of Motor Vehicles and a comprehensive computer system. The Jaguar was registered to a Ferdie Cartright. There was no reply at his home. A neighbour reported she had seen him leave – in the car – alone – at approximately eleven in the morning.

Leon spoke to the woman. He was good with witnesses. People trusted him.

'Did you see Mr Cartright in the company of this man?'

He produced two pictures of Deke. One the high school photo – and the other an artist's impression of how he would look today. Certain witnesses along the way had contributed to that look. Bald head, staring eyes, ragged clothes.

The woman studied them, squinting slightly. 'Mr Cartright does have a lot of male visitors.' She leaned close as if imparting a state secret. 'He's gay you know. But please don't say you heard it from me.'

Leon nodded sombrely. 'Certainly not.'

'What's Mr Cartright done anyway?'

'His car was in an accident. We're trying to locate him.'

'Is he all right?'

Leon swallowed impatience. 'That's what we're trying to find out. Please. Look at the photographs.'

The woman studied them again, screwing her face into contortions. 'I don't like the look of *that* one,' she said, pointing to the artist's impression of Deke.

'Was he here?' Leon asked urgently.

'Him? No, I'd remember him . . .' she trailed off. 'There's something about the other one . . .'

'Yes?'

'I'm not sure . . . it's not really like him at all . . .'

'Who?'

'This man who came by early this morning. Very good looking,' she laughed. 'This is going to sound crazy, but he was like an older, handsomer version of this one.'

She held up the year-book picture of Deke.

Leon felt a chill.

Buddy.

'You wouldn't remember what he was wearing, would you?'

'Black pants, a white shirt and a nice sports jacket – also black.' She roared with laughter. 'You're going to think I'm a dirty old lady glued to her window – but it's better than watching soap operas all day.'

'I'm sure it is,' agreed Leon, anxious to conclude the interview, already on his way to the door.

'I can remember thinking,' the woman called out. 'If this one's gay – what a dreadful *waste*!'

* * *

The detective in San Diego had given Buddy some numbers written on a piece of paper. But he had not been interested then, he had shoved the paper somewhere knowing full well he would never need to use it.

Feverishly he turned out his pockets – nothing. Then he vaguely remembered screwing up the piece of paper in the car and flicking it on the floor.

He raced from the apartment, into the elevator, down to the garage, scrabbled on the floor of his car.

HE COULDN'T FIND THE GODDAMN PIECE OF PAPER.

He turned out the glove compartment, dug around the

seats, swore aloud in frustration. Then he hastened back upstairs.

The door to his apartment was open as he had left it. He hurried inside and stopped short. There was someone there.

* * *

Deke was taking her to meet mother. It was a good feeling. So different from the time before.

This time they would get along. They would smile and speak to each other. They would sing his praises instead of criticizing him and laughing.

'And the Lord shall sing the praises of the dead,' he said aloud. 'For only in death shall the soul be cleansed of evil and the devils released.'

He thought carefully.

Kill.

Kill mother.

Kill Joey.

Kill self.

WHO IS BUDDY HUDSON?

He didn't care anymore. He had the solution.

It felt good knowing exactly what to do.

And nobody would ever laugh at him again.

Chapter Eighty-One

'What's your involvement with Ferdie Cartright?' Leon asked harshly, before Buddy could say a word.

'Hey—' Buddy grabbed his arm – not even curious about why he was there – just relieved that he was. 'Has Deke got Angel? Has that crazy sonofabitch taken my wife?'

'What are you talking about?'

'He was here!'

'How do you know?'

Buddy dragged him into the bedroom where he took in the ripped poster and the scrawled message.

'What does that shit mean?' Buddy demanded. 'Does it mean he's taken Angel?'

'Who is Angel?'

'My wife, goddammit. What are you going to do?'

'You'd better tell me everything you know.'

'Angel was supposed to meet me here at five. She came early for some reason, and now she's gone. I don't understand. How could he find me? *You're* the only one who knows my connection.'

'Who else has the poster?'

'Half of America. It goes on billboards coast to coast Monday.'

'Maybe that's the key.'

'What *fucking* key? Where's Angel?' Buddy screamed.

'We'll find your wife,' Leon said with more confidence than he felt. 'But I need information. Who is Ferdie Cartright?'

'What has *he* got to do with any of this?'

'Listen to me,' Leon said sharply. 'You visited him early this morning. Later his car was in an accident. By the time the police got there no one was in the wreck. But Deke Andrews' bag was in the car.' He paused. 'Talk to me, Buddy. Tell me what you know.'

'Ferdie works for my agent, Sadie La Salle. I stopped by to see him this morning. I wanted him to drop by Sadie's and give her a message for me.'

'Did he agree to do this?'

'Yes.'

'Was there anyone else there?'

'Some be-bop kid.'

'What was his name?'

'How the fuck would I know?' he exploded. 'Look, is any of this going to find my wife?'

'I hope so. Because it's all we've got.'

* * *

He was careful. You never could tell what forces would try to trap you. Even the air was dangerous. The heat. Enemies were always around.

This time Deke drove his van right up to Sadie's front door.

He walked around the grounds peering in windows.

The late afternoon sun was fading under low clouds. He hoped it would rain. He missed the rain. Water was a positive force. Heat came from hell.

Inside the house he could hear the telephone jangling, but nobody answered it.

He ran his right hand over the smoothness of his scalp. Then he took the keys he had stolen earlier from the pocket of his shirt and opened up the front door.

He had always known he would come back to mother.

Silence prevailed.

As it should.

* * *

She crouched in the back of the van and held back the screams which threatened to rip from her throat. The pain subsided, she unclenched her fists and breathed deeply. The van was almost airless causing her to choke on the thick dust. She was soaked in sweat and exhausted from the ride. At least they had stopped. Maybe he had gone away . . . left her . . .

Suppose she was trapped . . .

She struggled to the rear and began to hammer feebly on the double doors. 'Help me . . . Please . . . Please . . . somebody help me . . .'

* * *

How beautiful she was – his Golden Angel Of Hope. How different from the Joey he had first met.

She was sobbing as he helped her from the van. That was all right. Water . . . tears . . . all the same thing.

He half-dragged, half-carried her into the house. And knew that he desired her as he had never desired any woman on earth.

That was because she was truly his. He had guided her life, eliminated the evil from her body, cleansed her totally.

'Joey, sweet Joey,' he murmured, as he helped her up the stairs.

'I'M . . . NOT . . . JOEY.' she cried out desperately.

Immediately he was angry. Why did she want to make him angry?

Bitch.

Whore.

Prostitute.

Roughly he pulled her into Sadie's bedroom and pushed her on the bed. 'Don't say that,' he screamed. 'Don't *ever* deny who you are.'

He crouched over her and the hardness entered his body. There was nothing sinful about giving up his hardness to Joey. They were man and wife.

For a moment he couldn't remember where he was. Then the phone began to ring again, startling him into a frenzy. He leapt off the bed, grabbed the cord and yanked it violently from the wall.

WHERE IS MOTHER?

She would love Joey so pale and blonde and beautiful. Such a lady.

But a whore too. Mustn't forget that.

ALL WOMEN ARE WHORES.

He stopped to think.

KILL.

KILL MOTHER.

KILL JOEY.

KILL SELF.

But first . . . the two women must meet . . . He owed them that.

Abruptly he tugged a sheet from the bed and tore it into strips. Then he bound her once again, spread-eagling her across the bed.

* * *

He was mad. She knew that. His black eyes glared insanely at the world.

Who was he? And why did he bear such a horrible sickening resemblance to Buddy?

Buddy was handsome.

This man was ugly. A monster.

The baby had stopped kicking. She felt a dull throbbing ache.

He's killed my baby, she thought. And he's going to kill me too.

Her flesh crawled. She would never see Buddy again.

* * *

'Mother. Mother. Wake up, this is important.'

Deke's face swam before her. His eyes so like her own . . . nothing of Ross . . .

Poor Ross . . .

Sadie tried to speak through the pain. Her jaw hung slackly. She could feel the jagged edge of broken teeth and her eyes were no more than slits. At least he hadn't used the knife . . . yet. How long had she been unconscious? It seemed like a long time. Why was he still here?

Maybe it was only a few minutes . . . She felt herself going again and tried to hang on . . . but the pain was so bad . . .

He was untying her from the chair. Maybe he was going to let her go . . . Maybe . . .

She slipped back into unconsciousness.

He said, 'Mother. You're being very stupid.' Then he screamed, 'MOTHER. WAKE UP.'

When she didn't he kicked her. Joey was waiting. It wasn't right to keep her waiting.

* * *

Things fell into position.

Ferdie Cartright worked for Sadie La Salle.

Sadie La Salle was Buddy's agent.

Ferdie goes to see Sadie.

She lives on Angelo Drive.

She has the poster.

Ferdie vanishes.

Sadie not in Palm Springs where she should be.

Phone does not answer at her house.

Phone is pulled from the socket.

'Let's go,' Leon said urgently.

* * *

It was slow work pulling Mother upstairs.

She was heavy, but he persevered. After all, a promise was a promise, and he couldn't let Joey down.

* * *

Angel heard him approaching. 'You've got to let me go,' she called out desperately. 'I'm losing my baby. PLEASE. PLEASE. LET ME GO.'

When he entered the room she froze and despair washed over her. He lugged the body of a woman.

She began to scream hysterically.

* * *

'Mother. This is Joey. Joey, say hello to Mother.'

It was a shame that Joey would not behave. He was forced to gag her and it really wasn't right that she had made him do that.

His head hurt. He remembered Philadelphia, so long ago and far away.

He looked at Mother, propped in a chair beside the bed. Then he looked at Joey bound and gagged.

The two women in his life.

The two *special* women.

It had taken so long to arrange this meeting. And did they appreciate it.

DID THEY?

Furiously he stripped off his clothes, removing his boots last.

He fingered his knife, tested the point, smiled a death-mask grimace.

Desire flowed through him. Bubbling through his bloodstream, filling his mind. His head hurt, his eyes hurt . . .

Joey was waiting. Her legs spread.

WHORE.

Joey was waiting for him and she would never laugh at him again.

ANGEL.

He lifted her skirt, used his knife to cut her panties away.

WHORE.

Her face was contorted, her eyes huge. She wanted him. The Golden Angel Of Hope *wanted* to merge with The Keeper Of The Order.

He straddled her, prepared for entry, raised his arm with the knife in readiness to strike simultaneously.

AND THEY SHALL BE JOINED.

* * *

Buddy grabbed him from behind, a desperate lunge that threw them both off balance and onto the floor. They struggled for a few seconds, then Deke made an inhuman sound in the back of his throat and slashed the knife towards Buddy's face. The knife carved across the palm of his hand and blood spurted freely.

Buddy didn't feel the agony, he just felt the fury, and the fury gave him strength. With his right hand he grabbed the wrist of Deke's knife hand and bent it back . . . slowly . . . slowly . . . forcing it . . .

For a brief moment their eyes fused. Black on black. Different and yet the same. 'WHO IS BUDDY HUDSON?' Deke screamed, and his wrist went suddenly limp, causing the knife to swoop down and slit his own throat.

It was all over by the time Leon lumbered into the room.

Epilogue

The Sadie La Salle break-in, Ferdie Cartright's murder, and subsequent events caused shock waves to hit Hollywood which *really* reverberated when early Sunday morning Wolfie Schweicker was found shot to death by an intruder in his own bedroom. People panicked. Security was taken to new lengths. There was a run on attack dogs, personal bodyguards, armoured limos, and shotguns. Bibi Sutton started a trend by turning her bedroom into a fortress, complete with electronically controlled steel gates on the windows and a vault-like door.

Both Sadie La Salle and Angel Hudson were rushed straight to emergency. Diligent doctors were able to prevent Angel from miscarrying. She was allowed home after a few days with instructions to take it easy and rest.

Sadie was not so lucky. She had two cracked ribs, a fractured cheekbone, broken nose and multiple contusions. She was also suffering from shock and a total memory blank about what had happened.

When Leon Rosemont questioned her he was unable to learn anything. Angel had nothing to say either. Both women offered no clues . . . they seemed locked in a conspiratorial silence.

Leon had his suspicions, but even if they were right, what difference did it make now?

Deke Andrews was dead. But the mystery lingered on . . .

* * *

Oliver Easterne followed the weekend events on various televisions dotted around his house. He set off for the office early Monday morning mulling over the idea of putting a writer on it immediately.

What a movie it would make! And if he could only sign Buddy Hudson to play himself . . .

Seven a.m. precisely. And an eager parking attendant waited to take his car at the front of the building. No underground parking for Oliver Easterne.

The gleaming Bentley exchanged hands, and he hurried inside, stopping at the news stand to pick up the morning papers and three packets of breath mints. A morning ritual.

He jogged athletically up the stairs. Another morning ritual. He had no time for work-outs or gym. Running up stairs was the perfect cardio-vascular activity. Better than push-ups or skipping rope any day. By the time he reached the penthouse floor his heart was pounding at exactly the correct strenuous exercise rate.

He burst into the outer office full of the joys of screwing people on all sides. The big hustle. That's what life was all about, wasn't it?

His secretary did not appear until nine o'clock. This suited him fine, as it gave him time to shower and make his New York calls without interruptions. He opened the door to his office – a private sanctuary where he liked to sit behind his tooled leather desk, and admire the polished perfection of leather couches, fine rugs, and tasteful antiques.

He opened the door, sniffed suspiciously, then let forth a heart-rending cry of pure anguish. His desk was piled high with excrement.

He staggered back – a broken man.

Montana chose that moment to saunter through the outer

office. ' 'Morning, Oliver. Just came by to pick up a few things from my desk.' She paused. 'My God! What's that *smell*?' She moved towards him. He stood like a statue carved in stone at the entrance to his office. She peered over his shoulder. 'Oliver!' she exclaimed. 'Your desk is full of . . . bullshit. Oh . . . my . . . God!' She could not control her laughter. 'Oh . . . *Oliver*!!! Who can have done this to you?'

He had never been a physical man. If there was any punching out to be done he had always hired someone else to do it. But a rage came over him of such magnitude that he could not control himself. He turned and charged towards her.

A mistake.

Casually she stepped to one side, causing him to trip and sprawl on the floor.

He yelled out in frustration.

'Oliver,' she said, exiting gracefully. 'You know something? I think you've finally got all the bullshit you could ever hope to handle!'

By noon the story swept Hollywood.

* * *

Rats Sorenson flooded the news stands with copies of *Truth and Fact* the week after the Sadie La Salle headlines.

Ross Conti achieved greatness. Well . . . not exactly greatness. More a reputation for being the biggest cocksman since Erroll Flynn! There he was – in glorious colour on the front cover in all his natural glory. Accompanied by a very cooperative and very naked Karen Lancaster.

It did for Ross what *Cosmopolitan*'s centre spread had done for Burt Reynolds years before.

Instant superstardom. Again.

Full thrust back into the centre of the limelight. Just like old times.

It helped that he had a smile on his face and an erection that caused the magazine to be withdrawn from the stands by several angry pressure groups screaming about the obscenity laws. When the delivery trucks turned face and set about collecting the outlawed copies – there were none left.

Ross Conti was a sell out.

* * *

Little S. Shitz did not receive a photo credit, but he did receive a handsome payment.

He celebrated in a Marina Del Rey singles bar, where he met a girlish redhead who gave him herpes and stole his car.

* * *

Elaine ruled the roost. She became the wife of the year. What sort of woman sat through the kind of indiscretions Ross Conti had committed – publicly – and came up smiling?

Journalists clamoured for her quotes. *People* magazine devoted two pages to her – calling her warm, witty, and wise. Dear Merv had her on his show and discussed infidelity and understanding wives. *She was a celebrity in her own right.* The Contis were *the* hot couple in town. Bibi Sutton called *her*. They were invited to every opening, party, and event.

Together they enjoyed it. After ten years they had found each other and that's what really mattered.

* * *

Leon Rosemont returned to Philadelphia. Millie was not in their apartment upon his return. He waited weeks before contacting her. She was staying with her brother.

'Come home,' he said dully. 'It's over.'

'It'll never be over, Leon,' she replied, her voice tinged with regret. 'There'll always be another case . . . it's worse than there being another woman.'

Perhaps she was right. He was too weary to fight with her.

Maybe he was born to be a loner. Often he thought about Joey. Her cheerful disposition and her crooked smile . . .

* * *

Buddy Hudson achieved everything he had ever desired in life and more. His heroic rescue of Angel and Sadie and his bizarre connection to Deke Andrews made world-wide headlines.

His billboard was a sensation.

He had Angel back.

Everyone wanted him. The big agents, the most important producers, network television executives, plus every magazine, talk show and newspaper in the country.

The mass attention was exciting in one way – terrifying in another.

He turned to Angel. His beautiful pregnant wife – more wonderful and warm than ever, but with an extra gentle strength which he welcomed.

'Don't do anything,' she said simply. 'Wait for Sadie. After all, she is your . . . agent.'

Her advice was sound. When Sadie emerged from the hospital she went back to work with a vengeance. And Buddy received top priority. She never mentioned Deke Andrews, Ferdie Cartright, or that fateful Saturday at her house. She never allowed anyone else to mention it either.

* * *

Gina Germaine had a run of disastrous publicity. It started with the reporter she had lunch with the day of Ross Conti's car accident. The girl wrote an assassination piece of the first order. Gina sulked for a week.

Then the *Enquirer* ran an exposé of her former life. *T.V. Guide* killed her in a cover story. And several supermarket rags took up the cause.

Gina fled to Paris, where she had breast reduction surgery in a desperate bid to be taken seriously, and fell in love with an ageing *cinéma vérité* French film director who promised her real acting roles and starred her in a low budget black comedy about a dumb blonde American movie star. At last! She was being taken seriously as an actress. She cabled Oliver Easterne that it would be quite impossible for her to fulfil her commitment and return to America to star in his movie.

He hit her with a lawsuit.

She sent him a single word reply.

BULLSHIT.

* * *

Karen Lancaster left the country with her rock star. Daddy was unamused by her public indiscretion. Josh Speed found the whole thing hilarious.

She became groupie numero uno as she followed Josh around on his sell-out European tour. She enjoyed her new found celebrity for a while, and then the airplanes, hotels, different stadiums and parties parties parties became a boring routine.

She missed Beverly Hills. She missed Giorgio's and Lina Lee to shop in. She missed Ma Maison and the Bistro to lunch in. She missed Dominick's and Morton's to dine in.

She missed Bibi's wonderful Oscar night parties. And Sadie La Salle's star-studded casual dinners in her kitchen.

She missed valet parking, hot sun, tennis, the Polo Lounge. Hell – she missed *everything*.

It didn't take her long to persuade Josh that he *oughta be in pictures* and that she was just the lady with the right connections to arrange it.

He loved the idea. And he was no slouch in seeing the usefulness of being with a woman like Karen. When she discovered that she was pregnant a few weeks later they decided to get married.

Karen's eyes gleamed. 'We'll have the wedding of the

decade!' she announced. 'We'll give Beverly Hills a show the likes of which will have 'em talking about it *forever*!'

* * *

Beverly Hills was abuzz. The Karen Lancaster-Josh Speed wedding was an event that if you weren't invited you may as well leave town.

Venue: Disneyland.

Dress: Whatever.

* * *

Sadie La Salle decided a beige lace suit was okay. She had lost a lot of weight, and with her new svelte figure could wear anything she wanted. She peered closely at her face in the mirror. Not a sign of the damage Deke had inflicted . . . Outwardly not a sign . . . but inwardly . . .

She thought about Buddy. So handsome and vibrant. And then she thought about Angel. The girl was a gem, sweet, kind and genuinely nice. Sadie adored her. And the feeling was mutual.

Angel was expecting her baby any day . . . Sadie smiled a secret smile. *I'm going to be a grandma* – she thought, *only nobody knows it but me.* Ross would have a fit if he knew.

Ross Conti. Grandpa.

Only he would *never* know. Because finally she had her revenge. And now she could forget him. In fact she already had. She had something else instead . . .

Buddy had told his story to Angel, and she in turn related it to Sadie. The two women became very close. They had a silent secret . . . something they never mentioned . . . but it bonded them together in a very special way.

One day, Sadie decided, she *would* tell Buddy. In the future . . . when the time was right . . .

* * *

Montana read about the forthcoming wedding in Liz Smith's column. Reading about Los Angeles reminded her of Oliver Easterne, and when she thought of him she grinned. That classic Monday morning in his office was one of the highlights of her life. It had not been easy to arrange, but oh – the lasting pleasure! Neil would have been proud of her!

In a funny way she missed L.A. There had been many good times, and now she was going back to direct *Street People*. Oliver had been forced to relinquish the rights in exchange for Neil's other project – the film that Gina Germaine was supposed to star in. He had not been happy, especially when Gina backed out. He was left with an empty package. No director. No star.

Montana had shed no tears on his behalf.

She went out and personally raised the finance to make *Street People* a go project again. And now she was in control. All the way.

She was proud of herself.

* * *

Pamela London and George Lancaster flew in from Palm Beach.

'I hate this tacky little village,' Pamela announced hoarsely to the waiting press.

'Come on, you big-mouthed cow,' George said amiably, shoving her towards their limousine. 'Move your fat ass.'

Marital bliss survived – with the help of an insult or two.

* * *

Bibi Sutton wore a white brocade mink-trimmed gown which had set Adam back four thousand dollars, and made her look like the fairy on top of the Christmas tree.

She was lost without Wolfie. Poor, dear Wolfie . . . who had listened to her constant stream of gossip, escorted her to all the places Adam refused to go, and always – *but always* – picked out her clothes.

* * *

Maralee Gray attended the wedding with the new love of her life. An ageing Jesus-freak who wore flowing white robes, sandals, and was hung like a prize-winning stallion.

She was ecstatic. What more could one ask out of life? Religion and sex.

How nice if he could have had money too . . . But so what . . . she was getting used to paying the bills.

* * *

Elaine wore pink.

Ross wore white.

What a couple!

* * *

Buddy wore Armani. Of course. Angel wore maternity. What else?

Koko fussed around her, making sure that every hair was in place and that her make-up was perfect.

Buddy grinned, 'Hey – Koko. You can't make her look any better than she already does.'

Koko shook his curls. 'I merely embellish the rose,' he said kissing her. 'Have a wonderful time dreamheart. And don't forget – I want to hear *all* about it. Call me when you get back.'

Angel nodded and smiled. 'Thanks for coming over. Give Adrian a kiss for me.'

Downstairs Sadie waited in a sleek silver limousine. She exchanged hugs with Angel, kissed Buddy on the cheek, and once again he marvelled at how great everything was. Sadie had accepted Angel. No hassles. Nothing. The two of them got along wonderfully.

He leaned back in the car and closed his eyes for a minute. It had all worked out . . . the bad memories were behind him now . . . Even Wolfie had got his . . . No more nightmares.

Success. Angel. He felt so lucky.

Halfway to Anaheim and the wedding Angel clutched his arm. 'Buddy,' she whispered. 'The baby . . . I think it's happening . . .'

He didn't panic. Stayed calm. Leaned forward and tapped the glass separating them from the driver. After all he was a star now. Had to act the part.

'Get this wreck to the hospital like yesterday!!' he yelled excitedly.

Sadie sat bolt upright and pressed towards Angel, taking her hand. 'You're going to be fine, darling. Don't worry. We'll be there in no time.'

* * *

Angel gave birth at four o'clock in the afternoon. It was not an easy delivery. Nobody had expected twins. The first one was a breech birth and for a moment it was touch and go.

Buddy, who was in the delivery room, picked up on the anxious vibrations as they struggled to get the baby to breathe. He felt fear grip him. Angel moaned as the second baby entered the world.

Twins.

Boys.

Just in time the first one let out a healthy yell.

If you have enjoyed Hollywood Wives, *you will want to read all of Jackie Collins' bestselling novels available from Simon & Schuster. Here is an extract from the opening pages of* Hollywood Husbands . . .

The nightmare began for the child when she was fourteen years old and alone in the house with her father. Her brothers and sisters were long gone. As soon as they were old enough to earn a living they left – quickly – and never came back to visit. Her mother was in the hospital, 'women's problems', a neighbour had sighed. The child did not know what that meant, only that she missed her mother desperately, even though she had only been gone two days.

The little girl was an accident. Her mother often told her that. 'You're a late accident,' she would say, 'an' too much work for me. I should be restin' now, not raisin' another kid.' Whenever she spoke the words she would smile, hug her daughter, and add warmly, 'I wouldn't do without you, my little one. Couldn't. You understand me, darlin'!'

Yes. She understood that she was loved by the frail woman in the carefully patched clothes who took in other people's washing and treated her husband like a king.

They lived in a run-down house on the outskirts of town. It was freezing in the winter and too hot in the summer. There were hungry roaches in the kitchen and giant rats that ran across the roof at night. The child grew up with fear in her heart, not because of the vermin, but because of the many times her father beat her mother, and the terrified screams that continued throughout the night. The screams were always followed by long, ominous silences, broken only by his grunting and groaning, and her mother's stifled sobs.

Her father was big, mean and shiftless, and she hated him. One day – like her brothers and sisters before her – she would leave, just sneak off in the early dawn as they had done. Only she had more exciting plans. She was going to go out in the world and make a success of her life, and when she had enough money she was going to send for her mother and look after her properly.

Her father yelled for his dinner. She fixed him a steaming plate of tripe and onions just as her mother had taught her. It wasn't satisfactory. 'Slop!' he shouted, after he'd eaten most of it, belching loudly as she hurriedly removed the plate and replaced it with his fifth can of beer.

He looked her over, his eyes rheumy, his face slack. Then he slapped her backside and guffawed to himself. She scurried into the kitchen. All her life she had lived with him, and yet he frightened her more than any stranger. He was brutal and cruel. Many a time she had felt the sharp sting of his heavy hand across her face or shoulders or legs. He enjoyed inflicting what he considered his superior strength.

She washed the solitary dish in a bowl of water, and wondered how long her mother would be in the hospital. Not long, she hoped fervently. Maybe only another day or so.

Wiping her hands, she made her way through the cramped parlour where her father snored in front of a flickering black and white television. The buckle of his belt was undone, and his stomach bulged obscenely over a grimy tee-shirt, an empty beer can balanced on his chest.

She crept outside to the toilet. There was no indoor plumbing; a cracked basin filled with luke-warm water was the only means of washing. Sometimes she cleaned herself in the kitchen, but she wouldn't dare to do that with her father home. Lately he had taken to spying on her – creeping up when she was dressing and sneering at her newly developed curves.

Wearily she pulled off her blouse, stepped out of her shorts, and proceeded to splash water under her ams, across her chest and between her legs.

She wished there was a mirror so that she could see what her new figure looked like. At school three of her friends and she had crowded together in a toilet and examined each other's developing buds. It wasn't the same as seeing her own body – she had no interest in looking at other girls' breasts.

Carefully she traced the swell of her small nipples, and sucked in her breath because it gave her such a funny feeling to touch herself.

So intent was she on examining her new body, that she failed to hear the clump of her father's footsteps as he approached the out-house. Without knocking he flung open the creaking door before she had time to cover herself. The buttons on his fly were open. ‘Gotta take a piss,’ he slurred. And then, as if working on a slow fuse, he added, ‘What you doin’, girl, standin’ around naked?’

‘Just washin’, pa,’ she replied, blushing beet-red as she frantically reached for the towel she had brought in with her.

He was too quick for her. With a drunken lurch he stepped on the flimsy towel, and blocked the door with his bulk. ‘You bin seein’ any boys?’ he demanded. ‘You bin sleepin’ around?’

‘No.’ Desperately she pulled at the towel, trying to dislodge it from under his foot.

He staggered towards her, all beer breath and bloodshot eyes. ‘Are you sure, *missy?’*

‘Yes, pa, I'm sure,’ she whispered, wanting to run and hide in her bed and die of embarrassment.

He watched her for a long moment. Then he touched himself and grunted loudly.

Her heart was pounding – signalling DANGER DANGER. *She held her breath. Instinct told her she was caught in a trap.*

He fiddled with his thing until it was completely visible, sticking through his trousers like an angry red weapon. ‘Ya see this?’ he growled.

She stayed absolutely still and silent.

‘Ya see this?’ he repeated, his face as red as his weapon. ‘This is what ya gotta look out for.’ He stroked his erection. ‘This is what every boy ya ever meet is gonna want to stick ya with.’

As he reached for her she began to scream. ‘No! No! No!’ Her voice was shrill and unreal as if it belonged to someone else.

But there was no one to hear her. No one to care.

And then the nightmare really began.

About the Author

There have been many imitators, but only Jackie Collins can tell you what really goes on in the fastest lane of all. From Beverly Hills bedrooms to a raunchy prowl along the streets of Hollywood; from glittering rock parties and concerts to stretch limos and the mansions of the power brokers – Jackie Collins chronicles the real truth from the inside looking out.

Jackie Collins has been called a 'raunchy moralist' by the late director Louis Malle and 'Hollywood's own Marcel Proust' by *Vanity Fair* magazine. With over 400 million copies of her books sold in more than 40 countries, and with some twenty-eight *New York Times* bestsellers to her credit, Jackie Collins is one of the world's top-selling novelists. She is known for giving her readers an unrivalled insiders knowledge of Hollywood and the glamorous lives and loves of the rich, famous, and infamous! 'I write about real people in disguise,' she says. 'If anything, my characters are toned down – the truth is much more bizarre.'

Visit Jackie's website www.jackiecollins.com, and follow her on Twitter at JackieJCollins and Facebook at www.facebook.com/jackiecollins

This book and all of **Jackie Collins'** titles are available as eBooks, or as printed books from your local bookshop or can be ordered direct from the publisher.

Paperback	**ISBN**	**Price**
Goddess of Vengeance	978-1-84983-144-4	£7.99
Poor Little Bitch Girl	978-1-84983-546-6	£7.99
Drop Dead Beautiful	978-1-84983-544-2	£7.99
Lovers & Players	978-1-84983-422-3	£7.99
Hollywood Divorces	978-1-84983-547-3	£7.99
Deadly Embrace	978-1-84983-545-9	£7.99
Lethal Seduction	978-1-84983-421-6	£7.99
The World is Full of Married Men	978-1-84983-617-3	£7.99
The World is Full of Divorced Women	978-1-84983-619-7	£7.99
Sinners	978-1-84983-615-9	£7.99
Hollywood Wives	978-1-84983-625-8	£7.99
Hollywood Husbands	978-1-84983-623-4	£7.99
Hollywood Kids	978-1-84983-621-0	£7.99
Hollywood Wives: The New Generation	978-1-84983-522-0	£7.99
Lady Boss	978-1-84983-627-2	£7.99
Vendetta: Lucky's Revenge	978-1-84983-629-6	£7.99
Dangerous Kiss	978-1-84983-631-9	£7.99

Paperback	ISBN	Price
The Love Killers	978-1-84983-633-3	£7.99
Lovers & Gamblers	978-1-84983-635-7	£7.99
Rock Star	978-1-84983-637-1	£7.99
American Star	978-1-84983-639-5	£7.99
Thrill!	978-1-84983-641-8	£7.99
L.A. Connections	978-1-84983-643-2	£7.99
Chances	978-1-84983-610-4	£7.99
Lucky	978-1-84983-641-2	£7.99
The Stud	978-1-84983-646-3	£7.99
The Bitch	978-1-84983-648-7	£7.99

Free post and packing within the UK

Overseas customers please add £2 per paperback
Telephone Simon & Schuster Cash Sales at Bookpost
on 01624 677237 with your credit or debit card number
or send a cheque payable to Simon & Schuster Cash Sales to
PO Box 29, Douglas Isle of Man, IM99 1BQ
Fax: 01624 670923
Email: bookshop@enterprise.net
www.bookpost.co.uk

Please allow 14 days for delivery. Prices and availability are subject to change without notice.